Her Most Loyal SERVANTS

By Michelle Matteson

ISBN: 979-8-9899085-3-0 (Paperback)
ISBN: 979-8-9899085-1-6 (eBook)

Any references to historical events, real people, or real places are used fictitiously. Names, characters, and places are products of the author's imagination.

Front cover image by Ler (www.twitter.com/bifacialler).

Second printing edition 2023.

thosethatglowgold.tumblr.com
instagram.com/thosethatglowgold/

FOR MY MOTHER

Thank you for being my first customer
I'll miss you, Mom

PROLOGUE

May 2003

The slave felt the summons, and he grumbled.

He had just bought a hotdog and was chewing his first bite when the summons caused the itch from his middle finger to his shoulder blade. Really, if they wanted him to come at their beck and call, they could at least let him enjoy his food first. He sighed and looked at the rest of his dinner, wondering if he should finish it or throw it out and get his butt in gear. He felt another bolt of pain in his left arm and decided to get to the mansion first. Food could wait.

Thomas Monroe threw away the hotdog and started walking. Warm weather had brought everyone out of their homes, and the streets were crowded even as the sky darkened. Late shoppers, diners heading out for supper, lovers on dates. And musicians. Tommy's people. Singing, dancing, playing any instrument they could find. Guitars and drums and saxes and violins. He grabbed a roll of money out of his pocket and made sure to tip every person he saw. No bill was under twenty dollars. Some people nodded and smiled at him; most ignored him, lost in their music. Tommy didn't mind.

When he arrived at the mansion, a servant ushered him into the study without a word, closing the door behind him. Wilkes was sitting at the desk, but Tommy was surprised to see someone sitting in a chair in from of him. Generally, Wilkes met with Tommy by himself and kept him away from the other acolytes.

"Ah, Thomas," Wilkes greeted the changeling with a grimace. Wilkes's smile seemed forced, and Tommy noticed the overweight man was sweating. Tommy blinked as he put his hands in his pockets. Something was wrong. "Thank you for joining us. Do you remember Jozef York?"

Tommy looked at the seated figure and broke out in a malicious smile when the name finally clicked. He had not seen the man in eight years, but his haughty expression was the same. York was glaring at Tommy over tented fingers. "Yeah, I remember," Tommy drawled. "Not every day I get to throw one of you assholes off a landing."

Wilkes cringed and glanced at York, but York didn't stir. "Now, I don't think we need to mention that unfortunate night," Wilkes said. York continued to frown at Tommy while Tommy smirked back. Wilkes turned to Tommy. "It has been decided, for the honor of our Lady, York will now be the leader of the Acolytes. Your ring will pass to him, and you will serve him."

Tommy didn't say anything. They always acted like he had a choice and he should treat it as an honor when he literally had no option. Wilkes glanced at York and took the slave ring off of one fat pinkie. "Take off your jacket," Wilkes ordered, and Tommy complied. He had worn a sleeveless shirt that night and crossed his arms so both men could see the slave band.

Wilkes turned the ring in several directions, studying it. Tommy fought the urge to surge forward and try to snatch it. He didn't know why the magic of the ring worked on him, but it would stop him from getting close, just like it would block him from hurting whoever wore it. So he just had to wait while they went through their song and dance.

Wilkes brought out a short knife, made a small cut on his thumb, and smeared blood on the ring. "The blood makes you his master," Wilkes explained as he passed the ring to York. "He has to listen to you and only you. He can't harm you. But..." Wilkes trailed off as York took out a hidden knife from his cane to cut his palm. "He's been... stubborn for the last few decades. He doesn't always want to listen. Do with that information as you will."

York didn't comment as he watched the blood well from the fresh wound. He looked at Tommy as he smeared his blood on the ring. Both the ring and the band glowed for a moment, and Tommy tried not to grimace as it burned. Finally, both items stopped glowing, and York smiled as he put the ring on his pointer finger.

"Congratulations," Wilkes said with a smile as he stood up from the desk. "You are now the leader of the Acolytes."

York kept his smug smile for a moment, examining the ring on his finger. Tommy waited to see what he would do. Some acolytes sent him away; others wanted him to stick close. There was no telling which category York would be in. York's smile died a little.

"Tell me, slave," York started in a tight tone, "The night you injured me..."

"The night you killed a man in cold blood," Tommy interrupted, and York glared at him.

"...what were your exact orders?" York continued without commenting on Tommy's interruption.

"Now, I don't see why we have to talk about that night," Wilkes said with a nervous chuckle.

"Shut up," York told him in a cold tone, and Wilkes' teeth clacked with how fast he closed his mouth. He kept his glare on Tommy. "What were your orders?"

"To keep you alive," Tommy said.

"No orders to keep me safe?"

"None."

"Now, wait just one minute—" Wilkes started to object.

"Silence him," York told Tommy, and Tommy actually felt a flush of glee at Wilkes's frightened expression.

"Thomas, don't you dare," Wilkes said as Tommy took a step towards him. Wilkes tried to slash the short knife at him, but Tommy dodged the poor defense and transformed. He growled as he grabbed Wilkes's head and slammed it onto the desk. The man cried out but quickly fell silent as Tommy let out a snarl and bared his teeth.

York smiled as he used his cane to stand up, and he leisurely walked behind the desk and sat down. He tented his fingers again and looked at Wilkes as the fat man whimpered. "Looks like the slave's loyalty does not extend to former masters," he drawled.

"I couldn't have known that he would hurt you!" Wilkes cried out. Tommy tightened his grip on the man's head, claws cutting into the skin, but Wilkes just kept babbling. "It's like what I said before! He doesn't always want to listen. You have to give him a direct order to follow!"

"And you neglected to order him to protect me," York said. He was looking at his palm, and with a wave of his hand, the wound started to close. "I have often wondered if that was pure stupidity or spite on your part."

Wilkes groaned. "You were an enforcer. Your role was to go on dangerous missions! The slave was there to keep you alive, not keep you safe!"

"It's true. I was one of the ones to go out and perform the missions that others declined to do. Meanwhile, you sat here and grew fat," York said. He was examining the ring again, comparing it to the gold band on his ring finger. He looked Tommy in the eyes. "Kill him."

"No."

York blinked, and even Wilkes stopped panting for a moment. York's shocked expression gave way to anger, and he glowered. "You have to listen to me. I am your master."

Tommy winced as the band started to burn, but he just rumbled and bared his teeth at York. "I made a promise a long time ago. I wasn't going to kill anyone for you assholes anymore." He nodded at the fat man he was still holding onto the table. "Even this bastard."

York's eyes narrowed. "You hate this man."

"Yep."

"But you won't kill him, as I've ordered you to."

"Nope," Tommy said. He gave York a toothy smile. "Ain't it a bitch?"

Wilkes started to laugh, a high and unhinged twitter. York scowled at the sound and looked like he was chewing on something sour. "You see?" Wilkes asked in that high tone. "He's stubborn."

York moved so fast that Tommy barely saw him, but he took out the hidden knife from his cane and drove it into Wilkes's neck, nicking Tommy's finger as it pinned Wilkes to the desk. Tommy let go and jumped back, watching Wilkes twitch as blood gushed from the wound. York didn't look at the man as he glared at Tommy, sitting back in his chair. "A slave who will not listen is a useless thing indeed," he drawled as Wilkes made a horrible gurgling sound.

Tommy looked between the dying man and the new leader of the acolytes and felt a cold finger of fear run up his back. For as long as he had known them, the acolytes always surprised him with how cruel they could be. The smell of blood filled the air, and Tommy felt his stomach clench in hunger. York called out, and someone opened the door of the study.

Two men came in but paused when they saw Wilkes's dead body and Tommy in his other form. The blonde man turned green, but the redhead just smirked at the body and the blood pooling on the rug.

"Wilkes fought the exchange of power," York lied. He pulled the knife out of Wilkes's neck, and the lifeless body fell to the floor. York wiped the blade on a handkerchief before putting it back into the cane. York tossed the cloth onto Wilkes's body with a dismissive hand wave. "Frost, have someone clean this up."

"Yes, sir," the redhead said and made a slight bow before leaving the room. The blonde was studying Tommy, and Tommy made him jump with a snarl.

"Stop that," York snapped, and Tommy straightened up. "You are not to harm any acolyte unless I say so. You only listen to me. I will be moving my wife and daughter into this mansion. You are not to show up here unless I summon you. Now leave."

"Fine by me," Tommy replied. He transformed into his human form and grabbed his jacket, putting it on. Tommy snapped his teeth at the blonde, making the man jump again. He just smirked as he strolled out of the study and out into the warm night.

Tommy studied the wound on his hand as he walked down the city streets, debating what he would eat. The smell of blood was still in his nose, and it was making his stomach flip in hunger. Meat. Red meat. As raw as he could get it. And booze. Lots of booze. He stretched his arms behind his head and studied the night sky.

So there was a new leader of the Acolytes. It would take some time to see if that was a good or bad thing. The man was cold. That much was certain. And apparently, the guy was married. Tommy pitied his poor family.

But then, that wasn't his problem.

1

Tommy stretched and yawned. He put his arms behind his head, looking up at the star-filled sky as he walked through the gardens. It was late and cold, and it had been a long day, but it was nice to be going back to the Club, knowing some food and a soft bed were waiting for him. Then he looked down and saw Nyla Hafeez in the woods watching him, and the smile died on his face.

"Think she would attack me if you weren't here?" Tommy asked the hunter to his left, Smith.

Smith nodded. "Oh, yeah, definitely," he said.

"And would you stop her if she did?" Tommy asked the dark-skinned hunter to his right, Ellis.

Their eyebrows shot up. "Yes, because Burke ordered us to."

"I'm just scared of what your girlfriend would do to us if we let Nyla hurt you," Smith joked, and Tommy scowled.

And just like that, his good mood was gone.

It had been a long few days.

After he had taken Chrysta out into the woods to go stargazing, they went back to the club and crashed. "Being in the other form uses a lot of energy," he explained to Cross over a late breakfast the next day. "I haven't been forced to be in that form for that long before. Hopefully, I'll be okay with some sleep." He looked around the empty kitchen. "Where is everyone?"

"Gone home for a few days," Cross said. "Spending time with their families after swearing not to breathe a word about you and Chrysta."

"Good," Tommy said. "How about Chrysta?"

"Sleeping," said a voice, and he looked up as Rosa came into the kitchen.

"She used a lot of energy herself in the last few days," Cross said. "Once she gets some sleep, she will be right as rain."

"Yeah, don't remind me," Tommy grumbled.

"She didn't want to watch you die," Rosa said as she sat down and pulled her feet into the chair.

"Well, she shouldn't have gone back to that house," Tommy said in a low voice, glancing at his left arm. Seeing bare skin instead of the slave band was still an unfamiliar sight, but his mouth twitched up into a smile despite his anger at Chrysta for putting herself in danger while he was sleeping. He looked at Rosa across the table. "What about you? Avoiding your family?"

"Don't have a family to avoid," Rosa replied sarcastically. Her smile died, and she frowned. "My family was killed when I was ten."

Tommy winced. "Shouldn't have opened my big fat mouth," he said. "I'm sorry."

"Only have to be sorry if you killed them," she answered back.

"Rosa," Cross started to say, but Tommy made a wave with his hand.

"It's alright," he said. He looked at Rosa. "I'm guessing it was the Acolytes that killed your family?"

"Yes," she said, voice cracking slightly on the single syllable. She cleared her throat. "I didn't see them; my sister made me hide and then went back to try to save everyone else. It was her and our brother and our parents."

"I wasn't there," Tommy said. Rosa looked at him like she didn't believe him. "I swear. York didn't trust me, so he never sent me out on their little raids when he got into power."

"So you don't know what they were searching for?" Cross asked as Rosa looked down into her lap.

"As long as I have known them, the Acolytes have been looking for some magical paper ripped up centuries ago. They never told me what it was, but there were at least five pieces." He shrugged.

"Interesting," Cross said, and they fell into an uncomfortable silence as Tommy ate.

Later, when Chrysta woke up and stepped out of the girls' quarters, Tommy happened to be in the common room, trying to understand a book on curses. "Good afternoon," she said with a smile. Her hair was a mess, but she looked well-rested and absolutely stunning, but then Tommy knew he was biased.

"Good afternoon, beautiful," he said, returning her smile. "Feeling better?"

"Yes, I do," she said, sitting down in a nearby armchair. "Hungry, though. I feel like I could eat a four-course meal." Her smile died, and a frown took its place. "Is today Christmas?"

Tommy quickly did the math in his head. "Yep, it is." He frowned as she bit her lip. "What's wrong?"

"Nothing," she said, but he saw through the lie. He leaned over and touched her hand, and she gave him a grateful smile. "I would have spent the night at the Jackson house. We would have woken up to open presents and have pancakes for breakfast. They must be so worried about me right about now."

Tommy grimaced. He kept forgetting that York had turned Chrysta's life upside down when he tried to kill her, and everything she knew was gone. It wasn't her father she missed, though, but Chrysta was going to miss Mary and the Jacksons the most. "Sorry, beautiful."

"It's okay," she said, still lying through her teeth. "Mr. Cross said I can call them, but not right now. Getting in touch with Mary may put her in danger."

"He's right," Tommy said, nodding. He got an idea and gave her a grin. He got up, tugging Chrysta up with him. "Come on, help me make some pancakes for lunch." And she broke out in a smile so bright it made his heart ache.

Rosa and Cross came into the kitchen sometime later to Tommy mixing batter while Chrysta flipped pancakes (she couldn't crack an egg to save her life, but with a bit of practice, she made perfect pancakes). "Good morning!" Chrysta called out with a smile, all previous sadness gone. "Merry Christmas!"

"Merry Christmas," Cross returned the greeting, taking in the pile of pancakes already on the table.

"Sorry, do you celebrate Christmas?" Chrysta asked with a frown as she flipped a pancake.

"Oh yes, my mother loved the holiday; she couldn't get enough of it," Cross said as he sat down. "We generally try to stick with just celebrating the winter solstice here at the Club, but this year, you know, we were running around trying to save lives and all that."

"We thank you so much," Tommy said dryly, and Rosa laughed at his expression.

"We will probably celebrate when the others get back. I was thinking of a bonfire for New Year's Eve."

Tommy handed Chrysta the last of the batter and then dusted off his hands. "Hey, Torres, you have any movies around here?"

"Uh, yeah," Rosa said as she poured some syrup on her pancakes. "Kevin has a collection in the boys' room. He wouldn't mind if we borrowed one."

"Alright," Tommy said. He leaned over and kissed Chrysta on the temple before leaving the kitchen. Tommy saw Cross make a face but ignored it. Several minutes later, he was back in the kitchen with his hands behind his back. He gave everyone at the table a wide grin and then showed them his prize with a loud "Ta-da!"

"Oh, is that the *Blood House* box set?" Chrysta asked.

"Yep, movies one thru five," Tommy confirmed as he handed the set to Chrysta.

"Horror movies on Christmas?" Cross asked with a frown.

"It's my favorite series, Mr. Cross, but if you rather we watch some—"

"All in favor of watching the entire box set, raise your hand!" Rosa said with a grin, and her hand shot up with Tommy's. Chrysta laughed and put her hand up as well. "Outvoted, Mr. Cross, three to one."

"Well, you will forgive me if I don't join you," he muttered as they dug into their pancakes.

They all piled on the couch, covered in blankets, and watched all five movies, just as Rosa promised. Cross tried to watch with them, but he got up after the first disembowelment in the first movie. "Watching bloody horror movies on Christmas of all days," he murmured to himself as he left the room, and the teens and changeling laughed.

After eating pizza for dinner and finishing the last film, they started to head to bed. Chrysta leaned up and kissed Tommy on the cheek, quick and chaste. "Thank you," she said as Rosa yawned. "I know you were trying to distract me."

"From what?" he asked innocently with a grin, but she only returned the smile and turned to go into the girls' room as well.

That night, lying in bed on his stomach, Tommy spent way too much time thinking about the day and that quick kiss Chrysta gave him, running his right hand over his left arm without really thinking. She had said she wanted to restart their relationship, but he wasn't sure what that meant. Did Chrysta wish to be just friends? Did she want to be with someone else? He thought about Julien, the young man that had helped her at the York mansion. Julien, with his dark hair and bright blue eyes. Tommy scowled at the headboard. He was a handsome bastard. Tommy had to give him that.

Tommy sighed and tried to rein in his jealousy. If Chrysta wanted to move on, he had to let her. He knew it was for the best.

.....

The following day, Tommy, Chrysta, and Cross were in the kitchen while Rosa went for a run in the woods. Cross was reading a newspaper, Chrysta had picked up the book on curses, and Tommy had just pulled a frittata out of the oven when there was a knock on the door. Two men entered the kitchen, wearing hunter uniforms with swords on their hips. "Cross," one of them said to the head of the Disaster Club while the other sniffed the air, "we came to collect the changeling."

"Sorry, gentlemen, I'm not for sale," Tommy joked, but he was just trying to cover up his panic. Hunters coming for him was never a good thing. The first hunter scowled at him while the second walked to the counter to study the frittata and rub his hands.

"What's going on?" Chrysta asked, looking between Tommy and the two hunters. "Is something wrong?"

"Burke needs to question him," the second hunter explained. He pointed at the food. "May I?" he asked Tommy, and Tommy shrugged in fake indifference. The hunter grabbed a plate and started to take a slice.

"So, why the armed escort?" Chrysta asked in anger, glaring at the two hunters.

Cross put a hand on hers. "Now, I'm sure Headmaster Burke is just being cautious."

"He wants to ask me about the Acolytes," Tommy explained, and Chrysta turned to him with a worried look on her face. "Doesn't surprise me. At least he gave me a few days to rest up." Tommy grabbed a piece of the frittata and chewed thoughtfully. "These guys are just here to keep an eye on me. Wouldn't want the changeling to be running around unsupervised," Tommy said sarcastically.

The hunter next to Tommy snorted. He finished what he was chewing and swallowed. "You haven't been outside lately, have you?"

"Not in a couple of days. Why?" Tommy asked as the man laughed.

"Nyla is staking out the Disaster Club."

"Wait, what?" Cross asked. He scowled and stood up. "On Burke's orders?"

"No," the first hunter said with a sigh. "For her thirst for revenge."

"If she hurts him—" Chrysta started to say.

"You'll toss her across the forest again?" the second hunter asked with a grin. He leaned on the counter, and Tommy couldn't tell if he was truly that relaxed in the changeling's presence or just acting. "I have to admit, that was funny to see. Terrifying at the time, but funny after the fact."

"That's why we are here," the first hunter said, looking at Chrysta. "We have to keep Mr. Monroe safe from our colleague. Although I have to admit, I rather not raise my sword towards another hunter."

"So I have bodyguards? Sweet," Tommy teased, earning a glare from the first hunter and a grin from the second.

The second hunter finished the food and held out his hand. "Hunter Smith, third class." Tommy cautiously shook it.

"Hunter Ellis, second class," the first hunter flatly said. "Let's go." And with that statement, he turned and stalked out of the kitchen.

"He's a ray of sunshine," Tommy said.

"Them or they pronouns, dude," Smith said.

"My mistake," Tommy answered back. He saw the worried look on Chrysta's face and gave her a soft smile. "I'll be fine, beautiful. Burke said I would be safe here." He leaned in to kiss Chrysta on the forehead. "Just need to answer some questions."

She bit her lip. "Be careful," she told Tommy. She shifted to glare at Smith. "And you keep him safe."

"Ma'am, yes, ma'am," Smith said with a salute.

Cross stood up. "I'll see you two out. I want to have a few words with Hafeez."

Tommy got his leather jacket and boots on and went outside with Cross and Smith. Hafeez was in the forest, about fifty feet from the tree, with her caracal by her side. Ellis was talking to her, breath fogging the cold air. She glared at Tommy when she saw him and stopped talking.

"Just to let you know," Smith said in a low voice, "I don't think she's afraid of your girlfriend. I think she's waiting for you to do something stupid, so don't give her a reason to attack you."

"Got it," Tommy muttered, glaring right back at Hafeez. "And Chrysta is not my girlfriend."

"Do you think if I blast her again, she would be afraid of me then?" a voice asked behind them, and all three men jumped and turned around. Chrysta was standing behind them, Poe on her shoulder, wrapped in a blanket but barefoot, glowering at Hafeez as the caracal hissed at Chrysta.

"Miss York, go back inside; you will catch your death," Cross said. But he turned around and started walking towards Hafeez without making sure she did so.

Rosa jogged up to the tree, breath fogging in the air. She looked at the group of grown-ups standing in the trees. "What's going on?"

"Hunter Hafeez is getting a lecture from Hunter Ellis and Cross," Smith joked. "One is telling her that standing outside the Disaster Club in the cold is unprofessional and unbecoming of a hunter, and the other one is Ellis."

Rosa snorted and then reached out to touch Chrysta's shoulder. "Come on, let's head inside." Chrysta sent another glare at Hafeez but shifted around and went down the stairs with the other girl. After he was sure she had gone inside, Tommy started to walk towards the Academy, Smith following close behind. Ellis joined them while Cross stayed where he was, gesturing at the hunter who was ignoring him.

When they went into the Academy, Tommy had to pause to have a sneezing fit. "You okay?" Smith asked.

"Yeah, allergic to the bullshit," Tommy joked.

They climbed the tower, all of them using the stairs. Tommy went first, his instincts screaming at him not to let the hunters stay behind him, but they didn't give him much choice. When they made it to Burke's office, the headmaster was talking to a man with glasses. The unknown man looked at Tommy in surprise, nervously straightening his suit as Tommy took a seat. "Mr. Monroe," Burke drawled as he gestured to the unnamed man. "Norio Tomomasa. He is here to ask some questions about your time with the Acolytes."

Tommy just nodded at the agitated man, who didn't have the build of a hunter, current or former. Tomomasa adjusted his suit again and cleared his throat. "Mr. Monroe? I don't think I have ever heard of a changeling with a last name before."

"It's the name my mother gave me," Tommy said with a shrug, not giving any more detail.

"Yes, well," Tomomasa said as he took the seat across from Tommy, and Burke sat behind his desk, "shall we begin?"

"And who was your first master?"

Tommy sighed and rubbed his eyes. He had taken off his jacket hours ago and was slumped in his chair, his legs crossed. "For the fourth time, Felix Kristiansen, from 1866 to 1889."

Tomomasa looked over his glasses with annoyance. "We just went over this, Mr. Monroe. You need to be one hundred percent honest with me."

"And I already told you, Felix Kristiansen had the slave ring from 1866 to 1889."

Tomomasa sighed. He glanced at Burke, who was observing the conversation like he was watching the world's slowest tennis match, only his eyes shifting from side to side as man and changeling talked. "I thought you said he would cooperate."

"I know how you sorcerers operate," Tommy interrupted as he sat up and leaned forwards, making Smith and Ellis twitch. Tommy ignored them. "If I name the person who put the slave band on my arm, the whole family will be shunned for something that happened before they were born." He leaned back again, and the hunters by the door relaxed. "I'm not doing that to them."

Tomomasa blinked in surprise. "But if the person who put the band on you taught their family the spell, then they may be performing it illegally."

"They're not," Tommy said.

"But how do you *know?*" Tomomasa asked in desperation.

"Let us move on," Burke said loudly as Tommy opened his mouth to continue the argument. "Monroe is here to talk about the Acolytes. If he wishes to keep the identity of the person who enslaved him a secret, that is his choice." Burke made a gesture with one hand. "Continue."

Tomomasa shifted in irritation but made a note on a sheet of paper and fixed his glasses. "And after Kristiansen, who was in charge?"

"Daniel Torrance, 1889 to 1912," Tommy responded, settling back into the chair. "And then Frederick Britland, from 1912 to 1919."

"And then Jack Zannino, from 1919 to 1929."

Tommy sighed. "You keep forgetting William Shawcross," he growled.

"Shawcross doesn't count. He was in power for what? Four months?" Tomomasa argued.

Tommy sighed again and put his right arm over his eyes. "You keep asking me who was in charge, and as far as I'm concerned, whoever that was, was the one controlling this thing." And he pointed at his left arm, forgetting that the band wasn't there for a split second.

"Shawcross was so low on the acolyte hierarchy, he shouldn't even have been the leader in the first place," Tomomasa said.

"So, how did he get in charge?" Smith asked. Ellis threw him a glare, but he ignored it.

"He waited until higher-ranking acolytes were out of the country, poisoned Britland, took the slave ring, and started to bark orders. The others caught wind of it and came back to kill him and get power back," Tommy explained.

"What did he do during this period of four months?" Tomomasa asked, either genuinely curious or just to humor Tommy.

"Don't know," Tommy said, leaning back again and putting the arm back over his eyes. "He threw me into a cell and starved me for the entire time."

Tommy waited for the next question with some boredom until he realized the room was as silent as a tomb. He removed his arm to look around and saw four aghast expressions leveled at him, ranging from a cocked eyebrow from Burke to Smith's hanging jaw. "What?" he asked, not understanding their reaction.

"I'm sorry," Tomomasa said, "he did *what* for four months?"

"Starved me. Locked me up and didn't give me any food. *Someone* kept feeding me scraps, but I never saw who it was. Probably the only reason I survived."

"Why?" Smith asked, actually looking upset.

"I don't know. Wanted to kill me but was too chickenshit to do it himself, I guess."

"So you were abused by the Acolytes?" Tomomasa asked, looking unconcerned, but something in his voice made Tommy think he was only acting indifferent.

Tommy felt anger rising in his chest. "What? That surprises you? You thought those assholes were my friends? Half of them didn't even know my *name*. They just called me 'the slave.' You think that the band on my arm was a fashion statement?"

"We didn't know that the silver band you wore was a slave band," Tomomasa said defensively.

"Oh, so that makes it all okay?" Tommy asked. He leaned forward. "Maybe someone did realize it was a slave band. But they decided to ignore it. Because it wouldn't fit your story, would it? I was there because I wanted to be and not because *I was forced to.*" He leaned back in his chair, placing the arm over his eyes, ignoring the awkward silence around him.

There was a few moments of stunned silence, and Tomomasa made another note on his paper before he continued. "So Shawcross was the leader of the Acolytes for four months. Who was the leader after Zannino?"

.....

Several hours later, Burke finally stopped the questioning. "It's late," he simply said. "He needs to rest. We all do. We will pick this up tomorrow."

Tommy got up and stretched as Tomomasa put his notes into a briefcase. "Is Nyla still waiting outside the Disaster Club?" Burke asked the two hunters.

"Day and night," Ellis confirmed as Smith yawned.

Tomomasa looked at Burke. "Hunter Hafeez? Why isn't she here?"

"Nyla recognized Mr. Monroe as the changeling who was there the night her father was murdered," Burke explained, and Tomomasa gave Tommy a grim look.

"I didn't kill him," Tommy said quickly, guessing the man's question before he could voice it. "York did."

Tomomasa nodded. "I will have to ask you about that night."

"Joy," Tommy flatly responded.

"Let me escort you to the Disaster Club," Burke said to Tommy. He looked at Ellis and Smith. "Thank you, you two. I will see you in the morning."

"Aw, man, I was looking forward to eating more of that frittata," Smith whined.

Burke, his Irish wolfhound, and Tommy descended the stairs behind the others, making Tommy feel safer. Tomomasa and the hunters went one way while Burke and Tommy went the other. When they exited the Academy, there was a squawk, and Poe landed on Tommy's shoulder. "Chrysta. Worried," croaked the raven and clicked his beak as Tommy rubbed his head.

"That's not normal, is it?" Tommy asked, and Burke raised an eyebrow in question. "A familiar talking like this? Chrysta says he didn't talk until I met her, and that was about the time her powers started showing. Now he knows about a dozen words."

"Yes, it's peculiar," Burke responded. "Familiars are more intelligent than their non-magical counterparts, and they develop the ability to speak if they have the capability to, but I have a feeling that Poe is going to surpass all our expectations."

Poe took off, heading towards the tree. In the stillness of the cold late afternoon, Tommy heard a violin playing, and he smiled as he and Burke made their way through the snow.

"What is she playing?" Burke asked in a whisper as they got closer.

"*Salut d'Amour,* by Edward Elgar," Tommy told him, also keeping his voice low.

Burke looked at him, eyebrows raised. "'Hello, love?'" he translated.

"Yup," Tommy confirmed with a grin. "Written by an English dude, if you can believe it."

Chrysta came into view, sitting on the bench underneath the tree. The pixie lights had faded days ago, but there was enough light for Chrysta to see the sheet music in front of her, set on a painting easel. She spotted the two men walking towards her, and she flashed them a large smile as she played. They paused when they reached her, enthralled by her playing. Poe dropped down next to her and started swaying to the music.

Chrysta let the last note die out, and both men started clapping. She stood up and gave them a small bow in thanks. "Brava, Miss York," Burke said softly. "That was beautiful."

"Thank you, sir," she said. Burke's dog walked up to her and nuzzled her hand, and she started petting the familiar on the head. She looked at Tommy and smiled. "Are you done with your questions?"

"Unfortunately, no, I must borrow Mr. Monroe tomorrow, I'm afraid," Burke said, and Chrysta's face fell into a frown. Burke looked around, taking in the Disaster Tree and the rest of the forest. "I heard Nyla was here?"

"She was," Chrysta said with a sigh. "She finally left about an hour ago, but she stayed here most of the day, watching the club and the gardens. So I decided to break out my violin and play for her. Might as well practice if I have a captive audience."

"When I explained that Monroe was alive and staying here, I told her to leave him alone," Burke explained. "Regrettably, she did not listen. I will talk to her again."

"Thank you," Chrysta replied.

Burke gave the two of them a slight bow. "Good evening," he drawled, and then he turned back towards the Academy, his dog following close behind.

Chrysta turned to Tommy and bit her lip. "You look tired," she said.

"Tired and hungry," he replied. "We have been talking all day and skipped lunch."

"Let's get you inside and get you some dinner."

"Not sure if I'm up for cooking, beautiful," Tommy admitted.

"Rosa said she was making tacos," Chrysta said as she grabbed the painting easel and her music.

Tommy pointed to her violin as they made it down the stairs. "So, what did you play for Hafeez? Anything good?"

"Weeellll," Chrysta said with a grin. "I don't think she enjoyed my one hundred and twenty-one renditions of *This is the Song That Never Ends.*"

Tommy blinked at her as he held the door open, and then he was laughing. He laughed so hard tears formed in the corners of his eyes. When he calmed down and got his jacket and boots off, he threw an arm around Chrysta's shoulders and pulled her into a hug, kissing her temple. She leaned back with a smile, a blush on her cheeks that was not only caused by the cold.

"That is the evilest thing I have ever heard of," he said while she took his hand and tugged him towards the kitchen. "I approve."

.....

Tommy ate enough tacos to give himself a stomachache, and the soft bed waiting for him at the end of the day made him elated, but he still spent the night tossing and turning. Talking with Tomomasa had turned up some terrible memories, and many ghosts had shown up with them. So before dawn, he finally slumped out of bed and was showered, shaved, and dressed before the sky turned from its pre-dawn grey into winter blue.

Looking at himself in the mirror, Tommy thought about the Disaster Club as he checked his hair and face. True, it was underground and reeked of magic, but it was a hell of a lot better than living on the streets or in the basement of the acolyte mansion.

He was in the kitchen cooking bacon when Cross came in. "Coffee or tea?" Tommy asked the man as he sat at the table. "I didn't know what you would prefer."

"Both," Cross said, and Tommy thought he was joking until he got a good look at the bags under Cross's eyes.

"Long night?" Tommy asked, setting a tea kettle on the stove.

"My ability is psychometry," Cross started to explain. "But unfortunately, I can't completely control it. When I touch anything or anyone, I do a reading. Just as unfortunate, when I was helping Chrysta, Luca Guerra touched me."

Tommy winced. "I'm sorry," he said sincerely. He could only imagine what horrors Cross was going through right now. Guerra had a very long and bloody history, some of which Tommy had had a front-row seat for.

The empath shrugged. "The memories will fade eventually. But, in the meantime, I will have some nightmares waiting for me when I go to bed."

About twenty minutes later, the hunters came into the kitchen without a knock, looking for Tommy. The changeling already had a plate set up for Smith. "Lettuce or avocado with your tomato and bacon?" he asked the hunters before they got through the door.

"Avocado," Smith said with a grin, and Ellis rolled their eyes as Smith bit into the sandwich.

"What?" Smith asked as he used a thumb to wipe at the mayo on his lip. "It's good."

Ellis just shook their head and then put a hand up when Tommy offered them a plate. "No, thank you, I already ate breakfast," the hunter said.

"I ate breakfast too," Smith said defensively around a mouthful of food. "I just never turn down free food."

Tommy picked up his sandwich and then started heading out the door. "Make sure Chrysta eats," Tommy told Cross, and Cross waved a hand as he took a sip of coffee.

Hafeez was waiting in the trees when they got to the top of the stairs, and Tommy lifted a hand in greeting, a fake smile wide on his face. "Doesn't she have a home to get to?" Tommy asked under his breath just so the two hunters next to him could hear him.

"Forgive her," Ellis said, their voice just as low. "She's hurting. She's been hurting for a long time." Tommy felt the smile slide off his face. He could sympathize with someone who had lost her family.

They made their way into the Academy, Tommy's sneezing fit not as bad as the last one. They climbed the stairs, Tommy feeling a little better about the two hunters behind him. Once they made it to the top, Tommy sat down in the chair in front of Burke's desk that he had used the day before without a greeting to either Burke or Tomomasa, who waited for him.

"Gentlemen," he said brightly with the biggest shit-eating grin he could muster. Tomomasa looked at him in shock while Burke arched a brow. Tommy leaned back and put his hands behind his head, crossing his legs in front of him. "What fresh hell are we getting into today?"

.....

"What happened in 1972?"

Tommy cocked his head to the side and thought about the question. "What do you mean?" he asked.

"Helen Chambers," Tomomasa said, checking his notes but not elaborating further.

Tommy waited for a second for Tomomasa to continue, but he didn't. "What about her?" he asked.

"You helped her to escape the Acolytes. Why?"

"She passed me a note asking for me to help her save her son. I didn't feel like I could say no."

"She didn't tell officials at the time that you helped her, not until several years after the fact."

"I asked her not to."

"Why?"

Tommy sighed in irritation and rubbed his face. "I mean, what would it have accomplished? 'Hey, I know you guys hate and distrust me, but look, I helped a lady. Can you do me a solid?' You guys would have thought it was some kind of trick and may not have helped her. I wanted to make sure she got out, and her kid got a new life, that was all."

Tomomasa paused in writing his notes. "What did your master at the time do when he found out you helped her?"

"Beat the shit out of me, ordered me to keep what happened a secret, and threw me out of the mansion," Tommy replied. "I think the only reason West didn't kill me was that Wilkes stopped him. Said I still could be useful."

"All this for someone you barely knew?" Burke asked.

"Look, like I said, she asked for help, and I felt like I couldn't ignore her," Tommy explained.

"And if they killed you?"

Tommy shrugged with one shoulder. "I had been wearing the slave band for over a century. Didn't matter to me if I lived or died at that point."

"Were you in the habit of helping people even if it meant the Acolytes would harm you for doing so?" Tomomasa asked.

Tommy glanced at Burke, and the man gave a small shake of his head, slight enough that Tomomasa didn't catch it. So Burke hadn't told Tomomasa about Chrysta. Tommy shrugged, trying to look indifferent. "I did it once or twice. Mostly I helped normies. The Acolytes didn't care as long as it didn't mess with their plans."

"Why?" Tomomasa asked.

Tommy considered his question for a minute. Finally, he opened his mouth but snapped it shut and sighed. "Because someone once told me that I couldn't complain about the world being a shitty place if I was a shitty person myself." Tommy sighed again and rubbed his left arm without thinking. "I couldn't control what life threw at me, but I could control my reaction to it. That I could be a better person." He looked Tomomasa in the eye. "So I made a promise that day. I would try to help people instead of hurting them."

Tomomasa didn't say anything but kept writing notes for a few minutes. "And is that why you are here now?" he asked suddenly.

Tommy glanced at Burke again, but this time Tomomasa noticed. He glared at Burke. He put down his pen and rubbed at his eyes after taking off his glasses. "Neil, I am here as a favor to you. You need to be honest with me as well."

"I'm not at liberty to say what happened," Burke said, hands still tented.

"You called me during the holidays, asking me to keep this whole thing a secret, not telling me how you met this changeling, why you trust him, or even why he agreed to do all of this in the first place. How he came to be controlled by a slave band, or why it's gone now. But I'm supposed to trust you when you say I should ignore all that and continue my questions?"

"Yes," Burke mildly said.

Tomomasa paused, blinking for a few seconds. He put his glasses back on with a sigh. "Can you tell me about your time in France?" he asked Tommy.

. . . . .

"Do you remember Olinda?"

Tommy blinked at the question, mainly because it was coming from Burke and not Tomomasa.

They had taken a break for lunch, sandwiches. Smith had left the room to get them, and Tommy noted that the others seemed to be more relaxed with him, but they always had two hunters nearby to keep an eye on him. He tried not to feel insulted by that.

He had been chewing on a bite of sandwich, casually putting his boots on Burke's desk. Burke didn't say a word but coolly got up and walked around the desk to knock Tommy's feet off. Tommy just grinned. Burke was a serious man, so messing with him was fun. The former hunter leaned on the desk, folded his arms, and delivered the question with a neutral tone.

Tommy smiled, tapping his finger on his chin. "1954, right? Never been to the Carnival in Venice, but I bet it has nothing on the partying they do in Brazil." He took a bite of his sandwich and then started humming some samba music, dancing in his chair. Smith snorted at his antics.

"Yes, but what happened?" Burke asked.

Tommy didn't stop dancing as he took another bite of his sandwich. "You know," he said while chewing, "you guys keep asking these questions about what happened. How about you tell me what you think happened? I'll just let you know how far off you are."

Burke frowned at him, but Tomomasa shuffled some papers and brought out a ledger, leafing through it until he found the page he was looking for. "Hunters were dispatched to a church where unmagical humans found an alleged artifact of the Golden One. A changeling attacked them and tried to drown one of them in the ocean, but she claims another changeling came to her aid."

"I don't remember hearing about that," Smith said. "Who were the hunters?"

Tomomasa hummed as he checked the sheet. "The names have been redacted. Officials at the time ruled that the hunter was under stress and mistaken in regard to what happened. So they hid the hunters' names to protect their reputation."

"Let me guess," Smith joked with Tommy, "you were the one who tried to drown her?"

Tommy stopped dancing in his chair and put a hand to his chest like he was hurt. "No, I was not. I think I was the one that saved her."

"You think?" Ellis asked.

"I was too drunk that day to remember," Tommy confessed. "Totally wasted. I remember seeing the other changeling dragging her out of the church, realizing he had the statue I was looking for, following them to the beach, and then... I don't know. I guess I thought that drowning her was unfair somehow? That I should help her out because he was cheating. Even though she probably would have cut off my head in any other situation."

"So you're saying that you only saved her because you had too much to drink that day?" Burke asked.

Tommy lifted his shoulder in fake indifference. "What can I say? I'm an alcoholic."

"How do you know about this incident?" Tomomasa asked Burke, giving the other man a suspicious look.

Tommy grinned at Burke. "Were they friends of yours? If they are still alive, can you say hi for me? It's not every day I can say I saved a hunter's life."

Burke's lip twitched under his beard like he was fighting a smile. He got up from the desk and sat behind it again. "I will do so," he said cryptically. He looked at Tomomasa. "You can continue your questioning," he said.

.....

When Burke finally stopped the questions, it was long past sunset, and the windows around Burke's office showed that it was snowing. "Hafeez can't possibly be waiting for him outside," Smith said to Burke, Burke's dog getting up and stretching with a yawn. "That means Tommy can get back to the Disaster Club by himself, right?"

"No, best you two go with him, just in case," Burke replied, and Smith's face fell into a scowl.

They went down the staircase and out into the gardens, fighting to open the doors against the wind. Hafeez wasn't waiting for them, just like Smith predicted, but Tommy gave the two hunters a quick thanks anyway before he descended the stairs to get inside. He stamped his feet and then took off his boots and jacket before noticing that Cross was sitting in front of the woodstove, reading a book with a tumbler of amber liquid in front of him. "I hope you weren't waiting for me," Tommy told him as he sat down in the armchair next to Cross.

"No," Cross replied, closing his book and putting it in his lap. "No, I was avoiding going to bed." He looked Tommy over. "Done with your interrogation?"

"No," Tommy said with a sigh. "Burke said there is still more stuff to go over, but tomorrow is the last day."

Cross nodded. "Good. Abby said she wanted to come over and check on you. I'll let her know to come over the day after tomorrow." He suddenly leaned forward to grab a glass and pour a drink. He handed it to Tommy without comment, and Tommy debated drinking it. He had been sober since before Thanksgiving, a pretty long time for him. *Fuck it.* It would help him sleep. He accepted the glass and drank it in one gulp, wincing as it burned.

"Too many ghosts," Cross stated, sipping from his glass.

"Yeah, that's one way to put it."

They stayed like that for a few minutes, not talking, just staring at the fire. Cross finished his drink and poured a second glass for both of them. "You know the worst part of these dreams? I keep having the same one, over and over, of Guerra hurting a woman. And she looks so familiar, but I swear I don't know her."

"He was one of the main topics of discussion today," Tommy admitted, nursing his second drink.

"Oh? Well, you probably know him the best, as long in the tooth as you are. How long have you known him?"

"I met him in 1924. He was 15 then."

Cross choked on his drink. "He is that old?!" he nearly screeched.

"Yep," Tommy said, taking a sip. "The Acolytes have a rumor going around that killing people with his power gives him some of their life force or something."

Cross blinked and then shivered. "I try not to call people evil—"

"Oh, he's evil," Tommy confirmed. "You see him torture someone with a smile on his face, and there is no doubt." Tommy finished the last of his drink. "When he showed up at the York mansion as 'head of security,' I knew something was up."

Cross didn't say anything for a full minute, just watching the fire. "Chrysta is having nightmares," he told Tommy suddenly. "Bad ones. About the night you saved her."

Tommy grimaced. Damn Jozef York for putting his daughter through all the trauma. "Can you give her something to stop them? Some spell or potion or something?"

"Abby is worried that it won't work," Cross explained. He looked at Tommy. "Chrysta's lucky that you were there to save her."

"Nothing lucky about it," Tommy told him. He reconsidered and then shrugged. "Well, we're lucky Normandy decided to help."

Cross smiled, something warm and tender. "She fought both Burke and me to help you two. You won her over with your natural charm." He held up a finger and then refilled both glasses for the third time. "To the strong women in our lives," he said, holding his glass up for a toast. "May we always know them, love them, and never get in their way."

Tommy snorted but gently knocked glasses with the other man. "Amen to that." They sat in silence for a moment after their toast. "To the ghosts in our lives," Tommy said, voice low enough to be a whisper. "May they finally rest in peace."

Cross smiled and nodded. "Amen," he said, and they knocked glasses again.

3

Tommy made sure to drink some water with his leftover tacos, but he still had a headache when someone started pounding on his door the following day. He tried putting a pillow over his face to drown out the noise but finally got up when the offending party started yelling through the door as well. "Get up, Monroe!"

Tommy quickly opened the door to find an angry Ellis about to knock again. "Alright, alright!" he yelled at the hunter. "I'm up already!"

Ellis quickly took stock of the changeling. "Get dressed!" they cried.

Tommy looked down, checking to make sure the undershirt and sweatpants he went to bed with didn't disappear in the middle of the night. "I am dressed," he stated.

"No, you're not."

"Well, I'm not naked," he joked, and there was explosive laughing coming from one of the couches from the girls, witnesses to the entire conversation. Rosa was hugging herself, her head thrown back while laughing. Chrysta was giggling behind her hand, cheeks turning red. Tommy leaned against the door frame. "Ladies," he drawled, trying to lay as much charm in the single word as he could muster. It just made the girls laugh harder.

Smith and Cross came out of the kitchen, both men trying to keep themselves from smiling. "I dare you to go outside like that," Smith said with a grin.

"Alright, it's a bet," Tommy said with a smile, but before he could take a step forward to do so, Ellis started to pull their sword out of its sheath.

"Get dressed," the hunter ordered.

"Fine, fine," Tommy sighed.

With Ellis hounding him, Tommy barely had time to grab some bacon and toast and kiss an exhausted-looking Chrysta on the forehead before being pushed out the door. Hafeez was not waiting for them when they went outside, and Tommy took that as a good sign. They fought through the snow into the Academy, Smith and Ellis knowing to pause to let Tommy have his sneezing fit. Then, they climbed the stairs to find Tomomasa and Burke waiting for them.

"Monroe," Tomomasa greeted Tommy while making notes, and Tommy nodded at the man in return.

"After we finish," Burke said to the changeling as he sat down in his customary chair, "I need to speak to you about a private matter."

"Still keeping your secrets, Neil?" Tomomasa asked.

"Trust me, Norio, you don't want to be in the middle of this."

Tomomasa paused, looking thoughtful. "Fair enough," he said after a minute of thought. "Monroe, can you tell me about the Lorenzo Mancini massacre again?"

·····

Many hours later, Tomomasa's questions had finally run out, and he and Burke were finalizing the paperwork as the sky outside turned orange. Burke had not dismissed Tommy, so he just crossed his legs and leaned back as much as his chair would allow so he could study the ceiling. He wasn't sure, but he was almost positive that the silver stars were moving across the surface. A reflection of the night sky itself? It was a nice touch of magic if that was the case.

Tommy felt more relaxed than he had felt in ages. Burke and the others in the room believed him and seemed to trust him to a certain degree. It was a good feeling, knowing they were not judging him based on the fact he was a changeling. Tommy was thinking about what to make for dinner for Chrysta, hoping to play his violin that night, when Burke twitched. The headmaster grunted and shook his head. "Something wrong?" Tomomasa asked him.

"Someone just teleported onto the grounds," Burke said.

Tommy glanced at him. "Expecting company?" he asked, a bad feeling settling in his stomach.

"I am not," Burke said.

Tommy caught the sound of the door at the bottom of the tower opening, and Burke's dog perked her ears up as the racket of footsteps climbing the stairs started to drift up. Tommy leaned forward, and Burke threw him a look. "What is it?" Burke asked the changeling.

"People are climbing the stairs," Tommy murmured. He cocked his head to the side, trying to catch individual sounds. "Three... no, four people... I think they are carrying swords."

Burke pointed at Tommy. "Get behind me, do not say a word," he barked. Tommy got up and did so, heart starting to race. The office did not have another exit. If he had to run, there was nowhere to go but out a window, and it was a long way to the ground. Burke pointed at Ellis and Smith. "No matter what happens, you two do *not* get involved. No matter what. Understood?" The two hunters looked worried as they finally heard the footsteps ascending the tower, but they both nodded mutely. Burke looked at Tomomasa. "I have no authority over your actions, but if you can help, I would welcome it."

Before Tomomasa could respond, the unknown group finally made it to the final flight of stairs and scaled them into the office. Tommy recognized Hafeez, but the other three people were strangers. They all had on hunter uniforms, one of the men older than the others. "That's it," Hafeez said as she pointed at Tommy, her caracal hissing, and the other hunters drew their swords after she drew hers. Smith grabbed the hilt of his sword, but Ellis stopped him before he could remove it from its sheath and started tugging their partner so they both were out of the way.

The older hunter scowled at Tommy. "Burke," he growled, not taking his eyes off of Tommy. "What is the meaning of this?"

"Deputy Director Campbell," Burke said with a smile. The once-stoic man looked relaxed, his hands folded in front of him while he flashed the newcomers a warm smile. Tommy was uncomfortably reminded of Guerra and the creepy grin he always wore. Burke's dog got up from her bed and stood by the desk in front of Tommy, growling softly. "What a pleasant surprise."

"Don't start with me," Campbell gritted through his teeth. "Why am I just now hearing about a changeling living on the Academy grounds for the last *week* from Hafeez and not you?"

"My apologies," Burke drawled. "I was making sure everything was in order before I brought the situation to your attention. I was going to have a meeting with you and Director Zheng." Burke started to move his head around like he was trying to look behind the group. "Is she with you? Or is this little raid completely your idea?"

The older hunter started to puff up and turn red. He pointed at Tommy. "I am taking that thing and throwing it into a cell, and you will not stop me."

"No."

If possible, Campbell turned a darker shade of red. "How dare you, Burke," he shouted. "What possible reason do you have to stand in my way?"

"He is under protection," Burke said, voice staying even.

"Your word may be law at the Academy, but you are retired, Burke," the other man nearly shouted. "Just because you say it is under your protection doesn't mean you have the authority to shield a known, dangerous changeling."

"I didn't say he was under my protection," Burke said, still calm. "He is under the protection of a stronger sorcerer than myself. Harm him, and you face her wrath."

"Stronger sorcerer than you?" the man asked while letting out a bark of laughter. "How could that be? Does she glow gold?"

Tommy felt his face twitch, and he had to make a coughing sound to cover a laugh. Burke glared at him but continued.

"The fact you are barging in and threatening him is the exact reason I waited to contact you. Mr. Monroe was a slave of the Acolytes, and he has been cooperating and giving his statement of his time spent in bondage. I wanted to wait until I had all the facts before making his presence at the Academy known, as making threats against his life may have made him act unreasonable."

"Hunter Hafeez said that the changeling was using that story to protect itself, but how do you know it is telling the truth?"

Tommy glared at Hafeez and growled, making the new hunters jerk. Burke lifted a hand slowly, lazily, but Tommy got the message. *Now is the time for calm.* Tommy lifted his left arm, rolling down the sleeve so they could see the cuts and scars still there. "There was a magical device called a slave band on his arm," Burke explained. "He had to do whatever his master ordered him to do. He didn't have a choice."

Campbell scoffed. "And where is it now?"

"Removed," Burke said, that pleasant smile not slipping from his face. Campbell looked at Burke, Tommy, Hafeez, and back again, but when no one elaborated, he puffed up again.

"And what information did you need to gather before reaching out to me?"

"Mr. Monroe has been sharing details about the Acolytes that only someone from inside the organization could give," Tomomasa said calmly. He gathered some of his papers and handed them to Campbell. The hunter glanced at the report but went back to glaring at Tommy. "Headmaster Burke asked me to record this testimony and to make a report. It will be my recommendation that Mr. Monroe receives amnesty for the crimes he committed while enslaved by the Acolytes."

Tommy looked at Burke in shock while Campbell made a squawk of disbelief. He had assumed that Burke needed to ask the questions for the headmaster's peace of mind, but Tommy never thought it could be to his benefit. Burke didn't look at him.

"Amnesty?" Campbell barked. "Amnesty? For a changeling? Have you lost your minds?"

"How could you?" Hafeez said while frowning at Burke. "You know what that thing did."

"I didn't kill your father," Tommy said softly. Burke held up his hand again, and Tommy had to bite back the rest of his words.

"I asked him about that night," Tomomasa explained, "and he named Jozef York as the one to kill Hunter Hafeez's father." He gestured at the papers still in Campbell's hands. "You can read about it when I publish my report."

"How convenient," Hafeez sneered. "The one person who could confirm its story is the leader of the Acolytes. How do you know it is telling the truth?"

"I have verified any details I could, and he has been one hundred percent honest with everything he has shared," Tomomasa explained, stepping back when Hafeez glared at him but otherwise standing his ground. "I trust that he would be truthful in anything I can't check."

"Trust? *Trust?* You mean you trust that *monster?!*" Hafeez screeched, and she took a step forward with her sword coming up. Tomomasa quickly retreated to the other side of the desk so that he was behind Burke. Burke raised an eyebrow, and Hafeez stopped.

"I would like to hear this story," Campbell stated, carefully pulling Hafeez back as he put his sword away.

"As I said, it will be in the re—" Tomomasa started to say, but Campbell just sat down in the chair Tommy had been using.

"No, we will hear it now," Campbell said, his voice not leaving any room for argument. Campbell then turned his glare to Tommy.

Tommy shifted from one foot to the other; Burke turned somewhat and gave Tommy a slight nod. "Fine," Tommy growled. "I can tell you what happened that night." He sighed. "Although I don't think you will believe me."

4

August 1995

Tommy popped back into existence and heaved. He tried to keep his breakfast down, swallowing as best as he could to keep the bile from rising in his throat. Tommy thought his stomach was under control when his insides clenched, and the world spun. "Nope," he moaned. "Fuck this." And then he leaned on a tree and hurled.

How did sorcerers do it? How could they use transportation spells and not lose their lunch every time? He wiped his mouth and panted. Maybe it was because he was a changeling. Or perhaps it was the whole bottle of tequila he drank last night.

Tommy stood up and took in his surroundings. He was in a small grove near a stream, the air cooler under the leaves than in the sun. Tommy paused to drink from the stream and wash the sour taste of bile out of his mouth. When he finished, Tommy found the sun, made sure he was facing north, and then started walking. Wilkes had told him that his target would be north of where they were sending him and that it would take all day for him to walk there and meet the acolytes for their mission. He scowled. Wilkes had summoned him in the early morning, transported him across the globe, not telling him what country he was in, making him walk all day, and didn't even bother to come himself. Meaning the slave band would start burning soon. Wilkes was trying to make him angry and frustrated, and so far, it was working.

He found a small road and started following it, trying to aim north as much as possible. He finally found a town: identical houses as far as he could see, none over three stories tall, white walls and terra cotta shingles, roads barely wide enough for two cars to pass each other, just like most of the picturesque little cities in Europe. Tommy saw that the signs were in Spanish and felt his frustrations grow. He barely knew any Spanish and only had American money in his pocket, adding to the problems he would have to face.

Finally, Tommy found a modern gas station, although it was designed to look like the surrounding buildings, and went inside. He went up to the young attendant. "Excuse me," he said, not trusting his skills in speaking Spanish. "Where are we?"

"Dónde estamos? Where are you?" the attendant asked with a wide grin. He turned to his coworker and hit the man on the shoulder. *"Estúpido americano, actuando como si se hubiera caído del cielo. Debe estar borracho."*

Tommy tried to keep his face neutral as the first attendant grabbed a map, some brightly colored thing in simple English. He opened it on the counter and pointed to something in the corner. "Ronda," he said slowly. "In Spain. You know what Spain is, *sí?"*

Tommy didn't respond. He brought out a piece of paper, the only information Wilks gave him before throwing him across the ocean, and put it next to the map. "Do you know where this address is?" he asked.

The first attendant just rolled his eyes without even looking, but the second attendant glanced at it and then nodded. He pointed to the map. *"Aqui,"* he said with a smile, indicating the north part of the city.

"Thank you," Tommy said as he took the map. He glared at the first attendant as he turned to go back outside. "This stupid, drunk American will get out of your store," he drawled, and he was happy to see the first man look guilty as the second one laughed.

The map was cheap and simple, but Tommy used it to continue his hike north. The terrain started to slope, and the sun was getting hot, but other wandering tourists made it easy for him to blend in, even if he wasn't like one of them. Finally, he came to the *Puente Nuevo,* and he realized why the small town was a tourist attraction. Ronda was on the top of a mesa, a river splitting the city in half, houses and buildings situated right on the edge of 300-foot cliffs. Humans built the bridge in the 18th century before Tommy was born, so he wouldn't call it new, but it offered an impressive panorama of the surrounding valleys and mountains. Tourists lined the bridge as they took pictures and admired the view.

The town sported many old buildings and historical sites for sun-burnt travelers to gawk at—statues, churches, and bullfighting arenas mixed with American fast-food restaurants and shops lining cobblestone streets. Signs in English pointed to what people would find interesting, and the people of Ronda smiled as money changed hands. The crowds were annoying but also a blessing, shielding Tommy from suspicion.

By mid-afternoon, Tommy's stomach was growling, and his mouth was dry. He kept pausing by the food carts to look longingly at the food but didn't dare ask for any. Finally, an older lady waved him down from her small shop, and he stopped walking. "Pulled pork?" she asked in a thick accent, presenting an open-face sandwich with meat drenched in sauce. Tommy's mouth watered as his stomach clenched.

"Um, I'm sorry... *lo siento*. All I have is American money," Tommy explained, holding his empty hands open in apology.

"Nonsense, you eat. *Ponte las botas,*" she said with a smile as she thrust the sandwich at Tommy. Tommy had no choice but to take it. He didn't know what boots had to do with free food, but he bit into the meat and bread and moaned in pleasure. The older woman laughed and handed him a water bottle, and Tommy downed half of it in several gulps. He ate most of the sandwich before he could slow down and swallow. "Thank you... *gracias.*"

"*No tienes nada que agradecer.* You looked hungry."

He nodded. "I was sent here by a..." Tommy paused as he tried to think of something other than the word asshole to describe Wilkes, "...business partner, really quickly, and he forgot to give me money."

"By your face, he is not a good partner, no? Make sure he feeds you next time before he sends you here, *mi amigo.*"

Tommy finished his food, said a farewell to the grinning old lady, and resumed his way north. He was leaving the tourist areas behind him, the English signs disappeared, and the shops stopped selling overpriced knick-knacks. Now people watched him with open curiosity, a man with darker skin than theirs, with combat boots, black clothes, and hair up in dreadlocks. But he continued walking, trying to look bored and like he knew where he was going. *Nothing to see here, folks. I belong here, in this town, in your neighborhood.*

He found the address he was looking for just as the front door opened, and an old lady wearing a hijab and two young girls left the house. Tommy tried not to react or stare as the lady locked the door, and the girls chattered in a mixture of Spanish and a language Tommy didn't recognize. They started walking in the direction that Tommy came from as he continued to head north. Tommy turned onto another street and then ducked into an alley. He growled while he rubbed his face. No wonder Wilkes didn't give him any details. He knew Tommy wouldn't want to hurt anyone, especially some poor grandmother and her granddaughters.

He cautiously turned back to the house and then crossed the street to a park in front of it. It was a narrow three-story home, white, just like every house on the block. There was the slight smell of magic when he was close, but they were the only sorcerers in the neighborhood, as far as Tommy could tell. The park had a small playground, and parents watched as their children ran and screamed on the equipment. Nearby, a group of older men smoked cigarettes and listened to a radio, a soccer game if Tommy had to guess. He sat on a bench and watched the house, waiting for the small family to return.

Tommy tried to keep his mounting concern off his face and keep an air of relaxed calm instead. Still, the parents kept glancing in his direction, and even some of the older men glared at him between soccer plays. Tommy had a feeling that the *policía* would soon be visiting the neighborhood if he wasn't careful. Once the small family returned with groceries and let themselves into the house, Tommy got up and started walking.

He wandered around, not straying far from the house. Night finally began to fall, warm and humid, and the streets started to empty as people went inside their homes. Tommy passed a bright bar, the patrons inside celebrating something, maybe the soccer game results from earlier. He desperately wanted to go in and get a drink, but he doubted they would be as generous as the older woman from earlier. So finally, when the night had deepened to the point Tommy believed that everyone would be staying inside their homes for the evening and not likely to see him loitering in the streets, he returned to the house for the final time.

Tommy was waiting in the dark park, watching the house with dread growing in his stomach, when he finally sensed someone walking up to him. He caught a scent and frowned. "Ah, Mr. Monroe!" a voice said when the figure stopped by his side. "So good to see you!"

"Wish I could say the same, Guerra," Tommy growled back.

"Oh, don't be like that," Guerra said with that smile that set Tommy's teeth on edge. It never seemed to reach his eyes. "Any day that we get to serve our Lady is a day to celebrate."

"Yeah, she ain't my Lady," Tommy muttered, and Guerra looked annoyed for a moment. Tommy suddenly realized that there was a second figure behind them. Another enforcer by the look of him. What was his name again? York? The younger man studied Tommy as Guerra cleared his throat.

"What have you seen?" Guerra asked.

"One old lady and two young girls," Tommy said, glaring at the younger man behind him. York was looking at the changeling like Tommy was something he found on the bottom of a shoe. "Guerra, I swear, if you hurt them—"

"Relax, my friend," Guerra uttered as he studied the house. "We have our orders. Hunter Hafeez has something our leader wants. Our spy says that Hafeez is out on an assignment but will be returning tonight. We go in, convince him to give us what we want, we leave. Any violence that occurs will be his fault, not ours."

"Shouldn't we be going?" York asked impatiently, looking at the house now. Guerra lifted a hand.

"What are your orders?" Guerra asked Tommy.

"Keep you two alive," Tommy said flatly and then flashed the older man a brilliant smile while Guerra cursed. "What? What's wrong?" York asked while looking at Tommy's smile and Guerra's scowl.

"Mr. Monroe would have protected us if he was ordered to, but if Wilkes only told him to keep us alive..."

"As long as I keep you guys breathing, I don't get in trouble," Tommy finished for the older enforcer, and now it was York's turn to scowl.

"Do we abort the mission?" York asked.

Guerra examined Tommy for a long moment. "If you shield us, I will give you my word that no one will be killed tonight."

Tommy considered Guerra's compromise. He didn't know what Guerra and York wanted or how much Hafeez would fight to keep it from them, but he would consider protecting these assholes if he could keep the family safe. "Deal," he said, and he crossed the street, making the two men scramble to follow him.

They gathered around the front door, and Tommy caught the scent of magic again. He turned back to watch the cobblestone street as York examined the door. "Can you remove the wards?" Guerra murmured as the younger man ran his hands over the wood.

"Yes," York said lightly, and then his hands were glowing white. Red markings flashed on the door in response, pulsing as York closed his eyes. Then, after several minutes, the red markings winked out, and York stopped glowing. Guerra took out a lock pick and started working on the lock.

Tommy kept quiet, trying not to sneeze at the lingering smell of magic in the air, when he noticed a car turn onto their street. Tommy couldn't make out what the writing on the side said, but he had seen enough police cars in his lifetime to know what one looked like, no matter what country he was in. "Hey, as much as I don't want us to go inside that house, I hate the idea of spending the night in jail with you two assholes more," he whispered to the two men crouched by the door.

"Got it," Guerra whispered in triumph, and he quickly and quietly opened the door, ushering York and Tommy inside. The door was closed a second before the car's headlights washed over the front of the house.

The door opened into a small foyer in front of a flight of stairs. The living room was to their right, the older woman sitting on the couch watching TV, her back to them. Towards the back of the house was the kitchen. "Irman?" the older woman asked, starting to turn around on the couch. She continued asking her question in the other language Tommy didn't know, but the smile on her face faltered when she finally caught sight of the three strangers standing in her home. Tommy expected her to scream, expected her to run to the phone he could see on the kitchen wall, but she surprised him when she stood up and quickly formed a fireball in her hand and threw it at them.

Guerra ducked behind Tommy, who put his hands up instinctively. While Tommy flailed his arms to put the fire out before it ruined his clothes, York was vaulting over the back of the couch to tackle the woman. She put her hands up again to form another fireball, but York put his hand out, and the fire died at her fingertips. She was staring at her hands in shock when York wrestled her to the floor.

Guerra rushed to help York, and she started to yell, mixing her insults with English. *"Allah yakhthek!* Pigs! Get out of my house!" They finally got her standing, and Guerra clamped a hand over her mouth as she struggled.

"Find the girls. Bring them here!" Guerra ordered, and Tommy and York made a run for the stairs. There were three doors off of the landing, and Tommy burst through one door while York picked another. The older of the two girls was sitting upright in bed, her eyes wide in terror. She started shrieking when Tommy entered the room, and he winced at the assault on his ears. "Sorry, kiddo," he said as he grabbed the girl, and she started to punch and kick him as he carried her out the door.

York was pulling the younger girl out of her room by her hair, cursing when the girl bit him. He raised a hand to hit her, but Tommy stopped him. York glared at him. "Come on, York," Tommy joked as he took his struggling captive down the stairs. "Don't let a little girl beat ya up!"

The older woman redoubled her efforts to get free when she saw her granddaughters getting carried down the stairs. Guerra's hands started glowing red, not the bright red of a fire user but the deep dark color of blood, and the woman's eyes went wide as her back straightened from the pain. Guerra finally let her go after several agonizing moments, and she crumbled onto the couch, cowering as Guerra stood over her. "Do as I say, or I do the same to them," Guerra purred in a silky tone, that creepy smile in full force on his face. The woman nodded mutely, and her granddaughters were released and ran to her. They cringed on the couch as Guerra sat in front of them on the coffee table.

"Now," Guerra said in a low, calm voice. "When is your son due to come home?"

The woman just glared at the enforcer, but when Guerra reached out and put a hand on the eldest girl's knee, she finally answered in a shuddering voice. "In an hour."

"Good," Guerra said, smiling wide. "Your son has something we want. Do you know where it is?"

"We don't have anything you would want, *ant wahash,"* she spat, but if Guerra was insulted, he didn't show it.

Guerra looked up at Tommy and York. "Seal the windows and doors. Look around, see if you find anything."

York turned to the front of the house, laying a hand on the windowsill and muttering under his breath. Tommy climbed the stairs. The girls' rooms didn't have anything, and neither did the third bedroom on the second story. The third story was different, though. The bedroom at the front of the house was normal as far as Tommy could tell, but there was a second door that reeked of magic, so strong it made Tommy's eyes water. He tried the door handle, not surprised to find it locked. Tommy gave the door a swift kick, and the wood splintered, only for the door to glow red and become whole again. He cursed under his breath and tried again, lifting his foot high and bringing it down with all his weight, focusing on the door jam.

Tommy made a hole, but it only lasted for seconds before the door glowed again and fixed itself. Tommy turned as he heard someone climb the stairs behind him. "Stop making so much noise, you stupid creature," York hissed. "I haven't sealed all the windows. Someone may hear you."

Tommy growled at the man but gestured at the spelled door. "What do you make of this?"

York pushed past him and started waving his hands over the wood, his hands glowing slightly. Sparks popped in the air, and York scowled but kept his hands up. The sparks increased until one popped in York's face, and he flinched back.

"Well, this is the room," York grumbled, primarily to himself. "Come, we can't do anything about this, not until the master of the house arrives."

They went back downstairs, Guerra looking up with a questioning look. "The second bedroom on the third story is magically sealed," York explained. "It would take me hours to remove it, and he can't break it."

"What do we do now?" Tommy asked while rubbing his left arm.

"Now?" Guerra said with his cold smile. "Now we wait."

৫ 5 ৩

Irman Hafeez closed the door to the taxi he had taken home and sighed. It was good to be home before the girls started school so they could spend some time together. Irman would be stationed at the Academy this upcoming school year, the "babysitting duty," as most of the hunters put it, but it meant he would be working there before Akilah started her first year. Maybe he would move the entire family to America and take a permanent position at the Academy as the girls attended the school. He would have to talk to his mother about it.

He went to the door as the taxi drove away. He frowned. The wards were down. He unlocked the door and placed his bag inside. *"Am?"* he softly called out. The girls should have been in bed hours ago, but his mother would generally stay up to wait for him. He noticed someone sitting at the kitchen table in the dark. *"Ealayk 'an takun hadhiraan mae alhawajiz, laqad kan—"* He had been walking across the living room but stopped dead in his tracks when the kitchen light turned on, and he noticed that his mother wasn't alone. The Butcher was sitting with her at the table, smiling.

Irman stood still in shock for a long moment, but it wore off, and he formed a fireball in his hand. The bastard was in his kitchen, *in his home*, and was going to regret it. Before he could let the ball go, someone grabbed him from behind. The man to his right started glowing white, and Irman lost the ball. He was pushed forward and forced to sit in a chair while he struggled to make more fire. He looked at the men holding him in the chair and felt his blood run cold when he realized the man at his left was really the Acolytes' changeling. The man on his right reached into his jacket, grabbed the charm hanging on his neck, and snatched it away. Guerra casually reached out and put a hand on his mother's hand, and Irman froze, recognizing that fighting was futile. He slowly settled into the chair, glaring at Guerra as the other man smiled. Irman's mother looked at him in misery, her clothes a mess. Irman's anger made his vision go red for a moment; how dare they treat his mother like this in her own home?

"I swear, if you have hurt anyone in my family—" Irman started to growl as the younger man gave the charm to Guerra.

"Yes, yes, you will kill me, make me suffer," Guerra said, almost sounding bored. "I have heard that all before, Hunter Hafeez." Guerra kept his voice low and pleasant. "How about we talk about the reason we are here instead. Where is the paper, Hunter Hafeez?"

Irman felt his heart stop for a second, and then it started again, galloping in his chest. He kept his face blank, though, trying to stay calm. "What paper?" he asked.

Guerra's smile got wider, showed more teeth. "Now, let's not play this game, my good sir." His hand started to glow. Irman's mother whimpered.

"Stop, or I—" Irman said while he tried to stand up, only for the changeling to push him back down violently.

"Just do what he says," the changeling whispered in his ear, and Irman flinched away to look at him. There was something in the changeling's eyes, something that looked almost... sad?

Guerra, meanwhile, turned to the younger acolyte. "Get the youngest girl," he ordered.

Both Irman and his mother yelled "No!" at the same time while the younger acolyte stalked across the kitchen. He waved a hand, and the door to the pantry glowed for a second before he opened the door. The man reached in and dragged Nyla out by her hair, the girl screeching as he slammed the door shut behind him. The door glowed again, and the man dragged Irman's daughter to Guerra. Guerra pulled the girl to him.

"You said you wouldn't hurt them," the changeling growled. Guerra put up a hand, the one not holding Nyla's arm in a death grip, and waved his finger from side to side.

"I promised not to kill anyone," Guerra said. "Any harm that comes to the hunter and his family will be completely his responsibility."

"Irman," his mother pleaded while his scared daughter whimpered. "Tell them you don't have anything they would want."

"I don't know what paper you are talking about," Irman lied, and Guerra shook his head.

"Please don't insult my intelligence," Guerra purred. The hand holding Nyla started to glow red, and the girl screamed, putting a hand on her forehead. Irman's mother tried to get up, but the young acolyte stopped her.

"Please," Irman begged, also trying to get up, but the changeling held him back. "Let them go, and I will do what you ask."

"I thought you didn't have anything," Guerra said as his hand stopped glowing.

Irman's mother looked at him in shock while his daughter relaxed. "I have it. I have what you're looking for. Just please, please, let them go. Let them leave the house, and I will give it to you."

Guerra hummed. "I'm afraid not. They will call for reinforcements while you can try to stall us." Guerra looked at the changeling and the younger acolyte. "You two go with him; make sure he does what we want." Guerra smiled at Irman but put a hand on his mother's hand, making her wince. "I will stay here; keep an eye on everyone else."

. . . . .

Tommy climbed the stairs behind Hafeez and York, York holding the hunter by the upper arm. Once they got to the spelled door on the third story, Hafeez jerked his arm free and glared at them. York looked annoyed but folded his hands behind him and looked down his nose at the hunter. "Comply," he drawled, "or we go back downstairs, and I take your other daughter out of the pantry and hand her to Guerra."

Hafeez's cheeks darkened in anger, and he started to puff up. Before the man could attack the acolyte, Tommy grabbed his shoulder and leaned in. "Just do what he says," he whispered again. Hopefully, if the hunter listened, no one else would have to get hurt that night.

Hafeez looked at him; confusion, fear, and anger seemed to be fighting for control of the man's features. Finally, he gave a slight nod and went to the door. He put his hand on the doorknob, and the door started to glow red, bright enough to hurt the eyes. When the glow disappeared, the hunter moved the handle with ease and unlocked the door.

The door opened to a small study full of bookshelves and a desk. A portrait hung on the wall behind the desk, the whole family together, the girls smiling with Hafeez and a woman, probably the girls' mother. In front of the windows was a display case holding what looked like an arm. As Tommy got closer to inspect it, he realized that the arm was covered in fur, orange with black stripes. Black claws tipped long fingers. So it wasn't a human arm, but a changeling's arm, cut in the middle of the bicep and preserved as a trophy. The Hafeez household was one of the buildings hanging on the edge of a cliff, and when Tommy peered out of a window, all he could see was the valley floor, hundreds of feet below.

Hafeez went to the portrait and swung it to the side to reveal a safe. He waved a hand, and it glowed red, just like the door had. Hafeez turned the dial, and the safe unlocked with a *thunk*. York stopped Hafeez from opening the door. "I don't trust you," he said as he made Hafeez step to the other side of the room.

The safe was full of the things you would expect to see: jewelry, money, weapons, and essential documents. York spied a wooden box and carelessly grabbed it, placing it on the desk as other items fell out. Tommy watched Hafeez for a moment before turning to York. "Is that what you were looking for?" he asked while rubbing his left arm. He wanted to get back to the States. The band was starting to burn so much that it was becoming agony. The sooner they got out, the more likely everyone would survive the night, including the Hafeez family.

"I'm not sure," York confessed as he ran his hands over the box. It glowed white for a moment, but then a portion of it moved in the front, and the top popped open.

Tommy glanced at Hafeez, who was moving over to the table with the display case. Tommy's attention was drawn back to the box when York suddenly gasped. Inside was a piece of paper, old and yellowed, all the sides torn, but York picked it up reverently.

"Another piece of paper?" Tommy asked. "Is that why we're here?"

Before York could answer, Tommy glanced back at Hafeez, who had made his way to the table. Hafeez hit the side with a fist, and the bottom popped open, revealing a black sword. Before Tommy or York could move, Hafeez grabbed the blade with a shout and rushed at them.

Hafeez held the sword parallel to the floor, trying to run Tommy through. Tommy barely dodged to the side, feeling the blade cut his shirt and brush past his skin. Hafeez used his momentum to swipe the sword up and away from Tommy, almost hitting York's head. York scrambled towards the door as Hafeez turned on Tommy.

"Wait, *wait!*" I don't want to hurt you!" Tommy pleaded with hands held up.

"Then you shouldn't be in my home, monster," Hafeez hissed as he took another swing at Tommy. Tommy ducked again as the sword crashed through the display case, making the arm tumble to the floor. Tommy got up with a growl from deep in his chest, a warning for the hunter to stop. But before either of them could move, a knife shot in front of Hafeez and slashed his throat.

Tommy gaped as Hafeez dropped the sword and clawed at the wound, making an awful gurgling noise. Hafeez fell to his knees, revealing York cleaning the knife before putting it back in his coat.

"Why did you do that?" Tommy asked breathlessly as Hafeez collapsed on the floor.

"You should thank me," York drawled as he carefully folded the paper before it, too, went into his coat.

"He did what you asked him to," Tommy said, voice rising in anger as the shock wore off. "You didn't have to do that. We could leave, and no one had to get hurt."

"He was the one who took the sword," York said. Tommy stood up and then transformed, making York take a step out of the room. "W-wait, what are you doing?"

"You shouldn't have done that," Tommy rumbled, and he stepped over the dying Hafeez and grasped York by the front of his coat. The man gulped as Tommy lifted him in the air, feet kicking uselessly about a foot off the floor.

"Stop! *Stop!* Stop this at once! Put me down!"

"Don't have to listen to you," Tommy said with an evil grin, showing as many teeth as he could. He raised York over the railing and then dropped him so he fell to the first floor, tumbling down the stairs with a scream.

York landed with a crash and one final shout, and Tommy turned away, going back to Hafeez. The man had crumbled into a heap on the floor, and Tommy gently turned him over. The man stared lifelessly at the ceiling. "Fuck," Tommy cursed. If the hunter had just listened and let the acolytes go, he wouldn't have died because of an old piece of paper.

There was the sound of someone clambering up the stairs. Tommy turned, expecting Guerra, but it was Hafeez's youngest daughter. She screamed when she got to the door and rushed into the room, punching and kicking at Tommy.

"Leave him alone, you monster," she cried, and Tommy moved away from her father, letting her sit next to the body. She started crying, sobs that made Tommy's heart hurt in guilt, even if he wasn't the one holding the knife that killed the man. He backed out of the room, knowing that no apology would bring the girl's father back.

Tommy went down both flights of stairs to find York's broken form at the bottom, Guerra trying to get him to stand. The older woman gasped as she saw Tommy in his other form. "What happened?" Guerra hissed at Tommy.

"Hafeez had a sword and attacked us," Tommy explained.

"So Hafeez was the one that hurt him?" asked Guerra.

"No," groaned York. "The creature did."

"You didn't have to kill him," Tommy growled, ears going back.

There was the sound of something breaking in the kitchen, and the group turned. The older woman stood over a broken beacon charm, a knife in her hand, her granddaughter cowering behind her. "Get out of my house," she growled, and Tommy wondered if she was a former hunter, as brave as she was.

"I think we have overstayed our welcome," Guerra said sarcastically. "Grab York, we're leaving," he ordered.

"I don't want that thing touching me," York said through gritted teeth.

"Oh, shut up," Tommy said as he grabbed the injured acolyte. York groaned in pain. "Or I'm leaving your ass behind."

They flew out the front door into the dark park across the street. York was limping badly, holding onto his hip in pain. "Can you teleport?" Guerra asked the younger acolyte.

"No," York hissed. "I can't... I can't think because of the pain. I think my hip is broken."

Tommy looked up to see people running to the Hafeez household, running inside. Other hunters were coming to investigate the broken beacon charm. It wouldn't be long until they came back outside to look for them. "We have company," he murmured.

Guerra cursed. "York, you have to try."

York gulped, face pale from the pain. He closed his eyes and started chanting to himself. York began to glow white, and Tommy heard a shout from the house, wondering if the hunters saw the glow. Finally, Tommy felt the pressure building, and they winked out of existence.

❧ 6 ❧

The office was silent after Tommy finished his story. The windows had turned dark, and snow blew past them. No one talked for several minutes, but everyone looked at Nyla Hafeez to see her reaction. Hafeez looked around before she spoke. "Well, clearly, you can't believe it."

Tommy opened his mouth to say something, wanting to ask Hafeez what her problem was, but Burke put up his hand again. "Why would he lie, Nyla?" Burke asked, voice low and soft.

"To save its own hide!" she yelled, the scream echoing in the room. "It's trying to save its neck, right? You have to see what it is doing!"

Campbell glanced between Burke and Hafeez, looking slightly less sure of himself than he did when he stormed into the room. "What would you have us do, Burke?" he asked.

"As I said before," Burke said, tenting his fingers on the desk in front of him, "we don't have to do anything rash. I think we can wait for Tomomasa to finish his report, have a meeting with Director Zheng, and then decide what to do then." Burke looked at Nyla, face blank. "Let's not let emotion cloud our judgment."

Hafeez scowled, but to Tommy's shock, Campbell just nodded. "Fine then," he stated, standing from the chair and gesturing at the other hunters, making them put their swords away. He held up a finger and pointed at Burke. "But if this changeling hurts anyone..."

"Burke will personally detach my head from my body," Tommy flatly declared, making everyone, including Campbell, look at him. "I know the rules: one toe out of line, and I'm dead."

Campbell nodded again and then shifted on his feet uncertainly. "Come on," he ordered the other hunters, and the three of them started down the steps, the atmosphere of the room instantly relaxing as the footsteps faded. When the sound of the door closing behind the group echoed up the tower, Burke finally broke the silence. "Nyla—"

"*Don't,*" she hissed, voice wavering. "Don't even start to defend that... that thing standing next to you."

"Nyla, if you would only let me and Jiao explain—" Burke tired again, but Hafeez just turned around and started her way down the stairs, her caracal giving one last hiss before it followed.

When the door closed behind her, Ellis and Smith stepped forward. "Well," Smith said quietly. "That was fun."

Burke glared at the hunter but rubbed his eyes and sighed. "Thank you, you two, for your help this week," he said. "Could you wait for Mr. Monroe outside in the gardens to escort him to the club? After that, you can go home and get some rest. I may need your assistance in a few days."

Both hunters nodded and then bowed at the waist before they, too, left the office. Burke looked at Tomomasa. "And thank you for your help as well."

"Well, I didn't spend the last few days talking to Mr. Monroe just to see him cut down by hunters," Tomomasa joked.

"Did you mean what you said?" Tommy asked, and both men looked at him. "Are you going to get me amnesty?"

"That's the goal, yes," Tomomasa said. He started to rifle through his papers and put them into a briefcase. "Neil asked me to be a neutral party in all this, figure out what we should do with a changeling who was a former slave." He finished with his papers and looked at Tommy with his hands folded in front of him. "I may not know why you are here or how you got rid of the slave band, but I did mean what I said. I do believe you are telling the truth. Please don't make me wrong." And he held his hand out for a handshake. Tommy looked at the offered hand, not sure why he suddenly had a lump in his throat, but he shook the man's hand without saying a word. Tomomasa gave Burke a slight nod, and then he turned to take the elevator down.

Once the sound of the door closing drifted up for the last time, Burke cursed under his breath and pinched his nose between his eyes. He growled to himself, and Tommy sat down in the chair across from him, not saying a word. Tommy knew that this was a full-blown tantrum for a stoic man like Burke, and it was wise to stay quiet and let him calm down. When Burke finished, he tented his hands again and glared into the fire. His dog lay down with a whine and put her head on her paws.

"No offense, but I don't understand why Hafeez threatening me gets under your skin," Tommy said. He knew he was poking the bear, but messing with people was one of his favorite pastimes. Burke frowned at Tommy, and he almost regretted annoying the sorcerer with a sword within reach.

"I was hoping Nyla would be sensible and not drag anyone else into this. The more people know about you, the more likely someone will dig into how you came to be here and then learn about Miss York."

"Do you think she's doing it on purpose? Trying to out Chrysta?"

"No, I think she is just attempting to make you take responsibility for the crime she thinks you committed."

"You know her that well?"

"She came to me when she was younger, wanting a mentor to help her become a hunter. She is the best hunter in the Organization right now." Burke sighed and rubbed his eyes. "I may have made a mistake. I thought she could be professional and not let her anger cloud her sense of duty."

Tommy leaned forward. "And why do you believe me when she doesn't?"

Burke looked at him for several long minutes, face blank and hard to read. "Two things," he finally said. "One, I was one of the first hunters to report to the Hafeez household that night. The murderer clearly used a knife to kill Nyla's father. That never sat well with me. I had seen victims of changelings before, and their deaths are never... clean like that." Tommy nodded. "Two," Burke continued, getting up from his chair, "you have not once tried to use any of your good deeds to ask for leniency. You even offered to let Nyla kill you. Also, you are not using what you did for Miss York as a way to shield yourself from hostility." He shrugged. "If anything, you are trying to shield *her.*"

Tommy nodded. "Thank you," he quietly said.

Burke waved his hand, and the fire died in the fireplace with a whoosh. "Just as Norio stated," Burke drawled, "don't make me wrong in trusting you."

Burke got his coat on while Tommy shrugged his arms into his jacket. They started making their way down the stairs. "Tomorrow afternoon, I would like to see Miss York, Cross, and yourself," Burke murmured. "There is something that we need to discuss."

"More questions?" Tommy asked, trying to keep the annoyance out of his voice.

"No, this is a conversation I must have with Miss York. I just have a feeling she will want you there."

They joined Smith and Ellis at the bottom of the stairs, Smith trying to stifle a yawn. Burke went one way as the others went out into the gardens. Tommy stretched as they made a path through the snow, looking up to the star-filled sky. Then he looked back down and saw Nyla Hafeez in the woods watching him, and the smile died on his face.

"Think she would attack me if you weren't here?" Tommy asked Smith.

Smith nodded. "Oh, yeah, definitely," he said.

"And would you stop her if she did?" Tommy asked Ellis.

Their eyebrows shot up. "Yes, because Burke ordered us to."

"I'm just scared of what your girlfriend would do to us if we let Nyla hurt you," Smith joked, and Tommy scowled.

"She's not my girlfriend," Tommy growled.

"Just keep telling yourself that, buddy," Smith joked as Tommy started down the stairs to the club. Tommy didn't turn around but raised his hand lazily in silent farewell.

Tommy opened the door and took off his jacket and shoes, storing them by the entrance. He debated getting some food or going straight to bed. *Fuck it.* The changeling was too tired. He would wait until morning to eat something. He started to walk across the common room, heading to the guest room on the other side, when he passed the couch set closest to the woodstove. He was surprised to find that what he thought was a pile of blankets was actually Chrysta curled up and sleeping. Poe was sitting on the back of the sofa, head tucked under a wing. There were several piles of books on the table in front of her. Had she been waiting for him? He smiled as he leaned over the back of the couch and moved some hair off of her face.

He was debating on taking her to her own bed or leaving her where she was when sparks suddenly appeared, popping in the air and flashing as bright as a camera. Poe woke up and squawked, flapping his wings in surprise. Chrysta whimpered and started to curl in on herself, forehead wrinkling. Tommy panicked for a moment. Should he wake her up? But when the books and furniture began to glow and levitate, Tommy rushed around the couch and started to shake her shoulder.

"Hey. Hey, beautiful, you okay?" Tommy asked, trying to keep his voice low. Chrysta moaned in her sleep, so he shook her shoulder harder. Chrysta startled awake, breathing hard and eyes darting around the room like she didn't recognize her surroundings. Everything plummeted, the couch only dropping a few feet while the books fell from above Tommy's head. "Hey, you're safe, beautiful. It's okay," Tommy whispered, and she relaxed and rubbed her face.

"Tommy?" she asked while sitting up. "You're back." Poe croaked and landed in her lap. Chrysta looked around while she stroked Poe's head. "What time is it?"

"Late," he said while picking up the books. He happened to look down at the open book in his hands. The fall had opened it to a page towards the back of the book. There was a picture of a young girl holding hands with a woman who had to be her mother, with darker skin and long black hair. *The wife of Jozef York has shown no magical ability,* the picture's caption stated.

"People were watching us," Chrysta said bitterly, frowning. "They knew about my mother and me, but they didn't help us. You were the only one who helped me when I needed it."

Tommy took a deep breath. "As much as I hate to say it, you can't be mad at them, Chrysta." She gave him a confused look, and he sighed. "The Acolytes have controlled the city since it was founded. No other sorcerer can live or visit there without risking the acolytes attacking or killing them. I should know." He rubbed his left arm. "Sometimes I was the one to... gently remove them from the city limits." Chrysta looked down at the opened book and bit her lip.

"Yeah, sorcerers spied on the Acolytes, kept tabs on them, but it is a pretty secretive group," Tommy continued. "They wouldn't have been able to get to know you or your mother or find out that you two had no idea what was going on or that you needed protection from your father."

"Or that you were a slave and needed help," she added.

He gave her a soft smile. "I'm a changeling, beautiful. I never expected to get any help at all."

Tommy stood up with a grunt and then sat next to Chrysta, gently putting an arm around her shoulders and getting her to lean into him. She sighed when she settled into him. They sat in silence for a few minutes, Tommy gently rubbing Chrysta's back. "So what is the light show about?" he asked.

"I'm having nightmares," Chrysta explained. "I keep seeing my father standing over me with the knife." She gently put Poe next to her, brought her feet up, and wrapped herself in the blanket. Poe croaked and hopped to the table. "And this time, you aren't there to stop him. So whenever I have that dream, I make things float. That is why I was sleeping out here. I keep waking Rosa up."

Tommy stayed silent, not knowing how to provide any comfort. Chrysta started to rub her hands together, pulling the blanket this way and that. She glanced at him from the corner of her eye. "Was she part of the Acolytes? My mother?"

"As far as I know, no," Tommy replied, and Chrysta's shoulders slumped. She looked relieved, and her hands stopped pulling on the blanket. "She wasn't part of the old families, but she could have been a recruit. I don't know for sure. Your father ordered me not to mess with you or your mother."

"It makes sense," she said softly. "If she didn't know about magic or what father was doing, he wouldn't want her to know about you. She would have asked questions." Chrysta looked worried again and put her hands on her knees. "You told Mr. Smith I wasn't your girlfriend," she said in a low voice. "Is it because my last name is York?"

He blinked in surprise for a moment and then snorted. "What? No, of course not." Chrysta gave him a worried look. "I know you, Chrysta. You are nothing like your father. I don't hold anything he did against you. It's just when people find out your father is the leader of the Acolytes and that you glow gold, you will get a lot of grief for it. It's just how sorcerers work. You don't need 'changeling lover' added to that list. Trust me."

Chrysta scowled. "If people are going to shun me anyway, why does it matter?"

He studied her for a moment. She was so fierce and brave, even with everything that had happened in the last few weeks. He smiled at her. "Yeah, maybe you're right; fuck 'em," he joked, and she laughed. She tried to put a strand of hair behind her ear and then grimaced as her fingers became trapped in a knot. She started to run her fingers through her hair, trying to untangle it, and Tommy felt his fingers twitch, wanting to move his fingers through her hair as well. "Look, try not to obsess over what happened, okay? Probably why you are having nightmares."

"Maybe," she agreed. Chrysta was still running her fingers through her hair, so Tommy studied the books on the table instead, trying to ignore the urge to touch her. One hefty tome caught his eye, and he picked it up. *Her Most Loyal Servants* glinted up from the leather cover in gold leaf. He started to leaf through it and paused at the illustration of Camazotz. Tommy scowled. Not these assholes. "Do you know him?" Chrysta asked softly.

Tommy started and looked at her. He opened his mouth and shut it, trying to find the right words. "Yes," he replied softly. He shook his head. "No, I met him and the others. Once. A long time ago."

"Others?" Chrysta asked, tilting her head to the side. Her eyes went wide. "The other generals? The book is about them. The Golden One's generals."

"Yes," he answered. He didn't say anything else and stared at the illustration, lost in memories of screams and blood. Tommy started again when he felt Chrysta's light touch on his arm. She looked at him with sad eyes.

"I'm sorry."

"You're fine," he murmured. He took a deep breath and let it out. "It was a long time ago, but it was not a nice encounter."

"Is that why other changelings attack you?"

"You know about that?" he asked, wondering why she seemed to be so calm. She reached forward and grabbed another book, and opened it to a page towards the back. When she handed it to Tommy, he instantly knew the picture, even before reading the caption. "Australia," he said under his breath, running his fingers over the image of the dead lion changeling. They sat in silence for several minutes, Tommy not looking up from the book. Poe gave a soft, croaked "Tommy?" at one point, but Tommy didn't respond, mind lost in memories again.

"I'm sorry," Chrysta murmured. "I don't need to kn—"

"No, you need to know," Tommy interrupted her. "You deserve to know. Just," he paused, shaking his head, "not right now. I want to tell you. But not now." He looked at her, trying to give her a smile. "Okay, beautiful?"

"Okay," she agreed. "Whenever you're ready." And she suddenly yawned.

"Come on," he said in forced cheer. "You need to get to bed."

"Can we... can we stay out here?" She asked as he stood up from the couch. "Together?"

"I don't think that's a good idea," he said.

"Worried this changeling lover will take advantage of you?" she asked with a smile.

He snorted. "Uh, yeah. You glow gold. You're dangerous."

She laughed aloud and then slapped a hand over her mouth to silence herself. Tommy laughed with her, a genuine smile growing on his face, and she shushed him. He leaned down, kissing her on the forehead, not thinking about it. And then started to kick himself mentally. *Idiot,* he told himself, *you need to stop touching her.* But it was so hard to remember why he should keep his distance when she beamed up at him like that.

He added some wood to the fire and made sure the blanket covered Chrysta before settling on the couch himself. Chrysta burrowed into his side and laid her head on his shoulder. They both sighed at the same time, relaxing in each other's embrace.

"Burke wants to see you tomorrow," he mumbled. "He said to bring Cross and me with you."

"I wonder why," she said, but he could only hum in return.

Chrysta's breathing slowed down after a few minutes, and Tommy waited to see if the nightmare would return. Tommy wondered if Chrysta would still want to be with him once she learned more about his life and the things he had done. Would she still feel safe with him? Care for him? He sighed. He had made a promise. He would stay as long as she wanted him to.

When he was confident that she would not wake up again, he kissed her temple and fell asleep.

❧ 7 ❧

Brooke checked her reflection in the mirror for the third time in ten minutes. She made sure her blonde hair was still teased up, although how could it fall with the ton of hairspray she had used? She adjusted her shirt again, making sure it was still tired tight around her torso to show off her figure. Her shorts were still rolled up, putting her long legs on display. She wanted to make sure she looked perfect for her date that night.

Look perfect on the night she was going to sleep with a boy for the first time.

They had met at a rock concert a few nights ago, some underground punk show in an abandoned factory. Brooke went with her best friend Ashley, and they had danced and screamed with the other young adults on the dirty floor, ears ringing from the giant speakers in front of the makeshift stage. They didn't know the band, didn't even know the words to the song, but it didn't matter as they jumped up and down. It was fun rocking out in this dirty place while the crowd laughed and yelled and drank around them.

He had been leaning against a wall, tall and imposing, his mohawk adding to his height. He wore a black leather jacket, black shirt and jeans, combat boots, chains, and a single silver earring to round out his look. He caught her eye and smiled, and Brooke felt her stomach flip. For the next hour, she kept glancing his way, and although he wasn't always looking at her, sometimes she did catch him staring at her.

She was trying to scrounge up the courage to go talk to him when the screaming started. Not the happy yelling of punks singing a song but screams of anger and fear. Brooke looked in the direction the cries were coming from and noticed two dozen uniformed men running into the factory. "Shit! It's the cops!" someone yelled, and that finally made the crowd surge in the other direction. There were about two hundred people at the party, and there was no way the police would get all of them, but Brooke felt her blood run cold at the thought of getting arrested and having to call her parents. She would be grounded for life if that happened.

"Need help?" a voice said in her ear, and she jumped and whirled around. It was the rocker, a grin wide on his face as the crowd moved around them like water in a river moving around a rock. Ash was pulling on her arm, trying to force her to run.

"Um, yeah," she said, not quite sure what to say. His smile got larger, and he grabbed her other hand and started pulling her with Ash, the other girl looking at him in shock.

They followed the mob to the back of the factory while cops were wrestling the band to the ground. But the crowd ran into a dead-end, a wall with windows set high above their heads, blocking their escape. The party-goers were trying to climb up the wall, some of them trying to form human ladders, but the rocker pulled Brooke and Ashley to the side, to a door. He used his shoulder to break the door opened and motioned them to follow. They ran down a short hallway, a part of the crowd following close behind.

A boy suddenly pushed the girls to the side, making Ash trip and fall with a shout. The rocker stopped and turned around, cursing when the boy shoved past him. The rocker was helping them up as the boy opened a door at the end of the hallway. As soon as he stepped outside, a cop tackled him to the ground.

The rocker had the girls up and running, and he didn't even let them pause before they were vaulting over the two men on the ground. Brooke turned around to watch the boy and cop fighting and gave out a bark of laughter as others streamed out of the door and trampled them.

They kept running, the rocker helping the girls to clear a fence, not letting them stop as he made it over himself. They ran and ran, and only after they had run several blocks away from the factory did he let them collapse in an alleyway. He leaned on a wall with a crazy grin on his face as the girls sat on the ground panting.

"Holy shit," Ash was chanting. "Holy shit. Holy shit. Holy shit."

"Yeah, we aren't going to see that band play again anytime soon," Brooke said. Ash shot her a look, and then they were both laughing, the rocker joining them a minute later.

"Oh, I'm shaking," Ash complained. "I'm shaking."

"It's the adrenaline," the rocker said. He got up and held out a hand to Ash, helping her up. Brooke felt some jealousy until he held out a hand for her too, and she took it with a grin.

"Thank you," Brooke said with a smile, the nerves she felt earlier totally gone. "We owe you one."

"Buy me a burger," he said while pointing across the street to a 24-hour diner, "and we can call it even."

They got a table and quickly exchanged names. His name was Louis, from New York. He said he was in Boston for business, but he didn't say what kind. The girls chattered for a few minutes as they waited for their food, talking to get rid of the leftover adrenaline. They fell into silence after their food arrived, and they began to eat.

"So what were you two doing there?" he asked after devouring half of his burger. "Shouldn't you two be, I don't know, studying at home, listening to Yazz or Duran Duran?"

Brooke snorted. "You sound like my dad," she said and then mentally kicked herself for reminding him that she was just a silly teenager.

Louis just shrugged. "No skin off my nose if you get arrested, but maybe you should stay out of the underground party scene for a few years. Just 'til you graduate high school." He smiled and gave them a wink, and Brooke felt her face flush.

"Actually, I think you're right," Ash said, and Brooke gave her a sour look. "What? I don't need to call my mom from jail. She would kill me."

"Well, I was having fun until the police showed up," Brooke said haughtily, and now it was Louis's turn to snort. "So, how long will you be in town?" Brooke asked him.

"A couple of days," he answered.

"You should come to a party that a girl from school is having tomorrow night," Brooke told him, and she tried not to react when Ash kicked her under the table.

He started to rub his chin. "I don't know," he said. "Don't want to risk getting caught in another police raid."

"There won't be," Brooke told him.

"Well then, I guess I'll show up," he drawled with a grin. "I'll bring beer. Unless it's not that kind of party?"

"No, that would be wicked cool," Brooke said with what she hoped was a flirty smile. Ash rolled her eyes.

The girls paid, and they left the diner. "Where are you two heading?" Louis asked.

"Friend's house," Brooke said, and this time she hissed when Ash hit her arm.

"Don't tell him that," Ash growled, but Louis just nodded in agreement.

"No, no, I get it. Don't tell the stranger where you're going," Louis turned while raising his hand. "Stranger danger, girls." He wagged a finger, pointing up into the night sky. "Stranger danger is no joke."

The girls made it to Tina's house and crashed in her basement. Tina was annoying, but she wouldn't tell a soul that they were there, and then they could go straight to school in the morning. Ash turned to Brooke with a pissed-off expression once they were settled on the floor with the lights out. "Why did you tell him about the party?"

"Look, he saved us tonight. I figured we owed him a favor," Brooke hissed back.

"We don't know him," Ash argued.

"He's a cool guy," Brooke spat back.

"I don't like the way he was looking at you, alright?" Ash actually shivered. "Like an animal hunting for prey. It was creepy."

"Oh, calm down," Brooke told her best friend. "He's leaving in a few days. No reason to worry." She got as comfortable as she could on the floor and went to sleep while Ash stayed awake, worrying at her lip.

.....

The girls went to school the next day, where nothing happened until Brooke got her test back from Mr. Hyde in history, a big fat, red F on the top of her paper. She went home, showered, and changed, knowing she had to at least have dinner with her parents before leaving for the party. Her father was buried in a book while her mother was on the phone as they ate. Brooke could almost make it out of the dining room before her mom said anything to her. "Oh, honey, how was that history test?"

"I haven't gotten it back from my teacher yet," she lied. "But I'm pretty sure I got a B, at least."

"Good," her mother drawled, sipping on some wine. "We wouldn't want you to have to go to summer school; we have plans to go to Europe next summer, right, dear?"

Brooke's father just grunted, not looking up from his book.

"Going to, whats-her-name's, for a party tonight, right, honey?" Brooke's mom asked, not really reacting to her husband's non-answer.

"Yes, mom," Brooke sighed, wanting to get away from the conversation.

"Have fun, be back by 11," her mother said, and Brooke made her escape.

Once they got to the party, Brooke stayed close to the front door, looking up every time it opened. Ash frowned at her at one point. "He's not coming," she yelled over the music.

"Who?" Brooke asked innocently.

"Louis, from last night. He's not coming to a party full of high school kids."

Just then, the door opened, and a football star yelled into the crowd. "Look, everyone, punk rock Eddie Murphy is here!"

"Look, everyone, tall Danny DeVito is here!" Louis shot back without pause. The football star scowled as the teenagers around them laughed, and Brooke rushed to rescue Louis.

"Hey! You made it!" she said with a smile. She looked down at the two packs of beer he was holding. "And you brought beer!"

The crowd cheered at her statement, and Louis was allowed to make his way back to the kitchen. He grabbed two beers before the masses descended onto the rest like wild animals. Louis grinned as he handed one to Brooke, ignoring Ash's glare.

They stayed for a few hours, dancing and moving to the music—too much noise for them to talk.

"Would you like to hang out tomorrow night?" Brooke suddenly asked, leaning into Louis so she could yell into his ear. "My parents will be out of the house," she added. "We can have a nice night," she paused, reaching out to put one hand on his arm, "alone."

"Brooke!" Ash cried. She had leaned in close enough to overhear what Brooke said.

"Stop listening in on our conversation!" she yelled back but stopped when Louis touched her hand.

"No, she's right," he said with a sad smile. "You shouldn't be hanging out with someone you don't know."

Brooke pouted. "Fine," she said, fighting the urge to stomp her foot. She had a thought and then went to the bathroom, writing something down.

Soon, Ash was tugging on her arm to leave. "I have to go," Brooke told Louis, once again leaning in close to talk over the music. She pressed something into his palm, a scrap of paper with her address on it. "Hope to see you soon," she said, trying to give him a coy smile.

"You just want to sleep with him because he's black," Ash scolded her as they walked home.

Brooke scowled at her friend. "Racist much?" she spat back. There, that was mature, pointing out her friend's prejudice.

Ashley huffed. "No, I'm not. I am just trying to make sure you don't get hurt."

Brooke smiled at her friend. "Look, it's just one night. He's a cool guy, and I'm old enough to hang out with whoever I want to. I am 16."

Ash sighed. "I'm not going to convince you not to, am I?"

"No, you're not," Brooke said with a wicked smirk.

.....

Brooke waited for her parents to leave on pins and needles, worrying that Louis would show up before they left. But finally, her mother was dressed and ready to go, and she stood by the door to give them both a light kiss on the cheek before they took a limo to some gala the museum was holding. Brooke slowly made her way to the kitchen, making a snack before sneaking into a small office off the hallway. She flipped a switch, and the security system powered down, and she smiled. She would tell her father that the power went out; she had done it before.

She got ready, dressing in short shorts and a tight shirt, waiting for a sign that Louis had decided to come after all. When she heard a light knock on the door an hour after her parents left, she flew down the stairs. She checked the peephole and did a little dance in the foyer. She made herself calm down and then opened the door as cooly as she could. "Hi," she said.

"Hello," he purred back, tall and dark and handsome.

"Come in," she said, stepping back to let him inside. He strolled in but froze when he saw the camera in the foyer.

"Is that on?" he asked.

"Hell no," she replied. "I turned them off."

"You can do that?" he asked.

"Oh yeah," she said, taking his arm. "Come on, let's go upstairs."

She dragged him up the stairs, pushing him into her room. "When will your parents be home?" he asked.

"Later," she said. "The galas at the museum go on for *hours*." She studied him as he looked around her room, with its music and movie posters and pictures of her and Ash. "We will be alone for a while."

"Uh-huh," he said. He had found Brooke's boombox and was looking through her cassettes.

"There isn't any Duran Duran if that is what you're looking for," she joked, but he only grunted in return. He looked upset, and Brooke was losing the self-confidence that had made her invite him in the first place. She suddenly crossed the room and grabbed his hands, pulling him down so she could kiss him. He was stiff, and it was awkward, but suddenly he relaxed and brought his hands up to her face, kissing her back. She moaned and stretched up. Her nerve came back, and she felt like she had made the right decision. He broke off the kiss and leaned back, Brooke feeling her face burn.

"You have never done this before, have you?" he asked, running his thumbs across her cheeks. She blushed harder.

"Y-yes, I have," she lied.

He gave her a sad smile. "I'm sorry," he said before he pushed her onto the bed.

"H-hey!" she cried. "Easy! You don't h-have to be so rough!" She tried to smile, to show him that she wasn't upset, but her stomach dropped when he ripped the phone cord out of the wall and started to wrap it around his hands.

Oh shit.

She tried to scramble back to get some distance between them, but he grabbed one of her legs and pulled her closer. She started to fight, kicking wildly, and Brooke thought one of her feet connected with his stomach, but he didn't stop. She tried to scream while he flipped her, but once he finished tying her hands, he secured a bandana around her head. She kicked and struggled, but the gag didn't disappear, and he flipped her back on her back.

He looked down at her, a sad look on his face, while Brooke screamed and cursed through the gag. "I am *really* sorry," he murmured, and Brooke felt terror claw at her throat. But instead of hurting her, he got up and left her room, running down the steps.

Brooke felt some relief. He wasn't there to hurt her. Just to rob the house. She started twisting her hands, trying to get free.

·····

Tommy flew down the stairs, glancing at the cameras. He hoped that Brooke wasn't lying and that they were off. What he had to do wouldn't take long.

He found the office on the first floor and took a moment to look around the room after opening the door. There were movable panels against the far wall, each with three or four paintings hanging on them. He inhaled deeply, letting his nose guide him to the left. He moved the panels until he found the one that gave off the sour smell of magic.

He found the painting almost immediately. It was easy if you knew what it was: a woman walking through a forest, petite and blonde, with a red robe, her hair blowing out behind her. Animals surrounded her, but it was the weirdest menagerie ever to grace a painting. A bear was to her right, a bull to her left, a snake wrapped around her arm, a wolf by her side, and a bat on her shoulder. Three black dogs were walking in front of her, jumping and looking up at her in admiration. It seemed so wholesome and pure, but it made Tommy's skin crawl. "Hello, you bitch," he murmured as he picked up the tiny painting. "I really hope I get to burn this later."

He was stepping out of the office, not paying attention when the golf club whistled by his ear. He ducked as it became lodged in the office door. Brooke struggled to get it out, her eyes red, her hair an absolute mess, but Tommy was impressed he got out of her bounds so quickly. He was surprised that she was fighting him and not running or calling the police. "Brooke!" he cried.

"Don't you talk to me, you *asshole!*" she yelled, finally getting the golf club loose, and Tommy had to duck again as it went flying over his head. He felt it brush his mohawk this time. "You put that painting back right *now!*"

"I would if I could," he said, backing up towards the front door with his free hand up. "You don't have to hurt me."

"*Ha!*" she barked out. "And let my parents know I let you in? At least if I catch you for the police, they won't kill me for letting you take the painting."

"That's just it. You don't have to," he said softly. Brooke stopped and blinked, and he kept moving back slowly. "Tell them that the power went off, the cameras stopped recording, and someone broke in and took a painting. Just one." She glared at him, but he could see that the story was winning her over. "I get away with what I want, and you can play innocent victim to your parents."

She stepped forward and swung at him, but there was very little effort behind the swing. He was giving her a way out. They stood like that for a few long moments, a nearby grandfather clock ticking away the seconds. She finally let the golf club drop a few feet before she sighed. "I'll give you a minute before I turn the cameras back on and call the police."

"Thank you," he said. He kept backing up, not turning his back on her.

He had his hand on the doorknob when he heard her whisper. "Stranger danger, my ass."

Tommy gave her a sad smile. "It really is no joke." And he opened the door and ran into the night.

.....

Tommy ran to a nearby hotel as nearly old as him and expensive as hell. One of the workers kept a back door open for smoke breaks, and Tommy went in without hesitation. Kitchen staff and cleaners looked at him in curiosity, but no one stopped him. Maybe it was his murderous scowl that kept them from bothering him.

He took a service elevator to the top floor, and he pounded on a door to one of the most expensive suites available. An acolyte opened the door, and Tommy pushed past him, determined to talk to the leader of the Acolytes. He didn't have to look long.

Wilkes was eating in the main room, some steak smothered in a thick sauce, wine glass full, and a gramophone playing opera nearby. The man had only gotten fatter over the years, and Tommy glared as he took a bite of food and chewed. The acolyte tried to grab Tommy's arm and pull him back, but Tommy snatched his arm back and growled. The other man jumped and took a step back.

"It's alright, York," Wilkes called out with a smile. "Let him in. He has something for me."

Tommy stomped into the room and flung that painting at Wilkes. It hit the wine glass and made it go flying. Wilkes made a slight sound of distress over his spilled drink, but he was grinning when he picked up the painting and inspected it. "Don't fucking ever make me do something like that again!" Tommy shouted at Wilkes, pointing a threatening finger at the large man.

York glared, but Wilkes just gave the changeling a lecherous grin. "Oh, I was just making sure you had some fun," he said.

"She is sixteen years old!" Tommy yelled back, and he took a step forward, planning on punching Wilkes, knowing that the band on his arm would stop him, but dammit, he was going to try. York tried to stop him, and Tommy shoved the enforcer away.

"Hey now," Wilkes said loudly, still not looking concerned or angry. Instead, he took out a sharp blade and looked over the back of the painting. "There is no need to fight. The worst is over. The deed is done." He gave Tommy another oily grin. "Unless you didn't seduce her as I ordered."

Tommy lifted his left arm and pulled back the jacket sleeve as far as it would go, showing the glowing edge of the slave band. Wilkes threw his head back and laughed. "So you, what? Stole the painting with her knowledge?"

"I didn't have any choice," Tommy said.

Wilkes chuckled and made a motion with his free hand at York. York, looking like he had sucked on a lemon, went to grab a clean wine glass for his leader. "You always have a choice," Wilkes said. "Listen to orders, and the band will stop troubling you. Or don't, and the band will hurt more. Besides, would you rather I sent Guerra in and killed the whole family to get what we want?"

Wilkes ran the blade across the canvas, exposing a pocket behind the painting itself. He gently reached in and brought out a piece of paper. "Well, however you accomplished your goals tonight, Thomas, you did a wonderful job." He looked up and smiled at the changeling as York poured him a new glass of wine, Tommy just scowling back. "You can have the night off. Relax. We leave in the morning to go back home."

"Is that what you wanted?" Tommy asked, gesturing at the paper. "Not the painting but just a piece of paper?"

"Oh, it's more than a piece of paper, Thomas," Wilkes said as he cut a bit of steak and took a bite, humming at the taste. "It is the key to freeing our Lady. And I will go down in history as the one who brought her back."

"You know that will make you the most hated man in the history of sorcerers, right?" Tommy asked, crossing his arms.

"Ah, but my good changeling," Wilkes countered as he picked up his glass. "That means that everyone will have heard of me."

8

Guerra was passing by the second bedroom on the second story of the acolyte mansion when he happened to look inside to see the lady of the house furiously packing a suitcase. She looked upset. Correction, she looked infuriated, moving so fast from one side of the room to the next that her dress flared out behind her. He generally avoided talking to her as they had nothing to discuss, but curiosity got the better of him, and he stepped inside the bedroom. "Bella signora," he greeted her. "How are you this evening?"

"Don't you start that shit with me," she growled, rounding on him with a finger in his face. He blinked and leaned back, shocked at her behavior. She was generally a nice and calm woman.

Guerra hesitated at her tone but smiled at her, his brightest one. Unfortunately, it never reached his eyes. "What do you mean, my lady?"

"I just heard one of your associates talking about attacking someone, possibly killing them. I don't know what is going on, but I am out of here, and I'm going to the police," she explained while snapping the suitcase shut. She started to step past him, suitcase in one hand, but he reached out and grabbed her upper arm.

"I'm afraid I can't let you do that, bella signora," he stated, trying to smile even as rage surged through his veins. He didn't know who talked in front of her, but he was going to find them and teach them a lesson in secrecy.

She frowned, and then her eyes went wide in fear. She pulled her arm out of Guerra's grip, but he just seized her throat with the same hand instead. She made a gurgling noise, something that

probably would have been a yelp if he was not currently choking the life out of her, and dropped the suitcase.

She clawed at his hand at her throat and started to reach for his face with the other, but he just grabbed her wrist and kept her from scratching him. He continued smiling at her, even as he glowed red and set her nerves on fire. He felt most alive when he was causing pain to others, the fear and anguish in their eyes sending a thrill down his spine. He lifted her and hauled her to the balcony to make sure no one in the mansion could hear her.

Guerra stopped at the railing, pushing her so that she was leaning over the edge. Her feet kicked out even as he turned his power up. What she was feeling must be pure torture, but Guerra was impressed by her fighting spirit.

He held her there for several long and tense moments, reveling in her panic and fear. He wasn't an empath, but when he used his power like this, without restraint, and saw his playthings writhe, he could nearly imagine their agony. Ecstasy flooded his system even as the pain overwhelmed theirs. Guerra still wasn't sure why they died. Did their hearts stop? Did their brains overload from the sensation? Either way, she finally went limp, and he almost felt relief that her suffering was finally over.

Almost.

Guerra let her body go, and she tumbled over the edge of the railing to the ground below. He watched in detached indifference as her body landed with a thump. *She was beautiful at that moment, hair around her face like a halo. Her necklace had caught his hand and broken, the beads surrounding her, the only sign that something was amiss and that she wasn't currently sleeping. The fall should have broken her neck, which would be the story everyone would believe. She fell, she died, life went on.*

Now, to find the one who couldn't keep his mouth shut.

. . . . .

Akrur sat up, panting, rubbing at his throat as the dream faded. The same blasted one again, with the woman in the blue dress. Akrur could not shake the feeling he knew her, even as he swore that he had never met her before in his entire life.

Guerra knew who she was, and the sense of familiarity had made its way to Akrur; that was all it was. It had to be.

He slowly got up, groaning as he rubbed his eyes. It would fade; memories that he accidentally took from others always did. Soon this woman and her tragic demise would be a distant, unpleasant bump in his recollection.

Akrur stood up, stretching and yawning. He showered, shaved, and dressed with quick ease. Everything in his room was his and safe, from clothes to books to linens. He didn't have to worry about a sudden reading and learning a horrible secret. Even the things that did hold memories, like a pocket watch given to him by his father or the soft maroon sweater that Abby gave him, kept pleasant memories for him, not the severe shock of pain or suffering. The gloves were the last thing he put on, his armor against his uncontrollable ability. They saved him so much pain but caused so much at the same time.

He was crossing the common room to the kitchen when he spotted them—Chrysta and Tommy sleeping on the couch. The couch was the biggest one they had, but there was barely any room for two people to use it simultaneously. That didn't stop the two from cuddling together; Chrysta's head was on Tommy's shoulder, slightly snoring, Tommy's nose buried in her hair.

Akrur frowned at the two figures on the couch. Being in charge of teenagers meant sometimes you had to break them apart before things got too physical. He was no stranger to finding two kids in a heated snog session; he had even used a cold bucket of water on two separate occasions to break them up when he discovered the couples in the greenhouse. It was natural, really, with all the hormones in the air. He had been keeping an eye on Kevin and Rimsha for that very reason, with the way Kevin pined after the girl.

But this? This was different. Sure, they were touching, but they had their clothes on. Their hands were not on any inappropriate parts. But it felt so *intimate*, in a way that made Akrur feel a stab of jealousy for a fleeting moment.

He flicked one of Tommy's feet, making the changeling jerk. Tommy blinked and looked around the room, his eyes settling on Akrur. He glared but froze when Chrysta made a slight sound of distress. Akrur jerked a thumb towards the kitchen, and Tommy silently nodded in understanding.

Tommy started to get off the couch, slowly extracting himself like he was moving a ticking bomb and not a sleeping girl. Once he was vertical, Tommy made sure Chrysta was covered and then gently moved some hair off her face. She murmured but didn't stir. Poe clacked his beak and then tucked his head under his wing.

Once in the kitchen, Akrur propped the door open so he could keep an eye on Chrysta. "What exactly do you think you're doing?" he asked with a scowl.

The changeling scowled back. "I found her on the couch last night when I got back. She had a nightmare and was making things float, so I woke her up. She was having trouble getting back to sleep, so I stayed out here with her."

Akrur hummed. "Ah yes, stayed with her, on the couch. How very hospitable of you. I have a few rules here, Mr. Monroe, and 'no shenanigans' is on the top of that list."

"Is that what the kids are calling it these days?" Tommy joked, giving the empath a wide grin.

Akrur glared and held a finger up. "You know what I mean. May I remind you, if people find out about you, Chrysta will be the one to suffer if they think you two have a romantic relationship?"

Tommy winced and actually looked ashamed for a second. "I know, okay," he said while rubbing his neck. "I tried to tell her that last night. But I made her a promise; I wouldn't leave unless she wanted me to."

Akrur blinked. "Alright, fine," he said. "But I don't want to find you two on the couch again, you understand?"

"Fine," Tommy spat. "I get it. The dirty changeling will keep his hands to himself."

"That's not..." Akrur started to say but then sighed. "I'm sorry, that was not what I meant. I am just trying to make sure Chrysta doesn't get hurt."

Tommy relaxed, going back to rubbing his neck. "Yeah. Yeah, you're right. She doesn't understand how sorcerers work."

They fell into an uncomfortable silence. After a moment, Tommy held up a finger. "I have something for you," he said and walked out of the kitchen to the guest room.

By the time Tommy had returned to the kitchen, Akrur had started the coffee maker. Tommy reached out with something, and Akrur instinctively put his hand out for it. "Here," Tommy stated as he dropped a bundle in Akrur's hand. "For room and board for Chrysta and me."

Akrur studied it and blinked in surprise when he realized what it was: a whole lot of money rolled into a bundle. "What is this?" he asked as he peeled a fifty-dollar bill off the top.

"Money."

Akrur snorted. "Well, obviously. How much?"

"A thousand bucks," Tommy said nonchalantly.

Akrur replaced the bill and tossed it back to the changeling. "Keep it," he said. "The Academy pays for everything. It's not unlimited, but having two more people is not a burden on the budget." He paused after pouring some coffee into a cup. "How many of those do you have?"

"Ten," Tommy said, opening the fridge to inspect what was inside.

"Well, keep it hidden in your room, alright? None of the kids nick stuff, but that is a lot of money to have just lying around."

Tommy nodded as he grabbed the eggs. Akrur checked his watch and went to the front door, opening it to examine the welcome mat. He leaned on the door frame until a *pop* sounded, and a newspaper appeared out of thin air and dropped with a *thump*. "You're late," he scolded the paper before picking it up and returning to the kitchen.

Tommy was mixing the eggs in a bowl as Akrur sat down and opened the paper. "Is that the sorcerer newspaper?"

"The Rising Phoenix? You know about it?" Akrur asked.

"Yeah, some of the acolytes got it delivered to them. I would read them if they left them lying around."

Akrur scowled at the paper. "They can't teleport it to me on time, but they send it to members of an evil organization with no problems? Typical."

Tommy snorted and turned back to the stove. By the time he placed a plate of crepes on the table, Akrur had read through the main article *(Saving the Dragons of Asia: Keeping a Highway Project From Completion)*, skipped over the daily fluff piece *(Which Animals Make the Best Familiars?)*, and marked an article Abby may enjoy (*Magical or Non-Magical Cosmetic Surgery: Which Is Better?*). Akrur's stomach rumbled, and he patted it. "You and Kevin are conspiring to make me fat," he said while smiling.

Tommy gave him a grin while placing empty plates on the table. "Always liked cooking, just couldn't do much of it while living on the streets."

Tommy let Akrur get a few bites in of the fruit- and cream cheesed-stuffed crepe, humming in delight at the taste before he cleared his throat. "Burke wants to talk to Chrysta this afternoon. He said we should be there too."

"You and me?" Akrur asked. Tommy nodded. "Probably wanting to talk about Chrysta's training."

"Will he be able to help her?" Tommy asked.

"He may be the only one who can," Akrur said, and right on cue, Chrysta whimpered in her sleep from the couch. Tommy and Akrur watched as several items in the room glowed gold and started to levitate. Poor Poe, who had been sleeping on the back of the couch, squawked as he began to float too. Tommy got up from the table, possibly to wake her up, but Akrur grabbed his arm and shook his head. Chrysta took a deep breath and relaxed, and the items around the room dropped. Poe gave a loud croak and then flew to the kitchen table, clicking his beak at Tommy in distress. Tommy rubbed the bird's head and settled back down in his chair.

"Is that normal?" Tommy asked.

"Young sorcerers can have problems controlling their abilities, and strong emotions can make it worse. Of course, we are talking about someone who glows gold. Her level of normal is not something that anyone has seen in centuries." Akrur took a bite of his crepes. "Burke has had four apprentices that I am aware of. Each of them gained mastery of their abilities in an extremely brief amount of time. If anyone can help her, it's him."

Tommy didn't say anything. He just nodded and went back to eating. Several minutes later, Akrur heard a door close, and Rosa walked to the kitchen, giving Chrysta a curious glance. She leaned on the doorframe while stretching her arms about her head, dressed in her warm jogging gear. "Alright, Mr. Cross, I'm heading out for my run."

"Be safe, my dear," he responded, taking a sip of coffee.

Rosa paused and sniffed at the air. "Are those crepes?" she asked.

"Yep," Tommy said with a grin. He pushed the plate forward, still piled high with sugared goodness. "Have some."

Rosa nibbled at her lip. "Well, I do need the energy to run." And then she sat down to serve herself.

Akrur waited for a few minutes for Rosa to take several bites before asking. "So, how many times did Chrysta wake you up last night?"

Rosa held up three fingers as she chewed. After she swallowed, she added. "After the third nightmare, she said she would come out here to sleep."

Akrur hummed. "And she was making things levitate when you got back?" he asked Tommy. The changeling nodded. "That settles it then; after Abby checks on you, I'll have her give Chrysta a sleep potion."

"I thought you said that wouldn't work on Chrysta?" Tommy asked.

"It may work for one night, which we may need to make sure Chrysta doesn't hurt anyone. The others are due back this evening, and I don't want to risk any injuries if Chrysta's nightmares get worse."

While he was talking, Chrysta started to stir and sat up on the couch. Akrur stopped talking, and the trio watched as Chrysta got up and stretched. She began to walk to the girls' room, wrapping the blanket around her, turning her shape from a small girl to a lumpy creature. When she came back out and finished in the bathroom, she finally joined them at the table, and she tried handing something to Akrur. He put his hand out, and she dropped a bundle of money into his palm.

"What is this, Miss York?" he asked.

"Money for letting me and Tommy stay here," she said with a yawn. She shrugged shyly. "I know it's not much, but it's about half of what I have."

Akrur folded the money up and handed it back to her. Tommy was smiling with his eyebrows raised. *More alike than they realize,* Akrur thought to himself. "Keep it, my dear," he said with a grin. "Your money is no good here."

"Okay," she said quietly. She looked at the food and hummed. "Did you make these, Rosa?"

"Nope, they're mine," Tommy said.

Chrysta took a bite and moaned. "They're good," she told the grinning changeling. She tried to reach out to pat Poe on the head, but the bird hopped away from her. "What's wrong, Poe?"

"You were making him float for a little bit," Tommy explained. "He's probably just mad."

"Oh, I'm sorry, Poe," she whispered. "Can I give him an egg? He loves hard-boiled ones."

"I got it, beautiful," Tommy said as he got up and put his plate in the sink.

"So, Mr. Burke wants to talk to us later?" Chrysta asked Tommy as he started to boil some water.

"Yes, we will head out as soon as Abby gets to take a look at you two," Akrur explained.

Chrysta nodded, looking pensive. "Do you think she can help with the dreams?"

"I don't know, my dear, but if anyone can advise us on the best course of action, it's her."

Chrysta didn't respond and went back to her plate of crepes. By the time Tommy put a hard-boiled egg in front of the raven, Rosa had gotten up for her run with a promise to do the dishes when she got back. "Has she been treating you well?" Akrur asked Chrysta as soon as he was sure Rosa was gone.

"Rosa? She's been fine," Chrysta replied.

"Why would she bother Chrysta?" Tommy asked, looking back and forth between them.

"Rosa says it was my father that killed her family," Chrysta said softly. Tommy winced in sympathy.

"Both of Rosa's parents were former hunters and could control fire as their abilities," Akrur said. He drank the last of his coffee and examined the bottom of the cup like the solution to all their problems would be there. "It would have taken a powerful sorcerer to stop them."

"Or a sorcerer who can stop others' magic," Tommy said with a frown.

"Exactly," Akrur confirmed.

Just then, the door to the outside opened, and Abby came through. Akrur noticed her pink cheeks from across the common room. "Hello!" she called out as she took off her cloak and boots, setting a piece of luggage down next to the coat rack. She made her way to the kitchen and gave everyone a big smile. "How is everyone this morning?"

"Doing good," Tommy replied. He gestured to the crepes. "Sit down and have some breakfast."

"Oh, I really shouldn't," she said, sitting down next to Chrysta. "I'm on a diet."

"Oh, come on, Abby, you must try them. They're really delicious," Akrur told her.

"No, just coffee for me, thanks."

"She's rejecting the crepes," Tommy said, looking shocked. He turned to Akrur. "How can she say no to crepes?"

"I'm not sure; she may not be human," Akrur said seriously, getting up to grab a cup of coffee for Abby and to refill his own.

Chrysta giggled while Abby glared at Tommy and Akrur. "Fine, I will try just one," she said while finally taking a plate from Tommy. She took a bite and hummed. "Well, maybe more than one."

While Abby pulled Tommy into the common room to examine his arm better, Chrysta went into the girls' room to change. Tommy kept sipping his coffee while Abby twisted his left arm this way and that. Akrur sat on the arm of the couch to watch in fascination. It was the first time Akrur had seen Tommy's bare arm since Abby removed the slave band a few nights ago.

And boy, it was a bloody mess.

Dozens, if not hundreds, of scars crisscrossed his arm, newer dark, raised marks covering older light, flat ones. Some as thick as a finger, some as thin as a hair. It looked like he had inserted his arm into a blender. The only indication that the scars were abnormal was the fact that the injuries stopped right where the band ended, one perfectly straight line around his wrist and one line an inch from his elbow. Abby looked grim as she studied them, but Tommy's expression stayed neutral.

"Any pain?" she asked softly.

"Nope," Tommy answered. "It was kind of itchy for a bit, but that was it."

Abby hummed. "You said the arm was numb."

"Yeah, from the elbow down, but now it's mostly the fingers."

"Amazing," Abby murmured. "There were some open wounds on this arm just a few days ago, and now everything is completely healed." She finally let Tommy's arm go. "I'm afraid I can't do anything for the scars. My magic can't heal them. I can give you some medicine that may help, though."

"I would appreciate it," Tommy softly said as Chrysta came out of the bedroom. She had changed into a pair of jeans and a sweater, braiding her own hair as she joined them. "Although, it might be cool to keep them."

"Why is that?" Chrysta asked.

"Changelings don't get scars. We heal too fast," Tommy said, rolling down his sleeve.

Abby grabbed what looked like a hairpin from her bag. "Let's check the numbness real quick."

Tommy covered his eyes with his right hand, holding out his left one. Abby started to poke the appendage gently, beginning with the pinky finger. Tommy didn't react as Abby went down his palm towards his wrist. She tried the ring finger with the same results. It wasn't until she poked his middle finger did he say a flat "Ow." He twitched as she checked his palm and, finally, the pointer finger. Abby's lips were thin as she stopped and put the hairpin back in her bag.

"Why didn't you try the other fingers?" Tommy asked as he uncovered his eyes.

"I did them first," Abby admitted.

Tommy scowled at his hand. "Ah," he simply said.

"What does that mean?" Chrysta asked, looking between Abby and Tommy.

"Nerve damage. Probably caused by the band when it put Tommy in a coma. Again, if I could, I would use my magic to heal it, but unfortunately, only time can fix it." She shrugged sadly. "It could take days or weeks. I can't tell."

Tommy flexed his fingers. "I haven't tried to play my violin since I woke up," he said softly, and he left to go to the guest room. When Tommy came back, he put his instrument under his chin and started to play.

Akrur didn't know what he was playing, but it sounded beautiful. It was slow and started to build, Tommy swaying slightly as he played. A few moments after he began, he hit a sour note, and he frowned but soldiered on. He let the music die after he made a second mistake.

"That was beautiful," Abby breathed in the silence.

"It was shit," Tommy growled. And he looked like he was about to throw the violin, but he leaned it against his hip instead.

"He made a lot of mistakes," Chrysta confirmed. She bit her lip, studying Tommy's face as he frowned at the violin. "Do you think you will be able to play again?"

"Don't know," Tommy said. "I will have to practice, maybe change hands." He looked up, and his expression changed to surprise. "What's wrong, beautiful?"

"You can't play because of me," Chrysta said, looking miserable. "Protecting me is why you lost the feeling in your hand."

"Hey now," Tommy said while pulling Chrysta into a hug. "If it's being able to play the violin or having you around to play Paganini for me, I'll choose the

Paganini every time, beautiful." He kissed Chrysta on the forehead, and she gave him a small, sad smile.

Akrur glanced at Abby, expecting her to look upset at the small show of affection, but she just smiled at the couple. She reached out to squeeze Chrysta's arm. "I'm heading out of the country for a few days, but when I get back, I will help Tommy with some physical therapy, I promise."

"Come on," Akrur said. "Let's not keep the Headmaster waiting." Chrysta and Tommy nodded.

They went to the coat rack, Tommy getting his boots and jacket on while Chrysta put on one of Kevin's old parkas. It was so large on her that she looked like a giant marshmallow with arms and legs. Abby took her time with her boots and gloves, so Akrur stayed with her as Chrysta and Tommy went outside, Poe taking off with a loud croak. Finally, Abby picked up her luggage, and Akrur opened the door for her.

It had snowed the night before, leaving at least two feet of snow on the ground, but the sky was clear and bright. Poe was flying over them, making lazy circles. There was a path in the snow from where Tommy had pushed through it, Chrysta a few feet behind him, trudging through the snow with her arms out for balance. Tommy said something, and she laughed a light sound. She had been quiet the last few days, and it was nice to hear her laughter. Akrur watched them closely.

Abby poked him, making him jump. "Alright, what's up?" she asked.

"What do you mean?"

"The sour look. You look like you have something that's bothering you."

Akrur sighed. She was so good at reading him, always had been. "I found those two this morning," he said, gesturing at Chrysta and Tommy, "on the couch, sleeping." Chrysta almost fell, but Tommy caught her arm. Chrysta laughed again and took his arm, and they finally made it to the gardens.

Akrur expected Abby to look shocked, maybe angry, but she gave him a perplexed look instead. "And?" she asked.

"And what?" he shot back.

"And were they naked? Kissing? Something worse?"

"Well, no," he admitted. "But really, sleeping together like that is…" he trailed off, waving his hands around to try to make the correct word appear from thin air.

"Akrur, you were the one who invited him to stay here," she said.

"Yes, but as a friend. I didn't think I would have to worry about any exophilia going on."

She laughed, crossing her arms in front of her. "I seriously doubt that is what they are thinking about right now. You are talking about two people who have gone through a very traumatic experience together."

"One girl and one changeling," Akrur corrected her.

Abby glared at him. "Oh, don't you start that."

"Start what?" he asked.

"Judging someone based on what they are, not what they have done."

Akrur puffed up. "Bloody hell, woman, this is slightly different than what the kids go through."

Abby hummed, still glaring. Her eyebrows went up. "I know what this is," she said as she started to pull off one of her gloves. "You can't read him, so you don't trust him. Anyone else, you would have used your ability by now and know what their intentions were. Would it help if you had a character witness?"

Abby held out her fingers, a casual gesture but one that held so much weight to it. Akrur looked at her offered hand and sighed. He tugged his glove off with his teeth and, after some hesitation, gently laced his fingers with hers. She was one of the few people he trusted doing this, outside of his own family, because she was so careful with her emotions. He was transported to that night, and the imagery flooded his senses—

Tommy, in his other form, looking like something out of a nightmare, with teeth and claws and tail, and Akrur could sense the fear that Abby felt at that moment, mixed with a bit of pity and curiosity, of course, it would be like her to want to know more about someone in pain and not think about how there was a bloody changeling *in her kitchen*

"Let me die, turn me into dust. I don't care. But she doesn't deserve it."

—Akrur grunted and broke off his contact with Abby, trying not to think about how soft and warm her hand was. Instead, he glared at the two figures off in the distance. Chrysta and Tommy were in the gardens, turned to look at the two adults, probably wondering what was taking them so long. "I don't doubt his devotion to her, Abby," he said while getting his glove back on. "I just don't think their relationship should be *romantic*, that's all."

Abby gave him a soft smile. "She glows gold, Akrur," she said. "I hate to say it because I know your ego won't like to hear it, but at some point, your opinion will probably not mean that much to her."

He made a slight growl. "Maybe you're right," he admitted slowly. He considered the two figures. "But may the gods help him if he ever hurts her."

"Hurting her is the farthest thing from his mind," Abby stated with a smile, putting her glove back on. She picked up her luggage and sighed.

Akrur looked her up and down while she picked some lint off her arm, and she wouldn't notice his gaze. Dark jeans that hugged her figure, a blue sweater that brought out the color of her eyes, a dark brown cloak that matched her hair, with matching leather boots and gloves. He wanted to tell her how beautiful she looked, but he gestured to the luggage instead. "So, where are you heading this time?" he asked.

"Russia," she said. "A group of kids decided to play with curses and then couldn't reverse one of them. When they tried to break it, it went back to the one who cast the curse."

Akrur snorted. "Serves them right."

Abby glared at him. It was an old disagreement that they had had before. "Come on, Akrur, are you saying you never did anything stupid as a kid?"

"Oh, I did plenty of stupid things when I was a child," he said, offering his arm to the healer. "I just was never stupid enough to put a curse on anyone."

Abby hummed as she took the offered elbow. "Well, stupid or not, his parents reached out to me, so I'm heading there as a curse eater."

"Just be careful, yeah?" he asked.

"Always," she stated with a smile.

They plodded through the snow, using the trail Tommy and Chrysta left behind. Poe dropped from the sky and settled on Chrysta's shoulder as they entered the gardens. "Cold!" he cawed, and Chrysta smiled at the raven and scratched his chest.

They opened the doors into the Academy, Tommy pausing to let out a thunderous sneeze. "Are you okay? Are you getting sick?" Abby asked.

"No," Tommy said as he sniffed. "The scent of magic is too strong here."

"I'm sorry, the scent of what?" Akrur asked as he helped Chrysta shrug off the parka.

"Magic."

"Magic has an odor?" Abby asked, and the changeling nodded. "What does it smell like?"

"Sour," Tommy explained. "Like something rotting."

"Interesting," Abby said.

"So that is how changelings can find sorcerers," Akrur mused.

"Yep, you guys tend to stink to high heaven."

"Now you are making me want to take another shower," Abby joked, and while Chrysta was laughing, she turned with a wave, probably going to the front of the building, where a transportation spell would take her where she wanted to go. The rest of them turned to Burke's tower, bidding her farewell.

Akrur guided Chrysta to the lift while Tommy started to ascend the stairs. "I will not miss doing this climb," he grumbled, keeping himself level with the car.

"Do you think Mr. Burke trusts you after all those questions?" Chrysta called out to him.

"Well, he trusts me enough to let me keep my head," Tommy joked. Or, at least, Akrur hoped he was joking.

The lift had made it to the top of the tower, and Akrur rolled the door open for Chrysta but paused when he spotted a figure waiting for them at the bottom of the final flight of stairs. Tommy had made it to the landing and paused as well, eyeing the woman. Akrur felt a slight finger of fear go up his back.

"Good morning, Director Zheng," Akrur said brightly as he stepped off the lift. "It's a pleasure to see you today."

Director Zheng gave him a small smile, and he suddenly felt like a young child who was found with chocolate smeared on his face before supper. She was a lovely woman, even with the crow's feet at the corner of her eyes and the lines etched around her mouth. Her hair was silver with streaks of white in it, and she wore it in a long braid that almost reached her lower back. She was wearing the high-waisted black pants and the white long-sleeved shirt of the hunter uniform, but she had replaced the short black jacket with a long purple one, letting it hang off her shoulders unbuttoned. The black sword hung from her hip, and her left hand was lightly resting on the hilt. "Cross," Zheng said in the same tone he had used, "why are you always in the middle of trouble when it comes knocking at the Academy's door?"

"I'm innocent this time," Akrur said with a shrug, not sure how much the director knew at this point. "Just trying to support Abby in her hour of need."

"Spoken like a true man in love," Zheng said with a smirk, and Akrur blinked in surprise. Akrur opened his mouth to give a retort, but Zheng turned to Chrysta with a smile. "Hello, my dear. I'm assuming you are Chrysta York?"

"Yes, ma'am," Chrysta said, giving the older woman a smile in return.

"I'm Jiao Zheng, Director of the Hunter Organization. It is a pleasure to meet you in person." Director Zheng held out her hand, and Chrysta shook it.

"I thought Burke was keeping the fact that Chrysta was here a secret?" Tommy asked with a scowl as he stepped up to Chrysta and stood next to her.

Akrur opened his mouth again to calm Tommy down before the changeling said anything that would make Zheng angry, but Director Zheng just turned to Tommy and talked over the empath. "Oh, I knew Miss York was here. Neil told me the first night she was brought here who she was and what she could do." She looked Tommy up and down. "What he failed to mention was the fact she was brought here by a changeling. He shared that little detail with me this morning. Am I correct that you are Thomas Monroe?"

Tommy folded his arms, and his frown deepened. "Yes. I am. Are you here for more questions? Because I'm gonna be honest with you, I'm getting tired of answering them."

"Now, wait, no need to be brash—" Akrur started to say, worried that Tommy was going to offend the one person he really shouldn't, when Zheng put her hand up lazily.

"No, no questions, I promise. Norio's report is thorough enough for me." She looked Tommy up and down again, a smile still on her face. It scared Akrur how calm she was being. "I would like to ask one favor, however. Can I see your other form?"

Tommy blinked and leered. "Not going to offer to buy me dinner first? I don't usually put out like that."

The older woman smiled, the smile of a predator. She patted her fingers against the hilt of her sword—*tap, tap, tap, tap*. "Please, Mr. Monroe," she asked.

Tommy sighed and looked at Akrur and Chrysta. "You guys are my witnesses, she asked me," he said, and before Akrur could say anything to stop him, he changed.

Akrur jerked, fighting the urge to jump back. He didn't think he would ever get used to seeing Tommy change like that. One moment he was a tall African-American man in punk clothing, and the next moment he was a giant cat-like creature with grey skin in punk clothing. Chrysta barely reacted, silently looking between Tommy and Director Zheng. Zheng, to her credit, didn't move, but she squinted up at Tommy's face. Tommy rumbled in his chest, ears going back. Chrysta poked his arm, and he stopped the growl, looking down at the young girl. "Be nice," Chrysta told him.

"Well, Hunter Zheng, like what you see?" Tommy asked in his low rumble. He started to lean forward so he and Zheng were eye-to-eye, drifting into her personal space. Zheng raised an eyebrow, and Akrur was worried that a fight was about to break out until the older woman reached a finger out and touched Tommy's nose. "Boop," she said in a high voice, and then she turned to ascend the stairs to Burke's office.

Tommy jerked back, alien features frozen in shock for a minute. Chrysta laughed at the look on his face. "She *booped* me," Tommy whispered. Akrur was not sure if he was angry or just startled.

"Well, it wasn't the assault I was dreading," Akrur said as Tommy shook himself out of his stupor. "Come on, up you two go."

10

As they climbed the stairs, Zheng was next to Burke, one hand on his shoulder as she whispered into his ear. He gave a small nod and then tented his fingers as Akrur and Chrysta sat in the chairs in front of his desk. Akrur noticed a large wooden cube on his desk, something he had never seen before. Tommy stayed standing, already back in human form, glaring at Zheng. Zheng just looked back at Tommy, leaning against Burke's chair with a grin.

Akrur passed the book on slave bands back to Burke. Burke accepted it. "Oh my, is that where that went to?" Burke said sarcastically. Akrur just gave a slight shrug in apology. "Miss York, I hope you are feeling well?" Burke drawled as he folded his hands on top of the book.

"Yes, I am. Thank you, sir," she said. Burke's dog got up and sat by her chair, letting Chrysta pet her on the head. "Tommy said you needed to talk to us?"

"I needed to speak with you and Cross about your training. I have a feeling that you will want Monroe to be here when I do," Burke explained.

"You want to take Chrysta as your apprentice?" Akrur asked, and the other man slowly nodded.

"Given how powerful we believe she will become, I assume that we need to get her in command of her abilities before they grow out of control."

"I agree. Before things get worse," Akrur said.

Burke gave him a look with a quirked brow. "Worse?"

Akrur shifted in his chair, but before he could say anything, Chrysta answered for him. "I have been having nightmares about the night Tommy saved me. And I make everything float around me when I do."

"I see," Burke murmured. "Cross also said something about you cursing a classmate?"

Chrysta looked down at her lap for a moment. "Yes. She stole something from Tommy the day we met. She couldn't touch a violin without breaking it for several weeks until she returned it."

Director Zheng blinked in surprise. "Did you use a spell?"

Chrysta shook her head. "No. I didn't even know magic was real at that point."

Zheng just stared at the young woman for several moments in shock, and Tommy snorted. "Yeah, believe me, that was how I felt at the time too."

"So you have the power; we just need to make sure you can wield it before it becomes destructive," Burke said as the woman next to him shook her head in disbelief. "I can offer you the opportunity to accelerate your training, Miss York, if you like. But it is not without risks." He reached over to the cube and placed his hand on top. "Before I continue, I must let you all know what you learn here today stays in this room."

The box started to shine white, lines and runes lighting up along the dark wooden structure. Finally, there was a soft *click*, and the sides slowly opened. Burke picked up the top and set it aside. There was a glass ball inside, glossy and black, about the size of a basketball. Akrur and Chrysta leaned forward at the same time to examine it. "There is something inside it," Chrysta murmured, and Akrur could see the shapes she was talking about, although he couldn't quite make it out. "Is it a crystal ball?" she asked, and Akrur smiled at her. She was so curious about everything, and he loved seeing her curiosity.

"Crystal balls are generally clear quartz, my dear, and with nothing inside," he explained. "Looks like this is glass? And I don't know what that—" he was saying, and then the ball lit up.

It was the soft pink glow of morning light coming from the right of the ball. It started to become brighter, and the vague shapes became more defined—a castle, miniature in scale but beautiful in its detail, on the side of a mountain. Green covered the mountain, and as Akrur leaned forward, he realized it was a forest, light fog weaving between the trees in the lower elevations. A waterfall was next to the castle, creating a stream (or maybe a river? it was hard to judge the proportions) winding through the trees. It flowed to a lake on the left of the ball, the water the most beautiful blue Akrur could ever recall seeing. The light was shifting, causing the shadows to move in the ball.

"We don't know who created it," Burke said after Chrysta and Akrur had studied the ball for a few silent moments. "But it has been passed down from sorcerer to sorcerer for centuries."

"Is it... is it a pocket universe?" Akrur asked, voice low in awe.

"What's a pocket universe?" Chrysta asked, keeping her voice low as well.

"More sorcerer bullshit," Tommy muttered, and Akrur shot him an annoyed look.

"Sorcerers have figured out how to bend space," Akrur explained. Chrysta gave him a perplexed look, and he lifted his hands about fifty centimeters apart. "You can take a big space and fold it into a smaller space," he said as he brought his hands closer together. "You see them in houses that sorcerers live in and pass down the generations a lot. You open the door to something that should be the size of a broom closet, and instead is a room the size of a library or a ballroom." He turned to Tommy, who was leaning forward to study the ball himself. "They are not bullshit, I assure you."

"Messing with natural laws is bullshit," Tommy replied. "Aren't they known to collapse without warning?"

"Only if they are improperly made," Burke said, and Chrysta turned to him. "This one is stable and has been for a very long time."

"It's so small," Akrur murmured, mostly to himself. "I have never seen that much area condensed into that small of a container before." While they were talking, the light continued to move across the sphere. The light was now coming from the top of the ball. "How big is it?"

"Fifteen point six kilometers across," Burke said, his fingers tented in front of him. "Almost ten miles," he said to Chrysta.

"The castle is huge," Chrysta breathed, and Akrur nodded.

"A mile long and nearly a third of a mile wide," Burke confirmed.

"Why is the light moving?" Chrysta asked.

"Is... is time moving faster in the ball?" Tommy asked.

"Correct," Burke said. He put his hands down. "One hour equals ten days in the sphere." He lightly placed his hand on it. "Every six minutes is one complete day."

Akrur suddenly had a thought. "All the apprentices you have had, they all became masters of their abilities in such a short amount of time. You were taking them inside the ball and artificially accelerated their training."

"Correct," Burke said again. "It also has the added benefit of giving us complete privacy. No one could observe Miss York as she gains control of her powers. If there are any accidents or incidents that could gain too much attention, it will happen in there and not where others could see it."

"What's the catch?" Tommy asked.

"There are... dangers inside the sphere," Burke stated. He leaned back, and Zheng sat on the arm of his chair. "Also, the magic that maintains it is not kind to humans. Staying inside for long periods causes ill effects."

"What are the 'ill effects?'" Akrur asked, looking between the permanently neutral-looking Burke and a grim-looking Zheng.

"One sorcerer attempted to stay in the sphere for 120 hours," Burke said. "That is a little over three years inside the sphere. After two years, about seventy-two hours, he stopped sending messages to the outside world, so someone went in to find him. He had gone mad and tried to attack them. After an investigation, other sorcerers determined that it wasn't the isolation. He was used to living alone for extended periods of time. So they decided that no one would stay in the sphere for longer than a year."

"The ball is so small that it can be easily destroyed as well," Zheng added. "And if you smash the ball, you demolish everything inside."

"Including any people who are in there," Tommy said, and Zheng nodded.

"It is so dangerous to go into the sphere that Neil promised his poor wife that he wouldn't use it anymore," Zheng growled, and she glared at the headmaster.

Tommy blinked and then started to grin. He pointed between the two of them. "Wait, are you telling me you two are married? To each other?"

"Is that so hard to believe?" Zheng asked as she leaned into Burke. Burke just lifted one eyebrow at his wife as she kissed his temple.

"No, I shoulda guessed that the two most dangerous hunters in recent history would get hitched at some point," Tommy said with a chuckle. Chrysta gave him a curious look, and he pointed at the two hunters. "Those generals of the Golden One you have been reading about? These two killed one of them."

Chrysta's eyes went wide. "Wait, one of the generals is dead?"

"You are learning about the changeling generals?" Zheng asked Chrysta. Chrysta nodded. "What book are you reading?"

"Her Most Loyal Servants," Chrysta replied.

Zheng scoffed. "Paul Bulter, that bleeding heart prick," she growled and then added something in Mandarin under her breath.

Burke patted his wife's knee as if to calm her down. "My wife and Mr. Butler have an antagonistic relationship," he explained. He looked at Chrysta. "What do you know about the generals, Miss York?"

"There were six changeling generals," Chrysta robotically said, like she was reciting something from memory. "They were some of the first ones she created, the strongest and most devoted of all of her creations. Named for various gods of death from religions across the world."

"The first case of cultural appropriation," Akrur said sarcastically. Tommy snorted at his tone.

Chrysta kept going, starting to count on her fingers as she recited a name. "Camazotz, the bat god from the Mayas. Degei, the serpent god from Fiji. Yama can change into a water buffalo like the Hindu god of death rides. Hel, who can change into the wolf changeling Fenrir." She paused and looked at Akrur. "I don't understand that one. Is she a woman?"

"She is female in her human form and male in his changeling form," Akrur explained. "What probably happened when the Golden One made them is that she used a female human baby and a male wolf cub. No one knows if it was intentional or a mistake, though."

"A mistake," Tommy added. "Although the generals will say it was on purpose. Their god doesn't make any mistakes," he said sarcastically, almost bitterly. Akrur felt the prickles of curiosity go up his spine. Tommy's past, especially how the slave band ended up on his arm and how he became an outcast among changelings, was still a mystery, but Akrur felt those subjects were not ones he could broach with the changeling.

Chrysta looked at the ball, which had gone dark in the time they were talking. "Veles, a bear changeling, and Serapis, their leader, were the last two. No one knows what animal Serapis changes into." She looked at Burke. "Which one did you kill?"

"Back in 1981, Jiao and I were sent to Eastern Europe," Burke started to explain. "A creature was terrorizing the forests and countryside. It was killing everything: livestock, wild animals, and people. Campers were disappearing. It was carnage on a scale no one could explain. Witnesses said it looked like a bear, but it walked on its hind legs. It was smart too. It could avoid and destroy traps and open doors. It was no ordinary animal."

"We found the center of the destruction and started our search," Zheng continued. "One night, we found Veles attacking a cabin full of campers. We engaged and neutralized him."

Tommy snorted. "'Neutralized.' You killed him."

Zheng gave him a look. "Are you like Butler and think we should have captured him? Rehabilitate him? That a monster like that is deserving of humanity?"

"Fuck no. Kill the assholes, as far as I'm concerned," Tommy said, and Zheng broke out into an evil-looking grin. "Just don't sugarcoat it."

"It was probably a mercy killing anyway," Burke added. "The necropsy showed that Veles had a case of very late-stage rabies. He was delirious and very dangerous at that point. We probably would not have killed him otherwise."

"Rabies, huh?" Tommy asked with a surprised look. "I had heard you two had killed him, but not that he was sick at the time."

"Our superiors decided to keep it a secret from the public. They were worried that some might try to weaponize the disease and cause more harm than good," Zheng explained.

"Maybe I should look into getting some shots," Tommy joked.

"Soon after, Jiao and I decided to retire," Burke continued. "I accepted the Headmaster position here, and Jiao went on to become the director of the Hunter Organization."

"But you still have a lot of enemies who would love to crush a glass ball, killing you instantly," Tommy said.

Burke nodded. "Traditionally, the people going into the sphere have one person on the outside that they trust to watch over it. Jiao has done it in the past for me.

Miss York, you, of course, will have Cross there as your guardian, but you can have Monroe there as well."

Chrysta looked up at Tommy as if to ask for his permission. He shrugged. "I already told you, beautiful, you are not getting rid of me."

"I will also be asking Nyla to be there," Burke added.

Tommy let out one of those inhuman growls deep in his chest, and Akrur jumped in surprise. "Great," Tommy hissed through gritted teeth.

"Why?" Chrysta asked.

"Your father may be looking for you. For your safety and for my own, I can't take the chance that he won't find the sphere and destroy it. Her thirst for revenge aside, she is the most powerful hunter alive right now, excluding myself and Jiao."

"If she hurts Tommy—" Chrysta started to say.

"She won't," Zheng growled, and Akrur was shocked at the venom in her voice. For someone who had just met him, she was being very protective of Tommy, a changeling. "I can handle Nyla."

"So, is it settled then?" Burke asked, looking at Chrysta. "You will do it? Or would you prefer to think it over for several days?"

Chrysta looked down at her hands for several quiet moments. "I... Yes. Yes, I will do it." She looked up, looking at everyone. "I have to control these powers, no matter how strong they get."

"Where? When?" Akrur asked.

"Wednesday. New Year's Day. That will give you a few days to prepare. As for where," Burke hesitated. "I don't think the Academy would be the best place. Too many people work and live here. We need somewhere isolated and secured."

"Let me make a call. I may have a spot," Akrur said, and Burke gave him a nod.

"Your charges are arriving, Cross. We should get you back," Burke stated.

They all got up simultaneously and went down the stairs to the landing where the lift was waiting. Akrur reached out to open the doors when Zheng reached out and covered the buttons. "No elevator," she said with a wicked grin, "Use the stairs, Cross. You need the exercise."

"You're not my boss," Akrur pointed out, trying not to pout.

"I am," Burke said, voice even, but Akrur could have sworn he saw a smile tugging on the man's lips.

"Come on, beautiful," Tommy said while crouching down, and Chrysta hopped on his back with a giggle. The adults watched as the two of them started to descend the staircase circling the tower.

"She's reading about changelings?" Zheng asked in a low voice.

"Yes, and the Acolytes," Akrur confirmed as they, too, started to climb down the tower, Zheng going first and Burke taking up the rear. Zheng gave him a glare over her shoulder. "What?" he asked with a shrug.

"She should not be reading about such morbid subjects," Zheng growled at him in a low voice.

"She is curious. The world of magic is new to her. And it is only natural she would want to learn about the group her father leads and the race of beings Tommy belongs to."

"Her father tried to kill her," Zheng shot back. "She has been through enough trauma. Learning about those topics is not in her best interest."

"Acquiring knowledge is always in one's best interest," Akrur argued back. "We will not be able to keep who she is and what she can do a secret forever. She will be shunned, first for who her father is and then for her glowing gold, both things she cannot control. Better she learns that it's not her fault now than wait until the vitriol starts." Akrur puffed a little to get his breath before he continued. "And she needs to know what Tommy being a changeling means for her relationship with him."

"You may want to keep your voice down," Burke murmured.

"Why?"

"'Cause I have excellent hearing," Tommy called up from the bottom of the tower, and Akrur felt his cheeks heat up. Fantastic, he felt shame for a second time that day.

"What is it?" Chrysta asked. Tommy had put her down when they reached the bottom, and she was looking between him and the adults and back again.

"Zheng is worried about you obsessing over acolytes and changelings," Tommy explained. "Cross says you need to know what you are getting yourself into."

"Don't I have a right to learn all I can about magic?" she called up to the adults. "Especially since my father kept it a secret from me for so long?"

Zheng sighed. "Fair enough. But do try not to focus on just those two unsavory aspects of the magical world, alright?"

They headed outside, and they paused at the edge of the gardens. Two figures underneath the Disaster Tree started waving wildly. Chrysta smiled and started waving back, but the smile slowly died on her face, and she brought her hand down. Akrur followed her gaze, noticing that Hafeez was back performing her vigil in the woods, her and her caracal standing out against the snow.

Tommy growled, a more human-like sound than the one he let out in the office. "You would think after last night she would have learned to stop doing that."

"What happened last night?" Akrur asked.

"Nyla brought Deputy Director Campbell here to the Academy to arrest Monroe and take him away," Burke explained, and Akrur turned to him in shock. Tommy hadn't mentioned the incident, and Akrur was astounded that anyone would try to undermine the headmaster like that. Chrysta's head whipped around, and she glared at Hafeez.

"I'm sorry for that, by the way," Zheng said to Tommy as she closed her coat against the cold. "Campbell likes to throw his weight around and often goes for the theatrics."

Tommy lifted one shoulder in fake indifference. "Kinda comes with the territory," he said.

"Mrs. Zheng, I know she thinks Tommy hurt her father, but she shouldn't—"

"It's alright, my dear, I can handle it," Zheng purred in a low, dangerous voice and started to trudge through the snow toward Hafeez.

"Strong women," Akrur murmured to himself. Zheng was still a long way off from Hafeez, but the younger hunter seemed to have recognized her superior and slowly made her way into the snow to join Zheng. Hafeez did not look happy to see her leader there.

"May we never anger them," Tommy finished for him, and Akrur smiled.

~ 11 ~

It turned out to be Ichiro and Rimsha waiting for them at the foot of the tree, and Chrysta gave them both a hug when she, Akrur, and Tommy got close. Akrur looked in horror at Ichiro. "My word, boy, what did you do to your hair?" The young man cut it in a buzz cut and dyed it a bright purple since Akrur had seen him a few days earlier.

"Like it?" Ichiro asked with a grin. "I wanted to try something different."

"Well, it certainly is... different," Akrur muttered, and the girls laughed. Rimsha ruffled his hair, and Ichiro glowered at her.

Tommy looked at Zheng and Hafeez with a nasty grin on his face until Akrur grabbed his arm and started to pull him inside. "Hey," Tommy protested. "I wanna watch."

"Let Hafeez have some privacy while she gets her dressing down," Akrur said while sparing his own curious glance at the two hunters. They were too far away for Akrur to hear what they were saying, but a scowling Zheng had a finger in Hafeez's face. Hafeez's caracal almost looked chastised as well.

Once they were inside, Tommy sneezed. He pointed at Rimsha. "What spell is on you?" he asked with a frown.

"Um, nothing," she said softly, looking the changeling up and down in slight fear. Tommy's features softened, and he put his hands in his pockets, stepping away from her.

"Sorry, I smell magic," he explained. "Kinda plays havoc with my sense of smell."

Rimsha looked concerned for a second. "Magic smells bad?" she asked, and Tommy nodded. "I haven't done anything since I got—wait! Maybe it's this!" And she put her hand up to her hijab and stroked the hem. The color of the hijab changed from a soft baby blue that matched her sweater to a dark blue.

Akur raised his eyebrows in surprise while Chrysta gasped next to him. "Color-changing fabric? That is pretty expensive."

"Yeah, my brother had a client that had some extra fabric after he made her dress, so he created this for me," Rimsha explained. "This way, I can have one hijab that can match all my clothes." She smiled at Tommy. "But I can put this away for now and wear something that won't bother you." She turned to the girls' room, and Tommy opened his mouth to protest.

Tommy gave Akrur a sheepish look. "I didn't mean to make her change."

Akrur patted his arm. "I can't always promise that this will be a magic-free space, but we will try to keep you comfortable while you're here."

"How long are you staying?" Ichiro asked with a grin, and Tommy blinked in surprise at him.

"Not sure," Tommy murmured.

The door opened before Ichiro could say anything else, and Julien stepped inside. "It's freezing," he signed with a grin on his face. After getting his coat off, he gave Chrysta a small hug and fist-bumped Ichiro. Akrur was shaking his hand when the empath saw a sour look cross Tommy's face, but it was gone by the time Julien turned to Tommy and gave the changeling a nod in greeting. "Who is outside with Hunter Jerkface?" Julien signed.

Akrur smirked at the nickname Julien had given Hunter Hafeez. "Jiao Zheng," he explained, both signing and talking at the same time so Chrysta and Tommy could understand him. "Leader of the Hunter Organization. Hopefully, she can get Hunter Hafeez to leave Mr. Monroe alone."

Julien nodded and suddenly broke out into a wide smile when he saw Rimsha and Rosa coming out of the girls' room, Rimsha now in a black hijab. He gave them big hugs, and then Rosa went to Tommy and poked him. "You making dinner, Monroe?"

"Yeah, I was thinking gumbo," he said.

"Need help?" Rosa asked.

Tommy smiled. "Yeah, that would be... nice."

.....

Akrur loved the kids greatly. Each one had their own strengths, and different personalities. They could be so kind and open-minded, intelligent and accomplished, and he was proud of each of them.

But he wished they weren't bloody teenagers sometimes.

Almost immediately, there was a fight between Rosa and Ichiro. "I just don't get why you can't move the clothes from the washer to the dryer," Akrur overheard the younger boy complain in the kitchen as Akrur sat at the kitchen table reading his newspaper.

"Because I'm busy," Rosa shot back, gesturing at the vegetables she was chopping as Tommy mixed something in two pots on the stove. Chrysta had found a step stool and was looking over Tommy's shoulder, watching him stir. "I don't understand why you couldn't have done your laundry before you left. Or better yet, take it with you."

"We were kinda busy before I left to go home," Ichiro said sarcastically, wildly gesturing at Chrysta and Tommy. "And I don't like taking my dirty clothes back home with me. My mom acts weird when I do. She starts asking if I'm getting neglected here or something."

"I can help," Chrysta said before Akrur could intervene. "I'll need help doing my own laundry later anyway. I have never done it myself," she added shyly.

While Chrysta and Ichiro disappeared into the bathroom, Kevin finally arrived. He dropped a giant bag that would have made Santa jealous while taking off his parka and waving at Akrur. "Hello, Mr. Cross," he said as he entered the kitchen.

"Hello, Mr. Butler," Akrur said with a smile. "Good of you to join us. Dinner will be served soon."

"What?" Kevin asked and frowned when he noticed Tommy at the stove. Kevin made an audible gulp and went over to the changeling. Akrur watched the boy go like he was facing an executioner.

"Hey, Tommy," Kevin said nervously. "I, um, I'm the one who usually cooks."

"Don't mind me, just making something I haven't had a chance to cook in a while," Tommy explained as he grabbed the vegetables from Rosa and added them to both pots.

"Well, that's the thing. I usually make the food around here," Kevin said, trying to look into the pots. "No offense, but some people have food restrictions, and well..." Kevin trailed off like he didn't know how to continue.

"Well, Cross can't eat beef, so this pot has chicken, sausage, and shrimp," Tommy explained as he hit the bigger pot with a *thonk* with the wooden spoon.

"Well, yes, Mr. Cross doesn't eat beef, but Rimsha—"

"Rimsha is a vegetarian, so I'm making this one without meat," Tommy interrupted, hitting the smaller pot with the spoon as well, making a higher *thang* sound.

"But, I mean... But I..." Kevin sputtered. Akrur got up from his chair to rescue the flustered boy, but Rosa beat him to it, putting her knife down with a sigh and drying her hands on a towel.

"Por el amor del cielo," Rosa growled. "Come on, Kevin, leave him alone. You will like his cooking, trust me." She grabbed the younger boy and frog-marched him out of the kitchen.

Akrur joined Tommy and leaned against the counter. "Forgive him," he said softly. "Kevin's domain is in the kitchen, and it's where he feels most comfortable. He can get possessive of his territory."

"He's done an excellent job. I think some professional cooks could take lessons from him in organizing their kitchens," Tommy confessed, looking behind him. All the kids were in the common room, giving Kevin hugs and greetings. Chrysta sat in an armchair, Poe perched above her. "Looks like I'm just making everyone uncomfortable tonight," Tommy said.

Akrur studied the changeling for a moment. Tommy seemed relaxed, but Akrur couldn't help but notice the self-deprecating tone he had used for the second time that day. Maybe Abby was right; perhaps he was letting some prejudice color his perspective of Tommy's intentions with Chrysta.

Akrur then watched Chrysta for a moment. She looked between the other teens as they had a heated discussion about something, head going back and forth. Her future was uncertain, but she was alive and away from her father. He cleared his throat. "I don't know if anyone has told you this, but if they haven't, I think you should know something: you did the right thing, bringing her here. You put your life on the line for her, and you should be proud of yourself for making the right choice."

Tommy froze for a moment, and then it was his turn to study Akrur. He looked suspicious for a second like he wasn't sure if Akrur was making fun of him or not. But Tommy must have seen something in Akrur's face that showed how sincere the empath was. Tommy looked into the common room again, and the expression that softened his features as he stared at Chrysta was so genuine that it made Akrur smile. "Yeah, well," Tommy said softly, "I didn't do it for praise. I did it for her." He shrugged that slight lifting of his shoulder that Akrur was beginning to realize was his defense when dealing with a hurtful issue. "I didn't know what the band would do to me, the Acolytes would say that it would end badly for me if I didn't listen, but I couldn't stand by and let those assholes hurt her. Not like that."

Akrur grinned, but the smile slid off his face when he realized that the teens' voices were rising in a fight, something he should probably stop before it got worse. "Bloody teenagers," he growled as he got up from the counter. "They will be the death of me." Tommy chuckled as Akrur left the kitchen.

"You didn't do your laundry," Ichiro was saying, arms crossed in front of him. Julien looked back and forth, trying to follow the conversation as best he could. "You didn't do the floors. Did you do *anything* while we were away?"

"Hey," Rosa snapped back. "First, I'm not your maid. Second, Chrysta was here too. Why are you not yelling at her?"

"She just got here," Rimsha argued, putting a hand on Chrysta's shoulder. "She wouldn't know what to do like you do."

"Well, if she's staying permanently, she needs to help out," Rosa shot back, and Akrur noticed that one of the logs in the fireplace suddenly lit up. The air was getting hotter too. Rosa's temper was getting out of hand. He gently put a hand on her shoulder, knowing that the physical contact would help calm her.

"I'll get Chrysta on the rota next week once classes start back up," Akrur explained. "For now, how about everyone help in cleaning the floors before dinner."

There were groans and sighs and mutinous murmurs, but the teens started to file out of the common room. Julien hesitated and then signed to Akrur: "Can we talk for a minute?"

"Of course," he signed back, and he gestured to the kitchen.

They sat down, surrounded by the delicious smell of food cooking. Tommy gave them a curious glance but turned back to the stove as Julien began to sign. "My mother…" he started, letting his hands falter and then fall back to the table for a moment. Akrur gave him a minute to collect his thoughts patiently, and Julien picked up his hands again. "My mother came for a visit. I'm not sure how to feel about it."

"Did she show up unannounced?" Akrur asked.

"She called Dad and then showed up the day after Christmas," Julien explained. "If felt… wrong." Julien used the sign for "mistake" as he stuck his thumb and pinky finger out and brought the hand up to his face. "Felt like she shouldn't be in our home." Julien signed the word "home" aggressively, pinching his fingers together at his cheek and running them up to his ear and back, looking angry.

Akrur put his hand on Julien's. "It's okay to be upset," he signed back. "She's been gone for seven years. You can forgive her and still be troubled with what happened at the same time."

The young man huffed. "Okay," he signed. "I just hope she doesn't hurt Kat." He made the sign for the animal cat, the nickname he gave his younger sister, holding his forefinger and thumb apart in front of his mouth and pinching them together as he moved his hand to the side.

Julien looked at Tommy's back for a moment. "How were things here?" he signed.

"Here?" Akrur held both hands palm up, making circles with them as he raised his eyebrows like he was asking a question. "Never a dull moment," was his answer. Julien grinned in return.

"How are you doing, Tommy?" Julien asked out loud, and Tommy turned slightly so Julien could see his reply.

"Oh, just peachy," Tommy drawled, and Akrur chuckled at the changeling's dry tone. Tommy gestured between the two of them. "Everything okay? You two seem to be having a heated discussion."

"Julien was just asking for some advice on a family matter," Akrur said and signed at the same time. "Nothing serious." Akrur could hear the sound of voices rising in the other rooms, and he sighed, rubbing his eyes. Julien, who couldn't hear the commotion, gave him a questioning look. "The others are fighting," he signed as an explanation.

Akrur put his hands on the table to get up, but Julien shot up from his seat. "I got it, Mr. Cross," he said and left the kitchen. Akrur settled back into the chair, glad to let the young man supervise his peers.

"Is he a good guy?" Tommy suddenly asked.

"Who?"

"Julien," Tommy stated, still facing the stove. Akrur couldn't decipher his tone.

"Julien is a wonderful boy. Wonderful man, I should say. Smart. Kind. Brave. He hopes to apply for a teaching position opening for the fall. He would be a great addition to the teaching staff."

"He helped you guys that night, right?" Tommy asked, and he finally turned so Akrur could see his face. He looked grim. "He went with you guys to the mansion?"

"He did," Akrur said. "Tackled Guerra at one point."

Tommy stared at Akrur for a full minute, mouth open in shock. "I thought you said he was smart," Tommy nearly shrieked, and Akrur laughed until tears formed in the corners of his eyes.

12

Dinner was ready an hour later, and everyone piled into the kitchen. Akrur took his customary seat at the head of the table, Chrysta, Tommy, and Rimsha to his right, Rosa, Ichiro, and Kevin to his left. Julien took the other end of the table, watching the various conversations happening around him. Tommy had made rice and cornbread with the gumbo, which the kids dug into with relish. Rimsha declared the vegetarian gumbo a success, much to Kevin's chagrin, and everyone tried a few bites on her insistence. "When was the last time you made this?" Akrur asked Tommy after a few minutes of silence as everyone ate.

"Fifty years?" Tommy said after a moment of thought, and Akrur blinked at him. That's right. He kept forgetting that Tommy was four times older than himself.

"One hundred and seventy-seven years old," Chrysta said after swallowing her food. "Is it weird?" she asked, and Tommy arched an eyebrow as he chewed. "Knowing you will live longer than a human?"

"Sometimes," he admitted. "The years start to blur together, and you forget how long it has been since you saw someone, and it can be jarring when you see them after a lot of time has passed. But, mostly, it's meeting a kid bugging you for money for candy and then finding him fifty years later by accident, and now he's married with five kids and a dozen grandkids."

"Has anyone ever recognized you?" Rimsha asked.

"A few people," Tommy said with a grin. "It's hard to avoid. They always ask me if I'm the grandson of a guy named Thomas Monroe. So, I usually tell them the truth, but they never believe me. People rather think I am the descendant of the man they remember than a semi-immortal creature that they met decades ago." He shrugged.

Chrysta laughed. "Well, I didn't believe you, that's for sure."

"The things you have seen," Rosa said in wonder.

"The American Civil War," Tommy started to say, counting on his fingers, "the First World War, the Great Depression, the *Second* World War, the dropping of the bombs, African-Americans fighting for civil rights, the Vietnam war..."

"Man walking on the moon," Rosa offered.

"Doctors developing vaccines and new medicines," Rimsha said.

"Rise of computers," Ichiro added, buttering a piece of cornbread.

"Invention of cars and planes," Julien said.

"Movies!" Kevin added with a smile.

"The birth of jazz and rock and roll music," Chrysta said.

Tommy grinned and held up his hands in surrender. "Okay, so it wasn't all bad," Tommy admitted. "I still say the invention of toilet paper is the best thing humans came up with."

"Did you ever get to see anyone famous in concert?" Chrysta asked.

"Mostly jazz musicians," Tommy said. He seemed relaxed and was smiling from ear to ear. "Duke Ellington, who got me into the piano, John Lee Hooker."

Everyone finished dinner, leftovers were stored in the fridge, and the dishes placed in the sink. Everyone groaned at their full stomachs, and the only thing that would make Akrur's night better would be a cigarette, but Abby had confiscated his last pack. Instead, he popped a piece of gum into his mouth as the kids pulled Akrur into the common room, excited to open the presents that had been waiting since the winter solstice. Tommy draped himself into an armchair, Chrysta settling onto the floor in front of him.

Rimsha handed Akrur a couple of packages with a smile. "The blue one is from Miss Normandy," she explained.

"Oh, now, you kids didn't have to get me anything," he said in a disapproving tone, but he still had a giant grin on his face as he unwrapped the gifts. The one from the kids was an old leather book. "First edition Sherlock Holmes," he murmured. "You really didn't have to."

"What did Miss Normandy get you?" Ichiro asked.

Akrur tore off the wrapping paper and laughed. It was a paperback romance novel, one with a bare-chested man pawing at the heroine in a dress on the deck of a brig. He thumbed through the book as the kids laughed, and a note dropped out with a gift card. *For the man who needs a little romance in his life,* it read. "A little bit of an inside joke," he told Tommy as the changeling raised an eyebrow.

Julien and Ichiro opened their gifts: a deck of tarot cards for Julien and video games for Ichiro. Kevin opened his box as Julien inspected the black and white designs with their gold accents. "Sweet!" he exclaimed as he sorted through the movies inside.

"Is that a Hitchcock collection?" Chrysta asked.

"Yep. Are you a fan?" Kevin asked with a grin.

"Oh yes, my mom got me into his films," Chrysta explained. "She would cover my eyes at the bad parts. Although, *The Birds* did give me nightmares for a few weeks after we watched it."

"I'm surprised Poe didn't scare you then," Tommy joked.

"He did the first time I met him," Chrysta admitted, gently using one finger to pet the bird's head. "He dropped down from the sky when I was on the balcony. I screeched and ran inside, thinking he was going to scratch my eyes out." She laughed. "Next time he visited me, he brought me a button in apology, and we have been friends since."

Rimsha opened her gift and gasped. Three sets of earrings, all made with clips. "So I can clip them to my hijab," she told Chrysta as she handed a pair to her.

"So beautiful," Chrysta cooed as Rimsha clipped a pair to her hijab, peacock feathers with gold beads on the ends. She suddenly laughed and clapped her hands, looking at Tommy. "I can finally get my ears pierced! My father would never let me do it!"

"Want me to do it, beautiful?" he asked with a grin.

"Yes, as soon as possible, before Wednesday."

"What happens Wednesday?" Rosa asked.

"Chrysta, Tommy, and I will be leaving for a few days," Akrur explained. "Headmaster Burke will be training Miss York to get her powers under control, hopefully."

"Sounds like it could be dangerous," Rimsha murmured, looking worried.

"That's why Tommy is going," Ichiro said. "Keep an eye on his girlfriend."

"Chrysta is not my girlfriend," Tommy almost growled.

"That is the second person to say that I'm your girlfriend," Chrysta said in a sing-song voice, looking at Tommy over her shoulder. "If someone else says it, it's official."

Akrur glared at the changeling, but Tommy just opened his hands and gestured at Chrysta as if to say *She said it, not me*, making Chrysta and Rimsha giggle.

Rosa was last to open her present: a new workout outfit with shoes. She whistled. "Thanks, guys. I needed a new set."

"Just please don't leave them on the floor after you use them," Rimsha begged.

"Hey, Kevin," Ichiro whispered. Kevin hummed but kept looking at Tommy. "Hey, Butler, the bag?"

"Oh! Yeah!" Kevin said with a start, and he ran to the coat rack where he had left his bag. He came back with the entire bag, dropping off packages with each teen as he went, finishing with a green one on Tommy's lap and a red gift on Chrysta's.

"Oh, you didn't have to get us anything," Chrysta said, a sad smile on her face while Tommy studied his with a raised eyebrow.

"It's no big deal. My mom makes a sweater for everyone at the Club every year, and she can make a sweater in, like, a day."

"Wait, you told your mother about Chrysta?" Akrur asked angrily. "What happened to the promise of not telling anyone what happened during the solstice?"

Kevin looked guilty for a second. Keeping secrets was not his strong suit. "I didn't say anything to my parents," he said. Akrur gave him a look. "Honest! I just told my mom that someone came to the Disaster Club after she was saved from an abusive household by her boy—" Kevin paused and looked at Tommy, who was now glaring at him as well. "—friend! Her friend! I didn't give any details other than that! So she made sweaters so they would have some presents, I swear!"

"Well, thank her for me..." Chrysta trailed off as she opened the paper, and she grimaced.

"What's wrong?" Kevin asked.

"It's a lovely sweater," Chrysta started to say as she lifted the garment from the paper, and Tommy laughed, "I just hate pink."

"Oh, sorry," Kevin said.

"No, it's alright," Chrysta assured him. "It's a lovely gift. I'm happy to get it."

Tommy lifted up his own sweater, identical, except it was black and bigger than Chrysta's. He looked between the two sweaters and then leaned over, plucking the pink sweater from Chrysta and depositing the black one in her lap. "Yoink! Mine now!" he announced as the girls laughed.

"You can't wear pink," Kevin said with a frown.

"I happen to think I look stunning in pink," Tommy joked. He took off his old sweater, filled with holes, and put on the pink one, rolling up the sleeves since they stopped in the middle of his forearms. Kevin's eyes flickered to the scars on Tommy's left arm.

"I thought changeling's healed really quickly," Kevin asked.

"We do," Tommy confirmed, putting his arms above his head. There was a flash of his undershirt since the sweater wasn't long enough as he leaned back in the chair. "These were caused by magic, though, so I don't think they will heal."

"But magic doesn't affect changelings," Kevin stated, and Akrur looked up from his book to glance at the boy. Generally, he encouraged the kids to be curious, but he had a feeling this was a sore subject the teen was trying to navigate.

"It was weird," Tommy murmured, not looking upset. "The magic of the slave band always affected me." He shrugged with both shoulders. "Don't know why, though."

"What did it do?" Chrysta asked after putting on the black sweater, looking up at the changeling with a worried expression.

"Mostly, it hurt like hell, especially if I didn't follow orders. But it also kept me from hurting the person wearing the ring. Kept me from stabbing your father," Tommy admitted. Chrysta frowned, and Akrur wondered if she was more upset that Tommy had tried to harm her father or that he had failed in the task.

"Have you been hurt before?" Kevin asked. Now all the other kids were quiet, looking at Tommy.

"Stabbed, shot, beaten up," Tommy confessed.

"Alright, I think we shouldn't explore this topic any further," Akrur stated.

"Beaten up?" Ichiro said as if Akrur hadn't spoken. "By who?"

Tommy snorted and looked around the room like he had just noticed all the kids looking at him. "Hunters, acolytes, normies—"

"And other changelings," Kevin finished for him with a note of excitement in his voice.

"Mr. Butler," Akrur said in warning, but Kevin leaned forward and continued.

"So why do other changelings attack you?" Kevin asked.

Tommy blinked and leaned forward, his body language starting to change. "Kind of a personal question to ask, don't you think?" Tommy asked with a smirk.

"Is it because you're a mixed breed?" Kevin asked, not deterred by the note of warning in the changeling's voice.

"Mixed breed?" Chrysta asked.

"Different species of changelings can breed to have offspring. We don't know how," Kevin explained. Tommy glared at him and sighed, but Kevin, still clueless, continued. "But mixed breed changelings are rare, so we think that they are rejected."

"Wow. You know, this is why I hate sorcerers sometimes," Tommy said, voice holding a frosty note to it. He looked at Akrur. "You make up theories to fit what you think is going on and not the truth."

"Well, what did you do to make the other changelings hate you then?" Kevin asked. Ichiro actually facepalmed.

"Kevin," Rimsha said. "I think you should stop."

"Why do you think I did something to make them hate me?" Tommy asked flatly, leaning forward so he could rest his elbows on his knees.

"Well, changelings usually protect each other," Kevin said, now totally lost in talking. "So if they attack you—"

"I must have done something to deserve it," Tommy finished for him.

"Exactly!" Kevin exclaimed, looking excited. After a moment of silence, he finally seemed to realize that Tommy wasn't smiling, and he started to look ashamed.

Tommy stood up. "Well, this was fun," he said sarcastically. "But I think I can do with a little less of the interrogation."

"Tommy," Chrysta started to say, "are you oka—"

"I'm fine!" Tommy snapped, and Chrysta flinched. Poe squawked and flapped his wings, getting between Tommy and Chrysta. Tommy's look of anger softened when he saw how scared she was. "I... I'm sorry, beautiful." And with that, he turned around and stomped into the guest room, slamming the door shut.

Akrur rubbed his face and then frowned at Kevin. The kids were glaring at him too. "Smooth move, Butler," Rosa murmured.

"Mr. Monroe has been getting questioned by hunters all week long," Akrur explained to the group. Kevin's look of shame deepened. "So, unless he volunteers to talk about his past, keep that topic of discussion off the table, alright?" All the teens nodded.

"Maybe I should go talk to him," Chrysta whispered.

"I would leave him alone for now, my dear," Akrur said. "Let him cool down."

13

October 1982

Tommy was being stalked.

His kind had a scent. It was faint, but like the scent of magic, it let Tommy know that some people weren't just non-magical human beings. Sometimes they could use magic, and sometimes they could transform and try to rip his limbs off.

Of course, living in the city had the perk of keeping both groups out of Tommy's hair. This was the territory of the Acolytes. Trespass and you lost your life.

But as the weather had gotten colder and wetter over the last three weeks, he kept catching the scent of something following him. It lingered around the nightclub where he worked and always seemed to be there when he woke up on the street or hung in the air in the spot where he hid his instruments—unwashed human body odor mixed with fur. Canine.

He was getting ready for a shift on Halloween night when Lindsey paused by the door and leaned in. *"Psst,* Tommy," she said in a stage whisper. Her thick New Jersey accent made his name sound like Tom*may*. "Some guy was here earlier asking for ya."

"Oh yeah?" he asked with a grin. "Did he want to offer me a job, get me out of this hellhole?"

She grimaced. "He didn't say why. But listen, Mr. Rostami told him you were working tonight."

Tommy sighed and frowned, getting up from the bench he was sitting on. Rostami was a greaseball of a man, greedy and repugnant, but he didn't ask for minor things like social security numbers or tax information. He also paid in cash. Unfortunately, Tommy had gotten on his bad side almost immediately.

One week after he started working for Rostami, the man had pulled Tommy into the office and started cussing him out. "Do you know who you fucking threw out of the club last night?"

Tommy shrugged. "An asshole who was trying to drag a waitress into the back room so they could be alone even though she was saying no? You pay me to be a bouncer. I made him bounce out."

Rostami turned red. "That was the son of an old friend of mine. And you threw him out before he paid his tab. That's over three thousand dollars he now owes and won't pay. I should take that out of your hide."

Tommy studied the man's large gut making Rostami's shirt strain at the buttons. "I would like to see you try," he smirked.

Rostami opened his mouth, probably to continue the barrage of curse words, when the door busted open. Suddenly, all of the waitresses that worked in the club marched in. "What the fuck do you want?" Rostami growled.

"Well, we are here to say, if you fire him, we walk," Clarissa, the oldest of the bunch at 27, said as the others nodded behind her.

"What?!"

"Look, this is the first decent bouncer you've ever hired, and if he goes, we all go," Lindsey piped up. Several of the women nodded and murmured in agreement.

"I'll just hire someone else," Rostami said, but he looked scared.

"On a Saturday night? The busiest night of the week?" Clarissa pointed out. "Good luck."

"Well, the ladies have spoken," Tommy said with a grin as he stood up. "Can I go now?"

Since that minor mutiny several months before, Rostami had begrudgingly let Tommy stay at the club, although he never missed the chance to throw an insult Tommy's way. Knowing him, Rostami was hoping the stranger asking about Tommy was there to kill Tommy and take care of him for good. Tommy looked at Lindsey, who had added cat ears to her cigarette girl uniform for Halloween. "What did he look like?"

"Young," Lindsey, who had just turned 19, said. "White, red hair. Wearing ancient clothes that didn't match. Black leather jacket, pink corduroy pants, and a plaid shirt." She made a gagging noise.

"Anything else weird about him?" Tommy asked.

"He was sitting at the bar and asked for a beer. When he paid for it, he tried to use weird money," she said, putting a finger to her lips in thought. "Like, not American. It was different colors. The bartender yelled at him, and then he was able to find some cash in his pocket."

Tommy nodded. If it was a changeling, he was smart enough to avoid the Acolytes' wards but didn't know much about humans.

Lindsey lightly put a hand on his shoulder. "Look, I don't know why Mr. Rostami told him you would be here. It doesn't seem safe. Stranger danger isn't a joke. I just wanted to give you a heads-up. Do you owe the kid money? Is he going to hurt you?"

Tommy smiled and rubbed at his left arm. "No, money isn't the only reason people don't want me breathing, trust me."

She suddenly broke out in a brilliant grin. "By the way, I got the part!" she said while jumping up and down, making her heels click.

"Congrats! The main part?"

"Nah, the sister of the main character, but I have over a hundred lines." Lindsey cleared her throat. "Good day, kind sir," she said in a southern accent.

"Awesome," he said.

She folded her arms behind her, thrusting her chest forward. "Want to come over to my place some time to help me practice?"

"Nah, but let me know when the play's happening, and I'm getting a front-row seat."

Lindsey pouted. "You know, Tommy, you are young, handsome. So why are you always playing hard to catch?"

"Believe me, Lindsey," he said with a sad smile. "You wouldn't want me after you caught me."

.....

That night, Tommy traded with the other bouncer, so he was outside. The rain kept most people off the streets, but he kept an eye out for anyone who looked suspicious. Tommy didn't think that the mystery changeling would be so stupid to show himself, but halfway through his shift, he noticed someone loitering in the alleyway across the street. He was in the shadows, but Tommy saw enough of him to confirm that he fit the description of the man Lindsey saw. Oh man, he had the worst fashion sense Tommy had ever seen.

Tommy tried to act like the other changeling wasn't there as he opened the club's door for guests and helped the other bouncer eject anyone getting too rowdy. He was probably waiting for Tommy to be alone before he did anything. Well, let him cool his heels.

Tommy went in several hours later to get changed and get his money. Rostami gave him a smirk as he passed over some bills. "Any plans for this evening, Tommy?" he asked in a pleasant tone. The bastard was probably hoping Tommy would get jumped that very night.

"Nah," Tommy said, acting nonchalant. "May just go for a walk. Such a lovely night."

Rostami snorted. "You're a crazy son of a bitch, you know that?"

"Yeah, I heard that before," Tommy replied as he walked out of the office. He lifted an entire bottle of rum from the bar as he made his way out of the club and started walking.

If this changeling had been watching Tommy for weeks, he knew where Tommy liked to sleep. But Tommy headed in the opposite direction of his regular haunts towards the warehouse district. He didn't check behind him, but he got a whiff of his pursuer every time the wind changed. So the guy was a shitty hunter too. Tommy took sips directly out of the bottle as he walked.

He passed the prostitutes and the homeless and the drug dealers braving the rain-splatter streets, paying them no mind, finishing half the bottle by the time he got to the deserted warehouse he was thinking of. He scrambled over the chain-link fence, dropping his bottle but catching it before it touched the ground. He sauntered into the warehouse, not checking to see if he was still being followed.

Once inside, Tommy's relaxed demeanor dropped, and he climbed one of the support beams, settling into the rafters. He took off his shoes and blazer and waited.

The changeling stayed outside awhile before cautiously walking inside. He was sniffing the air loudly, not trying to hide that he was scenting the air like an animal. Tommy waited until the changeling was deeper into the warehouse before dropping from the rafters. The other changeling whirled around with a growl. Tommy just stood there with his blazer held over one shoulder, the bottle of rum in the other hand.

"You need to spend more time with humans," Tommy drawled. He gestured at what the other changeling was wearing. "Cause that outfit is..." He groaned. *"Bad."*

"Thomas Monroe?" the changeling asked, trying to deepen his voice.

"Friends call me Tommy," Tommy joked, "but I have a feeling you are not a friend."

"I'm here to kill you."

"Looks like I was right," Tommy muttered, taking a drink.

"Veles is dead. Hunters murdered him. There is an opening for the generals. If I bring Serapis your head, he will let me be one."

Tommy blinked at the kid's speech and snorted. And he could see that was what he was dealing with—a kid. The poor tracking skills, no knowledge of humans and their customs. The other changeling looked as old as Tommy, but Tommy knew that meant nothing. This changeling couldn't have been alive for more than two decades, three at the most. Tommy should go easy on him. "Did Serapis order you to kill me?" he asked.

The changeling shifted nervously. "What does it matter?"

"It matters because if Serapis finds out you are going around doing things without his orders, he won't be happy you're showing ambition. He will kill you."

The other changeling puffed up. "You are just trying to scare me."

"Yes, but I'm not the one you should be afraid of."

"Quit stalling," the kid growled, low and inhuman deep, in his chest. He transformed, becoming a giant wolf, growing a least a foot and sporting claws and grey fur. "Fight me. Or are you too scared?" He gestured at the bottle. "Or too drunk?"

Tommy sighed and stepped towards the wolf. "Look, Veles was killed by those great hunters, right? The one that glows white and his partner?" Tommy may have been thrown out of the Acolyte mansion by West, but he still hung around enough to hear the story of the general being killed last summer. "Serapis is not going to replace him because, knowing him, no one would be good enough to do it. Especially not a kid like you."

Tommy lifted his bottle to take a drink, but the wolf changeling backhanded it, so it flew to the side, shattering a dozen feet to Tommy's left. Tommy clicked his tongue in annoyance. "I wasn't done with that," he growled.

"Killing you may not make me a general," the wolf changeling rumbled. "But it will make Serapis pleased that you are dead. So now you die, mongrel."

"Now, why did you have to bring the slur into this?" Tommy asked. Suddenly, he whipped the blazer around so that it smacked the wolf changeling in the face, wrapping around his head. The wolf changeling struggled with the blazer, growling and snapping his teeth. While the wolf changeling cursed, Tommy transformed. Finally, the blazer was ripped in half, and the other changeling snarled in triumph, but now Tommy was a foot taller than him, and the wolf's ears dropped as he discovered that Tommy was towering over him.

"Yeah," Tommy rumbled. "You fucked up."

The wolf tried to drop his jaw, realizing too late that he had left his throat exposed, but Tommy wrapped his long fingers around his throat and pushed the wolf back. The wolf changeling snarled and grabbed Tommy's bare arm, drawing blood, but Tommy ignored the pain and slammed the wolf into a wall. He lifted the wolf off the floor, his feet kicking uselessly. Tommy lifted his own foot, placing it on the wolf's thigh and tearing through pants and skin with his claws. The kid punched him and tried to snap at his face, so Tommy threw him.

The wolf landed on his back, scrambling to get back on his feet. Tommy waited for him to launch himself in the air, timing a punch just right so he gave the wolf an uppercut to the jaw. The kid landed on his feet but faltered, so Tommy took the opportunity to wrap an arm around the wolf's neck. The kid tried to bite the arm, but unfortunately for him, it was the left arm. There was an audible *crunch*, and Tommy felt his teeth hurt in sympathy. *Idiot.* Either the kid was really stupid or really didn't do any homework. Tommy grabbed his own arm and started pulling it towards himself, forcing the wolf's jaws open to an uncomfortable degree.

The wolf growled and whined, but it was muffled and unthreatening. Tommy angled the wolf's head to the side, exposing the meaty part of his neck where it met his shoulder. "Change back," Tommy ordered, but the kid just growled back, trying to tear into any part of Tommy he could reach. "Change back, dammit," Tommy tried again but just got a grunt back in return. So Tommy bit him.

Blood gushed into his mouth, and the wolf changeling gave muffled howls and groans of pain. Tommy could continue with more pressure, tear into something vital, and make the kid bleed out on the dirty warehouse floor, but he didn't want to. But he had to make the kid believe he would do it. So he gnawed on the spot for a moment, lamenting his ruined clothes, and then let go, his jaws dripping blood. "Transform, now," he ordered, and this time the stubborn idiot did it.

If anyone came into the warehouse now, Tommy wondered what they would think. He, a seven-foot grey-skinned monstrosity, holding a poor human in the air, forcing the kid's mouth open by shoving his forearm in it. They wouldn't think he was defending himself; they would think he was the attacker, harming this poor man. Tommy tried to not think about it as he growled into the wolf changeling's ear.

"Listen to me," he rumbled. "You obviously didn't think this little meeting through. You are outmatched. And your best chance at survival is to tuck your tail between your legs and run. You probably will want to keep this little date a secret, or not, I don't care. But if you tell others, make sure to tell them this: I'm not going to just roll over and die, and if you come for my head, you bring your best, understood?"

Tommy shoved the other changeling and sent him flying before he could respond. The wolf scrambled away after landing on his ass, wheezing. Tommy changed as well, crouching down and panting, waiting to see what the kid would do. He spat out some blood and tried to wipe his mouth clean. But his clothes were ruined with dark blood. The wolf changeling just lay there, glaring, one hand over the wound that was still bleeding.

Tommy blinked in surprise. "Wait a minute," he muttered. "You look like him. Serapis." He cocked his head to the side. "Is that why you are trying to impress him? Make dear old dad proud of you?"

The wolf changeling sneered. "Knowing who your parents are doesn't matter; that is something only humans care about."

"And yet here you are, getting yourself beat up for that asshole," Tommy said mockingly, leaning his head on his hand.

"Knowing who your family is didn't turn out so well for your mother either, did it?"

Tommy felt his blood run cold, and the cocky grin on his face died. He quickly stood up and stalked up to the other changeling, whose eyes went wide in fear.

When Tommy was towering over the kid, he backhanded him. The wolf changeling seemed to realize how much trouble he was in and tried to backpedal as Tommy raised a fist. The kid started to cower, and Tommy felt the anger die in his chest. He suddenly just felt so tired. Tommy had made his point. He should just go. Tommy studied the leather jacket the other changeling was wearing. *Well*, he thought to himself, *I might as well.*

He grabbed the kid's collar, making him stand. The wolf cowered some more and yelped when Tommy started to rip the jacket off of him, but he didn't open his eyes. Once Tommy got the jacket off, he pushed the kid away, making him land on his ass again. The kid finally opened his eyes while Tommy put the jacket on, checking the fit.

"They will never accept you," the kid said, and Tommy glared at him and raised an eyebrow. "The humans. They will never let you live with them. No matter how much you try to be like them."

"Maybe," Tommy agreed. "But at least I'm not kissing Serapis's ass, trying to keep that sadistic bastard happy." Tommy grinned as he put his hands in the jacket's pockets and started walking backward out of the warehouse. "And at least I will have more style," he purred as he slipped into the night.

14

Tommy spent the next hour pacing the guest room as low-grade rage simmered in his blood. He could hear the teens getting ready for bed, and somehow the sounds of them doing everyday things made his anger worse. Tommy shouldn't be here. He didn't belong here. He was just a horrible changeling to them, not their equal, not their friend. He had been an idiot to think otherwise.

But as quiet descended in the basement of the fallen tower, a violin started playing. Bach's Violin Partita No. 2 in D Minor, and when Tommy recognized it, he felt himself begin to relax. He sighed and rubbed his face. "He's just a kid, Monroe," he muttered to himself. "Give him a break."

He sat on the bed, head leaning on his hand, listening to Chrysta play with a sad smile on his face. It was her way of saying sorry even though she didn't do anything wrong, her way of trying to make him feel better. And it did make him feel better, or maybe it was knowing she cared enough to play it for him that lifted his mood. When she finished, complete silence took over.

Tommy sighed. He needed to get out, go get some fresh air. Would Burke be upset with him for taking a walk in the woods? Screw it. He wasn't a prisoner. He should be able to go where he wanted.

When some time had passed, he got up and took off the pink sweater. He put on his black jeans and his last clean black sweater. He found a grey hoodie and put that on as well. He slowly opened the door to the darkened common room, not seeing anyone at first. When he stepped out of the room, his foot bumped into something. He looked down, and Tommy realized it was the black sweater from Kevin, folded with a note on top. Tommy picked them up while he read the message: a simple *Sorry* with a frowning face next to it.

He was almost at the coat rack when he spied her. Chrysta was on the couch next to the woodstove, wrapped in a blanket, with Poe sleeping on the back of the couch. Just like the night before. Tommy smiled and put the sweater over her, moving some hair off her face.

"She was worried about you," a voice murmured, and Tommy jumped. It was Rimsha, curled up on a nearby armchair. She smiled in apology. "Sorry."

"No problem," Tommy whispered. "Just didn't see you there." Rimsha hummed, closing the book she had been reading and putting it on the table in front of her. "What are you doing out here?" Tommy asked.

"Chrysta took the sleeping potion Miss Normandy gave her, but she still wanted to sleep out here just in case she has a nightmare," Rimsha explained. "Some people can have a bad reaction to the potion, so I was just making sure she was okay before I go to bed."

Tommy nodded. He rubbed the back of his neck and shifted his feet. "About earlier, I should apologize—"

"Don't worry about it," Rimsha told him. "Kevin likes knowing all he can learn about changelings, but he shouldn't force you to talk about stuff you don't want to. Mr. Cross talked to him about not bothering your anymore, but just let Kevin know if he goes too far, okay?"

Tommy nodded again. "Why is he so interested in changelings anyway?"

Rimsha didn't answer but leaned forward and grabbed a book off the table. She pointed to the author's name as she handed *Her Most Loyal Servants* to Tommy. "Paul Butler is Kevin's dad," she explained as Tommy glared at the cover. "I guess he inherited his fascination with changelings from him."

"Fantastic," Tommy muttered, kicking himself mentally for not making the connection sooner. "Who is this guy anyway?"

"Mr. Butler? He has been studying changelings almost his whole life and has written many books about them. So he's considered an expert."

Tommy snorted. "I seriously doubt that any sorcerer can be an expert on changelings."

Rimsha gave him a small smile. "I think that's why Kevin wants to ask questions so badly. You could be the key to solving a lot of mysteries that they still have."

Tommy sighed. "Maybe someday I will give them an exclusive interview." He looked at Chrysta. "But not right now."

Rimsha picked up the book she had been reading and settled in the armchair again. "Mr. Cross mentioned you were getting questioned by Mr. Burke all week. Don't worry about Kevin; I'll make sure he leaves you alone."

"I was going to take a walk," Tommy started to say, "but I can stay and watch Chrysta if you want to get to bed."

"Go ahead. I don't mind staying up." She gestured with the book with a shy smile. It was the romance novel Cross had gotten as a joke. "This is finally getting good."

Tommy snorted and turned back to Chrysta. He leaned down and kissed her forehead, taking a deep breath to enjoy her scent before leaving. He turned to the coat rack, and after getting his jacket and boots on, he opened the door to the outside while Rimsha gave him a soft "Be safe."

The sky was clear and full of stars. Tommy stood in the cold, taking several deep breaths, just examining the sky. It was beautiful. You certainly never saw the stars like this in the city. He looked around, making sure Hafeez was not in the trees waiting for him. Then, when he was sure he was alone, he picked a direction and started walking.

Tommy thought he had picked a random direction, but he found himself walking through the gravel parking lot in front of the Academy. He followed the small road to the entrance, two stone pillars with dragon statues on top and a manicured hedge separating the school grounds from the forest. Finally, the gravel path led to a paved road that winded into the woods, and Tommy followed it.

The road started to weave west, and Tommy walked with it, not rushing. Snow crunched under his boots, but otherwise, the woods were silent and still. Tommy, who had lived most of his life in the city, couldn't remember the last time he had been in a space that was so serene. He also wondered if he was crossing one of Burke's wards and if the headmaster would appear and tell him to go back.

He didn't mean to travel all the way to New Bendigo, but after an hour of walking, he crossed the train tracks and found himself on the outskirts of the small town. He considered turning back but noticed a nearby building that seemed open. Bikers were standing outside, talking and laughing and drinking while leaning on their motorcycles. A bar? Tommy stood in the dark, weighing his options. Should he go in? Get a drink? Go back and try to sleep? He had money. It had been a long week. *Fuck it.* A few drinks wouldn't hurt.

He made his way across the street, keeping an eye on the bikers. There were eight tattooed and bearded men, and Tommy hoped they weren't the racist type. They looked at him in curiosity but otherwise did not say or do anything as he walked toward them. The bar was a one-story brick building with windows covering the entire front, mirrored so that you couldn't look inside. Writing on the door identified is as *The Wandering Ostrich,* making Tommy pause and squint at the door before opening it and walking inside.

The space that greeted him on the inside bar was small and dim while still warm and clean. It was like most of the bars he had ever been in, walls covered in framed photos and flyers. There were dartboards and a pool table opposite the long bar. A mirror filled the wall behind the bar, reflecting the bright and colorful collection of spirits. The only thing that made this bar stand out from all the others Tommy had ever been in was the stuffed ostrich neck and head hanging on the wall. *Our Founding Father* stated a golden plaque beneath it.

Two older men sat at one end of the bar, one white and one black, with long grey beards and deep-lined faces. Tommy wondered that if they stood up from their stools, would the seats be molded in the shape of their asses. A younger man was tending the bar, wiping it down as Tommy settled on a stool. Tommy noticed someone sitting in the back, a woman in one of the booths with a cell phone lighting her face and nothing else.

"What can I getcha?" the bartender asked. He was clean-shaven, long hair pulled into a messy bun, a deep voice, and blue eyes that crinkled at the corners when he smiled.

"Rum," Tommy ordered, peeling a fifty off the money he had brought with him.

"Top shelf?"

"That would be fine."

The bartender grabbed a glass and poured two fingers of rum with some ice, placing it in front of Tommy with a smile. Tommy took a sip and grimaced at the burn but smiled as he felt the heat bloom in his stomach. Gods, how he had missed this.

The bartender put another glass in front of Tommy before he was done with his first one. "So, new to town?" he asked—no malice in his voice, just benign interest.

"Yep," Tommy confirmed, not elaborating further. He drained the first glass and grabbed the next one.

"Where are you staying? You came out of the woods. Only thing out there is the school."

Tommy paused. He was surprised that the Academy would let the ordinary townsfolk of New Bendigo know that they were there. Or maybe it made sense. The school was barely five miles out of town limits, after all. "Yeah, I'm staying there for now," he confessed.

"No offense, you look too old to be one of the students. Are you a teacher?"

Tommy snorted. "No. Helped a friend get out of a bad situation, and they are helping to protect her. I don't know how long they will let me stay before they kick me out, but I have a feeling that it will be soon."

The bartender chuckled. "Well, welcome to New Bendigo. Hope you have a good visit, however long that may be."

Tommy held up his glass. "This helps, trust me." The bartender smiled as he moved back down to clean the other end of the bar.

For the next few minutes, the older men started having an animated but low conversation, hands moving all over the place and occasionally hitting each other. Suddenly, they paused and studied Tommy for several long moments. Tommy, enjoying his third drink, chose to ignore them. Finally, with grunts and groans, they got up and joined Tommy at his end of the bar, the black man sitting to his right and the white man to his left. Tommy didn't say anything, just waited for them to talk.

"So you are from that school, huh?" the white man asked.

Tommy thought about the question for a second. "In a way."

"What is going on up there?" the other man asked.

"It's aliens, right?"

Tommy blinked. "Excuse me?"

"There has always been talk about that school," the black man explained. "Rumors about mysterious lights and smells. All the people there have exotic pets. I say it's a cult, but my friend here thinks they're aliens, teaching those kids how to act human." The white man was nodding enthusiastically.

Tommy continued to blink in surprise for a few minutes. "You wouldn't believe me if I told you."

"Oh, come on, we have a bet going on which one of us is right. All we are asking for is the truth."

Tommy gave them a cocky grin. He lowered his head. "Do you really want to know?"

Both men lowered their heads as well, leaning in closer.

"Magic," Tommy whispered, waving his fingers dramatically. "Everyone there is a sorcerer."

Both men looked surprised and scowled at the same time. "What, you mean like those Henry Pothole movies from a few years back?"

"Jim, Rich, leave him alone," the bartender said with a sigh.

"What? Just trying to get the inside scoop," the black man said.

"Nothing weird is going on there," the bartender told them as he grabbed another glass and motioned with it silently to ask if Tommy wanted another drink. Tommy nodded. "All the students and teachers are polite as hell, and this town is better with them around."

"Well," the white man grumbled, Tommy still not sure if he was Jim or Rich, "I still say it's aliens." He placed a five-dollar bill in front of Tommy as he got up. "If you ever decide to tell the truth, you let me know."

The other man got up, also putting money in front of Tommy and following his friend. "If you ever decide to tell the truth, you let *me* know first."

He was on his sixth drink when the woman hugged him from behind. For one alcohol-filled crazy second, he thought it was Chrysta with one hand on his chest and the other on his thigh, and he was so happy she was there. But before he greeted her, he looked in the mirror behind the bar and felt a stab of annoyance when he realized that this woman wasn't Chrysta.

The mystery woman was the exact opposite of Chrysta, really. Hair bleached within an inch of its life with pink streaks. Heavy makeup and flashy jewelry. Pink camo shirt with plunging neckline and short shorts. Skin so tanned it was turning into leather and manicured pink nails. "Hey, sugar," she whispered in Tommy's ear with a fake southern drawl. "You look lonely. Want some company tonight?"

"Nope," he flatly replied, finishing his drink in one gulp. "Just want to go solo tonight."

"Oh, come on," she said with a grin. She pressed her chest into Tommy's back. "I can't let someone so cute be so lonesome."

Tommy fought the urge to roll his eyes. Even before meeting Chrysta, women like this were not attractive to him, but now, comparing her to Chrysta, she was so fake it was a turn-off. Instead of answering, he knocked on the bar with a knuckle, and the bartender gave him another drink, scowling at the woman. "Go away, Megan. He said he wants to be alone."

"Oh, fuck off, Nick," she growled, fake accent dropping for a second. She put a smile back on her face as the hand on Tommy's thigh started going up. "What do you say, stranger? I think you and me could have a lot of fun," she purred in his ear.

Tommy grabbed her wrist, pinching it a little harder than he had to, to stop her hand on its journey. He turned around on the barstool, holding her hand away from his body. Megan hissed and glared at him, but she tried to replace her frown with a pout once Tommy let go of her wrist. He reached into a pocket of his jacket and got out his money. Tommy found a fifty-dollar bill and held it up. "Can we skip the part of trying to get into my pants?" he asked, offering her the money.

Megan's expression went hungry with curiosity, watching him get the money out, to a thunderous rage when he offered her the single bill. She slapped him across the face, and as Tommy blinked and rubbed his jaw, she snatched the bill out of his hand. "Asshole!" she hissed at him as she stalked out of the bar. The two older men chuckled and hooted at her antics from the safety of their end of the bar.

"Sorry about her," Nick said as Tommy turned around and grabbed his drink. Megan grabbed a parka and flounced out the door. "She likes to party, but only if she can use someone else's money."

"It's not like she's wrong," Tommy muttered. He watched as Megan started talking to the bikers, arms waving in agitation. Tommy happened to look beyond them and felt his stomach drop as he recognized the figure walking towards the bar from the woods. Not in her hunter uniform, Hafeez stalked to the bar, and Tommy had a feeling it was not to say a friendly hello.

"Aw hell," he muttered as she burst through the door, and she beelined to the stool right next to Tommy. The old men leaned around each other to get a better look at her. Nick was staring at her with wide eyes, probably too scared to leave the safety of the other end of the bar to see if she wanted anything to drink.

"What are you doing?" she hissed.

"Getting a drink," Tommy murmured back. "I would offer you a glass, but I have a feeling you would decline."

"You shouldn't *be* here," she continued like he didn't say anything.

"Burke never said I had to stay at the Academy," Tommy tried to reason with her. "I'm not causing any trouble. I'm not hurting anyone."

"I still don't know why he seems to trust you unequivocally," she said. "He should have thrown you in the deepest, darkest hole he could find, and I refuse to believe otherwise."

Tommy sighed, placing his empty glass on the bar. "Look, hate me if you want, but if you don't trust Burke for trusting me, that sounds like a problem with *you*, not me."

She blinked, and then her glare turned into something predatory. "If Burke won't see you as the monster you are, I will make him understand just how dangerous you really can be." With that, she put both hands on the bar and pushed away, stomping outside. She started talking to the bikers too, and fear began to settle in Tommy's stomach.

"Hey, are you alright?" Nick asked, watching the hunter gesture and point inside, fear on her face.

"I have a feeling I'm not going to be," Tommy said. Looking both and forth between the two women, the bikers were starting to look pissed. "Is there a back door here?"

"Yeah, past the bathrooms."

"Is it alarmed?"

"No. Good luck. I'll hold them off as long as I can."

Tommy quickly got up and immediately grabbed the edge of the bar, the room swaying. He had a little more alcohol than he realized. He made sure that the money the old men had left was still on the bar and started walking quickly to the back. "Gentlemen," he said with false cheer, "it's been fun." Nick watched the door as Tommy clapped Jim and Rich (Tommy still wasn't sure who was who) on the backs, and Tommy retreated.

He jogged to the exit, easing the back door open and letting it shut behind him when he heard Nick call out, "What's up, guys, need more beers?" The door was almost shut when he saw someone moving out of the corner of his left eye. Tommy jerked back and stuck out his foot, sending the man who was trying to punch him flying. Tommy tried to go back inside, but the door was completely closed and locked behind him. He glanced to his left and saw two more men trying to flank him. "Guys, this is just a big misunderstanding," he said but started to run before they could respond.

He vaulted over the man on the ground, made it around the building, skidded past a dumpster, and shot past the front of the bar, trying to make it into the woods. When he was in the middle of the road, there was a shout, and two more men joined the chase. Tommy was almost across the street before one of the men tackled him, and he went down, teeth clacking as his jaw hit the pavement. By the time he had gotten back some of his wits, the bikers had circled around him, and he picked himself off the ground, groaning.

Tommy put his hands up to show that they were empty. "Look, guys," he panted, "normally, I would agree that I deserve an ass-kicking once and a while, but this time I think I'll take a raincheck."

Megan and Hafeez were behind the ring of men. Hafeez was smirking with her arms crossed while Megan bounced up and down in excitement. A young man stepped up, bringing the number of bikers surrounding Tommy to eight. "Kick his ass, Charlie!" Megan crowed happily.

"Hey, stranger. I don't know where you're from, but here in this town, we treat women better," the man named Charlie told Tommy. He cracked his knuckles as the other men murmured in agreement.

"Usually, I would applaud you for your feminist ways, but I'm telling you, this is a misunderstanding."

The bar's door burst open, and Nick leaned out. "Charlie, I'm calling the sheriff! Don't you hurt him!"

"Just means we only have a few minutes to beat a lesson into you," Charlie muttered so only Tommy could hear him.

Tommy's shoulders slumped as he realized he wasn't getting out of the fight. "Alright, let's do this." And he put his fists up.

Charlie surprised him by coming at him directly, fists held up in a boxer's stance. Charlie swung at Tommy, and the changeling ducked. Charlie tried hitting with his other fist, but Tommy leaned back and let it sail by his nose. "Dammit, stop moving!" Charlie yelled when Tommy ducked for the third time. Tommy tried to circle Charlie to stay out of his reach but had to jump back when one of the others took a swing at him. Charlie took advantage of Tommy being distracted and got Tommy's temple with a right hook.

The bikers and Megan cheered as Tommy shook his head, eyes stinging from the blow, and a biker grabbed him from behind to pin his arms to his sides. Charlie grinned and moved forward, getting his fists up for another shot at Tommy, but the changeling surprised him when he brought up his feet, planting them on Charlie's chest, and kicking with all of his strength, making Tommy and the man holding him fall backward while Charlie went flying in the other direction.

Tommy was on his feet in a flash, but before he could get up to start running, a biker tried to kick him, and Tommy caught his foot and pushed him back, making the man stumble and land on his backside. Two men launched themselves at Tommy and stopped him from getting up, letting Charlie get a kick in. Tommy wheezed as the air was knocked out of his lungs.

Before Charlie could kick him again, Tommy elbowed one man in the face while pushing the other one away, catching Charlie's foot and throwing the man off balance. Suddenly, Tommy surged up, punching Charlie in the diaphragm, so Charlie let out a loud *oomph* as Tommy got his feet under him.

Once again, Tommy turned to the forest to make a break for it, but this time four men grabbed him before he could escape. They pummeled him: ribs, stomach, face, and Tommy cursed as he felt his lip split. The cut over his eye was freely bleeding, and the blood made him close his left eye, limiting his field of vision. He growled, not his threatening guttural cat rumble, but a human growl of frustration, and he started fighting back. The man holding his right arm got an uppercut to the jaw, and Tommy kept swinging until only one man was holding on. Tommy pushed him with all of his might, and the biker went flying, knocking Charlie on his ass again. If the biker hadn't been wearing a jacket, he probably would have had the worst case of road rash of his life.

There was a snarling sound behind Tommy, and he spun around to see Hafeez's caracal daring towards him for out of the woods. He put his arms up to protect himself as the cat landed on him. He grabbed a handful of the cat's skin and threw him, the caracal twisting in the air to land on his feet and hissing. The bikers all took a step back, looking between Tommy and the large cat.

"Hafeez, call him off," Tommy said, trying to stay calm as the cat circled him. Hafeez didn't say anything, but Tommy noticed her hand was in her jacket, probably holding a weapon. He realized that she was waiting for him to transform, and then she would have all the justification she needed to kill him. He didn't know why she was doing this in front of witnesses, especially normies. But Tommy wasn't going to give her the excuse she was looking for to attack him.

The caracal hissed again and rushed at Tommy, trying to swipe at Tommy's legs. Tommy jumped back, the bikers scattering as he avoided teeth and claws. He drew one leg back and kicked the cat in the ribs, making the familiar hiss as he twisted in pain.

"Siad!" Hafeez cried, and she started to take her hand out of her jacket, hand wrapped around the hilt of a hunting knife, just like Tommy assumed. Suddenly a brown SUV pulled up and screeched to a halt, red and blue lights flashing. Megan retreated to the bar, where Nick, Jim, and Rich stood, watching the fight. "It was eight against one, sheriff!" one of the older men yelled. "And now they got that cat involved!"

A taller man came running around the car's front while a shorter Latino man hopped out of the passenger seat. The sheriff slowed down as he took in the situation: Tommy still trying to stay out of the caracal's reach, Hafeez holding a knife that had to be at least six inches long, and eight bewildered bikers standing in a loose circle. The sheriff put his hand on his gun but didn't take it out of the holster. "Alright, everyone on the ground!" he ordered. The bikers complied immediately, kneeling and putting their hands above their heads. When Tommy tried to stop moving to follow the order, Siad's claws finally caught his thigh, and Tommy cursed.

"Call him off!" the sheriff roared at Hafeez, taking out his gun but keeping it pointed at the ground. She nodded and finally dropped the knife.

"Siad, down!" Hafeez called out, and the caracal finally backed off, joining her as she kneeled on the ground with her hands behind her head as well.

Tommy panted and slowly kneeled. The sheriff made his way over to the changeling and crouched down, knees popping as he did so. "Damn," he muttered. "You look like shit."

Tommy smirked. "Would you believe me if I said this wasn't the worst beating I've ever got?"

15

February 1972

Tommy stood in the back of the dining room of the acolyte mansion, leaning on the wall and scowling. It was packed, standing room only, as West made his speech. The people in the room cheered and murmured and gasped as West gestured wildly. Tommy had stopped paying attention to the words about a half-hour ago, but West had ordered him to stay, so stay Tommy did. It was dark in the back of the room, so Tommy couldn't see who had joined him, only smell the man. "Hey, Guerra," he whispered, "can you try to kill me? I don't want to listen to this shit anymore."

Guerra surprisingly chuckled. "Oh, don't be like that," he whispered back, arms folded behind him. He kept that disturbing smile on his face as he surveyed the room. "It's important that we all get together as a family and remind ourselves of our mission every few years."

"'We will bring our Lady back,' blah blah blah, 'we will be her chosen ones,' blah blah blah, 'we will prosper in her golden light,'" Tommy muttered.

"And as her creation, you will be blessed twofold for bringing your god back to you."

"I don't worship that bitch," Tommy muttered, and Guerra's fake smile dropped, and he looked at Tommy with rage on his face. Tommy broke out with a brilliant smile. "Oh, sorry, was that blasphemy?"

"You walk a fine line, changeling," Guerra growled. He opened his mouth, probably to continue to berate Tommy for his heresy, when West started to project the last of his speech.

"*—and with the knowledge to bring our Lady back to us, we will fulfill our promise to her and usher in a new age of prosperity for all!*"

The mob cheered, and Guerra turned to clap as well, watching Tommy out of the corner of his eye. West left the temporary stage and started to move through the crowd, shaking hands and offering a smile to everyone around him. Tommy stayed leaning on the wall, refusing to clap or smile. The whole show turned his stomach.

Tommy pointed at a group of acolytes crowding around a young man, shaking the kid's hand and clapping him on the back. "Who is the kid?" Tommy asked Guerra in a whisper.

"A new recruit," Guerra said in a purr. "He is young, but he glows white. The hunters have Burke, and now we finally have someone who will be just as powerful."

Tommy studied the kid as West's second in command, the overweight Wilkes, came up to him and shook the kid's hand. He was small and pale but wore a haughty expression that made him look older. The look of disdain on the kid's face as he shook Wilkes's hand made Tommy smile. "Doesn't look like much."

"Give me time," Guerra replied, a fake smile pulling on the edges of his lip again. "In a year, he will be the best enforcer ever."

West gestured to Guerra and Tommy to join him, and they both stood up from the wall and started to push through the crowd. West liked to have Guerra and Tommy nearby when the Acolytes were around, probably showing the power he wielded over the most feared acolyte alive and a deadly changeling. Soon, they would complete their show here at the mansion and move to a nearby restaurant for dinner, a display of the Acolytes' wealth.

Tommy was forcing his way through the mob when a body collided with him. He put his hands up instinctively, grabbing the figure by the shoulders, just to make sure neither of them fell. It was a woman, one of the wives of the Acolytes, and when she turned to him with rage on her face, Tommy felt his stomach drop. The wives were just as bad as their husbands, shrill and sharp, treating Tommy as a loathsome creature and not a person. She stepped back in shock and then slapped Tommy with an open palm. Tommy was actually impressed as his head rocked back.

"Don't touch me!" she shrieked.

A man put himself between her and Tommy and glared at the changeling. "Don't touch my wife!" he ordered.

"Now then, what happened?" West asked as he walked up to the small group causing a scene in the middle of the dining room. He was smiling, but it was strained.

"This creature dared to assault my wife!" the man cried. Tommy recognized him as someone who visited the mansion often but couldn't remember his name. "It should be punished!"

"Now, I don't think Thomas meant anything by it," Wilkes said as she slid up to the woman to pat her hand. "He knows better than to hurt anyone without due cause."

West looked Tommy up and down. "Well, if you would feel better, Chambers, I can have the slave stay here while we move to have dinner."

"Yes, yes. I think that would be best," the acolyte said, giving Tommy a smug smile. He put his arm around his wife, the woman just glaring at Tommy. "Have it stay here, away from us all."

"Thomas, go to the basement. Don't leave until morning. Understood?"

Tommy shrugged. It meant he wouldn't eat that night, but then he wouldn't have to stay around these assholes. "As you wish," he said and turned around and left the dining room as the other acolytes watched him go, laughing and talking behind their hands.

Tommy went towards the back of the house, passing the empty kitchen and opening the basement door. He went down the stairs to the small nook he was given to sleep in, taking off his tie and jacket as he descended. One bed, with a flat mattress and pillow, a small bookcase that housed his record collection and player, and his violin were the only belongings West allowed him to have. He flopped on the bed and waited for the Acolytes to leave.

It took a while for the talking and the laughing and the shuffling of feet to go away as the Acolytes left. But Tommy waited, listening for a deafening silence that pressed from above. Nothing. He leaned over to the bookcase and grabbed an Aretha Franklin record, putting it on the player, and turned the volume up to the highest setting. When no one came down to yell at him to turn it off, he knew he was truly alone, and he finally reached into his jacket to take out the piece of paper that Mrs. Chambers had put in there when they collided.

Mrs. Chambers had gone through a lot of trouble to get a message to Tommy, but it only contained one sentence: *Help me save my son.* Tommy blinked at it for a few minutes. The children of the Acolytes were forced to join the cult when they grew up, whether they wanted to or not. Some of them would try to escape. Very few of them would actually succeed in defecting. So what exactly did Mrs. Chambers expect Tommy to do? He couldn't even save himself.

He leaned on the wall, studying the paper. When no more instructions appeared, he grabbed a candle and lit it, tearing up the paper and feeding it to the flames. Save her son, she said, like doing so wouldn't mean instant death for him. When the message was ash, he laid down in the bed with headphones on, listening to Franklin sing her heart out. Although, it wasn't like death was not an appealing option at this point. No more slave band, no more suffering at the hands of men who didn't care about him.

And no more fucking boring speeches.

.....

By the following day, Tommy had pretty much forgotten about the piece of paper Mrs. Chambers slipped him. But, strangely enough, it was Chambers himself who served up the perfect way to help his wife a few weeks later.

West had a meeting in the study with some of the Acolytes, which meant he wanted Tommy to act as a bodyguard. So there he was, in a suit, staring at nothing as the men droned on about... something. He wasn't paying much attention. Chambers was there as well, complaining about the cost of buying an antique, Tommy finally remembering that he was the Acolytes' accountant. For the most part, the men ignored him, so Tommy was practicing music in his mind, playing jazz and blues on the piano in his imagination. Several hours later, the acolytes left, and West left the study, not even acknowledging the changeling. Tommy noticed a newspaper in the chair Chambers used, and he went over to investigate.

Chambers had left a copy of *The Rising Phoenix,* the sorcerer newspaper. West would have a fit if he saw it just sitting there. Most of the staff were normies, and a magical newspaper just lying around would attract the wrong kind of attention. Tommy picked it up. He didn't care what was going on in the magical world, but it would help relieve some of the boredom. Tommy headed to the basement.

The front page was covered in a photo of the hunters Burke and Zheng, dressed in formal wear. *Romance in the Ranks?* read the headline, and Tommy had to admit that the two looked pretty friendly. Something in the way Burke rested his hand on the small of her back as she placed a hand on his arm. The accompanying article claimed the two were more than just partners while also pointing out Burke's broken engagement to another woman. It was mildly interesting for the drama alone.

The rest of the newspaper was dull and uninteresting, but Tommy paused when he looked over the last page, covered in advertisements. Among the ads for spells and magical items, there was a small ad for the Hunter Organization: *See Something? Suspicious Behavior? Illegal Activity? Possible Changeling Sighting? Call the hunters today! We are here for your protection!*

Tommy ran his finger along the border of the ad, circling the phone number in red, and it gave him an idea.

"Alright, Chambers," he murmured to himself. "Let's see if we can invite some hunters to the party."

.....

West didn't need Tommy every day, so Tommy could leave the mansion sometimes. The next time he had the opportunity, he made sure no one saw him go with a big box.

He went to the nearest black neighborhood and found a pawn shop. Half an hour later, he left without the box and with a small ball of money in his pocket. He hated getting rid of his collection, but if he did survive this insane little plan he had, he felt that they would be the first thing West would destroy in a fit of rage.

Several days later, Tommy was back in the study, listening to the Acolytes talk again. He paid a little more attention to Chambers this time, especially when he was talking to West. The men hated each other as far as Tommy could tell (not surprising, none of the Acolytes really liked each other), but they were butting heads over money.

"We must release our Lady," West argued. "The artifact will free her."

"You *assume* it will free her," Chambers countered. "Meanwhile, we will bankrupt the entire organization on a hunch."

"Money is of no value to us. Once our Lady is given back to us, we will be rich beyond measure," Guerra purred.

"Either way, I am your leader, Chambers. You listen to me," West growled. "I weary of you fighting this." He stood up from his desk and straightened his jacket. "Find the money, make it work." And with that, he strode out of the office, Chambers glaring at the man's back as he left. Finally, it looked like Tommy was going to get his chance.

Once West went to bed that night, Tommy wasted no time changing clothes and letting himself out of the mansion, carrying his violin, the last possession he couldn't part with. There were guards posted at the gate, but Tommy jumped over the wall near the balcony on the second story. A tree there made the climb quick and quiet. Chambers walked to the mansion, meaning he had to live nearby. Tommy caught the acolyte's scent and followed it. He found a park on his way and hid his violin in a tree, hoping to come back for it later.

The Chambers mansion was larger than the one West was living in, and Tommy wondered briefly if Chambers was stealing money from the Acolytes. He found the wards at the front gate and paused. Once Tommy passed the threshold, there was no going back. West could find out he was here, and he wouldn't be happy. Tommy took a breath, scaled the gate, and started marching to the front door.

Tommy got to the entrance and kicked at it, breaking the lock quickly. He strolled into the foyer and waited with his arms folded. Lights turned on upstairs, and Chambers appeared with his wife in tow, both tying bathrobes around them. "What is the meaning of this?" Chambers called out, voice shaking slightly.

"West sent me," Tommy lied. The band started to burn, but he ignored it. "He's not happy with you right now."

Chambers snorted. "You stupid creature. You needed to come and break down my door to deliver a message?"

Tommy grinned, trying to make it look as evil as possible. "That wasn't the message." He transformed and growled, flexing his claws as Chambers paled and his wife screamed.

"N-now, no ne-need for t-that," Chambers stammered, taking a step back up the stairs. "We can come to an ar-arrangement."

"You don't have anything I would want," Tommy growled, and he started towards the acolyte. Chambers turned and ran, actually grabbing his wife and pushing her towards the changeling. Tommy ignored her prone figure and continued after her husband.

Chambers ran into what looked like the master bedroom. He went for a desk and rifled through the contents as Tommy ran into the room. Chambers had grabbed a beacon charm and was about to break it, probably to summon the other acolytes, but Tommy knocked it out of his hand. The changeling grabbed the man by the throat and lifted him up. Chambers made a motion with his hand, and Tommy felt the wind whip by him. The ability to move objects, only as a changeling, Chambers couldn't move Tommy. Chambers made another hand motion, and a chair moved from across the room and hit Tommy on the head. Tommy shook the pain away, growled, and punched Chambers, knocking him out cold.

Tommy went to the hallway after dropping Chambers, scenting the air to find the lady of the house. He cautiously moved to an open door, leaning inside to search the bedroom. After he cleared the threshold, he spotted her, but she threw several objects at him before he could say anything. They hit him *thwack-thwack-thwack*, sharp icicles several inches long and about an inch thick, in a line from hip to shoulder.

Tommy looked at the icicles embedded in his torso, shock keeping the pain at bay. "Dammit, woman," he rumbled. "Is this how you thank everybody who tries to help you?"

She blinked, and the icicle forming in her hand quickly melted. "Wha... What do you mean? You're not here to kill us?"

"No," Tommy said, and he grunted as he pulled an icicle out of his chest. "You wanted to get your son out. This is the best plan I could come up with."

Mrs. Chambers looked confused for a moment. "Killing my husband?"

Tommy took something out of his pocket and held it out to her. She cautiously took it. He pointed at the red number in the ad with one black claw. "Would be a shame if hunters decided to come here and stop me."

"They won't come here," Mrs. Chambers whispered.

"They will if they think I'm here to kill you. They will want to at least capture your husband and interrogate him. If your husband believes West doesn't want him alive anymore, he will talk to them. You will have to go into hiding, but your son will not be forced to serve the Acolytes. You're free."

She blinked at him again and then looked at the piece of paper in her hand. "What about you?" she asked.

Tommy shrugged with one shoulder. "The hunters' goodwill won't stretch to include me. Don't tell them I helped you. It will make you look crazy and not help the story we made up."

She studied him with shining eyes. "I'm sorry," she whispered, gesturing at his wounds. "I'm sorry for... I'm sorry for hitting you. I needed to get a message to you, but I... that was the only way I could think of doing it."

"I know," he murmured. "You did well. Very convincing, and that slap was awesome."

She laughed a sad sound. Suddenly her husband called out. "Helen!" he bellowed from the other room.

"You make the call," Tommy told her. "I'll keep him busy."

He turned to go back to the hallway, and she suddenly reached out and put a hand on his shoulder. "Thank you," she whispered. He didn't say anything but nodded and left.

Chambers was standing in the hall, holding his head and looking dazed. He blanched when he saw Tommy leave the room. "Wha-what did you do to my wife and s-son?" Chambers stuttered.

"Only what I was told to do," Tommy said. He growled, flashing as many teeth as he could. "Now it's your turn."

He let Chambers run downstairs, hoping his wife had a phone she could use upstairs. Chambers was halfway down the last flight of stairs when Tommy tackled him. "No, no, please," the man started to beg, sweaty and red in the face. "You don't have to do this. I will listen to West, I swear."

"Not my call to make," Tommy rumbled. A coatrack flew at Tommy, and he batted it away. Chambers gestured at a grandfather clock in the foyer, and it rattled and then flew at Tommy. The changeling had to stand up to catch it, and Chambers took the chance to get up and run. Tommy roared and smashed the clock on the wall.

Tommy tackled the man again, wondering if he should just kill the acolyte for being annoying. Suddenly, there was a *pop,* and four figures appeared in the foyer. Tommy registered their black hunter uniforms and roared, trying to sell the dangerous changeling act. The sorcerers drew their swords while one lit up a fireball in his hand.

"Please!" Chambers wailed. "Please help me!"

"Please help us!" Tommy heard a voice cry behind him, and he looked over his shoulder to see Mrs. Chambers on the stairs with a young boy cowering behind her. Tommy looked at the hunters and hissed but turned around to run towards the stairs.

"Stop!" someone ordered behind him, and the fireball connected with Tommy's head. It didn't hurt him, but it did stun him for a moment, and he had to stop to shake his head. Two hunters rushed at him, and he hopped out of the way, trying to stay out of the reach of their swords. He hissed and took a swipe at them, a claw actually catching one of them on the arm. Instead of continuing that fight, Tommy turned and ran upstairs, passing Mrs. Chambers and her son.

There was a window at the end of the hall, and Tommy crashed into it, landing on his feet. He transformed in the front yard and ran. Hunters yelled from the mansion, but he didn't look back as he ran to the gate and scaled it.

He ran towards West's mansion, hoping the hunters wouldn't give chase. He was traveling down an alleyway when he saw a group of people running toward him.

Tommy stopped and cursed under his breath when he recognized West and Guerra in front. The hunters teleporting to the Chambers's mansion caught their attention. West took in Tommy's appearance and scowled. "What happened?" he growled.

"The hunters have Chambers," Tommy said. "I think he was defecting."

West studied Tommy and walked up to him. West grabbed Tommy's left arm and held it up. "What did you do?" West growled.

"Nothing," Tommy lied, but the band lit up.

"Oh, Thomas," West said with an evil smile. "What have you done?"

. . . . .

West dragged Tommy back to the mansion while he ordered the others to check on Chambers. When they went down into the basement and West saw that the record collection and violin were gone, the look of rage on his face made Tommy both scared and pleased at the same time. Guerra came back and reported that the Chambers's mansion was empty. West's look of fury melted into something serene. "Send everyone home," West told Wilkes.

And then the beating started.

West, a former enforcer, took his coat off and started to hit Tommy with the power and precision of a boxer. Tommy couldn't fight back, not while West had the ring on, so he just took the blows the best he could, trying to keep himself from crying out or reacting. Punches, kicks, Tommy lost count of how many hits he took. Finally, his legs gave out from under him. He was panting from the pain, putting his forehead on the cool basement floor, when West stomped on his right hand. Tommy did scream this time, snatching his hand away and cradling it to his chest.

"What were you thinking?" West panted. "Hm? Did you really think you could attack an acolyte and not face any consequences?"

"Just hated his smug face," Tommy wheezed.

West lifted his foot again, aiming for Tommy's face, when Wilkes, holding a handkerchief up to his nose, grabbed his arm. "Maybe the slave can still be useful," Wilkes said calmly.

"Chambers is gone. He will be interrogated and spill all our secrets. We will lose all the money and assets he was in control of," West growled. He started to pace the basement. "How can this creature be useful? If the others think I can't control him, they will revolt, and demand I step down. Better I kill him now."

"Tell everyone that you sent the slave to kill Chambers. That he was stealing from us and needed to be punished. The slave failed and is now forced to live on the streets."

"Where we can't watch him," West countered.

"Where he can't meddle with anyone unless you order him to," Guerra added.

West paused in his pacing, hand to mouth, for several minutes. Tommy waited, trying to keep quiet as he held his injured hand to his chest. He had expected West to kill him for insubordination, but maybe Wilkes could get West to reconsider. Finally, West sighed. "Fine," West snarled. West grabbed the wound on Tommy's shoulder, pulling him up from the floor. Tommy tried to not react to the flare of pain. West leaned over to hiss in Tommy's ear. "Now listen here, you son of a bitch," he started to say.

"Actually, my mother was a leopard changeling," Tommy joked, and this time he did whimper as West tightened his grip on Tommy's damaged shoulder.

"You are going to leave the mansion," West continued, ignoring Tommy's pained gasp. "You will now live on the streets. You will not tell anyone what happened here tonight. But mark my words, another incident like this one, and you will be dead. Do I make myself clear?"

"Crystal," Tommy groaned, and he slumped over when West let him go.

West started up the stairs, passing Guerra. "Get him out of my home," he ordered. Wilkes followed, looking smug even as he kept his nose covered.

Guerra gave Tommy a moment to pick himself off the floor. "Oh, you used to be so valuable," Guerra said, smiling sadly. "A shining example of what our Lady's deadliest creatures could accomplish."

"You mean when I used to listen to you assholes?" Tommy asked. He tried to flex his hand and winced at the bones moving against each other. Definitely broken. "No thanks."

"Well, if the day comes when you are to be killed, I promise to make it quick and painless."

Tommy glared at the man. "Your kindness knows no bounds."

Guerra escorted Tommy outside, opening the gate for him and closing it behind Tommy. Tommy stood on the sidewalk, swaying slightly. His right eye was swollen shut, his right hand was broken, it felt like one of his ribs was bruised, and he was covered in his own blood. But, his plan had worked. Mrs. Chambers was free of the Acolytes, and he was free of the mansion.

He walked with no destination in mind. Maybe he should go to a hospital to at least get his hand looked at. He passed a homeless man sitting on the ground who called out. "Damn. You look like shit." Tommy glared until the man held out a bottle of booze. Tommy broke out in a grin and grabbed the bottle, taking a large gulp and wincing at the burn.

"You should see the other guy," Tommy told him.

16

New Bendigo's sheriff opened the door to the cellblock and let himself inside with someone in tow. Tommy was not surprised that it was Burke and his Irish wolfhound. But he was surprised when Burke paused with a look of wonder as he took in the cellblock, the most expressive that Tommy had seen him. Although they *were* all a sight to see.

New Bendigo's jail housed three cells, each big enough to hold four or five people comfortably. But all eight of the bikers were packed into the middle cell, sporting cuts, bruises, and black eyes. They all crowded into the middle, trying to put as much space between themselves and the bars as possible like they were scared of what the other two cells contained. Tommy was in the cell closest to the door by himself, blood crusted around his eye and lip, a white bandage wrapped around his thigh. Hafeez was in the last cell, her caracal pacing back and forth, occasionally hissing at the men in the middle.

"Well, isn't this a spectacle," Tommy heard Burke mutter under his breath, and Tommy snorted. He groaned as the snort made his head pound.

"Sheriff, you can't keep us in here like this," Charlie started to protest, but he stopped when the sheriff held up a hand.

"Don't worry, Charlie. I was just letting you cool your heels while I figured out what to do with you," the sheriff replied. He was as tall as Burke but broader.

His hair was dark and long, although his face was clean-shaven. He glanced at Burke, and the headmaster nodded. The sheriff put his hand up and snapped his fingers, causing orange sparks to fly in the air. Tommy's eyes watered at the smell of magic filling the small space, and all of the bikers stopped and stared at the man.

"Now, you guys got into a fight tonight, which is not surprising since you guys get into a fight once a month." The bikers all nodded at the same time, slow and robotic. "What was different this time is that the young man you jumped was innocent."

"Innocent," all the bikers droned at once. Tommy stared at them, but they only looked at the sheriff, faces blank.

"You will remember his face, and if you see him again, you will leave him alone. If anyone asks you what happened tonight, you will tell them you were wrong in jumping this man but fortunate that he didn't press any charges."

The bikers nodded, some of them looking upset and ashamed.

"Now, the only woman you saw tonight was Megan. You did not see another woman and her," he paused as he looked at the caracal, and it hissed at him, "very large cat."

"No cat," the bikers said together.

The sheriff got a set of keys out and went to the middle cell, opening the door. "Gentlemen, you are free to go. Don't ride your motorcycles. I called people to come collect you. Go home, get some sleep, and you can get your bikes in the morning, alright?"

The men all nodded at once and filed out of the cell, not talking.

"Are you a hunter?" Tommy asked as the last biker left the room.

"Me? Nope," the sheriff replied, closing the door behind him. "I'm just a sheriff of a small town. A small town that sometimes needs people to forget the weird shit they have seen." He looked Tommy up and down. "Although a changeling... that is a new one, even for me."

Burke was scowling between the two cells. "Can you give us some privacy, please, McClarnon?"

"Sure, Headmaster Burke," the sheriff said. "Just let me know when you're done."

McClarnon left the cellblock, and Burke just silently looked at the two occupants of the cells for several moments. Tommy dropped his eyes. "I can't believe how irresponsible you were tonight," Burke growled in a voice full of rage, and Tommy looked up, expecting the headmaster to be looking back, but to his surprise, Burke was glaring at Hafeez.

"What do you mean?" the hunter asked him.

"You instigated a fight for the sole purpose of attacking Monroe when he transformed," Burke said. Hafeez opened her mouth, but Burke cut her off. "No! Don't deny that was your plan. What were you *thinking?*"

"He will hurt someone!" Hafeez shouted. "Maybe not today, but he will! I don't know why you want to protect a monster like him!"

"I didn't kill your father," Tommy said softly.

"You didn't save him either!" she screamed, and her voice echoed in the small space and left a ringing silence.

There were several minutes of stunned silence. Tommy stayed seated, studying his feet, not daring to look up. Finally, Burke sighed. "I'm sorry, Nyla," he murmured. Tommy looked at the young hunter and noticed her eyes were shining, tears threatening to fall. "I have always had the horrible practice of expecting others to react the way I want them to regardless of their feelings or emotions. I should have realized that your grief could drive you to do something reckless." He shifted. "I will ask Jiao to transfer you, so you can leave New Bendigo and the Academy."

Hafeez looked at the headmaster in shock for several seconds. "No, I... I don't want that."

"Then what do you want?" Burke asked. He pointed at Tommy. "To kill him?"

"Yes," she said quickly. She glared at Tommy. "I don't care if York's daughter would be upset. He shouldn't be alive."

"He offered to let you kill him when he woke up," Burke admitted to Hafeez. She looked at Burke in shock and then looked back at Tommy.

Tommy shrugged. "I do feel bad for what happened that night. Your father attacked me, but he didn't deserve to die."

"But tell me, Nyla, what would it have accomplished to kill someone who was not your father's murderer?" Burke asked her. She looked down, studying the floor, not answering him. "And I wouldn't be so quick to cross Miss York if I were you, Nyla. She glows gold; she would be a formidable enemy to make."

"And you are going to train her," Hafeez said softly.

"I can't predict what kind of person she will be with her abilities, but I can at least help her control them, so she doesn't hurt anyone unwillingly."

Silence fell on the cellblock again while Hafeez weighed Burke's words. Then, finally, she sighed and looked up. "I want to stay at the Academy. I want to guard the sphere when you go inside."

"Then trust in Jiao and me," Burke responded. He went to the door and called out for the sheriff. When McClarnon came in, Burke gestured at Hafeez's cell. "She is free to go."

The sheriff glared at Hafeez. "If I had my way, she would be spending the next week in here." The caracal hissed at him. "Her and the cat both." He pointed at the hunter. "If you pull something like that again, I'm making a formal complaint and getting you demoted. Am I clear?"

"Yes," Hafeez whispered, and McClarnon unlocked her cell and let her out. She looked at Burke and opened her mouth several times, for several moments, but she said nothing and finally left, her caracal hissing one last time at Tommy as they went.

Burke sighed and rubbed his eyes. "Thank you, McClarnon, for making sure no one remembers her behavior tonight."

"No problem, headmaster. Can't have people circulating rumors of a feral cat running around. Might cause a panic."

Tommy expected the men to leave then, forcing him to spend the night in the jail, but Burke gestured at the door, and McClarnon unlocked it. Tommy cautiously got up. "Am I free to go?" Tommy asked.

"Well, as long as you didn't sexually harass Megan like she claims you did, I don't see why you shouldn't be," McClarnon said.

Tommy snorted and once again regretted doing so. "No, I gave her money, but it was for her to leave me alone."

"Yeah, that sounds about right for Megan. Likes to stir up trouble when she can. And she and Charlie aren't dating anymore, but boy, does she like it when he kicks someone's ass for her."

"Sounds like a fun couple," Tommy muttered as he gingerly walked out of the cell block.

"Ninety percent of my calls are about them, I swear."

They went out to the station's main room, which had three desks arranged so the owners could look at each other. The deputy from before sat at one, studying Tommy with wide eyes. Tommy didn't say anything but carefully kept walking as the man's hand drifted to his gun. Apparently, the deputy didn't share his boss's sense of ease while knowing there was a changeling in their midst.

"Anyone still here, Angel?"

"I think Charlie and his brother are still here, didn't hear their truck leave," the deputy replied, not taking his eyes off of Tommy. Tommy ignored him and hobbled to the front of the building. There was still a truck in the parking lot, two figures having an animated discussion inside.

"I can transport us back to the Academy," Burke told Tommy.

The changeling shook his head. "Transportation spells make me sick. Unless you want me to vomit all over you and your fancy suit."

"Well, we'll wait for them to leave then, and then I will drive you," McClarnon said. "The memory I planted should hold, but seeing you so soon might make it dissolve if we aren't careful."

Tommy just nodded and then went back to watching the truck. Burke stook with him, gently scratching his dog's ears as they waited. "Why are you letting me go back to the Academy?" Tommy suddenly asked the sorcerer in a low whisper.

"You did nothing wrong," Burke explained. "There was security footage that McClarnon took and destroyed, but not before he showed it to me." He sighed and shifted. "You are not confined to the Academy ground, Mr. Monroe, but I would appreciate it if you didn't set off all the wards in your quest for a stiff drink."

Tommy looked down for a second. "Would you believe me if I said I just went for a walk?"

"It's never just a walk for someone who has a vice, Mr. Monroe," Burke muttered. "I will not pretend to have the authority to tell you what to do," Burke continued in a low voice, "but if you care for Miss York as much as your previous conduct indicates, then you at least owe her better behavior than what occurred tonight."

Tommy flinched like Burke had hit him. He opened his mouth to defend himself but then shut it. Burke was right; Chrysta deserved better. He nodded.

"Once Miss York is out of that sphere, you can go and do whatever you want, but if I find that you have touched a drop of alcohol until then, I will dispatch you myself. Understood?"

"Understood," Tommy murmured. Just then, the truck peeled out of the parking lot, tires squealing.

McClarnon strolled up to the window and glared in the direction where the truck disappeared into the night. "Come on," he said. "It's getting late."

"Want me to go with you, sir?" the deputy called out, still not taking his eyes off Tommy.

The sheriff beamed at the other man. "Nope. Watch the phones. I'll be back."

Out in the cold, Tommy took a couple of deep breaths, the night air helping to clear his head a little. The sheriff unlocked the brown SUV and held a door open for Tommy, surprisingly, the passenger door to the front seat. Tommy would have thought the man would want him in the back.

"Goodnight, Mr. Monroe," Burke drawled. "Remember what I said."

"Yes," Tommy simply said. And with a *pop,* the headmaster and his familiar were gone. Tommy walked to the SUV and got inside.

The sheriff climbed into the car and started it, turning up the heat and putting it in drive. Tommy glanced at the clock and saw that it was after two in the morning. Was anyone still up at the Disaster Club? Would they care if they knew he was gone? They drove south down deserted streets in silence, the sheriff turning east to travel the same road Tommy had hiked just hours before. The heat and the hum of the road were making Tommy tired, and he fought the urge to sleep.

"I read the report," McClarnon suddenly said. Tommy glanced at him with raised eyebrows. "The report that is based on your testimony. It hasn't been released to the public yet, but they sent it to me. Since you are living at the Academy and all, I guess I'm on the 'need-to-know' list."

Tommy hummed, not trusting a snort again in his condition. "What does it say?"

"Not much, to be honest. The officials redacted a lot of it—whole pages in some spots. But there was something that caught my eye. The Chambers story, when you helped that woman escape the city with her son."

Tommy smiled despite the headache that was forming. "Helen Chambers," he muttered. "Haven't thought of her in years. I wonder what happened to her?"

"Well, that is why it caught my eye," the sheriff said. He gave Tommy a grin and then turned back to the road. "I got my ability from my dad. He would do official work for the hunters sometimes. We can sense when someone's memories have been altered, so we will interview people sometimes, especially sorcerers who have defected from the Acolytes." Tommy gave him a curious look, so McClarnon shrugged. "Acolytes would sometimes turn them into sleeper agents. They would alter a person's memory to make them think they defected. Then send them some spelled letter with a magic phrase, and *bam!* They would go on a rampage."

They had pulled up to the Academy, and the sheriff parked. Then, giving Tommy his full attention, he continued. "Anyway, one time, my dad was called in to talk to a woman. He never told me her name. I don't think he could. But she had this story about the Acolytes' changeling helping her leave the city. And no one believed her. They were so sure she was either lying or that her memories had been altered. It was just too farfetched.

"He told me later that when he sensed that those were her true memories, he couldn't help but think that the changeling who helped her, with nothing to gain for himself, was either the bravest son of a bitch ever or the stupidest."

Tommy chuckled. "Can't tell you which one it is, honestly."

"Why did you do it?" McClarnon asked.

Tommy glanced at the man and saw that he was genuinely curious. Tommy shrugged with one shoulder. "I didn't think I would ever make it out of slavery alive, so if I was going to die, I might as well make it on my terms." He paused, thinking for a moment. "Think you can find out what happened to her?" he asked.

"I can try, but I would think Headmaster Burke would have more luck than me," McClarnon said. He shifted and leaned over, holding out his hand. "Not the best way for us to meet, but as long as you don't partake in anymore bar fights, you are welcomed in New Bendigo."

Tommy looked at the offered hand, not sure why he suddenly had a lump in his throat. He didn't say anything as he shook the man's hand. "I won't make any promises," he joked when he felt like he could talk again.

McClarnon smiled and unlocked the car. Tommy climbed out and stepped back, letting the sheriff drive off, tires crunching on the gravel parking lot.

Tommy swayed slightly. The cold night air broke some of the lethargy that had settled in his limbs, and he started to hustle to the Disaster Club. When Tommy made it to the tree, he carefully descended the stairs. He opened the door and looked around, quickly closing the door behind him. The couch that Chrysta had been sleeping on was empty, the blanket she was using was on the floor. Poe was still asleep on the back of it, beak pointing straight down as he slept. Chrysta must have gone to bed. Good. She wouldn't see him in this state. He put his jacket up and headed to the kitchen for water. He had a feeling he would need it.

Tommy stumbled into the kitchen and froze when he saw Chrysta at the counter. She was wearing Kevin's gift, the black sweater. It was so large that one shoulder was falling down, so it showed her tank top's strap. Her hair was in a braid, pulled over the other shoulder. She turned around, her smile dying as she looked at him. She put the knife and jar of peanut butter she was holding down and rushed to him. "What happened? Are you okay?" she asked, gently putting her hands on his face.

Tommy wanted to tell her it was nothing, make some joke to put her at ease, but he couldn't do it; he was just too tired. So instead, he pulled her into a hug, crushing her to him. She didn't protest and put her arms around his neck. He buried his nose into her throat, taking a deep breath. Chrysta smelled like borrowed soap and weird laundry detergent, but underneath that was the smell of her, something warm and spicy, like cinnamon.

When he let her go, she looked him over and gasped when she saw the bloody bandage wrapped around his leg. "What happened?" she asked again.

"Went for a walk. Found a bar. Decided to have a drink," he explained. He took a deep breath. "Decided to have many drinks. And then Hafeez showed up." Chrysta's face fell into a scowl. "She convinced some bikers that I was a dangerous asshole molesting women, and they decided to beat me up."

Chrysta's hands had been lightly resting on his chest, but they curled up into fists, and Tommy heard a ringing sound from across the room. Tommy realized a glass of milk next to the sandwich Chrysta made was vibrating. Chrysta was slow to anger, but the few times he had seen her truly enraged showed him that the combination of her powers and her temper could be deadly. Burke was right: she needed to get her abilities under control.

"I'm okay," he murmured, putting his hands on her shoulders, trying to get her to calm down. "The local sheriff showed up, and we all went to the jail, including Hafeez. Burke sprung us and finally got her to back off."

The ringing slowly disappeared as the glass stopped vibrating, but Chrysta kept scowling. "As soon as I get out of the ball, I'm going to turn her into a toad."

Tommy snorted, felt a stab of pain go through his head, but still chuckled at the image of a toad dressed in a hunter's uniform, hopping around and croaking. Would Hafeez's caracal recognize his master, or would he chase her around and try to eat her? "I don't think that's possible, beautiful," he said, trying not to laugh.

"I glow gold. I'm sure I can figure it out," Chrysta said, crossing her arms and grinning.

"Sure, beautiful, whatever you say," Tommy chuckled. And he finally lost the battle with the mental images of a hunter toad hopping around, trying to bite Tommy's ankles, and started laughing, pulling Chrysta into a hug.

If you asked Tommy later, he would say Chrysta initiated the kiss, but honestly, he didn't know who started kissing whom. All he knew was that one minute he was laughing, and the next minute he was kissing her, one hand cupping her face, his other arm wrapped around her waist. At that moment, he couldn't remember the reason he had been avoiding her all week, scared to touch her. Kissing her just felt so *right*.

He pulled away, putting his forehead on hers. "You okay?" she asked.

"Yeah," Tommy said. Then he yawned, jaw popping. "Just really drunk and really tired."

"Go sit on the couch. I'll bring you some water."

Tommy nodded numbly and did as she ordered. He was barely able to get the hoodie over his head as he walked across the common room, but once it was off, he flopped onto the couch. Poe woke up from all the movement and croaked a pissed-off-sounding "Tommy!" Tommy leaned his head back and put an arm over his eyes, fighting a headache that was pounding at his temples. The raven dropped to Tommy's leg and started pulling at the bandage.

"Poe, stop it," Chrysta told the bird. Tommy took the arm off his eyes and saw Chrysta standing there with a tray. He accepted a glass of iced water from her, and she put the tray on the table. He gulped down half of the glass of water while she placed a plate of her sandwich's crust for Poe. Finally, she settled onto the couch, wrapping herself in the blanket as she picked up her sandwich and the glass of milk.

"What are you doing up so late?" Tommy asked, finally wondering why he found Chrysta in the kitchen in the first place.

"Nightmare," Chrysta grimly said. "I think the couch was all the way at the ceiling when I finally woke up this time. It scared the crap out of me when it dropped." She sighed. "I don't know if I will be able to get back to sleep tonight." She gave him a smile. "Last night sleeping with you was the first time I was able to get any rest in a while."

"I think Cross will skin me alive if he catches us on the couch together again," Tommy joked.

"I will talk to him," Chrysta said after finishing a bite of her sandwich. "I need to get some sleep. Mr. Cross will understand."

Tommy chuckled. "So I'm your emotional support changeling then?"

She gave him a brilliant smile. "Exactly." The smile died a little as she gingerly touched his split eyebrow. "I wish I could fix this," she murmured.

"Magic doesn't work on me," he reminded her.

"Transportation spells do," she pointed out. "And the slave band did."

"Transportation spells grab everything in their circle," Tommy explained. "I get transported because I simply exist. Sorcerers have to be careful what is near them. I once saw a sorcerer take half a table with him because he wasn't paying attention. Jacobs and your father are lucky you didn't leave one of their limbs behind when you yeeted them across the city." Tommy rolled up his sleeve to look at his left arm. "And like I said before, I don't know how the slave band affected me, but it did."

She looked thoughtful at that, and they fell into silence as she finished her sandwich. Tommy leaned his head back again and dozed, getting startled when Chrysta grabbed his glass, which he had almost let spill. He was rubbing his face when she got back from the kitchen, trying to get himself to get up and go to the bedroom, but Chrysta grabbed his feet and dropped them on the couch, forcing him to lie down.

"What are you doin'?" he asked thickly.

"Making sure we get some sleep," she explained like it was the most natural thing in the world.

"Cross won't be happy," he muttered.

"Mr. Cross isn't here right now," she said lightly, and Tommy decided not to argue with her.

She made sure he was covered in the blanket and then got another one for herself. They shifted on the couch until they were both comfortable, Tommy tucking Chrysta to his chest as he wrapped himself around her. Poe settled back on the back of the sofa, tucking his head under his wing. She sighed, and he felt her relax. "I think everyone should have an emotional support changeling," she joked.

He chuckled. "Just don't forget that while you're in the ball."

"I couldn't forget you," Chrysta sighed, and Tommy felt his heart melt at her soft promise.

Their breathing slowed, and Tommy felt himself drift into sleep.

17

Guerra was passing by the second bedroom on the second story of the acolyte mansion when he happened to look inside to see the lady of the house furiously packing a suitcase. She looked upset. Correction, she looked infuriated, moving so fast from one side of the room to the next that her dress flared out behind her. He generally avoided talking to her as they had nothing to discuss, but curiosity got the better of him, and he stepped inside the bedroom. "Bella signora," he greeted her. "How are you this evening?"

"Don't you start that shit with me," she growled, rounding on him with a finger in his face. He blinked and leaned back, shocked at her behavior. She was generally a nice and calm woman.

Guerra hesitated at her tone but smiled at her, his brightest one. Unfortunately, it never reached his eyes. "What do you mean, my lady?"

"I just heard one of your associates talking about attacking someone, possibly killing them. I don't know what is going on, but I am out of here, and I'm going to the police," she explained while snapping the suitcase shut. She started to step past him, suitcase in one hand, but he reached out and grabbed her upper arm.

"I'm afraid I can't let you do that, bella signora," he stated, trying to smile even as rage surged through his veins. He didn't know who talked in front of her, but he was going to find them and teach them a lesson in secrecy.

She frowned, and then her eyes went wide in fear. She pulled her arm out of Guerra's grip, but he just seized her throat with the same hand instead. She made a gurgling noise, something that

probably would have been a yelp if he was not currently choking the life out of her, and dropped the suitcase.

She clawed at his hand at her throat and started to reach for his face with the other, but he just grabbed her wrist and kept her from scratching him. He continued smiling at her, even as he glowed red and set her nerves on fire. He felt most alive when he was causing pain to others, the fear and anguish in their eyes sending a thrill down his spine. He lifted her and hauled her to the balcony to make sure no one in the mansion could hear her.

Guerra stopped at the railing, pushing her so that she was leaning over the edge. Her feet kicked out even as he turned his power up. What she was feeling must be pure torture, but Guerra was impressed by her fighting spirit.

He held her there for several long and tense moments, reveling in her panic and fear. He wasn't an empath, but when he used his power like this, without restraint, and saw his playthings writhe, he could nearly imagine their agony. Ecstasy flooded his system even as the pain overwhelmed theirs. Guerra still wasn't sure why they died. Did their hearts stop? Did their brains overload from the sensation? Either way, she finally went limp, and he almost felt relief that her suffering was finally over.

Almost.

Guerra let her body go, and she tumbled over the edge of the railing to the ground below. He watched in detached indifference as her body landed with a thump. She was beautiful at that moment, hair around her face like a halo. Her necklace had caught his hand and broken, the beads surrounding her, the only sign that something was amiss and that she wasn't currently sleeping. The fall should have broken her neck, which would be the story everyone would believe. She fell, she died, life went on.

Now, to find the one who couldn't keep his mouth shut.

.....

Akrur sat up, panting. That bloody dream again. This one was not fading like it should; it was still clear and vivid. He flopped backward on the bed and rubbed his face. Maybe it was time to go to a professional? Maybe get the memory cleared from his head? Generally, he did not like having memories removed, but he didn't think anyone would blame him for having this nightmare erased for good.

He got up and started getting ready. Although, he thought to himself as he brushed his teeth, maybe there was a reason this one wasn't fading. The woman, she seemed so *familiar*. Like he knew her. But he didn't. Did he? He glowered at his reflection as he moved his toothbrush around his mouth. Maybe an investigation was in order? If he found out who she was, perhaps the memory would finally leave.

He left his bedroom, heading to the kitchen, wondering if he should check on Tommy when he spotted them on the couch. Tommy and Chrysta. On the couch. Together. Bloody hell. Akrur scowled at the two figures on the couch. Really, did they think this was a joke? Just sleep where they damn well please? He stalked over to the sofa to do something (Exactly what, he wasn't sure. Perhaps a good hour-long lecture was in order) but stopped short when he took in Tommy's appearance.

A cut on his lip and eyebrow, already healing but fresh enough to be from last night. A bandage on the leg not currently covered by the blanket. Poe woke up at that moment and let out an alarmed, "Chrysta!" His mistress stirred then, and Chrysta blinked at Akrur.

"Good mornin', Mr. Cross," she mumbled and then started the process of getting off the couch without waking up Tommy.

"Good morning, Miss York," Akrur responded. He waited until she was vertical to gesture at the couch. "I really can't let this continue, my dear."

She winced. "I'm sorry, Mr. Cross," she whispered. And then she started to pull on the sleeve of his sweater towards the kitchen. "I had a nightmare and couldn't get back to sleep. Having Tommy on the couch with me seems to really help me sleep. And he needed it too. Tommy went for a walk last night. He was at a bar when Hunter Hafeez convinced some men to beat him up."

Akrur groaned and rubbed his neck, studying the sleeping changeling. "That's it. I'm making a formal complaint. He may be a changeling, but that doesn't give her the right to hound him."

"The sheriff came and arrested all of them, and then Mr. Burke showed up at the jail and told her to leave Tommy alone," Chrysta explained. She looked over at Tommy. "But... Mr. Cross, I'm worried. What if she hurts him while Mr. Burke and I are in the ball?" She started to rub at her braid and bit her lip. "Maybe I should tell Tommy not to guard the ball? But then he might get upset. My father has been telling him what to do for so long. I don't want to force him to do something he doesn't want to do just because it's me asking him to do it—"

Akrur put his hands on Chrysta's shoulders, and her flow of words stopped. She looked up at him with shining eyes, and he gave her a small smile. "Deep breaths, Miss York," he said. She nodded and did as he said, and as she let out a shaky exhale, he felt her relax. "I would like to try something if you don't mind." He gathered her hands in his. "Close your eyes."

She did as he instructed. "Now, imagine you're going into the sphere. Who do you want to see before you go?"

"Tommy," she said in a quiet voice.

"And now imagine it has been a year. You're coming out of the ball. Who do you want to see when you get out?" Akrur asked. She smiled, and Akrur could see why Tommy fell in love with her. "It's alright if you say it's me. You wouldn't be the first student to have a crush on me."

She laughed, and she opened her eyes and wiped at them. "Tommy. I want Tommy to be there."

He gave her a smile. "I want you to know that I am aware that you are making a sacrifice, my dear," he explained, taking his hands back. "You deserve to have whoever you want there for support. And if Tommy is that individual, he will be there, no matter what Hafeez thinks. And honestly, I doubt Tommy sees it as a burden. On the contrary, he would want to be there."

Chrysta nodded. "I'm sorry, Mr. Cross, for all of this trouble."

"No need to be sorry," he said. "I find the whole thing fascinating, really. It's not every day you get to see a magical item of that magnitude. Keeping Hafeez and Tommy from killing each other... now that will be the challenge."

The door to the girls' room opened, and Rimsha came out. She gave Tommy a curious glance as she joined Chrysta and Akrur by the kitchen door. "What happened? He just went for a walk last night."

"Hafeez started an old-fashioned bar fight, apparently," Akrur said.

"Oh, I didn't even think of her trying to hurt him last night. I shouldn't have let him go," Rimsha whispered.

"No worries, my dear," Akrur said. "You are not Tommy's keeper."

Slowly, the Disaster Club started to rouse, the kids coming to the kitchen for a breakfast of cereal, yogurt, and leftover crepes. The teens all had the same reaction as Rimsha: curiosity about what happened, criticizing Hafeez's behavior, and then giving Tommy plenty of space. At one point, Kevin leaned over to talk to Rosa at the kitchen table. "Hey, Rosa, can you help me with practicing my fireballs?"

"No one can help you with your fireballs, Kevin," she shot back.

"No, I think that is a good idea," Akrur told her over the top of his newspaper. "Get us all outside and less likely to bother Tommy. Ichiro, can you help them?"

The kids finished breakfast and went to get dressed and ready for the day, thankfully keeping their voices low. Chrysta made sure Tommy was covered again, and then the whole group went outside. Poe took flight with a croak. Rimsha had enlisted Julien's help in bringing her easel, stool, and paints outside. The day was bright and clear, and there was a foot of snow left on the ground, patches of bare earth showing. Julien and Chrysta took the bench as Kevin, Ichiro, and Rosa formed a triangle a dozen meters from the tree. Akrur stayed standing, getting ready to intervene if the kids needed him.

Kevin took off his gloves and started to stare at his hands. He tried waving them, snapping his fingers, but nothing formed. "See?" he told Rosa after several fruitless minutes. "I can't get it."

"It's easy, Butler," Ichiro said, and he put his hand out. *"Honō!"* he cried, and a ball of flames formed in his hand.

Rosa put her hand out, and her own ball formed. It was bigger than Ichiro's but not as well-formed, dripping licks of flames onto the ground.

"Mr. Cross," Chrysta asked, "why do different words do the same spell? And why does Rosa not need a word?"

"It's not the words or the language that matters, my dear," Akrur explained, not taking his eyes off the group in front of him. "It is the *intent* that is needed."

"If you do magic that is not your ability, then words or a spell help you to form it," Rimsha explained as she started to mix paints. "For most sorcerers, using another language helps you to give the right intent."

Akrur smiled at Rimsha but quickly put his attention back to Kevin, who had finally formed a fireball but was tossing it from one hand to the other like it was hurting him. "Rosa's ability is controlling fire, so she can use that magic without words. You will be the same someday, my dear, able to perform any magic you want without spells."

Chrysta lifted her hand and wiggled her fingers. "Should I try words?" she asked.

"You can give it a go," Akrur told her.

"*Ignis,*" she said, and a fireball formed, smaller than anyone else's but still a perfect ball. Chrysta laughed and put her other hand out to hold the flames, Julien leaning away from her. "I did it!" she cried in joy.

"Hey now, Kevin is supposed to be learning how to do that," Ichiro joked. Kevin glared at Chrysta's work and then put his focus back on his fireball, actually sticking his tongue out in concentration.

"Come on, Butler, you can do it," Rosa said. Finally, Kevin's fireball grew in size and shaped itself into a perfect ball. He gave a shout in joy.

Rimsha and Chrysta gave cheers of encouragement, but then Chrysta frowned. "Mr. Cross," she said nervously, holding up the fireball with two hands. "What do I do with this?"

"Toss it here!" Rosa yelled, and before Akrur could stop her, Chrysta was throwing the fireball at her. Rosa caught it, and she pulled at the flames, and the ball lost its shape, coating her arms with fire. "Alright, your turn Kevin!"

Kevin winded up the fireball like he was about to throw a baseball, and he let it fly, Rosa catching it with ease. She added it to the flames she was already holding. "Want some, Takahashi?" she asked Ichiro.

"Hit me!" he responded. Rosa threw some of the flames, and he caught them, forming them back into a ball and then making it disappear.

"Easy, Rosa," Akrur cautioned the older girl. "Remember that you can handle more than them."

For several minutes, they continued like that, the boys throwing flames and fireballs at Rosa, Rosa throwing them back at the boys, or adding them to the fire she maintained on her arms and hands. She wasn't careful, though, letting the flames drip to the ground. If the ground wasn't covered in snow, Akrur would have been worried that the grass would be ablaze by now.

Rimsha suddenly stopped painting her landscape and turned to Julien. "Hey," she said, making sure he could see her face, "weren't you going on a date?"

Julien blushed but nodded. "Yes," he said while making a knocking motion with his right hand.

Rimsha gasped and put down her paintbrush to sign with her hands. "Oh, details, now!" she ordered.

Julien glanced between Rimsha and Chrysta, shrugging shyly. "Nothing much to report," he said with a small smile. "We went out to dinner. Had ice cream afterward." His blush deepened until his ears turned pink. "His sign language is getting good. That's how we met." He held his hands in front of him, opening them up like a book and then making a pinching motion and pulling his hands apart. "In a bookstore. I was looking for something, and he helped me."

"Awwww," Rimsha cooed. "You will have to bring him here when you're ready. I wanna meet him!"

Akrur tore his attention away from their conversation when he heard Kevin shout. Rosa had thrown a larger ball at his head, and he had barely caught it. "Easy, Miss Torres," Akrur called out, but she just waved him off.

About ten minutes later, the door at the bottom of the steps opened, and Tommy climbed the stairs. He was dressed in just jeans and a shirt and shuffled past Akrur to the bench. His eyes were almost closed, squinting in the bright daylight. Julien and Chrysta moved so he could sit down, Chrysta sitting between the two boys. Poe dropped down from the sky and landed on Tommy's shoulder. Tommy waved at the bird but without much force.

"Hello, Mr. Monroe!" Akrur chirped. Tommy winced and glared at Akrur, although it was not threatening as the changeling probably wanted, considering his eyes were almost closed. "So glad you could join us! How is your head?"

"Poundin'," admitted the changeling. Chrysta put her hand on his as he rubbed his face.

"Want some of the hair of the dog that bit you?" Akrur joked.

"How do your people put it?" Tommy growled. "Sod off, Cross."

Akrur smiled as the girls giggled. "Oi, don't let me ruin your morning," Akrur said, thickening his accent while grinning.

Suddenly, Kevin let a fireball go, and Rosa had to duck to let it sail past her head. It landed in the snow and sizzled. Rosa turned to the boy and glared.

"Sorry!" Kevin cried.

"Pay attention!" Rosa barked back, and she threw a fireball for Ichiro to catch. The younger boy grabbed it, but barely.

"Rosa, keep calm," Akrur warned Rosa.

"Is that normal?" Tommy asked. "She doesn't seem to have much control of her flames."

"Rosa has always had problems with limiting her ability," Akrur explained, not taking his eyes off the trio. Rosa's throws were getting more aggressive, and it was making him uneasy.

"Mr. Cross?" Rimsha called out nervously. "I think you should stop them."

Akrur stepped forward to do just that, but just as he opened his mouth to order the kids to stop, disaster struck. Kevin threw a fireball at Rosa, and she caught it and threw it toward Ichiro. But instead of a small ball, she threw all the flames sitting on her arms at the young boy. Ichiro put his hands up to catch it but realized a second later that what was coming towards him was really a wave of fire. So he put his arms up, and a magical purple shield formed. The flames hit his shield, and it bowed inwards, so instinctively, he pushed the fire to the side.

Towards the bench.

If the flames were launched at Akrur, he might have been able to stop it, but he could only give a shout in warning before a flash of light blinded him. Akrur blinked for a few moments and finally regained his sight. He gasped and gaped at the scene in front of him.

Chrysta and Julien were on the ground, Julien protecting Chrysta with his body. Not that he needed to. The golden flash was from Chrysta bending the Disaster Tree's roots to point to the sky to shelter them. The roots still had spots of fire on them. Akrur wondered why Tommy wasn't protecting Chrysta until he realized Tommy had gotten off the bench and pulled Rimsha to the ground to shield her. Tommy's shirt was still on fire, and Akrur took his coat off and rushed to them to put it out.

Poe was in the tree, croaking and flapping his wings in alarm, while Akrur made sure Tommy and Rimsha were okay, and Ichiro kicked snow on the fire in the roots. "Are you alright?" Akrur asked the pair once the fire was out.

"Y-yeah," Rimsha said, voice shaking. Kevin rushed over and put a hand on her shoulder, and she gave the boy a small smile.

Tommy scowled at his shoulder, inspecting the new holes in his shirt. "Yeah, I'm good," he growled. "You okay, beautiful?"

"I think so," Chrysta said. She was looking at the roots in wonder. "Did I do this?"

"Yeah, you did," Ichiro said, putting one hand on the roots. He then looked down and gave a yell.

Julien was still on the ground in the same position, and as Chrysta leaned away from him and gasped, Akrur could finally see why. A root, as thick as a candlestick, had curled and stabbed Julien in the back, coming out from his stomach. Julien was shaking, one of his hands hovering over the root, like he couldn't believe that it was there.

Tommy sprang into action, going to Julien and grabbing his hands. He made sure Julien could see his face. "Don't touch it," the changeling ordered, and the boy nodded.

"J-Julien, I'm so sorry," Chrysta said, eyes shining.

"Apologize later, beautiful. Right now, I need towels," Tommy told her. She numbly nodded and ran inside.

Tommy inspected the root as Akrur crouched down next to them, holding Julien's hands so he didn't aggravate the wound. "My knife won't cut through this," Tommy said. "I need something else."

"There's a saw in the greenhouse," Rimsha said, and she got up and ran inside as well.

Akrur looked at Ichiro, standing by the roots, looking sick. "Get the healer, now," Akrur ordered the boy. Ichiro nodded and ran off towards the Academy. That was when Akrur saw Rosa, who had her arms crossed over her chest and tears streaming down her face. "Rosa?" Akrur called out to her. "Are you alright?"

"I... I didn't mean... I-I didn't think..." Her voice trailed off into a sob, and she turned around and ran off into the woods.

"Rosa! Where are you going?" Kevin called after her. He got up like he was about to follow her.

"Leave her for now!" Akrur ordered him. He shared a grim look with Tommy. "I can only focus on one wounded soul right now," he muttered to himself.

18

Rimsha and Chrysta rushed back, Rimsha handing the saw to Tommy, Chrysta wrapping the towels around the root sticking out of Julien's stomach, which was already dripping blood. Tommy grabbed the wood with his left hand and set the saw with his right. He made sure Julien could see his face. "I will keep this from hurting if I can, but I have to do this quickly. Stay still."

Julien, face pale and sweaty, nodded. Akrur grabbed one of his hands while Rimsha took the other one.

Tommy started sawing quick, hard strokes that swiftly cut through the wood. It took Tommy a dozen slices to get through the root; each one made Julien gasp and shudder. Julien started to lean forward when Tommy was done with his eyes fluttering. Both Akrur and Tommy caught him, keeping him from falling onto the root.

"Inside," Akrur said, and Tommy nodded in agreement. Tommy put Julien's arm around his shoulder and got the injured boy standing. They all hurried inside, coats and jackets being shed and left on the floor in their haste. Kevin got towels set on one of the couches, and Tommy gingerly laid Julien down on his unhurt side, facing the back of the sofa. Chrysta rushed into the bathroom while Kevin backed away, looking green at all the blood. Rimsha sat down and got Julien to put his head in her lap.

"You okay?" she asked when Julien opened his eyes and could see her face.

"Hurts," he gasped, sweat on his face. Chrysta came back with a bowl of water and a washcloth and started to wipe his face.

Akrur touched Julien's shoulder so he would look at the empath. "Ichiro will be back with the healer soon," Akrur told the young man.

Right on cue, the door to the outside opened. Ichiro came inside, quickly followed by the Academy's head healer, Paulson. Her eyes widened when she saw Julien on the couch. She closed the distance while taking off her coat, leaning down to study the wound in his side. "What happened?" she asked.

"I moved the roots outside, and one of them hurt him," Rimsha lied.

Paulson poked the root, making Julien hiss in pain. "Why?" she asked Rimsha.

Rimsha shifted. Lying had never been her strong suit. "I accidentally threw some fire at her, and she put the roots up to protect herself," Ichiro said, leaning over the back of the couch.

"Fire?" Paulson asked. She checked Julien's pupils. "You wouldn't have been playing with fire with the Torres girl, would you?"

"I don't see how that is relevant," Akrur growled at the woman.

"Oh, it is relevant," she said. She glared at Akrur and then picked at Tommy's shirt, showing the fresh burn marks. Tommy glared at her, but she kept her eyes on Akrur. "When children are hurting each other trying to protect themselves from a fire user, it is *very* relevant." Akrur squared his shoulders and glared back. "Where is she, Cross? Are you hiding her?"

"She ran into the woods," Kevin said, and Ichiro hit him.

"So she at least knows what she did was wrong," Paulson said, setting her bag on the floor next to the couch.

"Mr. Cross? Can I go looking for her?" Rimsha asked.

"Yes. Just be safe." He didn't look at Rimsha as she left, glowering at the healer in front of him. Chrysta sat on the couch and took Rimsha's place, getting Julien to put his head in her lap. "Well, are you going to help him? Abby would have had him up and about by now," Akrur told the woman.

Paulson frowned at him, mouth puckering at the insult. "Fine, but we will be discussing this further," she said.

The healer kneeled on the floor, getting a pair of scissors out of her bag. Julien's jacket and shirt were pinned to his body, and she had to cut through them to expose his back. Her hand glowed orange for a brief moment, and she made a circle on his spine. Julien sighed and visually relaxed.

"What did you do?" Chrysta asked.

Paulson looked at her and sniffed. "Blocked the pain," she explained in a clipped tone. She looked Tommy up and down. "You seem to have your wits about you. You will be helping me." Tommy raised an eyebrow at her tone but didn't argue.

She got some gloves on and had Tommy hold Julien down while grabbing the root. Finally, she pulled the root out from Julien's back, and Kevin made a distressed retching sound and ran for the bathroom. Paulson removed the rest of Julien's clothing and inspected the wound. "Well," she murmured, "it didn't hit any organs." She looked over her shoulder at Akrur. "At least we can be happy for that," she said sarcastically.

Paulson grabbed a pair of forceps and a jar of liquid from her bag and started to clean out the injury with gauze. When she seemed happy that the wound was clean, her hand would flash orange, and the wound started closing. Then she would go back to inspecting and cleaning the damage. Tommy kept her view clear, wiping away the blood as it flowed. Poor Kevin was conscripted into taking dirty towels to the bathroom and coming back with fresh ones. Ichiro and Chrysta watched Julien, keeping him distracted.

"Ichiro," Julien murmured at one point. "That shield was awesome."

Ichiro smiled. "It was, wasn't it?" The smile died a little. "Just gotta make sure I watch where I deflect stuff next time."

Paulson glanced at the younger boy but didn't say anything as she kept working.

Finally, after half an hour of intense work, Paulson finished. There was a red ring on the skin of Julien's stomach and back, but otherwise, he looked normal. Tommy leaned away and sneezed, eyes shining. Akrur wondered how long he had been holding it in. Paulson touched Julien's shoulder so he would look at her. "I'm turning the nerves in your spine back on. It will hurt for a moment."

Julien nodded and held Chrysta's hand as Paulson's hand glowed orange, and she made the circle on his spine again. Julien hissed and flinched, but he looked more comfortable than he did before. He gingerly turned onto his back and stretched.

Paulson got a small vial out of her bag, handing it to the young man. "Two drops every four hours for the pain. No heavy lifting for the next three days." Julien nodded, and she turned to Akrur. "I expect Miss Torres in my office as soon as possible for the wasting curse." Tommy, who was washing his hands in the bowl of water Chrysta got, looked at her in shock.

Akrur frowned at her. "No." Paulson opened her mouth, and he interrupted her. "I will report the incident to Burke, but it is not your job to judge if the wasting curse is required in this case."

"It is my job to protect the children of the Academy. It is your job as well, if you haven't forgotten." Paulson stood up, and Akrur was bothered that she was a few inches taller than him, giving her the ability to look down her nose at him. "The wasting curse is the only course of action here."

Akrur straightened his shoulders and gave Paulson his most potent glare. "No," he said again, and before she could argue, he continued. "She is a minor, and as her guardian, I will not let anyone even think about using the wasting curse on her until her seventeenth birthday. And that, madam, is my final say."

Paulson scowled back. "She turns seventeen in the summer. Do you really think she will improve that much in that short amount of time?"

Akrur opened his mouth to give a retort, but suddenly the door to the outside opened. Rosa came in with Rimsha in tow, and she froze at the scene in front of her. Her face twisted into a mask of grief, and she ran to Julien and tackled him. He gave out an *oomph* as she kneeled on the floor and hugged him. "I'm okay," he started to sign. "I'm okay." When she didn't lift her head so she could read his hands, he hugged her back and murmured, "I'm okay."

"Miss Torres, I will have you know—" Paulson started to lecture, but Akrur grabbed her by the elbow and tugged on it. She snatched her arm back and glared at him.

"Not now, Paulson."

"Fine. *Fine*. But if she hurts anyone else, it is on your head, Cross," she shot back.

Paulson leaned down and touched Julien's shoulder to make sure he looked at her. "I will be reporting this," she explained. "You do not have to press charges if you do not want to, but it will go on record." Julien didn't say anything but glared as she left.

"Well, she was a ray of sunshine," Tommy muttered. He looked at Akrur. "Is she serious about the wasting curse?"

"Unfortunately, yes," Akrur said.

"What is a wasting curse?" Chrysta asked, getting up from the couch as Rimsha took her spot.

Akrur rubbed his eyes. "It is a curse that will slowly take a sorcerer's ability to perform magic away." He sighed and folded his arms in front of him. "It will essentially make the sorcerer into a nonmagical human being, a normie. Also, it shortens their lifespan and makes it so their children may be nonmagical as well."

Chrysta looked at the members of the Disaster Club, from Rosa, who was still hugging Julien, shoulders shaking, to Rimsha, then Ichiro, and Kevin. Then she looked back at Akrur. "That sounds horrible. Why would they do that to Rosa?"

"It is only used in cases where a sorcerer has been deemed a danger to themselves or others," Akrur explained.

"Or by the Acolytes to make sure people couldn't perform magic against them," Tommy added.

"I should go through with it," Rosa said, voice muffled. She sat up, eyes shining and cheeks wet. "I should have my ability taken from me."

"Rosa, that is not the answer," Akrur told her, hating to see the girl look so defeated. Chrysta walked past him to stand next to Tommy. She stretched up to whisper something in the changeling's ear.

"Mr. Cross, it's the only thing I can do," Rosa said, looking up at him in misery. His heart hurt to see the pain on her face. "What if I hurt somebody worse next time?"

"I was the one who deflected the fireball," Ichiro murmured.

"And I made the roots move," Chrysta added.

"It doesn't matter!" Rosa yelled. "It was *my* fault! It was all my fault!" And she crumpled onto the floor, sobbing. Rimsha and Ichiro rushed to her and hugged her. Julien reached out a hand and put it on her shoulder, and Kevin put a calming hand on her back. Akrur leaned down and put a hand on her other shoulder. They stayed like that for a few moments, Akrur only looking up when he heard the door to the outside softly clicking shut.

❧ 19 ☙

Rimsha was able to get Rosa to go to the girls' room after several minutes, so the older girl could calm down and have some privacy. Kevin went to the kitchen to make a late lunch while Ichiro stayed with Julien on the couch after getting the older boy a sweater to wear. Akrur went outside to see where Chrysta and Tommy had disappeared, wondering if Chrysta had gone looking for Poe, but they were nowhere in sight. Akrur glared at the tree's roots, still in their skyward position, and then went back inside.

"Where did they go?" Ichiro asked while Julien inspected his ruined clothes with a scowl.

"I'm not sure," Akrur admitted, slightly upset that they left without telling him where they were going. "If they aren't back in several hours, we will have to go looking for them."

After an hour, Rimsha came out of the bedroom. "Mr. Cross," she said softly. "Rosa would like to see you."

He joined Rosa in the bedroom, sitting at the foot of her bed. Rosa sat cross-legged, looking grim, glaring at her hands. "What can I do for you, my dear?"

"I want to go see Mrs. Paulson," she said, voice firm. "I need her to do the wasting curse."

Akrur sighed and looked away, trying to find the right words. "If that is truly what you want, my dear, then we will do it. But I implore you to wait."

"Waiting is not going to help," she said. She sniffed and squared her shoulders. "It's the right thing to do, Mr. Cross. I appreciate you trying to help me the entire time I've lived here. But it's time to face facts. I'm not getting better." She looked at him with shining eyes. "What if I kill someone next time?"

Akrur opened his mouth to counter her argument, but the door to the bedroom opened, and Rimsha stuck her head inside. "Mr. Cross?" she called. "Mr. Burke is here."

Akrur blinked at her. "What?"

"Mr. Burke is here. And he wants to see you and Rosa."

Rosa gulped, making her throat click, and Akrur had to help her stand up. She was pale as they walked out to the common room. Chrysta and Tommy were there with Headmaster Burke and Director Zheng. Burke looked incensed, probably the angriest Akrur had ever seen him, even more furious than when Abby went to him about Tommy breaking into her house. "Cross," he growled. "We need to talk."

Akrur looked at Chrysta, trying to keep control of his surprise and fury. He didn't know why Chrysta had brought the headmaster into this, but it was a severe overreach on her part. He nodded, not trusting his voice, and went to the kitchen, opening the door and letting everyone file in. Rosa stood at the table, not looking up from the floor. Burke and Zheng went to the other side of the table while Chrysta and Tommy stayed on the other. Akrur stood by Rosa. No one sat down.

"Headmaster Burke," Akrur started to say, "I was going to inform you—"

"I'm not here to talk about what happened earlier today," Burke said. He was frowning at Chrysta, and Akrur didn't understand why. "I agree with you: Miss Torres's seventeenth birthday is the appropriate time to talk about applying a wasting curse." Rosa finally looked up, looking at Burke with shining eyes.

"Then why are yo—"

"I'm being extorted," Burke growled, folding his arms in front of him. "And I do not approve."

"Extorted?"

"Miss York," Zheng said calmly, "had informed us that she won't do her training unless Rosa can join her."

"What?" Rosa breathed, and she looked at Chrysta in shock.

Chrysta shrugged, looking embarrassed. "It's not right that I get training that would help Rosa too. She should get the same opportunity that I am getting."

Akrur shifted from foot to foot. "I appreciate the sentiment, my dear, but it is not the same thing."

"Isn't it?" Chrysta argued. "I need to control my abilities, and so does she."

"I am not a miracle worker," Burke explained. "You are new to magic; you can be taught. Miss Torres has had years to attempt to control her ability."

Chrysta scowled at the man. "And going with us still gives her the best chance to avoid losing her abilities for good. I can't go while she is forced to stay. If she can't come with me, I'm not going."

"If you decline this opportunity, I may be forced to make you leave the Academy if your abilities grow beyond your control, Miss York," Burke said while glowering at her.

"Fine. Do it," Chrysta said, folding her arms and making herself as tall as possible.

"And what do you have to say about this?" Zheng asked Tommy.

The changeling shrugged. "I go where she goes. If she leaves, so do I."

"And if you do, we can't protect you," Zheng pointed out.

"Like I was protected last night?" Tommy shot back.

Akrur put his hands up. "Wait, wait. Everyone, just calm down." He got a glare from Burke. "Please. Let's discuss this rationally. What disadvantage is there to Rosa going?"

"It's dangerous, Cross," Burke explained, looking at Rosa briefly. "We are not talking about a week on holiday. This is a whole year of isolation."

"All the more reason for Rosa to go," reasoned Akrur while Rosa looked at the headmaster in confusion. "The girls can watch out for each other."

Burke shifted, looking a little calmer than when they had entered the kitchen. "You are their guardian, Cross. Are you saying you are comfortable with both of them going into the sphere?"

"Sphere?" Rosa asked.

"I don't think this is a conversation Miss Torres should be a part of," Burke said.

"Rosa's only choice shouldn't be a wasting curse," Chrysta argued. "If I have a way to get my abilities under control, she should be able to use it too."

Burke looked at Akrur. "How do you survive living with teenagers?" he asked.

Both Akrur and Tommy snorted, and some tension left the room. "You are the one running this school, right?" Tommy asked sarcastically.

"I run the school," Burke drawled. "I let the teachers handle the students." He pulled a chair out from the table for his wife and then sat down himself. Tommy did the same for Chrysta but stayed standing. Rosa sat at the head of the table, and Akrur remained standing by her side.

"There is a sphere," Burke explained. "A glass ball that contains a pocket universe with a large amount of land compressed inside of it. Time also moves differently in the sphere. Every hour is ten days, meaning you would spend three hundred and sixty days in the sphere after only a day and a half passes outside. It also means that we would be completely isolated. No one would get hurt if anything went wrong, and no one could see Chrysta use her abilities. It could be dangerous. Cross may give you permission, but you have to make the decision to go on your own."

Rosa looked at Akrur, and he gave her a shrug. It may be their last chance to get her powers under control, but it had to be her choice. "I'll do it," Rosa said after a brief moment of thought. "I'll go with you two. And if I can't control fire after I get out, I will do the wasting curse."

Burke sighed in resignation. "Fine, Miss Torres. You have a deal." He wearingly looked at Chrysta. "And you have your way, Miss York." Chrysta smiled.

"More supplies will be needed," Zheng pointed out. She looked at Akrur. "You have to make sure both of them get ready."

"I was going to go shopping with Chrysta today, but... well. The incident this morning made everything else just slip my mind."

"What about a guard?" Tommy asked. "I'm going to be there for Chrysta. Doesn't Rosa get to choose someone to watch over the ball for her?"

"The rest of the Disaster Club," Rosa said, this time saying it without a pause.

"Now, maybe Julien can do it. He's old enough to make that choice. But I can't allow the others to join us, my dear. It's much too risky," Akrur told her.

"I want them all to be there," Rosa argued.

"Absolutely not," Burke said. "This needs to be a small operation. More people means less secrecy."

"The children may keep Nyla in line," Zheng added, and her husband gave her an annoyed look. "After last night, I think Monroe will need as much protection as the sphere."

Tommy put a hand on his chest. "Hey now, I'll have you know that I fought some really angry bikers last night, all by myself. And didn't transform at all."

"See, Tommy needs the Disaster Club, too," Rosa said with a smile, and Tommy shot her a glare.

"No, definitely not," Akrur said. "I won't let the kids put themselves in that kind of jeopardy."

Tommy twitched suddenly and leaned back. He gave Akrur a smile and then grabbed the door handle. "You may not have a choice," Tommy told the empath and opened the door. Ichiro stumbled inside, Kevin almost joined him on the floor, but Rimsha grabbed him before he fell. Unable to eavesdrop, Julien was leaning on the back of a couch a few feet away, rubbing his face at the other kids' antics. Ichiro recovered and stood up, and gave everyone a bright smile. "Hullo!" he cried.

Burke groaned and tented his hands on the table, leaning forward so his hands hid his mouth. "Fantastic," he muttered darkly.

Zheng was chuckling at his expression. "Laugh all you want," Burke told her. "You will have to deal with them while I'm away." Her face fell into a frown.

.....

After discovering the kids spying on them, Akrur invited them into the kitchen to further discuss the sphere and what it meant for Chrysta and Rosa to go inside.

"So if the ball is destroyed while anyone is in there..." Rimsha started to say.

"Then they die as well," Ichiro finished for her.

"Hence why guards are essential," Zheng clarified.

"You could just go into the ball and not tell anyone where it is," Kevin pointed out.

"Last time someone tried that, he was injured and almost died," Burke explained. "So the guards are for the threats inside the sphere as much as the ones outside of it."

"Who made it?" Rimsha suddenly asked.

Burke shifted and looked at his wife. She shrugged. "Miss York is the one inheriting the sphere," Zheng said. "Let her decide if she wants to share that secret."

"Me? Why me?" Chrysta asked.

"The sphere has been passed down from the strongest magic user in a generation to the next since its discovery," Burke said. "It stands to reason that you will become the next sorcerer to receive it."

"So, who made it?" Chrysta asked.

Burke raised an eyebrow but continued anyway. "The consensus is that Strifelaughter constructed it. Perhaps as a prison for the Golden One. Sorcerers found it in his home after his final battle with her."

The room was silent in shock for a few minutes. "To destroy the ball after trapping her inside?" Akrur asked.

"Or have her die in the sphere," Zheng said. "That would explain the accelerated time."

Burek sighed and put down his hands. "I think we are getting off-topic here. The question now is, Miss York, Miss Torres, what would you have us do?" Burke asked.

Chrysta and Rosa looked at each other for a minute. "We will go together," Chrysta stated, Rosa nodding in agreement. "Mr. Cross, Tommy, and the Disaster Club are the people we want guarding it." She looked at Director Zheng. "I understand why Hunter Hafeez needs to be there, but please make sure she doesn't hurt anyone."

Zheng and Burke shared a look. "I could ask Ellis and Smith to be there as well," Zheng said. "They have a rapport with Monroe and can help protect everyone."

"Protect us from what?" Ichiro asked.

"The Acolytes are presumably looking for Chrysta," Zheng explained. "And if they can't have her back, they will not pass up the chance to kill her instead."

"But they would have to find her first, right?" Kevin asked nervously. "I mean, they don't know where she is, right?"

"They can't find her while she is on Academy grounds or in New Bendigo, yes," Mr. Burke explained. "But once she leaves, they can find her through scrying."

"Actually, I don't think they can," Tommy suddenly said. "I think they had to scry for Poe when we were running from the mansion."

"The statement still stands," Zheng said. "If they scry for her or something they know she has, they can find her." Chrysta bit her lip and started to wring her hands.

Akrur put his hand on Chrysta's shoulder and gave her a small smile. "I have a plan to make sure that doesn't happen," Akrur said. "But there is still a chance that something nasty may happen." He looked up and glanced at each of the kids. "So there is still a risk. That's why if anyone wants to back out of this, now is the time. No shame in wanting to stay behind."

The kids paused, looking at each other. "The Disaster Club doesn't run from a fight, not when one of the members needs us," Kevin declared. The others nodded in agreement.

"We will see you Wednesday, then, Cross," Burke said while standing. He looked at Rosa and Chrysta. "Make sure you two prepare yourselves tomorrow."

The girls nodded, and the headmaster and director left. Rosa put her hand on Chrysta's, and Chrysta turned to her. "Thank you," Rosa said softly. "You didn't have to do that."

"I'm a member of the Disaster Club," Chrysta said with a grin and a shrug. "We help each other."

"So, if the ball is destroyed, we lose both of them," Ichiro said with a frown. He sighed and looked at Kevin. "So Kevin 'Butterfingers' Butler can't touch it."

"Screw you, Ichiro."

.....

After Kevin made dinner (Akrur suspected Kevin was trying to show off his cooking skills by making lasagna rolls) and the others cleaned the kitchen, Chrysta approached Akrur. "Mr. Cross, can Tommy and I sleep on the couch again?"

"No," he replied, barely looking up from his book.

"Please, Mr. Cross," she asked with a slight pout. "He helps me sleep, so I don't have any nightmares."

"I'm her emotional support changeling," Tommy joked, not looking up from the book on curses.

Akrur glared at him but looked back at Chrysta with an apologetic look. "It's not proper, my dear. I can't let everyone just cuddle up with someone they fancy whenever they want."

Chrysta sighed. "It was worth a shot. I guess I will sleep on the couch by myself tonight."

There was a weird tension in the Club that night. Rosa was subdued, barely talking to anyone and occasionally shooting Julien guilty looks. Julien would sometimes wince and hold his side. Tommy kept to himself, only letting Chrysta be next to him. Kevin would glance at Tommy but then quickly look away, trying to avoid another outburst from Tommy. When the kids finally started getting ready for bed, Akrur felt relief that they had avoided any more drama.

"I'll be glad when all of this is over," Akrur confessed to Tommy. "Then things will hopefully go back to normal."

"I'll just be happy to get a full night's sleep," Chrysta muttered darkly from the couch.

"Nah, I don't want to go back to my normal," Tommy said while kissing Chrysta on the forehead. She smiled and burrowed into the blankets. "I like having a bed to sleep in now."

❧ 20 ❧

Guerra was passing by the second bedroom on the second story of the acolyte mansion when he happened to look inside to see the lady of the house furiously packing a suitcase. She looked upset. Correction, she looked infuriated, moving so fast from one side of the room to the next that her dress flared out behind her. He generally avoided talking to her as they had nothing to discuss, but curiosity got the better of him, and he stepped inside the bedroom. "Bella signora," he greeted her. "How are you this evening?"

"Don't you start that shit with me," she growled, rounding on him with a finger in his face. He blinked and leaned back, shocked at her behavior. She was generally a nice and calm woman.

Guerra hesitated at her tone but smiled at her, his brightest one. Unfortunately, it never reached his eyes. "What do you mean, my lady?"

"I just heard one of your associates talking about attacking someone, possibly killing them. I don't know what is going on, but I am out of here, and I'm going to the police," she explained while snapping the suitcase shut. She started to step past him, suitcase in one hand, but he reached out and grabbed her upper arm.

"I'm afraid I can't let you do that, bella signora," he stated, trying to smile even as rage surged through his veins. He didn't know who talked in front of her, but he was going to find them and teach them a lesson in secrecy.

She frowned, and then her eyes went wide in fear. She pulled her arm out of Guerra's grip, but he just seized her throat with the same hand instead. She made a gurgling noise, something that

probably would have been a yelp if he was not currently choking the life out of her, and dropped the suitcase.

She clawed at his hand at her throat and started to reach for his face with the other, but he just grabbed her wrist and kept her from scratching him. He continued smiling at her, even as he glowed red and set her nerves on fire. He felt most alive when he was causing pain to others, the fear and anguish in their eyes sending a thrill down his spine. He lifted her and hauled her to the balcony to make sure no one in the mansion could hear her.

Guerra stopped at the railing, pushing her so that she was leaning over the edge. Her feet kicked out even as he turned his power up. What she was feeling must be pure torture, but Guerra was impressed by her fighting spirit.

He held her there for several long and tense moments, reveling in her panic and fear. He wasn't an empath, but when he used his power like this, without restraint, and saw his playthings writhe, he could nearly imagine their agony. Ecstasy flooded his system even as the pain overwhelmed theirs. Guerra still wasn't sure why they died. Did their hearts stop? Did their brains over—

"Mr. Cross!"

Akrur jerked away, feeling his heart, already pounding from the dream, galloping in his chest. Rimsha was in his room, by his bed, fear etched on her face. "Fire!" she screamed, and he was scrambling out of bed, not even bothering to put his gloves on.

They rushed to the common room, and the sight of the couch on fire greeted Akrur. Tommy, Julien, and Rosa tried to beat the fire out with blankets. Ichiro was with Chrysta several feet away, Chrysta clutching her arm. Poe was on a bookcase across the room, croaking loudly while flapping his wings. As Akrur was trying to get his wits about him, Kevin came rushing out of the kitchen with a large pot of water. He threw it on the couch but only managed to douse the flames on the arm of the sofa.

"*Bujhaana!*" Akrur yelled, and his hands glowed blue as he concentrated on putting the fire out. The fire flared up for a moment and then went out with a *whoosh,* leaving only smoke and soot in its place.

Everyone was coughing and blinking in the haze. "What happened?" Akrur asked the kids, looking at each of them in turn.

"Don't look at me!" Rosa cried. "I was dead asleep."

"It was me," Chrysta panted from the floor. She looked miserable as Tommy rushed to her and inspected her arm. "It was my nightmare again. Only I guess instead of making everything float, I set the blanket on fire. I'm so sorry, everyone."

Akrur went to her and had her hold out her arm. The flames had severely burned her forearm, her skin red and weeping. Rimsha kneeled next to her, inspecting the wound as soon as she secured her hijab.

"Should I get a healer?" Ichiro asked.

"No," Akrur said. "Mrs. Paulson will think it was Rosa again." He looked at Rimsha. "Do you think you can heal it?"

"Maybe," the young girl said. As she screwed her eyes shut and started glowing green, Ichiro sighed and looked at the smoldering couch.

"What do we do with this?" he asked.

"Take it outside when we're sure it's not hot anymore," Akrur told him. Chrysta suddenly hissed and squeezed Tommy's hand. Akrur looked at a nearby clock as Tommy rubbed Chrysta's back. Akrur winced. Four fifteen in the morning. He doubted any of them would get back to sleep at this point.

While Rimsha worked, Kevin went up to the bookcase Poe was perched on, gently shushing the bird. Kevin's hand glowed orange for a moment, and a glow appeared around Poe's head. The bird stopped flapping and cocked his head at the boy and then dropped down to Kevin's offered arm. Chrysta tried to crane her neck to look at them. "Is he okay?" she asked Kevin.

"I don't know," Kevin replied. He started to chat, "easy, easy, easy," to the raven as he gently made Poe hold out a wing to inspect it. "Looks like his feathers got singed."

"Oh no," Chrysta mumbled. "Will he be okay?" she called out.

"I don't know. Let me get him some water. We will have to see if he can fly later."

"There," Rimsha murmured as Kevin headed to the kitchen. She moved her hands and examined her work. Chrysta's arm was slightly red but otherwise markless.

Akrur held out a hand to help Chrysta up, momentarily forgetting that he didn't have his gloves on. He winced when a few raw emotions flooded his head at her touch—

phantom pain from the burn on her arm, pain in her heart, she hurt Poe, she injured one of her oldest friends, she could have killed him, he could have died!

—but he tried to ignore them. Once Chrysta was vertical, he put his hands on his hips and sighed. He surveyed the damage. "Alright, everyone," he said. "Let's get to work."

.....

They broke out mops and rags and towels and got to work, scrubbing the floors as well as the ceiling. Tommy and Rosa carried the couch outside, and when they got back inside, Ichiro used a blast of wind to send the smoke out. Unfortunately, that meant he sent the heat with it, and they had to get the woodstove going to try to get the Club warm again. The rug was mainly untouched, just soaked, so Rimsha took out the carpet cleaner to get it dry. Finally, once everyone was done cleaning and dressed, Rimsha grabbed all of their smoke-filled clothes and washed them together, trying to eliminate the smell. Poor Tommy constantly sniffed and sneezed as they worked, his heightened sense of smell working against him. It was only six in the morning when they finished, and Kevin started breakfast as soon as they were done.

Chrysta was quiet throughout the entire morning, not talking to anyone and just drifting from one cleaning project to the next. Akrur kept an eye on her and wasn't surprised to see Tommy watching her as well. When they sat down for a breakfast of bacon and eggs, Akrur put a hand on one of Chrysta's. "Are you alright, my dear?" he asked.

"I... I'm okay," she said. Akrur glanced at Tommy, and the changeling scowled. "Are you sure?" Akrur asked.

"Yeah, I'm okay," she replied. "Just... just glad I didn't hurt anyone, that's all."

After breakfast, Akrur excused himself to go outside. He climbed the stairs and sat on the bench, throwing glares at the burnt couch and upturned roots. He got his mobile out of his pocket and thumbed through his contacts. His thumb hovered over the picture of Abby, smiling at the camera, weighing his options for a few minutes. "Oh, sod it all," he muttered to himself and finally touched the icon.

The line trilled for several seconds, and Akrur was wondering what the hell he would say in a voicemail when she finally picked up. "'ello?" she asked, voice thick with sleep.

"How's the case going, Doc?" Akrur asked with a grin.

"Oh, it's too early for that nonsense, Akrur," she groaned, but he could hear the smile in her tone.

"Sorry, couldn't resist," he said, still grinning. He paused as Abby yawned. "Did I wake you?"

"Yeah, just getting a nap in. This time change is murder. What time is it there?"

Akrur hummed as he checked his pocket watch. "Just ten past seven here," he replied.

"In the morning? That's kinda early, is everything okay?"

Akrur hesitated. Now that he had her on the line, he realized that he couldn't talk about what was happening at the Disaster Club. The sphere had to remain a secret, at least for now. Tommy's barfight, Julien's injury, Rosa being threatened with a wasting curse, Chrysta's nightmares. Telling her about any of it would make her feel like she had to cut her trip short and run back. And maybe that was why he had called in the first place. To know that she would come back to help if he needed her. He was quiet for so long, thinking, that she spoke again. "Akrur," she said with concern in her voice. "Is everything okay?"

"Yes," he said quickly. Then, Akrur sighed. "No. It's complicated."

"I can be there in an hour," she said without hesitation, and he smiled in gratitude.

"No! No, no, no, my dear. You stay right there where you are needed."

"Are you sure?" she asked.

"Yes," he added without pause. "I can't talk about what is going on, not right now. I guess I just needed to hear your voice."

There was a long pause on the other end of the line, long enough that Akrur was about to ask if she was still there, but she suddenly laughed. "Well, I don't know how to respond to that. Literally, I have no clue what to say now that you said that."

Akrur laughed. "How is your trip going?" he offered.

Abby let out a groan that would make a teenager proud. "Oh my lord, Akrur, you would not believe what these little idiots have done."

"Oh, I can't call them idiots, but you are free to do so."

"I'm the one treating them, Akrur. I can call them idiots if I want to." Abby sighed, and Akrur could imagine her rubbing her eyes, something she did when extremely stressed. "So get this. They found a book on curses. And then started to use it. Page by page. Every single curse."

"Oh, my, Abby," Akrur muttered in shock. "What were they thinking?"

"That they would be able to reverse the curses. And they did. For some of them." She sighed again. "When I got here and started helping my original patient, the others started coming out of the woodwork. One of them is *shrinking*, one breaks out in *hives* every time he talks, and the last one is *green!* I don't know what would have happened if they got to the high-level curses like a wasting curse."

At the mention of the wasting curse, Akrur felt his smile fade. It just made him worry about all of the things he couldn't tell her again. Abby was still talking, but he didn't listen. "Akrur?" she suddenly asked. "What's really wrong?"

"It's... something I can't share yet," he said with a sigh. He glared at the scorched couch and the tree's skyward pointing roots again. "But when you get back, boy, do I have a story for you."

She chuckled. "Well, if you change your mind, let me know. And if you need to hear my voice again, you know how to get ahold of me."

Akrur felt himself blush, and he cleared his throat. "I'll try not to abuse the privilege," he drawled. "I don't think I can afford your doctor's fees." And he smiled when she started laughing.

21

After his call, Akrur gathered the kids to head into town. Kevin said he had to remain to work on a project to help Poe. Julien declined to go, saying that his back was hurting. Rimsha said she would stay to keep an eye on the injured young man and try to fix the roots of the Disaster Tree. As the others were leaving, Rimsha was forcing Julien to lie on the couch to rest.

They walked to the gravel lot where the faculty parked their cars. Akrur went up to his late-model van with his keys in hand to unlock it. Tommy snorted behind him. "Is that yours?" he asked.

"Yes, it is," Akrur answered, slightly offended. "What is wrong with it?"

"Nothing. I just wonder if it's as old as I am."

Akrur snorted. "Hardly."

As Akrur unlocked and opened the doors, Rosa turned to Tommy. "Rock, paper, scissors," she announced with no other explanation, holding out her fist. Tommy looked her up and down and then tentatively put out his fist as well. "One, two, three," Rosa counted, and she flashed a rock while Tommy did scissors. "Ha!" she cried and knocked Tommy's hand with hers.

"Okay, I'll bite. What just happened?" Tommy asked.

"You were fighting over the passenger seat," Akrur explained. Rosa was climbing into the front as he spoke. "It has the most legroom." Rosa closed the door and smiled brightly at the changeling.

"Oh joy," Tommy muttered as he studied the tiny third row. He climbed in, Chrysta and Ichiro climbing into the second row by themselves.

New Bendigo was busy, people bustling from one store to the other. Akrur parked in a spot in front of the town's square. New Bendigo was a small town but not lacking in amenities. There was a department store, the bookstore where Abby got his gift card, and an active coffee shop. A movie theater, a pizzeria, and a diner. An antique shop, craft store, and barbershop. There were plenty of places to find what they were looking for. They all got out of the van and stood on the sidewalk.

"Now," Akrur started to explain to the group, "Headmaster Burke is handling the day-to-day necessities. Food, laundry soap, dish soap, and some medical supplies. What you ladies need to worry about are the personal supplies: soap, deodorant, toothpaste, toothbrushes, the works. It would be best if you got enough for a year, but keep it to the bare essentials" He nodded at Chrysta. "I recommend that you get more clothes, my dear. The small amount you were able to take with you probably won't last a year."

Chrysta bit her lip. "I don't have much money, Mr. Cross," she said.

"No worries." Akrur held up his wallet. "Headmaster Burke has given a little extra to the Disaster Club budget. So don't worry about the price; I will cover it."

They started in the pharmacy. The girls grabbed a cart and started throwing the items they needed. Akrur would occasionally remind them that they needed enough for the entire year.

The poor cashier's eyes bulged when they finally got to the front. "Gosh, why do you need so much stuff?"

"Long trip," Rosa said just as Chrysta said, "Donations." The cashier blinked but got to work scanning and bagging everything. They threw everything into the van. "What's next?" Tommy asked.

"Clothes," Akrur stated, pointing at the department store.

"Oh, how about there?" Chrysta asked, pointing to the thrift store.

"Save some money by buying secondhand. Bully idea, my dear," Akrur said with a smile and offered his arm to the giggling teen as they crossed the street.

Once in the thrift store, the kids scattered. Tommy looked at shirts, taking out the black ones and draping them over his arm. Rosa and Ichiro started trying on odd things, like hats and heels, earning a glare from the lone cashier. But they cleaned up after themselves, so Akrur didn't stop them. Chrysta wandered around in the women's section, grabbing shirts, jeans, pants, and skirts. She kept glancing at Akrur every time she took something, but he just kept looking at the kitchen appliances, hoping to find a cheap toaster. Finally, after Chrysta's fifth time glancing in his direction, he went over to Tommy. "Why is she looking at me like that?" he asked, making sure Chrysta couldn't see him talking.

"You know her concert dress, the black one?" Tommy asked, continuing to look through the racks.

"Yes."

"She picked it without her father's permission. He took it away when he found it. She's probably worried you're going to make her put everything back." Tommy paused in his search in the racks and flashed Chrysta a large smile. She smiled back and seemed to relax.

"Well, I won't let her wear anything inappropriate, but really, she can pick whatever she wants. They are for her, after all."

"Well, you and Jozef York have different opinions on what is appropriate," Tommy growled.

When Chrysta picked out a simple black dress for herself, Akrur wandered over to her and grinned. "That looks lovely, my dear," he said.

Chrysta glanced at him again, studying his face. She smiled shyly. "You like it? Is black okay?"

"Black is fine. You should try it on."

Chrysta went to the changing room, the others waiting for her to emerge. They would clap every time she came out, Rosa giving her wolf whistles. Chrysta blushed, but she started to laugh and model off her clothes as time went on. Some were too long or too big for her. "I wish I weren't so small," she lamented at one point, trying to hold a skirt up so it wouldn't fall off her hips.

"Rimsha can help you with that," Ichiro told her. "She helps me with my clothes all the time."

Finally, Chrysta had enough outfits to fill a small wardrobe, smiling from ear to ear. They went to the counter to pay, and Akrur took Tommy's selection from him and added it to Chrysta's pile. The changeling looked at him. "Why?"

"Consider it a thank-you gift for protecting Miss Khalil yesterday," Akrur explained.

Tommy shifted from foot to foot and tried to grab the pile of shirts back. "You know I can afford that, right?"

"Yes, you can," Akrur agreed while putting his hand on the pile and keeping them in place as the cashier rang them up, still scowling. Finally, Tommy gave in and pouted, the others laughing.

Once they took Chrysta's new clothes to the van, Akrur clapped his hand together. "Alright, what's next?"

Rosa looked at the coffee shop. "Coffee," she stated.

"Really, my dear, we don't have the time."

"Please, Mr. Cross. I won't be able to get a caramel latte with a double shot of espresso when I go into the ball."

Akrur sighed and glared at the girl. "Fine, but after that, we have to find you some books to bring with you. Headmaster Burke says that electronics sometimes don't work in the sphere, so you may not be able to watch movies in your downtime."

Rosa grinned and ran across the street with Ichiro. Akrur turned to Chrysta and Tommy while Chrysta studied something in the distance. "What is that store, Mr. Cross?"

Akrur squinted at the store in question. "The Song of Miriam? It's a music shop, although I confess, I have never gone inside myself."

"May I go, Mr. Cross? I would love to buy some supplies for my violin to take with me."

"Of course, my dear," he said, and they started to move as a group down the street, Chrysta taking Tommy's offered arm. Akrur started to slow down as they passed a store. "Head on without me. Need to run an errand first."

Tommy raised an eyebrow at the liquor store, covered in ads for booze and tobacco products. "Gonna get some cigarettes?" he asked.

"Well, need something to keep me busy for 36 hours," Akrur joked as he went inside. Then, he suddenly stuck his head back outside. "Don't tell Abby."

After making his purchase, Akrur strolled outside to join the couple in front of the music shop. They were still on the sidewalk, Chrysta peering through the door and Tommy through the window. "What's wrong?" Akrur asked.

"The sign says they should be open, but the door is locked, and it's dark inside," Chrysta explained.

"Strange," Akrur said, peering into the dark store with them.

There was a shout, and the group turned around. Crossing the street towards them was two older men. Akrur's face fell into a scowl as he recognized them: Jim Hunt and Richard Henson. The two biggest nosy parkers of New Bendigo, known to all the Academy staff and faculty for their horrible habit of trying to pry as much information about the school from anyone they could corner. Right now, they were focused on Tommy, giving him identical bright smiles. "Well!" Jim cried as they made it to the sidewalk. "We were worried Charlie ran you out of town, stranger!"

Richard grabbed Tommy's face to examine it when he was close enough. "I thought he did more damage, but you barely have a scratch on you!"

Tommy knocked the older man's hands away. "I'm a fast healer," he growled. He held his hand out. "Thomas Monroe. Friends call me Tommy."

Richard smiled and shook the changeling's hand. "Richard 'Rich' Henson," he said. He gestured at his friend, and Jim tipped an imaginary hat. "Jim Hunt." When Tommy let go of Richard's hand, he turned to Akrur and wagged a finger in the empath's face while Jim shook Tommy's hand. "I knew he had something to do with that school, and seeing you proves it."

"Not that it's any of your business, sir," Akrur grumbled.

"Don't worry. He didn't give away any of your secrets," Jim said. "Said that the school is full of wizards, so your mystery is still safe."

Akrur felt his stomach drop, and he glowered at the changeling, who gave him a shit-eating grin. "Yes, wizards. What a ridiculous concept," he muttered.

Richard spied Chrysta, and his bushy eyebrows shot up. "Well, who is this enchanting creature?" he asked as he put out his hand.

"Chrysta Angelos, sir," she said, shaking Richard's hand.

"Please, you can call me Rich," he said with a smile and then kissed Chrysta on the back of her hand.

"Rich... Rich, you are old enough to be her grandfather. Stop traumatizing her," Jim scolded his friend as Chrysta gave a nervous smile and Tommy scowled.

"Control yourself, old man," Tommy growled, pointing at the man as he put a hand on Chrysta's shoulder.

Richard let go of Chrysta's hand and held his up in surrender. "Alright, tough man, I get it. I have seen what you can do in a fight. I don't need that type of trouble."

"Were you guys trying to get into Micha's?" Jim asked, gesturing at the dark shop.

"Yes, sir," Chrysta said while nodding. "The sign says the shop should be open, but the door is locked."

"Micha is older than us and semi-retired," Jim explained. "Wait here. I'll get him." The old man headed to the back of the building.

The group waited on the sidewalk, Richard studying Tommy's face. Akrur leaned closer to Chrysta. "Angelos?" he asked in a whisper.

Chrysta blushed. "My mom's maiden name. I figured if people hate the York name, then I will use another name instead."

Akrur smiled. "Good idea, my dear. Very smart. I wish I had thought of it."

"Not a scratch on ya," Richard muttered, almost to himself. Tommy didn't comment and just stood there with his arms folded. "I wouldn't even know you were in a fight unless I saw it happen with my own two eyes. What about that cut on your thigh, the one from the cat?"

"What cat?" Tommy asked.

"That big cat with the lady," Richard said incredulously.

"I don't remember a cat," Tommy replied, giving the old man a quirked eyebrow. "You must be going senile."

Richard opened his mouth like he was going to argue when Jim showed up with a man, ancient-looking and bent over. The man adjusted his glasses and looked at Tommy and Chrysta. "No. No children. No children in the shop. You two know that." He jabbed a crooked finger in Tommy's direction. "And that one looks like a delinquent."

Akrur opened his mouth to defend them, but Jim beat him to it. "Hey now, he's a good guy. And they aren't children, you curmudgeon. They're customers."

Chrysta grabbed a roll of cash out of her pocket and showed it to the older man. "I just need some strings and music for a violin, sir. If you have them."

Micha glared at the money and moved his jaw around, thinking. "Come on, Micha," Richard scolded him. "You're always complaining that you don't have customers."

"Fine! Fine, fine, fine," the older man said, taking some keys out of his pocket and opening the door. He held the door open, letting everyone inside. He poked Tommy when he got close. "I'm keeping an eye on you, punk."

"I'm also watching you, old man," Tommy joked with a forced smile, and Akrur laughed.

The small shop was full of instruments, racks of sheet music, and various supplies. A baby grand piano took over half of the floor space. Tommy went over to it while Chrysta went to a wall full of violins. Micha shuffled behind the counter, and Jim and Richard stood at the counter, leaning on it. "Don't you touch that!" Micha yelled at Tommy when he noticed the changeling at the piano, wagging a finger threateningly.

Tommy glared at the older man. He took off his leather jacket. "Don't you dare!" Tommy moved to stand in front of the keys. "Touch it, and I call the police!" Tommy sat down. "You don't even know how to play!" Without breaking eye contact with Micha, Tommy lifted his hands and started to play. Chrysta laughed when she saw the older men's jaws drop in shock.

"You think that is good?" she asked the dumbfounded men. "You should hear him play the violin."

"I'm not nearly as good as her, though," Tommy confessed as he continued to play, letting his eyes rest on the keys he was playing.

"Mozart's Piano Sonata No. 16 in C Major," Micha said in awe. "Nearly perfect too."

"Looks like your left hand is doing better," Akrur said to Tommy.

"Fingers are still numb, but most of this is muscle memory," Tommy explained.

Just then, the shop door opened, and Rosa and Ichiro walked inside, both holding overpriced coffee. Their jaws dropped as well. They joined Akrur by the piano. "I think you should buy a piano for the Club, Mr. Cross," Ichiro whispered to Akrur.

Tommy finished the song, everyone clapping lightly. Tommy just inclined his head and started to play something else. "My apologies, young man," Micha called out to him. "I think I learned a lesson in not judging a book by its cover." He suddenly rounded on the two teens standing by Akrur. "But if you spill a drop of that in here, you're buying whatever you ruin."

"They won't ruin anything, you old bat," Akrur told him, and the shop owner scowled.

Chrysta finally went to the counter with a small package. She put it down and then started to count her money. Ichiro picked it up and gasped. "One hundred and twenty-five dollars?" he asked.

"Yes, for strings," Chrysta said, not looking shocked about the price. She started to press her lips into a thin line in worry. "I was hoping to buy some sheet music too, but I think I only have enough money for the strings." She looked at Tommy. "Do you have any sheet music I could borrow?"

"Only jazz music and piano music, beautiful," Tommy answered, not pausing his song.

Chrysta bit her lip and studied the racks of music. "It wouldn't hurt to look," she said and walked over to the other wall.

Tommy got Ichiro's attention and started to jerk his head. The young boy went over to him. Tommy quickly reached into his jacket and brought out some money. He let Ichiro see it and then nodded toward Chrysta. Ichiro grinned and nodded.

For the next few minutes, Ichiro stood next to Chrysta and watched as she scanned the shop's music collection. Every time she put something down, Ichiro would pick it up like he was studying it, then he would quickly and quietly hand it to Tommy. Somehow, Chrysta didn't realize what the others were doing, but the collection of music sitting next to Tommy grew as time went on. Finally, Chrysta got her selection down to two books and headed back to the counter.

Tommy stopped playing his song and joined her. He tugged the music she held into his pile and put it on the counter. He also grabbed the strings and then smiled at the bewildered girl. "I got this, beautiful," he said with a grin.

"Oh no, Tommy, that's too much."

"Like I said, beautiful. I can make more money. Good friends are hard to come by."

Micha was adding up the total, putting the music in a bag as he worked, when Jim hit Tommy's shoulder. "Where did you learn to play like that?"

"I taught myself for the most part," Tommy explained. "Although I have worked with a lot of jazz musicians too."

"Anyone we would know?"

"Ever hear of Duke Ellington?" Tommy asked, and Jim gave him a baffled look.

Suddenly, Tommy clapped his hands. "Oh! You have any Paganini, old man?"

Micha glared at him, although the large amount of money the changeling was spending kept him from saying something rude. "Violin Concerto Number 4," he said.

Tommy ran to the wall full of music, found what he was looking for, and added it to the pile. "Learn this, and we will call it even," he said to Chrysta.

The group left the shop, Chrysta thanking him loudly even as the older man glowered at them from the front door. The kids went ahead, talking to each other in excited tones, as Jim and Richard stopped Akrur.

"Hey," Jim said in a low voice, "Tommy said something about helping a friend the other night. Is she the one he helped? What happened?"

"Chrysta?" Akrur asked. The older men nodded. He glanced at Chrysta as she walked away. She was smiling, all the melancholy from earlier gone, as she wrapped an arm around Tommy's after he got his leather jacket on. Akrur didn't know how much he should tell the two gossipmongers. "She was in a bad situation. And Tommy helped her to get out." That was all he wanted to say.

Richard nodded. "I had a feeling that was a fine fellow." He held up a finger. "Don't brainwash her to join your cult, okay?" He clapped Akrur on the shoulder and started to walk away.

Jim snorted. "Cults. He is losing his marbles. Do you know he thinks he saw a jungle cat the other night? At the bar brawl. Can you imagine?"

Akrur smiled, but it felt strained on his face. "A jungle cat in North America. How absurd."

"Well, gotta go. Don't let that girl get kidnapped by aliens." And then he clapped Akrur's shoulder on the exact same spot and wandered in the direction of his friend. Akrur just stared at them and shook his head, and then started walking in the direction of the van.

Akrur was walking up with his keys out when he addressed the group waiting for him. "Alright, everyone, we need to go to the bookstore and then to the grocery store."

"Why the grocery store, Mr. Cross?" Ichiro asked.

"Well, I thought we would let the two adventurers choose what to have for dinner."

Rosa and Chrysta looked at each other. "Steak," Rosa said. "As raw as I can get it. Sorry, Mr. Cross."

"No apologies needed, my dear. Miss Angelos?"

"Sushi?" Chrysta asked, looking at Ichiro.

"Oh, because I'm Japanese, I must know how to make sushi?" Ichiro said with a scowl.

"Um, I'm sorry, it was just a thought..."

"I'm messing with you," Ichiro said with a bright smile. "I can totally make you some sushi." He took Chrysta's arm as she laughed. "To the grocery store!"

22

After they finished their epic shopping trip, they headed home, Rosa allowing Tommy to take the front seat. When they got back to the Academy, they left almost everything in the van but carried Chrysta's new clothes and the food back to the Club. They found Rimsha outside, covered in dirt and mud, but she was grinning as she glowed green and reset the last root back into the ground.

"Good job, my dear," Akrur told her, giving her a pat on the back.

"Wasn't easy, but at least I didn't have to cut them off," she said with a smile. She looked down at her sweatshirt. "I need a shower, though."

"Hey, guys!" Kevin called out as he climbed the stairs. Poe was on his shoulder.

"Hey, Poe," Chrysta said. The raven croaked and jumped to her shoulder. She scratched his chest. "How is he doing?"

"Good. He only lost a few feathers this morning. He can fly, but probably not for long distances. I asked my dad to send me some more if he can find them."

"You can replace them?" Tommy asked.

"Yep! It's called imping. You take some spare feathers and superglue them to the damaged one." Kevin reached out and held his hand out to the raven. Poe held it with a leg and started to nibble at the boy's fingers. "Then, next time he molts, he gets brand new feathers." He pointed at the grocery bags. "What are those?"

"Rosa and Chrysta want steak and sushi for dinner," Ichiro explained with a grin. "Sweet!"

With Tommy, Ichiro, and Kevin in the kitchen, dinner was whipped up in no time, and the whole Club sat down to eat that night. Steak with salsa for Rosa and several types of sushi for Chrysta. "Thank you, Ichiro," Chrysta said after taking a bite. "This is delicious."

"And this steak is awesome," Rosa said with her mouth full.

"Anything for you ladies," Kevin replied with a leer, and Ichiro and Tommy gave him a look.

They continued eating, the kids talking about the sphere. "I wonder what's inside?" Kevin asked.

"There's a castle," Chrysta started to explain. "And a waterfall pouring into a river that flows into a lake. And trees. But the light is so weird. It moves so fast."

"I'm still amazed at all the land that they got into that small space," Akrur admitted.

"Oh, Mr. Cross, are we still doing the bonfire?" Julien signed after finishing his bite of steak.

"I don't see why we can't still do the bonfire," Akrur said and signed, keeping the chopsticks away from his face.

"Let's just please not burn the whole forest down," Rimsha said and signed, and Julien made the sign that he was laughing.

After dinner, the kids stayed in the common room, waiting for it to get late. Rimsha helped Chrysta with her clothes, hemming pants and tightening shirts and dresses. Kevin got a text and then went to the door and gave a loud "Ha!" as a package appeared.

"What's that?" Rosa asked from the sofa as she played video games with Ichiro.

"Feathers from my dad," Kevin explained. He opened the box and started laying out the contents. Poe flew over and cocked his head at the pile, clicking his beak together. The raven began to pick up the feathers, Kevin trying to get him to stop. Finally, Kevin put his hand out, and it briefly glowed orange. A glow appeared around Poe's head, and the raven stopped trying to grab the feathers.

"What was that?" Chrysta asked.

"His ability," Rimsha explained, using pins to hem a pair of jeans for the other girl. "He talks to animals."

"'Talks' is not really the right word," Kevin said. He pulled at Poe's wing, and the raven let him, croaking. "Animals kinda... feel the thought you send to them? It's hard to explain abstract concepts to them. Like, he doesn't know that I'm trying to help him, but I told him the feathers are 'mine,' so he shouldn't touch them."

When the clock finally read eleven, Akrur gathered the kids. They got dressed in coats and jackets, gloves and hats, boots and thick shoes. Chrysta finally had her own jacket and boots, brown leather ones she had found at the thrift store. They headed outside, walking into the woods.

Akrur went ahead with a small ball of light hovering above his hand, Rosa by his side. Then Chrysta and Tommy, Kevin and Rimsha, and Julien and Ichiro brought up the rear. They talked in hushed tones, breath fogging in the night air. Akrur offered his arm, and Rosa took it. "So, my dear, did you have a good day?" he asked.

Rosa scowled. "I think I just realized that I won't be able to have a latte whenever I want. So you better send me some for me when you can."

Akrur chuckled. "I'm not getting you coffee for every day you are in there, my dear. Three hundred and sixty cups sounds like too big of an order." Rosa snorted.

Akrur looked over his shoulder. "And you, my dear?" he asked Chrysta.

"I had a good day," Chrysta said. "I just wish I could..." She trailed off. "Nevermind."

"Nevermore?" Tommy asked. Chrysta smiled at him, and Akrur had a feeling he knew what that meant in the back of his mind, but its meaning eluded him.

"I just wish I could call Mary," Chrysta confessed.

"Mary?" Rimsha asked.

"My friend. My best friend. More like a sister to me. She is probably worried sick about me. And I know for you guys it will be thirty-six hours, but knowing that for me, it will be a year before I get to talk to her again..." She trailed off again and frowned.

Akrur caught Tommy's eye. Tommy cocked an eyebrow, and Akrur caught his meaning. He gave a slight nod, and the changeling grinned.

They found a clearing in the woods, with several stone benches set in a circle around a giant stone basin. The kids started to gather wood, small sticks, and limbs at first, and then large logs that Tommy carried with ease. At one point, Rimsha started smacking Julien with a stick. "Sit down! You're injured!" she ordered, and he finally retreated to one of the benches.

When they had a pile of logs almost as tall as Akrur, he nodded to Ichiro when his pocket watch said it was midnight, and the young boy made a fireball and lit the wood on fire. The kids cheered and sat down. Akrur stayed on his feet and looked around. "To the new year!" he cried.

The kids yelled and whooped and applauded.

"To new friends!"

The Disaster Club roared for their new member and new changeling friend.

"To new adventures!"

They yelled even louder, the quiet woods the only witness to their joy.

"To the Disaster Club!" Akrur finished and threw up his hands, and the kids went wild, howling into the night, Chrysta joining them and Tommy just grinning at their antics.

They all sat and settled down, talking and laughing. Kevin had brought the ingredients for s'mores, and they made the sweets, daring each other to get as close to the fire as possible. Finally, Akrur watched as Tommy reached into his jacket, brought out his cell phone, unlocked it, and dialed a number. Tommy handed the phone to Chrysta, who was talking to Rimsha. "It's for you, beautiful," he said with a grin, and Chrysta's eyebrows furrowed in confusion.

"For me?" she asked, putting the trilling phone to her ear. The phone stopped trilling, and Akrur could hear a squawking start over the line. Chrysta's face lit up, and she smiled. "Hi Mary, it's me," she said.

The rest of the kids fell silent as Chrysta talked. "Yes, I'm okay... No, I can't tell you where I am... I just don't want my father to hurt you... What? What do you mean he's missing?" She glanced at Akrur. "Don't go over there anymore... No, I don't trust the other men. If he's missing, they had something to do with it, I'm sure." She paused and listened. "No, I'm *okay*, I swear... No, I don't know when I can go back to the city... I'll come back when I can... It may just be a while."

She listened for a moment and then laughed. She handed Tommy's phone back to him. "She wants to talk to you."

Tommy pressed a button to put the phone on speaker. "Yeah?" he drawled.

"Thomas Monroe!" a voice yelled back, and Tommy winced and pulled the phone away from his ear. "You asshole! You bring my fri—Wait, do you have a middle name?"

"My mother never gave me one," Tommy replied.

"I'm mad enough that I need a middle name," the voice growled.

"I've gone by the nickname Louis a few times," Tommy offered.

"Thomas Louis Monroe!" the voice yelled, and the kids laughed, Chrysta putting her hands up to her face and shaking her head. "You bring my best friend home, you hear me?"

"'fraid I can't, Mary," Tommy drawled, not cowed by the girl's demands. "She's safer where we are."

There was silence on the phone, long enough that Akrur was worried that the call had dropped, but when Mary spoke again, it was in a much softer tone. "Is she safe, Tommy? Really safe?"

"I am, Mary, I promise," Chrysta answered for the changeling.

"Well, as long as you are out of danger, that's the important thing," Mary said gently, all of her anger gone. "I'll forgive you this time, Tommy."

"Your absolution means the world to me, Mary," Tommy said, and the other girl laughed over the line.

Chrysta took the phone back and continued talking for several minutes, taking her friend off of speaker, what sounded like general school gossip. She brought her feet up and leaned against Tommy, and he wrapped an arm around her. The other kids kept eating s'mores and talking, letting out the occasional laugh.

Akrur brought out his pocket watch and tapped it, catching Chrysta's eye. "Listen, Mary? I need to go. I have something I need to do tomorrow, but when it's over, I'll visit you, okay? So you can meet my new friends." She paused and sniffed. "Say hi to everyone for me, okay?" She listened and laughed. "Even Chloe."

Chrysta finally gave Tommy back his phone. She wiped at her eyes but smiled when Rimsha rubbed her back. "Thank you," she whispered to Tommy.

Tommy smirked and put the phone up to his ear. "What's that, Mary? Where are we? Well, if you believe some people, I took Chrysta to a cult or some aliens. Take your pick."

Akrur could only snort and shake his head.

"Don't worry, Mary," Tommy joked, "I don't work with cults or aliens... Just Krampus."

23

December 1966

Tommy walked down the dark sidewalk, going fast and with purpose. It was almost one in the morning, and he was afraid that someone would call the cops on the random black man in their neighborhood if they noticed him. But, of course, Tommy couldn't blame them for thinking he was dangerous. He was there to beat someone up, after all.

The air was crisp and burned his lungs as he jogged. The neighborhood was not the richest, but it wasn't a complete ghetto either. Cars were old and cheap but in good condition. Houses were not large but clean and neat. Kids' toys dotted the small yards. All the signs of the middle-class dream, something that Tommy could never be a part of. He was an outsider, only here to ruin someone's Christmas.

Tommy finally found the address that Penmark had given him. He opened the front gate slowly, wincing at the screech it gave. It was a small brown two-storied home. There was a late-model car in the driveway, a boy's bike on the porch— nothing remarkable, and no signs that made Tommy think that it was a sorcerer's home either. No wards, no scent of magic. He rushed to the back door.

The door was unsurprisingly locked, but a quick search of the flower pots around the back porch yielded a key, and he slipped inside without a sound. The kitchen was dark, and Tommy wandered to the front of the house, looking for the stairs. The family had tidily decorated the home for Christmas. The front room had a small tree covered with an obscene amount of tinsel, presents waiting for Christmas morning in a few days. He rounded the banister and slowly climbed the stairs.

The man of the house was lying in bed with his wife in the master bedroom, their young son and daughter in another room, all asleep, probably with gumdrops and sugar plums dancing in their heads. Tommy studied the overweight man snoring in the bed with a scowl. What had this man done to piss off the Acolytes, Tommy wondered. Penmark hadn't told the changeling why he was here, just that he was to find Benjamin Ross and beat him until the acolytes got what they needed, whatever that was. Tommy didn't like this. It felt like a trap.

Tommy didn't want to include the man's family in this mess. The best thing would be to tail him for a few days and learn his schedule. And then attack when he was alone. There was a twinge of pain in his left arm. Penmark had made it clear he wanted this done tonight, but he wasn't the one that was attacking innocent people, was he?

"Santa?"

Tommy jumped in shock, vertically like a cat, whirling around and gawking at the young girl standing in the hallway when his feet landed on the floor. She was dressed in pink PJs, carrying a white rabbit toy. People rarely surprised him, and he took a few deep breaths to slow his heartbeat before responding to her. "Kid, do I look like Santa?"

She rubbed her eyes and yawned and then looked him up and down. A black man dressed in a black sweater and pants. The farthest thing from a fat, jolly, white man. "No," she admitted. "But if you aren't Santa, how did you get into our house?"

Before Tommy could respond, a voice called out from her bedroom. "Susan? What are you doing?" Her brother appeared and froze when he spotted the changeling. He was probably a year older than his sibling, but he seemed to have enough sense to step between Tommy and his sister. "Who are you?" he asked.

"My name is Tommy," Tommy whispered as he approached the kids and crouched down, mind racing to come up with a story to soothe the children before they started screaming for their parents. "I'm not with Santa. I'm with the other guy, Krampus."

"Krampus?" Susan asked, her forehead furrowing in confusion.

"Yeah, you American kids don't hear about him because he works out of Europe. But, sometimes, he asks people in other countries to help him find horrible kids."

"Horrible kids?" Susan asked in wonder, her brother scowling.

"Santa brings toys to good kids and leaves coal for the bad kids. But the horrible kids? Krampus comes to beat them. Sometimes even to kidnap them." Tommy mentally kicked himself. He was supposed to be putting them at ease, not freaking them out more.

Susan seemed delighted, though. "I told you!" she cried out, hitting her brother's arm. "I told you that pulling that cat's tail was bad and you wouldn't get any presents!"

Tommy put his hands up to calm the kids, sparing a glance behind him to the two adults who were thankfully still sleeping. "Now, don't worry. I can see that you two are *good* kids. I don't think I'm here for you two. I'm looking for a kid named Benjamin."

Susan's grin got bigger, and her brother's face started to crumble. "B-but, I'm B-Ben," the young boy stuttered, and Tommy felt his stomach drop.

No wonder Penmark was so vague about what Tommy was doing here tonight. He wanted Tommy to beat Ross's son, not hurt Ross himself. Tommy glowered when the truth hit him, and poor Ben gulped and stepped back.

"You know what, let me check my paperwork," Tommy said, trying to force a smile back on his face. He removed a piece of paper from his pocket, some advertisement for a department store, covered in red and green ink. "Now see," Tommy said, flashing the stricken boy a bright smile. "I'm supposed to find a *Bobby* Ross." He put the ad back in his pocket before the kids could study it. He smiled at the two kids. "Looks like a big mix-up. I'll contact head office, and find the right house. But no more messing with cats, just to be safe, yeah?"

Susan seemed disappointed, but Ben visually relaxed. Tommy stood up and rubbed his hands on his thighs, sparing a glance at the kids' parents. "Hey, let's go to the kitchen. You guys can have some milk and tell me a little about your dad, okay?"

.....

Ronald Ross was sleeping peacefully when suddenly his daughter jumped into his bed and landed on his diaphragm. "Daddy! Daddy! Daddy!" she chanted as he groaned. "Daddy! My new friend wants to talk to you! He's in the kitchen!"

Ronald looked at the clock by the bed and groaned louder. "Jellybean, it's two in the morning. It's not time for presents yet."

"No! He's not Santa! He's with Krampus!"

"Go to bed, Susan," June muttered and rolled over, making Ronald responsible for their daughter.

"I can't go to bed. You have to meet him first," Susan explained, still bouncing on her father's chest.

"I thought we were past the imaginary friend phase," Ronald grumbled. "Alright, alright, I'm coming," he said a little louder, and the girl cheered.

They started to descend the stairs, Ronald only pausing to look into the kids' bedroom. Ben's bed was empty as well. So one of them woke up and bugged their sibling in the middle of the night. And knowing them, they would argue and not fess up on who did it.

Susan took his hand when they got to the foot of the stairs and tugged him toward the kitchen. The door was swinging shut behind him, and Ronald was opening his mouth to yell at his only son to get his ass to bed when he registered the stranger standing in his kitchen. He froze and gaped like a fish, his brain trying to understand the scene in front of him.

A black man was leaning on the island, holding a glass of milk. Ben was sitting next to him, and before he could react, Susan skipped to grab her glass to finish her drink. The stranger just raised one of his eyebrows, waiting for Ronald's reaction.

"Wha... Who are you?" Ronald wheezed.

"This is Tommy," Ben said with a bright smile. "He works with Krampus."

Ronald's paralysis was starting to wear off, and his eyes darted around the kitchen, trying to find a weapon within reach. But the stranger was too close to his kids and could hurt one of them before Ronald could move. The stranger just stared, like he could read Ronald's mind and see his panic rising. "Krampus?" Ronald asked through dry lips. He didn't care what the hell that meant; he just didn't want the kids to panic.

"Krampus hits bad kids," Susan said with glee, always the morbid one. "Tommy was here to find a bad kid, but he got the wrong house."

"Hey, guys," Tommy murmured. "I think it's time to head to bed. Before you get in trouble with Santa."

Susan whined, but she surprisingly got up and put her and Tommy's glass in the sink. She never put her dishes in the sink. Ben downed his milk and followed suit. They started to file out of the kitchen. "Hey, kids," Ronald said, and the two siblings paused. "Your mother..." he began to say, but the stranger shook his head ever so slightly. "Don't wake your mother. Keep Tommy's visit a secret, okay?"

The children grinned but nodded in agreement. "Straight to bed," Ronald said sternly, not taking his eyes off of the black man.

"'Night, Tommy!" Susan called in a stage whisper.

"'Night, kid," Tommy responded, not taking his eyes off of her father.

Ronald didn't move, watching the stranger as the kids climbed the stairs. A heavy and tense silence settled in the kitchen, but Ronald waited for a few minutes, making sure the kids wouldn't return. He suddenly dived for the knife block, but the stranger intercepted him. He clamped a hand on Ronald's mouth before he could shout and pinned him to the corner of the counter.

"Ssshhhh," Tommy hissed. "I think we can both agree that the kids don't need to be a part of this conversation."

Ronald was breathing hard, heart racing, but he just gave the briefest of nods. Tommy slowly removed the hand. "What are you doing in my house, asshole?" Ronald growled.

"Well, that's the thing," Tommy muttered as he slowly backed away. "I was just about to ask you the very same thing." Ronald looked at the black man in confusion as he leaned on the island and sighed. "I'm... employed by some nasty people. I don't like what they make me do, but I can't say no, so I have to do what they want."

Ronald snorted. "You take money to do bad things to people and try to play the victim?"

Tommy winced and rubbed at his left arm through his sweater. "Oh, if you only knew," he muttered. "But tonight was different. Tonight, I was given this address and told to do one thing when I got here: beat Benjamin Ross until they got what they wanted."

Ronald felt his stomach drop. "If you touch my son—" he started to growl.

"Don't worry, I won't. I don't hurt kids." He stood up and crossed his arms. "But now the question is, are you going to give them what they want, or do I have to beat *you* for it?"

Ronald gulped. "I... look, I don't have anything that anyone would hurt my son for, I swear."

"The guy I'm working for, his name is George Penmark. Does that ring a bell?" Ronald shook his head. "What about Guerra? Did you meet him?"

"That wop? Yeah, that guy I met."

"What did he want from you?"

Ronald shifted nervously, and Tommy raised an eyebrow. "Look... no one can know about this. I could lose my job."

"Buddy, Penmark sent me here to hurt your son until you gave him what he wants." Tommy started to lean into the other man's personal space. "I could leave and tell him I couldn't do the job, and I will probably get a thrashing myself if I don't get killed for failing. And then that guy you just called a 'wop?' He will show up here instead. And trust me, after he gets through with you, you will wish I beat you instead."

Ronald gulped but slowly nodded. "I work for a shipping company in a warehouse. As a manager. We accept shipments on the docks and then make sure they get to their final destination." He sighed and rubbed his neck. "As the manager, I sign off when stuff gets damaged. So if a shipment of, say, televisions comes in..."

"You mark a new television as damaged and then turn around and sell it," Tommy muttered and finally stepped back.

"Look, I have a family to support, and I don't do it often. Maybe once every couple of months."

Tommy rubbed his eyes. "I don't really care about your illegal activities. How does Penmark come into the picture?"

"I guess the guy that I sell the stuff to told Penmark I could get him something from a shipment that just came in. A collection from an art museum from Asia. It's going to be touring America, and he wants one of the pieces."

"Oh gods, it's her again," Tommy muttered, and Ronald started to worry about his sanity. "So, where is this warehouse?"

Ronald started shaking his head. "No. This is not just a television or a fur coat going missing. If we lose something for a fucking museum, then the whole company will go under."

"I don't think you understand," Tommy growled. "These men, if they don't get what they want, will hurt you. Maybe *kill* you. I would tell you to leave tonight, but that will look suspicious." Tommy sighed and rubbed his left arm. "The best thing for you and your family is for me to get that artifact, and then the people who employ me may forget you exist, and you can pick up and live somewhere else."

Ronald sighed and started to pace the kitchen, trying to think of a better solution. The stranger was right. If these guys were as dangerous as Tommy said they were, it was better to let him take what they wanted and get them all out of his life. He went to a drawer and took out a pen and some paper. He wrote something down and handed it to Tommy.

"The address of the warehouse and the serial number of the box that they wanted," he explained. "My next shift is after Christmas, so no one will think I helped you. The guard working tonight to too good at his job. He will catch you. If you wait until tomorrow, then you will have more luck. The guard working has a bad habit of falling asleep during his shift."

Tommy sighed and rubbed his arm again as he took the paper. "Noted." He glared at Ronald. "When this is over, stay out of trouble, alright? Those kids need you."

"I... Yeah, alright," Ronald said. He went to the back door and opened it. "Now get out."

Tommy went to the door and left, disappearing into the night. Ronald closed the door behind him and then, after a moment of thought, got a chair from the dining room and edged it under the door handle. He doubted he would get back to sleep tonight. He probably would not get much sleep until after Christmas, and they could move somewhere else.

But at least the stranger had given him the heads up. And even though he took money from bad people, at least he didn't stoop so low as to hurt the kids.

He sighed and started making a pot of coffee.

·····

Guerra descended the basement stairs, late morning sunlight streaming through the small windows set high on the wall. He smiled when he caught sight of Tommy, the changeling bare-chested and sitting on a chair. Tommy was sporting two holes in his left shoulder and was digging in one of them with a pair of forceps and hissing in pain. His left forearm was in a bowl of water. "My, what a sight this is," Guerra purred to the enforcer behind him, a man named West. "How did you end up like this, Mr. Monroe?"

Tommy glared at the acolyte and finally pulled the forceps out of his shoulder. He deposited a bloody slug on the table with a wet *plonk*. "What brings you down here, Guerra?" he asked, ignoring Guerra's question. He gestured at his cot and small record collection. "The music? The ambiance? Sorry I don't have tea and cookies ready for you."

Guerra chuckled and then held out his hand. Tommy glanced at the offered hand and reluctantly handed the forceps over. Guerra clicked his tongue as he looked at the other hole. "I smelt blood and came to investigate," Guerra murmured and then started to dig around for the other slug. "Let me see your arm," he ordered as Tommy hissed.

Tommy ignored him. Technically, he did not have to listen to Guerra. Guerra moved his thumb to put pressure on the other wound, smiling at Tommy's sharp intake of breath. "Your arm," he growled, keeping the unsettling smile on his face.

Tommy lifted his arm out of the bowl, and Guerra was not surprised to see the slave band glowing. He made a tsking sound and continued his work. "So, you didn't beat the boy," he said.

"The children weren't at the house," Tommy said.

"Lies," Guerra hissed. He wasn't upset, not really, but he wasn't happy either. Tommy not doing the job right the first time meant the enforcer would have to go in and clean up the changeling's mess. He finally got a hold of the slug and pulled it out, examining it as Tommy took some deep breaths. "You are getting too sentimental for your own good, Mr. Monroe. Keep messing up, and we may have to reevaluate your usefulness."

Tommy glared and stood up, getting into the enforcer's personal space. Guerra didn't flinch, however, and just kept that wide, disturbing smile on his face. Tommy pushed past him without a word and grabbed a small box, handing it to Guerra. "Who said I messed up?" Tommy said with a smile, looking way too proud of himself. "I just had some trouble with the guard. He was a better shot than I was expecting."

Guerra took the box and opened it. He carefully removed a protective covering and then gasped. Guerra gently placed the box down and then hastily grabbed the bowl of water to scrub his hands. He dried them and then turned back to the box. He gently lifted the contents out, revealing an antique hanfu made with silk. It was orange in color and intricately embroidered. The scene on the back was a woman with pale skin and blonde hair, surrounded by black creatures with glowing blue eyes twisting around her like smoke. Tommy grabbed a cloth and pressed it to his wounds, watching the enforcer with a frown.

"The battle of the Golden One and the Shadow Demon Queen," Guerra breathed. "It was my favorite story when I was growing up. I would ask my father to tell it to me every night." He ran his hand reverently down one sleeve, sighing in pleasure. "Can I keep it, I wonder?"

"If you don't, I'm burning it," Tommy growled as he bandaged his shoulder. Guerra glowered at him.

Guerra placed the hanfu on the bed, running his hands along the inside. When he got to the bottom, he took out a knife, and with the precision of a surgeon, he opened a hole in the silk at the hem. Next, he took out a piece of paper and unfolded it. "I stand corrected, Mr. Monroe," Guerra said in a breathy tone of wonder. "You acquired what we wanted with minimal bloodshed." Guerra looked up from the hanfu and glanced at the bloody bandage on Tommy's shoulder. "Other than your own."

"Shouldn't he be punished?" West suddenly asked. Guerra looked at the enforcer like he had forgotten the other man was there. "The slave, for not following orders?" West explained.

"I think, in this case, the end justifies the means," Guerra said, his smile growing in size. Tommy got a sweater on with no comment, glaring at the acolytes. "Penmark will be pleased to go down in history as the leader of the Acolytes to find two pieces of the Tree during his tenure." Guerra gently folded the hanfu over his arm. "The Lady's artifact is in our possession, as it should be." He smiled at Tommy, and the changeling frowned back. "Good job, Thomas. I will have a bottle of scotch sent down. You have earned it."

Guerra turned and climbed the steps, West following him. Tommy waited until he heard the door close and started to clean up the mess. Tommy almost didn't want to accept Guerra's gift. Although, maybe he should. He did save the kids, after all.

"Merry fucking Christmas to me," Tommy muttered to himself. "May Krampus find up where you live, Guerra."

~ 24 ~

ommy slowly woke up, Christmas carols strangely playing in his head. He started to stretch but froze when he heard Chrysta groan next to him. That's right; they had slept on the sofa last night.

Cross surprised him when they returned to the Disaster Club after the bonfire. He turned to the couple as they went down the stairs. "You two can sleep on the couch," he had growled. "But I'm staying out here, you, so no—"

"No shenanigans," Tommy interrupted him with a grin as Chrysta broke out in a beautiful smile. "What changed your mind?"

"Not wanting to wake up to the entire Club on fire, thank you very much," Cross explained with a scowl. "I'm not happy about it, but you do seem to keep Miss Angelos calm enough to sleep through the night."

Tommy looked over at Cross, who was currently snoring on a nearby chair, book in his lap. The sorcerer seemed not to trust Tommy completely, but he did have all the kids' best interests at heart, including Chrysta's, and Tommy did respect him for that.

The sofa they were sleeping on wasn't as big as the couch Chrysta had set on fire, so Tommy barely fit on it, his feet almost hanging off the arm. Chrysta, meanwhile, was using Tommy as a pillow, curled up by his side comfortably. He smiled at her while she slept, deciding to indulge himself while he could. He gently ran his fingers through her hair, making her murmur in her sleep.

Like the night he had first kissed her, Tommy tried to commit every detail of this moment to memory. He knew that a whole year away from him would finally help Chrysta see what was wrong with their relationship. She would come out of that sphere not needing him, and Tommy would never get the chance to hold her like this again. And he understood it was for the best. He did.

But it didn't make it hurt any less.

Chrysta shifted and slowly woke up. She blinked and then gave him a sleepy smile. "Good morning," she mumbled.

"Morning," he said, removing his fingers from her hair reluctantly. "How did you sleep?"

"Mmmm, just fine," she said. She burrowed under the blanket, rubbing her face on his chest. "Everyone needs an emotional support changeling."

Tommy snorted. "Whatever you say, beautiful."

They stayed like that for several minutes, Tommy gently rubbing Chrysta's back. "Do you think I'm doing the right thing?" Chrysta suddenly asked in a whisper. Tommy glanced at her, but she wasn't looking at him but at her hand on his chest. He grabbed her hand and laced their fingers together.

"Going into the ball or taking Rosa with you?" he asked.

"Both."

He sighed and cocked his head to the side, trying to choose his words wisely. "I agree with Paulson. Without being able to control her ability, Rosa is a danger to herself and others." Tommy paused when Chrysta turned to glare at him. "Hey, you asked for my opinion."

"And do you think Mrs. Paulson was right about the wasting curse?" she whispered fiercely. "Would you want someone to take your ability to change away from you? Your fast healing? Your long life? Just because they thought you were dangerous?"

"Beautiful, that's what I have been trying to tell you," Tommy sighed. "They *can't* take a changeling's ability to shift away from them. So generally, we just lose our heads when they get ahold of us because we *are* dangerous."

She winced and looked pensive for a moment. "But to answer your question, no, I don't think a wasting curse is a solution either. Some of the Acolytes were sorcerers who had a wasting curse placed on them. The Acolytes told them that the Golden One would get their abilities back for them—only if they joined and gave everything they had, including their lives, of course.

"As for whether or not you should go into the ball," he started to say. She looked up at him, and Tommy realized that he could tell her to stay, and she trusted him so much, she would. Without any question, she would stay, and there would be a chance that she wouldn't want to leave him after all. He took a deep breath. "You should go," he said, letting out his breath in an explosive sigh. "Burke is right;

you can work on your abilities in secret. And when you get out, it will be easier for you to hide them."

She nodded, and before he knew what she was doing, Chrysta stretched until she could kiss him. He should have stopped her, pushed her away, but he found himself cupping the back of her head and pulling her closer instead.

Suddenly, there was a croak, and Poe dropped onto Tommy's chest. "No!" he squawked as Tommy gave out an "Oomph!"

Chrysta giggled as the bird flapped his wings. "Looks like Mr. Cross had nothing to worry about," she said while petting the bird's back. Poe calmed down and cocked his head to the side. "Poe could protect me this entire time." Tommy glared at the raven while Chrysta scratched his head. "Take good care of him while I'm gone, okay?" she whispered.

"What do you mean?"

"I don't think I should take him into the ball with me," she whispered. "What if he gets hurt again?"

"I doubt I could keep him away if I wanted to," Tommy said. "What do you say, you ball of feathers? Do you want to stay with me?" he asked the raven.

Poe cocked his head to the other side, clicking his beak as he thought. "No!" he finally answered. "Ass!"

"See?" Tommy said as Chrysta laughed. "Poe is a bird who knows what he wants."

Across the room, Cross gave out a groan. He twitched, and the book he had been reading fell off his lap. Chrysta turned to look at him. "Must be a bad dream again," she said.

"Yeah, I don't envy him right now," Tommy murmured. "Being in Guerra's head has to be the worst thing ever."

Chrysta got up and walked over to the man, Tommy sitting up and stretching. Chrysta gently reached out and shook the empath's shoulder. "Mr. Cross?" she said lightly.

Cross jumped and gasped. Chrysta pulled her hand back as Cross looked around in fear for a few moments and then visually relaxed as he noticed his surroundings. "Oh, that bloody dream," he rasped.

"Is it the same one?" Tommy asked.

"Yes," Cross said as he rubbed his face. "Guerra killing a woman. Unfortunately, I still don't recognize her, although I swear I should."

"Is there anything we can do about them, Mr. Cross?" Chrysta asked.

"I will look into getting the memory removed when we get back," he said with a sigh.

"That may not help," Tommy said as he stood up from the sofa. "That old geezer still remembered Hafeez's cat attacking me from the night of the bar fight."

"Some people are immune to their memories being altered," Cross explained as he picked up his book. "Plus, there is the fact the sheriff was trying to remove something as memorable as a large cat attacking someone. Things like that tend to stick in someone's mind." He looked at Chrysta and studied her. "How did you sleep, my dear?"

"Very well," she replied with a smile.

"Good," he responded, returning her smile. He winced as he stood and rubbed his neck. "Let's get everyone else up and get ready to head out."

.....

Tommy had lived in the Acolyte mansion must of his life and then on the streets afterward but living with teenagers was a whole other annoyance, he was quickly learning. As Cross woke up the Disaster Club and started getting ready to leave, there was a frantic, organized chaos that was both irritating and amazing to watch at the same time. Tommy was happy that the guest room had a private bathroom as he heard Ichiro and Kevin fight in the bathroom. By the time Tommy came out of the bedroom with a backpack full of everything he would need for the next few days, the girls were throwing the boys out to use the showers, loudly protesting that the boys had used all the hot water.

Breakfast was a free-for-all; Cross wanted the kids to eat the leftovers before leaving. The steak and eggs Tommy ate seemed like a breakfast fit for a king, and Chrysta gave him a grin as she finished the sushi. "Alright," Cross said once the plates were cleared from the table, his hands also signing for Julien's benefit. "Is there anyone who is going to stay here?" The teenagers all looked at each other and shook their heads. "Fine. Just remember that this could be dangerous. There is no shame in staying behind. I'm starting the van at 10 o'clock. Anyone not in it by then will not be going."

The kids got ready in a blur. Kevin started the painstaking task of getting the feathers ready for Poe's wing. "I have to cut the calamus in half without cutting off the vane," he explained while he worked, cutting the feathers with a sharp knife as Poe looked at the feathers greedily. "Then I superglue the shaft onto the damaged feathers."

"And it will help him fly?" Chrysta asked as Poe clicked his beak.

"Yep," Kevin said with a smile.

Cross put a hand on Chrysta's shoulder. "Get ready, my dear," he gently said.

"Can you help?" Chrysta asked Tommy as she ran off to get ready.

Tommy held Poe in his lap and held the bird's wing out as Kevin operated with feathers and super glue. Poe would croak a "Tommy" once and a while, but otherwise, he patiently waited as the glue dried. After about an hour, Kevin leaned back with a smile and surveyed his work. "Looks good," he said as Poe preened his new feathers. Finally, Kevin held out the remaining feathers. "You can have the rest."

Poe took the feathers in his beak and flew across the Club into the girls' room. Rimsha yelped and then laughed. She came out with Poe on her shoulder.

"No boys allowed," she growled playfully, making a knocking motion with her right hand, and the bird cocked his head to the side.

"Want to add the feathers to your collection?" Chrysta asked as she carried a backpack out of the girls' room and opened it on a couch. She brought out a drawstring bag and laid it out for the bird. It was packed with buttons, feathers, shiny stones, and the blue beads that Poe seemed obsessed with. Tommy picked up a bauble, and Poe croaked in outrage, beating his wings in agitation. Tommy quickly put it down and put his hands up as the girls laughed.

"Mine!" the bird squawked.

"Easy, Poe! Damn!" Tommy yelled over Poe's croaks of protest. "Is this Poe's collection?" he asked Chrysta.

"Yeah, everything I could take with me," Chrysta explained. "This, my violin, my dress, and my picture of my mom were the most important things to bring with me." Chrysta bit her lip and took the framed photo out of her backpack, studying it for a full minute. "Do you think I should leave this here? I don't want anything to happen to it."

Cross was passing nearby with a suitcase of his own when he glanced Chrysta's way. He did a double-take and slowly came to stand next to Chrysta. He reached for the photo, and she handed it to him instinctively. Cross had a strange look on his face as he examined the image. "Your mother was a lovely woman, my dear. I see the resemblance," he said softly.

Chrysta smiled and took the photo back. "Yes, she was."

"I think you should take it, my dear. Let your mother watch how strong you become."

Chrysta nodded and put the frame back into the backpack, closing it once she put Poe's collection away.

Cross shook his head slowly and headed to the door to the outside, placing his suitcase down by the coat rack. He then took the case of cigarettes out of his jacket and went outside, not saying a word. Tommy watched him go, feeling like something was wrong but not knowing what.

Ichiro brought a box to Rosa and Chrysta, opening it to reveal about a dozen silver disks. "I copied as many movies as I could," he said with a smile.

"What are they?" Chrysta asked as he took one out so she could see it.

"Information disks," Ichiro explained. "It's what sorcerers use to store a lot of information." He held up the disk to show her the glass embedded inside. "Sorcerers were turning info into zeroes and ones before normies even dreamed of computers." He showed her a square stone with a modern cord attached. "Play the disk on this when it's connected to the laptop—a great way to have a large collection of movies in a small space."

While the girls finished getting ready, Tommy went outside and climbed the stairs to check on Cross. The man was smoking and looking off into the distance, looking pensive.

"Are you alright?" Tommy asked the empath.

Cross nodded slowly, still looking off into the horizon. "Still a little tired," he murmured. "Not looking forward to all the driving."

"Where are we heading?" Tommy asked.

"South," Cross said. He cleared his throat and then put the cigarette out in the snow. "A warehouse district, just outside of Philadelphia."

"That's your secret? A warehouse?"

"Owned by my family business," Cross explained with a grin. "And you will see why it's the ideal location when we get there." Cross climbed down the stairs and stuck his head inside. "Thirty minutes!" he cried, and Tommy heard the sound of distressed screams. He joined Tommy again underneath the tree, smiling. "Oh, how I love to torture them sometimes."

Once Cross announced that it was ten minutes until he left and they all should head to the van, the kids filed out of the Disaster Club with their suitcases and bags. The back of the vehicle had stuff stacked from top to bottom, to the point Tommy doubted Cross could see out of the back window.

"Mr. Cross?" Chrysta started to ask at one point, letting Poe settle on her arm and stroking the raven's chest. "Why don't we use the transportation crystals?"

"The crystals only have so many charges to them, my dear," Cross explained as he studied the cargo in the back of the van. "Better to drive than waste a trip with the crystals. Besides, I set up the return circle here at the Disaster Club so that we have a way of getting back home if there is an emergency." He smiled. "It's a short trip. Only about five hours."

Rosa snorted. "Only five hours," she muttered.

Tommy turned to Rosa. "Let me guess, and we have to Roshambo for the front seat again."

"Nope," she said with a grin. "I'm in the second row with Rimsha and Chrysta. So you have to fight Julien for the front seat."

Tommy turned to Julien, and they held out their fists. Tommy threw out paper while Julien threw scissors. The deaf man grinned and took the front seat. "Great," Tommy growled as he glared into the compacted third row.

Tommy climbed into the back row, with Kevin close behind him. Kevin suddenly yelped as he was pulled backward. Ichiro took his place, climbed into the van, and sat next to Tommy. "Wanna listen to Baby Metal?" the younger boy asked as Kevin took the last seat in the third row, and the girls started to climb into the second row.

"I would love to," Tommy said as he took an earbud from Ichiro.

"Alright, everyone," Cross chirped from the driver's seat. "Let's get this circus on the road." And with that, the van was moving.

.....

The road trip went on for several hours, the girls chattering in the second row, Tommy and Ichiro listening to music, and Kevin keeping Poe entertained with a ball that the raven tossed into the air and caught with ease. Tommy kept glancing at Chrysta, glad to see her smiling and happy. Good. Let her have fun while she could.

"Mr. Cross," Rimsha asked at one point. "Can we take a break?"

"Yes, my dear, just waiting for... ah, yes." Cross hummed as he merged into the exit lane. "Just needed to find a place for us to eat."

They pulled into the parking lot of a truck stop with a diner. Poor Rosa looked uncomfortable as the other girls climbed out of the van. "Out of my way, gotta go," she said as she ran inside, probably to the bathroom. Tommy was the last one out, stretching to get the blood flowing in his legs.

Chrysta scratched Poe's head as he rested on her forearm. "We'll be leaving in an hour. Be safe, and don't go far," she ordered the bird, and he took off with a croak. She gave Tommy a bright grin and took his arm as the group went inside.

The diner was like every restaurant built in America in the 50s and 60s. Chrome details, red leather on the stools and booths, and a counter spanning the entire length of the building. Truckers sat at the counter, eating, reading newspapers, or just taking a break before they got back on the road. They looked at the group of teens with curiosity, but no one looked hostile as the Disaster Club claimed two booths. Tommy sat next to Chrysta with Rimsha and Kevin across from them, Cross sitting with a more comfortable-looking Rosa, Ichiro and Julien sitting together. A dour-looking waitress came over, handing them sticky menus. "I'm paying for both tables," Cross explained with a smile, but she just sighed in return.

"What can I getcha?" she asked sourly.

"Burger and fries, please," from Chrysta.

"Burger, rare, please," from Tommy.

"Burger, medium, with fries," from Kevin.

"Is fries the only vegetarian option?" Rimsha asked.

The waitress snorted. "Yeah, everything else has meat."

"Just the fries, please," Rimsha said with a sigh.

"You can't have the fries by themselves. You have to order a burger," the waitress droned without looking at Rimsha. Both Cross and Tommy gave her a look and then glanced at each other. The waitress was quickly getting to the point where Tommy would give her a penny tip, just out of spite.

"I'll add fries to my order then," Tommy said, and the waitress frowned but said nothing as she scribbled on her pad of paper.

"Burger, fries, and coffee," Rosa ordered, glaring at the woman.

"Chili, please," from Ichiro.

"Burger, medium rare, please," from Julien.

"I'm sorry, I didn't catch that," the waitress yelled back, Julien blinking at her reaction and the rest of the Club glaring openly at the woman.

"Burger," Cross said loudly, cupping his hands together into a ball, "medium rare, please." He gave the woman a large, strained smile. "If you have hearing problems, I recommend sign language."

The woman turned red as some of the men at the counter laughed and chuckled. "The chicken sandwich, please," Cross drawled, handing her the menus. "Thank you so much."

Their food came out quickly, Tommy keeping an eye on the window into the kitchen to make sure the waitress didn't mess with it. She put their plates down without a word and stalked off. Kevin raised his hand and opened his mouth, but the woman was gone before he could get a word out. "Ketchup?" he asked weakly.

"I got you, Butler," Ichiro said as he passed the bottle over his shoulder to their table. Tommy passed his fries to Rimsha, and the girl accepted them with a smile. Tommy then stole some from Chrysta, laughing when she huffed.

"So you can eat more than meat, right?" Kevin suddenly asked. He jumped, and Tommy realized that Rimsha must have kicked the boy under the table.

Tommy studied the teen, debating if he should answer Kevin's question or not. "Well, yes," he answered after a moment of thought. "I can eat anything I want, just like you." He picked up the burger with both hands and took a bite, humming at the taste. "Although the rarer the meat, the better," he explained with his mouth full of food.

"What about..." Kevin started to ask, and then he leaned forward and lowered his voice, "your other form?"

"Kevin," Rimsha growled in warning.

"Well, I have only eaten meat in the form," Tommy said, also lowering his voice. "I mean, my mom was a leopard, and my father was a shark, so I doubt veggies would agree with me."

"What kind of meat?" Kevin asked.

"Oh, for crying out loud," Tommy heard Rosa mutter.

"Fish mostly, a sheep once, and human," Tommy said with a grin. If he was going to satisfy Kevin's curiosity, Tommy might as well give the kid what he wanted.

"You've eaten a human?!" Kevin practically yelled. The diner went quiet, some of the men at the counter turning around to glance at the teen. Tommy just tried to keep a smile on his face while the Disaster Club did a collective facepalm. Cross started signing, probably telling Julien what happened since he had his back to the other table. Julien turned in his seat and scowled at Kevin, who was turning red in embarrassment.

Tommy leaned over the table, folding his hands on the top. "Yep, I have. So keep that in mind if you ever think of pissing me off," he whispered and then flashed Kevin a toothy grin, one that he hoped was more creepy than comforting. The young boy gulped.

"I'm sorry, but *why?*" Rimsha asked, looking a little disgusted.

Tommy cleared his throat and glanced at Chrysta, surprised to see her glaring at Kevin and not at him. "One of the Acolytes named Shawcross poisoned his leader and took over, stealing the ring in the process. But then he locked me up for four months and starved me."

"What?! Why?" Rimsha fiercely whispered.

Tommy shrugged. "Don't know. But when the rest of the Acolytes showed up and knocked him out of power, the new leader killed him and then offered to let me eat the body. I wasn't going to say no to a free meal, as hungry as I was."

Rimsha looked grim for a moment, and then she started to push her fries back onto Tommy's plate. He put his hands up. "Whoa, whoa, it's okay. This was a very long time ago. It was actually the perfect lesson in not trusting those assholes. They never had my best interests in mind."

"Serves him right," Cross muttered, and Tommy realized he was talking about Shawcross. "Letting someone starve like that. Sounds like karma."

They went back to eating, their waitress not coming back the entire time they ate. Finally, Cross gestured to another waitress for their check after they finished their food. The teens got out of the booths and headed to the restrooms while Tommy and Chrysta stayed with Cross, examining the bill. "What are you thinking? Leave a penny tip?" the changeling asked the empath.

"Maybe she is just having a bad day," Cross muttered.

"Or she's a bigot," Tommy offered.

"Or she's a jerk," Chrysta growled.

"I think the best thing, in this case, is to kill her with kindness," Cross said with a smile and left a sizeable pile of cash on the table. "Come on, let's get ready to get back on the road."

The group used the restrooms and then headed outside. Cross opted for a cigarette, so the kids took the opportunity to walk around the truckstop, keeping the van in sight. Rimsha saw someone selling plants on the side of the road and went over to investigate. She came back a few minutes later with Ichiro, holding up a small but healthy tree. "Everyone, meet Punchi! Ichiro named her."

"Do you really need another plant, Rimsha?" Cross asked her.

"You can never have too many plants," she responded with a smile.

As Chrysta called Poe back to the van, Julien tapped Tommy on the shoulder. "You can have the front seat," he said.

"You sure?" Tommy asked. Julien was as tall as Tommy, and he would be just as uncomfortable in the third row as the changeling had been.

The young man shrugged. "Better to take turns," he simply said and started to climb into the back.

Tommy settled into the front seat, immediately thankful for the room for his knees. He grabbed his phone and examined the stereo, happy to see an auxiliary cord he could use. While Cross and the kids settled in the van, Tommy hooked up his phone and started looking for a song. Cross raised an eyebrow when he saw what Tommy was doing. "I hope you don't plan on playing anything objectionable," he said.

"Oh, so because I'm a black man, I must have offensive taste in music?" Tommy asked while placing a hand on his chest like he was offended. "Now, who is the racist?"

Cross just glared as Tommy finally picked something, and the first notes of Brahms' Violin Concerto started to play over the sound system. Chrysta paused and leaned forward into the front seat. "Is that my performance?" she asked with a smile.

"This is you playing?" Rimsha asked.

"Nope, this is," Tommy said, and he pointed to his phone as Chrysta started her solo in the recording.

"Wow, that's beautiful," Ichiro announced from somewhere in the back.

"Yes, it is," Tommy agreed. He turned to a blushing Chrysta. "See, beautiful? This is why I rather have you around to play for me."

25

They continued south, the group getting more vocal about Tommy's classical music tastes as time when by. He finally switched to jazz, but then Kevin complained that the music was going to put him to sleep.

"We're almost there," Cross growled. "Just a little longer."

The highway became busier, and the forest dissolved into suburbs and then into city streets. Finally, they went through a city and went over some train tracks, ultimately driving through a warehouse district. "Thank goodness we made it in time," Cross muttered. "I would have never heard the end of it if we were late."

Cross drove down one row of warehouses, every one of them dark and deserted. Finally, they arrived at the last one in the row, pulling up to the front. Tommy noted that Burke, Zheng, Smith, and Ellis were waiting for them. Smith was sitting on the bed of an old and beaten-up truck, dressed in jeans, a holey and worn shirt, and a jacket. Meanwhile, his partner Ellis was leaning on an expensive-looking sports car, not wearing the hunter uniform but a three-piece suit, as impeccable as his partner was shabby.

Zheng wore a purple A-line dress, which ended at her knee, just as flawless as Ellis. The only thing that made her outfit unsuitable for a boardroom meeting was the black sword on her hip, although the black leather belt matched her black boots and gloves. Burke, surprisingly, was in a pair of jeans, a flannel shirt, and boots, although they all looked brand new and spotless, and he had tucked his shirt into his jeans. There were three pallets piled high with boxes, waiting to go inside.

The hunters watched as the van pulled up, and everyone started to file out. Smith flashed Tommy a large grin as Ellis gave him a nod. Tommy looked for Hafeez but didn't see her, a flush of relief going through him.

"You're late, Cross," Burke said as he crossed his arms.

Cross glared at his pocket watch. "You said you wanted to go into the sphere at six o'clock. It's only five minutes past five o'clock." He gestured around them. "Besides, you seem to be missing one of your hunters."

"She should be here," Zheng growled. As Tommy walked up to Smith and Ellis, inspecting their vehicles, Zheng sighed and brought out a large bag. "We have to get started without her. Alright, everyone, cell phones in the bag."

"What?!" Ichiro cried. "Even *our* cell phones?"

"Yes, I mean everyone," the director confirmed. "All the cell phones, in the bag. Now."

"Why?" Rimsha asked even as she handed over her phone. Ichiro held his phone to his chest, glaring at the older woman.

"I don't want to risk anyone giving away our position," Zheng explained as Kevin and Julien gave her their phones.

"I seriously doubt anyone here is a spy," Cross muttered, even as he placed his cell phone in the bag.

"It only takes one social media post for someone to figure out where we are," Zheng clarified. "And I don't know about you, but I'd rather be safe than sorry." She held the bag out to Ichiro, and the boy finally relented and gently placed his phone in the bag.

Zheng walked over to the hunters. Ellis gave up their phone without comment, but Smith was almost as theatrical as Ichiro, actually kissing the phone before handing it over. Zheng held the bag out to Tommy, and he surrendered his phone, only hating the idea of not being able to listen to music as they waited.

"Shall we head inside or wait for Hafeez?" Cross asked.

"Go inside. I don't want to gain any more attention than we probably already have," Burke said.

Cross took out some keys, opening a door on the side of the building. A second later, the main warehouse entrance started to roll open. Everyone filed in as Smith, Ellis, and Cross brought their cars inside. Big printing machines filled the floor, an office with large windows along the left side of the building. The kids looked around in curiosity, barely moving from the door like they were afraid to go deeper into the warehouse. "This is your family business?" Tommy asked Cross as he locked his van. "A printing company?"

Cross scoffed. "Hardly. The warehouse is just a front. Easier to have vans coming and going making deliveries if people think it's just a printing company."

"Deliveries of what?" Chrysta asked.

Cross put a finger up in a "wait a moment" gesture and grinned. He walked to the back of the warehouse, selecting a key from his collection. He kneeled on the floor next to a machine and stuck the key in its base. "Mind the gap," he grunted as he turned the key, and the sound of gears and metal moving filled the air as the machine lifted in the air and turned on its side, revealing a hole in the ground. Once the printer stopped moving, Cross gestured to the ladder leading down. "Ladies first," he said with a smarmy smile.

Burke gave Zheng his hand, and she went first, followed by Chrysta, Rosa, and Rimsha. Cross followed them, and a light turned on. Ichiro poked Kevin. "You first. I don't want you falling on me."

Kevin made a face but went down the ladder without a comment. There was a yelp. "I'm okay!" Kevin called out, making Ichiro facepalm.

Ichiro climbed down, followed by Julien. Burke gestured to Tommy. "You next."

"Don't want me to lock you in?" Tommy asked with a grin, but he descended the ladder without further complaint.

Tommy whistled as he went down. Cross stood in front of a vault door, something that looked like it should be in a bank, all gears and levers. The small room was full, but Cross waited for the hunters to climb down the ladder with a smile on his face. Burke followed Tommy, able to see above everyone. Smith stayed on the ladder, his partner above him, both hunters watching Cross as they hung on the ladder.

"Welcome, potential customers!" Cross loudly proclaimed in the voice of a barker at a circus. The girls giggled as he wiggled his eyebrows. "The Cross family has been the primer company in cataloging, storing, and testing magical items since 1578. We can examine your article of supernatural origin, remove any harmful spells or enchantments, and stow your valuables in one of our many safes located all over the globe."

The smell of magic hit Tommy's nose suddenly, and he let out a thunderous sneeze, the sound echoing in the small room. Cross gestured at the sniffling changeling. "Why, yes sir, we boast the latest and strongest enchantments known to sorcerers to protect your relics." He motioned to the walls, and runes lit up on the wall in blue, pulsing light. "No one will be able to scry for the site of your item or teleport into the safe even if they divine the location. So rest assured, your item," here he leaned closer to Zheng, "in this case, your sphere," he leaned back, "is perfectly safe in Cross hands."

Burke nodded at the door. "And that?"

"The same kind of vault door that you would find in a normie bank," Cross explained, knocking on the door, producing a hollow metal sound. "But that's not all!" He reached over to a keypad, and after putting in a 5-number code, the door started to open inwards. When the door was completely opened, it revealed a second door.

"Two doors?" Smith asked. "Isn't that overkill?"

"Two doors would be reasonable. *Four* doors are overkill. Guess how many we have."

"Four?" Rosa asked with a smile.

"Five!" Cross announced with glee, and the teens laughed as he ran to open the next door.

Tommy rolled his eyes as the group moved inside, only pausing to let Cross open each door. True to his word, there were five of them. Tommy thought it was excessive, but maybe the clients that Cross's family catered to found it comforting. Finally, Cross opened the last one, and he made a show of turning to the wall to some switches, the kind you would see in old black and white monster films, switches that would wake up the fearsome monster. Lights turned on with a hum, and Tommy whistled again, taking in the large space they revealed.

It was two stories, and they were on the top floor looking down. The space was the size of a football field, full of shelves that filed into the back. The first floor also had tables running down the middle of the room into the back, and a few couches sat between them.

"Magical items have to be removed and rotated every few years," Cross explained as he leaned on the railing that looked over the first floor, his barker voice abandoned for now. "If they stay in one place for too long, their magic starts to bleed into the space that houses them. So we move them to several different locations. This one is empty for a cleaning." He pointed to the teens, who were looking around in wonder. "If you see something here, it's probably no longer under enchantment, but still don't touch it. It may be more dangerous than it looks."

"Nothing can be teleported in?" Burke asked, joining his wife at the railing.

"Well, I'm sure someone who can glow white can figure it out," Cross said with a shrug. "Or someone who can glow gold," he said with a grin at Chrysta. "But it would take several hours at the very least."

"This is the only entrance?" Ellis asked, pointing at the five opened vault doors behind them.

"Correct," Cross said. "There are several vents that let fresh air in, so it is not completely sealed, but the pipes that lead to the outside are only fifteen centimeters thick." Cross held his hands in a circle that was about six inches across. "Even if someone could find them and seal them, we would have several hours of air."

"The sphere could stay in here," Zheng murmured. She looked at Burke. "If anything happens, we close all five doors."

"And we are at the end of the row of warehouses," Smith added, standing next to his partner, hands on the railing. "We can see if anyone tries to sneak in."

"Your family won't drop in for a visit?" Tommy asked.

"Nope," Cross confirmed. "My brother is watching our location in Asia, and my father is in Europe. So we have the space all to ourselves.

"There is the office space upstairs to sleep in if we want, although the couches down here will probably be more comfortable," Cross continued with a smile.

"And a large bathroom with showers everyone can use. It's unisex, though, so everyone would have to take turns. If anything should happen, the transportation circle in the office upstairs will be a backup. The return circle is at the Disaster Club. That will be for the kids if they need it in an emergency."

Burke slowly nodded. "Alright, I think this is the best solution for us," he said. "Everyone, let's get the supplies into the vault."

They formed a bucket brigade, one person passing a box to the next, all the way down to the vault. Meanwhile, Zheng brought the wooden box to the lower level, placed it on the floor, and opened it, the box glowing purple. Next, she drew a large circle on the cement with chalk. Once the group stacked all the supplies by the chalk ring, the teens gathered around the sphere to ogle it. Ellis and Smith went upstairs to keep watch.

"It's so small," Rimsha said in awe, Kevin standing next to her. "I was expecting something bigger."

"Whose castle is that?" Ichiro asked, leaning over the line Zheng had just finished. She glanced at him in annoyance but didn't respond. "I mean, someone should notice when their whole freaking castle disappears."

"How fast is time going?" Rosa asked as the light moved from one side of the ball to the other.

"Every six minutes is a day," Burke started to explain, rubbing his familiar's ears. "One hour is ten days. Twenty-four hours will be two hundred and forty days."

"And we will be in there thirty-six hours," Rosa said softly, looking upset. "A whole year."

Cross put a hand gently on her shoulder. "If you don't want to go, now is the time to say so."

"I don't have a choice," she replied. She gestured at the ball, which was completely black. "If I can't get my shit together in there, I should just go to Mrs. Paulson and do the wasting curse."

"Language," Rimsha said lightly, with very little force.

"We may not be in there the whole year," Burke told the young woman. "If yours and Miss York's training goes well, we can leave at any time."

"See?" Cross said as he rubbed Rosa's back. "Study hard, and you will be out for a latte in no time." Rosa gave him a weak smile in return.

Zheng placed a large digital clock on a nearby table. "You three will go in at six o'clock," she explained, addressing Rosa and Chrysta. "We will wait two minutes and then send the first set of supplies in for you."

"Two minutes... That is eight hours, yes?" Chrysta asked.

"Yes," the older hunter said with a smile. "We will send in the next set of supplies in twelve hours, six o'clock tomorrow morning."

"Aw, man, do we all have to get up that early?" Kevin whined.

"Then we will transmit the final supplies tomorrow evening," Zheng explained, ignoring the teen. "If you stay the entire year, you will come out the next morning at six."

"And we are camping in the woods?" Chrysta asked.

"Or are you guys staying in the castle?!" Ichiro asked, eyes lighting up.

"There is a cottage we will be inhabiting," Burke explained, and Ichiro's face fell.

Six o'clock was rapidly approaching, so Chrysta and Rosa gathered their stuff and put it in the circle with the sphere. Then, they started saying their goodbyes, hugging the other members of the Disaster Club. Rosa held a tearful Rimsha. "I don't know why you're crying. It's only going to be a day and a half for you," Rosa muttered.

"Yeah, I know, but I worry," the other girl said, sniffling.

Cross hugged Rosa, getting the girl to lean down to embrace each other fully. "Take care of yourself, yeah?" he said with a sad smile. He gave Chrysta a half hug. "Take care of each other, I should say."

"Will do, Mr. Cross," Chrysta said softly, and then she hugged Julien.

Tommy had hung back, leaning on a shelf to give the teenagers some room as they said goodbye. When he saw Chrysta hug Julien, he felt his stomach tie itself into knots. He looked away and saw Zheng approach her husband, who was kneeling on the floor to tie an ax to his hiking backpack.

"Husband," she purred, and the Headmaster stood. Zheng was only a few inches taller than Chrysta, and Burke towered over Tommy. But at the moment, they seemed to fit together somehow.

"Wife," he murmured back.

She hooked a finger into his front pocket and pulled him down for a kiss. It was quick and chaste, but it was full of love. Anyone could see that. "Make sure you return in one piece, husband," Zheng ordered when they parted.

"Tommy?"

Tommy jumped and turned to see Chrysta in front of him. "What's wrong?" she asked.

"Nothing, beautiful," he lied.

She smiled, and then she hugged him, forcing him to unfold his arms and wrap them around her. "Liar," she whispered into his chest.

He buried his nose in her hair and closed his eyes. Something chanted in his head, *don't go, don't go, don't go*. And he knew he just had to say it, and she would stay. "What's wrong?" she asked again, but he could only shake his head, not wanting to voice his fears.

"I'll be okay," Chrysta said. She leaned back and put her hands on his cheeks, making him open his eyes. "It's only going to be a day and a half," she added hopefully. "Maybe less if we train hard. And I will feel safe knowing you are out here waiting for me," she said with a smile.

"Anything for you, beautiful," he replied, and he kissed her on the forehead.

"Spare me," a voice said above them, and Tommy looked up to see Hafeez and Smith standing at the railing. Hafeez was scowling at the couple, and Tommy glared back.

"So good of you to join us, Nyla," Zheng drawled, sounding sweet but looking pissed.

"After we got everything downstairs," Cross joked.

"I know, right?" Smith joked with him.

"Miss York?" Burke said. "It's time."

Chrysta let go of Tommy and walked back to the circle, glaring at Hafeez the entire time. When she joined Rosa, Burke, and Burke's dog, she picked up her backpack, and Poe landed on her shoulder. Tommy kissed his fingertips and held out his hand toward her, and Chrysta gave him another smile. Zheng took out a tuning fork, hit it on the floor, and held it to the sphere. A ringing noise started, and the ball began to glow purple. Zheng got up and stepped back, standing outside the circle she had drawn on the floor.

The light kept getting brighter and brighter until it hurt to look at it. Everyone had to put their hands up to shield their faces. Finally, the light winked out, revealing that the group had disappeared entirely.

26

Chrysta expected the extreme pressure that happened when teleporting, but she didn't feel anything push on her as the purple light finally faded. She slowly opened her eyes and looked around while blinking. The vault was gone, and they were standing in a stone circle in the middle of the woods. There was a stone ball between them, right where the sphere had been on the floor in the vault. Poe croaked and took off flying.

"Whoa," Rosa said softly. "This is freaky."

"Tell me about it," Chrysta said. The trees around them looked like aspen trees, and the pattern on the bark looked like eyes staring blankly at them.

Mr. Burke put on his backpack. "Ladies, follow me," he said and started to hike through the woods. Rosa and Chrysta scrambled to follow him.

They walked for what felt like an hour, Rosa walking in front of Chrysta. At one point, Rosa stopped and pointed to their left. "Look," she said in awe. Chrysta squinted and finally made out the shape of the castle through the fog in the trees. "It's huge," Rosa breathed. Mr. Burke's dog barked at them, and they started walking again.

Finally, they walked out of the woods and walked through hills covered in tall grass. There, nestled between two hills, stood a cottage made of dark wood, its roof covered in grass. It was two stories tall and had a chimney coming out of its middle. Mr. Burke led them to the front door and opened it for the girls.

It was dark inside, and Chrysta and Rosa hesitated to go in. Finally, Mr. Burke opened the shutters outside, letting in the morning light. Furniture became visible, and the girls ventured deeper into the cottage.

The fireplace was massive, so large that Chrysta could walk inside without ducking, although Mr. Burke would have to crouch. There were two walled alcoves, one to the left and the right, with no doors to separate them from the main room, but they did have curtains. Chrysta went to the left room and saw a bed frame, fur for blankets, and a small table with a chair. Poe landed on the windowsill outside and tapped on the glass with his beak. She smiled and waved at the bird and put her backpack on the floor before walking back to the main room.

Towards the back of the cottage was a kitchen with a wood stove and deep sink. The fireplace opened on this side, too, cast iron pot hanging from a bar that could swing in and out of the fire. A large round window was set high near the roof, probably to catch the afternoon sun. Across the kitchen was a round table for eating. A bedroom loft was above the wooden table, reachable by a spiral staircase. The loft looked down on the kitchen and main room. Mr. Burke went upstairs, putting his pack down and claiming the bedroom as his own.

"Where's the bathroom?" Rosa asked as she came out of the other alcove. Mr. Burke smiled and climbed down the stairs. He gestured to the back door, and Rosa opened it. Outside was an outhouse.

"Oh great," Rosa said sarcastically. "Pooping outside, what I have always wanted."

"Wait until you see the shower," Mr. Burke muttered. He went to a curtain by the outhouse and opened it. Inside was an open-air stall with just a metal basin set on the wall. Chrysta and Rosa were short enough to stand underneath it, but it would hit Mr. Burke in the face. There was also a metal tub on the ground, although it looked like even Chrysta would be folded in half to use it.

"Fill the basin with water, and then pull the rope," Mr. Burke explained with a smirk. He pulled on the rope to demonstrate.

"Will it be hot?" Rosa asked.

"Once you have mastered magic, you can heat the water then," Mr. Burke drawled.

"Fantastic."

They all went inside, Mr. Burke heading into the dining room. He took out a piece of chalk and started writing on a section of smooth black slate on the wall. They were numbers, small and neat, and after each multiple of six, he went down to the following line.

"We will do six days a week," he said while writing. "Today and every first day of the week will be for cleaning and chores. Then we will do four days of training and study. The last day of the week will be a day of rest. You can do whatever you want as long as you follow the ground rules."

"Ground rules?" Rosa asked, but Mr. Burke put his finger out in a "wait" motion.

"That will be a total of sixty weeks, three hundred and sixty days in total," he continued. "If your education goes well, we will leave early, so I suggest you two apply yourselves."

Once Mr. Burke was done writing on the wall, he turned around. "Alright, the ground rules."

"The sphere maintains a status quo," he started to explain. He paused when both girls gave him identical confused looks. "It keeps the natural habitat the same from day to day." He picked up an ax from the table. "I can go out and cut a tree down for firewood; in the middle of the night, the tree, even if it's burning in the fireplace, will disappear from the fireplace and reappear as a living tree in the forest."

"Cool," Rosa said. "What about the castle?"

"The castle and this cottage seem to be under the same enchantment. No matter how much time has passed, the buildings stay the same.

"Weather also never changes," Mr. Burke said. "It is always cold in the morning, warmer in the afternoon, and cool in the evenings. It does rain, but rarely, and once it starts raining, it will continue for several weeks. Let's hope it doesn't rain because otherwise, we will be stuck inside the cottage for the duration."

Mr. Burke gestured to a map on the wall in the dining room. "The stone circle we arrived in is in the sphere's center. It is the only way to go in and out. I will teach you how to use it to leave on your own in case of an emergency. Everything in the circle will go with you, so be aware of your surroundings when you use it.

"We are here," he stated, pointing to the lower right of the circular map. "There is nothing here that can hurt you. There are no wild animals here, no fish in the river or lake, no deer or predators. Miss Torres, I believe you like to run?"

"Yes," she replied.

"Then, stick to the fields until you get a lay of the land. I don't want you risking an injury in the woods.

"Finally, do not go towards the castle," Mr. Burke said. He gestured to the north of the map, where someone had drawn the castle, and a red area encircled it. "There are guardians that will attack you if you do. There are markers in red to warn you before you enter the area, but to be safe, avoid the north portion of the sphere."

"Guardians?" Chrysta asked. "What are they?"

"No one knows. Magical automatons made by the former owner of the castle, most likely. They don't allow anyone to study them," Mr. Burke explained. "I may show you someday, Miss York, but for now, do not let curiosity get the best of you."

He looked between the two teens. "Alright, we have several hours until the supplies are here. So let's get to cleaning, shall we?"

.....

"*Hijo de perra!*"

Chrysta jumped and turned around, making sure Rosa and Mr. Burke were alright. There was a sapling on fire about fifty feet away from them, but otherwise, everything was okay. Rosa was pacing, muttering under her breath, and if Rosa were closer, Chrysta wouldn't be surprised if she was cursing in Spanish. Mr. Burke was in the same position he had been that morning when they arrived: sitting on a fallen tree, holding a branch between his legs like a cane, and stoic expression still on his face.

"Try again, Miss Torres," he drawled. "And do try to leave the poor trees alone."

Rosa didn't respond, just glaring at the Headmaster and stopped pacing. She put her right hand out and pointed at a candle 100 feet away. About ten seconds later, another sapling in the treeline started to burn instead. Rosa began to curse again, much louder this time.

Chrysta sighed and turned back to her book.

She was starting to think she had made a mistake.

They had spent their first day cleaning the cottage and bringing the supplies from the stone circle, just as Mr. Burke said they would. Chrysta almost hoped that he would ask her to try to teleport something, but he did all the magical heavy lifting by himself. Rosa automatically took over the cooking duties, although she wasn't happy about it.

"Powdered milk, powdered cheese, vegetables in cans, dried meat," she muttered over the stove. "It will be a miracle if I can make anything edible."

"You will do a better job than I could," Chrysta admitted, trying to at least pay attention to what the other girl was doing in case she would have to try her hand at cooking.

Even with all her complaining, Rosa did an excellent job making a good meal, and Chrysta cleaned up as best as she could, although Rosa pointed out the dishes were still dirty when she was done. "I never had to do chores at home," she explained as Rosa scowled at a messy plate.

Rosa sighed. "Come on, let's teach you how to clean dishes."

Chrysta nodded, feeling stupid. Rosa spent the next few weeks not talking to Chrysta unless it was to tell her what to do while cleaning. Maybe the other girl still didn't like Chrysta because her last name was York? Chrysta couldn't really blame her if that was the case.

On their second day in the sphere, they followed Mr. Burke back into the forest, and they stopped when they came to some ruins in the trees. "What was this?" Chrysta asked as Poe landed on a nearby branch and croaked.

"No one knows," Mr. Burke said. He took five candles out of a bag and placed them on the stone pillars that rose out of the underbrush.

"Oh no," Rosa moaned.

"What is it?" Chrysta asked, looking between Mr. Burke and Rosa, feeling very lost.

"Fire aptitude test," Rosa responded.

"Creating fire at your fingertips is effortless," Mr. Burke explained as he walked back to the teens. He held up his hand to demonstrate, and flames licked at his fingers.

"But controlling fire at long ranges is different. It looks simple, but it's rather difficult."

He snapped his fingers, and the closest candle lit up. *Snap. Snap. Snap. Snap.* Each candle lit up in turn. "Also, extinguishing the flames at this distance is part of the challenge." He waved his hand dismissively, and the flames went out.

He studied Rosa. "How many times have you attempted the test?"

She shifted from foot to foot. "Seven," she confessed. "The last two candles always get me."

"Then this will be your assignment. Pass this, and consider yourself a functioning magic user, Miss Torres."

Rosa glared at the candles. "Great. I have only been trying to do it for the last five years," she muttered.

"What do I do?" Chrysta asked, looking forward to performing some magic intentionally and not by accident.

Mr. Burke reached into the bag that had the candles and took out a book. He handed it to Chrysta. "You will be studying for the next few weeks, Miss York. Magic theory and ethics," he told her.

"Oh," she said softly, taking the book. "Okay."

And so, that is how their time had passed for the last twenty days. They would get up in the morning, Rosa making breakfast, and Chrysta cleaning up. Then, they would travel to the ruins, Rosa trying to light the candles until she got too upset to continue working or the light faded. Chrysta would read and work on writing assignments, feeling like her time was being wasted, completing one book just to have Mr. Burke hand her another out of his seemingly endless stock. Shouldn't she be performing magic? Learning how to control it? Finally, they would walk back to the cabin, Rosa making dinner, and then it would be silent for the rest of the evening, both Mr. Burke and Rosa going back to their bedrooms and ignoring Chrysta.

They had had three free days so far, and Chrysta had gone off on her own with a promise not to go near the castle for Mr. Burke. It was beautiful, and Chrysta slowly learned the area and the forest's layout. It was so weird being in a place where there were no people: no car horns, no traffic, no planes, no music, no children, nothing but the sound of the river or the wind in the trees every day.

The only good thing to come out of their schedule was Chrysta was too exhausted to dream at night, and she enjoyed the uninterrupted sleep.

But as Mr. Burke had gone up to the calendar last night and crossed out the "20" written there, Chrysta couldn't help but feel some small amount of panic. She didn't think she could continue this way for the next three hundred and forty days. She felt so isolated and alone and just wanted to leave.

But they did all of this for you, she scolded herself that night, Poe sleeping next to her bed. *Trust Mr. Burke. He knows what he is doing.*

Chrysta sighed and closed the book, stretching and yawning as she got up. She walked over to Mr. Burke as Rosa stood silently with her hands on her head, glaring at the candles like they had intentionally humiliated her. Chrysta handed Mr. Burke the book, and he glanced at the sheet she had filled out. He didn't say anything and looked at Rosa. "Are you done for the day, Miss Torres?"

"No," Rosa snapped. She took a deep breath and let it out. "No," she said again, softer this time. "I think I almost have that fourth candle."

"Then continue," Mr. Burke drawled. He gave Chrysta the book back without a word, and Chrysta took it without comment. She was hoping that he would have at least acknowledged the work she had done, but he had barely looked at her.

Just like my father, she bitterly thought to herself. She walked back to the sunny spot she had been sitting in, curling up and leaning on a tree. Chrysta was now confident all of this had been a mistake. She wasn't doing anything in the sphere that she couldn't have done outside of it.

She yawned. Mr. Cross had mentioned that Rosa's parents were hunters. Maybe Mr. Burke was ignoring Chrysta because he wanted to work with Rosa more than he wanted to help Chrysta?

Chrysta closed her eyes. She just needed to be patient. Mr. Burke would help her soon. He had to.

A small creek babbled to itself nearby. Poe was talking to himself in a tree nearby, his new favorite pastime. "Nevermore, nevermore, nevermore," he chanted. Finally, Chrysta's head lulled forward, and she slipped into sleep.

.....

Chrysta is back on the table in the mansion's third-story bedroom that used to be her home. She is tied with so many ropes that she can't move, can barely breathe. The Acolytes surround her in robes, faceless, featureless, their chanting ringing in her ears. Her throat is burning from the liquid they forced her to drink, still sore from coughing. Her father is next to her, his features twisted in a snarl, holding a knife over her.

She is trying to scream through the rag stuffed in her mouth, asking her father why he is doing this. "For our Lady, of course," her father purrs, somehow reading her mind.

He starts to raise the knife over his head, with no light touch to her forehead this time, no small comfort as he is about to kill his daughter. Instead, his face contorts into a mixture of glee and rage. And then the knife plunges toward her chest.

The knife pierces Chrysta's chest, and it hurts. IT HURTS, and the gag is somehow gone, and she is screeching in pain. There is no flash grenade, no Tommy, no escape.

And throughout her screams and her cries of pain, her father is watching with a mad grin. "Why?" she gasps. Her father only smiles and twists the knife.

27

"Miss York!"

Someone shook Chrysta's shoulder, and in her fear and panic, she threw up her hands and pushed them away. Only, she also felt the flex of magic in her chest, and there was a flash of golden light, and the person went flying.

Chrysta panted and looked around in confusion. Rosa was a few feet from her, looking at Chrysta and then back to the person Chrysta had thrown across the woods. Poe was still in the tree, flapping his wings madly and croaking loudly. Mr. Burke was crumpled against a tree, groaning and holding his head. Chrysta looked at him in horror, tears burning the back of her eyes. She carefully got up, and Rosa stepped back in fear.

"Mr. B-Burke, I'm so-sorry, I didn't m-mean..." she started to stutter, but she couldn't finish her apology and let out a sob.

Rosa ran to help Mr. Burke up, and his dog put herself between him and Chrysta, growling low in her throat. Guilt made Chrysta's eyes burn more, and the scene in front of her wavered as tears fell down her cheeks.

I want to go home, she thought, and with that feeling, she popped out of existence.

With a great deal of pressure and a loud *pop,* Chrysta found herself in the cabin, gasping as the breath got knocked out of her lungs. She panted for a few moments and then ran to her bedroom, throwing her things in her backpack. She was leaving the sphere, and she was going to go home.

But you don't have a home to go to, a voice whispered in her head, and Chrysta sobbed. She couldn't go back to the mansion with her father. That much was sure. But she couldn't go to the Jackson household, not while she was a danger to them.

She would leave the sphere. Mr. Burke had shown them how. She would leave and take Tommy and go... *somewhere.* Somewhere secluded. And when she was better, she could come back, be with her friends and not hurt them.

What if Tommy doesn't want to go with you? the traitorous voice whispered, and she slowed down and almost stopped packing. *What if you don't get better?*

She started packing again. Then Chrysta would leave and be by herself. She was dangerous, and if she had to be isolated to protect others, then so be it.

The cottage door burst open, and Mr. Burke marched in with Rosa in tow. Poe flew in, landing on the bed and grabbing the shirt Chrysta was packing, tugging it back out of the backpack. She snatched it back from the bird and finished stuffing it in the pack while Poe flapped his wings in irritation. Mr. Burke looked around and spotted Chrysta, and frowned. Chrysta felt her eyes prickle with unshed tears, but she tried to swallow past the lump in her throat. "I'm sorry, Mr. Burke, but I think I need to leave," she said, trying to keep her voice from shaking.

"Of course, Miss York, if that is what you want to do," Mr. Burke said gently.

When Chrysta realized what he had said, she stopped her frantic packing and stared at him. "You're not going to stop me?" she asked softly.

"You are not a prisoner. You are free to go whenever you want," he said. He started to step towards her slowly, putting his hand up. "But are you certain that is what you want?"

"N-no, I want to st-stay," she said. "But I want to st-stop hurting people, and I need to learn h-how..." She paused and took a deep breath, trying to keep herself calm. "I need to learn how to control it before I r-really hurt s-some... someone..." She finally lost control and broke down crying, burying her face in her hands and sobbing.

She was trying to calm down several moments later, hiccupping as she took several deep breaths when she felt someone hug her. It was Rosa, and the taller girl let Chrysta put her head on Rosa's shoulder. It was awkward, being held like that and soaking the girl's shirt, but Chrysta felt instantly better and didn't pull away. Mr. Burke was standing nearby, looking extremely uncomfortable. "Really, Miss York, I'm fine. The theatrics are not needed."

Rosa sighed. "It's not that," she said while Chrysta rubbed her face, feeling embarrassed for her outburst. "Chrysta lit a couch on fire while sleeping at the Disaster Club before we came in here. She hurt herself and Poe."

Mr. Burke blinked and then scowled, and Chrysta cowered. "She used fire? In her sleep?" he asked, and Rosa nodded. "I thought you were just making things float, Miss York."

"I was, but then it got worse," Chrysta whispered, and she felt her cheeks burn in shame and tears threaten to fall down her face again.

Mr. Burke sighed, and Chrysta felt her stomach drop. So this was it; he would say he could do nothing; she was a lost cause. And then what would she do? He reached into his back pocket and brought out a handkerchief, holding it out to Chrysta. She blinked in surprise at the piece of cloth. "Come now, Miss York, you would do better to wipe your eyes on this, not Miss Torres's shirt." Chrysta nodded numbly and accepted it, wiping her face. "And why, pray tell, did Cross not inform me of this event, Miss Torres?" he asked the other girl.

"I think he was worried that everyone would think I did it," Rosa said with a shrug, letting Chrysta go as she blew her nose.

Mr. Burke sighed again and started pinching the bridge of his nose like he had gotten a sudden headache. "They warned me," he growled, making his dog perk up her ears and look at him. "They warned me when I became the headmaster, 'Watch the Disaster Club, they will be the end of you, you will see.'" He looked at the teens. "And they were flecking right."

Rosa snorted, and Chrysta felt the corners of her lips lift in a smile. "I'm sorry, Miss York," he said in a much gentler tone than his growl from before. "I focused on Miss Torres because I thought her getting control of her powers took priority. I was misinformed."

Chrysta blinked and nodded. "I understand, Mr. Burke," she said. "But I would like to start learning how to control magic, not just read about it." She squared her shoulders and pushed forward. "I understand that phasing into people's homes is wrong, and changing people's DNA can be dangerous, and... and cursing someone is bad, but can we skip all that?"

"It's basic stuff that they have to teach kids that grew up in nonmagical households," Rosa explained, and Chrysta blinked at the other girl. "When you grow up in a magical household, you get that stuff drilled into your head when you're young before your abilities start showing."

"Really?" Chrysta asked.

"You see, Miss York," Mr. Burke explained, "you may think it is common sense that sorcerers shouldn't use their abilities to harm people, but sometimes it is safer to teach someone restraint before developing their abilities. Before they do permanent harm."

"Ichiro was like that," Rosa admitted. "When he started school last year, he got obsessed with potions. He started making love potions and selling them."

"And when those are used without supervision, that can lead to more than heartache. You can have problems with consent and obsessive behavior," Mr. Burke added.

Chrysta bit her lip and thought about what the others were saying. "I'm sorry, Mr. Burke," she said softly. "I'm sorry I freaked out."

"It's alright. Everyone has an episode when they are in the sphere. Isolation is difficult for everyone. But, I confess, I thought Miss Torres would have had an incident before you would, though." Rosa shot him a look.

Chrysta gestured to the book that Mr. Burke was currently holding, which she had been reading earlier. "I'll go back to studying if you say it will help me."

Mr. Burke glanced at the book in his hand. "Actually, with the new information you just divulged, I think ridding you of those nightmares is our next course of action."

"How do we do that?" Chrysta asked.

"Dream walking."

Mr. Burke turned around and went up to his bedroom, Chrysta listening to him climb the stairs. "Miss Torres," he called out. "Can you clear the floor?"

"Yes, sir," Rosa responded, and she started to move the furniture in the large main room. Chrysta stood blinking at her for a moment and then started to help.

"Dream walking?" Chrysta asked the other girl. "Isn't that Julien's ability?"

"Yep," Rosa said. She flashed Chrysta a smile as they rolled up the rug. "Don't worry, it's kinda dangerous, but that's why you go with someone else."

"Have you ever gone dream walking, Miss Torres?" Mr. Burke asked as he climbed down the steps.

"Just once," Rosa said, standing up and dusting off her hands. "Julien took several of us dream walking while Mr. Cross watched. Me, Rimsha, and a kid named Yung-See." She broke out in a huge grin. "We got to meet the whale."

"The whale?" Chrysta asked, feeling lost.

"There is a world that runs parallel to ours," Mr. Burke explained. He leafed through a book, and when he found what he was looking for, he began to draw on the floor with a piece of chalk. "It's the astral plane, and as sorcerers, we can pass into it while sleeping. It is possible to see the past, and sometimes the future there, and visions can be clearer than any other form of divination." He finished a large circle on the floor and made a smaller circle that bisected it. "There are beings there, creatures of spirit with no physical form, immortal beings of cosmic origin. They take the form of several animals when they appear to us: the whale, the turtle, the elephant, and the spider."

He finished one small circle and shifted to make another. "Unfortunately, they are not all benign, so you have to be vigilant while dream walking." Finished with the second shape, he started to write runes along their edges and say a poem simultaneously.

To walk in your dreams
Is not what it seems
There are Old Ones there
So you must take care

The whale is a giant
But very reliant
The turtle will aid
If you make a trade

The elephant is cruel
He will make you a fool
Avoid the spider
She kills outsiders

"I like what my dad used to say better than that old poem," Rosa said wistfully.

"What's that, Miss Torres?"

"The whale is your friend, the turtle is lazy, the elephant is an asshole, and the spider will rip you in half," she said. Mr. Burke paused in drawing and shot her a look.

When Mr. Burke finished, he pointed to one of the circles. "Miss York, if you please."

Chrysta went to the circle and took Mr. Burke's offered hand to lie down on the floor, making sure her skirt was still covering her legs. Mr. Burke lay down in the other circle. Poe landed on Chrysta's chest and laid flat, a heavy and comforting weight. Mr. Burke's dog set down between them, placing her head near her master's and giving him a lick on his cheek. He reached up and scratched at her ears.

"What's her name?"

"Pardon me?"

"Your dog, Mr. Burke. What is her name? I have never asked."

"Willow." The familiar whined and wagged her tail in response to hearing her name.

"So, how long should I wait?" Rosa asked.

"Two hours," Mr. Burke replied. "That should be plenty of time."

Rosa nodded. Mr. Burke reached out and placed his fingers on the bigger chalk circle, and it began to glow white. The whole design started to rise in the air until it was several feet above them, and then the markings began to move, twisting and turning like they were gears in a clock, following some pattern and speed that they only knew.

The nightmare had chased all desire to sleep from Chrysta's mind, but now, watching the circles move, she felt tired again. She blinked and sighed and felt her body relax.

"Don't fight it, Chrysta," Rosa said. The girl was sitting on a table with her head resting on her hand. "Just let go." And with that advice, Chrysta did just that.

❧ 28 ❧

Even though Chrysta could still feel the stone floor under her head and back, there was a weird sensation of falling. It felt like she was going backward until she stood back up, as strange as that feeling was. She opened her eyes and looked around without moving her head. There was inky blackness everywhere, nothing in sight as far as she could see. Chrysta thought it was complete darkness until she brought her hands up to study them. They were brightly lit, although Chrysta couldn't see a light source anywhere.

She looked down and saw that she was wearing a dress like the one her mother was wearing the night she visited. Her hair was down when it was in a braid before. She wiggled her toes as she examined her bare feet and giggled. She gasped, however, when she saw ripples move out from her feet.

She crouched and put her hand down. The surface felt smooth and slightly cold, but it moved like water when she touched it. She brought her hand back up to her face and wiggled her fingers. They didn't feel wet. She picked up one bare foot and moved it around. It seemed dry as well.

"Such an eerie sensation, isn't it?"

Chrysta looked up and saw Mr. Burke walking towards her. He looked very different, though. His hair was a dark brown, the highlights red instead of his usual white and grey. He still had his beard, but it was shorter and brown as well.

His face was unlined and wrinkle-free. The strangest thing about his appearance, however, was his clothes. Jeans with a hole in the knee and a buttoned-up shirt untucked and with the sleeves rolled up. Chrysta couldn't remember the stoic man ever looking so rumpled.

Mr. Burke paused and looked down when he saw the look on Chrysta's face. "Ah, yes. It's been a while since I was here. I forgot you have to think about your appearance if you want to alter it." He put his hand to his chest, and his clothes shifted, turning into the tan and white suit the Headmaster seemed to prefer, although his younger face and brown hair stayed the same.

"You didn't have to change on my account," Chrysta joked.

"I have a reputation to protect, Miss York," he drawled, and she smiled. He gestured around them. "So, what do you think?"

"It's not what I imagined," Chrysta admitted. She peered into the darkness, trying to see something, anything in the black. "I was expecting bright colors and abstract shapes. More like a dream. This endless blackness is creepy."

"This world is whatever you make of it," Mr. Burke explained. "Maybe we can go exploring one day. But for now, let's see that nightmare of yours."

The floor suddenly lit up under Chrysta, beautiful gold that swirled and twisted around her like it was liquid swirling in water. It spread, and where it went, figures and objects started to rise from the floor. It was the scene of the nightmare again, Chrysta blinking at her double tied up on the table. The figures began moving, and the chanting started at the highest volume, like someone had pushed play on a movie. Chrysta flinched at the loud noise and her double's frantic cry as the men forced her to drink the liquid.

The Not-Chrysta choked, and Chrysta felt her own throat burn in response. Her hands flexed, wanting to undo the ropes that tied the poor girl, and grab the knife out of her father's hands. *This isn't real,* she told herself. *She is not real.* But the Not-Chrysta's muffled screams still made her heart race as her father showed Not-Chrysta the knife and leered.

Mr. Burke was watching, walking around the table, still cool and calm. *He's probably seen much worse,* Chrysta told herself.

"For our Lady, of course," her father hissed, the answer to the silent question of "Why?" His features were exaggerated, nose longer and pointed, cheekbones so sharp they looked like they could cut glass, eyes dancing with mad glee.

And he raised the knife, and Not-Chrysta struggled, but there was no hope, no flash grenade, no Tommy, no chance to survive. And the blade came down swiftly, a plunge into the heart, and the gag in Not-Chrysta's mouth disappeared, and she is screaming, screaming, screaming. Shrieking so loud it hurt, and Chrysta fought the urge to bring her hands up to cover her ears.

"Wait," Mr. Burke said, and the scene paused like someone pushed a button. Chrysta let out a breath she didn't know she was holding. Although Chrysta didn't remember shedding them, her cheeks were wet with tears.

"Are you alright, Miss York?"

"Y-yes," she lied, wiping at the tears so Mr. Burke couldn't see them. "I'm sorry, I know it's a dream, I know it is silly to be—"

She stopped talking when she felt the hand on her shoulder. It was heavy and sudden but still a comforting weight. She looked up at the impossibly tall man beside her to see him looking down at her, features soft. "You survived a terrible ordeal, Miss York, and then chose to go back to your tormenters to help Monroe. Your fear is both natural and nothing to be ashamed of. On the contrary, you should be proud of yourself. Remember that."

Chrysta nodded and took a deep breath. Mr. Burke walked to the other side of the table, behind her father. Poor Not-Chrysta was frozen beneath him, tears going down her face as she looked at the blade in her chest in shock. "The good news is that we are going to fix all this, Miss York."

"How?"

"Well, you are standing here in front of me, ribcage intact," he joked, and Chrysta snorted in surprised laughter. "So I know that your father didn't complete his plan to take out your heart, and this nightmare is a falsehood. So focus on what really happened that night."

Chrysta nodded and closed her eyes. When she opened them again, the scene had changed. Guerra and Frost were about to force Not-Chrysta to drink the liquid again. But this time, there weren't as many ropes wrapped around her, her father's features weren't so severe, and the hooded figures around the table looked more human. When the chanting started this time, it didn't seem as loud and jarring as before. Once again, the men made Not-Chrysta gasp to open her mouth and pour the swirling liquid down her throat.

Chrysta reached out her hand, and the scene paused. "Why did they do that?" she asked, and Mr. Burke quirked an eyebrow up. "What was that liquid? Why did I have to drink it?"

He hesitated for a moment, taking in the scene before him. "Purification, most likely," He murmured after several moments of thought. "Did they make you fast before they brought you here?"

"Yes!" she cried. "They didn't bring any food to me for an entire day."

"Human sacrifice calls for the victim to be as pure as possible," Mr. Burke explained. "No food, no alcohol. The liquid is part of that process."

"I'm surprised that you didn't say they needed a virgin sacrifice. That is so cliche," Chrysta joked with a smile. But Mr. Burke didn't share her smile. "Wait, really?" she asked while a blush burned up her neck to her ears.

"To be fair, even someone who has had sex can be a part of a sacrifice," Mr. Burke explained. "The closer to unsullied and untainted innocence you can get, the better."

"No wonder my father never let me go out to date anyone."

"It does raise the question, though. If he had been isolating you for years—"

"Then was he planning to use me as a sacrifice for most of my life?" Chrysta finished for him in a whisper, and the Headmaster nodded. Chrysta went silent, Mr. Burke letting her have a few minutes to think and process the revelation. She put her hand out, and the scene started again.

Guerra was shushing Not-Chrysta as she screamed. "Hush now, *bella ragazza*," he cooed after clamping a hand on her mouth. Frost came up to her with the bowl of liquid, and they were trying to force her mouth open to drink it. Only after they had pinched her nose shut and made her take a breath did they finally get the concoction down her throat.

"Fighter to the end," Mr. Burke said.

"I... I didn't know what was going on, what they were doing," Chrysta said as Not-Chrysta coughed and had the gag shoved back into her mouth. "I just knew I didn't want anything to do with it."

Jacobs was handing the bundle to her father, and he uncovered the stone blade, although it didn't look as long and threatening as it did before. The red crystals winked as her father held it up.

"Brothers," Jozef York said in a loud voice. "Seven hundred and eighty-two years ago, the Lady was taken from this plane. We, her loyal followers, have kept the faith and have made her return our only mission." He lifted his hands, the knife pointed down at Not-Chrysta's chest, and Chrysta felt her stomach drop like it was her on that table again. "May this offering tonight bring her to us. For her alone!"

"For her alone," the other robed figures echoed, and Not-Chrysta started fighting her bonds in earnest as her father looked at her.

Her father was leaning over Not-Chrysta, the knife hovering over her chest as she pulled at the ropes. Suddenly, the cords started to glow gold, making Guerra and Frost jump to hold Not-Chrysta down. "Quickly, York!" Frost hissed. "She is going to get free!" Chrysta's father placed that single hand on her forehead as she struggled.

Mr. Burke stood next to her father, one hand covering his mouth, forehead furrowed. Chrysta couldn't tell what he was thinking or feeling from his aloof expression. Suddenly the *thunk* came from the group of acolytes watching, and one of them stumbled. Mr. Burke jumped in surprise. "What the hell was that?" he asked.

Chrysta's face broke out in a smile. "Tommy," she simply said, and the Headmaster looked at her in confusion.

"Bomb!" someone shouted, and the chaos began. Mr. Burke walked forward, trying to study the ball even as everyone else was pulling away from it. "Quickly!" Jozef York yelled. "Get it out of here!" But before anyone could react, the red dot flashed, and then the world exploded in white.

It was just as bright and loud as before, but it didn't stun Chrysta like it did that first time. However, all the acolytes were stumbling around blindly, grabbing each other and tripping over their own feet. It made Chrysta laugh, watching the men doing pratfalls in their robes, yelling uselessly at each other. Tommy suddenly appeared, shoving his way through the crowd, stopping at the table to pull at the ropes holding Not-Chrysta down.

"Wait," Mr. Burke said, and the scene froze again. "Can you go back? I want to see what he did."

"I couldn't see him from the table," Chrysta said. "I can't show you what happened."

"That is the whole purpose of dream walking, Miss York," Mr. Burke explained. "To witness something we wouldn't be able to see otherwise." He walked around the table and gestured at Chrysta. "Follow me."

They walked towards the door of the room, the scene rewinding like someone had hit reverse on a video. The Acolytes writhed on the floor in reverse before the flash. After the explosion, the gray ball wiggled on the floor, its victim holding his head but straitening up as the ball jumped in the air. It sailed towards the door, its victim acting like nothing was wrong as he turned, facing the table once more.

The door slowly came into view, rising from the floor like everything else in the vision. Part of the wall joined it, but it was low enough that Mr. Burke stepped over it, offering a hand to help Chrysta climb over it as well. The ball landed in Tommy's hand, and he pulled the door almost close, just leaving it open a crack. His mouth was moving, but Chrysta couldn't hear anything. About six men were around him, unconscious or injured. Chrysta assumed they were left to guard the door. One of them sat up from the floor, Tommy's foot lifting to rest on his shoulder. It was going back down after the man reached for Tommy. Tommy pulled his hands apart, and he now had the grey ball in one hand and a red crystal in the other. Tommy did something with his fingers, and a part of the red crystal flew from the floor and fused with what was in his grip.

"He didn't," Mr. Burke murmured, primarily to himself.

When everything started moving forward again, it was in the middle of her father's speech. "—her loyal followers, have kept the faith and have made her return our only mission."

"Yeah, keep talking, asshole," Tommy muttered. He flexed his hand, and the red crystal cracked, and the bottom portion fell to the floor. He placed the crystal into the ball, and it flashed.

"That, Miss York, is a magical bomb," Mr. Burke explained. "But I have never seen anyone use it as a flash grenade."

"One-one thousand, two-one thousand," Tommy was saying. The man next to him tried to grab Tommy's jacket, but he lifted his leg and placed his boot on the man's shoulder, callously kicking him down. The man cried out, and some of the acolytes at the back of the group turned around.

"Three-one thousand, four-one thousand," Tommy continued, not even looking at the man he kicked. "Five one-thousand, six-one thousand." He opened the door wider and brought his arm back, throwing the ball into the room.

Chrysta wondered if he meant to hit anyone or if it was an accident, but Tommy did smile when the struck man shouted in shock.

Tommy turned away from the door. "Seven one-thousand, eight one-thousand," he whispered.

"Quickly!" her father was yelling. "Get it out of here!" But it was too late, and Tommy covered his ears.

"It's brilliant, really," Mr. Burke said as the flash made the world go white again. "There was no way he could have stopped all of them at once." Tommy was barreling through the door as Mr. Burke talked, and they followed him. "So he incapacitated all of them without harming you."

Tommy shoved acolytes aside and reached the table. Guerra was the one who had Not-Chrysta by the hair, and Tommy ripped his hand away and pushed him back. Guerra took Frost and Jacobs with him as he fell. Tommy started to pull at the ropes that held Not-Chrysta. She was still struggling and fighting, and when her legs were free, she kicked and kneed Tommy in the face. He paused and shook his head, but instead of looking angry, he grinned and started working on the ropes on Not-Chrysta's arms. When her hands were free, she began to punch out as well as kick. Tommy just grabbed one of her hands and placed a kiss on the palm of her hand.

"That was when you realized it was him, didn't you?" Mr. Burke asked, and Chrysta nodded. "Then that is how we stop your nightmares, Miss York."

"How?" she asked as Not-Chrysta stopped fighting on the table and grabbed Tommy's jacket in desperation.

"Your nightmare is primarily based on feelings of helplessness," he explained as Tommy picked up Not-Chrysta and ran out of the room, dodging the acolytes who were still yelling and running into each other. "You need to remind your dream self that you did not die that night. So the next time you have that dream, remember that kiss. That contact proves that you are alive and safe, and it is all thanks to Mr. Monroe."

Chrysta nodded in understanding. "Like lucid dreaming," she replied.

"Exactly," Mr. Burke responded. The vision suddenly started to disappear around them, the table, the stilling stumbling acolytes, Chrysta's father, who was blindly feeling the table and banging his fist on it when he realized Not-Chrysta wasn't there. All of it melted and vanished into the inky black floor below them.

"Thank you, Mr. Burke," Chrysta said, taking in the endless dark around them. "I appreciate you helping me like this. I'm sorry I freaked out earlier."

"And I apologize for not being clearer in my plans for your education," he replied, folding his hands behind him. "Again, I just run the school and let the teachers handle the students. We will add some practical training to your studies soon."

The floor beneath them suddenly lit up, swirls of blues, purple, and greens, getting brighter by the second. Chrysta looked down in panic and started trying to walk backward away from it, but Mr. Burke reached out and touched her shoulder to stop her from moving away.

"Looks like the whale is coming to say his welcome," Mr. Burke told her.

The luminous colors moved until they were in front of them instead of below them. Then, something broke the surface, and a whale slowly floated into the air. It looked like a blue whale, massive but floating in the air like it weighed nothing. Chrysta gasped and grabbed Mr. Burke's arm but didn't dare move as the whale moved through the air like he was swimming. Weirdly enough, the floor rippled as he rose, but it wasn't giant waves like one would expect from a large mass breaking the surface of a body of water. The whale was not grey but a mixture of bright colors that whirled and eddied on his skin, reflecting on the black floor. He completed one slow lap around them before he spoke.

"Neil Burke, former hunter, current Headmaster of the Academy," he rumbled. His mouth didn't move, but Chrysta felt the vibration in her chest. Like she was sitting too close to a concert bass drum. He moved until his head was closer to them, studying them with one large eye. "Chrysta Angelos, formerly York, she who glows gold. It's a pleasure to see you both."

"It is a pleasure to see you as well," Mr. Burke lightly said like they were at a cocktail party exchanging greetings. He gently removed Chrysta's hand from his forearm but placed a hand on her shoulder for reassurance. "I hope we did not disturb you."

"I'm afraid that Miss Angelos gives off a very intense light in the dark here," the whale stated. He lazily moved one of his flippers and started another lap around the humans. "I would warn you not to wander around here by yourself, my dear, but I have already had a vision of you doing just that, so I will save you the lecture you will ignore."

"I'm sorry? Sir?" Chrysta said, unsure if she should apologize for something she had not done yet.

The whale chuckled, a deep rich sound. "'Sir!' I have not been called sir in a while. So polite. Unlike your father."

"My father has been here?" Chrysta asked.

"Most sorcerers have been here," the whale explained while slowly ascending. "Some unmagical people as well. Although you will be the first to bring changelings here."

Chrysta looked at Mr. Burke in confusion. He shrugged. "The Old Ones have the gift to see the future. The whale is the only one who will tell you what he sees without receiving anything in return, but it's always in sections and never what you truly want to know."

"Asking nicely will help," the whale joked, high above them. "For your good manners, Miss Angelos, I will let you know something about the future. I like you more than your father."

Chrysta thought hard for a few moments. The chance to know the future. It seemed like an extraordinary gift. "I... I don't know what I should ask about," she admitted after thinking for a full minute.

"Sleep on it," the whale said, arching his back so that his head pointed straight down at them. "I'm sure you will have a burning question for me next time we meet."

Suddenly, the whale pumped his tail and started dropping at them at an alarming rate. Chrysta gasped and put her hands up, bracing to be crushed—

—and then she was sitting up from the cabin floor, gasping and panting. Rosa looked over from a chair and grinned. "You met the whale," she said while getting up.

"I thought you said he was nice," Chrysta panted, gladly taking Rosa's hand so she could stand up. Poe croaked and landed on her shoulder, clicking his beak and rubbing his head on her cheek.

"I said you could believe him and trust him," Mr. Burke said, still on the floor. Willow whined and licked his face while he rubbed his eyes. "I never said he was nice," he continued as he sat up and scratched Willow's ears. "He likes to scare people the first time they meet him."

"He hit us with his tail when I met him," Rosa said with a smile. "What did he do to you?"

"Flatten us like pancakes," Chrysta muttered.

"And promised to answer a question of Miss Yo—Miss Angelos's choosing," Mr. Burke added.

Rosa whistled. "That's nice. What are you going to ask him?"

"I'm not sure," Chrysta confessed.

Mr. Burke sighed as he stood up, knees popping. "I think that is enough excitement for the day. I will retire until dinner. Miss Torres, what concoction are you creating this evening?"

"Chicken alfredo," Rosa said.

"Lovely. Until then, ladies," he said and headed to the loft.

Later, as Chrysta helped Rosa make dinner, the other girl cleared her throat. "Hey, you feel better?"

"I do," Chrysta said. "At least I feel better about spending the next three hundred and forty days in here as long as I don't have to read the entire time."

Rosa shuddered. "I just hope I don't have to do the proficiency test every day the entire time we are in here." The other girl stirred the boiling pasta in the fireplace and then cleared her throat again. "Wanna... I don't know, play some games after dinner?"

"Um, sure," Chrysta said. "You don't have to, you know. I understand why you don't like me."

"What? Why do you think I don't like you?"

"My last name is York," Chrysta explained, trying to sound calm even as a lump formed in her throat. "I understand if you don't want to spend any time with me because of that."

"Nah. Your last name isn't York. It's Angelos."

Chrysta blinked and then broke out into a smile. "Yeah, you're right. So what do you want to play?"

"Well, do you know how to play poker?"

"No."

"Then you're the perfect victim," Rosa joked, and Chrysta laughed.

29

Mr. Burke stayed true to his word, and he started letting Chrysta train with magic just as much as she had to read about it. The day after meeting the whale, Mr. Burke had Chrysta try the fire aptitude test before Rosa. Chrysta was surprised that she could only light two of the candles.

"Ha! See?" Rosa barked with a grin. "Not that easy, is it?"

"Give her time," Mr. Burke said. "Miss Angelos is proving to be a fast learner."

Now that Chrysta felt that she was making progress and Rosa was much friendlier, time was starting to move fast, and they settled into a comfortable routine. Rosa began jogging in the mornings while Chrysta went to a nearby stream to get their water supply for the day. Rosa would shower and then cook breakfast, and they would hike into the forest for practice. Once the light started to die, it would be a hike back to the cottage, where Rosa would cook dinner, Chrysta would clean up, and then she would shower.

"How is the quest for a hot shower advancing?" Mr. Burke asked Chrysta one night, not looking up from his book.

"Lukewarm at best," Chrysta groused while toweling her hair. "You would think that warming up water in a metal basin wouldn't be that hard."

"At least you can manage lukewarm," Rosa growled.

The girls would usually go out exploring on their day of rest, with the promise of not going north to the castle. Unfortunately, they ran into the barrier of the ball on one of those days, poor Poe crashing into it as he flew. The girls ran to the raven as he picked himself off the ground. "Fuck," he croaked as Chrysta looked him over gently, checking the bird for any injuries.

Rosa knocked on the glass. "Wild," she murmured. "Still looks like we could walk for miles."

Chrysta placed Poe on her shoulder, and she put her face up to the invisible barrier, wrapping her hands around her face to block out the light. The land beyond it was there, but it did seem blurry. "Wild," Poe croaked in her ear.

"So now we know," Chrysta breathed in wonder. "We really are in a glass ball."

Rosa gave her a look. "Like you had any doubt before?"

. . . . .

Chrysta noticed Rosa pulling at her hair a lot a few weeks later. She seemed annoyed as it got in her eyes and kept putting it up in buns and ponytails. Finally, she went up to Mr. Burke on one of their rest days. "Your hair is always neat, Mr. Burke."

The Headmaster put his book down and looked at the girl with a raised eyebrow at the random compliment. He didn't say anything, so she cleared her throat and continued. "Do you think you can cut my hair? Please?"

"I'm not a hairdresser, Miss Torres," he drawled. "If I cut your hair, you would probably end up looking like me."

"Okay."

He raised eyebrows now. "You want to chop it off."

"Yep."

"All of it?"

"All of it."

He studied Rosa for several long moments. "I will do so," he finally said, "But I want video evidence that you are requesting this so you don't claim that I forced you to do it later."

"Video evidence?"

"A video on your cellphone should do."

"My cellphone? I don't have my cell phone here," Rosa said nervously.

"I know you have it and have been making videos, Miss Torres," Mr. Burke said dryly. "Just promise not to show them to anyone, and you can keep them."

They moved outside, Rosa giving Chrysta her phone, and Chrysta opened the camera app.

"Rosa, how do I know it's on?" she asked.

"It's on," Rosa said.

"You su—Oh yeah! It's on!" Chrysta smiled at the camera and waved. "Hi, guys! It's day fifty-four, and Rosa wanted you guys to see this." Chrysta said with a grin.

She changed the view on the camera, and Rosa, sitting on a tree stump, filled the screen. Rosa waved at the camera. "Rosa wants a haircut," Chrysta explained.

"Not a haircut. I want to chop it off," Rosa said. Mr. Burke grinned and opened the pouch he was holding, revealing a set of scissors and straight razors. "And no one can stop me."

Mr. Burke took out a straight razor and sharpened it on a leather strap. "Say it, Miss Torres," he ordered.

Rosa sighed. "I, Rosa Maria Torres, of sound mind and body..."

"I still challenge the sound mind part," Mr. Burke muttered, and Chrysta laughed.

"Hereby resolve Mr. Burke of the consequences of his actions," Rosa continued as Mr. Burke folded his arms with the blade still in his hand. "I have asked him to do this, and do not hold him responsible for my bad decisions." She glanced behind her to the Headmaster. "Okay, I said it. Now what?"

Mr. Burke didn't say a word, but he grabbed a portion of Rosa's hair on the side of her head and, with the swipe of the straight razor, cut it off. He offered the hair to Rosa, who looked at the long strands in shock. "Now the screaming starts," he drawled, and Chrysta laughed as Rosa gaped.

Rosa started to yell. "Oh my Lord, you took *so much of it off!* What are you *doing?!*" she screeched. Chrysta was laughing so hard she had to turn off the video and hold onto her sides.

"Stay still, Miss Torres, unless you want me to skin you."

When Mr. Burke finished with his razors and scissors, Rosa looked very different. He had buzzed her hair on the sides of her head but kept the top long.

"Damn," Rosa murmured as she studied herself in the mirror Mr. Burke had handed her. "If you ever retire, you can become a barber, Mr. Burke."

The corners of Mr. Burke's mouth twitched like he was about to smile, but he frowned when Rosa handed him the mirror. "Jiao is the one who keeps me looking clean, I'm afraid," he confessed as he tugged on his beard, which was looking shaggier than when they'd entered the sphere. He glanced at Chrysta. "Would you like a haircut, Miss Angelos?"

Chrysta held her braid like she was trying to protect it. "No, thank you. I was planning to grow it longer, actually." She blushed a little. "My father never let me wear it too long, and now that I can do what I want..."

"You want to grow it out," Rosa finished for her. "Hell yeah, long hair is nice," she said, even as she ran her fingers through her shorter hairdo.

·····

Mr. Burke crossed off the number 60 on the board. "One-sixth of the way through," he drawled.

"How long has it been on the outside?" Rosa asked.

Chrysta did the math in her head. "Six hours."

"So it's only midnight for them?" Rosa asked, and Mr. Burke nodded. "Wow, that's weird."

"Sixty days until we get our supplies," Mr. Burke reminded the girls.

"Mr. Cross better include a caramel latte," Rosa growled, and Chrysta laughed.

.....

Chrysta is back on the table in the mansion's third-story bedroom that used to be her home. She is tied with so many ropes that she can't move, can barely breathe. The acolytes surround her in robes, faceless, featureless, their chanting ringing in her ears. Her throat is burning from the liquid they forced her to drink, still sore from coughing. Her father is next to her, his features twisted in a snarl, holding a knife over her.

Wait. Wait. Wait.

This is a dream.

And Chrysta knew how to stop it.

Chrysta closed her eyes. She tried to slow her breathing even as the chanting got louder like the acolytes around her knew that she was trying to stop them. She focused on the ghost of a sensation instead: the feeling of lips pressed into her palm. The sign that Tommy had untied her, saved her, and that she was alive and no longer in danger.

The chanting faded, the feeling of the ropes wrapped around her weakened, and without opening her eyes, she sat up and then moved to the edge of the table. She stood up and just started walking, not surprised that her father and the other acolytes didn't stop her. They weren't real, after all.

She walked for a bit, not opening her eyes, just letting the scene disappear behind her. She paused after several moments when she felt a presence. Chrysta cracked an eye open and, to her shock, saw Tommy standing in front of her with a smirk.

"Hey, beautiful," he said, flashing her a smile, and Chrysta couldn't help but smile back. "Hope I didn't break up your father's party. It seemed like a real rager."

She knew this was only a memory, but she was still so glad to see him that she wrapped her arms around his neck and kissed him. He kissed her back, chuckling as he hugged her.

She leaned back, opening her eyes, but her smile died when she realized that Tommy was gone. She brought her arms down, feeling foolish. Oh, but it had been so good to see him.

"Good job, Miss Angelos," a rumbling voice said. Chrysta turned and watched as the whale slowly floated up from the floor.

"Hello, Mister..." Chrysta trailed off. "I'm sorry, I don't know your name."

"No name, I'm afraid to say," he replied, still rising. "Mr. Whale will do."

"Hello, Mr. Whale," she said with a smile. "I didn't mean to come here by myself," she quickly added.

"Oh, I know. That is why I'm here. The others won't bother you while I'm around. But it was quick thinking coming here to stop that nightmare." He turned so that his eye was examining her. "Have you thought of a question for me yet?"

"I haven't," she admitted. "Can I have some more time to think it over? I don't want to waste your gift."

He chuckled. "So polite. It has been a while since I met someone like you, Miss Angelos. Have all the time that you need." He lazily moved a flipper and started a low circle around her. "Would you like help waking up?"

"Only if you promise not to flatten me again," she said, and he laughed, a sound that made Chrysta's whole body vibrate.

"How about I teach you how to do it yourself?" he offered.

"I would like that," Chrysta replied.

"Close your eyes."

Chrysta did as he said, and she could still see that light he gave off through her eyelids. "Count down from ten," he said. "And try to let yourself drift backward."

"Ten, nine, eight," she started, "seven, six, five..." Chrysta wasn't sure, but it felt like her feet had left the floor.

"Until next time, Miss Angelos," the whale said.

"Four, three," she leaned back, feeling like she was drifting. "Two, one." She finally touched her bed and settled onto her side.

Chrysta woke up, the sun barely shining through the window. She sat up and looked around. Nothing had moved. Nothing was burnt. Chrysta smiled when she realized that it had worked.

She put her feet on the floor and stretched. Poe stirred next to her and clicked his beak. "Looks like I will finally be getting a decent night's sleep from now on," she stated as she scratched the raven's head.

. . . . .

It was day eighty-three when Rosa finally had a breakthrough.

They were at the ruins. Chrysta was trying to make water in a bucket move. Chrysta was learning that handling water and wind was easier than controlling fire and earth, but moving any element without touching it still took a lot of concentration. Rosa was still working on the fire aptitude test, although the last two candles were still eluding her. She had sat down on the ground half an hour ago and was just glaring at the unlit candles while their lit counterparts slowly melted.

"I give up," she muttered.

"Are you sure, Miss Torres?" Mr. Burke asked, seated on his usual log. Willow was at his feet, sleeping. "We still have several hours of daylight yet."

"No, I give up completely. I can't do it," Rosa replied, her voice sounding hollow. "I should just give up now, go outside, and let Mrs. Paulson do the wasting curse."

"Don't give up," Chrysta told her. She picked herself off the ground and knocked some dirt off of her jeans. "We have only been here a few months, and you still have time to try," she said as she walked over to the other girl.

"It doesn't matter how much time I have; I'll never get it," Rosa said with a sigh. She flopped down on the ground, and Poe joined her, croaking as he hopped up and down.

"What are you trying to do, Miss Torres?" Mr. Burke suddenly asked her.

"Light the candles and put them out at a distance," Rosa responded, almost sounding bored.

Mr. Burke waved his hand, and the candles went out. "And what makes the first three candles easier than the last two?"

"They're closer. It's easier to see them and light them in your mind's eye."

"Light them now," he said.

Rosa waved her hand, and the candles lit, even without her looking directly at them.

"And the fourth and fifth candles? What makes them so hard?"

"Being further away means it's harder to control the magic and not set fire to anything else around them," Rosa explained. "My father said he was able to do the fire aptitude test when he was 13. My brother did it when he was 12. Here I am, about to turn 17, and I can't do it." She opened her eyes and stared at the sky, eyes shining. "I guess I'm just defective."

"Try again, Miss Torres," Mr. Burke gently told her.

Rosa threw up her hands. "Why?" she asked, voice almost breaking. "It's pointless."

"Just try," he ordered her.

Rosa waved her hands, and suddenly the fourth candle lit up, although nothing happened to the fifth one. Chrysta gaped at the sight, but Mr. Burke put a finger up to his lips before she said anything.

"I once knew a mimic; peculiar man. He could not change his appearance while anyone was watching him. Had to be completely alone. If anyone watched him morph, he would turn blue instead."

"Good for him," Rosa said sarcastically.

"Do you know how he fixed it?"

"How?" Chrysta asked with a smile.

"One day, he went into an office to change," Mr. Burke said while getting up from his log. "What he didn't know was that someone was already in there. It was Jiao, actually. She watched him change, and when he left the office, she got up, found him, and told him, 'I watched you change, and you didn't even turn blue.' He never had that issue again."

Chrysta laughed, but Rosa sighed, still lying on the ground. "What is your point, Mr. Burke?"

"My point, Miss Torres, is you just did something you didn't think you could do without even knowing you were doing it."

"What do you me—" Rosa started to ask, finally sitting up and stopping mid-question when she saw the fourth candle flickering. "I didn't do that. Did I? Did you?" she asked while pointing at Chrysta. Chrysta smiled and shook her head. "I did *that?* No... Did I?"

"You are not defective, Miss Torres," Mr. Burke said. "Just need to get out of your own head."

Rosa smiled. She waved a hand, and all the candles went out. She twisted her hand again, and all four lit up again. "Alright," she announced with a grin as she got up from the ground. "Four down, one to go."

.....

"I just miss him, you know?" Chrysta confessed.

Rosa sighed. "Yeah, I know what you mean. I miss everyone too."

It was day one-hundred and eight, and they were outside on one of their rest days, enjoying the sun. Rosa and Chrysta were cross-legged on the ground, playing poker. Chrysta was getting good at the card game, and she folded when she saw Rosa run her fingers through her hair. She only did that when she had a straight.

Mr. Burke was nearby in a wooden chair, leaning back with his feet crossed at the ankles, open book on his chest, eyes closed. Chrysta noticed he was spending more time in their company; although he didn't interact with them, he just seemed not to want to be alone all the time. He had come outside with a bottle of amber liquid and a bucket of water. After freezing the water with a wave of his hand, he relaxed and took small sips out of the cold bottle while the girls played their game.

"I mean, I don't miss sharing a bathroom with everyone or Rimsha getting up at the crack of dawn, but I do miss them," Rosa continued.

"I wish Tommy could have come with us," Chrysta murmured. "But asking him to give up a whole year of his life just because I wanted him to seems selfish."

"I'm sure Mr. Monroe wouldn't have seen it that way," Mr. Burke replied, not moving from his position.

Rosa looked at the Headmaster. "I'm surprised you haven't tried to tell Chrysta off for having feelings for a changeling," she admitted.

"Miss Angelos glows gold, Miss Torres. At some point, no one will be able to 'tell her off' and have her listen to them," he said dryly.

Both girls laughed. "That's probably why Mr. Cross hasn't tried to lecture you yet," Rosa told Chrysta. "I can feel him wanting to, though." She shifted and then deepened her voice, mimicking a British accent. "'You can't be attracted to a changeling, my dear. It's unnatural to want a relationship with a creature who could snap you in half.'"

Chrysta looked down, examining the playing cards as she shuffled them. "Actually, Tommy has been saying we shouldn't be... together." She glanced at Mr. Burke to see if he would be mad at the mention of an unconventional relationship with a changeling, but he didn't stir. "That I don't want to be labeled a 'changeling lover.'

And he was upset before we left." She studied Mr. Burke, wondering if he would hate it if she asked for his advice. "Do you think Tommy is upset because of who my father is, Mr. Burke?"

"I think if he were upset, he wouldn't have done what he did to protect you, Miss Angelos. Getting you away from your father and bringing you to the Academy almost cost him his life. You don't do that for someone you despise."

Chrysta nodded, digesting the Headmaster's words, and dealt out the cards. Rosa had taught her Texas Hold'em, and she was happy when she saw she had a four-of-a-kind at the flop. She tried to keep her face neutral as she raised Rosa. "Mr. Burke," she started to ask, and the Headmaster raised an eyebrow to show he was listening, "why do you trust Tommy so much?"

"I didn't," he acknowledged. "Not at first. But everything he had told us is the truth, as far as we can verify. And you are not the first person that he has helped. He also came to the aid of Helen Chambers and Jiao. So, therefore, I feel that saving you three proves that we can trust him."

Chrysta and Rosa paused, looking at each other with confused looks. They both put their cards down and gave the Headmaster a bewildered look. "Who is Helen Chambers?" Chrysta asked, trying to sound nonchalant.

"A woman that Tommy helped to leave the Acolytes," Mr. Burke explained, still not opening his eyes.

"And how did he help Mrs. Zheng?" Chrysta asked.

Mr. Burke's eyes popped open. "Beg your pardon?"

"You said Tommy saved Mrs. Zheng," Rosa said.

"Did I?" Mr. Burke asked. He picked up the bottle and inspected it. "I think I have drunk too much of this."

"Mr. Burke," Chrysta said with a smile. "Are you hiding something?"

"No," he stated. He slowly sat up. "I mean to say, I don't think Jiao wants to keep this a secret per se." He hesitated, looking at the bottle. "But I don't think this is a conversation to have while inebriated."

"Well, everyone keeps saying that Chrysta needs to know more about Tommy before getting into a relationship," Rosa said slowly. Chrysta glanced at her in confusion, but the other girl gave her a wink. "Think of it as giving Chrysta all the information she needs to decide for herself."

Mr. Burke glared at the girls, his face not moving for several long moments. Then he sighed, took another sip from his bottle, leaned back, and crossed his feet at the ankle again. "Fine," he growled. "But if my wife asks, you did not hear this story from me."

Akrur's phone started going off, and he groggily reached for it. He finally found it and turned it off, groaning at the time—four in the morning. He rubbed his face as he sat up from the couch. His brother was the one who insisted on using sofas in their vaults, claiming it added some warmth to the otherwise cold, sterile space, but as Akrur looked around at the sleeping teenagers around him, he was happy for the added furniture.

After Burke and the girls disappeared into the sphere, things had settled into an uneasy quiet in the vault. Zheng had taken Hafeez for a walk, saying that they needed to talk with an air of cool anger. Akrur, Ellis, and Smith watched the two women go after Hafeez had brought her SUV into the factory and closed the main door. "Man," Smith said with a grin. "That is a conversation I'm glad I'm not a part of."

"Why was she late?" Akrur asked Ellis.

"She said something about not being sure she should come," they said, glaring in the direction the hunters had headed. "I just hope this doesn't turn into a constant conflict over the next few days."

Akrur went out to get dinner soon afterward, going to a nearby Indian restaurant. It was one of the few located in America that his mother had deemed satisfactory to eat at. It was also one of the few places he knew that could cover all their dietary needs.

"Thank you, Mr. Cross!" Rimsha said brightly as he handed her some aloo gobi. The other teens descended on the takeout containers like a pack of hyenas. Akrur reached into the fray and grabbed some chicken tikka masala and naan. "Where are the others?" he asked Ellis.

"Monroe and Smith are in the vault," they replied. "Mrs. Zheng and Hafeez are still off talking."

"Well, eat up." Akrur glanced at the teenagers and grimaced. "If you can find anything left, that is."

Ellis smiled at him. "Thank you," they said. "Really, you didn't have to."

"Well, you need to keep up your strength," Akrur said. "I'm just here to support the people doing the heavy lifting."

When he entered the vault, he found Tommy and Smith on the lower floor, near the sphere. He handed the food containers to the two of them. "You two should eat too. It will be a long watch."

"It's been an hour and a half," Tommy suddenly said, face set in worry. "Fifteen days for them."

"They will be fine," Akrur said, for his own peace of mind as well as the changeling's. "The Headmaster will keep them safe."

Tommy nodded but still picked at his food. "A year is just... a very long time."

"Worried she won't want to be with you after she comes out?" Smith asked with a cocky grin.

Tommy glared at the hunter. "That is none of your business."

"No, it's not," Smith agreed while taking a bite of food. "But I get why you're worried," he continued while chewing. He swallowed and then resumed talking, waving his fork around. "Girl meets boy, and girl likes boy, boy likes girl, boy saves girl, the girl finds out that boy is a changeling." He took a sip of water out of his bottle. "Only you thought the girl would hate you for being a changeling, but she didn't, and now you are worried she won't want you when she gets out of the sphere." He took a bite of his food. "Did I guess right?" he asked with his mouth full.

Tommy just kept glaring at Smith. "You are a smartass. Anyone ever tell you that?"

"Oh yeah," the hunter said. "All the time." Akrur just rolled his eyes.

They finished eating, Zheng and Hafeez joining them in the vault at one point. Hafeez refused to look at Tommy when she patrolled the vault to look around. Akrur took it as a good sign.

"Smith, you will take first watch," Zheng told the hunter. "Ellis will take the morning watch. Nyla and I will patrol outside tonight."

Smith gave her a lazy salute. "Yes, ma'am."

Zheng then studied Tommy for a moment. His leg was moving up and down, a bouncing motion Akrur had not seen him use before. "How are you doing?"

"Good," the changeling lied.

"Want to rest or stay up with Smith?"

Tommy scowled at the grinning hunter. "Guess I will stay up. Doubt I would get much sleep anyway."

The kids kept themselves busy, watching movies on a laptop Ichiro had brought. At one point, Kevin went off exploring deeper into the vault. "Whoa!" he cried out, voice echoing from the back of the vault. "There's an iron maiden in here!"

Akrur jumped. He had forgotten about that particular artifact being stored here. "Don't touch it!" he yelled back.

"An iron maiden? What kinky stuff are you into, Cross?" Smith asked with a smirk, looking up from the card game he was playing with Tommy.

Akrur glared at the hunter. "It was from the state—evidence from a murder investigation. A sorcerer was prolonging his life by killing his victims in the iron maiden and taking their life essence. We aren't sure if the enchantment is completely removed from it, so we keep it here for safe-keeping."

Smith winced. "Oomph, I'm sorry I asked."

"Well, it's still a torture device with spikes," Akrur explained. "So don't touch it!" he yelled at Kevin. He couldn't see the boy, but he wouldn't be surprised if the teen had been reaching for it as he spoke.

The kids finally turned in around midnight, choosing to use the sofas in the vault over going upstairs to the offices to sleep. Julien walked over to the sphere, studying it for a bit. "It's weird," he signed after a few minutes. "Knowing that for us, it's only been six hours."

"And for them, it's been sixty days," Cross finished for him, both signing and saying the words out loud.

"One-sixth of the way there," Zheng added.

"Is it normal for them not to send notes?" Akrur asked.

"Neil will have them send something when we send in the supplies," Zheng said with a smile. "Don't worry. It means they are hard at work."

Akrur set his alarm and went to bed, settling on a couch in the back, away from everyone else. He would have liked to get more sleep but wanted to get up early enough to grab breakfast for everyone before they brought the next batch of supplies into the vault.

The alarm jarred him awake, and he shuffled to the front of the vault, heading for the stairs to go up. Tommy and Smith were sitting close to the sphere, both looking very tired.

"You snore like a chainsaw," Smith told Akrur as he passed to go outside. Tommy snorted in amusement.

"Keep that up, and I won't let you have any breakfast," Akrur shot back, and Smith looked hurt.

He found a coffee shop that was open and put in his order. "Eighteen assorted bagels with cream cheese, eighteen assorted donuts, two large containers of coffee, and a mountain of cream and sugar," the attendant at the counter verified his order in a way too loud and chipper voice for that early in the morning. "Are ya feeding an army?" she asked.

"Oh no, just teenagers," he joked, and she laughed. "Oh, and one of those caramel lattes as well, please."

Akrur returned to everyone mulling about in the office space, Ichiro the only teen not awake. Once again, Akrur put the food down on a desk and stepped away before losing a limb. Tommy and the hunters stepped in to get their share once the teens were done. Tommy sat with the teens while Zheng and the hunters sat by themselves at another desk. There were lots of muffled and mumbled thanks yous and the food seemed to perk everyone up. Rimsha pointed at the latte. "Is that for Rosa?"

"Yes," Akrur confirmed with a grin, eating his donut before tucking into a bagel. "I reason she deserves a treat, no matter what her progress has been so far." He looked at Tommy. "What do you believe Miss York would like?"

Tommy picked up a donut. "A donut for her and a bagel for Poe," he said.

Akrur nodded. "Done." He glanced at his pocket watch. "It's five-oh-nine. Fifty-one minutes until we have to send the supplies in." He looked at Rimsha as he put his watch away. "Do you have to take some time to pray this morning?"

"At five fifty-five," Rimsha confirmed. She glanced at Hafeez. "Would you like to join me?" The hunter shot her a glare as she placed a plate of chicken down for her caracal. "Praying? Would you like to join me?"

"Considering he didn't answer my prayers last time I prayed to him, I don't have anything else to say to him," Hafeez said flatly. Poor Rimsha flinched but nodded. Akrur squeezed the girl's shoulder, a silent sign of support, while the rest of the Disaster Club glared at the hunter for her rude tone. Tommy leaned over and whispered something in Rimsha's ear, and the girl laughed. That just made Hafeez's frown deepen.

Zheng wiped her hands and mouth with a napkin and looked at the donuts with disdain. "Really, Cross, you couldn't have brought some better pastries?" She took one of the fried desserts, however.

"Sorry, Director Zheng, I'll remember to make it the continental breakfast next time," he replied, grabbing a second donut and taking a bite as the Director sighed in resignation, and the kids laughed.

Ichiro finally appeared, yawning and stretching as he headed to the bathroom. "Hurry up, Mr. Takahashi. We have to be moving the supplies down to the vault soon," Akrur called out to the boy. "All hands on deck."

"That means you too, Hafeez," Smith said to his associate. "You ain't getting out of it this time."

"I'm not going down there if that thing is up here," she growled, and Tommy shot her a glare.

"What? Think I will lock you all down there?" Tommy asked her sarcastically.

"I'm not taking that chance," Hafeez fired back.

"Alright, this is not happening," Zheng snapped as Akrur reached out and put a hand on Tommy's. The kids were wide-eyed and looking back and forth between them. Ichiro finally joined them, silently grabbing a bagel and chewing it thoughtfully. "Nyla," the Director continued. "if you want to, you can stay up here. But you *will* be helping to move the supplies."

Hafeez ignored her superior and continued talking directly at Tommy. "You just can't help yourself, can you?"

"What are you talking about?"

Hafeez gestured at Rimsha. "Seducing young women. That is what you do, right? It's how you have been shielding yourself with York this entire time."

Tommy scoffed. "I'm not messing with Rimsha," he explained with an icy tone. "I just told her that asking you to pray was like asking your cat to pray: completely useless."

"Besides, Tommy is with Chrysta," Kevin interrupted, earning him a glare from the hunter. He leaned back in his chair but continued with a slight tremor in his voice. "He wouldn't mess with s-someone else."

"You think that thing knows anything about love?"

"Well, he wouldn't have done everything he did to save Chrysta if he didn't love her," Rimsha argued.

"Wow, you have these fools deceived, don't you?" Hafeez jeered.

The office got as silent as a tomb for several long moments, and then everyone started talking at once in an explosion of sound. The teens yelled at Hafeez, except for Ichiro, who was chewing his bagel and glaring at the same time. Akrur was trying to quiet the teens down but wanted to tell the woman off simultaneously. Ellis was pulling on Hafeez's arm, possibly to get her away from everyone before she said anything else to start a fight.

Surprisingly quiet through the uproar, Tommy got up with an icy smile. "Come on, guys," he yelled over the kids. "Let's get started moving those supplies. It looks like we will be doing it by ourselves," he shot at Hafeez.

The teens grumbled but got up to follow the changeling, Ichiro staying to finish his breakfast. Director Zheng fiercely whispered at Hafeez, but the younger hunter ignored her, glaring at Tommy's back. "Maybe I'm wrong," Hafeez called out, raising her voice so the changeling could hear her. "Maybe Chrysta York has seduced *you.*"

"Nyla, that is *enough,*" Zheng ordered, but Hafeez continued and disregarded her.

Hafeez stood up slowly from the desk. "Isn't that what the Golden One did? Use changelings for any of her whims?" Tommy didn't react, so she started yelling. "Didn't the Golden One *consort* with her creations? Maybe glowing gold makes them sexual deviants, willing to *sleep* with *monsters.*"

"Seriously?!" Smith yelled at her, even Ellis looking disgusted with their associate's behavior. Zheng just rubbed her forehead like she had a headache. All the teens froze and turned around, except for Julien, who couldn't hear the hunter's insults.

Rimsha shouted something in Arabic, Kevin grabbing her shoulder so she wouldn't get closer to the hunter. Whatever Rimsha said, it must have been insulting if Hafeez's face was anything to go by.

Akrur glanced at Tommy and felt his stomach drop when he realized that the changeling had frozen, his spine ramrod straight. Suddenly he let out an unmistakable growl, deep and inhuman, and started to change as he turned around. Poor Julien, still not aware of what was going on, jumped in surprise as the changeling transformed before him, but Tommy just pushed him aside and stalked toward Hafeez.

All the hunters stood up, Hafeez grabbing her sword's hilt as she smiled in mad glee. Ellis also reached for their sword, but Smith rushed to stop Tommy, placing a hand on the changeling's shoulder. Tommy just batted it away.

"Take it back," Tommy growled in warning. Akrur went up to him, trying to break the changeling's gaze.

Hafeez just smiled, pulling her sword out slowly.

"Nyla, apologize now," Zheng ordered while pointing at the younger hunter.

"No," Hafeez coldly replied.

"Take it back!" Tommy roared, and everyone jumped.

"No!" Hafeez yelled back.

Tommy snarled and tried to jump at Hafeez, only to be stopped by Akrur, Smith, and Julien grabbing onto him. Hafeez unsheathed her sword entirely and held it at the ready, getting ready for the attack. Suddenly her sword started glowing purple, and with a loud *pop,* it disappeared out of her hands. "Mine!" Ichiro shouted, and Akrur looked at him in shock as the younger boy held up the black sword in triumph.

"Not helping!" Akrur bellowed as Hafeez blinked at her hands in confusion. Tommy growled again and surged forward, realizing Ichiro had disarmed his target.

Hafeez glared at Ichiro, probably debating how to retrieve her weapon, but Ichiro was standing behind a very large, pissed-off changeling. Hafeez started to back up, her caracal hissing at Tommy. Tommy hissed back, and the cat cowered.

Ellis finally unsheathed their sword, but Zheng pulled on the hunter's arm, making them back up. The kids also backed away, but Akrur, Smith, and Julien kept their hold on the growling changeling.

"Well, Nyla," Zheng called out with a grim smile. "You wanted to fight him. Now is your chance." She looked at the men holding Tommy. "Let him go," she ordered.

"Ma'am?!" Smith asked. Akrur whipped his head around, shooting the Director a skeptical look.

"Let him go!" she repeated, louder this time. Now Nyla was looking at her superior in shock.

Akrur and Smith glanced at each other, and they both let go simultaneously. Akrur pulled Julien to get him out of the way.

Tommy charged, and Hafeez slid across a desk to get a straight shot to the door, running past Zheng and Ellis. Tommy tried to get himself to stop but skidded across the floor, crashing into the wall. When he finally got the traction to go after the running hunter, Kevin and Rimsha were in the way. They ducked as the changeling rushed past them. Akrur was just happy that Tommy didn't hurt them, as focused as he was on catching the hunter.

Ichiro whooped and then raised the sword into the air. Ellis ran to the boy and grabbed the weapon before he hurt himself. "A tip for the future," they growled. "Never, *ever* touch a hunter's sword." Then they ran out of the office, Zheng and Smith hot on their heels.

Akrur stopped at the door and turned around, trying to keep the kids from exiting the office. When he finally faced the factory's main floor, he groaned. Tommy had cornered Hafeez in the back of the factory, and she was trying to weave through the metal shelves to keep Tommy from grabbing her. They were knocking over boxes and pallets of paper. Luckily Cross's family was getting rid of everything anyway to make way for a new business to be a front for the vault. Akrur just didn't know how he would explain the mess to his brother.

Tommy thrust an arm through one of the shelves and finally caught the hunter. Akrur could see Hafeez uselessly kick her feet as Tommy lifted her in the air by her uniform jacket. Hafeez reached into her jacket, and there was a flash as she swiped at Tommy in a wide arc. Tommy roared and let her go, Akrur finally seeing the wicked-looking hunting knife in her hand.

Hafeez ran towards the front of the factory, pushing past the other hunters and knocking Smith over. Tommy was close behind her, running past the hunters too, surprisingly not knocking any of them to the ground in his haste.

Hafeez's caracal, who had been close behind his master through all the commotion, decided to turn around and launch himself at Tommy. Tommy hissed and batted the cat to the side. The caracal recovered and flew at the changeling again, using a chair to propel himself at Tommy's head. The changeling roared and sent the caracal flying again. "Don't hurt him!" Rimsha yelled from the office; Akrur was unsure if she was asking the caracal or the changeling to show mercy.

Ellis, who was helping their partner off of the floor, thrust the two swords they were holding into Smith's hands. They then took off their suit jacket while Smith looked at the swords he was now holding in confusion. Ellis wrapped the jacket's sleeves around their hands and then caught the caracal while it concentrated on Tommy. It hissed and spit at him, probably ripping the jacket to shreds, but Ellis grimly held onto the writhing bundle.

Hafeez glanced at them in fear but quickly looked back at Tommy. "Let him go!" she ordered her peer.

"I'm keeping him from getting hurt!" Ellis yelled back, keeping the enraged animal close to their chest.

Hafeez kept retreating towards the front door, not turning her back on Tommy. "Cross!" she yelled when she reached the vehicles. "Open the door!"

Akrur hesitated, staring at Tommy's back. He wasn't happy with what the hunter had said either, but would the changeling let Akrur help her? Or would he attack Akrur too? Zheng grabbed his hand and shook her head, and he gaped at her.

"But what if he takes this too far?" Akrur fiercely whispered to the older woman. "What if he kills her?" Zheng just shook her head again, and Akrur turned back to the drama unfolding, feeling helpless.

Hafeez, realizing that no one was coming to help her, stopped her retreat. She started to swipe at Tommy, the changeling dodging easily. The cars were close enough together that Hafeez didn't have the room to swing correctly, but neither did Tommy. He waited until she thrust the knife at him, and he sidestepped it, grabbing her arm. She started to punch and cut at the changeling, concentrating on the hand holding her arm. Tommy ignored all of it, hitting her hand on Smith's tuck until she cried out and dropped the knife.

"Not my truck," Smith whined under his breath. He put one of the swords down, and when Tommy grabbed Hafeez by the throat, he started to walk toward them with his sword up, ready to strike. Zheng put a hand out and stopped him.

"Tommy, that's enough!" Akrur called out, trying to put as much authority as he could in his voice. Tommy's ear twitched, but he didn't say anything. "The kids don't need to see a murder today! Not hers and not yours either!" he yelled, finally getting Tommy's attention. He looked at Akrur and growled, but at least the snarl on his snout seemed to soften. He walked towards the other hunters, ignoring Hafeez kicking at his legs.

"Let me make one thing very clear," Tommy growled, snarling in the hunter's face. "You keep Chrysta's name out of your mouth from now on. Or next time, I will let them give you your sword back so it's a fair fight when I wipe the floor with you."

Tommy suddenly let her go, and Hafeez fell to her knees and coughed. Director Zheng went to her, putting a hand on the younger hunter's shoulder. Hafeez knocked her hand away.

"Are you quite done?" Akrur asked Tommy, sounding stern as he put his hands on his hips. Tommy huffed in response.

"She started it!" Tommy yelled, gesturing at the hunter on the ground.

"Well, you are cleaning up the mess you made," Akrur ordered, and the changeling rolled his eyes and sighed, a great impression of a teenager as far as Akrur was concerned.

"Why?" Hafeez growled, glaring at the Director, voice rough with emotion. "Why are you protecting it? I thought you would want to destroy it as soon as you knew it was at the Academy, but you have shielded it instead. And you won't tell me *why*."

Zheng sighed and stood up. She folded her arms and stared at the younger hunter for several long minutes in silence. No one moved or breathed. Akrur's curiosity was killing him, but he tried not to stare at the Director while she studied everyone in the room, from Hafeez and the other hunters to the kids who were gingerly leaving the office.

"He saved my life," Zheng said quietly.

"What?" Hafeez asked. Tommy also looked at the Director in confusion.

"He saved my life, Nyla. And for that, I will protect him as long as I can," Zheng explained.

"When?" Tommy asked. "I think I would remember something like that."

Zheng sighed. She glanced at Ellis and Smith. Akrur wasn't sure, but she looked almost embarrassed. "Olinda," she softly said, and Akrur blinked in bewilderment.

Smith and Tommy also blinked, but they burst out laughing when they glanced at each other. They started leaning on each other for support, making a sight indeed. Tommy, still in his monster form, cuts all along his arms, leaning against the hunter, who was doubled over in his mirth.

Ellis stared at Director Zheng with a look that Akrur couldn't place. Pity? Disappointment? "Ma'am," they said. "No offense, but *how?*"

Akrur and Hafeez glanced at each other with identical looks of confusion as Zheng sighed again. "I'll tell you how," she said. "But this doesn't leave this factory." She pointed at Akrur. "Understood?"

31

March 1954

Tommy looked over the railing and grinned. The streets were clogged with masses of people singing, dancing, drinking, and living life to the fullest. Tomorrow they would have to slump into the churches, hungover and lethargic from their celebration, but that was a problem for their future selves. Right now, it was time for revelry, and Tommy wanted to join them.

"Savages," a voice said behind him, and Tommy wiped the smile from his face before he turned around.

George Penmark, leader of the acolytes, stood on the hotel balcony with a handkerchief over his mouth, looking at the people below with disdain. Tommy wanted to point out that Fat Thursday was a Catholic tradition, but he didn't think Penmark would care.

"If I didn't think that the hunters would be here any day now to search the church, I would have waited for a time when the city wasn't full of these... festivities," Penmark sneered, contempt dripping from the last word. He looked down his nose at Tommy. "Do you know the church's location?"

"Yes," Tommy replied flatly.

"Then get going," Penmark ordered and then turned to go inside.

Tommy blinked at the acolyte's back as the man returned to his food platter from room service. "With everyone out partying, wouldn't it be better if I broke into the church at night?"

"No!" Penmark called back. "I refuse to stay here longer than needed." The man primly grabbed a fork and started picking fruit off of his breakfast. "You find that artifact and return as soon as possible."

The slave band on Tommy's arm constricted, and he nodded grimly. Penmark wiped his mouth with a napkin and gestured with it. "Well? What are you waiting for, you stupid creature? Get to it."

The band started burning then, and Tommy sighed and turned to head out. Once he closed the door to the hotel suite, he felt a hand on his shoulder and jumped. Guerra gave him a wide smile. "Is our leader being unreasonable?"

Tommy gave the enforcer a smile despite himself. "That's one way to put it," he grumbled. "He wants me to break into the church as soon as possible and not wait for nightfall."

Guerra gestured down the hallway, and they started walking together to the elevator. Tommy didn't know how the Acolytes had taken over a whole hotel floor during Mardi Gras, but Tommy was grateful for the privacy. "Well, it will take you most of the day to get there on foot with these crowds anyway, so it will probably be dark by the time you get there," Guerra said as he called the elevator to their floor. "As always, stealth and speed are what we need, and that is why you are the one we rely on, Mr. Monroe."

Tommy fought the urge to roll his eyes as the door to the elevator opened, and the attendant gave them a large smile. "Go ahead, Guerra, pull the other leg. I need a laugh."

Tommy got on the elevator with a scowl, putting his hands in the bomber jacket he wore, but he looked at Guerra in surprise when the enforcer held out his hand. Tommy took it slowly, not entirely trusting the man. "May the Lady give you luck," Guerra said with that creepy grin still plastered on his face. The enforcer leaned back, letting the attendant finally close the door. Tommy looked down at his hand and was surprised to see money pressed into his palm.

"Well, now I have a reason to party," he muttered. He wasn't sure how much money it was, but hopefully, it was enough to enjoy the "festivities" in the city.

Tommy tried to melt into the crowds once he made it to the lobby and pushed his way outside. He felt his skin crawling, Penmark probably watching him like a hawk. Tommy felt better once he was out of sight of the hotel. He was studying the bills in his hand, unsure how much Guerra gave him or what he could buy with them when a stall caught his eye.

A young boy was selling masks, cheap papier mache ones. They mainly were caricatures of human faces with exaggerated smiles and frowns, but the boy had made some to look like animals. Among the monkeys and gators and parrots, Tommy spotted a weird one. From the feline shape and spots, he assumed that it was supposed to be a snarling jaguar and not a leopard, but instead of being a bright yellow, someone had painted it grey with black spots. Nevertheless, it seemed too good to pass up, so he picked it out and gave the boy a crisp bill. From the way the boy's face lit up, Tommy probably gave him more money than he was asking for, but Tommy didn't mind.

He slipped the mask on and pushed his way back into the crowd.

. . . . .

Burke leaned on a car with his familiar sitting next to him, watching his partner argue with a man across the lot. She knew more Portuguese than Burke, so she had insisted on trying to barter with the man renting out cars so they could try to drive to the church instead of walking through the crowds with swords on their hips. Lady whined at Burke's side, and he reached out to scratch her ears. "Yes, I know," he murmured so only the wolfhound could hear him. "She's upset."

Unfortunately, Burke was starting to think he was the reason she was so upset and not the overweight man in front of her.

Ever since they were in school together, Zheng seemed to hate him. He still remembered the hot embarrassment he felt when she would throw him around like a ragdoll as they sparred, other students laughing at such a small woman kicking the ass of such a large man. He tried to tell himself that it was just practice, that she wasn't going easy on him because she wanted him to get better, and that she treated others the same way. But when she would offer her hand to help him up, the grim smile on her face told him differently. She despised him and was not afraid to show it.

He racked his brain for a reason Zheng would dislike him but never came up with a good cause. Since he had started to glow white when he was thirteen, people tripped over themselves to get in his good graces. But, of course, he had learned at a young age that people didn't do that because they liked him as a person but for what they thought he could do for them as a sorcerer. But Zheng was different, showing open hate for him, not scared to cross a man who glowed white while she glowed only purple.

But, for all her animosity, something just clicked when they worked together. In every training exercise that they had together, they exceeded all expectations. They completed the objective quickly, fought swiftly and without remorse, and could improvise with anything their instructors threw at them. During their last year in school, Burke sometimes bested Zheng in sparring, although he was left with a bruised ego more often than not.

When it came time for their scores, it was not surprising that Zheng was given the first-class title while Burke only had second-class. She had worked hard and deserved her status. What did surprise him was their superiors insisting they become partners.

"It just makes sense," the Director told Burke when he complained. "You two work so well together."

Burke shifted from foot to foot. "No offense, sir, but I feel that Hunter Zheng would rather work by herself."

"Did she tell you this herself?"

Burke shifted again. "Yes," he lied.

"Well, technically, as a first-class hunter, she could work independently. But even first-class hunters have to listen to orders. And Zheng has been ordered to have a partner. You! The hunter that glows white! Most hunters would be thrilled to have you at their side." And the Director clapped Burke on the shoulder, making him grimace.

If Zheng was upset by their forced proximity, she never told Burke. She was, in fact, utterly professional in all of their dealings in the last five years. Of course, they had done some grunt work at the beginning of their careers, but they had quickly gained a reputation for working well as a team. For example, they had stopped several changelings attacks and tracked one of them in the Canadian wilderness. Zheng had even followed some acolytes through Europe and prevented them from sacrificing a poor girl. There were rumors Burke would be the next Director, although he planned to decline the position if they asked him to take it. Zheng deserved it more than he did.

She had a horrible sweet tooth, taking spoonfuls of sugar in her tea while he went with just milk. No matter the mission, she would find a sweets shop in whatever city they were in and indulge in the local desserts. She rotated between several perfumes, sweet fruits in the spring and summer months and musk and vanilla in the fall and winter. She wore the latest fashions out of uniform, always cool and collected when journalists cornered them with cameras.

But as other hunters grew close to their partners and became friends and family, Zheng kept Burke at a distance. It was so frustrating to learn so much about her and know absolutely nothing at the same time. He knew nothing about her family, if she was an only child. He did not know why she was a hunter, although her fighting ability spoke to years of training. She often had cuts and burns on her hands, and he didn't know what caused them. Cooking? Potion making? Why did she have a love for fashion? Did she want children one day? Did she have a spouse waiting for her when she went out on missions?

Burke winced and shifted on the car. Well, he already divined the answer to that particular question. Zheng was a beautiful woman, and depending on where in the world they were, her exotic appeal lured men in. She would openly flirt with them, accepting meals or drinks with a dazzling smile. And then she would take them back to her bedroom at whatever hotel they were staying in or go willingly into theirs. And he wouldn't see her until hours later, hair and makeup a mess, or maybe it would be her gentlemen callers he would catch in the hallways, looking dazed and drunk on love.

He told himself in the beginning that it was none of his business who she consorted with. It was not his concern whether she was in a relationship with them or even if it was one night of passion. But as the years went by, he noticed that his sense of unease grew with each encounter he witnessed. A knife would twist in his heart as he imagined what happened behind closed doors. It was getting harder to tell himself to leave well enough alone.

Maybe you love her.

And really, that was the rub, wasn't it? Maybe he cared about the random men she invited into her bed because he was not one of them. Perhaps if he found out why she hated him so, he could overcome the invisible barrier she had put up and, finally, learn more about her. But what would that do to their partnership, their careers, her chance at being Director, or even his own betrothal?

His musings were interrupted when Zheng finally stomped in his direction, keys in her hand. The lot owner stayed where he was, scowling at her retreating back. "Asshole," she spat as she threw the keys at Burke's head, his quick reflexes the only thing that kept the keys from doing permanent damage.

"Did you at least get a discount?" Burke asked sarcastically, and she shot him a glare. She held the door open for Lady to jump in the back seat and climbed into the passenger seat as he put their luggage in the car's trunk, swords hidden for now. Zheng was pouting when he settled in the driver's seat, wincing as his knees hit the steering wheel.

"He was trying to charge us double because he said he would have to clean the car after a dog was in it. Like every car in the lot didn't smell of wet pig. I told him that Lady was cleaner than most of his family probably," she said darkly with her arms folded, and Lady huffed like the familiar was insulted.

"Well, thank you for procuring the car," Burke said. Zheng didn't respond and just looked out the window. Lady whined again from the back seat. Burke sighed.

It was going to be a long mission.

.....

The streets were so congested with people that Burke found his patience quickly eradicated. The map from the lot owner was outdated by a few years if Burke had to hazard a guess. People did not want to move for them. He had to double back several times because of parade routes. Olinda was laid out like many European cities, with cobblestone roads barely wide enough for their small car to squeeze through, even before adding the mass of people. Zheng did not say a word or offer any help the whole time, staring out of the window.

By the time they got to the church, the sun was setting, Burke had a headache from the stress, and he put the car in park with a growl. The church was under renovation, and scaffolding was set up outside. The neighborhood was mostly deserted because of the holiday; most residents were attending the parties and parades several blocks over. In the distance, you could see the ocean, sea salt heavy in the air.

"What is the plan?" he asked Zheng, studying the church and not looking at her.

"Leave the swords in the trunk, go into the church, find the artifact, see if it is what people think it is, and then take it if it is."

"So we steal it," Burke murmured.

Zheng shrugged. "Can't let it fall into the wrong hands. We will wait for nightfall. Don't want people suspicious of a Chinese woman and a white man wandering around."

The inside of the car fell into an uncomfortable silence. Burke glanced at his partner, but she was staring at the church with a scowl. It was the first time they had been alone for weeks. He cleared his throat. If he was going to talk to her, now was the time. "Zheng," he started to say, "I'm sor—"

"Not now," she snapped back.

"I'm trying to apologize for that night, Zheng." He waited for a response, but she refused to look at him. "Jiao..."

"Don't," she snapped again.

"Jiao, please."

"I'm going to ask for a new partner as soon as this mission is over."

He blinked at her in shock. "Why?"

"Because our relationship is no longer professional," she explained. She finally looked at him, and Burke could see the contempt in her eyes. "You crossed a line, Neil, and I don't want your feelings to jeopardize my career."

Burke felt panic settle in his stomach. "I'm sorry, Jiao. I don't want another partner." She scoffed and turned her scowl at the church again.

"Do you even remember what happened that night?" she asked. "Do you know what you are apologizing for?"

"Yes."

"Do you?" she asked again, her tone as brittle as ice.

He opened his mouth to argue but closed it with a snap. In truth, he had lost part of that evening, which seemed to be the part that upset her. "I... no, I don't remember," he admitted.

"You showed up at my apartment absolutely drunk," she explained. "How did you even know where I live?"

Burke winced. He had never been good at making personal connections and never could get a handle on any relationship that required more than a shallow contact. So he had been surprised when some of the other hunters had asked him to go out drinking. He had been even more stunned when he agreed. He had not drunk alcohol to that degree before and found himself stumbling to Zheng's apartment hours later.

"I found out where you lived, so I would know if there ever was an emergency," he said.

"Your first overstep," she growled. "The second was trying to kiss me."

Burke's stomach dropped. "I don't remember that."

"When I pushed you away, you complained that you should be marrying me, that we were good together," she continued, rubbing her eyes. "You then threw up on yourself and passed out."

"So that is why I woke up naked on your couch," Burke replied sarcastically.

"Your third overstep," she growled. She sighed. "Don't you have a fiancée, Neil? Shouldn't she be the one you go crying to when you have a bad day?"

The car fell into silence again. "I think she had been with another man," Burke said softly.

"Excuse me?"

"I think she is in a relationship with another man," he said again, a little louder.

"You can't believe everything you see in the *Rising Phoenix*," she told him.

"It isn't just the gossip in the *Rising Phoenix*." He sighed, upset that journalists had plastered his private business all over the sorcerer newspaper. "And I can't blame her. We were betrothed when we were 16, but our marriage was postponed when I decided to become a hunter."

"Eleven years is a long time to wait for someone," Jiao said, her voice losing some of its icy tone.

"I have," he responded.

"You have what?"

"Waited for her," he explained.

She looked at him in shock. "You haven't been with anyone? That entire time?"

"Not even her," he said. "She said she wanted to wait for marriage." He snorted. "That must have been a lie," he said bitterly.

"Do you love her?"

He paused at Jiao's question. "No," he admitted. And just like that, it felt like a weight had been lifted from his chest. "No, I do not. But it still hurt, thinking that she had been with someone else," he confessed.

"Then break your engagement," Jiao said, not unkindly. "You have cause to."

Burke looked out the window and scowled at the church as he weighed his options. Jiao was right, of course. Better to break off their commitment, let her be with someone else. It would upset his father and probably become fodder for the tabloid section of the Rising Phoenix for several weeks, or maybe even months. But it would be a clean break—no more drama.

Burke looked at Jiao, studying her. He stared for so long that she looked back at him and frowned. "What?" she growled.

"Why do you hate me?" he asked. If they were going to be candid, then he might as well go for broke.

Jiao blinked at him. "I don't hate you."

"Yes, you do."

"I don't..." She stopped and blew some air out of her nose. "I don't hate you," she continued in a softer tone. "I hate that you have had everything handed to you. You never had to work for anything you have ever received."

He opened his mouth to argue but snapped it shut again. She was right. He scowled at the church instead. "You're right. Everyone keeps falling over themselves to get in my good graces because I glow white. Except you."

Jiao snorted. "The best I can ever hope for is this Deputy Director position. Meanwhile, they will give you the Director position without a second thought."

"I'll decline it," he acknowledged quickly, and he felt her eyes on him, probably trying to see if he was serious.

"Bullshit."

"I will. I don't want it. Never did."

"Then why did you become a hunter if you didn't want to become the Director?" she asked.

Burke didn't answer for a few moments as the sun finally sunk below the horizon. The car darkened, and it was silent for an excruciating amount of time. "Your brother," she whispered.

"Yes," he replied, suddenly hating their frank conversation.

They waited for a few more minutes. Nearby, a couple walked down the road, laughing and talking as they made their way toward the parade route. Once they were gone from sight, Zheng broke the silence, making Burke jump. "Come on," she said. "Let's go."

32

They left the car, not bothering to lock it. "Swords?" Burke asked Zheng, and she shook her head.

"I don't want to risk scaring some poor priest," she replied. "But be ready to teleport them."

They quickly crossed the street, keeping an eye out for any late revelers. Burke felt naked; at least with the uniforms, they had protection spells sewn into the fabric to keep them safe. But like the swords, being in uniform would bring too much attention to them, more than their nationalities and the familiar did. He reached into the pocket of his jeans and fingered the beacon charm, their only means to summon help if needed. They climbed the stairs to the church, and Zheng reached for the door but paused. She pulled the handle up, slowly revealing a broken lock. They shared a look. *Someone had beaten them to the church.* She quietly pulled the door open, only to the point that they could squeeze through. Zheng went in first, Burke and Lady following closely.

The church was dark inside, and as Burke closed the door, the sound of banging reached them. *Thang! Thang! Thang!* It was loud and rhythmic, too steady to be accidental. They slowly made their way to the altar, studying each shadow as they walked past them.

The altar was covered in tarps and masonry, under construction, just like the outside of the church. That is what had brought them to Olinda. Several weeks ago, in the middle of Mass, a priest had been in the midst of his sermon to the faithful when the stones beneath him opened up. The priest was alright, although he had had a massive scare and was sent to the hospital. The congregation, meanwhile, examined the new hole in the floor to find, much to their shock, an unknown crypt. The church was closed for the safety of the parishioners, and the local museum called to explore this discovery.

The crypt was dated back to the 17th century, probably when the church itself was built. The skeletons inside were dressed in their finest robes, holding crosses in bony hands crossed on rotted breasts. Also present was gold from native cultures in the area, stolen from their owners and hidden in the tomb. So naturally, the museum seized the sight for study, much to the ire of the Church. Unfortunately, no Ash Wednesday would be celebrated at this church this year.

The story was intriguing, only reported internationally for its shock value and humor. But what caught the attention of sorcerers was a single photo of a statue. If you knew what to look for, it was easy to see the figure for what it was: a woman with a man-sized bat above her, its wings stretched wide. The Golden One and her changeling general. Also present was the strange writing of the Golden One; her "language of the Angels," she had called it, was still untranslatable even after centuries of study. Artifacts of the Golden One were rare but could be dangerous with enchantments on them. So it needed to be found and isolated right away.

And if the hunters had noticed it, then the Acolytes probably had as well.

As they approached the altar, Lady let out a whine. Burke examined her. Her tail was not tucked between her legs, but it was down. Her hackles were up. She was staring at the hole in the altar, nose twitching at some scent in the air. He leaned down to whisper in Zheng's ear. "She smells something," he murmured when the *thang* rang out so that his voice was masked by the sudden noise. "Swords?" he asked at the next *thang*.

Zheng shook her head. "Wait," she whispered back as the next *thang* rang in the air.

They reached the hole, and Burke craned his neck, trying to see if anyone was waiting at the bottom of the ladder. The pounding was at its loudest, but now Burke could hear muffled grunting and cursing, confirming that the pounding was not accidental but someone trying to break something. Zheng put her foot on the top rung of the ladder and started down, Burke trying to not hold his breath as she descended. He motioned to Lady to order her to wait and followed Zheng when she was at the bottom.

The space was lit with harsh electric lights that chased away all the shadows and revealed the strange scene in front of them. At the other end of the tomb, a man had a crowbar and was hitting a stone column that the statue was embedded in, maybe a tactic by the tomb's occupants to keep their earthly possession with them in death. It was hard to say how long he had been working on it, but the remaining stone had the circumstance of a broom handle and looked ready to go at any moment. The man had stripped down to just his pants, and his dark skin glistened with sweat.

Burke glanced at Zheng with a raised eyebrow. Was the stranger an acolyte or a local unmagical person trying to rob the crypt on a day he knew no one would notice? "Swords?" he mouthed to the other hunter, and she shook her head once again. Defeated, he sighed and took a deep breath, summoning all the authority he could to his voice.

"What do you think you're doing?"

The man jumped and whirled around, panting slightly but not as out of breath as Burke expected him to be. He studied the hunters for a few silent moments, eyes darting between the two of them. Zheng had leaned into Burke, trying to make herself look small and scared. "Who are you?" he demanded roughly in accented English.

"We are from the museum!" Zheng lied. "And that is a priceless artifact you are trying to steal! Leave now, or we will have to call the police!"

If the man was a local or a graverobber, the threat of the law should have shaken his resolve and sent him running. But he just grinned and wiped the sweat off of his bald head. "Call the police. See what happens."

Burke felt a cold finger of fear go up his spine, even in this warm, cramped space. The man was behaving suspiciously. Burke put his hand out to shield Zheng, genuinely feeling threatened by the man's demeanor.

"We're serious!" Zheng continued shrilly. Burke hoped she was still acting and the fear in her voice manufactured.

"I will take a break. And break your neck. Then it will be quiet again." The smile on the man's face grew until all of his teeth were displayed in an obscene grimace.

The finger of fear had changed into a cold fist around his heart, and Burke was about to put his hand up to blast the man away, ready to turn and hurry Zheng out of the tomb, when Lady started barking shrilly from the hole behind them. He knew that bark. She had been trained to use that bark when—

The man's nostrils flared like he took a deep breath, catching a scent in the air. "Hunters!" he hissed, and suddenly he wasn't a man anymore. His form shifted and grew until his head scraped the ceiling. His skin turned to scales, the rough skin of a lizard. He hissed again, this time the hiss of a large cold-blooded predator. A tail lashed behind him, hitting one side of the cramped space and then the other.

—when a changeling was nearby.

The changeling rushed at them, thick, disgusting drool dripping off sharp teeth as it opened its mouth to an unnatural degree.

Burke didn't think; he just went into action. He reached out with his mind and grabbed the swords in the car's trunk. He flexed the magic and pulled the swords to them, leaving the sheaths behind. He dropped his hands, summoning his weapon back into existence so that it was pointed up and with his right palm on the hilt. He manifested Zheng's sword behind him and to his left, knowing that is where she would prefer to seize it.

The changeling was right in front of Burke, hands reaching out with curved black talons when Burke surged forward and drove the sword into its shoulder, using the changeling's momentum against it before it registered that the sword was even there. He braced his arms to keep the blade steady as the changeling hissed in pain. Zheng stepped up from Burke's left and lunged at the changeling's thigh. Its skin deflected the blow, so she didn't embed the blade in its leg like Burke knew she wanted, but the blade did leave a deep gash that immediately started bleeding.

Usually, Burke would pull the sword upwards to release it from the changeling's body, do as much damage as possible, and give Zheng time to set up another strike. But in slow motion, he saw the changeling reach out for his head, and he had to duck to prevent the creature from gouging his eyes out. He held onto his weapon, pulling it down and out of the changeling's shoulder, not doing any more damage.

Zheng swiped her sword over Burke's head, trying to get the force behind it so it would cut into the changeling's arm, but it just bounced off again, leaving a shallow wound. Zheng cursed in Mandarin. They had been taught that a lizard changeling's skin could be thick in school, but this was the first time either of them had seen it in person. Burke thought to himself, *we have to stab it*, but before he could reset his hands to thrust the sword again, the changeling finally got a hold of his shirt and tossed him deeper into the tomb.

He crashed into the stone column that held the golden statue and continued into the wall when that broke. He shook his head and picked up the artifact, and looked at it dumbly for a second. Zheng was still trying to swipe at the changeling, little droplets of blood on the tomb floor telling Burke that she was doing damage, but she wasn't doing enough to slow it down. Finally, it hissed and was able to grab her, picking her up by the throat.

Burke felt his blood run cold, and he flexed, trying to transport the statue out of the tomb and into their car. He felt resistance and realized there was an enchantment on the figure that stopped him from teleporting it. Burke could try to run past the changeling, completing the mission and keeping the statue out of the changeling's possession, but he heard Zheng choke, and the figure quickly dropped out of his hands. He was not leaving her behind.

He rushed at them, setting his weapon up so that he would run the changeling through the abdomen, hopefully near the spine and not into Zheng. The changeling, either sensing the attack or just a lucky bastard, moved at the last second so that the sword impaled him in the side, away from all major organs. The changeling yelled in pain, though, and swung Zheng so that she flew in the small space. She landed on one of the shelves with a skeleton on it. She gasped and choked on the dust, but she was alive.

The changeling turned on him, and before Burke could react, he found himself with a hand around his throat, and the changeling rushed him into the back of the tomb, slamming him against the wall. The changeling wound up for a punch, but Burke jerked his head out of the way, and it became a glancing blow off of his temple.

The lizard changeling opened his mouth, impossibly wide, Burke wondering if the changeling would crush his head like a melon as rancid breath washed over him. There was the sound of furious barking, and a grey ball of fur landed on the changeling's back, Lady trying to tear into the thick neck of the changeling. It hissed and let go of Burke, trying to scratch at the familiar on its back.

Burek gasped for breath and rubbed at his throat. "Burke!" Zheng cried, and he saw her standing at the ladder with her hands outstretched. He grabbed the statue and threw it as hard as he could.

Zheng caught it and started towards the ladder. The changeling looked over its shoulder and saw her retreat, and he hissed. He finally got a hold of Lady and threw her into another shelf, pulverizing a second poor skeleton and making the dog yelp. The changeling turned and started towards Zheng, who was barely halfway up the ladder.

Burke had an idea. *"Light!"* he roared, hoping both Zheng and Lady caught his meaning. He focused on making a ball of light in front of the changeling as bright as possible. The ball formed, white and blinding, about the size of a baseball. Zheng had covered her eyes with her arm, and Lady had buried her head between her paws. But even with the changeling blocking his view, Burke lost his vision as the ball flashed brighter for a second.

The changeling roared, but Burke couldn't wait for his eyesight to return. He could see black and grey shapes moving as he ran towards the ladder, trying to dodge the changeling's swinging arms. "Down!" Zheng called out, and he ducked, using his momentum to slide across the floor, praying that he was still heading the right way.

He must have hit the ladder when he crashed into the wall because he heard it clatter next to him. Zheng cursed above him, so he stood up and grabbed her legs, boosting her out of the hole. Suddenly, he felt a presence next to him, and he reached out and felt Lady by his side. He put his arm around Lady, tried to remember the church's layout, and then teleported them out of the hole.

He had meant to get them to the middle of the church, but as Burke blinked and took in their surroundings, he realized he had deposited them at the front door, about a hundred meters from Zheng, running from the hole. "Zheng! Sword!" he bellowed, reaching out with magic and grabbing their weapons. His sword popped in front of him and landed in his right hand, and he held it at the ready. Zheng held her hand out, and he angled her sword in front of her, prepared for her to grab it.

It was now dark in the church, so the electric lights in the crypt cast a glow that Burke could see, although it was still extremely blurry. He could see something hoist itself out of the hole, a massive black shape backlit with the lights. It rushed at Zheng at an alarming rate.

"Zheng!" he cried out, but just as she wrapped her fingers around the hilt of her sword, the shape barreled into her. Sword and statue went flying as she fell, and before she could roll over, the changeling stopped and stomped on her leg. Zheng cried out in pain, and Burke could hear the changeling laugh, a low, dark, evil sound.

Protocol told Burke that he should grab the artifact and run, but he wouldn't leave Zheng behind. He ran past the statue and put his foot on Zheng's sword to kick it toward her. He rushed the changeling, aiming at its chest. It saw him coming and grinned, deflecting the blade easily. But, it was concentrating so much on him that it didn't see Zheng seize her sword and roll over to attack him. She thrust her sword into its thigh, finally piercing the changeling's thick hide. It hissed in pain.

Not enough, Burke thought to himself. They hadn't damaged it enough. It was still too strong, too fast, still able to fight. Burke wound up to swipe at the changeling, hoping to take off its head in one blow. The changeling caught the blade, and although blood flowed from its palm, Burke couldn't remove his weapon from its grip. It grinned at him and snatched the sword out of his grip. *Not enough.*

Zheng used the distraction to crawl backward, and she started to tug on her sword, trying to do more damage as she removed it. The changeling hissed and looked down, grabbing her sword by the blade. He threw both weapons over his shoulder with a grin and then backhanded Burke, so he went flying.

Burke landed on his back, the breath knocked out of him. As he writhed on the ground, fighting to breathe, the changeling stepped over Zheng's body to get to him. The changeling chuckled darkly as it picked Burke up, ripping his shirt to shreds with its talons. Burke hissed in pain as he felt the claws raking into his skin.

"You fight good," the lizard changeling rumbled. "I make your death quick, yes?"

"You're so kind," Burke gritted out between his teeth.

There was a howl, and Lady crashed into the changeling, biting and clawing frantically. It roared and dropped Burke, grabbing Lady and throwing all 180 pounds of her across the church. She hit one of the pillars and yelped, landing in a heap on the floor.

A purple glow developed above the changeling, and by the time it looked up, several sharp icicles had formed, and they dropped. The changeling tried to dodge into the pews, but they embedded into its chest and shoulders. It roared a guttural sound mixed with hissing, trying to knock the icicles away. *"You!"* it hissed as it turned towards Zheng. "You die slow!"

Surprisingly, instead of going back to hurt Zheng, the changeling reached down and scooped Burke up. Before the hunter could react, call his sword, or form his own icicles to fight, the changeling threw him. He flew through the air and came down in the pews, breaking several before coming to a stop. He tried to move, to get up, but got dizzy and collapsed on the floor.

He could see the statue, but the changeling's feet came into view, and Burke saw it pick up the artifact. The changeling's disappeared from his field of view, and then Zheng was screaming. "Burke!" she cried, fear and panic clear in her voice. "Neil!" But he couldn't move, couldn't help her, as he heard a smacking noise, and her voice was cut off. The changeling was leaving. Burke was not sure if it was taking Zheng with it or if she was already dead. His vision started to darken despite his best efforts to stay awake, and he finally fainted.

.....

Tommy had slowly made his way to the church, the band on his arm slowly getting hotter, but he didn't care. The dancing, the laughing, the drinking, the *music*. This was the best celebration he had ever been a part of, and he planned on enjoying every minute of it. Penmark could choke for all Tommy cared.

When he finally got to the church, it was dark, and he just meandered down the street, taking his time. He had a bottle of cachaça in one hand, taking pulls from it ever so often, lifting his mask up just enough to uncover his mouth. He was drunk, and Penmark would probably say something about it later but screw him. Fuck him, and fuck all the acolytes. He took a sip of the liquor. Well, Guerra was alright for giving him money to get the booze. Creepy and a psychopath, sure, but an okay guy.

There was a roar, and even in his drunken haze, Tommy realized something was off about it. It was loud, and he couldn't figure out what kind of animal made it. He paused by a car, debating what to do, when the church door was kicked from the inside with such force that Tommy was surprised it didn't fly off.

Tommy dove behind the car, almost losing his bottle. A reptile changeling stalked out of the building with a woman over its shoulder and something gold in its hand. Tommy felt a weird combination of emotions at the sight of his kind here. A little fear mixed with annoyance. Tommy squinted as the changeling turned and started down the road. Was that the statue Penmark wanted? Tommy couldn't see it, but he doubted it could be anything else. And who was that woman?

Tommy waited for the changeling to charge down the street, heading for the ocean, and he cautiously approached the church. Inside was dark, but he could see the carnage. The smell of blood was thick as Tommy inspected the broken pews, the smell of magic just as heavy. He heard growling to his right and saw an Irish Wolfhound guarding a man who was a crumbled mess lying in the destroyed pews. The dog was holding her paw up, blood flowing from a wound on her shoulder. Tommy crouched and held his hand out. "Easy now," he told the growling dog. "I'm not here to hurt you."

The man groaned and opened his eyes. He was bleeding from a dozen cuts on his body, the worst one on his head, with enough blood pouring out of his scalp to obscure his features. "Jiao," he murmured thickly, trying to pry his eyes open. "It has Jiao."

"Easy, dude," Tommy told him. The dog (probably a familiar if the man was a hunter like Tommy assumed he was) continued her growling. "What are you doing here fighting a changeling?"

The man just moaned and lost consciousness again. Tommy weighed his options and then cursed under his breath. Looked like if he wanted the statue, he was going to have to go get it from an enraged changeling. And maybe deal with an angry hunter if that woman was this man's partner.

Tommy sighed, stood up, and almost fell over. Oh wow, this booze packed a punch. He took off his jacket and mask and transformed, making the familiar snarl and snap her jaws. She didn't rush at him but stayed where she was, protecting her master.

"Don't worry," he rumbled. "I don't want you two." He took a deep breath to catch the other changeling's scent, fishy and rotten, and then ran out of the church, still clutching the bottle. He ran towards the ocean, wondering what he would find.

33

Jiao slowly woke up, bouncing around on something that felt like a living rock. Cold and rough and as hard as a stone. She tried to lift her pounding head to see what was going on and to figure out why it appeared she was two meters off the ground when she was thrown. She was flying through the air when everything came back to her. And then she slammed into the water.

She gasped, losing precious breath, and pushed to the surface, causing her leg to scream in pain. She looked around and saw that they were in a dark, isolated cove, the moon just a splinter of light in the sky. Nevertheless, it was enough moonlight to see the changeling grinning from the shore. It chuckled and started to walk towards her, tail swishing lazily behind it in the water.

Up to her waist in saltwater, Jiao gingerly tried to put her feet down and winced. The leg that the changeling had stomped on felt like it was broken. And if she couldn't place both feet on the sandy ground, she wouldn't be able to support herself to fight. She had to use magic to finish this thing off if she was going to have a chance at survival. She smiled grimly at the changeling, and it actually paused with a look of surprise on its reptile face. Now that they were alone, it thought it had her trapped and helpless.

But without Lady and Burke around, she could really let loose.

She swung her arm, and a solid wall of water formed and slammed into the changeling from the side. It sputtered, and she formed icicles above its head again.

It saw the glow, so it jumped back, looking smug, but Jiao reached out and grabbed a small boulder from the shore and pulled it towards her, aiming for the changeling's head. When the large stone connected with its skull, she pushed with her other hand, sending another solid wall of water to hit it in the face.

The changeling swayed for a bit after the water retreated, looking dazed. Jiao formed lightning in her hands, filling the air with a copper smell. She put her hands in the water, focusing on the magic so it didn't hit her.

The changeling bellowed as the lightning hit it, every muscle in its body seizing up. Its eyes rolled into the back of its head, and Jiao stopped, watching with a smile as the changeling's body went slack and it started to slide into the water. Jiao relaxed because she believed that it was either dead or knocked out, and she could run for safety.

Jiao saw the changeling's eyes roll forward, but before she could form electricity or icicles or even a fireball to protect herself, it rushed through the water at her, knocking her off her feet when it crashed into her.

Jiao tried not to panic, holding her breath as she fought her way to the surface. The changeling kept swimming past her, letting its tail wrap around her torso. She struggled to get free, but it turned to the shore, lazily dragging her with it. She gasped when her head broke the surface.

"How would you like to die?" it asked as it walked towards the shore, pulling a sputtering Jiao behind him. "Water? Or tear your throat out?"

"Cào ni mā!" she spat.

It was knee-deep in the water when it growled and snatched her up. It brought her face up to its face, rotten breath making her gag as it hissed. "You drown now," it rumbled, and it dunked her into the water and held her down.

Jiao kicked, trying to fight even as she strained to hold her breath as long as possible. She felt one of her shoes go flying. Her lungs started to burn, but Jiao still fought, tearing at the hands holding her torso under the water. The changeling lifted her up, and she gulped air, only to swallow some water when the changeling submerged her under again. It was toying with her.

Her hands started to glow in her panic, trying to force the changeling's hand off of her, but it didn't work. She began to fight less and less, trying to stay calm. It was no use. The changeling had her, and it wasn't letting go. Unless someone found them, she was going to die in this cove, all alone.

Jiao's vision began to fade, and the burning in her lungs was starting to disappear. Jiao could feel her heart slowing down, and she wondered if the changeling could feel it too, if it got some perverse pleasure from feeling her pass away. Finally, the last of the air in her lungs bubbled out of her mouth, and she felt a wave of peace wash over her.

I'm sorry, Neil.

Suddenly, the hands holding her down disappeared, and Jiao felt herself float. Was the changeling playing with her, letting her have some hope before killing her?

She knew it was only a few feet of water, and she should kick up and get some air before she passed out, but she couldn't do it. Her limbs felt too heavy.

Something grabbed her again, but she was lifted out of the water instead of being held under it. She was carried to the sandy shore, turned over like a lifeless doll, her vision still fading. Something struck her back, making Jiao jump and then cough. The coughing turned violent, and she was vomiting up saltwater, eyes, nose, throat, and lungs burning as her body rejected the water. She took several breaths of cool air when she could, gulping it greedily.

"Easy now," a voice rumbled above her. Whoever it was turned her over, and she blinked, expecting another hunter. But she weakly gasped when she saw it was a strange feline face looking down at her.

"You alright?" it asked. Jiao gawked at the changeling, wondering why it was helping her. She dumbly looked around and spotted the reptile changeling about a dozen meters away, sputtering as blood ran down its face. "Yeah, he's not happy that I hit him with a bottle of booze," the feline changeling said as he followed Jiao's gaze. "I'm not happy either. I wasn't finished with it."

"Why?" she hoarsely asked. It looked back at her. "Why are you... saving me?"

"Don't get sappy. I'm here for that thing," it explained, pointing at the golden statue that the reptile changeling had left on the shore.

"Mongrel!" the reptile changeling bellowed. "Traitor! You die for that!"

"I don't suppose you would let us go without a fight, would you?" the feline changeling asked wearily. The reptile changeling hissed in response. "Guess not."

The feline changeling put Jiao gently down in the sand before he started to approach the other changeling. The changelings began to close in on each other, hissing and growling. The lizard changeling realized that the feline was between it and the statue. It paused, mouth open, claws at the ready, when it suddenly rushed for the figure. The feline changeling caught it, and they started to fight in the shallows, ripping and tearing at each other. The water started turning red from their blood.

Jiao watched in horrified fascination for a few moments. The lizard changeling started to drag the other one into deeper water, maybe hoping to drown it. The feline changeling fought back, kicking with bare feet to try to rip into the lizard's stomach. The lizard didn't react, taking the opportunity to lift the feline in the air and then submerge it in the water. However, the lizard suddenly bellowed and tried to retreat, but Jiao saw the feline changeling had sunk its teeth into the lizard's arm, not letting go.

Jiao glanced at the statue and then back at the two fighting changelings. Should she grab it and run? She gingerly got up and limped to the golden artifact, scooping it up from the sand but not running just yet. She started to back away from the water, not able to tear her eyes away from the fight.

The feline changeling still had the lizard's arm in its mouth, so the lizard tried to wind up for a punch. The feline caught the fist and held onto it, not letting the lizard have it back. The feline reached out with its other hand, trying to wrap it around the lizard's throat, blood flowing from the wounds its talons made.

They stayed like that, locked in a tie when the lizard changeling jerked its fist free and then slammed it into the feline's temple. It staggered, letting go of the lizard's other arm. The lizard laced its fingers together and then hit the feline changeling in the jaw, making its jaw close so hard that Jiao heard the crack of its teeth from a dozen meters away.

The lizard changeling glanced in Jiao's direction and then did a double-take, finally noticing that she held the statue. It hissed and rushed at her, abandoning the fight. Jiao put her hand up, getting ready to summon more icicles, when the feline changeling tackled the lizard from behind. They wrestled in the water, the waves they created blocking Jiao's view. She hesitated. If she sent icicles into the water, Jiao risked hitting the feline changeling. She blinked. It felt wrong to worry about a changeling's safety.

Finally, the two monsters stood up from the water. The feline changeling held the back of the lizard's head in its jaws and held its arms behind it. The lizard changeling tried to jerk away, but the feline clung on, a low growling sound coming from its chest. Both of their tails lashed behind them, the only thing the lizard could move.

"Wait! W-wait!" the lizard changeling cried. "You can't! You can't protect a human! *Please!*"

The feline changeling didn't say anything. It just started to work its jaws back and forth. The lizard hissed in pain, trying to jerk free, but suddenly there was a horrible crunching noise, and the lizard froze. Its eyes rolled up into its skull, and the body went limp, but Jiao knew it wouldn't get up this time. The feline changeling waited, blood flowing from its mouth until, it was sure that the lizard was dead. Then, it dropped the body into the water and spat out the blood.

It started walking towards the beach, and Jiao tried to run but cried out as her legs gave out from under her. She could try to teleport, but that would mean leaving the statue behind. As the feline changeling walked up to her, it casually crouched down in front of her. It was panting and bleeding from dozens of wounds, but it didn't say a word as it held out its hand. She expected it to snatch the statue, but it stayed still, only looking away to spit out more blood. She held the golden statue to her chest.

"Now, don't be like that," he rumbled, holding his hand out patiently. Jiao looked at the claw-tipped hand and back to his face several times, studying him. What would he do if she refused to give it to him? She didn't really want to find out. She slowly held the statue out, and the changeling took it gently. "Thank you," he said.

Jiao expected him to leave then, leaving her all alone, but she gasped in surprise when he gently picked her up to sit in his arms, supporting her hurt leg. Then he started up the beach, heading for a paved road, only pausing to scoop up a pair of boots. She looked over his shoulder at the body of the other changeling floating in the cove.

They traveled down the road, the only noise being music from the parades several blocks over and his bare wet feet slapping on the pavement. She openly stared at him, a weird sense of surrealism washing over her. She had never seen a changeling like him before. Grey skin, no fur, a few spots on his neck and through the holes in his black shirt. Jiao didn't understand why he was saving her, helping her, when if the situation was reversed, she wouldn't lift a finger to aid him. He glanced at her a few times from the corner of his eye but didn't say a word.

Finally, they came to the church, and the changeling walked inside without a word. Jiao saw Neil lying in the broken pews, and she felt a flood of relief when she saw his chest moving. He was alive. The changeling gently placed her next to him, and she checked his wounds. Lady kept her eyes trained on the changeling, but she wagged her tail and licked Jiao's face.

"Do you have a beacon charm?" the changeling asked. Jiao checked her pockets but couldn't find hers. She searched Neil's pockets, finding his and holding it up so the changeling could see. "Give me a few minutes to disappear, and then call your people." He stood up to leave, picking up a jacket off the floor as he walked away.

"Thank you," she called out.

The changeling growled a playful sound instead of an angry one. "Don't know what I'm thinking, saving a hunter," he muttered. He turned around and studied her for a few moments. "I'll probably hate myself in the morning when I'm dealing with my hangover."

And with that statement, the changeling turned and slowly walked out of the church.

.....

Tommy made his way through the crowds barefoot, surprised that he didn't cut his feet on anything on his way back to the hotel. Some people stared at him, wet, clothes torn, some blood running down his arms, but most partygoers were too far gone to care about him and his appearance. Finally, he arrived at the hotel and was across the lobby before someone from the counter shouted at him in accented English. "Sir! Sir! You can't be here!"

Tommy calmly put his boots on the elevator floor and then reached into his pocket for the last bit of the money Guerra had given him. "It's not like they will let me keep it," he told the attendant. "Top floor, please."

The attendant's eyes went wide, and he quickly took the money and closed the door even as a man was stalking across the lobby, yelling at them to stop.

The door opened to the top floor, and Tommy left the elevator. He meandered to Penmark's suite and pounded on the door. It was thrown open about a minute later, and Penmark scowled at the swaying changeling. "You are late," Penmark said.

"You were supposed to be here hours ago." He turned his nose up. "And you're drunk! How did you get money? Or did you steal your libations?"

Tommy sighed. "Well, if you're going to lecture me, I'll just take this and leave." He moved his arm so that the statue wasn't covered by his jacket so Penmark could see it and then started to turn away. Penmark squawked in a way that reminded Tommy of a seagull, grabbed the changeling's arm, and tugged him into the suite.

Guerra was there, sitting primly on the couch. There were several plates of food in front of him, and Tommy felt his stomach growl. He suddenly realized that he hadn't eaten all day and plopped down in an armchair and started to shovel food into his mouth. Tommy lazily held out the statue with his other hand without a word, and Penmark snatched it away. "My, what a mess you are," Guerra said brightly, like he was commenting on the weather and not the bloody and bruised creature in front of him. "What happened, Mr. Monroe?"

"Changeling was at the church," Tommy said through a mouth full of food. "I had to fight him for the statue."

"Oh, how fortunate you got there when you did," Guerra purred. "How is your colleague?"

Tommy glared at the enforcer. "He's dead."

"Pity."

Penmark still didn't say anything, studying the statue, turning it this way and that. "Guerra," he finally said in a huff. "I can't find it."

Guerra held out his hands and accepted the artifact. He twisted it as well, looking over the runes engraved in it. "It's this one," he murmured and started to run his thumb over one of the runes. It started to glow red. "It's the five circles together, her symbol for her followers."

"Whose symbol?" Tommy asked as a compartment in the artifact opened up on the bottom.

Guerra smiled as he took a piece of paper out of the opened compartment. "The Golden One."

"Is that it?" Penmark asked. "One of the sections of the Tree?"

"Yes," Guerra said in a soft voice. "Good job, Mr. Monroe." Tommy didn't know what they meant by a section of the Tree, but it must have been important because Guerra was reverently running his fingers over it.

Penmark glanced at Tommy like he just remembered the changeling was still there, eating his dinner. "Were you seen?"

"No," Tommy lied and felt the band on his arm constrict. He shifted his arm so that it was covered by his jacket so Penmark wouldn't see it glow.

"Did you leave behind any evidence?"

"Well, the church is a wreck," Tommy explained, which was true but not his fault.

"And the other changeling, will it be found?"

"Last I saw him, he was floating in the ocean." Also true, although Tommy suspected the hunters would collect it as soon as they found their friends in the church.

"Leave him be," Guerra admonished his leader. "He has done what he was told. Let him relax."

Tommy grinned at the leader of the acolytes as Penmark frowned. He sat back in the chair, putting his filthy feet up on the coffee table. Penmark sneered at the sight.

"Today was one hell of a party," Tommy said with a content smile, and then he let out a belch.

·····

Burke and Lady got off the elevator and greeted the receptionist on the medical floor. Burke signed in and then started walking down the hallway. He had been held overnight for observation but had been released the next day. Zheng, meanwhile, was held for a few more days. He had debated what to bring for her, thinking flowers would be too intimate, but ultimately settling on getting a box of cookies from a bakery he knew she went to regularly.

A man was outside Zheng's room, looking at a clipboard with some papers, a healer with his dog familiar if Burke remembered correctly. The healer smiled as Burke walked up. "Ah, Hunter Burke," the healer said. "So good to see you. Here to see your partner?"

"Yes, I am, if that is alright... Mister?"

"Mr. Normandy," the man said warmly, holding his hand out with a smile. Burke shook it while Lady and the healer's familiar greeted each other with tail wags and sniffing. "Visiting hours ended about an hour ago, but I have never been known to follow the rules."

"How is she?" Burke asked.

"Quite fine," Normandy replied. "Well, physically, at least."

"Still claims it was a changeling that saved her?"

"Yes. We will have to keep an eye on her and clear her to return to duty, but I'm sure that will be no time at all." Normandy smiled and opened the door for Burke, ushering him inside.

Zheng was sitting up in bed, looking out the window. Burke still felt a rush of relief at seeing her alive, just like when he woke up and she was sitting by his bedside. He was overjoyed that she survived, even if they would not be partners for much longer. "No more tests," she growled, not looking away from the window. "You have poked and prodded me enough."

"No more tests, my dear," Mr. Normandy agreed, smile still on his face, not taking offense to her tone. "As long as you have no signs of infection, you will be cleared to leave tomorrow, in fact." Normandy gestured at Burke. "I come with a visitor, though, and he comes bearing a gift."

Zheng turned then, stunning with her hair down. She smiled, and Burke felt something in his chest melt. "Hello, Neil," she purred, and Burke felt breathless.

"I'll leave you two be," Normandy said, either not noticing the warmth between the two hunters or not caring about it. Finally, he turned and left the room, closing the door behind him.

Burke stared for a few silent moments and then suddenly cleared his throat and approached Jiao's bed. He placed the box of cookies at her side. "I'm sorry if they are the wrong flavor," he quickly explained as she undid the twine that held the box together and inspected the contents. "The woman at the counter said she knew you, and these were your favorite?"

"Samantha? Yes, she is the best person working there. I'll have to thank her next time I see her." She picked up a chocolate cookie loaded with chocolate chips and walnuts. Taking a bite, she hummed, eyes closing in pleasure, and a small smile appeared on her face.

"I wanted to let you know," he said as she continued eating, "when you request a partner change, I will not object. You were right; my feelings are becoming unprofessional." She looked at him then, that small smile not leaving her lips. "I meant what I said before, though. If they offer me the Director position, I will decline. You deserve it more."

She hummed, chewing thoughtfully for a few moments. "No, I don't think I will ask for a new partner," she finally said. "You and I make a great team. I shouldn't break it up."

Burke shifted uncomfortably. "I'm sorry, but as much as I want that, we shouldn't. My inappropriate feelings could endanger your career."

"Neil," she said in a silky tone, "sit."

He obeyed, taking a seat in the chair by her bed. She finished her cookie and rubbed her hands together, dropping any crumbs on the floor. Lady sniffed at the remains and then huffed when she didn't find anything of value. "I have been viewing our relationship adversarially," she confessed in a light tone. "I thought that no matter how well I did, I would always be lost in your shadow." She shrugged. "And maybe I still will be. But if we stay partners, we can help people, Neil. Stop Acolytes and changelings from hurting other people as well."

He nodded. "Do you think we can still be partners? That I will just have to deal with my emotions?" That was fair. It wasn't her fault he had developed feelings for her.

"Now, I didn't say that," she said, and he looked at her in confusion. "I was worried that if people thought we were in a relationship, it would reflect badly on me." She looked into the box and let her fingers hover over the cookies like she was debating taking another one. "But if we *both* want a relationship, we can *both* work to hide it," Jiao explained as she took a second decadent cookie.

Burke felt a thrill in his chest, and a smile tugged on his lips. "Jiao Zheng, are you saying you want to break regulations and enter into a romantic relationship with your partner?"

"We make a great team. But, I have to wonder what a personal connection between us would be like," she purred, and Burke smiled for real. She hummed and held up a finger. "You do have to break your engagement, though."

"Already done this morning," he answered. "I reasoned that even if you and I weren't partners anymore, I shouldn't stay in a commitment that didn't benefit either party. It was the right thing to do. I think she was relieved."

"Good," she said. "We can all start with a clean slate."

They sat in silence for a few minutes, Jiao finishing her second cookie. She offered the box to him, but he put up a hand. "So, if you don't want to be Director of the Hunter Organization, what do you want to do?" she asked after knocking the crumbs off her hands for the second time, and Lady huffed at the lack of sustenance again.

He shrugged. "I will probably apply to become the Headmaster of the Academy next time the position opens."

"Headmaster? You want to teach children?"

"Heavens, no. I want to run the school, not teach," he explained.

She chuckled. "Headmaster of the Academy for Adroit Youth that glows white and Director of the Hunter Organization that glows purple. People will accuse us of trying to take over the world," she joked.

"Jiao, with you by my side, I will already have all I want," he said with a smile, and she laughed and blushed.

34

Chrysta waited nervously, watching the circle with its stone sphere like a hawk. Rosa sat next to her on the log, looking bored with her elbows on her knees, holding her head in her palms. Poe was on her other side, croaking to himself. Mr. Burke stayed standing, and even though his face was blank, Chrysta sensed he was anxious. Rosa sighed. "How much longer do you think they will be?" she whined.

"I'm not certain," Mr. Burke confessed, and Willow whined next to her master. "Jiao is never late."

"It's been two hours," Rosa said with another sigh.

"But for them, that is only thirty seconds," Chrysta explained, having already done the math in her head. She glanced at Mr. Burke. "Do you think something is wrong? Should we go out and check on them?"

"I wouldn't say that is required just yet, Miss Angelos," Mr. Burke said. "If the supplies haven't appeared by tomorrow, we will make the trip. Otherwise, we can wait."

Just then, there was a flash of purple, and a mound of boxes and supplies appeared. "Finally!" Rosa shouted. She got up from the log and jogged over to the pile. She suddenly gasped and picked something up. "Coffee!" she cried, holding a cup up in triumph. She took a sip and moaned. "It's still warm! Oh, this is so good!"

"What else did they send?" Chrysta asked when she noticed a bag.

Rosa grabbed the bag and opened it. "Donuts! Three of them! And a bagel!" She laughed. "It's like Christmas morning!"

"Is that it?" Chrysta asked, looking in the bag when Rosa handed it to her. She looked over the boxes. "No notes?"

Rosa hummed as she searched the boxes. "Just one," she said after a minute of searching. She picked it up and looked it over. "It's addressed to Mr. Burke, though." She handed the letter to Mr. Burke, and he opened it up.

"Jiao is saying there was an incident, and she apologized for the delay in receiving letters. She says they will send the notes in six days if you ladies can come back for them then."

"Incident?" Chrysta asked, a sense of dread settling in her stomach. "Is everyone okay?"

"Yes, they're fine," he said, face blank, folding the letter and putting it back in its envelope. "Miss Angelos, would you like to do the honors?"

"Honors?"

"Transport the boxes, if you please."

Chrysta blinked in surprise and then broke out into a grin. She had been training with Mr. Burke to do teleportation and really enjoyed the thought of finally putting it to good use. Rosa backed up with her coffee and the bag, Poe landing on her shoulder while Chrysta put her hands up. "Start with one box," Mr. Burke instructed her. "Imagine the spot you want it to go."

She did as he told her, feeling the flex in her chest as she weighed the box in her mind, feeling its edges, imagining it outside the cabin, waiting for them when they got back. Her hands glowed for a second, the box shining gold as well, and then there was a loud pop as the box disappeared. Rosa whopped as Chrysta jumped up and down in excitement. Even Mr. Burke had a slight smile on his face.

"Nice work, my dear," he said. "Wish to try the rest?"

Poe croaked and flew to the boxes, landing on top of the rest of the supplies. He hopped up and down. "Me! Me! Me!" he chanted as he bounced.

"Want to go for a ride, Poe?" Chrysta asked. Rosa tossed the bagel to Poe, and he caught it and brought it back to the top of the boxes. Chrysta reached out again and concentrated. With the raven perched where he was, she could better sense the boxes' weight and feel their shape easier. Her hands glowed once again, and with a louder *crack* than last time, the whole pile vanished.

"Alright, let's get back," Mr. Burke said, and he turned away.

They walked towards the cottage, Rosa sipping at her coffee and moaning in pleasure. They opened the bag and selected their donuts. "So," Rosa said after eating half of her donut, "do you think Tommy will send you a letter?"

"I think so. I hope so," Chrysta admitted, feeling her cheeks heat. "I know it's silly, but—"

"No, I get where you are coming from," Rosa interrupted. "It's such a short time for them, but we have been here for so long that you can't help but miss them.

I miss them too. You live with a bunch of people, and they get under your skin, but when they aren't around anymore, you get lonely." She looked at Mr. Burke's back. "How much longer do you think we will be here, Mr. Burke?"

"Both of you are progressing faster than expected," Mr. Burke responded. Chrysta thought he had a note of pride in his voice. "I feel that a few more months are all we need."

"Then I can stop with the freaking fire aptitude test," Rosa grumbled. She got quiet for several minutes and then cleared her throat. "Mr. Burke, why did you become a hunter?"

Mr. Burke froze and turned around. Chrysta couldn't read his expression, but something in the way he held his shoulders told her he was upset. "Why do you ask?" he asked, avoiding Rosa's question.

"My dad and mom were hunters, but dad didn't want us to join the Organization," Rosa explained. "But I have been thinking if I get control of my abilities, maybe I can try to enlist."

Mr. Burke looked thoughtful for a few minutes. Then, finally, he turned and started walking again, the girls hurrying to stay close behind him. "When Hunter Hafeez's father was killed, there was a concern that a spy in the Hunter Organization told the Acolytes where the family lived and when they would be at their most venerable."

"Another hunter?" Rosa asked in a small voice.

"Yes," Mr. Burke said. He stopped. "A majority of the hunters quit, citing concerns for their safety, and your father was one of them. It was a mess. The Organization almost folded, sorcerers didn't feel safe, and Jiao almost lost her position. Your father presumably didn't want you to go into the Organization to protect you." He studied Rosa for a moment. "If you can control your powers and still want to be a hunter after that, I will help you to the best of my ability, Miss Torres."

"Thank you, Mr. Burke," Rosa said.

"Did they ever find the spy?" Chrysta asked.

"Unfortunately, no," Mr. Burke acknowledged. "Either they left the Organization with everyone else, or they remain at their post to this day, although as far as we know, they haven't fed any more information to the Acolytes." He started walking again. "But mark my words, if Jiao or Nyla ever finds them, they will regret not running when they had the opportunity."

.....

Six days later, Rosa and Chrysta made their way back to the stone circle, Chrysta leading the way and trying to rush their hike. However, when they came across the stone sphere in the clearing, a stack of letters was already waiting for them, and Chrysta felt her heart beat faster in excitement.

"Aw, they do miss us," Rosa joked, but Chrysta didn't say anything as she went through the letters. One was addressed to Rosa, one was addressed to Mr. Burke, and one was addressed to both girls. The last one was for Chrysta, her name written in a looping script. She paused as she felt the letter. Had she ever seen Tommy's handwriting before? She tore into the envelope, a small disk landing on her palm. She showed it to Rosa.

"An information disk? Did he record a message?" Rosa asked.

"Don't know," Chrysta murmured. She looked into the envelope. "He didn't write a note. We have to go back to the cottage to use the disk reader, don't we?" Before the other girl could respond, Chrysta was already walking back to the cottage.

"Hey!" Rosa called out when Chrysta was about two dozen feet away. Chrysta turned back around to see Rosa still standing in the clearing with Poe on her shoulder. "Forgetting something?" Rosa said.

Chrysta felt her forehead wrinkle in confusion until it hit her. "Magic!" She rushed back to Rosa, the taller girl laughing. She held Rosa's hand and then concentrated on teleporting them, thinking of the cottage, setting them up so they would land outside. The magic flexed in her chest, and they popped out of existence.

When they popped back, they were in front of the cottage. Poe took off squawking. Mr. Burke was outside, reading a book. He looked up in surprise with his usual raised eyebrow, but he didn't say anything as the girls rushed past him. In passing, Rosa dropped his letter in his opened book, but she didn't pause to say anything. "Is this all?" he called out as Chrysta continued to Rosa's bedroom.

"Chrysta got a disk," Rosa called back as she grabbed the laptop Ichiro gave her. Christ handed her the disk, and they went to the table in the common room to set it up.

Chrysta always laughed at the strange setup when Rosa brought it out so they could watch the movies Ichiro copied for them, an odd collection of magical artifacts with modern components. But today, she didn't say anything while the computer booted up. A white crystal, Rosa called it a solar crystal, had a modern charging cable coming out of it, the only power source for the laptop in the sphere. There was also a round stone circle covered in runes, with a cord ending in a USB connector.

Both Mr. Burke and Rosa opened their letters as the laptop turned on. Rosa smiled at hers, eyes shining. "Everyone say hi," she said, voice slightly thick. She passed the note to Chrysta as she opened the other one. Chrysta smiled at the collection of good wishes from the Disaster Club, decorated with smiley faces and cute drawings. "And Mr. Cross says he's proud of us, that we should be proud of ourselves."

"He is right. You should be," Mr. Burke added, crossing his arms with his letter in one hand. He had a slight smile on his face but didn't say anything about his letter. Instead, he motioned at Tommy's envelope. "What does Mr. Monroe have to say?"

"He didn't write anything," Rosa explained as she placed the disk on the stone. She started clicking on the computer and opened something. "Looks like an audio recording." She looked at Chrysta. "Can we play it?"

Chrysta nodded. "Yes," she said, and Rosa clicked a button.

There were a few moments of silence, but then Ichiro's voice broke in. "Alright, Tommy, we're recording."

Tommy sighed. "Fuck, I wish I had more time," he growled. Chrysta smiled and sat down. She suddenly realized that she had missed his voice so much.

"Twelve minutes and counting," Kevin said.

"I know."

"It's now or never," Ichiro said.

"I know."

"Only time you will get to something for Chrysta," Kevin added.

"I kno—listen here, you assholes..." Tommy started to say.

"Leave him alone," Rimsha told the others. "What's wrong?" she asked Tommy in a softer tone. "Is it something you have never played before?"

"No, I have played this before. I just don't know if I can do it with my arm being shit like this."

Rosa and Mr. Burke looked at Chrysta in confusion. "Tommy's arm is still numb from the slave band," she explained. "It makes playing the violin difficult for him."

"I shouldn't do this," Tommy said on the recording, sounding upset. Chrysta looked at the computer with a frown. "It's just going to be a bunch of shit."

"Just play for her," Rimsha said gently. "She will appreciate whatever you can do."

"And if it's shit, I can delete it," Ichiro added cheerfully.

"Language," Rimsha said sternly, and Rosa laughed at Ichiro's huff of frustration.

Tommy sighed again. "Alright, alright," he said after a moment of silence. "I'll give it a shot. Ichiro, can you start over?"

"Yeah, totally," Ichiro lied. "Start whenever you're ready."

"Hey, beautiful," Tommy said. "It's been a while since I played this, and I think I do better with the piano, but I know Saint-Saëns is your favorite composer, so here is something for you." First, there was the sound of shifting and then the sound of the glide of a bow across strings.

Tommy launched into the song, and Chrysta gasped. She leaned closer to the laptop, like doing so would make it louder. "What is it?" Rosa whispered like she didn't want to disturb Tommy's playing.

"*Romance* by Camille Saint-Saëns," Chrysta explained, also keeping her voice low. She leaned on the table and closed her eyes. It was a beautiful piece by her favorite composer, and she couldn't think of a better present.

It was a short song. Maybe that was all Tommy felt comfortable playing, but he did beautifully. When the last note died, everyone was still for several seconds. Then, "Whoa," Ichiro said on the recording, and Rosa snorted.

"Oh, that was wonderful," Rimsha said. "Chrysta will lov—" But the recording ended there.

Rosa touched Chrysta's arm, and she looked at the other girl. "You okay?" Rosa asked.

"Yeah," Chrysta said, realizing that her eyes were burning slightly. "It was nice to hear him play. I missed it." She cocked her head to the side. "Do you think we can send a disk out to them?"

Rosa's eyes went wide. "Um, Ichiro is the one good with technology, but I can, um, I can try," she said. "What do you want to send him?"

Chrysta smiled. "Something I'm sure he would love."

.....

A few weeks later, Mr. Burke took them past the ruins. "I feel Miss Torres needs a break," he told them as they walked.

"Damn right I do," Rosa muttered under her breath.

"So, where are we going?" Chrysta asked.

"To the lake."

The lake was huge, taking up a quarter of the sphere; the river running through the forest fed it on the north shore. You could barely see the other shore, although Chrysta knew from the map in the cottage that the sphere cut it in half. If you took a boat and tried to cross the lake, she wondered when you would crash into the invisible barrier.

Mr. Burke looked at Rosa when they reached the shore. "Magical fire, wind, and electricity can't affect changelings," he stated without preamble.

"Well, they can," Rosa said.

"How so?" Mr. Burke asked lightly.

"If you set something else on fire, you can use it to hurt them," Rosa explained, holding up her hand and counting on her fingers as she talked. "You can't move them with wind, but you can move something else and hit them. And you can use electricity, but you have to pass it through water first and make sure not to hurt anyone else."

"Who taught you that?" Chrysta asked the other girl, Poe landing on her shoulder with a croak.

"My parents," Rosa said with a grin.

"We hunters are trained on how to overcome the changelings' invulnerability to magic," Mr. Burke added. "Often, that means using the elements to your advantage." He gestured at the lake. "Ice and water are generally the best to use. Water can stun a changeling and then drown it. Ice can form a weapon." He held out his hand, and a long icicle formed. He let it fall from his hand, and it embedded itself halfway into the ground.

"Magical fire is the result of exciting the molecules of oxygen in the air until they form a flame," Mr. Burke started to explain. "With that logic, how is ice formed?"

"Slowing down water molecules until they freeze?" Chrysta guessed.

"Exactly," Mr. Burke said. He looked at Rosa. "Try to freeze the lake."

"Me?" she said, pointing at herself. Mr. Burke simply nodded. "But I can barely control my own ability."

"To become at least a level three hunter, you have to control at least two elementals proficiently, one of them being your natural ability. So if you are serious about becoming a hunter, you need to practice controlling the elements." He motioned at the lake again.

Rosa went to the edge of the water, holding out her hands. She took a breath, held it for a few seconds, and then let it out through her nose.

"Rosa," Poe croaked.

"Hush, Poe," Rosa said, but she didn't sound upset.

They waited for several minutes; Rosa just stood there with her eyes closed and hands in front of her. Suddenly the temperature dropped noticeably. The ground and the water in front of Rosa froze about a foot in front of her. She cracked an eye open, noticed the ice on the water, and let out a bark of laughter.

"Now, Miss Angelos, it's your turn," Mr. Burke said.

"I doubt I could do any better," Chrysta said as she stepped to the water's edge. "I can only do three candles in the fire aptitude test."

Chrysta waited with her hands out. She tried to think of the water, the frigid cold of ice and snow. Poe croaked somewhere behind her and said something, but Rosa hushed him.

Suddenly, Chrysta felt something flex, and she understood what Mr. Burke had tried to tell them. Fire magic made molecules dance; ice magic made them stop moving entirely. So she let the magic go, and Rosa gasped behind her. When Chrysta opened her eyes, she saw that a half-circle of ice had appeared in front of her, reaching out about two dozen feet. She hopped up and down and laughed.

When she turned around, Mr. Burke was smiling with his arms folded. Rosa was also standing with arms crossed but wearing a scowl. "Show-off," the taller girl growled playfully.

.....

It was day 184, and they were at the ruins, Rosa working on the fire aptitude test. Strangely enough, Rosa was quiet and calm as she worked, lighting four candles and then trying for the fifth one over and over. Chrysta was reading and playing with Poe and Willow at the same time. Both familiars had found sticks, and Chrysta was either throwing or teleporting them into the woods to make both bird and dog go crashing through the undergrowth to find them. At one point, Chrysta stopped playing and sat up, her forehead furrowing.

"Something amiss, Miss Angelos?" Mr. Burke asked her.

"Yes," Chrysta murmured, running her finger over a paragraph in the book she was studying. "The more I learn about magic, the more I realize I was doing things I shouldn't do when my powers first showed up."

Mr. Burke raised an eyebrow. "How so?"

"Summoning a spirit, does it really hurt them?" Chrysta asked.

"Not necessarily," he replied. He then blinked. "What spirit do you think you harmed?"

"My mother," Chrysta explained. Willow had brought the stick back and dropped it at Chrysta's feet. The girl reached out and absentmindedly rubbed the dog's ears. "The night my mom showed up and helped me get my dress back with magic. At the time, I thought I was dreaming, but reading this section on summoning, I think I called her to me."

"I keep forgetting that you did more magic when you were ignorant of it than most sorcerers can perform after decades of study," he said, impressed. Chrysta felt herself blush. "To answer your question, summoning or calling a spirit does not hurt them. However, you can mine them for energy, and if you take too much, you can actually destroy a soul. It sounds like you didn't harm her when she answered your call, though."

"Good. I don't like the idea of hurting my mom," Chrysta said, feeling relieved. In the dirt on his back, Poe held the stick in his talons as he waved it in the air. "So is that what happens after we die? We just wander around aimlessly?"

Mr. Burke turned back to watch Rosa for a few moments, his face blank. "We don't know what is in the afterlife," he confessed. "The spirits we talk to tell us a bright light calls to them, but some choose to stay here, and we can commune with them."

"So my mother is a ghost?" Chrysta asked.

"In a way," he said. "You would have to ask her why she is still here, but I would imagine it has something to do with your father and keeping you safe."

"She did tell me to trust Tommy. That he would protect me from my father," Chrysta explained.

Mr. Burke nodded. "Spirits can see the future better than we can, even individuals who were not sorcerers when they were alive. So it's wise to take their advice."

"Have you ever called a spirit?" Chrysta asked and then blinked when Mr. Burke scowled. Suddenly his anger made sense, and she dropped her eyes to the ground. "I'm sorry. I shouldn't have asked something so personal."

They were quiet for a few minutes when Mr. Burke sighed. "My brother," he said in a soft voice. Chrysta looked at him, and his expression was back to being blank. "I tried to reach my brother, but he did not appear. I believe that he had moved on."

"I'm sorry," Chrysta apologized again.

"No need to apologize for your curiosity," he replied, still in that soft tone. "I doubt you could find a sorcerer who hasn't tried to talk to a loved one once they pass away. And if you do find one that says they haven't, they're lying."

Before Chrysta could respond, there was a shout from Rosa's direction. Chrysta and Mr. Burke looked over to see the fifth candle lit. It flickered for a few seconds and then winked out, a thin column of smoke rising from the burnt wick. Rosa turned around with a wide grin on her face. "Did you see it?!" she cried.

"Good job, Miss Torres," Mr. Burke said, giving Rosa the widest smile that Chrysta had ever seen on his face. "Now, do it again."

Rosa's face fell into a frown.

❧ 35 ☙

Marigold pulled the car into the dirt parking lot, put it into park ,and turned off the engine. Dorothy immediately popped up from the back seat and grabbed the rearview mirror to check her makeup. Delilah yelped and leaned out of the way. "Watch my hair!" Delilah cried, and she started to fuss with her curls, making sure the other girl didn't mess them up.

"You hair is fine," Dorothy shot back and then got some lipstick out of her clutch and expertly applied it. She was dressed in red, and her lipstick matched, bright and seductive. "You're the daughter of the richest black man in the county. So you don't have to worry about how you look. Guys will be buying you drinks all night long."

Delilah huffed and looked at Marigold. "Why did we bring her again?"

"Because I'm beautiful," Dorothy said with a grin, not waiting for Marigold to answer. Marigold just shrugged when Delilah shot her a look again.

They climbed out of the car and into the humid night, all three girls adjusting their dresses and studying the club. It wasn't much of a club, just a small barn out in the middle of nowhere, an hour from the city. But it was owned by black people, ran by black people, kept a secret from white people, and therefore, *their* club. First, it had simply been known as The Club for years, then The Garden of Eden, which some people had objected to, so it was finally christened Xanadu, a paradise to come and play in.

They walked across the lot, linking arms. Several men stood outside and nodded at them. The club was a secret, its location was shared with only a few people, but that didn't mean it wasn't without danger. If certain men found out where Xanadu was, they would appear with guns and burning torches real quick, so guards were posted, just in case. A doorman stood in the front and smiled as they walked up, opening the door for them, music spilling out into the night. "Ladies," he said brightly. "Welcome to Xanadu."

The barn was full of people, some sitting at tables lit with candles, but most of the crowd was on the dance floor, moving to the loud rock and roll song that the band was playing. Lit lanterns were attached to the columns supporting the roof, adding to the stifling heat. There was a loft area, but no one was allowed to go up there. But, of course, that wouldn't stop some inebriated men from climbing up and hanging out in the rafters, hooting and hollering at the band or dancers. The makeshift stage was at the back, the loud music the only thing covering the loud groans the old wood would give as the musicians played. A bar was to the left, where people leaned over the counter to yell their order to a grinning barman. The girls were barely 18, but it didn't matter at Xanadu. If you had the money, you could get the booze.

The crowd was a mixture of people, from white-collar to blue-collar, young to old, rich to poor. Some nights, you could find a heated debate on philosophy happening next to a table with a card game. People came to the club to enjoy booze and music but mostly to enjoy their own space. Still, Marigold adjusted her dress, a simple cotton thing that did not compete with Dorothy's red pencil skirt or Delilah's pink frilly ensemble, but it was the only nice thing she owned. She was surveying the mass of moving people, trying to see if there was anyone she knew when Dorothy grabbed her arm. "He's here!" she cried and pointed at the band.

No, that wasn't right. She was pointing at the man at the piano.

He went by Louis, or sometimes the nickname Louisana, but Marigold suspected that wasn't his given name. A few months back, he had shown up and had quickly gained the reputation of being a good, if bad-tempered, musician. Not socializing or talking to anyone, for the most part, just showing up and playing and then drinking for the rest of the night. But Dorothy had made it her mission to get to know him better.

"Think he would like a drink?" Dorothy asked with a grin. "He looks thirsty. He needs a drink."

Marigold rolled her eyes. Louis already had a drink in front of him, and if she remembered correctly, the musicians got to drink for free, but Dorothy was like a dog with a bone. She wouldn't let it go until she got her way.

They pushed their way to the bar, Dorothy getting two glasses right off the bat and then heading off to the stage and her target. Delilah didn't have to wait long before a man bought her a drink, lost in their conversation a few minutes later. Marigold grabbed her water and sighed, entirely forgotten by her friends.

She didn't drink, and Delilah didn't want someone drunk driving her father's car. She was just there to be the driver for the evening, and she wasn't happy about it.

"Marigold Freeman?"

Marigold turned towards the voice and smiled at the tall man next to her. "Abraham Jackson! What are you doing here?"

Abraham gave her a shy smile and lifted his own glass of water. "I imagine the same thing that you are doing here tonight. Playing chauffeur to a bunch of your friends this evening." Someone knocked into him, and he grimaced. "Come on, let's get a table."

They were lucky to find an empty table, and they sat down, Abraham pulling her chair out for her. "So, how are you?" she asked when he took the seat next to her. "It looks like college is treating you well."

Abraham laughed and patted his belly. "I swear I gained fifteen pounds, but my mom says I look too skinny. Other than the weight, I'm doing well. How are you doing?"

"Good! Delilah and I have been accepted to Bennett College. Her father is helping us to move there next year."

"That's great!" he cried. He threw his arms out wide for a hug, and she closed the gap between them to return it, laughing. "You will have to let me take you out to dinner for a proper celebration."

She leaned back, feeling her cheeks heat. "Yeah, it's a little scary, moving to another state and everything."

"Still, you should be proud of yourself!"

The band stopped playing, and the dancers clapped for them. At the front of the stage, Dorothy presented a glass to the piano player with a flirtatious grin. He took the offered drink but didn't return Dorothy's smile.

"And I see Dorothy is doing well," Abraham joked, looking towards the stage.

"She's decided to not go to college and stay here to help her father with his business," Marigold explained. "This may be the last night we spend some time together." She glared at her friend across the club. "And Dorothy is trying to get lucky."

"Well, that just lets me get you all to myself," Abraham said, and Marigold felt the heat in her cheeks move to her ears.

The band started playing again, something slower than their last song. It sounded like the Ink Spots, one of Marigold's favorite bands, and she suddenly wished she could be on the dance floor. Abraham suddenly got up, and for a second, she thought he was leaving her to go find someone else to dance with until he held his hand out with a grin. "Want to dance?" he asked, and Marigold felt butterflies in her stomach as she accepted his hand.

"I would love to."

.....

With Abraham dancing with her, the night flew by, and Marigold was upset when she realized it was midnight, time for her to gather her friends and start heading home. "This was fun," he said with a grin. "We should do this again. Before you head out of the state."

"Yeah, we should," she agreed.

They headed to the bar, where Delilah was surrounded by several men, hanging on her every word. "Come on, Delilah, we have to head home."

"Aw, Come on, Mari, the club will be open for several more hours," Delilah whined.

"Sometimes until the sun rises," one man said with a leer, and Delilah twittered.

"It's an hour's drive to the city," Marigold said, Delilah's argument not changing her mind. "You made me the driver. That means I get to say when we go."

Delilah pouted and whined but then noticed Abraham standing next to Marigold. "Abraham! I'm surprised to run into you here at Xanadu and not at church!"

"Funny, I seldom see you at church, so I'm not surprised to see you here at Xanadu," he joked, making Delilah's smile fall into a scowl.

Abraham frowned and glanced at a table. His friends had been playing cards all night, ignoring Abraham just like Marigold's friends had forgotten about her. "I don't like the idea of three women traveling by themselves this late at night. I would go with you if I could."

Marigold smiled at his concern. "We will be fine," she assured him. She glared at Delilah. "As long as we leave now."

The band stopped playing, and everyone in the club clapped and hooted at their performance. The musicians left the stage, Dorothy closely following the piano player. He got to the bar, and she leaned on it, trying to look seductive. Instead, he accepted a drink from the bartender and started drinking it, ignoring Dorothy.

"So," she purred. "Can we have that date now?"

"Look," he said. "I appreciate the drinks, I really do, but I ain't interested."

"You said you live in the city," Dorothy continued, undeterred. "Come on, you can pay me back for all the drinks I bought you."

Louis sighed. "Is that what you want? Dinner?"

"Among other things," Dorothy replied, and he rolled his eyes.

"Dorothy, let's get going," Marigold said, lightly touching her friend's arm.

"In a minute," Dorothy hissed in response.

"No, Dorothy, we are leaving now."

"Oh, what happens if we stay another hour? You turn into a pumpkin?"

Marigold opened her mouth to respond, but Louis interrupted. "You should go with your friends. I doubt you would want to catch the ride I have back to the city."

"I'm not leaving until I get your number." Dorothy firmly stated.

"I don't have one," he flatly replied.

"Then let me write down mine," Dorothy pressed, stubborn as hell.

"Dorothy, leave the poor boy alone," Marigold snapped, finally done with her friend's antics.

"Marigold, leave me be," she hissed back.

"Hang on, ladies," Louis said. "I think I know how to solve this." And then he held a finger up in a "wait a minute" motion as he downed his drink. Then, when he placed the empty glass back on the bar, he roughly grabbed Dorothy and kissed her.

Dorothy yelped when he grabbed her, but her eyes closed in bliss, and she let out a moan as the kiss lingered. Marigold was not experienced in the ways of the bedroom; hell, she could count the number of boys she had kissed in her lifetime on one hand, but this kiss was heated, carnal, and it made her uncomfortable to watch like she was a voyeur. Abraham must have felt the same way because he let out a soft cough of embarrassment. Other bar patrons started to howl and laugh, which didn't faze the couple at all. Delilah let out a faint twitter of a laugh, looking between her two friends.

The kiss seemed to last forever, and finally, the musician leaned back. Dorothy stayed where she was, a look of joy still on her face. Suddenly her knees gave out, Louis's arm around her waist the only thing keeping her from falling.

"Now, can we leave?" Marigold growled, trying to ignore the blush on her cheeks.

"Mmmmmmm, no," Dorothy said, finally opening her eyes to look around. "I'm staying with him."

"Alright, that's enough," Louis said, and he roughly pushed Dorothy away. She yelped as Marigold caught her. "Go home before your friends leave you behind."

"Hey, I'm not that kind of girl," Dorothy growled, picking herself up and straightening her shoulders. "You can't just kiss me like that and make me leave."

Louis turned back to the bar and nodded at the bartender for another drink. "Looks like I just did," he drawled. He gave the girls a giant smile and then started his new drink.

Dorothy started to puff up and glared at the piano player, making Marigold hide a smile. Dorothy stuck her nose in the air. "Asshole!" she hissed and stalked off.

Louis just grinned and winked at Marigold. "I did warn her."

Marigold gave him a small smile. "Thank you for that. Now she will be complaining about this for weeks."

Louis just shrugged and turned back to the bar.

"Come on," Marigold ordered Delilah. "It's getting late."

Marigold pushed through the crowd, keeping Delilah in front of her, so the other girl couldn't stop to talk to anybody. Abraham followed close behind them, throwing glances at Louis sitting at the bar. "What just happened?" he asked over the noise of the crowd.

"He gave her the attention she wanted," Marigold explained, still pushing Delilah forward. "But he made her feel like that was the *only* thing he wanted from her, making her feel like a loose woman. So now she's mad at him and will avoid him in the future. Really smart if you think about it."

Abraham went silent for a few moments. "Women are strange," he said after a minute of thought, and Marigold laughed.

Abraham accompanied them to the door, but then someone yelled his name from inside, and he hesitated. Marigold reached out and touched his arm as one of the doormen opened the door, the night air outside just as muggy and hot as it was inside. "It's okay," she assured him. "We will be fine. You stay here and have fun for the rest of the night."

He grinned, and without a word, he grabbed her hand and kissed it. It wasn't the passionate display that Dorothy and Louis had, but Marigold still felt butterflies dance in her stomach. She blushed and smiled. She turned and went outside before she was tempted to stay longer.

<h1 style="text-align: center;">⌒ 36 ⌒</h1>

Delilah took Marigold's arm, slightly unsteady from all her drinking. She twittered and poked Marigold's shoulder. "I never thought you would have the hots for a preacher," Delilah joked.

"He's not a preacher," Marigold growled. "He's studying to be a teacher, and religious studies is just one of his minors."

"Still, you two looked good together. Too bad his mother would never let you two get married."

Marigold frowned, but she knew her friend was right. There was a small list of women who could marry Mrs. Jackson's sons, and Marigold was not on it and probably never would be. She didn't have the money or the class as far as the matriarch of the Jackson clan was concerned. Maybe Marigold would decline that final date with Abraham if he asked her. It would be a waste of time.

Dorothy was leaning on the car and frowning, waiting for them. She let herself into the back seat and pouted when they arrived. Delilah flopped into the front seat, laughing her high twitter as she got settled. Marigold just started the car and began their way home, feeling a little more depressed than when they arrived.

There were two main ways into the city from Xanadu, and Marigold debated which way to go. She could either get on the interstate or take the back roads.

Each route took the same amount of time. She finally chose the back roads, wanting to avoid the bright lights on oncoming traffic and the risk of being pulled over.

They traveled through the dark roads, mostly made of dirt and gravel, some of them paved with asphalt. Delilah turned on the radio and caught a faint signal. She hummed to the music, tapping her fingers on her knees and smiling. The song playing was *If I Didn't Care* by the Ink Spots, and Marigold thought it was an appropriate song for her dilemma.

Suddenly there was a loud *POP*, like a gunshot, and Marigold felt the wheel jerk to the right in her hands. All the girls yelped in surprise, and Marigold started to tug the wheel in the opposite direction, overcorrecting and almost making the car fishtail. She turned the wheel right again and then started applying the brakes. The car slowed, shuddering as Marigold pulled to the side of the road. They sat panting for several moments, Marigold watching her hands shake as she pried them off the wheel. "Everyone okay?" she asked in a shaky voice.

"I think so," Delilah said in a small voice. "What happened?"

"That was the tire," Dorothy said from the back seat. Marigold glanced over her shoulder and saw that her friend was tangled in a heap. Dorothy slowly sat up, rubbing one of her shoulders. "We have a flat."

"Can you fix it?" Delilah asked.

"Have to see the damage."

They slowly got out of the car into the humid night air, Delilah crying out as she stepped into a mud puddle on the side of the road. They had broken down in the middle of the woods, the moon the only thing illuminating the scene. Delilah moaned in distress as she saw the shredded front tire. "Oh, Daddy is not going to be happy," she cried.

"I can replace it before your father gets back to the city," Dorothy said as she walked to the front and crouched down to inspect the tire. "He won't even know it was flat."

"Oh, thank you," Delilah said in relief. She shifted and pulled at her dress. "I know I asked earlier why we brought you with us, but Dorothy, I didn't mean it—"

"Yeah, no one likes me until they remember I can fix their car real cheap," Dorothy drawled. She flashed her friends a big smile. "It's okay, Delilah. What are friends for?" She looked at Marigold. "Can you get the jack and the spare?"

Marigold nodded and headed to the trunk, grabbing the lug wrench and jack. She went back to the front of the car and handed the tools to Dorothy. "I need help with the tire," she told Delilah.

"I don't want to get this dress dirty," Delilah whined.

"And I don't want to change a flat in heels," Dorothy shot back. "But I hate the idea of being on a dark road in the middle of the night even more, so hurry up."

Marigold gulped. Dorothy was right. They did not want to be caught with a flat tire in the middle of nowhere. She tugged on Delilah's arm, and the girl followed without further complaint.

They got the spare out without marking either of their dresses and brought it to the front of the car while Dorothy took off her shoes and nylons in the front seat. She rolled her skirt as high as it would go and got to work trying to get the lug nuts off the wheel. After eight minutes of cursing, grunting, and sweating in the dark, Dorothy got the first lug nut off. She started loosening the second one and got it off after fifteen minutes. Finally, she stopped to take a break, leaning on the car.

"Can't you go faster?" Delilah whined.

"Sorry, your royal highness, I'm going as fast as possible," Dorothy panted. She held up the lug wrench. "Unless you would like to try."

Marigold sighed and rubbed her forehead. "I should have gone on the interstate. Someone would have stopped to help us by now."

"Nah, they wouldn't. We would be stuck on the side of the road with cars rushing past us, and I would be more pissed off than I am now," Dorothy said. She got up and rolled her shoulders, setting the wrench up to work on the third lug nut.

After several minutes of fruitless grunting and pushing, car lights appeared in the distance from the opposite direction of Xanadu. Marigold looked up, a mixture of hope and fear warring in her mind. Delilah studied the incoming lights with her. "Think they can help us?" she asked hopefully.

Dorothy got up and joined them, panting. She gripped the lug wrench tightly until her knuckles lightened. "We should hide in the woods," she whispered.

Marigold bit her lip. "They could help us," she argued weakly.

"Or they could hurt us," Dorothy countered.

"Well, I'm not hiding in the woods with this dress on. I'll tear it to pieces," Delilah said. "Let's at least talk to them and see if they can help."

As the lights got closer, Marigold could see they belonged to a dirty truck. She wasn't as knowledgeable about cars as Dorothy was, but it seemed ancient, rust eating at its body. The truck slowed down as it approached and just as slowly pulled over on the other side of the road. The doors opened, and two men climbed out.

Two white men.

The driver brought a lantern with him, and he lit a match as he walked, lighting the lantern and illuminating him and his passenger. The driver was taller, with blonde hair, dressed in a plaid shirt and jeans. The passenger was shorter, with black hair and ears sticking out from his head, only wearing a pair of overalls. They slowly walked to the car, studying the women with open curiosity.

"Well, well, well," the taller of the two men said with a grin. "What do we have here? Three negresses in trouble?"

Marigold felt her cheeks heat in anger. She always hated that word, but she tried to ignore it and gave the two men a big smile. "Yes, it's the tire. We have a flat, and we're trying to change it."

"Well, that is a shame," he replied. He looked at the tire, but his eyes widened as he noticed Dorothy frantically trying to get her skirt back down her thighs. "All dressed up but stuck on the side of the road."

"We are heading home, actually," Delilah explained. The shorter man was standing next to her, openly leering at her. She pulled at the top of her dress, making sure it was covering her chest.

"Well, let's see if we can help you get home then," the driver said, grin still on his face. He suddenly gasped. "Now, where are my manners? I'm Fred, also known as Freddy," he gestured at the other man, "and this fine fellow is Raymund. He goes by Ray."

Delilah giggled, totally charmed by Fred, although Marigold's instincts were screaming at her that something wasn't right. "I'm Delilah, this is Marigold, and this is Dorothy."

"Delilah!" Fred cried. "The woman who cut off Samson's hair!" He sounded cheerful, but something in his smile unsettled Marigold.

Delilah laughed and nodded, totally won over by the white man. He smiled at Marigold, and she tried to return it, the uneasy feeling in her stomach not going away. He put one hand behind his back and held the other out to Dorothy. "If I can have the lug wrench, we can get you ladies sorted."

Dorothy hesitated; Marigold was secretly relieved that the other woman was clearly as troubled as she was. But after a long moment, she handed the wrench over. Fred and Ray went to the tire and started their work.

Between the two men, two of the remaining three lug nuts were removed in under ten minutes, although with as much grunting and cursing as Dorothy had done. The girls stood a few feet away, Dorothy and Marigold throwing meaningful looks at each other. Fred stood up and wiped the sweat from his forehead. "I'll be damn, those nuts are being as stubborn as a mule," he panted. "I'm surprised you could get two off on your own."

Dorothy sniffed, obviously trying to not be pleased by the compliment. "If I had the right tools, I would have done it faster," she said.

"Oh?" Fred asked, giving her a smirk. "And how could you do that?"

"Her father owns a car repair shop," Delilah explained, still not sharing her friends' unease with the two men.

"Really?! A nig-negro-owned garage?" Ray asked. Marigold glared at the man, sure that his stutter was because he was about to use another word before correcting himself.

"Will wonders ever cease," Fred agreed, and Marigold couldn't tell if he was being genuine or patronizing.

Dorothy gave them a haughty expression. "If you come to the city sometime, we can fix that old truck of yours," she said. It sounded like a friendly offer, but it was a challenge. Marigold was sure of it.

"Oh, I couldn't be a bother," Fred replied. His smile was gone, tone suddenly icy. He knew Dorothy's proposition was not friendly. He softly kicked Ray, who was still crouched down by the tire. "You know, Raymund, I think we need to sort something out before we get that last lug nut off."

"What's that?"

"Payment," Fred purred, and Marigold felt her stomach drop.

"Oh! I have some money in my purse!" Delilah cried, and she reached for the passenger door.

Fred grabbed her arm and kept her from opening the door. "No, I don't think money will do."

"Then what do you want, Freddy?" Ray asked.

Fred rubbed his chin with the hand that wasn't holding Delilah's arm. "I think we should get a kiss." Ray looked at the women and leered.

Delilah snatched her arm back and took a step back. "N-no, I don't think we should do that," she quietly, looking scared. "I can pay you, really."

"Why not?" Fred asked, putting a playfully hurt expression on his face. "Didn't we help you ladies tonight?"

"Yes, you did," Marigold said carefully, choosing her words wisely. She was dealing with a time bomb, she knew it, and one wrong word could set it off. "And we greatly appreciate it. But helping others should be its own rewards, not physical affection."

Fred scowled at her. She had chosen her words poorly, apparently. "'Physical affection?'" He gestured at their dresses, Dorothy's still bare calves. "And tell me, how much 'physical affection' did you show other men tonight?"

Delilah flinched as Dorothy puffed up. "We just went dancing," Delilah said, still looking scared.

"And it's none of your business who it was with," Dorothy added with a growl.

Fred smiled, but it was a hard and brittle thing. He stepped up to Dorothy and suddenly slapped her, the sharp sound almost as loud as Delilah's yelp. Dorothy held her cheek and glared at the man for one long moment and then moved towards him. Marigold grabbed her friend's shoulder before she could do anything foolish.

"Don't be a stuck-up bitch," Fred growled, and Marigold tugged at her friend before she could launch herself at the white man.

Marigold saw Ray stand up quickly, and she cursed under her breath. They were not only in the middle of nowhere, but now they were at the mercy of two men who had the lug wrench and were preventing them from getting to the car. "Now, wait a minute," she said, trying to muster as much authority in her voice as she could. "We thank you for your help, but if you won't take our gratitude or our money, please give us the wrench, and we will finish changing the tire ourselves."

Marigold hoped that her words would anger Fred and make him leave, probably taking the wrench, maybe even the spare, leaving them stranded by the side of the road. They would have to wait for someone else to find them, maybe even walk back to Xanadu, but they would be safe and still alive. But Fred smiled and then grabbed Marigold's arm, jerking her towards him.

"And after we went through all the trouble to help you?" he sneered, all his previous charm gone. "And how dare you tell me what I should do?"

"Now wait a damn min—" Dorothy started to say, and she took a step forward, but Ray swung the wrench out and caught her in the stomach. Dorothy let her breath out in a *whoosh* and went down to one knee, clutching her stomach. Ray whooped and laughed, Delilah crouching down to help her.

Marigold tried to go to her friends, but Fred kept his hold. "Well," he said with a leer, "how about you and I go into the woods and talk more about that physical affection?" Fred pointed at Ray. "You stay here with these two. If this one doesn't play nice, you can hurt her friends."

Marigold started fighting harder, knowing that going into the woods with Fred would be a mistake, maybe her last. Lights appeared on the road from the direction of Xanadu. It was a truck, just as ancient as Fred's. Marigold opened her mouth, hoping to call for help, but Fred covered it. The vehicle came closer, the cab dark, so Marigold couldn't see who was inside, but they had to realize what was happening. Fred's lantern clearly lit the scene: Dorothy kneeling on the ground, holding her stomach with a pained expression, Ray standing over her with a wrench, Fred with his vice-like grip on Marigold, hand over her mouth.

The vehicle slowly passed them, between the girls' car and Fred's truck, and Marigold felt fear and frustration claw at her throat. But the truck came to a complete stop once it passed. Three large hogs stood in the truck's bed, grunting to themselves as the passenger side door opened. A figure leaned out of the cab, and Marigold felt a rush of relief so strong her knees got weak. "Do you need help?" the person called, something familiar about the voice.

Marigold twisted away from Fred. "Yes!" she called out. "We do!"

Marigold yelped as Fred yanked her back to clamp a hand over her mouth again, but it was too late. The man was already closing the truck's door and knocked on the side. The hogs squealed as the truck jerked back into drive, and it drove off slowly. The figure walked towards them, coming close enough that Marigold could finally make out the man's face in the lantern's light.

It was Louis.

He had his shirt and jacket off, stripped down to his undershirt, holding his discarded clothing over his shoulder. As he walked into the circle of light, there was a glint of light, and Marigold realized he was wearing a weird band on his left arm. He strolled up to the car, posture relaxed and expression looking almost bored. Both white men watched him with identical looks of surprise and shock. And Marigold could see why. She couldn't recall ever seeing a black man act this way in the presence of white men before. Not even her father would use this kind of body language. *I'm not afraid of you,* it said. *You can't scare me.* Fred was so startled that his hand slowly left Marigold's mouth, much to her relief.

Louis paused when he reached Fred and Marigold, Louis looking at her and not the man holding onto her arm. "Flat tire?" he asked in a light tone, like he was asking about the weather.

"Y-yes," she replied, focusing on him and ignoring Fred. "We could use some h-help," she added, praying that he would catch her meaning.

"Look, boy, the ladies don't need—" Fred started to say.

"Well, I didn't ask you, did I?" Louis growled, finally fixing Fred with a glare, and Fred flinched. "If you were helping, they would be back on the road by now, wouldn't they?" Louis stepped up to Fred, and Fred took a step back, letting go of Marigold. She gladly hid behind the musician. Fred's expression kept shifting from anger to shock to something that looked like fear.

"Let me get you back on the road," Louis said. He was talking to Marigold but was giving Fred a glare that could melt ice. "You don't need to be out here in the middle of the woods at this time of night."

"Thank you," Marigold stammered. Louis slowly turned to the car, and Marigold followed, keeping Louis between her and Fred.

Ray was standing with the wrench by his side, mouth gaping. Louis once again stepped up to be in the white man's personal space, forcing Ray to step back. Delilah and Dorothy joined Marigold, looking as relieved as Marigold felt. "You ladies okay?" Louis asked, again talking to the girls but glaring at Ray, making the man look highly uncomfortable.

"I'll feel better once we get back on the road," Dorothy said, still holding her stomach.

"Well, let's get you going," Louis said, holding out his hand for the wrench.

Ray looked dumbly between Louis's hand and face and back again. "Freddy?" he called out. "What do I do?"

"*Don't* give him the wrench, Ray," Fred growled.

"No, Ray, give me the wrench," Louis argued flatly.

"Ray, I swear, you give up that wrench, I am making you walk home," Fred growled.

"And if you give me the wrench, your legs will still work when you walk home, Ray," Louis said brightly with a giant smile. Ray looked at that smile and must have seen some truth in it because he handed the wrench over quickly. He scrambled to Fred's side, and the taller man hit him in the shoulder.

Fred scowled at the musician. "You need to leave, boy. Now."

"I don't think I will," Louis said dryly. He crouched down and inspected the flat tire after handing his jacket and shirt to Delilah.

"If you don't—"

"I'll leave when I'm done with this tire," Louis said, tone not changing. He fit the wrench over the last lug nut, and with barely any effort, he started to turn it. Fred and Ray gaped at him.

"How'd you do that?" Dorothy asked.

"I'm stronger than I look," Louis said with a grin. Marigold didn't know how that could be. He was muscular but lean, and Marigold's grandmother would have tried to fatten him up if she had known him. But, surprisingly, he made short work of the lug nut and picked up the flat tire with no effort.

"Now listen here, boy," Fred said. He was trying to deepen his voice to add more authority to it, but it reminded Marigold of a child trying to boss an adult around. "You need to get back on the road and start walking. Or I will make you regret stopping."

"You talking about that gun in the back of your truck?" Louis asked, still not looking up as he put the spare tire on the car, grunting as he picked up the tire but still swinging it around like it weighed nothing. "You can try to go for it if you like. But you will regret it if you do."

Fred's face turned into a mask of murderous rage, and he turned around on one foot and stomped toward his truck. Ray looked between his friend and Louis, looking like a lost little boy. Marigold knew they weren't out of trouble yet, but Ray's expression was so funny that she almost laughed. Delilah must have found it funny as well because she did giggle, a high twitter. However, all three girls gasped and started backing up when Fred returned with a shotgun.

Fred stalked back up to the girls' car, pumping the shotgun and aiming it at Louis's face. Louis looked at it, appearing bored.

"Yeah, not so tough now, huh, boy?" Fred asked, looking smug.

Louis sighed like a gun being held to his face was a minor annoyance and not life-threatening at all. "You made a really big mistake," he stated.

"What's that, nig—"

But before Fred could finish his question, Louis quickly stood up, grabbed the shotgun, and hit Fred in the face with the barrel. The shotgun went off, but it was pointing straight up and not a threat to anyone. The girls screeched, but Louis didn't hesitate, punching Fred in the stomach with his other hand. Fred folded in half, the air leaving his lungs in a *woof* sound. Louis took the shotgun away from the coughing man, breaking it open so he could take out the ammunition. "You don't get that close to someone so they can disarm you." Louis studied Fred for a minute as the white man glared, blood running down his face from his broken nose. Louis then brought the gun up and hit Fred with the butt of the gun, making Fred fly back and land on his backside.

Dorothy gave out a bark of laughter, and Delilah joined her by giggling. Even Marigold smiled at the white man writhing in pain on the ground, glad to see him getting what he deserved. Ray was looking between Louis and Fred, face frozen in shock. Louis rested the shotgun on his shoulder and grinned. *"Boo!"* he shouted at Ray, and the man jumped and ran, barely pausing to pick Fred off the ground. The girls fell into peals of laughter.

Ray dragged Fred to the truck, and they scrambled inside. The vehicle started, and its tires squealed as it pulled away, making a wide turn to go back the way it came. Louis watched the truck go, standing in the middle of the road with a scowl on his face. "Holy shit," he suddenly hissed when the truck's taillights finally disappeared. He tossed the gun into the woods and then threw the ammo on the other side of the road. "Where did you ladies find those assholes?"

"They found us," Marigold explained.

"Yeah, well, let's get the hell out of here before they get back," Louis growled. His calm demeanor was gone, and he almost ran to the car and started tightening the lug nuts on the spare tire.

"You think they will come back?" Dorothy asked. "You did just rearrange Fred's face."

"Oh, they will be back," Louis said. He finished with the tire and started to lower the car. "Only they will have a whole bunch of their friends with them, and I don't want to find myself hanging from a tree, thank you very much."

Louis opened the trunk and put the wrench, jack, and flat tire away while the girls got into the car. Marigold felt him close the trunk and started the car when she noticed Louis in the rearview mirror, walking down the road towards Xanadu, his clothing hanging from his shoulder again. She rolled down the window and stuck her torso out of the vehicle. "Hey!" she yelled at the musician. "Where are you going?!"

"Back to Xanadu," he called back. "If I'm lucky, I can get another ride."

"Just get in the damn car!" Dorothy called out while leaning out of the car.

"Quickly! Before they come back!" Delilah added, leaning out of the passenger side.

Louis shrugged and ran back, climbing into the back seat with Dorothy.

Marigold drove faster than she usually would on the dark roads, but she didn't want to be out once the lynch mob Louis warned about appeared. She found a road that led to the interstate and felt relief when they turned onto the wide freeway. Louis relaxed as well and leaned back with his eyes closed. After a few minutes, he started to snore softly, Dorothy watching him sleep with a strange look on her face.

Marigold's mind wandered as she drove, and before she knew it, they turned onto Delilah's street. She pulled over and shut off the car. "You two head inside," she said to her friends. "I'll get Louis home and come back." Delilah was already climbing out of the car, but Dorothy hesitated, looking between Marigold and Louis. "What's wrong?" Marigold asked her.

"She doesn't want you to be alone with me," Louis suddenly said. Marigold didn't realize he was awake. He stretched like a cat and yawned, joints popping. Suddenly he grabbed his clothes and opened the door. "It's okay. I can walk from here."

"Wait!" Marigold told him, but he was already getting out of the car. So Marigold climbed out and started to follow him.

"Mari!" Dorothy called out, and she paused on the sidewalk. Her friends were by the car, both of them looking worried. "Be careful, okay?"

"He saved us," Marigold said. "I have to at least thank him." And before Dorothy could answer, she turned around and ran to the walking musician.

Louis was already a block away, walking slowly. He didn't say anything as Marigold fell into step next to him. "I'm sorry," Marigold said as she joined him. He raised an eyebrow. "We didn't thank you for your help. We owe you a lot. Dorothy didn't mean to insult you."

"I'm not insulted," he said flatly. He shrugged with one shoulder. "She just saw me hurt someone, and now she's scared of me. It's okay, really." He stopped and turned to her. "I just couldn't pass you guys without stopping. We both know what could have happened."

Marigold nodded, not sure of what else she could say. She pulled at her dress until Louis sighed. "Go home," he said. "It's late, and your friends will worry about you."

She nodded again. "If you ever need anything, please, let me know."

"Just don't go on that stretch of road anymore," he warned her. He looked up at the sky for a moment. "And do you want some advice?" She gave him a perplexed look. "That guy you were dancing with tonight?"

"Abraham?"

"Yeah. Take it from someone a lot older than he looks: you two belong together."

Marigold laughed. "I'll consider it."

"Seriously," he said and flashed her a bright smile. It was the warmest and most genuine smile she had ever seen on his face. "Get married, have a lot of babies, live happily ever after. Have the life some of us can only dream of."

"Well, now I can. Thanks to you."

His face softened, and he gave a small salute before turning and walking off. He started to whistle when he was a dozen feet away. It was The Ink Spots's *I Don't Want to Set the World on Fire,* and Marigold smiled as she turned towards Delilah's home and started walking.

37

Zheng told her side of the events in Olinda, everyone listening with rapt attention. Tommy listened closely as well. Most of the story was as new to him as it was to the others. "So you could have grabbed the statue and run away, but you decided to save a hunter instead?" Ellis asked him when Zheng was done.

Tommy shrugged. "If I didn't help her, he would have killed her. Just didn't seem fair."

Hafeez didn't say anything, scowling as she looked away from the Director. Then, suddenly, she stomped off, kicking the door open and letting the cold morning air into the warehouse. Zheng sighed, watching the younger hunter stomp off. "I will go talk to her," she said, and then she walked off after Hafeez.

There was a few moments of strained silence after the Director left. "Well," Cross chirped, clapping his hands together and making the kids jump. "Let's get those supplies downstairs. Mrs. Zheng can send them in when she's ready."

Tommy got up with the kids, expecting to help with the boxes, but he stopped when he felt a tug on his sleeve. He turned to see Rimsha holding onto his sweater. "You aren't going anywhere until I look at those cuts," she ordered.

Tommy looked at the cuts on his arms from Hafeez's knife. There were a lot of them, but they were shallow and had already stopped bleeding. "They're fine," he told the teen. "Really, they will be gone by tonight."

"Nope, come on. We are cleaning them. Now."

Tommy looked at Cross for help, but the empath just shrugged. Tommy sighed but let Rimsha pull him into the office.

Tommy sat down on a desk that wasn't covered in discarded breakfast food and let Rimsha tend to his arms. She cleaned them and then put bandaids on his arms, dozens of them. Tommy was upset, but only because the sweater was one of the new ones he found at the thrift store, and now it was all cut up. He watched Rimsha work for a few minutes, not talking. Then, finally, he cleared his throat. "I'm sorry," he said.

"For what?" she asked.

"For losing my cool with Hafeez," he confessed. "Cross was right. I shouldn't have attacked her in front of you guys."

Rimsha shrugged. "I don't blame you. She was out of line. But you shouldn't let her get under your skin like that. She's obviously trying to get you to fight her."

Tommy didn't respond, just studying the girl next to him for a few minutes. "And you don't agree with Hafeez?"

Rimsha gave him a confused look, and she smiled. "Of course not. The important thing is that you and Chrysta love each other. Somebody just has to spend some time with you two to see it." She finished with the last bandaid and gave him a large smile. "That's good enough for me."

Tommy shifted on the desk. "Don't you think Chrysta would be better off with someone else?"

"Like who?"

"I don't know," Tommy said. He looked down. "Julien seems like a good guy. Maybe Chrysta would be happy with him."

Rimsha blinked and then started laughing. Tommy folded his arms and waited for her to calm down. "What?" he asked, trying to frown but failing.

"Julien is dating someone," she explained, still giggling. "And he's gay. So I don't think you have to worry about him taking Chrysta away from you."

Tommy rubbed his neck, not sure why he felt a rush of relief. "Well, okay, so maybe not him." He shifted on the desk again. "But another sorcerer would be better for her, right?"

Rimsha cocked her head to the side, thinking. "My father thought the same thing about my mother when they met. Islam says that practicing magic is haram. It's a sin." She started to clean up, putting the unused band-aids away. "My father was worried that if he told my mum what he was, she wouldn't want to be with him."

She finished, holding the first aid kit to her chest, and leaned against the desk he was using. "But the abilities that sorcerers have are a gift. And like all gifts, you can either do good or you can do evil with them. So my father believed being a sorcerer was an important part of who he was, and he shouldn't hide it. So he was honest with my mother. And she loved him for *who* he was and not *what* he was, so they married."

Tommy thought about what she said for a moment. "So you're saying that as long as I'm honest with Chrysta, she will decide what is best for her."

Rimsha smiled brightly at him. "Exactly." She stood up. "And besides, she will need you, even if it's just as a friend."

"What do you mean?"

"Didn't the Golden One live for several centuries? Longer than any other sorcerer ever? Right now, the only creatures that can live that long are dragons—"

"And changelings," Tommy finished for her. He suddenly had a vision of Chrysta, still young, finding a sorcerer to be with, who would be very much human, but who would age as time went on. And then, one day, they would die. Tommy could see Chrysta, still her young self, mourning the loss of her human lover at the side of a grave. Would she fall in love again? Knowing that they would just pass away someday?

"And I'm sorry, but I don't think Chrysta could have a dragon as a lover," Rimsha joked.

Tommy snorted as the teen left the office. He followed her and started to head to the vault. He noticed that Rimsha was going in the other direction. "Hey, not going to help with the supplies?"

"Sorry. I have to go do the Fajr. Morning prayer." She stopped to grab a mat from the van and started to head outside.

"Hey!" Tommy called out to her, and she turned around. "By the way, what were you yelling at Hafeez earlier? When she insulted Chrysta?"

Rimsha looked embarrassed for a second. "It was a quote my father taught me when I was young. 'All the evils have been locked in a room, and its key is lying.'" She shrugged. "Seemed to fit the situation." And with that, she turned and went outside.

Tommy climbed down the ladder, finding Ichiro, Kevin, and Julien moving the last boxes into the vault. Ichiro studied Tommy and grinned. "Did Rimsha use every bandaid in the kit?"

Tommy held up his arms, looking at the dozens of bandaids that dotted his arms. "I don't know why she bothered. They will be gone by tonight."

"Rimsha is a good healer. She knows what is best," Kevin said brightly, and he turned to go deeper into the vault. Julien and Ichiro looked at Tommy, shrugged simultaneously, and followed the other boy. Tommy grabbed the last box and went in as well.

The boxes were all stacked on the lower floor of the vault, already in the circle. The bag full of donuts and bagels sat on the top next to the caramel latte. Tommy felt a heavy weight settle in his stomach when the two hunters stopped what they were doing and glared at him. *Great job, you idiot,* he told himself. *You just pissed off the only two allies you had.* He cleared his throat when he put the box down and then rubbed his neck as he stepped up to the hunters. "I'm sorry about... I understand if you guys hate me after that whole fight—"

"We don't care about that," Smith said, but he still glared at the changeling. "I'm pissed that we had to move all those boxes without you and Hafeez. *And* Rimsha. Look, I'm here because having the Director of the Hunter Organization owe you a favor is great, but I didn't sign up to be an errand boy."

Tommy snorted, feeling a flood of relief, as Cross rolled his eyes a few feet away. Tommy looked at Ellis. "And why are you so sour?"

Ellis went over to one of the tables and grabbed a bundle. They shook out their jacket, now torn to shreds. "I shouldn't have worn this suit," they huffed. "This was my favorite suit. Although," they held up a finger, "please don't go after a hunter like that again. She was in the wrong, but I rather not deal with Miss York if I have to hurt you."

"Noted," Tommy said with a smile.

Suddenly, the digital clock near the sphere went off. It was six in the morning, time to send the supplies. "Should we go get Mrs. Zheng?" Ichiro asked just as the Director appeared at the vault's door.

"My apologies, everyone," she said as she quickly descended the stairs. "We don't have time to send letters."

The teens erupted into excited and disappointed chatter, Cross trying to shush them. Tommy felt another stab of guilt. This would be their only chance of sending letters in. Would Chrysta think he didn't care about her?

Zheng waved a hand at the teens, moving quickly. "Calm down, everyone. I'll send a letter in with the supplies for Neil saying we will send them later. Thirty-six minutes from now. That will be six days for them."

Zheng quickly wrote a letter, grabbing the tuning fork and placing the envelope on the top of the supplies, under the latte so it would be seen. She stuck the sphere with the fork, and the ringing started, the supplies glowing purple. The light grew until it was blinding, and everything disappeared, just the smell of magic hanging in the air. Zheng relaxed slightly. "If we waited too long, Neil would have thought something was wrong and come out to investigate."

"Alright, everyone," Cross said. "Thirty minutes and counting. Now is the time to write it if you want to send something in."

The teens grabbed a sheet of paper and loudly started to talk about what they would write. Cross and Zheng took a sheet as well, quickly penning their notes. Tommy took his sheet to one of the couches, trying to get some privacy. He spent way too long staring at the blank page, wondering what the hell he was supposed to write.

Hey, beautiful, how are you? How's the weather? Practicing the Paganini music I bought you? I almost ripped a hunter's face off this morning because she accused you of being a sexual deviant. Still think I'm a great guy? Told you, you can't trust a changeling.

He groaned and rubbed his face with his hands. He was vaguely aware of someone sitting next to him. "You okay?" Rimsha asked him softly. He didn't know when the teen finished her prayers or entered the vault, but he was happy that she was here now.

"Yeah," Tommy confessed, not looking up from his hands. "I just don't know what to write."

"What would you tell her if she was right next to you?"

Tommy brought his hands down and stared at the blank page, thinking about it for a minute. "'I miss you,'" he finally said. "Not a very exciting letter."

"Well, maybe some poetry then?" Rimsha suggested hopefully.

Tommy grimaced. "Never liked poetry, really. Rather use music instead of poetry." He suddenly had a thought and broke out in a wide smile. "Actually, that gives me an idea. Takahashi, I need some help," Tommy called out to Ichiro, and the boy jumped up.

"What's up?"

"I need to record something and send it into the sphere. Think you can manage that?"

The young boy smiled. "Of course," he said and grabbed his laptop.

They went up to the office for privacy. Tommy stayed standing, nerves making his stomach flip as he picked up his violin. Ichiro tapped on the laptop for a few silent moments while Rimsha and Kevin sat down. "Alright, Tommy, we're recording," the younger boy finally said.

Tommy sighed. "Fuck, I wish I had more time," he growled.

"Twelve minutes and counting," Kevin remained the changeling.

"I know."

"It's now or never," Ichiro said.

"I know."

"Only time you will get to do something for Chrysta," Kevin added.

"I kno—listen here, you assholes..." Tommy started to say.

"Leave him alone," Rimsha told the others, glaring at the boys. She gave Tommy a soft smile. "What's wrong?" she asked Tommy in a gentler tone. "Is it something you have never played before?"

"No, I have played this before." Tommy brought up his left arm and pointed at it. "I just don't know if I can do it with my arm being shit like this." He rubbed his neck and groaned. "I shouldn't do this," Tommy said. "It's just going to be a bunch of shit."

"Just play for her," Rimsha said gently. "She will appreciate whatever you can do."

"And if it's shit, I can delete it," Ichiro added cheerfully.

"Language," Rimsha said sternly, and Ichiro huffed in frustration.

Tommy sighed again. "Alright, alright," he said after a moment of silence. "I'll give it a shot. Ichiro, can you start over?"

"Yeah, totally," Ichiro said. He turned to the laptop and seemed to mess with something on the screen. "Start whenever you're ready."

"Hey, beautiful," Tommy said. "It's been a while since I played this, and I think I do better with the piano, but I know Saint-Saëns is your favorite composer, so here is something for you." Tommy shifted, brought the violin up to his chin, and glided the bow across the strings.

Tommy launched into the song. It was a short song, the only thing Tommy felt comfortable playing, but he did alright, considering his fingers were still numb. When the last note died, everyone was still for several seconds. "Whoa," Ichiro said.

"Oh, that was wonderful," Rimsha said. "Chrysta will love it."

Kevin checked his watch. "Hopefully she does because we are almost out of time."

Ichiro finished with the disk, giving it to Tommy with a smile. They rushed to the vault with seconds to spare. "It's not a poem," Tommy admitted as he sealed an envelope, put Chrysta's name on the front, and handed it to Zheng. "But it's how I feel."

"Then I'm sure she will cherish it," Zheng said as she accepted the envelope. She hurried it over to the circle, and when her watch went off, she used the tuning fork to activate the sphere. Once again, the letters lit up with a purple glow and disappeared with a flash of light.

Tommy tried to not think about the song he sent so he wouldn't expect a response, so when the sphere flashed about ten minutes later, he was just as surprised as everyone else. Zheng grabbed the envelope. "For you," she said and handed the envelope to Tommy with a smile. He spent a few moments just staring at Chrysta's looping script spelling out his name on the front.

"Well, what are you waiting for?" Rimsha asked. "Open it!"

Tommy tore into it and took out a disk. Ichiro let him sit down in front of the laptop and started to play it for him as he put some earphones in. There was silence for a few seconds, and then he heard Chrysta's voice. "Are we recording?" she asked.

"Yep," Rosa replied. "You can start anytime you want."

Chrysta cleared her voice. "Alright. Um, thank you for the solo, Tommy. It was beautiful." Tommy smiled, a mixture of joy and relief blooming in his chest. "So, here is something for you. I hope you enjoy it. Um, I know this piece is for guitar, but it's Paganini, so I'm sure you will love it."

She started to play the song *Romanze,* and Tommy's smile grew. He noticed that the teens had crowded around him, so he unplugged the headphones so they could listen. It was short and light and entirely in Paganini's style, and Tommy loved every second of it.

Rimsha leaned down so she could whisper in his ear. "I think you have your answer," she said softly, and he smiled.

.....

Tommy went to take a nap, going deeper into the vault and finding a couch in the back to get comfortable on. He put headphones in the laptop that Ichiro let him borrow and fell asleep to Chrysta's solo put on repeat. The changeling woke up sometime later, feeling unsettled. When he sat up and looked around, he saw why.

Hafeez was sitting on a table nearby, watching Tommy sleep with a glare on her face. Smith was somewhere behind her, snoring loudly, but otherwise, Tommy didn't see anyone around making sure Hafeez didn't kill him in his sleep. He slowly got his boots on, not taking his eyes off the hunter. Her sword was by her side, within reach. Siad sat next to his master, looking like a regal statue until he hissed loudly.

"So what you said in Burke's office," Hafeez said with no preamble, "was all true? My father attacked you, but York killed him?"

"Yes," Tommy said, keeping the annoyance out of his voice and staying calm.

Hafeez didn't respond, just studying him for several long, tense moments. Then, finally, her posture relaxed, and even the caracal seemed to lose some of his rigidity. "Why?" she asked, pain showing on her face.

"I don't kn—" Tommy started to say. But he considered her question. "York and Guerra were looking for a piece of paper."

"A piece of paper?" she asked. "They broke into our home, tortured my family, and killed my father, all for a piece of paper?"

"It wasn't just your family," Tommy said. His leg started to bounce, and he tried to ignore it. "One time, they wanted me to break into a normie's house and torture his son so he would help the acolytes steal an artifact from a museum. It was a gown with a piece sewn into it. The fight in Olinda? The statue of the Golden One had a section at the base of it. The Mancini Massacre? All because Mancini stole a book with a piece inside of it, and Guerra and I were sent to make an example of him."

Hafeez looked down, arms still folded, weighing Tommy's words. He paused before continuing. "And one time, I was ordered to seduce a sixteen-year-old girl so I could steal a painting that had the paper hidden in it." Hafeez looked at him in horror. "No, I didn't do it. I tied her up and stole it instead. Which probably earned me a lot of these," he added, pointing to his left arm, with its many scars.

"What were they?" a voice asked behind him, and Tommy watched as Zheng and Ellis joined Hafeez by leaning on the table. Cross joined him on the couch, all of the sorcerers looking grim.

"I don't know," Tommy confessed. "They pointed in a direction and just said, 'fetch.' I wasn't given any more details than that." He thought about it for a moment. "They did call it the 'Tree' sometimes."

"And you shared all of this with Neil?" Zheng asked.

"Of course," Tommy said. "I have no reason to keep their secrets. Never did."

"The Tree," Cross mused. He reached into his coat and brought out a cigarette case, not taking out a cigarette just yet. "A magic spell created by the Golden One?" he asked Zheng.

"Has to be," the Director responded. She looked at Hafeez. "And you would have been too young to know what your father was guarding."

"It had to be important," Hafeez said softly. "He wouldn't have risked our safety for nothing." Her shoulder suddenly slumped. "But why all of that pain for just a scrap of paper?"

"You would have to ask a leader of the Acolytes about that," Tommy responded.

"Now that I know York is the one who killed my father," Hafeez growled, "I intend to." She looked at Tommy. "I'm sorry."

Tommy blinked, surprised by the apology. "Just leave Chrysta alone," Tommy warned the hunter. "She is a victim of her father as much as your family was."

"Well, if you two have kissed and made up," Cross said, and both Tommy and Hafeez threw identical glares his way, "I'm going to go get lunch. Any requests?"

"Steak, as rare as you can get it," Tommy joked and grinned as the sorcerer frowned at him. "What? I'm hungry."

"Italian it is," Cross said and stood up. Nearby, Smith snored loudly. Cross pointed in the hunter's direction. "He does not get to complain about my snoring anymore."

38

Cross left and returned by noon, bringing in pizzas and containers full of food. Everyone dug in, staying in the vault, Tommy grabbing a plate of spaghetti with giant meatballs. Smith woke up with the smell of food, stretching and yawning as he dug into a plate of chicken cacciatore. Tommy kept Hafeez in his line of sight, not trusting her to be behind him, but she seemed to be satisfied with leaving him alone as she ate with the other hunters.

Slightly after one in the afternoon, there was a *pop*, and something appeared on the ball. Ichiro was closest, so he ran into the circle, grabbed it, and ran back out. "It's an envelope!" he shouted, holding it high.

"Open it!" Kevin said, and Ichiro tore into the paper. An information disk slid out.

Ichiro sprinted to the laptop to load it, and the other teens gathered around him. Cross and Tommy joined them. "Who do you think made this one?" Tommy asked the empath.

"Don't know," Cross replied. "Hopefully, it is good news."

The blank screen lit up, and Rosa's face appeared out of the blurry background, grinning at the camera. "Hey guys!" she cried, waving at the camera. "It's day thirty-nine in the ball, and I wanted to do a check-in." She looked around and then started walking, lowering her voice slightly. "I don't think Mr. Burke would want me to be doing this, so just *shhhh!*"

The teens laughed as Rosa dramatically put a finger up to her lips. "But I wanted to show you something, so... ah! There it is!"

Rosa swung the camera around to show the castle through the fog and the trees. "Whoa!" Kevin whispered as Rosa continued talking.

"Yeah, we can't get too close, something about guardians, but isn't it cool?"

The camera switched back to show Rosa's face again. "It's been good here. I'm learning a lot; Chrysta is learning a lot." She paused. "It's quiet here. Bizarre to have no one else here. But we're staying busy and everything." There was a croak in the distance, maybe Poe, and Rosa looked off-camera. "But well... I just wanted to say I miss you guys." She did the sign for "I miss you," pointing at herself, then her chin, and then at the camera.

"Miss you too," Rimsha said, smiling over Ichiro's shoulder.

The camera went dark, and when it came back, Chrysta appeared on camera, looking into the lens in confusion. "Rosa, how do I know it's on?" she asked off-screen.

"It's on," Rosa said.

"You su—Oh yeah! It's on!" Chrysta smiled at the camera and waved. "Hi, guys!"

"Hi!" the teens answered back and laughed, making Tommy shush them as Chrysta continued talking on the screen.

"It's day fifty-four, and Rosa wanted you guys to see this," Chrysta said while grinning. Then, the view on the camera changed, and Rosa filled the screen. She was sitting on a tree stump with Burke standing behind her. His arms were crossed while holding a leather pouch. Rosa waved at the camera. "Rosa wants a haircut," Chrysta explained.

"Not a haircut. I want to chop it off," Rosa said. Burke grinned and opened the pouch he was holding, revealing a set of scissors and straight razors. "And no one can stop me."

"Oh no!" Rimsha cried and then giggled. Burke had taken out a straight razor and was sharpening it on a leather strap.

"Of course, the first thing she would do is cut off her hair," Cross said with a growl. But Tommy glanced at his face, and he was grinning just as much as the kids. Zheng joined them, smiling at the picture of her husband on the screen.

"Say it, Miss Torres," Burke drawled, still sharpening the blade.

Rosa sighed. "I, Rosa Torres, of sound mind and body," she started to say.

"I still challenge the sound mind part," Burke muttered, and the teens laughed with Chrysta on the screen.

"Hereby resolve Mr. Burke of the consequences of his actions," Rosa continued as Burke folded his arms with the blade still in his hand. "I have asked him to do this, and do not hold him responsible for my bad decisions." She glanced behind her to the Headmaster. "Okay, I said it. Now what?"

Burke didn't say a word, but he grabbed a portion of Rosa's hair on the side of her head and, with the swipe of the straight razor, cut it off. He offered the hair to Rosa, who looked at the long strands in shock. "Now the screaming starts," he said, and Chrysta laughed off-screen as Rosa gaped like a fish.

Rosa started to yell. "Oh my Lord, you took *so much of it off!* What are you *do—*" When suddenly, the scene cut off. When the camera was turned on again, Rosa was preening in front of it. Her hair was buzzed on the sides of her head but still long on the top. She was grinning from ear to ear, all her previous rage gone.

"Chrysta, aren't I beautiful?" Rosa asked. She turned the camera so that Chrysta appeared in the frame, reading a book while leaning on a tree. The sunlight was behind her, and Tommy's heart ached at the sight of her.

"Yes, Rosa, you are beautiful," Chrysta said in a tone of bored indifference.

"Aren't I handsome?"

"You are handsome," Chrysta confirmed, not looking up from her book or changing her tone.

"Don't you want to be my girlfriend now?" Rosa asked, throwing her hair over her shoulder.

"Oh, yes."

"Wait? Really?"

Chrysta rolled her eyes. "No, Rosa, I don't."

Rosa pouted for a second and then started preening again. "Well, I look better than your boyfriend, that's for sure."

Chrysta's eyebrows shot up, and she started smiling. "I'm sorry. What did you say?"

"I said I look better than Tom—" Rosa stopped talking, mouth still open for a second. "Shit," she cursed in a softer tone.

"Ha!" Chrysta said. She closed her book and stood up. She leaned towards the camera, smile bright and eyes dancing. "Hear that, Tommy? A third person called you my boyfriend. It's official."

"Tommy, I'm so sorry—"

"Thanks, Torres, I owe you for that one," Tommy told the teen on the laptop screen, the other teens laughing at his growl.

"—I didn't mean to say that. Chrysta, tell him you're not serious."

"Nope!" Chrysta chirped. She held the book in front of her chest and walked away from Rosa. "I don't think so!"

"Chrysta, wait!" But the smaller teen was laughing and still walking. Rosa started to follow her, but Chrysta suddenly disappeared, just a *pop* signaling that she had teleported away. "No fair, Chrysta!" Rosa yelled into the thick forest. "You can't just teleport like that! Come back and talk!"

"She did that without slowing down," Cross murmured, and Tommy glanced at his face. He was looking at the laptop in wonder. "I have never seen anyone do that while moving like that."

"Neil can't even do that," Zheng confirmed. "He has to be still when he teleports."

Meanwhile, Rosa yelled for Chrysta a few more times on the screen, but she didn't return. Finally, Rosa sighed and looked back into the camera. "Well, at least I still look good," she said with a grin, and the screen went black.

Chrysta was next to a giant rock when the screen came back to life. Burke was also there, walking around it. Chrysta looked nervous, jumping up and down, looking at the stone with a look of concern and worry. "Well, guys, it's day one hundred and thirty-four," Rosa announced off-camera. The screen blurred as Rosa quickly turned the camera to her face. "Thank you for the coffee, Mr. Cross," she added. Then, the screen went back to Chrysta. "And Chrysta is trying something insane."

"Nothing insane about it, Miss Torres," Burke said as he continued to study the stone. "Miss Angelos is just testing herself."

"Walking through that rock seems insane to me, Mr. Burke," Rosa responded.

"Miss Angelos?" Ellis asked. They and Smith had joined the group, Smith chewing on a breadstick.

"Chrysta's mother's maiden name," Cross explained. "Looks like she has decided to update her identity."

"Good for her," Zheng murmured.

Meanwhile, Burke stopped his inspection of the rock. He stopped in front of Chrysta, putting his hands behind him. "I estimate that the stone is at least two meters thick. At least seven feet," he said. Chrysta looked at him with wide eyes. "Are you sure you wish to still attempt to phase through it?"

"I do," Chrysta said, nodding solemnly.

"Whoa, wait, what did he say?" Smith asked.

"What's wrong?" Tommy asked, not liking the worried look on the hunter's face.

"Seven feet is a lot for someone new to phasing," Smith explained.

"Can she get hurt?" Tommy asked as Chrysta took several deep breaths on the screen.

"Well, the main thing about phasing is remembering not to breathe while doing it," Smith said. "You'll start to breathe what you are going through and not air. And, of course, if you get tired and unphase halfway through, you're screwed."

"And Burke is letting her do it?" Tommy asked, but of course, Chrysta couldn't hear him in the recording, and Tommy's stomach dropped as she stepped into the rock.

Rosa and Burke rushed to the other side. Tommy realized he was holding his breath as the seconds ticked by, and Chrysta didn't reappear. "Shouldn't she be out—" Kevin started to ask when Chrysta's arm shot out of the rock. Burke grabbed it and tugged Chrysta out of the stone, the girl laughing and gasping. Everyone watching the screen let out a collective sigh.

"I think I got turned around," Chrysta confessed. She stood up. "I'm gonna do it again," she said with a grin, and before Burke could stop her, she spun around and went back in.

"Ha!" Smith laughed, chuckling at Tommy's scowl. "She's a natural!"

"And how would you know?" Tommy asked the hunter.

"Phasing is my ability," Smith said. "You are actually looking at the sorcerer who holds the world's record for phasing. Fifteen feet through steel, thank you very much."

"You know the fact that Chrysta glows gold means she will break that record, right?" Tommy asked as Chrysta walked out of the giant stone again. Smith's cocky grin fell, and Ellis laughed.

The screen went dark, and when the picture came back, it was a close-up of Chrysta's face. She was messing with the camera, and when she was happy with it, she took a step back and waved at the camera. "Hey, everyone. It's day one hundred and eighty-nine. We will hopefully have something exciting to show you."

She turned around and walked away, joining Rosa and Burke. There were broken stone walls and columns overgrown with plants in front of them, five candles set on top of them. Rosa was standing with her eyes closed, taking several deep breaths. Burke crossed his arms and watched the teen. "Whenever you're ready, Miss Torres," he said.

Rosa didn't respond, just standing with her eyes closed for several long moments. Tommy looked at Cross. "What is it?"

"Fire aptitude test," Cross explained. "Rosa has never been able to manage it. If she succeeds, she will have mastery over her ability."

"Come on, Rosa," Rimsha murmured, watching the screen and biting her lip. "You can do it."

Finally, Rosa opened her eyes, face set in a determined grimace. She snapped her fingers. *Snap.* The first candle lit up. Two more snaps, *snap, snap,* and the second and third candles acquired a flame. Rosa paused and shifted on her feet. She snapped for the fourth time, *snap,* the fourth candle lit up.

"Come on, my dear," Cross whispered. "Show that harpy Paulson that you can do this."

Rosa snapped one more time, *snap,* and the final candle lit up. Rosa waited for one tense moment, and then she whopped, jumping up and down. Chrysta joined her, both of them laughing and dancing together. The teens watching the screen yelled in excitement with them, and Cross gave out a bark of a laugh. Meanwhile, Burke watched the girls celebrate, a smile tugging on his lips under his beard. The girls stopped dancing and hugged briefly, and then Rosa let out a gasp. Her shoulders started shaking, and Chrysta patted her back.

"You ladies and your waterworks," Burke joked, not unkindly. He reached into his shirt pocket and handed Rosa a handkerchief.

"She did it!" Kevin cried. Julien and Rimsha were hugging, Rimsha's eyes shining. "Shouldn't they come back now?"

"Neil will want them to stay in the sphere as long as possible," Zheng said. "Miss Angelos seems to be gaining control of her abilities quickly, but the longer they stay inside, the better she will be at hiding them when she comes out."

Tommy felt a slight pang of guilt as he watched Chrysta on the screen run to the camera with a giant smile on her face. She reached off-screen, and it went black, no new scene replacing it. He wanted her back out of the sphere so bad. But at least she was learning while she was in there.

"No worries, everyone," Cross said brightly. "They will come out when they are ready. Meanwhile, let us keep up our vigil."

The group broke up, the kids excitingly talking about what Rosa and Chrysta had done on the video. Zheng looked at Tommy, studying his face for a moment. "Be happy for her," she said. "She is doing what she set out to do. She will be a fine sorcerer at this rate."

"Yeah, she will be," he agreed. *A fine sorcerer who won't need me,* he thought to himself.

~ 39 ~

Rimsha worried at her lower lip as she watched Kevin study the iron maiden. She didn't know why the boy seemed so fascinated with the evil thing, but he could barely stay away from it as time passed in the vault.

"Kevin," she said softly. "I don't think you should touch it."

"I'm not touching it," he argued. "I just want to look at it." But right after he said that, he started to reach for it.

Rimsha sighed. The whole thing had sounded fun when Mr. Burke and Mrs. Zheng explained what the sphere was and why they would watch over it for Rosa and Chrysta. It reminded her of her father's stories from when she was younger, of sorcerers going on adventures and creating new and fantastic magical spells and objects. But in reality, it was getting boring, waiting for the girls to come out. It could be soon; it could be tomorrow at six in the morning. There was no way to tell.

Ichiro wandered up to her, watching Kevin with her, chewing on some candy. He offered her a bit of the sweet, and she accepted, slowly chewing as Kevin leaned as close as he could to the iron maiden without touching it. Julien was behind them, sitting on a couch with a table in front of him, using his new tarot set. Tommy and Mr. Smith were in the middle of the vault, both sleeping on couches. Tommy had headphones in his ears, probably still listening to that beautiful song Chrysta sent him.

Rimsha smiled every time she thought about it. If only someone would do something like that for her.

Mr. Cross, Mrs. Zheng, and Miss Hafeez were gathered around the sphere, watching it, Mx. Ellis patrolling outside by themselves. Although, there wasn't much to do when you watched the sphere. It just sat there, the light appearing and disappearing with the passage of the days, as interesting as... how did Kevin put it? Watching paint dry. That was why Kevin was currently playing with a medieval torture device and not protecting the sphere.

"I don't think he could hurt himself," Ichiro told her. "Mr. Cross said that enchantments were gone."

"But it had enchantments on it at some point," she pointed out. "You never trust an item that used to be spelled. Everyone knows that." Ichiro shrugged, and Rimsha huffed. He just didn't know about stuff like this. He never had anyone to teach him the rules of magic when he was younger. "Magic just doesn't fade away gradually. It can come back without warning." She raised her voice a little so that Kevin could hear her. "It could still be dangerous."

Kevin lazily raised a hand, dismissing her concerns. "I'll be okay," he said. "I don't even know how to open it." As he said that phrase, though, the front of the iron maiden split in half with a screech, opening up and revealing rows of spikes on the inside. Rimsha tried to not think about the stains that covered the sharp points. "Cool!" Kevin cried, excitedly bending in to examine the spikes.

"No!" Mr. Cross yelled, and the teens jumped and whirled around. Mr. Cross was jogging to join them, a scowl on his face. "Mr. Butler, do *not* mess with that! It's dangerous!"

"I told you," Rimsha fiercely whispered to Ichiro as Mr. Cross grabbed Kevin's arm and made him step back.

"You said that it was safe, Mr. Cross," Kevin said.

"I said that the enchantments that drain your lifeforce were gone, Kevin," Mr. Cross explained. "But the enchantments that allow you to control the door are very much active." Mr. Cross took another step back, dragging Kevin with him. *"Band karana."*

The door of the iron maiden snapped shut with a *boom*, a noise so sudden and loud that it made everyone jump. Even Julien looked up, feeling the vibrations through the floor. Poor Tommy and Mr. Smith started awake, the hunter so startled that he grabbed the sword lying next to him on the floor. "What the fuck was that?!" Tommy yelled, glaring at the group in the back of the vault.

"Sorry, gentlemen!" Mr. Cross called out. "Just showing the kids how nasty the iron maiden can be." Rimsha felt her cheeks heat up, even though Kevin was the one playing with it. Kevin, meanwhile, looked ashamed, and he shuffled over to Rimsha and Ichiro with his head down.

"I know you guys are bored," Mr. Cross started to say. "But it's only fourteen hours until we are done. So do try to stay out of trouble until then."

"Actually, Mr. Cross, it's fourteen hours, twelve minutes, and," Ichiro checked his watch, "forty-seven seconds until they get out. That's if they come out right at six in the morning."

"Thank you, Mr. Takahashi. Your accuracy is appreciated. Go do something else, please."

Ichiro and Kevin went towards the front of the vault, Ichiro grabbing his laptop from a scowling Tommy. Rimsha heard Kevin mumble something to Mr. Smith and Tommy as he passed, hopefully an apology. Mr. Smith settled back on the couch he was using, but Tommy stayed sitting, rubbing his face. Rimsha was going to join the boys, maybe watch a movie with them, or even go outside for some fresh air, but she hesitated when she saw Julien's face. He was frowning at something on the table in front of him. She gently knocked on the table so he would know she was there. "What's wrong?" she signed when he looked up.

"I keep getting the same cards when I do a reading," he signed back. "That's very rare, and with the card I keep getting, it's worrying me."

"What cards do you get?" she signed. He picked up the cards and started shuffling them. He even let her mix them for a bit. Finally, she held the deck out, and he chose three cards, laying them on the table.

Julien's frown deepened. "These cards bother me," he signed and then pointed to two cards.

Rimsha studied the cards and tried to think back to her divination class. It was not her strongest subject. As much as she squinted into tea leaves and bones, she couldn't see what others could. But at least the tarot was a little clearer. One was The Tower, the illustration showing two people falling from a tower as it was struck by golden lightning. "Something is coming," she signed, remembering her lessons. "It will be a shock, but it may not be a bad thing."

"It's a card for change," Julien agreed. "But it's getting paired with this one." And he pointed to the Three of Swords, three black swords like the sword of a hunter, sitting on a golden background. "The loss of something, often though—" Julien made a sign that Rimsha didn't know, holding his pinky and pointer fingers out on both hands and moving them in front of his chest so that his left hand was above his right. He fingerspelled the word when he saw her look of confusion. "—betrayal." He pointed at the last card. "The magician is good. He means solving your problems with your own resourcefulness."

"Do a reading for me," Rimsha asked him. He shuffled the deck, and she chose three cards. She winced when she saw The Tower again, but now it was joined by The Death card. "I remember this one," she signed, pointing at the gold skeleton riding a horse. "Something is changing, sometimes for the better? What is this one?" she asked, pointing to the last card: a man lying facedown on the ground, multiple swords stuck in the back.

"The Ten of Swords," Julien explained, and Rimsha counted the swords and was shocked that ten of them fit in the poor man's back. "Another card that predicts a surprise coming, something bad. Also caused by betrayal."

"So someone is going to betray us?" Rimsha asked.

"Or already has betrayed us," Julien added, and he turned in his seat. Rimsha followed his gaze and realized that he was looking at Hunter Hafeez. Were the cards warning them that Hafeez would hurt Tommy? Maybe that they would fight again, and she would injure him?

"Tommy!" Julien called out. "Can you come here?"

The changeling raised an eyebrow, but he got up and walked to them, passing a snoring Mr. Smith. "What's up?" he asked as he sat down.

"Let me do a Tarot reading for you," Julien said.

Tommy shook his head. "Magic doesn't work on me. It won't work."

"Tarot cards are influenced by fate," Julien explained as he shuffled his deck. "It is affected by our decisions and actions, human and changeling alike."

Tommy studied Julien for a minute, but he just shrugged and picked three cards when Julien offered the cards to him. Rimsha and Julien shared a grim look when The Tower showed up again. Tommy just snorted and pointed to the card in front of him. "I don't know much about tarot, but I think everyone knows this one."

Julien smiled at the androgynous couple embracing on the card. "The Lovers is certainly a popular card, but it doesn't always predict romantic love. It can also show that a decision will have to be made, generally about a relationship."

"Like Chrysta deciding if she wants to be with me or not?" Tommy asked, looking grim.

"It could be that," Julien admitted. "Or the lovers will share a strong bond that will empower each other. Like when one does everything in her power to save the one who recused her from her father, for example."

Tommy pointed at Julien while glowering. "You and Cross should never have taken Chrysta back to that mansion. Nothing you say can change my mind," he growled. Julien just gave Tommy a small smile and shrugged. Then, Tommy turned his attention to The Tower. "What about this one?"

"Something bad is going to happen," Julien explained. "Someone's plan is going to fail. It keeps showing up, over and over, and that's not a good sign."

"And this suicidal idiot?" Tommy asked, pointing at the last card.

"The Fool," Julien said, studying the man about to take a step off a cliff as he looked up to the sky. "It's the beginning of a journey or a new relationship, but he is naive and has to be careful, or his first step could be his last."

Tommy hummed, looking at the cards in front of him. "Interesting. So my new relationship with Chrysta is doomed to fail before it even starts? Wonderful job. I feel so grateful that I have that information." Rimsha giggled at his dry tone.

Julien smiled. "Or, Chrysta has to be careful in her new adventure, but with you by her side, she will be empowered and can weather any storm that the crumbling tower will cause."

"That's just too vague," Rimsha said.

"You're right," Julien said. He started to sign. "That's why I should go dream walking, see if I can get more information."

"Are you sure?" Rimsha signed back, keeping her hands low so Mr. Cross couldn't see their conversation. "That's dangerous. Mr. Cross probably won't want you to go dream walking right now."

"He will just think I'm taking a nap," Julien signed. "Keep an eye on me while I'm sleeping, okay?"

Tommy was looking between the two of them. "What? What is it?"

"Julien is going to dream walk," Rimsha whispered, still signing so that Julien could understand her.

"Walking dreams is that thing you sorcerers do to see the future, right?"

"Yes," Rimsha said. "How do you know about it?"

"The Acolytes had a guy who could dream walk. He was total shit, though. He had the acolytes invest in a whole bunch of stocks and companies that he swore would pay off big, but they always fell through. Dumbass ended up killing himself a few decades back. Used too much chloroform to make himself sleep and didn't wake up."

Julien nodded grimly. "Dream walking can be addictive," he said softly, remembering to keep his voice low. "People will live the same moment over and over or try to discover the future." He gave Rimsha a grin. "I'll be careful, I promise."

Rimsha glared at the older boy. "Be careful," she ordered him as he laid down, his hands glowing blue slightly as he made himself go to sleep. Tommy sniffed and got up, avoiding the magic that seemed to bother him so much.

Rimsha got up and grabbed one of her books, and by the time she got back to the chair across from Julien, he was fast asleep on the couch, mouth a little open as he slept. Rimsha settled as she opened her book. The hero had just gotten to his lover's castle, determined to find her and save her from her abusive father and cruel fiancé before they were married. Rimsha thought of Chrysta's gift to Tommy as she glanced at the changeling and sighed. Maybe someday, someone would do something like that for her.

Chrysta was twirled and then dipped, and she laughed. Tommy gave her a roguish smile and then picked her back up to spin her around on the dance floor. She was dressed in her concert dress, Tommy in his black and red suit, and Chrysta couldn't remember ever being this happy.

Too bad it wasn't real.

Chrysta's nightmares had slowly faded with time, the traumatic memory losing its power over her every time she stopped it. Mr. Burke's trick of reminding herself that Tommy saved her from her father was the key she needed to break the nightmare's hold on her. But as she got more comfortable with dream walking, the more she found herself filling her time asleep with pleasant visions and dreams. Breakfasts and Christmases in the Jackson household, playing violin with her mother, exploring all the locations in the world she had learned about at school that she never thought her father would let her see. And, of course, her favorite dreams, the ones with Tommy.

In the beginning, the dreams were mainly memories of the last few months. Their first meeting in the park by her school, playing in the jazz club, Tommy in the front row at her concert. Then, as time went on and she got better at controlling them, she could change them to be whatever she wanted them to be. He would play *Romance* on the piano while she sat next to him. She would be at the jazz club playing *Romanze* for the crowd as he sat at a table with a smile. They would make pancakes in some small apartment as the early morning light streamed through a window. Tonight's fantasy was dancing at a ball, a crowd of faceless people watching as they stepped around the floor. She didn't even know how to dance. Maybe she was copying a movie her mother had watched with her when she was a child.

"I don't think it's a bad thing," Rosa told her a few days ago when Chrysta confessed what she was doing at night. The dreams weren't hurting anyone, but she still felt a lingering pang of guilt every time she found herself dream walking with a vision starring Tommy. "Julien says that you have to be careful because people will start replacing reality with dream walking. Always sleeping to stay in the fantasy that they have created. But you aren't doing that, right?" Rosa waved a hand casually as she talked, and a fire roared to life in the hearth, heating the pot already there. Ever since Rosa had passed the fire aptitude test, she never passed up the chance to use her ability.

Chrysta bit her lip in thought. "No, I don't," she said. "But I don't know; using Tommy like that feels creepy somehow."

"Are you making him do something he wouldn't do otherwise?" Rosa asked.

"No."

"Then don't worry about it. It's just like a daydream. Remember that it's not an actual memory, no matter how real it feels."

The music in her dream changed, something slower and jazzy, and Tommy tugged her to him, placing a kiss on her forehead. Chrysta sighed and swayed with him to the music. No, not a memory, but someday they would go out and dance like this. They would play music for each other or make those pancakes. Tommy loved her, and when she got out of the sphere, she would make sure they did all of those things.

The song ended, and Chrysta smiled with her eyes closed. Tommy still held her, one hand lightly resting on the small of her back. "Love you, beautiful," he murmured.

"Love you too," she replied, and she looked up so he could kiss her, eyes still closed.

"Chrysta?"

Chrysta jumped in surprise at the unexpected voice, and the vision melted quickly into the floor. Her concert dress disappeared and was replaced with the simple one based on what her mother wore. She whirled and saw someone standing in the blackness. Julien, dressed in jeans and a shirt, looked as surprised to see her as she was to see him.

They stood like that for a few silent moments, and then they both yelled and threw up their arms simultaneously. Chrysta rushed to him, and they hugged while laughing. "Oh, it's good to see you," Chrysta said, speaking into his chest.

"Good to see you too," he said.

She blinked, feeling like something was off. Then she realized that there was no way for him to see her face. She looked up in confusion. "How did you know what I said?" she asked.

He gestured to the side of his head as they stepped apart. "This isn't the physical plane. My 'ears' work in here, and I can hear just fine. When I started to walk dreams, I needed someone to come in with me to help me identify sounds." He stopped and rubbed his neck. "I know that I still talk funny. There's nothing I can do about that."

"You sound fine," Chrysta said with a smile. "I'm just glad you can understand me. What are you doing here?"

"I was using my Tarot set and kept getting the same cards. I wanted to do some dream walking and see if I can divine the future."

"How... how do we see each other right now? Isn't time moving faster in the sphere?"

Julien gave her a grin. "And time moves differently here. Ever go to sleep and have a dream that seemed to last for an eternity, but you were only asleep for a few minutes? We just happened to be here at the same time on this plane, and we happened to find each other." He gave her an understanding smile. "What were you doing? Dancing?"

Chrysta felt her cheeks heat in embarrassment. "I was dancing with Tommy," she admitted.

He chuckled and made a sign, pointing his pointer fingers at each other in front of his face, thumbs held straight up, and then pulling his hands back towards his ears a couple of times. "Having some fun while dream walking? It's okay, it's fine, just remember, they aren't real—"

"And don't replace reality with them," Chrysta finished for him. "I know. Rosa has already warned me." She looked around. "I have looked at memories here, but how do you see the future?"

"It's a little complicated," Julien explained. He waved a hand, and the floor below them glowed blue, the light blossoming out around them. Building from the inky black, a scene started to form, all the figures frozen in place like they were a painting. It was the vault. Julien was asleep on a couch with Rimsha sitting in front of him. Tommy and Mr. Smith formed next, Tommy glaring at the hunter as he slept on the couch with his mouth opened, probably snoring if Tommy's expression was anything to go by.

The vault kept forming until the sphere was revealed, completely dark. Mrs. Zheng and Miss Hafeez sat around the sphere, watching it with identical bored expressions. Ichiro and Kevin were watching a movie on Ichiro's laptop at a nearby table. Mr. Cross sat in a nearby chair, hands folded on his stomach and chin on his chest, eyes closed. "This is the present," Julien explained. He pointed at the sphere. "It was just a coincidence that we came here at the same time."

Chrysta went over to Tommy, glad to see him. She frowned, though, when she saw his arms. She leaned down to study the many band-aids that now spotted his arms. "What happened to him?" she asked the older teen.

Julien looked uncomfortable for a moment before answering. "Hunter Hafeez said something about you... something bad, and she and Tommy got into a fight. So that was why we were late getting supplies to you guys and had to send the letters a little later." He quickly put up his hands. "Everyone is okay. And I think Hunter Hafeez apologized."

Chrysta turned to glare at the hunter sitting in the front of the vault. "Oh, I'm going to get her for that."

"What will you do to her?" Julien asked, looking nervous.

"Not sure," Chrysta growled. "Maybe I should make her cat cough up a ton of hairballs."

Julien seemed to relax and gave her a smile. "How can you manage that?"

"I glow gold; I will figure it out," she said. She crouched down and put her hands on Tommy's arms, studying his face. "Tell him I miss him," she said softly.

"I will," Julien promised. "I think he misses you as much as you miss him."

Julien went over to his sleeping self and held up his hands. They glowed blue, and the scene around them faded until just sleeping Julien was left. "When you divine the future, the closer you are to the person, the easier it is," he explained. "Doing your own future is the simplest, then family members, friends, and then people you know. Strangers are almost impossible unless you can bring someone they know into this realm with you."

"So I could see my father?" Chrysta asked.

Julien blinked but then nodded slowly. "Yes. But why would you want to?"

"I feel that I may want to keep tabs on him when I get out of the ball," she explained.

Julien nodded again and then stepped up to her. "Close your eyes," he said, and she did as he said. "Think of your father. Try to reach out to him and see where he is right now."

She concentrated on her father, how she remembered him—

always in a suit, never smiling, never asking how she was, coming to pick her up from school on the day her mother died to tell Chrysta that she was dead in an accident, not upset at all, not giving her any comfort as she cried

—and she felt the flex in her chest. When she opened her eyes, the floor beneath her was glowing gold. It spread, and then her father materialized out of the blackness. He sat on the floor, his suit jacket nowhere to be seen, his white dress shirt crumpled and dirty. He had several metal restraints on his arms, chained to the floor, the runes on them glowing different colors: from reds to greens, blues to purples. His head was tilted back, his face set in a scowl, his eyes closed.

Chrysta felt a swirl of emotions at seeing him again. Fear, anger, and red-hot hate rolled in her stomach, and a sharp metallic taste filled her mouth. "He's still alive," she said. "He said the others would kill him if I got away, but he's still alive."

"He glows white," Julien said. Chrysta looked at him, and he shrugged. "They may not want to kill him until they know that they don't need him anymore."

Chrysta looked at the scene of her father. "I hope it's a dark place," she said, almost surprised at the vitriol coming out of her own mouth. "I hope they never let him out."

"Well, let's see," Julien said, stepping forward. His hand glowed for a moment, and the vision morphed and changed. Jozef York's sitting figure was replaced by Tommy's tall monster form holding the acolyte about a foot off the ground by the throat. But, unlike the first vision, this one was moving, and Chrysta could hear Tommy's growling as her father kicked his feet uselessly. "How is it hanging, York, ol' buddy, ol' pal?" Tommy rumbled, muzzle set in a snarl.

Chrysta laughed as the scene froze. "When is *that* going to happen?" she asked.

"Don't know," Julien said. He made a slow circle around the two figures, studying them. "Your father doesn't look older, so maybe soon? That's if it happens at all."

"What do you mean?"

"Fate is not fixed. It changes with our choices all the time. So even small decisions can have big impacts on what can happen in the future."

"Like if my father never gets out of that prison..." Chrysta started to say.

"Tommy will never get the chance to threaten him," Julien completed her thought, gesturing at the changeling. "But considering that this is the scene that came up, means there is a good chance it will happen."

"So my father *will* get free," Chrysta said. "But we don't know how or when."

"The art of seeing the future," Julien said with a rueful smile. "Tea leaves, the Tarot, bones, dream walking..." Julien was moving his hands around, and Chrysta wondered if he was using sign language on purpose or because it was a habit. "Doesn't matter what you use; they are all vague."

"So, what is in your future?" Chrysta asked.

The scene of Chrysta's father and Tommy faded from view as Julien turned back to his sleeping self. He held up his hands, and his sleeping self and the couch disappeared. It was replaced with Julien standing with Kevin, both boys looking scared. Julien was holding onto Kevin, keeping the smaller teen from running forward. "Leave her alone!" Kevin yelled, but Chrysta couldn't see who he was shouting at.

The scene froze, and Chrysta turned to Julien with a frown. "Who is he talking to?" she asked. "And who is he trying to protect?"

"I'm not sure," Julien said, returning her frown. "Can you try to expand it?"

"I don't even know how to."

"Close your eyes again. Try to focus on Kevin. Maybe we can see who he is talking to."

Chrysta did as she was told, trying to think of Kevin: his voice, his interest in changelings, the food that he had made for everyone. She felt the flex in her chest again, and Julien gasped a strangled sound. She opened her eyes, expecting to see something different in the scene in front of them, but Julien was looking down. Chrysta followed his gaze, and the floor was glowing red, the colors growing brighter and getting bigger by the second. Julien waved his hands. "Stop! *Stop!* Stop glowing! He's coming!"

Chrysta looked at her hands dumbly, realizing that she was glowing gold from trying to read the future. "Who's coming?" she asked, trying to wave her hands like that would make the light go out faster.

"The elephant!"

Julien waved his hands, and the vision of himself and Kevin disappeared into the floor. He grabbed Chrysta's hand and led her away from the light. Like the whale, the light kept getting brighter until a figure broke out of the inky black floor. The elephant's skin glowed like the whale's, but his color was red and oranges shining through his rock-like skin that had the texture of cooling lava, deep cracks forming as the creature moved. This creature was bigger than a real elephant. Its tusks were massive, almost as long as its body, curling upwards. When the elephant fully emerged from the ground below them, he looked down his trunk at them, eyes red and full of malice.

Julien stepped in front of Chrysta like he was trying to shield her. "Don't talk," he ordered her.

The elephant snorted. "Do not speak, deaf mute. Your voice is grating," the elephant rumbled, his voice making Chrysta's chest vibrate. Julien winced at the elephant's cruel words. "My dispute is with the girl, not you."

Chrysta glared at the creature in front of them. "I'm sorry. What dispute do you have with me?"

"You're glowing!" he thundered, shaking his head so his tusks cut through the air. "It's bright and disturbs me. I demand you leave at once!"

Julien nodded. "We can do that." The elephant rumbled at him. "We *will* do that."

"But we just started," Chrysta said to Julien. He turned to look at her slightly, face set in fear. "We didn't get to see anything."

"What?!" the elephant roared. He picked up his front feet and slammed them down, shaking the black floor. "You dare to defy me?!" The elephant started to walk towards them, trunk waving in agitation.

"Please, sir," Julien said, pushing Chrysta back and keeping her behind him. "She's new to dream walking. We didn't know her glow would disturb you. We will leave. Right now."

The elephant snorted and swung his trunk. "No," he rumbled. "She needs to learn to not disturb me again." He lunged forward with his trunk, reaching for

Chrysta and knocking Julien over in the process. Chrysta yelped as the appendage wrapped around her, and she was lifted into the air. She tried to throw some sparks into the elephant's face, but he just turned his head and scrutinized her with one red eye.

"You will find that I am not like my brother," he growled. "I do not suffer humanity as he does." Chrysta didn't respond and just kept struggling, kicking her feet at the elephant's tough hide. "You truly wish to see the future? Then I will show it to you. As a lesson to never return."

Chrysta cried out as the elephant started to glow brighter, his rock-like skin getting hotter and burning her. Suddenly, he tossed her, and she went flying. She landed on the black floor in a heap. Julien tried to run to her, but the elephant caught him with a tusk, and he went sailing in the other direction.

Chrysta started to pick herself up, but the floor was no longer black but grey concrete. When she got vertical, she noticed that she was no longer wearing the dress but a pair of jeans and a red sweater. Suddenly, something heavy landed on her back, and she stumbled. Something dark was wrapped around her, and before she could fight it off, there was a searing pain where her neck met her shoulder.

Chrysta screamed and collapsed. She blasted the dark shape away, but it was too late. She reached up to her neck, and when she pulled her hand away, it was covered in blood. She pressed her hand back to her neck, even as she felt warm liquid pouring down her sweater.

"Chrysta!" Julien yelled, and he ran to her. But before he made it to her, the elephant reared up and brought his front feet down on top of the teen, making him disappear in front of Chrysta's eyes.

Chrysta panted, her vision going dark. The elephant snorted and then trumpeted, and finally, Chrysta passed out.

·····

Chrysta screamed, scrambling to sit up in her bed. She frantically looked around the room for a few seconds, looking for the elephant while holding her injured neck. By the time Rosa made it to the curtain to her room, she had realized that the elephant was gone, she was awake, and her neck was intact. She crossed her arms in front of her as Rosa rushed to her side.

Mr. Burke appeared a moment later, holding his sword and with Willow by his side. "What happened?" he asked. "Another nightmare?"

"No," Chrysta said, trying to calm down so she could talk even as she started to shudder. "N-no, it was the elephant."

Mr. Burke relaxed, lowering his sword. "You went dream walking? I don't want to say that I told you so, Miss Angelos, but—"

"You don't understand. I was dream walking, but then Julien showed up, and I was helping him to see the future, and the elephant was upset that I was glowing."

"Why was Julien there?" Rosa asked.

"He said he needed to see the future. But the elephant didn't just wake us up. He said he wanted to teach me a lesson, so he showed me the future. And then—" she stopped, and Rosa squeezed one of her hands. "—I was somewhere else, in different clothes, and something attacked me and t-tore my throat open."

Mr. Burke blinked at her. "You think the elephant showed you how you will die, Miss Angelos?"

"Y-yes," Chrysta stuttered. "And it's going to be soon."

"How do you know that?" Rosa asked.

Chrysta got up and went to the chest of drawers she used for her clothes. She found the sweater and jeans that were in her vision and showed them to Rosa and Mr. Burke. "Because this is what I will be wearing when it happens," she explained softly.

Suddenly there was a roll of thunder, and rain started to hit the window, the first rainstorm they had seen since entering the sphere.

41

ulien had only been asleep for a few minutes when suddenly Tommy heard a moan behind him. He turned around on the couch and saw Cross in the chair, face screwed up in a frown. He got up and walked over to the man, planning on waking him up.

"What's wrong?" Zheng asked, looking at the empath in curiosity.

"Bad dreams," Tommy simply said, not wanting to explain any further if Cross would prefer to keep the nightmares a secret. He reached out to shake Cross's arm when the sorcerer jumped with a yelp, almost falling out of his chair. "Holy shit, Cross," Tommy said as the man panted. "You need to get that memory out of your head."

"I... I know," Cross said. "As soon as we're finished here, I'll get the death of that poor girl's mother erased for good."

Tommy paused and blinked, a sudden feeling of unease settling in his stomach. He leaned closer to Cross, making sure they were eye to eye. "Wait a minute, what do you mean? You know who that woman is?"

Cross jerked guiltily and opened his mouth to reply, but there was a shout from behind them before he could answer. This time it was Julien, flailing on the couch. He was so loud that Hafeez and Zheng got up to investigate, and even Smith woke and grabbed his sword in confusion. Cross got up and went to the older teen, even as Rimsha was trying to wake him up.

"What is wrong with you and your charges, Cross?" Zheng asked as she, Tommy, Ichiro, and Kevin followed the empath to the couch.

"Chrysta!" Julien cried as he sat up.

"What about Chrysta?" Tommy asked, temporarily forgetting that Julien wouldn't hear him. Rimsha looked up, gave Tommy a look of fear, and then started signing. Julien signed something back.

"He says that he met Chrysta while he was dream walking," Rimsha said, interpreting as Julien's hands flew through the air. "They were trying to see the future when the elephant showed up."

So many questions came to Tommy's mind, but he fought the urge to ask them as Ichiro and Kevin sat down on the couch with Julien, and the older teen took a couple of deep breaths before he continued signing. "The elephant wasn't happy that Chrysta was glowing gold," Rimsha continued to translate, "so he…" Her voice trailed off, her eyes going wide. She put a hand to her mouth and looked at Julien in horror.

"What?" Tommy asked, looking between Rimsha and Julien. "He what?"

"He said that he wanted to teach Chrysta a lesson," Julien said out loud. "So he showed her the future." Julien gulped and then looked right at Tommy. "He showed her how she was going to die."

.....

It took a while to give Tommy a crash course in walking dreams and what had happened. How Chrysta and Julien met up in the first place, what the vision with York meant, why Julien saw Kevin in his dream, what the elephant was, and why he had attacked Chrysta.

"Are you certain that all of this is going to happen soon?" Zheng asked Julien.

Julien nodded, slightly calmer than when he woke up. "Yes, as certain as I can be with dream walking."

Cross and Zheng shared a look. "The boy yelling at someone to 'leave her alone,' Monroe threatening York, and a large dark shape attacking the girl," Hafeez murmured. "Barely anything to go by."

"Nyla, *something* is coming. Something is going to go wrong," Zheng said. She glanced at the table where Julien's Tarot set had been knocked over, with the card with the tower hit with lightning now on top. "The signs are there if we wish to see them. The question now is how we proceed."

Cross looked over at the sphere. "Apparently, Headmaster Burke doesn't share your worries, or he would have been out with the girls by now."

"Neil knows that whatever it is, it's not happening right this minute," Zheng argued. "I know how to signal to him that there is an emergency that justifies him leaving the sphere. He will wait until I use that signal or their time in the sphere runs out, whatever comes first."

"Could the visions be wrong?" Tommy asked. He really wanted to ask if the vision of Chrysta dying could be wrong.

Julien got up without a word and went to a backpack. He rifled in it until he found something and brought it back. "Kevin was wearing this in my vision," he said, handing Kevin's new sweater to the young boy.

Kevin gulped as he held the sweater. "I-I was going to wear this tomorrow," he said softly.

"And the vision that this elephant showed Chrysta?" Tommy asked. "Could it be fake? Since it sounds like he is some kind of asshole?"

"Aren't the Old Ones supposed to always know what will happen?" Smith asked from a nearby couch, leaning on his sword.

"They can see the future better than any human can," Ellis said to their partner. "But the elephant didn't say Miss Angelos would die. He just wanted to teach her a lesson." They looked at Julien. "Is there anything else you can remember?"

Julien's forehead furrowed in thought. "No. She was just standing in jeans and a sweater. Something large and dark landed on her back. She blasted it away, and then she was bleeding from her neck. And then she fell."

Cross groaned. "Too vague," he muttered.

"Let's be glad that we have that much to go on," Zheng said. She glanced at a watch on her wrist and then the digital clock by the sphere. "We have an hour and thirty-nine minutes to get the supplies down here and send them in. Once that is done, you're sending your charges back to the Academy, Cross."

Ichiro and Kevin exploded at her words.

"What! We want to stay here!"

"We have to stay for Rosa and Chrysta!"

"Yeah!"

"They would want us to stay!"

"Enough!" Rimsha yelled at them, and Tommy blinked in surprise at the girl's outburst. Rimsha shifted when she realized that everyone was looking at her but continued in a softer tone. "This is serious! If something bad happens, we need to leave so we're not in the way."

"She's right," Cross told the younger boys. "I am not only responsible for Rosa's and Chrysta's safety, but the safety of you lot as well." He pointed at the boys. "If I know you are safe, I can focus on getting the girls home in one piece, understood?"

Ichiro and Kevin shifted, looking ashamed. "Yes, sir," they both mumbled.

"Will you use the transportation circle?" Ellis asked Cross.

"No, I need to keep that here if we need it for an emergency," Cross explained. "I hate to send you all out driving this late in this weather, but I don't have much choice," he said while looking at Julien.

Julien nodded. "I can drive."

"Alright, you have your orders," Cross said, looking at the boys. "Hop to it."

Ichiro and Kevin grumbled, but they got up and started for the vault's door. Rimsha and Julien were close behind them. Tommy waited as Smith and Ellis went with them, watching Cross rub his eyes as Zheng picked up the Tarot set.

"Who is the woman in your dream, Cross?" Tommy asked the sorcerer.

"Not now, Tommy," Cross said warily, not removing the hand from his eyes.

"You said you didn't know who she was yesterday morning," Tommy continued, ignoring Cross's warning. "But just now, you called her the 'poor girl's mother.' So whose mother is she?"

"What dream is this, Cross?" Zheng asked. "Were you dream walking too?"

Cross sighed. He glanced behind him, probably to make sure the kids weren't nearby. "No," he said, looking at the hunter. "No, it's not a vision from dream walking. When I went to the mansion with Chrysta, Guerra grabbed me. It triggered a reading."

Both Zheng and Hafeez winced in sympathy. "So you saw—" Zheng started to say.

"Almost every murder and torture session that man was a part of," Cross finished for her. "At first, it was mostly abstract images and feelings. Pain and fear of his victims." Cross shuddered. "And his joy. The man is a certifiable sadist.

"But one memory was more vivid than the others—Guerra torturing and killing a woman. The memory wasn't fading, and I felt like I knew her. And now I know why."

Tommy felt fear settle in his stomach, something oily crawling in his belly. "Who did Guerra kill, Cross?"

.....

The rain didn't stop the next day or the day after that.

"It will last several weeks, I'm afraid," Mr. Burke told them as he crossed the number 224 off the board. "Generally, the weather stays constant, but it will be for a very long time when it does rain."

"I wonder why," Chrysta murmured while she looked out the window.

"Just another mystery of the sphere, Miss Angelos," Mr. Burke replied.

For the first few days after the encounter with the elephant, Chrysta was nervous. She didn't dare dream walk and found herself picking up the clothing from her vision many times, wondering if she should burn them in the fireplace. "Would you like to leave, Miss Angelos?" Mr. Burke asked her over breakfast one morning.

"I... I'm not sure," she confessed. "What the elephant showed me, it's going to happen for sure, right?"

"What visions the Old Ones show us generally come to pass, yes," Mr. Burke said.

"But Chrysta may not die, right?" Rosa argued. "You were still alive after getting attacked, right?" she asked Chrysta.

"I'm going to get my throat ripped out, Rosa. I doubt I will survive that," Chrysta replied.

"But maybe we can get you to a healer," Rosa said. "Or maybe it won't happen at all."

"Mr. LeBlanc will tell Jiao and the others what he saw," Mr. Burke said gently. "It will give them an advantage if and when the danger comes. Trust that our protectors will do their duty."

Chrysta nodded. "Better to stay in here and finish what we started."

"Exactly."

So they continued to read and learn, stuck inside the cabin as the rain continued. Chrysta studied mental abilities while Rosa was stuck reading legal texts and documents.

"Why do I have to study these again?" Rosa growled one night. There was a roaring fire in the fireplace, and they gathered their chairs close to it for warmth. The rain came down the chimney and made the flame spit and sputter.

"A hunter needs to know the laws they are upholding," Mr. Burke explained, leaning back in his chair with his feet up, Willow at his feet. Poe was on the other familiar's back, sleeping with his beak under one wing. "You still want to become a hunter, correct?"

"Yes," Rosa replied.

"Then you have to learn the laws you will uphold."

"I think I would rather go back to the fire aptitude test," Rosa muttered, and Chrysta laughed.

While Rosa memorized laws and legal procedures, Chrysta worked on anything she could while staying indoors. Levitation was fun, as well as talking to Poe and Willow. Force shields were entertaining and useful when she ran through the rain to the outhouse.

Mr. Burke only had one thing that he required Chrysta to learn. "Most sorcerers are multi-lingual," he explained. "I won't say you are required to learn a new language, but I do recommend you study xenoglossy."

"Xenoglossy?"

"Being able to listen to and comprehend any language," Mr. Burke explained. "Not all sorcerers speak English, but you will want to be able to communicate with them."

"Ichiro had to have a xenoglossy spell put on him when he first got to the States," Rosa said with a giggle. "But the spell was by a sorcerer from Britain, and he started saying all these British phrases and words. It was *hilarious*. Hold up a flashlight and ask him what it is. He gets so mad when he says 'torch.'"

"I always wanted to learn Spanish," Chrysta said with a grin. By the time Rosa had dinner ready that night, Chrysta was able to ask for *estofado be ternera* and *panecillos* from a smiling Rosa.

Telepathy scared her only because she learned too many secrets when she used it. One night she made the mistake of listening in on Rosa's thoughts as the other girl made dinner—

Tommy is right, she is beautiful, he is so lucky

ay, Dio mío, *what am I thinking?*

probably just horny, stuck in this fucking sphere with a talking bird, a dog, and a 90-year-old married man, she's the only one I could hook up with, but then I would have a jealous changeling wanting to rip my head off when we get out of here

I wonder if she's a good kisser?

—and Chrysta had to leave the kitchen, her face burning at the feelings she overheard. It took two days before she could look Rosa in the eye again.

She felt pretty confident in phasing, so she decided to try to make herself invisible.

"Good luck, Miss Angelos," Mr. Burke said to her when she shared her plans with him. "Even *I* can't turn myself invisible. Only a few sorcerers in history have been successful."

By the end of the first day, Chrysta had figured out how to make her arm invisible, watching in wonder as she picked up items and turned them this way and that, feeling her fingers but not actually seeing them. She made her whole body transparent the next day, although her clothes were still visible, making a frightened Poe squawk at her walking shirt and jeans. But on third day, she finally made anything she touched disappear, too, even though it was challenging to flex her magic muscle and keep it tense as she walked through the cottage completely clear.

"Excellent work, Miss Angelos," Mr. Burke praised her as she disappeared and reappeared from sight several times to prove she had mastered the ability.

"I'm over here, Mr. Burke," she giggled after she had quietly walked behind him while invisible, making the Headmaster jump and whirl around.

"Great, now we have to put a bell on her," Rosa growled, and Chrysta laughed so hard she lost her concentration and reappeared.

Psychometry was her next project, and just like telepathy, it became easy for her after just a few hours of study. "Be careful," Rosa warned her as she walked about the cottage, touching items and reading them for practice. "Mr. Cross says you never know what will have a bad memory until you read it."

"Would you like a test, Miss Angelos?" Mr. Burke asked. He reached into his buttoned-up shirt and took out a necklace, a gold ring hanging from it. "What color was Jiao wearing on our wedding day?"

Chrysta gently took the offered ring and read it, letting the scene flood her senses—

they had to keep their wedding a secret, finding a small chapel in the middle of nowhere where an unmagical preacher agreed to officiate, and Neil is at the altar, sweating and nervous, and is this the right thing to do? but when Jiao starts to walk down the aisle, all doubt leaves his mind, and he is confident they are doing the right thing, and Jiao stands by his side in a red dress, looking stunning

—and Chrysta smiled as she handed the ring back to its owner. "Red," she said confidently. "She was beautiful."

"She is," Mr. Burke agreed, a very warm smile tugging at his lips.

Chrysta wandered to her room, looking for more items to read. Poe was on the bed, the bag holding his collection open. He liked to go through it, picking up feathers and marbles and bits and bobs and placing them in patterns only he understood. "Chrysta!" he croaked at her but went back to studying his collection.

Chrysta spied one of the beads in his carefully crafted circles, and she smiled. "Can I see this real quick, Poe?" she asked. "I can finally see where you got these from."

"Yes!" he said, clicking his beak.

Chrysta's hand hovered over the blue beads, and she picked up one of the cool glass baubles. She frowned as some memory flooded her mind—

She moved across the room so fast it made her dress flare out behind her, determined to get out of the mansion that night. They had to leave that night. There was no way she would wait. "Bella signora," *a voice said behind her, making her insides jump in surprise.* "How are you this evening?"

that sounds like Guerra's voice

"Don't you start that shit with me," *she growled, rounding on the man with the dead smile. She pointed a finger at his face, making him blink and lean back in shock. She generally tried to be friendly to all of Jozef's associates, but not tonight.*

Guerra blinked again, covering his shock with a smile. A smile that didn't reach his eyes. "What do you mean, my lady?"

who is he talking to? do I know her?

"I just heard one of your associates talking about attacking someone, possibly* killing *them."* *It had been a detailed and gruesome conversation that she sensed wasn't friendly or said as a joke.* "I don't know what is going on, but I am out of here, and I'm going to the police," *she explained while snapping the suitcase shut. She started to step past him, suitcase in one hand, but he reached out and grabbed her upper arm.*

"I'm afraid I can't let you do that, bella signora," *he stated.*

She frowned, her anger making her see red for a moment. But when she saw the cold smile he gave her, one full of malice and glee, her stomach dropped in fear. Her eyes went wide in fear as she snatched her arm out of Guerra's grip, but he just seized her throat instead. She yelped, but it came out as a gurgle, and the suitcase dropped.

oh no, oh no, no, no, no, don't hurt her

She clawed at the hand at her throat and started to reach for his face, but he just grabbed her wrist and kept her from scratching him. He continued smiling at her; holy shit, was he enjoying this? Then, suddenly, he glowed red, and she would have been in awe at the sight if her body didn't suddenly feel like every nerve was on fire. Fear and anguish clouded her mind, and she could only weakly kick at Guerra as he lifted her and hauled her to the balcony outside.

leave her alone. she didn't do anything! stop!

Guerra stopped at the railing, pushing her so she was leaning backward over the edge. The pain somehow got worse, like every inch of her skin was burned, every bone broken, every muscle torn. She had to fight, though, to get her daughter and get them both out of the mansion.

wait, what?

She fought. She tried to kick. But her heart was pounding so hard that it made it hard to think, to plan, to fight back. She couldn't let this monster kill her, however he was doing it. She had to save her daughter. She had to protect Chrysta.

no! it can't be!

She couldn't think, she couldn't breathe, just let me breathe. *Chrysta! Chrysta, I'm sorry! Please don't hurt my daughter! Please!*
And then the pain is excruciating, and her heart just stops, and her last thoughts are of her daughter.
—Chrysta screamed, throwing the bead across the room like it was burning her. Poe squawked as she ran out of the room. She could still feel the physical pain that Guerra inflicted, but the knowledge of who the woman could be made her run out of the cabin, like running away could protect her from the truth. She heard Rosa and Mr. Burke yelling her name behind her, but she continued running.

She ran through the hills in the rain, thunder rumbling above her. She didn't even have boots on but paid no mind to the rain soaking her socks. Finally, she made it to the trees and collapsed, crying and gasping for air. She heard someone splash behind her and turned to see Rosa standing in the rain.

"What is it?" Rosa asked, panting. "What did you see?"

"Guerra," Chrysta said, shivering. "G-Guerra ki-killed her."

"Who?"

"My mom," Chrysta said miserably. And then she crumpled into a pile, and Rosa rushed to her to hold her while she wailed.

.....

"Guerra killed Chrysta's mother."

The admission Cross made hung in the air. Tommy felt his stomach drop, and then he saw red. "Dammit," he cursed under his breath. "I should have killed that bastard years ago."

"Are you sure?" Zheng asked softly.

"Chrysta has a picture of her mother that she took with her into the sphere. I saw it when she was packing yesterday." Cross looked at Tommy. "I wanted to tell her; I *will* tell her. I just didn't see a point in telling her before she went inside." He folded his arms and looked down. "Let her have one more year of not knowing."

"Why did he do it?" Zheng asked, looking grim.

"She was threatening to go to the police," Cross explained, suddenly looking exhausted. "He had to stop her. Secrecy is their highest priority, after all."

"Did Jozef York know?" Hafeez asked, directing her question at Tommy.

"He would have to, wouldn't he?" Tommy spat. "Guerra would have told him after it happened. Cruel bastard not only planned on killing his daughter, but he also let his wife die horribly too."

"Another deplorable crime in a long list of sins," Zheng stated.

In the front of the vault, the others were starting to bring the supplies in. "Hafeez! Monroe!" Smith called out. "Get over here and help, dammit!" Hafeez rolled her eyes but got up to join her fellow hunters.

"You did the right thing," Zheng told Cross softly, shuffling the Tarot cards in her hands. "Chrysta didn't need to know what happened before she went into the sphere. She couldn't do anything about it until she got out anyway."

"I just worry what she will do when she finds out," Cross murmured. "Chrysta does glow gold, after all."

"Do you blame her?" Tommy asked. "Guerra deserves whatever is coming to him."

Zheng picked a card out of the deck and grimaced when she looked at it. She showed it to Tommy and Cross. It was The Tower being struck by lightning again. "If this means that the Acolytes are coming like I fear, we may just see what Miss Angelos is capable of when she gets out sooner than later."

"Is that what you think will happen?" Cross asked.

"It has to be," Zheng said. "The Acolytes know how strong she is. So they will want to destroy Chrysta before she gets even more powerful."

"They will have to go through me first," Tommy growled.

"Us," Zheng purred, giving Tommy a cold smile. "They will have to go through us first."

. . . . .

Chrysta cried into Rosa's shoulder for what felt like hours. The rain completely soaked them, but Rosa never said a word. She just held Chrysta while she sobbed. When the taller girl was finally able to get her to stand and walk back to the cabin, she felt numb and hollow, like she had cried her heart out, lost a bit of her soul that afternoon. Mr. Burke was in the main room when they walked in, book open in his lap, but his eyes were looking off into the distance, not even glancing at the girls as they entered the cabin. Mr. Burke had tented his hands in front of his face, and Chrysta could see one of the beads in his palm.

Rosa gently guided Chrysta to her bedroom and stopped short. Someone had moved the beads from Chrysta's bed to the small table by her bed. Poe was hitting them with his beak over and over. He had already destroyed two of them and seemed determined to destroy the rest. He paused as Chrysta entered.

"Sorry," the raven croaked. "I'm sorry."

Chrysta felt her eyes burn, and tears threatened to fall again. Instead, she reached out and rubbed Poe's head. "It's okay, Poe," she said, voice raw from crying. It wasn't okay, not really, but the raven didn't know. She looked at the beads that remained. "She must have been wearing a necklace when she died."

"Who was she, Miss Angelos?" said a voice behind them.

Chrysta turned slightly to look at Mr. Burke, standing at the entrance of her room. "My mother," she explained in a small voice. "Guerra killed my mother."

Mr. Burke didn't react, but he turned to Rosa. "Miss Torres, could you give us a moment?" Rosa just nodded and left after squeezing Chrysta's arm. Mr. Burke pushed his way into the room, picking up all the beads. Poe squawked at him, but both he and Chrysta ignored the raven. "I'm sorry, Miss Angelos," he said.

"You didn't hurt her," she said, watching as he put the beads back in their bag.

"No. But maybe if we had kept the Acolytes under closer surveillance, we would have realized that you and your mother were under threat." Chrysta shivered, and he reached out and touched her shoulder lightly. "Would you like to leave, Miss Angelos?"

"No," she whispered. "I don't. I want to stay."

"Are you sure?"

"I want to learn all that I can while I am in here," she explained. "So I can go after that monster as soon as I get out of here and make him suffer like he made my mother suffer."

Burke studied her for a long moment. "Alright," he finally said. Rosa came back, dressed in dry clothes and holding a towel. "Be careful, Miss Angelos. It's natural to feel that revenge is the best way to heal your pain. But don't become the monster you are trying to stop." He finally left the room.

Rosa helped Chrysta get out of her wet clothes, turning around so she could get dry PJs on. Chrysta curled up on her bed while Rosa blew out the candle that lit her room. She finally noticed that Willow was still in her room, primly sitting by the entrance. Rosa patted the dog's head as she passed, leaving Chrysta alone, and then the giant dog got up and climbed into the bed with her. She was huge, pressing Chrysta into the wall, but Chrysta let out a laugh that was almost a sob and then pressed her face into the dog's grey fur.

Poe joined them, settling on Willow's back. Chrysta tried to concentrate on breathing to keep the dark thoughts away. But as she heard Rosa and Mr. Burke eating and then retiring to bed, she remembered the reading she had experienced earlier. Her mother's anger and fear and pain overwhelmed her, and she cried, cried for the loss of the woman she loved, cried like she would never be happy again.

~ 42 ~

July 1929

Lorenzo Mancini smacked his lips as he ate. The *ragù* was absolutely delicious today, the pasta divine, the meatballs almost the size of his fists. The waiter came over to refill his glass, and he made a show of sniffing the red liquid, loud sniffs that almost resulted in Mancini snorting the wine up his nose. The waiter was trying to keep his face blank, but Mancini could see his disgust rolling under the surface of his face. Let him disapprove of Mancini's manners. He had helped the kid's father buy this restaurant, so if Mancini wanted to come in a couple of hours before they opened and get a plate of pasta, well, it was his prerogative. He had guests to entertain. He might as well get lunch while he did.

The front door opened, and Mancini's guests finally arrived. Mancini's eyebrows shot up when he got a good look at them. A white man flanked by two young kids. Mancini waved as they walked up to his table, the mob boss chuckling to himself even as he chewed his food. "Well, isn't this a sight to see?" he asked with a smile. "You guys can't afford to hire proper bodyguards down in the big city, Mister?"

The white man frowned before taking a seat. "I assure you, my men can handle themselves, just like yours," he said while gesturing to Mancini's two guards.

Mancini looked at the "men" in question and snorted. A black-haired, pale-skinned boy that barely looked 15, and a dark-skinned monkey that was currently glaring at Mancini. "I'll take your word for it," he said. "So, your boss, Jack Zannino, wanted to talk?"

"Actually, I am Jack Zannino," the man explained. "This situation was so dire that I felt I needed to appear in person to rectify it."

Mancini blinked and then beamed at the other man. "Oh, so *you* are the big shot, huh?" He grabbed his napkin and wiped at his mouth and then his hands, holding one out when he was satisfied that it was clean. Zannino sneered at the offered hand but shook it with a haughty expression. "I think my mom dated a Zannino, any relation?"

Zannino just glowered. "I doubt it," he drawled. "Mr. Mancini, can you tell me why you have decided to steal our property?"

Mancini shook his finger back and forth with a smile like the other man was a naughty child. "No, not stolen. Stealing it would mean I took it from you. It was en route to you, so it wasn't in your possession."

Zannino returned the smile, although with none of the mob boss's warmth. "A shipment of items we were paying you to transport."

"Ah! But you didn't pay enough, did you?" Mancini asked, and Zannino's fake smile fell, the scowl deeper than before. Mancini wiggled his eyebrows and clicked his fingers, signaling to the waiter that he wanted more wine. The kid returned with the bottle reluctantly, watching the newcomers with fear.

"You see, Mr. Zannino, I don't know how you guys do it in the big city, but here? Upstate? When we make a deal, we stick to it." Mancini snorted at the wine again, just doing it at this point to annoy the other man, letting the waiter retreat. "Now, is our forty percent rate based on the value of the items we transport a little steep?" He shrugged as he grabbed his fork. "Perhaps. But my guys are risking their necks to get stuff over the lake from Canada. So it's only right that we are compensated fairly for it."

"We paid you," Zannino growled. "I don't know how you do things here in the north part of the state, but when you pay for something where we are from, you receive it."

"You paid for a box of moonshine," Mancini stated, all the warmth gone from his face and voice. "You forgot to mention the book made out of gold."

To anyone else watching, Zannino didn't react, but Mancini was able to see the man's hand tighten on the table, his lips getting a little thinner in anger. Mancini chuckled, and the smile returned to his face. "The box, I'm afraid, got smashed, and the booze with it. But then, you knew that your items might not survive the trip. But imagine my surprise when my guys bring the box's other item to me. A book made of gold! Real pretty, by the way, What are the pages made of?"

"They are made of gold as well," Zannino said.

"No shit?" Mancini asked. He took a large bite of his meatball and chewed, not bothering to keep his mouth closed. "Are the pages coated in it or...?"

"They are gold threads woven together," Zannino said through gritted teeth.

"Well, that kind of thing," Mancini paused to gulp some wine, "that kind of thing must be priceless." He smiled over the rim of his glass at the other man. "What's forty percent of priceless, I wonder?" He laughed, and his guards joined in.

Zannino shifted in his chair. "How much do you want?"

Mancini slapped the table with one meaty hand, making his plate rattle and making the poor waiter jump. "Now that's what I like, someone who gets straight to the point!" He grabbed his napkin and wiped his mouth again, humming for several moments. "Let's say, five thousand dollars. To start with, of course."

Zannino looked at him for several long moments, face blank, before gesturing to the black kid next to him, and the kid nodded. He took a deep breath, eyes closing slightly and nostrils flaring. He leaned towards Zannino and whispered in the older man's ear when done. Zannino suddenly broke out in a smile, a genuine one this time. "No, I don't think we will be doing that, Mr. Mancini," he purred.

Mancini blinked in surprise and slowly lowered the fork wrapped in pasta back down to the plate. "You don't want your book?" he asked, actually shocked that the other man was throwing in the towel so soon. "I mean, if you don't want it, I can always melt it to make some jewelry for my wife."

The pale-skinned boy next to Zannino twitched at that, and he leaned over to urgently whisper something in Zannino's ear. Still wearing the smile, Zannino patted the boy's shoulder to calm him down. "I think you will give us the book back, Mr. Mancini," Zannino said. "Without us paying a dime."

Mancini blinked again, and then he started to laugh. His guards joined him, big barks of laughter. They laughed so long that Mancini began to choke, actually spraying the man across from him with spit before he got his napkin to his mouth. Zannino flinched when the spittle hit him, but he didn't say anything as the mob boss recovered. "See, I wasn't upset when I found out you tried to get the book into the country without me knowing," Mancini wheezed when he finally got some air into his lungs. "That's understandable. Who would want to pay that money if they didn't have to? But you're crazy if you think I'm giving it back without getting paid for it. That's just business."

Zannino nodded as he wiped at the lapels of his suit. "Yes, business," he agreed. "I am a businessman myself, Mr. Mancini. I understand why you do what you do. You are providing alcohol to the masses for a very steep price. Supply and demand and all that."

Mancini finished his drink but didn't click his fingers to ask for more. A feeling of unease was starting to settle in his stomach. Mancini had just told this man that his precious book was not being returned to him without paying a lot of money. He should be upset, begging for it back, trying to bargain. But he wasn't, and that made Mancini nervous.

"But the book isn't just valuable for what it is made of, Mr. Mancini," Zannino continued. "It's priceless for the *knowledge* it contains. Knowledge that I must possess, Mr. Mancini, at all costs." He gestured to the black man next to him.

"Thomas has just informed me that the book is here. So I see no reason to keep up the charade. You will return it to us at once."

Mancini smiled, but most of his previous confidence was fading. Now, how did they know that? "Oh yeah? Are you telling me that your man *smelled* it? That would be a neat trick if it were true."

"Smelled it, and the two guys you have in the back with it," Thomas said, looking almost bored. "You got to get your guys some better cologne."

Mancini glowered at him. "Alright, let's say you're right," he finally growled. "So you know where it is. But how are you going to make me give it up? Huh? With these two?" He gestured at the two "men" that Zannino had brought.

Zannino smiled. "They can be quite persuasive when they want to be," he simply stated.

Mancini scoffed. This meeting wasn't going the way that he had planned. This *coglione* was too relaxed, too unfazed. Mancini felt like he needed to teach the other man a lesson. "Go get my money," he growled, placing his fork on the empty plate. "Or you and your 'men' will be leaving here without your kneecaps."

"Or you can bring the book out, and we can leave with it now," Zannino countered.

Mancini saw red. "You really are dense, aren't you? So now you owe me ten thousand dollars."

"No."

Mancini glared. "Tony," he said, voice low in anger. "Show these gentlemen out, will ya?"

Tony moved to do just that, going for Thomas. He tried to grab the kid, but the kid ducked and punched Tony in the ribs. Tony let out a whoosh of air and stumbled. Once he recovered, he threw a punch, but the kid ducked in the other direction and gave Tony an uppercut to the jaw. Tony staggered, and before he could recover, the black kid grabbed the back of his neck and slammed his head into the table in front of Mancini, the motion unbelievably fast. The mob boss jumped and pushed back from the table, but Zannino didn't move, just giving Mancini a cold smile. "See?" he asked. "Perfectly capable of handling himself."

"Boys!" Mancini roared. He reached for his gun but then cursed when he realized that it was still in his coat which was currently over the back of another chair. While he dove for his jacket, his other guard went for the pale-skinned kid. Once Francesco got a hold of the kid, some weird red light started where their skin touched, and Francesco screamed, body going rigid like the kid was electrocuting him. The kid just smiled, something cold and lifeless, as the larger man fell to his knees and started to scream.

Mancini wrestled with his jacket while his other two guards came running from the back, the waiter running past them, but then Zannino held up his hand, and Mancini could have sworn that he didn't have that much wine, but now Zannino was glowing too, a pale green color. Mancini felt like something grabbed him, not just his outstretched hand but his whole body, and he froze, grunting from the effort to move again. His boys glowed too, and they stopped moving, their eyes the only thing moving as they looked around in shock and fear.

"Now," Zannino said, voice light like he was having a pleasant conversation, "was all of this necessary?" Mancini wouldn't have given him an answer even if he could move, not that Zannino was expecting one. Zannino waved his hand again, and now Tony and Francesco were glowing green, allowing both of Zannino's men to let them go. Francesco was whimpering and blabbering, tears running down his face. Thomas went to one of the others and snatched the Thompson gun he was holding, checking the magazine before putting it back in the gun.

"Check the back," Zannino ordered while standing up from the table. "Find the book. Bring it here." He went to the counter where the waiter had been and opened a cabinet, finding the remaining supply of illegal wine. He smiled as he inspected a bottle and brought it back to the table with a glass. "I'll keep the others entertained," he purred as he sat down and poured himself a glass of wine.

·····

Tommy went running to the back with the kid hot on his heels. The kitchen was sweltering, vegetables waiting on the chopping block, a pot of boiling water on the stove, probably abandoned when Mancini showed up with his goons, and the waiter had to drop everything to serve him. They looked everywhere, but the scared waiter wasn't in the kitchen, and Tommy's sense of smell was pulling him through a door to the back room.

The back room was small, halfway full of food and ingredients and half full of illegal goods like booze and guns. A small table was covered in a deserted card game and money. There was an open door, letting heat and humidity sneak in from the alley, and the kid ran to it. "He's escaping!" he cried, and before Tommy could stop him, he ran outside.

Tommy was going to go outside and get the little idiot when a box of tomatoes suddenly fell over. The waiter had squeezed himself behind it, and when Tommy spotted him, he started to cry and whimper. Tommy instantly crouched down to talk to him, and he screamed. "Please, please, please don't hurt me, *please,*" he begged.

Tommy shushed him as he put the tomatoes back in the box. "I'm not going to hurt you," he whispered. "But if Zannino sees you, you're dead. Where's the book they were talking about? I can take it, and we will leave."

The waiter pointed to a satchel on the floor by the small table with a shaking finger. Tommy nodded and then started pushing the box back in place. The waiter gave a small sigh of relief but fell quiet once Tommy was done.

Tommy got up and picked up the satchel, and before he even opened it, he could smell the book. It was exactly as Mancini and Zannino had described; a book made entirely of gold. The front cover had the emblem of a tree on it, but Tommy didn't study it any further. Instead, he put it down and then took off his jacket, rolling up his sleeves before picking up the gun and heading outside.

Tommy could see a thin figure at the end of the alley. "Hey!" he called out, leaning out the door with a grin. "Forget him! He's long gone!"

"He will report us!" the kid yelled back.

"They won't believe it!" Tommy tried to reason with the kid. He looked up and saw a car at the other end of the alleyway, two men inside. One was holding a camera pointed at Tommy, and he couldn't be sure, but he had the feeling that the man had taken a photo of the changeling. Tommy grinned and pulled the hammer back on the gun, and both men jumped and looked terrified. The driver started the car, and it tore away.

"Come on, kid!" Tommy yelled. "We have more to worry about than some normie waiter!"

The kid jogged back, and Tommy pulled him inside. The changeling handed over the book and satchel, and the kid just stood there holding it for a few moments, mouth opened in awe. Tommy grabbed a pallet of moonshine but then noticed an odd-shaped box. A violin case. He gently picked it up and opened it, stroking the violin gently. It was seventy years since he even had the chance to touch a violin. He shook his head and closed the case, putting it on top of the case of booze.

Tommy made sure he had his jacket over his arm before hitting the kid with an elbow. "Come on," he said. "Let's get going." The kid just nodded dumbly, all thought of finding the waiter gone. Tommy resisted the urge to look at the waiter's hiding place as they went up front.

Zannino was sitting at the table, his posture relaxed as he sipped from his glass of wine. The five men were still frozen, eyes rolling in their heads, grunting as they tried to move, but none even twitched. The kid gave the acolyte leader the book, and Zannino smiled as he studied it. Tommy put the pallet of moonshine down on a nearby table. "The waiter is gone," he told Zannino, feeling a twinge from the band on his arm but ignoring it. "And someone was in the alley, taking pictures."

"Yes," Zannino murmured. "Our intel mentioned that Mr. Lorenzo 'Trigger' Mancini typically had the police following him. We will have to hurry then." He got up and downed his glass. He gestured at the pallet of booze. "To add to your private collection, Thomas?"

"Make it look like a robbery," Tommy explained.

"Ah, a robbery gone bad," Zannino agreed. "Makes sense. Why look at what happened in Chicago back in February. I wonder what they will call this? The Mancini Massacre?" He looked at the struggling mob boss. "If you had admitted to finding the book but not tried to extort me, you would have lived. Of course, I would have made sure you forgot about it, but you would have lived a long life of being a small-time crime boss." Zannino shrugged. "But such is life."

"*Li mortacci tua!*" Mancini gritted out, but Zannino ignored him as he turned to leave the restaurant. Zannino took the book, the kid grabbed the pallet with the violin case on top, and Tommy sighed as he picked up the gun. Tommy tried to tell himself that these were evil men, men who had hurt people, and if they had to die so the boy in the back lived, it wouldn't be a significant loss to the world. But unfortunately, the green glow was fading, so Tommy didn't have much time to agonize over what he was doing as he raised the gun and peppered the room with bullets.

Tommy made a pass in one direction and then the other, hitting every man before emptying the magazine. They crumbled, and Tommy paused to make sure that he didn't see any of them moving or breathing before he dropped the gun on the floor and grabbed his jacket. He sighed as he turned, ignoring the slight feeling of guilt that now settled in his stomach.

Zannino and the kid were waiting in the car for Tommy, and he climbed into the driver's seat with no word. "Good job, Thomas," Zannino cooed. "I'm sorry you can't have one of them to eat."

Tommy rolled his eyes. "That happened a decade ago. So when are you going to let it go?"

"Never," Zannino said with a chuckle. He was smiling ear to ear, obviously happy with how the day turned out.

"What is it?" the kid asked as he examined the book in his lap.

"A book full of knowledge from our Lady," Zannino explained. "It is rumored to hold the key to bringing her back to us. And it is the key to me stepping down as leader of the Acolytes."

Tommy felt a finger of unease go up his spine. "You're stepping down?"

"Yes, I think I will go back to being an enforcer," Zannino confessed. He held up a finger and wagged it at the kid. "Never become the leader, Luca. You will never have a moment's rest." He settled back into the seat with a sigh and a smile. "And I will make sure you are taken care of, Thomas. You have my word."

Tommy felt annoyance replace the guilt he felt earlier. Zannino could joke and make promises all he wanted, but in Tommy's experience, not every Acolyte leader was someone to be trusted. But maybe, just maybe, the next leader would be the one to release him from his slavery. As Tommy pulled the car away from the scene of the Mancini Massacre, he heard police sirens in the distance, coming closer.

43

The teens moved the last supplies quickly, Mr. Smith beaming at them as they worked as a group. "You see?" he asked with a grin. "If we all work together, it goes so much faster."

They also penned a letter to Rosa and Chrysta in record time. "It's not fair," Ichiro moped as Rimsha sealed it. "We should stay. We made a promise to Rosa."

"We need to leave, so Mr. Cross and Mrs. Zheng won't have to worry about protecting us *and* the sphere at the same time," Rimsha argued, annoyance starting to bloom in her chest. She didn't have to fight with her own brothers as much as she had to with Ichiro.

"But—" Ichiro started to say, but the heavy hand of Mrs. Zheng landed on his shoulder, and he jumped.

"If Jozef York has been ousted as Chrysta's vision shows," she said, a cold smile on her face, "then the Acolytes are in a state of transition and are at their most volatile. This is not a game. They will not give mercy. Just because you are children doesn't mean that they will let you live."

"Or let you live with all your limbs," Mr. Smith joked, but his smile was also grim.

"Alright," Ichiro pouted. "But you better keep them safe."

"No worries, kid," Mr. Smith said. "We are trained for this, and they don't have the element of surprise now." He winked. "We will have the ladies back home by noon tomorrow. You'll see."

Rimsha saw Tommy sealing a letter of his own, so she went over to him. She gestured at the letter in his hand. "What did you tell her?" Rimsha asked.

"Just that I promise nothing will happen to her while I'm here. Anything trying to hurt her will have to go through me first, and I'm not easy to move," Tommy explained as he stood up and folded his arms. He was deathly serious, no smile pulling at his lips.

"Keep both of them safe," she asked and gave him a quick hug, forcing him to unfold his arms. "And yourself too, okay?" she added, pulling back and smiling as he blinked in surprise.

As the alarm went off several minutes later, Mrs. Zheng sent the supplies, the letters attached to one of the boxes. The light had barely faded before another flash blinded everyone, and a letter appeared on the sphere. Mr. Cross grabbed it and tore it open. "Rosa says she understands why you all have to leave," Mr. Cross said after a few moments of reading. "She absolves you of your responsibility." He looked at Tommy. "Chrysta says the same thing. But she realizes you are stubborn enough that you will probably stay."

Tommy smiled. "She knows me so fucking well."

"See?!" Ichiro yelled, making both changeling and empath look at him. "Tommy's staying, so we should be here too!"

"When you get to be one-hundred and seventy-seven years old," Mr. Cross said sarcastically, "you can then consent to stay and fight the murderous cult of sorcerers, my boy."

.....

Mr. Cross pushed them to get ready to leave, and thirty minutes after they sent the supplies, he was forcing the teens to the van, handing the keys to Julien. "Just keep driving," he ordered them. "The sooner you are back at the Academy, the better." He handed a bag to Julien. "Everyone's cell phones. You can give them back once Rosa and Chrysta are out." He held up a finger. "Only contact me if there is an emergency; Mrs. Zheng will have my phone and monitor it."

"We can't even have our phones?!" Ichiro yelled.

"It's for the girls' protection," Mr. Cross explained, obviously getting irritated at the boy's attitude. "You can watch your laptop on the way home, yeah?"

They left, Mr. Cross and Tommy standing outside the warehouse, watching them go. Ichiro folded his arms and pouted in the back seat. "We should have stayed," he said.

Rimsha, who was in the front seat with Julien, rolled her eyes. Julien raised his eyebrows at her expression. "Ichiro is sulking," she signed, and Julien just smiled and shook his head.

They drove, the roads clearing of traffic as they left the city, and continued on the highways. Kevin played a video game while Ichiro leaned on the door, either asleep or pretending to be. At some point, Kevin paused his game and leaned forward. "Hey, are we stopping for food?" he asked, signing his question as well.

"The diner we stopped at yesterday is nearby," Rimsha signed. "We can stop there and then continue to the Academy."

Julien nodded in agreement.

"You sure about that?" Kevin asked Rimsha. "They didn't have anything for you to eat last time."

Rimsha smiled at him. "Some fries will tide me over until we get to the Academy and can eat something else. I just hope we don't have to see that horrible waitress again."

They pulled off the highway to the truck stop with its small diner. The lot was empty at the late hour, the woods quiet as snow gently drifted down. They exited the van, Ichiro still scowling, and headed into the brightly lit diner.

"Oh no!" Rimsha cried. Ichiro and Kevin whirled around, wearing identical expressions of fear. Julien saw their faces and spun, too, searching Rimsha's face. "Punchi! I forgot her!"

"You're worried about a plant?" Ichiro growled, posture relaxing.

"If Mr. Cross forgets her in the vault, she's dead," she explained. "Can you text Mr. Cross to get her, please?" she signed at Julien.

"When we leave," Julien signed with a small smile. "I'm hungry. Let's eat."

They entered the diner and approached the counter; Rimsha's stomach dropped when she noticed the rude waitress from before cleaning the countertop. The woman gave them a leer as they settled on the stools. "Well, look what the cat dragged in. Isn't it past your bedtime?" she asked.

"Hey, we're old enough that we don—" Kevin started to complain but stopped to yawn in the middle of his complaint.

Ichiro shook his head. "We just need to get something to eat," he said. "Can we do that?"

The waitress sighed and grabbed her pad. "Sure," she said sullenly. "But you have to pay," she added.

The teens ordered, Ichiro ordering fries to give to Rimsha. They waited for their food, watching the cook through the window to the kitchen. Ichiro sulked, putting his head on the counter. "I can't even listen to music," he muttered darkly.

"You poor thing," Rimsha said dryly.

"Can't check Instagram, can't text anyone."

"Who you gonna text? All your friends are right here," Kevin joked, and the younger boy shot him a glare.

"We shouldn't have left. All the good stuff is happening without us," Ichiro said, and before Rimsha could reply, the bell about the front door rang. She glanced behind her to see who was entering the diner but did a double-take.

Living at the Academy, Rimsha was used to seeing all the different cultures of the teens who studied there, but the man standing in the threshold was bizarrely dressed even by Academy standards. Dark-skinned and bald, tall and lean, barefoot, wearing a long-sleeve shirt and a sarong. Rimsha looked around the parking lot and didn't see any cars other than the van, which meant the stranger must have walked to the diner on foot. He had to be freezing, but he didn't look bothered by the cold.

"No!" the waitress suddenly yelled. Kevin and Ichiro whipped around to see who she was shouting at, Julien joining them after noticing everyone looking at the door except him. "You get out of there! No shoes, no service!"

The stranger smiled, cold and oily. He put his hands up and pressed the palms together. "Please, ma'am," he said in a thick accent. "The cold. Let me stay inside."

"No! I already told you and your friends to get out!" the woman shouted. "Roy!"

The cook glanced through the window, scowling as he put the teens' food down. "Hey, man, you need to go." He disappeared and then emerged out of the kitchen, wiping his hands on a towel. "Do we have to call the cops? They get coffee here all the time."

The stranger was still smiling, putting his hands up in surrender and bowing his head slightly as he backed out of the diner. "No, no police," he said as he opened the door, not turning his back on the cook. "I go, see? I go, I go."

Suddenly, Rimsha saw the stranger's nostrils flare like he was taking a deep breath. His eyes flickered over to the teens, locking on Rimsha, and she shuddered. His expression changed slightly, his smile getting larger, showing more teeth. Rimsha thought of the nature documentaries Kevin liked to watch, the predator homing in on his prey, and she grabbed Kevin's arm in fear.

"I go," the stranger repeated softly, not taking his eyes off Rimsha. "I go." He finally turned to the door and opened it, retreating outside.

"Good riddance," the waitress said under her breath.

"What is it?" Kevin asked Rimsha, looking at her hand on his arm and then outside to the stranger.

"He was creepy," Rimsha whispered, not knowing how to voice her concern. Or even if she should in front of the nonmagical waitress.

"He and his friends have been loitering around here all day," the waitress explained. She scowled as the man walked towards the road. "Coming and going. Ordering food but not having the money for it." She grabbed the food waiting in the window and gave the plates to the teens. "Weird clothes, weird accents."

A car appeared on the highway and stopped in front of the man. He climbed in quickly, and the car drove away, and Rimsha felt a flood of relief.

"Good riddance," the waitress said again, and Rimsha couldn't help but agree with her.

The teens ate their food, Julien paying for all of them when they were done. Kevin and Ichiro kept talking about the stranger. "Did you see what he was wearing?" Kevin asked at one point.

"Yeah, a dress," the waitress said.

"A sarong," Ichiro corrected her. "I don't know why he wears it, though; it must be freezing in this weather."

"He must have a good reason," Julien said with a shrug, counting the money Mr. Cross had given him and handing it to the waitress.

The boys started to head out, getting their coats on, when Rimsha felt a touch on her hand. She looked back to see the waitress with a frown on her face. "Hey," the older woman murmured. "Can I ask you a question?"

Rimsha felt a stab of annoyance. With the woman's behavior so far, she was sure the question would be about her hijab. Sorcerers at the Academy and even the nonmagical population in New Bendigo were very open-minded and tolerant, but in Rimsha's experience, the rest of America was not. She tried to force a smile on her face, giving the woman the benefit of the doubt. "Yes?"

"Where are the other girls who were traveling with you before?"

Rimsha blinked at the question; it was so unexpected. "They're not with us right now," she replied, not wanting to give any more detail than that.

"Those weirdos," the waitress started to explain, gesturing to where the car disappeared into the night, "they also asked a lot of questions before we threw them out. I kinda forgot about it until you guys came back. They were looking for a girl. A girl with black hair? Didn't one of the girls with you have black hair?"

Chrysta. "She does," Rimsha replied. She tried to keep the fake smile on her face, but her mind was racing. It was a bad sign if someone was looking for Chrysta in the exact diner they ate in yesterday.

She looked at the waitress. "Um, no one should be looking for my friend, but thank you for the heads up," she said.

"Don't know why those creeps would want a group of teens," the waitress growled while folding her arms. "But be careful driving home, okay?"

"Rimsha?" Kevin called from the door, and Rimsha jumped. She gave the waitress a real smile and hurried to join Kevin. "Something wrong?" he asked her in a whisper as she got her coat on.

"Not really," she murmured.

He started to look between her and the waitress. "Did she say something?" he hissed.

"No, no, she's fine," Rimsha explained as they exited the diner into the cold night. Ichiro was already in the van, watching them climb into the vehicle through the windshield. As soon as Rimsha settled into the passenger seat, Julien started the van and backed away from the diner. "I need my phone," Rimsha signed, and Julien scowled.

Julien made a pinching motion with his thumb, forefinger, and middle finger, the sign for no. Then, he put both hands on the wheel and pulled onto the road that would lead back to the highway.

"No, please, listen. I need my phone to call Mr. Cross."

Ichiro popped into the front seat so Julien could see him. "Hey, if she gets her phone, so do I." Julien glared at the younger boy and shook his head, not even taking his hands off the wheel to sign.

"Listen!" Rimsha hissed, violently bringing her open hand up to cup her ear, so Julien could see how serious she was. "That weird man? He and the people with him were asking questions about a black-haired girl."

"So?" Ichiro asked.

"So they are looking for Chrysta," Rimsha explained urgently. "Let me have my phone; I have to warn Mr. Cross."

Julien shook his head again, but he looked more unsure than before. "How do you know that the girl they were looking for is Chrysta?" he asked aloud.

"He is a changeling, in the same diner that we ate at yesterday, asking about a girl who looks like our friend. Who else could he be looking for?" Rimsha explained.

"Wait, what?!" Kevin cried, launching himself into the front seat and crushing Ichiro. "He was a changeling?!"

"He smelled us, like how Tommy could smell magic on me," Rimsha said, starting to feel panic. Why didn't they believe her? "He knew we were sorcerers, I'm sure of it. I'm telling you, the changelings are looking for Chrysta."

"Why would the changelings be looking for Chrysta?" Ichiro asked, shoving Kevin to the side. "How would they even know anything about her?"

"I don't know!" Rimsha cried, finally losing her battle with her panic. "I just know they were looking for her! Please! Let me have my phone, so I can warn Mr. Cross and the others!" Rimsha held her hand out to Julien, scowling at him to show how serious she was.

Julien looked between Rimsha's face, her hand, the road, and back again, looking worried and lost. But he finally made a decision and started to reach for the bag that held their phones. Just as he began to hand it to Rimsha, lights turned on in front of them.

It happened so fast that Rimsha barely registered it. The lights were blinding, in the middle of the road, and way too close. Julien jerked the wheel to the left, and when the van started to slide sideways, he dropped the bag with the cell phones and began turning the wheel to the right with both hands, overcorrecting. They somehow missed the lights on the road, and as they sailed into the dark woods, Rimsha saw the tree they were hurtling towards, brightly lit by the van's light. She braced for impact just before they slammed into the tree on the passenger side, right where the door was.

Rimsha stayed in a tight ball for several long moments, trying to catch her breath as her heart pounded. Finally, she slowly uncurled, looking around her. Her window was destroyed, letting in the cold night air. Julien was slumped over the wheel, so she reached out with a shaking hand to touch his shoulder. He stirred, and Rimsha felt relief flood her system. Julien winced and touched his forehead, his fingertips coming away with blood on them.

"Everyone okay?" Julien asked thickly, and Rimsha nodded even as she felt herself start to shiver. She looked into the second row to check on Kevin and Ichiro. Ichiro, who didn't have a seatbelt on as they talked, was crumpled in Kevin's lap; both boys sprawled on the door on the right side of the van.

Rimsha unhooked her seatbelt and reached into the back, wincing at a pain in her shoulder but ignoring it. "Hey," she said, shaking Kevin's shoulder. "You two okay?"

Kevin stirred and slowly started to move. "Um, y-yeah, I think so," he said, pushing on the door to sit up. "What happened?"

"Someone was in the road," Rimsha said, and that is when she looked up and froze in fear.

The thing on the road that had blinded them was a car with its brights on, but as Rosa looked through the van's back window, it turned off its brights and switched to the hazard lights. Rimsha could see two figures step out of the car, human-like silhouettes in the yellow light. The lights blinked, and the figures were closer to the van when the lights turned on. The light turned off again, and when they came on this time, Rimsha swore that the two figures were bigger. The light flashed for the last time, and when the yellow light highlighted the creatures again, they were not human; Rimsha was sure of it.

One stomped to the vehicle's passenger side, and the van leaned back towards the road. The door screeched open, and Kevin yelped when two hands grabbed him and Ichiro, snatching them into the night. Rimsha caught sight of the creature's massive outline with two horns curling upwards. The van was let go, and it rocked back into the tree with the sound of screeching metal and breaking glass.

Julien yelped, and Rimsha turned to see something yanking him out of the driver's door. She yelled something about leaving Julien alone, but as she scrambled over the driver's seat and leaned out the door, she froze at the sight that waited for her.

The creature that held Julien was snake-like, the face elongated and alien. Its skin was now scaled, alternating in black and white. It was wearing the same clothes that the man at the diner had been wearing, and Rimsha suddenly realized why the man needed a sarong. Anything else would interfere with the six-foot tail that the changeling now had, curling around Julien and pushing him into the van.

"Where is the black-haired girl?" the changeling hissed in Julien's face. Julien flinched at the changeling's breath, which Rimsha could smell several feet away. Unfortunately, Julien couldn't read the changeling's misformed lips, and when he didn't respond, the changeling raised a hand with fingers tipped in black talons as a threat. *"Where is the girl?!"*

"Wait!" Rimsha cried, and the changeling stopped, its diamond-shaped pupil focusing on her. "He's deaf! He can't hear you, and he can't read your lips!"

The snake changeling slowly turned to her, his hand still up to strike Julien. Whatever had the boys walked around the back of the van, and Rimsha could see Kevin struggling on one shoulder while Ichiro hung limply from the other shoulder. She could see that it was massive, bull-like, with horns and black hair. "Then I will talk to you, not the deformed one," the snake changeling hissed at Rimsha. "Where is the girl?"

"Who?" Rimsha asked. Maybe if she acted like she didn't know what the changeling was talking about, she could get it to let them go.

"The black-haired girl," the snake changeling hissed. He grabbed Julien's throat, and Julien grimaced. "The one with Neil Burke. Where is she?!"

"Who's Burke?! We don't know anyone by that name!" Rimsha cried, hoping the changeling would believe her lie. But the snake changeling grinned at her evilly, as much as his reptile mouth would allow.

"Oh, come now," he hissed. "You know who we are looking for. I can see it in your eyes." He leaned forward, and Rimsha leaned back in fear. "Tell me where she and Burke are, or I kill your friends."

He flexed his fingers over Julien's throat, and Rimsha could see blood well up where the talons pressed into Julien's skin. "No!" Rimsha cried, but the snake just smiled and pressed into Julien's throat. He knew that they were there because of Chrysta. And if she didn't tell them where Chrysta and Mr. Burke were, they were all dead.

Forgive me, Chrysta.

"Wait!" she cried out and grasped the changeling's arm, and his skin was so smooth and so cold, how could he stand it? He paused and glared at her, eyes narrowing at her hand, tongue flicking in and out of his mouth quickly. "I'll... I'll take you. But my friends stay here."

"Rimsha! No!" Kevin called out and started fighting the bull changeling. The changeling huffed and knocked a horn into the boy's side, making him yelp.

"Don't hurt him!" Rimsha yelled, making her voice stronger than she felt, even as she shivered in fear. "If you hurt them, I won't help you!"

The snake changeling's lip curled, but he barked something to his friend in a language Rimsha didn't know. The bull responded, and the snake said something back, his tongue flicking between sentences. The bull huffed again and then made his way around the van again. Julien's eyes were wide, trying to watch the changelings and Rimsha simultaneously. "Alright, sorcerer," the snake changeling hissed. "You and your friends are safe. For now. We will all go together. Yes?"

"N-no," Rimsha tried to argue, but the changeling squeezed Julien's throat again, and the older boy wheezed in pain. "Okay! Alright! We will all go together!"

The snake changeling's lip barely moved, but Rimsha could see him smile. Then, he shifted back to his human form. "You drive, sorcerer. I want to be able to talk to you as you drive."

Rimsha numbly nodded, and the changeling pulled Julien to the front of the van, heading for the passenger seat. Meanwhile, the bull changeling threw Kevin and Ichiro into the second row, Kevin yelling as he hit the side of the van and

Ichiro moaning. The bull changeling grunted and groaned and then pushed the van back towards the road.

Once the van was back on the road, the snake changeling pushed Julien into the passenger seat and then climbed into the second row with the other boys. Kevin froze, staring at the changeling in fear. The changeling brought a knife out from the folds of his sarong and showed it to Rimsha, grinning. "You drive, you take us straight there, you live. That is the deal, yes?"

"Y-yes," Rimsha agreed. When the bull changeling was done pushing the van onto the road, the bull opened the back door and settled in the back, staying in his monster form. He rumbled something, and the snake answered in the other language.

Julien started signing. "What is happening?"

"I have to take them back to the warehouse," Rimsha signed back to explain, but the snake changeling barked when he saw her hands moving.

"No! You speak! You don't use your hands to talk, only to drive!" he ordered. He took the knife and inserted it into the car seat, and Julien jumped when he felt it poke him in the back. "Drive! Now!"

"Okay!" Rimsha cried. She turned the van on, thankful that it started. She made a U-turn in the road, avoiding the changeling's car, which was still in the middle of the road with its hazard lights still flashing. Then, she headed back to the highway, back towards the warehouse, and hopefully, back towards the only people who could help them.

↶ 44 ↷

Chrysta was being stalked.

She could hear the heavy footsteps of her pursuer crunching in the leaves. She stopped moving and crouched by a tree, making herself as small as possible. The hunter's champion paused and sniffed the air, and Chrysta covered her mouth to silence her breathing.

Another figure joined the first two. "Chrysta!" it called.

Chrysta gasped and then felt her stomach drop as she heard the second figure growl. How did she get herself into this mess?

.....

Chrysta spent a week after finding the truth about her mother's death in her room, barely eating, barely sleeping, and crying until she felt dry and wrung out. Willow and Poe stayed with her at all times. And Mr. Burke and Rosa left her alone, leaving to train in the woods without her during the day. Rosa would bring her food, taking away any untouched food without comment or reproach. At one point, the rain stopped, and the weather turned back to warm and sunny skies, but Chrysta still stayed inside.

One day, Rosa sat on her bed before leaving with the plates. "They will be sending the supplies tomorrow," she said.

"It's day 240 already?" Chrysta asked, and Rosa nodded. She sat up in bed, and Willow lifted her head from her spot on the floor and yawned. "I'm sorry, I have been in here too long."

"Don't worry about it," Rosa said softly.

"I don't know why this hurts so much," Chrysta confessed. "She's been gone for ten years."

"Because somebody took her from you," Rosa said, and Chrysta blinked at her. "If it was an accident, that would hurt too. But when you know someone hurt them, killed them..." She trailed off and looked down at her hands. "They won't be there because someone took them away. No more birthdays, no quinceañera, they won't see your wedding day..."

"They can't teach you to play the violin," Chrysta added and stopped when her eyes started to burn.

"That's why I want to become a hunter," Rosa explained. "Stop the Acolytes from hurting anyone else. No kid should have to grow up with that kind of pain."

"I'll make sure of it," Chrysta promised. "My father is dealing with the consequence of his actions, but we have to make sure Guerra and the others do too."

Rosa smiled at her. "Well, you glow gold. I'm glad you're on our side." She got up. "I'm going to send a letter to the others. Tell them that they should leave the vault before they get hurt if your and Julien's visions come true. If you want to send a note to Tommy, let me know, okay?"

Chrysta considered Rosa's words that night, and by the time the sun rose the following day, she had made a decision. Rosa returned from her run and smiled when she saw Chrysta coming out of the shower stall. "Well, I'm glad to see you up. And my nose is glad you showered."

Chrysta smiled and stuck out her tongue. "Ha ha," she flatly said as she passed the other girl to go inside. She paused by the door. "Thank you," she called out, and Rosa stopped filling the shower basin with water and turned around. "Thank you for being patient."

"Anytime," Rosa said with a grin.

As they walked to the middle of the sphere with Mr. Burke, Rosa walked ahead, and Mr. Burke cleared his throat as Chrysta walked next to him. "Feeling better, Miss Angelos?"

"I am," she said and was surprised that she meant it.

He nodded. "I'm pleased," he said. "I'm aware that you will be stronger than me, and any authority I have over you will wean as your abilities expand." She looked up at him in surprise but then nodded as she thought about it. "But allow Jiao and the Hunter Organization the opportunity to apprehend Guerra on their own. It would be best if you did not try to serve your own justice, no matter how powerful you have become."

Chrysta looked ahead and thought about what the Headmaster had said. Willow was walking between them, and she looked at Chrysta and whined. "I promise,

Mr. Burke," she said after a few moments of silence. "But I also promise that I'm not letting the Acolytes hurt any more people when I get out of the sphere."

"Fair enough, Miss Angelos," Mr. Burke replied as they finally reached the clearing with the stone sphere.

They had barely left the treeline when there was the building of the blinding purple light, and the supplies appeared once the light faded. Poe landed on the top, squawking. "Mail! Mail! Mail!" he cried while picking up two letters. He brought them down to Chrysta.

Chrysta tore open the letter addressed to her and handed the other one to Rosa. "Julien told everyone about the visions. Mrs. Zheng is making Julien take the others back to the Academy for their safety," Rosa said after a few minutes of reading.

"Good," Mr. Burke murmured.

"Ichiro is mad about it, but Rimsha and Julien think it's for the best. Good thing I told them to leave," she said while waving her letter. She looked at Chrysta. "What does Tommy say?"

"He says he is not going to leave," Chrysta replied. "That anyone who wants to hurt me will have to go through him first." She smiled. She didn't want anything to happen to Tommy, but knowing that he would be there when she got out of the sphere made her feel so much safer.

"Wish to teleport them, Miss Angelos?" Mr. Burke asked, gesturing at the supplies.

"Sure," Chrysta said with a smile. Poe started to click his beak on Chrysta's shoulder, making the popping sound that transportation spells made. Chrysta waved her hand, barely having to think about the boxes and their weight and where she wanted to send them. There was the flex in her chest, and they were gone instantly.

"Excellent work, Miss Angelos," Mr. Burke said, and Rosa held her fist out to let Chrysta bump it. "I declare you a functioning sorcerer. You can leave the sphere if you want."

Chrysta thought about it, nibbling on her lower lip for a few moments. "Twelve hours. One hundred and twenty days."

"Indoor plumbing, proper food, hot showers," Rosa said. "You can see Tommy again," she added with a leer.

Chrysta looked at her. "What will you do?"

"Miss Torres can start her hunter training soon," Mr. Burke said. "Tomorrow if she wants."

"I'll stay then," Chrysta said. "Every day I stay to practice in here is better than out of the sphere."

Mr. Burke gestured at the stone ball. "Then send your letter, and let us get back to the cabin."

Chrysta stopped Rosa from stepping up to the stone ball. "Can I add something for Tommy?"

"Of course," Rosa said with a grin and handed her letter to Chryata. Chrysta took out a pen and wrote a quick note to Tommy, using Rosa's back to write on. "What are you telling him?"

"That he can leave too if he wants," Chrysta replied.

"Do you think he will?" Rosa asked.

"No," Chrysta said with complete confidence. "He's way too stubborn to listen to me." Rosa chuckled.

Rosa took the letter when Chrysta finished and put it on the stone ball, hitting it with the tuning fork. She quickly ran out of the circle when the ringing became its loudest, and the letter disappeared with a red flash.

They turned around to head back to the cabin, the girls in front and Mr. Burke following behind them. "So what will I learn with the hunter training, Mr. Burke?" Rosa asked the Headmaster.

"Fighting, swordsmanship, mastery of at least one more elemental, tactics against changelings," Mr. Burke said. "It should take at least several months."

Rosa was quiet for a long time, and Chrysta looked at her, wondering if the girl was reconsidering becoming a hunter. "Can I go back to the fire aptitude test?" Rosa suddenly asked.

Chrysta laughed and realized that it was the first laugh she had made since finding out about the true nature of her mother's death; she felt her eyes burn, but the tears didn't fall, and she just laughed harder.

⤳ 45 ⤵

unter training involved less magical instruction, Chrysta soon realized, and more physical exercise. Rosa would no longer get up in the morning to run but get up to spar and fight with Mr. Burke instead.

"Boxing, Karate, Krav Maga, Wing Chun, Kalari. The Hunter Organization will help you find a fighting style that works for you and help you to master it," Mr. Burke explained on the first morning. He took out his sword and pointed it at Rosa. "But your sword will always be your greatest weapon. Especially against changelings." He let the blade drop and offered the handle to Rosa, and she gingerly took it.

Chrysta studied the sword along with Rosa. Black with a subtle wavy design in the metal. "Damascus steel," Mr. Burke explained. "Not the modern mixture of steel with iron, but the ancient wootz steel. Shatter-resistant, extremely tough, and does not become dull with frequent use."

"You get a sword when you graduate the hunter school," Rosa said softly, primarily to herself and not to Chrysta.

"Correct," Mr. Burke answered, holding his hand out for his weapon. Once Rosa handed him his sword, he turned around and grabbed a wooden sword. "This one is for you, Miss Torres. For now."

They practiced for hours, parries and strikes and swipes, sometimes with each other and sometimes with a seven-foot-tall man made of sticks and straw.

Chrysta was always amazed to watch Mr. Burke fight, reminding herself that he was older than her own father. He moved quickly and effortlessly, and Rosa could barely keep up with the former hunter.

Occasionally Mr. Burke would enlist Chrysta's help in training, having her throw stones at the other girl, starting with rocks the size of Chrysta's fist and slowly working up to human-sized boulders. Chrysta took the opportunity to begin learning about healing magic, feeling a little bit better about hitting Rosa with a stone when she could heal the girl's wounds later with the wave of her hand. "I don't think Miss Normandy could heal wounds this fast," Rosa told her one night, watching as a large cut on her arm closed in under a minute.

For the last week, Mr. Burke taught Rosa how to track Chrysta deep into the forest, using traditional methods like looking for tracks on the forest floor or working with Willow. Then, that morning, Mr. Burke had handed Rosa a crystal on a chain. "For dowsing," he explained. "I doubt you can use it to find Miss Angelos, but it will be good practice."

"So, how do I find her?" Rosa asked.

"Like you would find a changeling," he said as he patted Willow's head. "I'll even make it a competition between the two of you. You will get a prize if you can find Miss Angelos at least ten times before dinner. If you don't, Miss Angelos will receive it."

"What's the prize?" Chrysta asked and then gasped when Mr. Burke pulled a chocolate bar from his back pocket. They had sweets sent in with the rest of the supplies, but the girls had to ration them to make them last.

"Oh, that chocolate is mine, Angelos," Rosa growled.

Even with her taunting, Rosa struggled to track Chrysta without Mr. Burke's help. By lunchtime, Rosa had only found Chrysta four times. "Do you give up?" Chrysta asked the other girl while they took a break for lunch by a stream.

"No," Rosa grumbled. "I swear you are cheating."

Chrysta laughed, and Poe squawked. "Nope, I'm just walking into the woods, like I promised."

"No teleportation spell?"

"Nope," Chrysta replied again. She got up and dusted off her jeans. "Well, if you don't give up, let's see if you can find me again."

Rosa sighed and held out the crystal, letting it hang from her finger on its chain, and closed her eyes. The crystal seemed to twitch a little, but not at Chrysta. Rosa cracked an eye open and sighed when she saw the crystal hanging uselessly. "Well, at least I have Willow." The familiar huffed.

Chrysta started to walk into the woods. "You can do it! I believe in you." She pointed at Poe. "Help her, Poe! She needs it." The raven clicked his beak and flapped his wings to land on a sour-looking Rosa's shoulder. "Count to one hundred!"

Chrysta walked and kept walking until she couldn't hear Rosa counting anymore. She tried to keep her footfalls light, stepping on roots as much as possible.

She wanted Rosa to do well, but she wouldn't make it easy for the other girl. Chrysta thought she heard Rosa yelling, but she knew that meant Rosa had finished counting, so she hurried. Chrysta was now being stalked.

Rosa was at least getting better at tracking quickly and quietly, and Chrysta barely had any time to crouch behind a tree by the time she heard the hunting party approach, making herself as small as possible. She could hear the heavy footsteps of Rosa's boots crunching in the leaves. Willow paused and sniffed the air, and Chrysta covered her mouth to silence her breathing.

Poe joined them, landing on Willow's back. "Chrysta!" he called.

Chrysta gasped and then felt her stomach drop as she heard Willow growl playfully. She shouldn't have let Rosa have both familiars. How did she get herself into this mess?

Chrysta considered teleporting away, but that would break the rules they had agreed on. Chrysta thought she heard the group moving away. Well, maybe she would win after all. When she thought she was alone, she started to look around the tree.

"Gotcha!" Rosa yelled right in Chrysta's face. Chrysta shrieked and fell back, almost throwing up some sparks in surprise. Rosa started laughing. "Oh! The look on your face!" Rosa said, holding her sides.

Willow trotted up to Chrysta, wagging her tail and licking Chrysta's face. The familiar started to jump up and down, her whole body wagging from side to side in her excitement. "You got me," Chrysta admitted.

"Play!" Willow was saying, her joy so infectious that it made Chrysta smile even as Rosa helped her off the ground. "Play! Again!"

"Well, someone is excited," Rosa commented, watching Willow as she did some circles around the trees.

"She thinks it's a fun game," Chrysta explained. "Want another turn?"

"Sure, I would love the chance to scare you again," Rosa said with a grin.

Before Chrysta could get ready to go into the trees to hide again, Willow suddenly took off running. Chrysta laughed at the giant dog as she disappeared into the woods.

"Hey!" Rosa called out. "We have to find Chrysta, not you!"

"Come on," Chrysta said with a laugh. "Let's find her and do another round."

They jogged after Willow, calling her name, but she didn't slow down, still running and barking in the woods. They started to run faster, Chrysta barely keeping up with Rosa. Poe flew above them, croaking. "Willow!" Chrysta called. "Slow down!" But the familiar kept going.

"Where is she going?" Rosa asked, but before Chrysta could answer, she saw the red trees. Rosa noticed them too, and they slowed down as they approached them.

The trees weren't painted red, which is what Chrysta imagined when Mr. Burke described them to the girls, but the trees were entirely red, from the roots burrowing into the earth to the leaves high above them. They formed a line to the left and the right, but Chrysta had a feeling that if they chose a direction and followed the trees, they would go in a circle around the castle.

"Don't cross the red trees," Chrysta murmured to herself, remembering one of the most crucial rules Mr. Burke had given them. Poe landed at her shoulder, clicking his beak. "The red trees mark the circle around the castle."

"You don't think Willow went this way, do you?" Rosa asked. She didn't wait for Chrysta to answer but put her hands around her mouth and yelled into the woods. "Willow! Come back!" Willow barked in response, but it was faint and distant.

"Willow!" Poe called, flapping his wings, but he didn't even want to cross the red trees.

Chrysta took out the dowsing crystal and let it hang from her finger. It barely took a second of her concentrating on the familiar for the crystal to twitch and pull until it was almost parallel to the ground. It pointed past the red trees and towards the castle.

"Do we go after her?" Rosa asked, but then there was a terrible screech, the sound of a dog in horrific pain. The girls didn't hesitate and ran past the trees and towards the sounds of a struggle, Poe taking to the air after them.

Rosa was faster than Chrysta, but Chrysta almost plowed into the girl when she stopped suddenly. They were in a clearing, and a metal monstrosity had a giant hand wrapped around Willow, holding her above its head. It looked like a suit of armor, almost ten feet tall, but it wasn't a flesh and blood creature that filled the pieces, but black smoke that rolled and moved like water. *"Hey!"* Rosa yelled, forming a fireball in one hand. "Let her go!"

The creature didn't respond or even acknowledge their presence, and it lifted Willow, who was trying to bite her metal attacker, higher in the air. Rosa let the fireball fly, and it hit the armor, clinging to the metal. The creature screeched and dropped Willow, trying to brush the fire off of its front. Chrysta reached her hand out and caught Willow, making sure she gently placed the dog on the ground. Willow collapsed when she tried to stand up, so Chrysta threw sparks into the air, as bright as fireworks, knowing that Mr. Burke would see them and come help them.

The creature put up a hand, trying to block the bright light, roaring a high-pitched scream. Chrysta winced at the sound, hearing the creature's pain in that cry. Poe landed on the ground in front of Willow, squawking and flapping his wings at the metal monster. Rosa made another fireball, but before she could throw it, there was a loud *pop,* and Mr. Burke appeared, sword at the ready. He took in the scene and pointed at the girls. "Fire!" he roared. "Burn it!"

Rosa threw the ball, and it coated the creature, sliding off its armor like oil. It screeched and screamed, and Chrysta put her hands down, all thoughts of forming a fireball leaving her mind. It was a horrible sound, and she felt pity for the creature.

"Wait!" Chrysta yelled when she saw Mr. Burke form his own fireball. "Stop! It's hurt!"

"Miss Angelos, it will kill us if it gets us," the Headmaster said. The creature put its arms down and started walking toward them, still crying in pain. The scream started to form words in Chrysta's mind, loud and shrill.

kill, it hurts, kill, the light, kill, it burns, it burns, itburnsitburnsitburns

"It's screaming!" Chrysta cried. "The light is hurting it!"

"Chrysta, it's not making a sound!" Rosa yelled. She formed a fireball in her hand, and Chrysta could sense that the creature could feel it—

it burns, it burns, IT BURNS

—but it couldn't stop itself from moving towards them. Rosa let the fireball go, and Chrysta winced as the screaming rose in volume, but the creature didn't stop.

Chrysta panicked, not knowing what to do. She couldn't let the creature hurt anyone, but its screams of pain pulled at her heart. Both Rosa and Mr. Burke were leaning back, winding up to throw another volley of fireballs, and Chrysta didn't think she had enough time to teleport them away to safety. So she did the only thing that she could think of.

She ran at the creature.

"Chrysta!" Rosa screamed, but she ignored the other girl. She needed to touch it, to figure out what it was and how she could help it. It stopped dead as she approached it, probably just as shocked by Chrysta's actions as she was. She was barely half its height, but that gave her the best angle to thrust her right arm through a crack in the armor. When her skin touched the black smoke that filled the suite, it burned. Not the burn of fire, but the burn of touching metal so cold that her skin instantly froze. She tried to ignore it and read the creature.

There were magical chains that helped the creature move the armor. But the chains were also keeping the black smoke trapped inside the armor. The chains hurt to touch and made the creature insane with pain. Chrysta had to wonder how long it had been trapped like this. How many years and centuries and millennia? No wonder it wanted to hurt the humans, even kill them. It was like a panicked animal striking out in distress. Chrysta grabbed the chains, pulled and yanked on them, and the armor stuttered to a stop as it sensed freedom.

Chrysta closed her eyes and concentrated on getting the creature free. It hurt, it burned, but if she could just—

can't break them, the magic is too strong, but maybe she could move them, just enough so the black thing could move, get out, get free,

wait, wait, there, THERE, the magic was vulnerable here, a weak link in the chain, and she flexed, and it broke, and her arm was burning from the cold, but Chrysta broke the chain

—and the armor started to fall apart, the black smoke bleeding out. The creature shrieked again as the sunlight hit it. But the screaming stopped as the smoke melted into the trees, into the cool shadows. Chrysta scrambled back, trying to avoid the falling armor. She yelped as her arm struck the ground, pins and needles erupting from where she hit. She looked down at her arm and was surprised to see a layer of frost clinging to her skin, her skin grey with patches of white. Poe landed next to her, croaking "Chrysta! Chrysta!" over and over.

Rosa rushed to Chrysta's side. "Are you alright?" she asked but winced as she looked at Chrysta's arm.

"I-I don't k-know," Chrysta replied. She tried to flex her fingers and grimaced as a bolt of pain traveled to her elbow, the fingers not moving.

"We will retreat to the cabin and regroup there," Mr. Burke said. He placed a hand on Willow's back. "Miss Angelos, are you able to teleport?"

Chrysta nodded. "I think so." She grabbed Rosa's hand, Poe landed on her shoulder, and they teleported, disappearing in a *pop!*

.....

They popped in front of the cabin, Poe taking off and flying into the open front door. Mr. Burke and Rosa carried Willow inside, and he examined the familiar as he barked an order to Rosa. "Warm water. We need to combat any frostbite Miss Angelos may have received." Rosa nodded and headed for the kitchen. "What happened?" he asked Chrysta as Willow whined.

"We were working on my tracking skills, and Willow got excited and ran away from us," Rosa explained as she hurried back with water and towels.

"Got too enthusiastic, you silly thing," Mr. Burke murmured as he felt Willow's leg, sounding stern but looking at the familiar with a fond expression.

"Can I help?" Chrysta asked, feeling guilty that Willow got hurt because of their training. She put her uninjured hand on Willow's fur, and the dog wagged her tail weakly.

"Rest, Miss Angelos," Mr. Burke ordered her, but it was too late. She was already glowing gold. She could feel the broken bone in Willow's front leg and gently and quickly fixed it. Willow whined, but Mr. Burke hushed her.

"I think that's it," Chrysta said when the bone felt healed entirely.

"Good work, Miss Angelos," Mr. Burke said. "Let us inspect your arm." He nodded at Rosa, and she handed him the bowl of water, but he paused when he studied Chrysta's arm.

Chrysta looked at her arm and gasped. The skin that had been white and grey was slowly turning pink. The pins and needles were getting stronger, stabbing as the nerves warmed up and healed.

"What is happening?" Rosa asked, voice low in wonder.

"It appears that Miss Angelos has the ability of spontaneous healing," Mr. Burke explained.

"Spontaneous healing?" Chrysta asked. She tried to flex her fingers, and it hurt, but at least the fingers actually moved this time.

"It means all damage your body sustains will heal itself."

"Does it mean I'm immortal?" Chrysta asked.

"I wouldn't recommend testing that theory, Miss Angelos."

"So what about the vision elephant showed you?" Rosa asked.

"Are you sure you actually died in the vision, Miss Angelos?"

"I... I don't know how to answer that."

"Fair enough." Mr. Burke leaned back, looking pensive. "What did you do to that guardian, Miss Angelos?"

"There was magic, like chains, keeping the black thing trapped in the armor," Chrysta explained. "I found a weak spot and broke it."

"What was that thing?" Rosa asked.

"The guardians have been a fixture of the sphere since the beginning. Sorcerers who have analyzed the sphere theorize that the castle's owner created them." He studied Chrysta for a few moments. "This is the first time anyone has been able to dismantle one." He leaned forward again. "Do you think you could do it again, Miss Angelos?"

"Maybe," she said. She looked down at her arm, which looked better by the minute. "I think I can break the chains faster next time, but I have to touch them."

Mr. Burke thought in silence for a few moments. Then, "Miss Torres, I think we will be halting your training for the time being."

"Did we do something wrong?" Chrysta asked, worried that Mr. Burke was upset that Willow got hurt.

"No, I am actually very proud of both of you for how you handled yourself today." Mr. Burke smiled. "No one has been able to get close enough to the castle to explore it. I think we should rectify that."

46

Mrs. Bellaund's carriage stopped in front of the house, and she waited for the coachman to open the door. She held a lace handkerchief briefly to her nose as she climbed down. It had rained earlier, and the dirt street transformed into thick, foul-smelling mud. Hopefully, this seer processed the true sight, and Mrs. Bellaund wasn't wasting her time here.

She went up the stairs and used the lion-shaped door knocker to announce her arrival. She was annoyed when a young dark-skinned man opened the door. He gave her a giant smile and moved inside, and bowed. "Mrs. Bellaund," he purred. "Welcome to Lady Sibyl's humble home. We were expecting you."

Mrs. Bellaund scowled at him and held her purse closer to her chest as he took her shawl off her shoulders and hung it up. Generally, she would have the young man whipped for addressing her in such a friendly manner, but she needed to speak to the lady of the house first. "If you were expecting me, where is your mistress?"

"I am here," a voice said, and Mrs. Bellaund looked up.

An old woman was moving her way down the stairs, a young woman helping her. She was bent over her cane, white hair pulled into a bun on the top of her head and dressed in a black dress and purple shawl. She moved slowly, carefully, to the first floor. "I apologize," she said, her voice surprisingly strong for a frail old woman. "I do not move as fast as when I was younger."

Mrs. Bellaund shifted. "I should be the one to apologize," she responded. "This is your home, after all."

Lady Sibyl hummed and continued her slow descent. "Can we offer you refreshments, Mrs. Bellaund? Wine?"

"Water, please," she responded. She wanted to ensure she had all her wits for this meeting.

Lady Sibyl finally made it down the steps, and she turned to the parlor as the young man opened the doors for them. "Thomas," she said to the black man, "water for our guest."

The parlor was all dark wood and wallpaper, the fire just low embers barely giving any light. Thomas lit a mirrored wall sconce, and it helped to chase some of the shadows into the corners, but not by much. Lady Sibyl made her way to a table in the middle of the room while Thomas poured water into a crystal glass. The table had a crystal ball in its center, quartz clouded by white streaks. Lady Sibyl sat down in a chair with a high back, and the young woman moved to pull a chair out for Mrs. Bellaund across from the old woman. She sat down, and the glass was placed in front of her, but she didn't acknowledge it or the young man who had brought it.

"I am here—" Mrs. Bellaund started to say but stopped when the older woman put her hand up.

"I do not need the details, Mrs. Bellaund. The spirits will provide me all the information I require." She placed both hands on the table. "I do, however, ask for half now and half after we are finished."

Mrs. Bellaund felt her lips press into a firm line, but she nodded and reached into her wallet. This was not her first seance, but she always hated how these men and women demanded money for their services. And some of them were fakes! Deceivers who only wanted to steal! It was so shameful.

Mrs. Bellaund held the money out, and the young woman took it, Lady Sibyl not moving from her position. She tucked the money into her sleeve, even as she pulled a scarf out of the other. Lady Sibyl accepted the scarf and covered her eyes with it. "Put an item that the spirit owned in life in the box, please," she said, and the young man held out an opened silver box. Mrs. Bellaund hesitated but then put her late husband's pocket watch in the box. It was closed and placed on the table next to the crystal ball.

"Let us begin," Lady Sibyl said, placing one of her hands on the box and the other on the table, palm up. "Complete the circle, please."

Mrs. Bellaund put one hand in the older woman's grip and the other on the box. Thomas blew out the candle and closed the door to the hallway, and the room was plunged into darkness. The seconds ticked by as Lady Sibyl let her head roll around on her neck, the young woman standing next to her silently. "Spirit," Lady Sibyl hissed after several minutes. "We wish to speak to you."

Mrs. Bellaund waited, keeping her eyes open to watch both young people for any signs of deception. Both of them stood by the table, hands in the open, but Mrs. Bellaund still didn't look away. "Spirit," Lady Sibyl called again. "We beseech thee. Make your presence known." The older woman's forehead furrowed in concentration. "The veil, it's thick tonight. It is difficult to see who you are searching for."

Mrs. Bellaund's lips pressed back into a thin line. Here it was. The point when the old woman would request more money. *That* would help; *that* would make the spirits talk. Well, she wouldn't fall for it, not for one second. She was about to break the circle, get up and march out of the house, but suddenly there was a glimmer in the crystal ball, a purple glow getting brighter. A trick of the light, maybe? But then the air in the room became frigid, and Mrs. Bellaund felt herself shiver. All the room occupants developed clouded breath, but the young man and woman didn't react. "Wh-what... what is this?" she asked weakly.

"He is here."

The purple glow was growing in the crystal ball, but it was also coming from Lady Sibyl's hands. Mrs. Bellaund tried to snatch her hands away, but the older woman held firm, stronger than Mrs. Bellaund expected. "Don't break the circle!" Lady Sibyl fiercely whispered. "I can almost se—*AH!* Yes! The spirit is here!"

Mrs. Bellaund waited for Lady Sibyl to continue as the old woman's head rolled on her shoulders again, the uncanny purple glow not fading. "Henri," Lady Sibyl hissed. "His name is Henri." Mrs. Bellaund froze, only her heart galloping in her chest. Lucky guess, perhaps? But then, the old woman paused. "He says hello, his little bird."

Mrs. Bellaund gasped and leaned forward, watching the older woman intently, the room's other occupants totally forgotten. Little bird had been his pet name for her years ago, before the children were born and when their marriage was new and loving. No one knew that. This woman was a *true* mystic! "Henri?" she asked. "Is it truly you?"

Lady Sibyl hummed. "Yes, it is him." Her head leaned to the side. "He wishes to speak to you."

"Oh, Henri! I have missed you so!" Mrs. Bellaund cried. "Henri! Henri, please! I need you to tell me where the will is!" She knew she was giving away too much information, but the excitement of finding an actual seer was overpowering her reason. "Your brother is trying to take over your business, and I *need* that will!"

Lady Sibyl didn't respond, humming to herself. Suddenly the young woman next to her closed her eyes, and then she started to glow as well, a pale green color starting on her hands. She opened her eyes again, but her pupils were gone, pale green light seeping from her eyes. Thomas jerked in surprise, looking at the young woman and back to Mrs. Bellaund, looking shocked. Finally, the young woman opened her mouth. "Nancy," she croaked, but the voice she emitted was deep, too deep for a girl to use. Mrs. Bellaund thought for a second that it was Henri's voice. Lady Sibyl stopped moving, her forehead furrowing again.

Was the young woman a seer too? Mrs. Bellaund addressed the young woman. "Henri? Henri, can you help me?"

"Nancy..." the young woman hissed in Mrs. Bellaund's late husband's voice. "*Go.*"

"Go? Go where?"

"Go home," the young woman said, looking upset. Lady Sibyl was squeezing Mrs. Bellaund's hand tightly, scowling.

"Home? Is that where the will is?"

"Noooooooooo," the young woman hissed. Her eyes were still completely white, but she looked directly at Mrs. Bellaund. She could *sense* it. "Leave this place." The young woman shuddered. "Leave and never re—"

Suddenly the whole table jumped, and Mrs. Bellaund flinched as her water glass fell and drenched her. She yelped, and she stopped holding Lady Sibyl's hands. The girl jerked and blinked, her eyes becoming normal as she looked around the room dumbly.

"*Oh!* Oh no! Can you bring him back?" Mrs. Bellaund cried, looking around the room like her late husband would be standing in one of the dark corners.

"Not tonight, I'm afraid," Lady Sibyl sighed as she removed the scarf from her face. She put a hand to her temple like a headache settled there. "The veil has fallen. Henri will not be talking to us again tonight." Her voice was calm and even, but she glanced at the young woman next to her, frowning. The poor girl looked upset like she was about to cry.

"When can we try again?" Mrs. Bellaund asked excitedly. "Soon?"

"In one week, it will be the night of the full moon," Lady Sibyl explained as she stood from the table using her cane. "We will attempt contact that night. Do you have friends that can join us?"

Mrs. Bellaund was ushered to the front door, almost forgetting her husband's pocket watch but taking it with a smile when Thomas handed it to her. She fawned over the older woman, trying to pay her but being graciously rebuffed every time. "Next week," Lady Sibyl explained. "I will take payment when we find the secrets you seek."

Mrs. Bellaund left through the door, standing outside, feeling elated. Finally, finally, a true mystic! Finally, she had found an authentic seer! And now she would have the answers she sought from beyond the grave! She went to her carriage with a spring to her step.

.....

Tommy closed the door and turned to the lady of the house dressing down her granddaughter. "Stupid! Imbecile! You nearly ruined the whole thing!" Cybill Léandre was yelling in Celeste's face. The young woman flinched but didn't respond.

"She didn't mean anything by it," Tommy argued.

The old sorcerer rounded on him, standing taller now that Mrs. Bellaund was gone, although she still held the cane. She may be one-hundred and twenty-four years old, but Léandre was much stronger than she led unmagical people to believe. "Don't you *dare* speak!" she shouted. "Your little trick was almost as bad!"

"It was the only thing I could do," Tommy reasoned. "If I didn't break Celeste's concentration, that dead man would have told the truth, and then we would never see Mrs. Bellaund again. Or her friends."

The slap was loud in the hallway, and Tommy's head rocked back as Celeste gasped. He bit back a growl as he squared his shoulders and glared at the old woman. She jabbed a finger in his face. "I said not to speak," she hissed.

"I'm sorry," Celeste whispered, earning her grandmother's glare again. "I couldn't control it. He was so insisted on talking to his wife."

"What am I paying that tutor for? Hm? Isn't he suppose to help you to control your ability?"

Celeste blushed and looked down at her hands, twisting them in front of her. "He is helping me," she whispered in response.

"*Bah!*" Léandre cried, throwing up her free hand and turning to climb the stairs, going much faster than she had before. "Clean up your mess and get out, Thomas," she barked. "And hope that Mrs. Bellaund brings enough friends with deep pockets to make up for tonight's disaster, or I may just sell *you* to make up for it."

Tommy waited for the sound of Léandre's door slamming shut, and then he made a face, sticking out his tongue. Generally, the small act of defiance would make Celeste laugh, but when he looked at the young woman, she was still upset, twisting her hands and eyes shining with unshed tears. Tommy touched her hand and gave her a soft smile. "Go to bed," he told her. "I can handle cleaning up some water."

"No, I will help," she said. "You got punished because of me."

The table was righted, and the tablecloth was cleaned and dried in a few minutes. Tommy started heading to the back of the house, Celeste following him. "Go to bed," he said again.

She shook her head. "I want to feed Ami. I... I would like to see her tonight."

The house was aged and run down but was large enough to have its own stable, where Tommy slept with the family's single mare, Ami. The old animal whickered as they entered. Celeste went over to rub her nose as Tommy got the horse's dinner ready. Suddenly, Celeste clamped a hand over her nose. "Oh, that *smell*," she moaned.

Tommy took a breath. It was a stable, with all the smells that came with it. "I don't smell anything. I mean, I have been sleeping here for the last four years," he said. "You have to get accustomed to the smell of manure pretty quickly."

Celeste made a distressed retching sound and ran outside. Tommy ran after her, finding her throwing up in the yard. He put a hand on her shoulder as she finished emptying her stomach. "Are you alright?" he asked as she wiped her mouth.

"No," she moaned. "I have b-been sick almost every day. I'm tired all the time, but I can't sleep" Celeste's eyes filled with tears. "M-my ability is getting out of control." The tears started to fall. "Y-you got hurt because of m-me."

Tommy sighed as Celeste softly cried. "That sounds serious. You need to see a healer." He looked up at Léandre's bedroom window. "But that old witch wouldn't pay for one if you asked her to, would she?" He didn't wait for an answer but went inside the stable and came out several minutes later with a bundle. He handed it to Celeste, and she blinked at the roll of money. "Oh, Tommy," she whispered. "I can't take this. Grandmother barely pays you as it is."

Tommy leaned down so Celeste could see his expression. "I can always make more money," he explained, "good friends are harder to come by." He glanced back up at Léandre's window and thought he saw the curtain twitch. "You aren't feeling good and need to see a healer, alright?"

Celeste nodded, standing up a little straighter. "I will," she promised.

"Go to bed," Tommy said for the third time. "Get some rest, and I'll make crepes for you in the morning," he promised and was happy to see her smile. She finally went inside, and Tommy turned to the stable, glancing at the window one last time. Once he was inside, he made sure Ami had all the food she would need for the night. The horse huffed at him and tried to bite his sleeve.

"Yeah, I know," Tommy said surly. "She needs to get out of here as soon as possible." Ami whickered. "Yeah, well, there is not much I can do, is there? I know it's bad in that house." He rubbed the horse's nose. "But she doesn't know how bad it can be out there."

.....

Two nights after the disastrous seance with Mrs. Bellaund, Celeste eased the door to her room open, holding her breath as she listened to the house around her. It was silent as a tomb, so Celeste could only hope that her grandmother was asleep and wouldn't see her leave the house. She quickly left her room and moved through the mansion, fast but quietly. Celeste knew which steps to avoid on the servant's stairs, stepping over the ones that would creak and groan. Once she reached the back door in the kitchen, she eased Tommy's boots onto her feet. Her grandmother wouldn't notice fresh mud on them. She unlocked the back door and rushed outside.

The sky was dark and cloudy, and although it wasn't raining right now, the black sky lit up with lightning in the distance, turning the dark clouds into purple towers bigger than anything man had built. The thunder rolled in half a minute later, a promise of rain to come. Celeste rushed to the stable, praying to any gods listening that her grandmother wouldn't look outside and see her.

Ami heard her open the door, and she huffed at Celeste as she closed the door behind her. Celeste hushed the horse but paused to rub her nose as the mare sniffed at Celeste's hair. She smiled and quickly walked to the last stall. Celeste paused at the door and knocked. "Tommy?" she whispered into the dark. "Tommy, are you there?"

Celeste heard him take a deep breath and sigh. "Where else would I be?" he asked thickly. Then, there was the sound of something moving around in the stall, and the top portion of the door opened. Celeste waited as he lit a lantern and then hung it on her side of the door. "What are you doing here, Celeste?" he asked, frowning at her. "Couldn't this wait for tomorrow morning?"

"I'm sorry, Tommy, I really am," Celeste started to say. She handed the remaining money to him. "I-I went to the healer today with Cyprien. I... I have something to tell you and... and I want to make sure grandmother doesn't overhear us."

Tommy took the money, barely glancing at it. Celeste felt horrible that she had used almost all of it. She silently vowed to pay him back. "Alright," he said. "What's wrong, Celeste? Is it serious?"

"I'm pregnant."

Tommy blinked at her for several seconds of stunned silence. *"How?!"* he asked when he had recovered. She gave him a look, and he lifted a hand. "No, don't answer that. I know *how*, but *how* are you with child?"

Celeste looked down for a moment. "It's Cyprien Leonard. He's the father."

Tommy sighed and rubbed his face, but he smiled, something tired but mischievous. Celeste smiled back, happy that her instincts to entrust Tommy with her secret were right. "Does that idiot know Cybill Léandre will kill him when she finds out?"

"Hopefully, we will be far away in Europe when that happens."

Tommy sighed again. "Come on, tell me everything," he said and opened the bottom portion of the door so she could enter the stall. She sat down on his bed as he blew out the lantern, plunging them into darkness. He sat in the straw in front of her but didn't say anything. The thunder rolled again, louder this time. It would rain again soon.

"Um," Celeste hummed, thankful for the dark that hid her blush. "It started a few months ago. We... we are in love, Tommy. I would have wanted to get married before we... before I became pregnant, but I'm happy that it is his child."

"So the old woman doesn't trust me to be alone with you, but she should have been worried about that bookworm this entire time," Tommy muttered. "What does your beau have to say about all this?"

"He didn't want me to come back here, but I had to," Celeste confessed. "I know if I disappeared, Grandmother would try to find me. So I want to ensure she can't come after us if we flee."

"What is the plan?" Tommy asked.

"Cyprien thinks we should go to the Hunter Organization," Celeste explained. "Grandmother is using magic in front of non-magical people. That could be enough to get her arrested and keep her from hunting us. Cyprien has family in France. We can go there and be safe."

"You have to be careful," Tommy growled, and Celeste blinked. She didn't know where his sudden anger came from. "The law that would incriminate her could affect you too."

"Not if we take her books on curses with us," Celeste argued. "Cyprien says that having them could give me amnesty with the hunters."

Tommy suddenly grabbed her hand and squeezed it so hard it hurt. "Celeste, those books are protected. Your grandmother will know if you try to take them, and she will hurt you for trying to steal them." He let go of her hand. "You need to do the best thing for you and your child. You need to save yourself, and hunters be damned."

"But Tommy, those books can help so many people if we can get them to the right sorcerers."

"The hunters should help you, even if you can't get those books," Tommy growled in reply.

"They will, but I don't want to leave without at least trying to do some good before I go." It was dark in the small building, but she could see his outline in front of her. She reached out and put her hand on his cheek. "You can come with us, Tommy. Please. You don't have to stay here with my grandmother. It's so bad here, and you deserve so much better."

Tommy went still, and the silence stretched between them, the sound of Ami sleeping the only thing surrounding them. But, suddenly, the thunder cracked above them, making Celeste jump, and the sky opened up in a torrent. Tommy grabbed her hand but held it in his. "I can't do that, Celeste," he said softly, barely loud enough for her to hear over the rain. "Hunters are the worse people for me to work with, trust me."

Celeste felt her eyes burn. She knew her friend was hiding here from the outside world but never thought he would prefer to stay here than leave for a better life. "I can talk to them. Let me talk to them," she begged. "If you help me take the books with me, the hunters will give you amnesty for whatever crime you're worried about."

Tommy sighed again and let go of her hand. "Let us worry about getting you away from here," he said. "I can take care of myself, but we must get you and that child out first."

"Alright," Celeste agreed. "But please go with us, Tommy."

"I'll... I'll think about it."

They talked, and by the time Celeste left the stable to run to the house, she felt better than she had in weeks. Tommy said he would help her the best he could, even consider coming with her. Knowing that her most trusted friend would leave this place with her made her feel at peace, and when she put her head on the pillow, she fell asleep quickly.

Meanwhile, Tommy lay awake in the dark stable, unable to rest.

⤬ 47 ⤬

ybill "Lady Sibyl" Léandre was a complex woman.

She had started to glow purple when she was thirteen years old. That would have been a fantastic development for many sorcerers, opening doors for any career they pursued or allowing her family to negotiate a hefty bride price for when she was old enough to marry. But for Léandre, her only concern was how she could use her abilities to make money for herself.

Her natural ability was cursing people, a power she couldn't monetize in sorcerer society, at least not legally. If she wanted to be rich, she needed to figure out how to make a fortune in other ways. So, when she was old enough, she left home and started to tour the country. She found that non-magical people were obsessed with mysticism, the occult, and being able to talk with the dead in particular. So, if non-magical people wanted to talk to dead loved ones and "Lady Sibyl" could provide that service (for a fee, of course), then how could that be a bad thing?

She started to stage fake seances. She wasn't talking to the dead, not really, but a box that had a psychometry enchantment on it helped her to get enough information from the deceased person's belongings that she could give solace to their living relations. What was the harm in that?

She traveled the country for decades, amassing a fortune, avoiding her family, and keeping her illegal activities hidden from the authorities. At one point, she crossed the ocean and started a tour in Europe, and Léandre met her child's father one day, a man she didn't love, but he warmed her bed for several months as she toured the continent. When she found out she was pregnant, she decided to retire from the transient life and settle down in Louisiana in America.

She continued her seances, Léandre's daughter becoming a part of the hoax early in her life. She would dress in white and play the role of a friendly ghost, using spells to float and walk through walls in front of surprised guests. Lady Sibyl gained a reputation of being an actual seer quickly, but as her daughter got older, finding and keeping clients became harder. Money started to become scarce. Eventually, Léandre decided they needed to add a proper medium to their group, a sorcerer who could gather even more information to persuade wealthy patrons to hand over their money. That man would become Celeste's father, much to Léandre's vexation, and it was from him that Celeste got her ability.

Celeste remembered her parents as loving people, but her grandmother had always been an imposing force in her life, someone to obey and please. Celeste had vivid memories of the adults fighting, but it wasn't until she was older that she realized what they were about: Léandre, in her quest for more money, was offering more illegal activities to their clients. Curse an enemy, enchant an object, poison a cheating spouse, Lady Sibyl could provide it all for the right price. But Celeste's parents argued that the lifestyle would get them all in trouble sooner rather than later, and they tried to convince Léandre to stop her life of hoaxes and scams.

When Celeste was ten, her parents became ill, catching the same ailment that made them cough blood and ultimately die in bed. Her grandmother became her only family, a fact Léandre frequently rubbed into the young girl's face.

"I could have made you live on the street," the older woman would say. "You could be begging for your supper, you know that? Instead, I feed and clothe you. Never forget that."

So Celeste helped her grandmother in her fake seances, sometimes dressing as a ghost or acting as a servant for her grandmother and guests. When she was fifteen, she started glowing green and talking to spirits like her father. But she struggled to control it. She couldn't always ignore the spirits who wished to speak to her, mad at Lady Sibyl for scamming their living loved ones. Her grandmother made her stay in their house as a result, never going outside and never having friends. She cleaned and cooked, and she helped her grandmother in her business. It was a lonely existence.

Until Thomas Monroe arrived.

Many people came to Lady Sibyl's home to seek her favor, but Tommy just wanted one thing: to live and work in their home.

"Why?" Léandre asked the young man. She sat behind her desk, her gnarled hands on her staff, her white hair piled high in a bun on her head.

"I need a place to live and work protected by magic," Tommy explained. "If you let me stay here, you don't have to pay me much."

The older woman looked him up and down, studying him. "So it is protection you are after?" she asked.

"Yes," he admitted but didn't explain further.

Léandre didn't talk for a long time, so long that eighteen-year-old Celeste began to fidget in her chair. Not Tommy. He stood tall and quiet, letting the older woman examine him. Finally, Léandre got up from her chair, using her cane to stand. Celeste quickly got up and helped her walk to the young man. They stared each other down without saying anything. Suddenly, the old woman snapped her twisted fingers, and a purple spark appeared between them. Celeste yelped, Tommy didn't flinch, and Léandre blinked in surprise. "The curse didn't adhere itself to you?" she asked. "Is that your ability?"

"You could say that," he said, still not explaining himself.

Léandre huffed. She turned her back on the young man and started to leave the study. "You are strong enough to repel my magic, but you wish to live here as a servant to protect yourself instead." She lifted a hand and waved it dismissively as she slowly moved out the door. "You can stay in the stable. Muck out the stalls. Do the manual labor. But be aware, if whatever nightmare you are running from comes here to darken my doorstep, I will be feeding you to it."

·····

Celeste became fast friends with Tommy, the man with a bright smile and easy-going nature. He was strong and willing to do the manual labor that Celeste struggled with, and he even helped her with the chores inside. He could read, and they shared books and stories, pooling their meager earnings together to grow Celeste's library.

"Ever hear of the story *Frankenstein?*"

"Of course," Tommy said, accepting the book with a grin.

Celeste reached over and retrieved another book from her collection in the parlor. "You might like Jules Verne. Although, I recommend reading the French version if you can."

"Sorry, just the English for me." Tommy suddenly sniffed and glanced at the glass cases in the middle of the room. "What about those books."

Celeste followed his gaze and grimaced. "Those are not for reading. They are Grandmother's books. They contain all the knowledge she has collected and created over the years. They are curses mostly."

"So not light reading," he joked.

Surprisingly, her grandmother didn't say anything about Celeste being friends with the strange man. She would glare and loom over them, but she never ordered Celeste to stop talking to Tommy. Maybe, Celeste hoped, the older woman realized that Celeste was lonely and needed someone to bond with. Léandre had nothing to worry about, in Celeste's opinion. She had no romantic interest in the man; he was more like an older brother to her.

Tommy was the one who helped Celeste with her abilities. One night, Léandre yelled at Celeste for not creating a curse properly, making her grandmother recreate it for their client. Tommy asked her about it the next day as they peeled a small mountain of potatoes for dinner. "Why did you have so much trouble last night? Doesn't it come naturally to you, like it does that old crone?"

Celeste gave an unladylike snort in amusement but quickly looked around the kitchen to see if Grandmother heard them. She had just turned 20, but tiny acts of rebellion still scared her. "It's not my natural ability," she explained. "I can talk to spirits, like my father, but barely. I have never been able to develop it, and you can't learn other spells until you master your natural one." She briefly wondered why he didn't know this already. He was a sorcerer, after all.

"So, what would help you to master your ability?" Tommy asked.

Celeste looked down for a moment so he wouldn't see how upset she was. "I'm too old. I can't go to the school up north; they only allow children to learn there." She sighed. "I may be able to learn more magic if I had tutors, but Grandmother would never agree to that." She felt a wave of sorrow hit her, and she stopped peeling her potato as her cheeks heated. "It would cost too much money."

That night, Celeste and Léandre were eating a silent dinner. Tommy, who wasn't allowed to eat with them, came in to clear the plates. "So," he calmly said to Léandre, "when do you plan to retire?"

Léandre, who was wiping her mouth with a napkin, glared at him. "What business is it of yours, boy?"

Tommy didn't react to her insult. "You plan on retiring, correct? You should let Celeste run the seances at some point, and she can make money while you enjoy your twilight years and not work." He poured the older woman some wine. "Or had you really not thought of that before?"

Celeste felt a slight sense of panic. She didn't want to continue her grandmother's business of running fake seances and cursing people, but Tommy gave her a mischievous smile and a wink behind her grandmother's back, and she suddenly understood what he was doing. If Celeste could learn magic, she would be able to take care of herself.

Léandre glared at Celeste as she took a sip of her wine. "The stupid girl can barely control her ability," she growled, and Celeste blushed in embarrassment. "I wouldn't trust her to run a seance alone."

"You can always get her tutors," Tommy said lightly, and the older woman's eyebrows shot up. "Think of it as an investment on your retirement. Money well spent on the future of your business."

"What is it to you?" Léandre asked, suspicion blooming on her face. "I have never seen you *use* a spell."

"Well, unless you plan on leaving your empire to me," Tommy joked, "I suggest you do something to help your granddaughter continue your legacy." He left the room, Léandre glaring at his back.

But, several weeks later, Léandre announced that Celeste would be starting lessons with the best tutors Léandre could afford. Celeste was so excited with the news that she gave Tommy a kiss on the cheek as soon as they were alone, his cheeks darkening in a blush. "Thank you," she whispered. "Now I can take care of myself."

And so, for the last two years, Celeste studied, learning as much as she could. She finally mastered her ability, but the best byproduct of her training was becoming friends with other sorcerers and discovering their cultures and homelands. Celeste shared their stories with Tommy, who seemed just as excited about her studies as she was. But he always declined when she offered to teach him what she had learned.

For the last few months, her tutors were a woman teaching her healing magic and Cyprien Leonard, a sorcerer training Celeste on how to call on and talk to the dead. He was originally from France but had traveled all over the world. He had read Jules Verne and even seen one of the author's plays in Paris. He was intelligent, funny, and kind. He was, in Celeste's opinion, perfect.

"Oh, you fancy him," Tommy teased her one day.

And Celeste couldn't argue with him because he was right. She fancied the sorcerer. And so, when she was alone with Cyprien one day, he suddenly took her hand and kissed it, telling her how happy he was to know her and how he couldn't imagine his life without her...

Well, it was no wonder she found herself with child.

.....

Several days after her confession to Tommy, Celeste was in her room when there was a knock. Léandre entered the room carrying a bundle of clothing. "I canceled the seance with Mrs. Bellaund," she said without a greeting and with no preamble. "I am holding an important dinner that night instead." Her grandmother wrestled the bundle until it was hanging in the wardrobe, still trying to use her cane. It was a bell-shaped deep, emerald dress, its color matching Celeste's eyes, with white lace and a slight train. "I got you a new dress for the occasion."

Celeste felt a weird mix of emotions. It was a beautiful dress, but expensive looking. That was money Celeste could have used to see the healer, not Tommy's savings. "Who is coming?" Celeste asked, trying to cover her concern.

"New clients," Léandre said, but she didn't elaborate.

Celeste fingered the material of the dress. "I think this is the same cloth used for the drapes in the dining room," she joked.

Her grandmother chuckled. "You shouldn't make fun of it. I'm told it is the latest fashion in Paris."

Celeste tried to keep her face blank at the mention of Paris. France meant freedom for her, and she wanted to leave soon, but she needed to get the books from her grandmother first. And convince Tommy to leave if she could.

"Thank you," Celeste said. She liked the dress, even if she didn't understand why her grandmother got it.

Suddenly, her grandmother grabbed her hands and tugged Celeste into a hug. Celeste froze, not knowing what to do. Léandre never showed any physical affection, and the hug was out of character for her. "Remember, child, everything I do is for this family," her grandmother murmured. "And one day, it will all be yours."

Celeste just nodded, not daring to voice her deepest thoughts. *I don't want to take over,* she thought. She wanted to run away to some quiet space where she didn't have to worry about money. Free of the older woman's greed.

Léandre let her go and turned to leave, her face wearing her customary scowl. Celeste waited as she slowly walked out of the room, leaning on her cane. "Whatever I do, child," she added before finally closing the door, "it's for the best."

48

On the day of the full moon, the night that they would have had the fake seance with Mrs. Bellaund, Celeste and Tommy spent the day cleaning and getting ready for Léandre's special dinner. Tommy was just as unaware of who Léandre's guests were as Celeste was. But, like Celeste, he assumed that they had to be very important to pass up the opportunity to fleece Mrs. Bellaund and her friends.

"She made me get a whole buck for this dinner," Tommy whispered to Celeste. "She must be trying to impress *someone* important."

Celeste went to feed Ami, passing Tommy in the kitchen, who was at the stove stirring something in a pot. She saw him still at the stove when she went upstairs, but by the time she bathed and put on her new dress, it was her grandmother at the stove when Celeste returned to the kitchen.

"I sent Thomas on an errand," her grandmother explained, stirring the contents of the pot. "He will not be back before dinner." She finally looked behind her and smiled. "You look beautiful, child."

Celeste smiled and blushed. "It is a lovely dress," she admitted.

Celeste rushed to finish setting up the dining room. However, she paused when she heard something thump in the parlor. She almost went to investigate, but her grandmother called out, making her forget about the mysterious noise.

A carriage drove up to the house, three men climbed out of it, and Celeste ushered them inside. Her grandmother waited at the foot of the staircase, standing tall and proud with her cane in front of her. "Lady Sibyl," the man in front said as he handed his coat to Celeste. "It is a pleasure to meet you finally."

"Cybill Léandre," the older woman corrected him as she offered her hand. He took it with a smile and lightly pressed his lips to it. "How was your journey, Mr. Kristiansen?"

"Call me Felix, please," he responded. "It was a long trip, but I hope a fruitful one."

"Hopefully, a profitable one for me," the older woman purred, and she showed the men into the dining room.

Celeste put the men's coats away and rolled a serving cart into the dining room to serve wine and the first course. It wasn't until she put the main course of venison in front of the men and Kristiansen bowed his head in prayer that she understood who they were.

"Thank you, O Golden One, for this meal and the many blessings you bestow. May we be bathed in your golden light," he murmured over his meal, the other two men mirroring him.

"You're acolytes," Celeste said, slight dread settling in her stomach at the revelation. She may have been sheltered and isolated from the sorcerer community, but even she knew who the acolytes were and who they worshipped.

"Yes, my dear, we are," Kristiansen replied with a smile. "I assure you, our reputation is not deserved."

"You hurt people," Celeste argued.

Kristiansen's smile became strained and cold. "So does your grandmother," he replied.

"I provide services for money. If the person I provide those services for is hurting someone else, that is their responsibility, not mine," Léandre reasoned, sipping her wine.

"We just want to worship Our Lady in peace," Kristiansen said while nodding. "Our goal is to bring her back." He looked at Léandre. "And we welcome anyone who helps us find a way to reach that goal." He held his wine glass up with a smile, and Léandre tapped her glass against his, and Celeste felt disgusted, trying to keep her face blank.

After a dessert of sorbet, Celeste cleaned up the dishes. When she left the kitchen, her grandmother opened the door to the parlor and guided the acolytes inside. Celeste froze at the door when she saw what was waiting for them.

Tommy was tied to one of the high-back chairs at the table. He was gagged and unconscious, a cut bleeding freely on his forehead. Celeste gasped and ran to him. *"Tommy?!"* she cried. "Tommy, are you alright?" He moaned but didn't stir.

"Would one of you gentlemen be so kind as to restrain my granddaughter?" Léandre asked cooly. One of the men got an evil grin and grabbed Celeste's arm, pulling her away from Tommy. "Gently, now."

"Grandmother, what are you doing?" Celeste cried, trying to fight the man who was holding onto her.

"Hush, child," her grandmother ordered. She walked to her bookcases, her hand glowing purple. The case also shone, and Léandre opened it up, grabbing one of the books. Then, she slowly turned around and returned to the table. "Have you ever made a spell, Felix?" she asked.

"Can't say that I have," the acolyte leader admitted. He looked between Léandre, her grandmother, and Tommy, a bemused look on his face.

"Every spell holds a little of the person's magic who created it," the older woman explained. "It is rumored that your lady, the Golden One, created countless spells in her lifetime." She placed the book on the table and started leafing through it. "Unfortunately, most have been lost to history, but we know some of the curses she created."

"Wasting curses," Kristiansen said while nodding. "Used for neutralizing her enemies."

"I believe, although I can't prove it, that she created slave bands too." Léandre found the page she was looking for, and then she gathered some items closer to her: a knife, a bowl, and a block of silver.

"Grandmother, please," Celeste pleaded. This conversation seemed very bad for Tommy.

"I have to ponder why she constructed both spells," Léandre continued like Celeste didn't say anything, "when one would be just effective as the other in keeping your enemies in check. And which one would be worse, I wonder? Losing your ability or your freedom?"

"No offense, Léandre, when you reached out and said you could help the Acolytes make an unstoppable army, I gathered that it would be full of more than just people, magical or not," Kristiansen drawled.

"I do have a way to make your army the strongest that ever existed," Léandre said in a cool tone. "Just as your lady intended."

"Then let's see it."

Léandre started pouring a liquid into the bowl. "I knew there was something about this boy when he arrived, but I couldn't tell what it was." She put her hands on the silver, which glowed purple, forming two flat pieces when Léandre removed her hands. "I have been watching him, trying to solve his mystery these last four years. He's strong, too strong for a human. He heals fast. And he doesn't use magic. And magic doesn't affect him." She approached Tommy in the chair with the bowl and the knife. "You are not human, boy, but I think I know what you are. And if I'm right, your Lady's spell will work on you."

"Grandmother, don't!" Celeste yelled. She almost got free of the man holding her, but he grabbed her arm again. "Please!"

"Silence her!" Léandre yelled, and the man clamped a hand over Celeste's mouth, crossing his arms over her chest to hold her to his torso. "I would have let you stay here, with your secret," Léandre continued, addressing Tommy, still ignoring Celeste's struggles, "but now that my granddaughter is with child, I can't allow you to remain unpunished."

Celeste felt her stomach drop, and she fought harder to get free. Léandre took the knife and cut at Tommy's left arm, cutting his shirt and skin. The pain finally woke him up, and his eyes flew open. Tommy looked dumbly between Léandre, Celeste, and the men watching. When he realized Celeste was being restrained, he started to fight his bonds. Blood welled up in his wound, and Léandre used the blade to gather it and add it to the bowl.

"Not that this family drama is not riveting," Kristiansen drawled as Celeste and Tommy fought to get free, and Léandre brushed the liquid onto the silver. "But I fail to see how this is the start of my unstoppable army."

"Just wait."

Léandre went back to Tommy, holding the two pieces of flat silver. They glowed purple, and as she pressed them onto Tommy's arm, he screamed through the gag. Celeste stopped fighting, watching in horror as the young man writhed in pain. Léandre finally stood up and held a shard of silver up. It flowed into the shape of a ring, and the old woman smiled.

Léandre waved a hand, and the ropes holding Tommy glowed purple and fell away. He dropped onto the floor to his knees, panting. Celeste finally kicked the man holding her on the shin, and he let her go with a shout. She rushed to Tommy, helping him to get the gag off. She looked at the band on his arm, slowly losing its glow. Then, Celeste rounded on her grandmother. "Why?!"

"I told you, you are with child."

"He's not the father!" Celeste hissed back, and if she weren't so enraged with her grandmother, she would have laughed at the older woman's surprised expression.

Léandre blinked for a few moments, looking uncertain. "Well?" Kristiansen asked with a note of annoyance in his voice. "What now?"

Celeste saw the internal debate that her grandmother had with herself. She could either commit to helping the Acolytes with whatever plan she made or throw the men out of the house, gaining them as enemies for life. Léandre slipped the ring onto her finger and looked at the young man on the floor. "Transform," she ordered.

Celeste looked between her grandmother and the young man, not understanding what her grandmother meant. Then, suddenly, Tommy hissed as the band lit up. "What is this?" he gritted out of clenched teeth.

"The punishment for not listening, boy," Léandre said with an icy tone. "Now transform. You don't want to know what will happen if you ignore a direct order for too long."

"What are you talking abo—" Celeste started to ask, but she yelped when Tommy changed next to her. Grey skin with no hair, a feline-like face, long claws, and large, *he was so big*. She scrambled away from Tommy as Kristiansen let out a bark of laughter.

"He's a changeling?" the acolyte leader asked. Tommy was looking between him, Léandre, and Celeste, although the snarl on his face softened when he looked at Celeste. His face looked almost... sad? "And the slave band works on him?"

"Yes," Léandre replied. "That will be our arrangement. You bring me gold and the changelings; I can build an army of enslaved creatures who listen to only you."

"Imagine if we can just get hundreds of changelings," one acolyte said as Celeste picked herself off the ground. "Hunters wouldn't stand a chance. We would be invincible."

Kristiansen slowly walked up to Tommy, and Tommy growled and snapped at him. "Stop!" Léandre commanded, and Tommy did, although he stood up so he was towering over the sorcerer.

"Finally, changelings can be used to their full potential," Kristiansen said with a smile. "Obeying the orders of her true followers and no longer being the loose cannons they have been for centuries." He held a hand out to an acolyte, and the man removed a bag from his jacket to place in Kristiansen's open palm. "You have a deal, Léandre."

"Grandmother, no!" Celeste begged, but the old woman didn't listen. Instead, she cleaned the blade she was still holding and then cut her palm, smearing blood on the ring. She passed the piece of jewelry to the acolyte leader, who handed over the money bag. He produced his own knife and cut his finger, spreading blood on the ring. Ring and slave band glowed, and Tommy snarled again, snout curling in pain.

Celeste looked around the room, tears burning her eyes. She felt so powerless at that moment. Celeste had seen her grandmother do many horrible things in her lifetime, but to take away someone's freedom? That was an atrocity she didn't think her grandmother would ever do.

Léandre opened the bag and started counting the coins in it while Kristiansen studied Tommy. Finally, he looked over and saw the book on slave bands open on the table. "How much for the book?" he asked in a silky tone.

"It's not for sale," was the growled response.

"Oh, everyone has a price," Kristiansen said. The older woman scowled at him, and he smiled. "If we had those books, we would be able to make our changeling army *and* control our enemies as well."

"It's not for sale," Léandre growled again. She quickly closed the bag and then slammed the book shut. "This is not part of the deal, Kristiansen. Knowledge like this is not to be shared."

"You said so yourself that you think that Our Lady made the spell. Doesn't that make us the best suited to hold that knowledge?"

"No," Léandre answered, and Kristiansen's smile fell into a frown. "My books are spelled to remain mine until the moment I die and not a minute before."

"Well," the acolyte leader said, "then I imagine you have to die."

It happened so fast. One of the acolytes, the man who grabbed Celeste, formed a fireball and launched it at Léandre. She created a shield and deflected it, sending it into the bookshelves. As Celeste's books started to burn, the acolyte threw a fireball at Celeste. She put her arms up, but before the flames hit her, she was jerked backward, and something covered her. She blinked, realizing Tommy was protecting her. He turned and snarled at the fire-using acolyte, and the man jumped.

"Enough!" Kristiansen commanded the changeling. He pointed at Léandre. "Attack!"

"Gladly," Tommy rumbled, and he let go of Celeste to step up to her grandmother. He snarled and picked the old woman up, making her shout and drop her cane.

Léandre dangled a foot in the air, but she glared at Kristiansen, face full of fury. "You dare?!" she hissed. "You dare to come to *my* home and attack me?!"

"Yes," Kristiansen responded, folding his hands behind him. "I mean to have that book, Léandre."

Léandre suddenly raised one hand and snapped her fingers, purple sparks flying toward Kristiansen. The acolyte beside him put his glowing orange hands up, and the sparks fizzled in the air. "Do you think I would come here, to a curse maker's home, with no protection?" Kristiansen asked, his smile getting wider. He pointed at the book, and the acolyte who could make fire went to collect it. "We will take your books now."

The acolyte grabbed the book on slave bands but paused after turning around. He suddenly blanched, and Celeste grimaced as he vomited violently. He lifted his shaking hand, looking at it dumbly as sores started forming on his skin. He dropped the book, but it was too late; the curse was running its course. He collapsed, crying in pain as the sores spread and blood started to weep from them. He reached out to Kristiansen, but the acolyte leader stepped back instead of helping his subordinate, not that he could do anything. The man finally crumpled, blood pouring from his eyes, nose, and mouth.

Léandre smiled grimly at the acolyte leader. "And did you think I would invite men like *you* into my domain without protection?" she asked, still held in the air by the changeling.

Kristiansen scowled at the older woman. He turned to the other acolyte, visibly shaking as he looked at his colleague lying on the floor. "Can you neutralize the protection spell?" Kristiansen asked.

The acolyte reluctantly got down on one knee and put his hand out over the book, still looking at the dead body on the floor. His hands glowed orange, and he winced. "It's too strong," he explained. "It would take me hours to dispel it."

"It would take you *days,*" Léandre hissed, and then she laughed a maniacal and unhinged sound.

Kristiansen looked at the spreading fire. He suddenly pointed his finger at the changeling. "Kill her and kill the girl," he ordered Tommy. He then gestured at the acolyte. "Stay here and make sure to seize that book, or I will kill you myself." Finally, he turned and left the room.

Tommy growled once the front door slammed shut, bringing Celeste's grandmother closer to his face. "What happens if I don't do as he says?" Tommy asked, baring a lot of teeth.

"The band will burn and cause you immense pain," the old woman explained. She looked at the remaining acolyte out of the corner of her eye. "But he didn't order *you* to take the book."

Tommy's ears went back, and he looked at the man. The acolyte took a step back, looking fearful. "Now, wait for just a mo—" the man started to say, but before he could finish, Tommy grabbed him. Tommy's whole hand covered the acolyte's face, and the changeling's fingers wrapped around his head so his claws dug into the man's scalp. Tommy growled and pulled the man to him, placing his teeth on his throat. Celeste cringed as Tommy twisted his head, and blood arced into the air. Celeste gagged as Tommy dropped the lifeless body.

Tommy let Léandre go, and she stumbled, catching one of the chairs to keep her from falling. Celeste was staring dumbly at the bodies on the floor until Tommy put a hand on her shoulder, and she smiled at him in relief. Léandre looked at the fire which was spreading.

"Thomas, get some water and help us—"

"Can you remove this band?" Tommy asked.

"I cannot," Léandre said after a moment of silence.

"Then I'm not helping you at all, you witch."

Léandre glared, but then she squared her shoulders and stood up as tall as possible. "Well then, get on with it," she said.

"So ready to die?" he asked.

"I'm not afraid of death."

"What about the death of your granddaughter?" Tommy asked. Her grandmother blinked at that question and then looked at Celeste. "Do you think Kristiansen will let Celeste live? He will kill her with you and let your bodies burn with this house."

Léandre looked down, looking thoughtful as the books crackled behind her.

"Grandmother," Celeste started to say, fear beginning to claw at her throat, and the older woman raised her hand to quiet her.

"What would you have me do?"

"You have damned us both tonight," Tommy rumbled. "But she can be free from all this. Her and the baby." He leaned toward the older woman and reached out with talon-tipped fingers. "Let me kill you, and she can run with the books. Kristiansen will have me, but not her or the books."

"Tommy, no, there has to be another way," Celeste said, and she sobbed.

He looked at her. "You need to get out of here, Celeste." He winced and looked at the band on his arm, which had started to glow. "Quickly! Before he comes back."

Right on cue, there was a shout from outside the house. "Slave!" Kristiansen yelled. "Bring me those books before they burn!"

Léandre looked in the direction of the acolyte leader and nodded. "You're right," she said softly, face serene. "It is the only way." She looked back at the changeling and smiled grimly. "But I did it. I did something that no one else could. I enslaved a changeling."

"You shouldn't be proud of that," Tommy growled, and he snatched Léandre again, by the throat this time.

"Tommy!" Celeste cried.

"Wait until my heart stops," Léandre gritted out. "And then run, child."

"Don't look, Celeste," Tommy said, and Celeste turned around and cringed when she heard a snapping sound and a thud.

Celeste slowly turned around and let out another sob when she saw her grandmother's body lying on the floor. Tommy was back in his human form, frowning as the band glowed brighter. He gestured at the books. "Take them."

Celeste looked between him and the books. "I'll help you, Tommy, I swear."

"Don't worry about me, Celeste," he said with a sad smile. "Go be free." They both looked up as the ceiling groaned, the flames weakening it. "Go! Now!"

She nodded, resolving to survive the night and help Tommy later. She gathered the books in her arms, horrible spells and curses, the legacy she never wanted, but at least they would be out of the acolytes' hands. Tommy rushed her out of the room, and they parted. Celeste ran to the kitchen while Tommy ran toward the front. There was a shout. Celeste glanced over her shoulder to see Tommy keeping Kristiansen from getting back into the house. Kristiansen was yelling and gesturing at Celeste, but Tommy ignored him, the band glowing brighter by the second. Celeste turned around and kept running.

Celeste rushed to the stable. She tugged a frantic Ami out of her stall and climbed onto the horse's back, cursing the tight dress as she struggled to hold the books. She guided Ami out of the yard, and they galloped through darkened streets. Celeste's clothing was torn, and tears streamed down her face. She ran to Cyprien's hotel, begging the man at the front counter to find him, and collapsed into his arms when he appeared. Celeste babbled about curses, and slave bands, and acolytes, and changelings. Oh, what a sight she must have made.

Hunters would go to the Léandre household in the morning and confirm it was burnt to the ground, although there was nothing to prove Celeste's story other than the burnt corpses in the ashes. The hunters would return to the hotel and tell a resting Celeste about what they saw, and she smiled. She was free.

Her smile turned into a frown. But Tommy was not.

49

Julien had taken several hours to drive from the warehouse to the diner, but with the snake changeling in the second row pushing her to go faster and then faster still, Rimsha made the trip in under two hours, much quicker than she thought was safe with the weather, but she didn't have much choice. The changeling would sometimes stick the knife into Julien's back to make him hiss, evilly smiling as Rimsha felt her anxiety growing. The bull changeling was quiet, lying in the back, occasionally moving his head so that Rimsha could see his horns outlined from the light streaming from the back window.

At one point, Ichiro woke up, groggily holding his head as his eyes opened. *"Nani?* Wha' happened? he asked, then he yelped as he noticed the stranger sitting with him and Kevin. "Who's that?! Who are you!?"

A giant hand reached from the back and wrapped around Ichiro's head, silencing the young boy. Ichiro's eyes went wide, and he kicked, clawing at the hand holding him against his seat. "Quiet," the bull changeling rumbled, the only word he had spoken that Rimsha understood.

"If he hurts my friend, I stop," Rimsha warned the changeling in the second row with as much authority as she could muster in a shaking voice.

The snake changeling clicked his tongue in annoyance, but he said something in another language, and the bull changeling let Ichiro go. Both boys cowered, leaning away from the snake changeling. The van was tensely quiet for an hour as Rimsha drove.

When they reached the city, the snake changeling started snapping at Rimsha, asking where they were, what road they were on, and how much further they had to go. Rimsha was just relieved that the way from the highway to the warehouse was a straight route. She didn't want to think of what the changelings would do if she got lost. The changeling didn't even seem to mind that she stopped at as many red lights as she could, squinting at the street signs and texting on the phone he produced from his sarong.

Rimsha turned onto the row of warehouses, her heart pounding as she brought the van to a crawl. Would anyone be awake? Would one of the hunters be patrolling outside? The snake changeling crouched down while trying to look out the front window simultaneously. "Which one is it?" he asked.

"The last one on the end," Rimsha said, not seeing any good reason to lie.

"Good," he hissed. "Drive up and park. Turn the van off." His face lit up as he texted something, probably telling someone where they were. "Not a sound from you two," he growled at Ichiro and Kevin, "or the girl will lose her life."

As they approached the warehouse, Rimsha saw that the large front door was open, with light spilling from inside. Someone stood outside, and the cigarette glow told Rimsha that it was Mr. Cross, not one of the hunters. Rimsha drove as close to the warehouse as she dared and turned the vehicle off as the snake changeling had ordered her.

"Who is that?" the snake changeling asked as Mr. Cross approached the van, holding his hands out in a "what happened" gesture.

"Mr. Cross," Rimsha explained as she rolled down the window. "He's a teacher."

"Get us inside," the snake changeling whispered. "And don't get any ideas."

Rimsha turned as Mr. Cross made it to the window. "What happened?!" he cried. "You should be at the Academy by now!" He looked at the van. "What trouble did you kids get into?" he asked, finally seeing the damage from the accident the changelings caused.

"We had an accident," Rimsha lied, surprised that her voice was even and calm. "Julien slid off the road, and we hit a tree."

"Aw, bloody hell," Mr. Croos growled. He walked to the van's passenger side, inspecting the damage. Julien didn't dare move, both he and Rimsha watching Mr. Cross with their eyes, not saying anything. Rimsha heard Mr. Cross sigh as he came back to her window. "You should have gone home."

"I'm sorry, Mr. Cross. We didn't know what to do. Julien said his back was hurting, and I thought it would be better to come back here than continue to the Academy."

"Why didn't you call me?" he asked.

"We... we didn't want to use our cell phones like you told us."

Mr. Cross sighed again as he looked at Julien. "You okay?" he asked, and Julien just nodded, probably scared to move his hands. Mr. Cross frowned. "What's the matter?"

"I'm okay," Julien said, but he made the sign for "help," closing his left hand into a fist and then placing it on his right palm and pulling them both up.

Mr. Cross blinked but didn't say anything. Instead, he looked into the second row at Kevin and Ichiro, unable to see the snake changeling crouching behind Julien from his angle. "How about you two? You're being awfully quiet."

"I hit my head, Mr. Cross," Ichiro said. "I thought I saw a monster when I woke up," he added, and Rimsha felt Julien jerk next to her, and she hoped that the changeling didn't hurt him.

Mr. Cross opened his mouth, but Rimsha placed her left hand out of the van and started signing before he could say anything. Generally, you finger-spelled with your right hand, so Rimsha prayed that Mr. Cross could understand her clumsy spelling. *C-H-A-N, please, Mr. Cross, please understand, G-E-L, we are all in danger, I-N-G.* Rimsha snatched her hand back into the van when she finished and put it on the wheel, not wanting to push her luck.

Mr. Cross's face went blank, closing his mouth and nodding slowly. "I'm glad you guys are unhurt," he said, voice even. "Pull inside, and we'll check you guys out... make sure you're safe." He slowly backed away from the van and then turned to go inside.

"What did you tell him?!" the snake changeling fiercely whispered from his hiding spot.

"I didn't say anything," Rimsha lied.

"His voice changed. You told him something," the changeling argued.

"You could hear me the whole time. I didn't say a word," Rimsha argued back.

Meanwhile, Mr. Cross walked to the door slowly. Someone appeared in the doorway, and Rimsha realized it was Tommy's silhouette. She felt a surge of relief at the sight of the changeling. Maybe he could smell the others and get the hunters. "What's wrong?" Rimsha heard him ask Mr. Cross, but Mr. Cross just put a hand on his shoulder and leaned close to his ear to say something.

Suddenly, the bull changeling stuck his nose in the air and took several deep breaths, scenting the air. "Mongrel," the changeling rumbled from the back.

"What do you mean?" the snake changeling hissed in a whisper.

The bull changeling said something in the other language Rimsha didn't know, and the snake changeling hissed at his response and transformed, the lower half of his body pinning Kevin and Ichiro to their seats. "You didn't say the mongrel was here!" he yelled at Rimsha.

"Who?!" Rimsha screamed back, so confused and panicking.

Ichiro and Kevin were yelling, which got Mr. Cross and Tommy's attention. They both rushed to the van, but Rimsha saw a flash of metal and realized that the snake changeling was about to stab Julien. Rimsha grabbed him with one hand and opened the driver's side door at the same time, pulling Julien as she tumbled out of the van, helping him narrowly miss the blade sticking out of the passenger seat. She felt a bolt of pain go up her arm as she landed on the pavement and yelped.

Tommy transformed as he stepped over her, grabbed Julien by his sweater, and pulled him out of the van. Julien landed next to Rimsha, getting the wind knocked out of him in a *whoosh* of air. The snake changeling pulled himself into the front seat and then launched himself at Tommy, and Rimsha helped Julien up as they dashed towards the warehouse to get out away from the fighting changelings.

Mr. Cross ran to the van's passenger side, and as Tommy wrestled the snake on the ground, he opened the door. He shouted when a giant hand shot out of the back, the bull changeling keeping him from helping Kevin and Ichiro. Mr. Cross flew back, and the boys screamed as the van rocked.

"Get inside!" roared a voice, and Mr. Smith and Mx. Ellis ran past Rimsha and Julien, swords at the ready. Rimsha just dumbly watched as Mr. Smith went to help Tommy as Mx. Ellis took a swing at the arm reaching out of the van. The snake looked up from pinning Tommy to the ground to see the sword aimed at his head, and he hissed and dodged it, Mr. Smith's blade hitting his shoulder instead. Tommy grabbed a brick and hit the snake. The snake shook his head and hissed, opening his mouth impossibly wide to bite Tommy. Tommy shoved the brick into his mouth, and the snake made a choking noise as Tommy scrambled away.

Mx. Ellis, meanwhile, had cut the bull changeling's arm, and he bellowed inside the van. The arm vanished, and then the van rocked as the changeling struck the back door from the inside. Several hits, and the door flew off its hinges with the sound of breaking glass. The bull changeling climbed out of the back and advanced toward the hunter.

Mx. Ellis put himself between the bull changeling and Mr. Cross, who was trying to help the boys out of the van. The bull lowed, his hoofed feet clicking on the pavement, and he brought a fist back to punch Mx. Ellis. The hunter waited for the last possible second to duck, and the changeling's fist connected with the van, making it rock on two tires. Ichiro and Kevin scrambled out of the van as it teetered back onto four wheels, and Mr. Cross pulled them towards Rimsha and Julien.

"Go!" Mr. Cross shouted, breaking Rimsha out of her stupor. *"Go!* Get to the transportation circle!"

Julien started herding them inside, and Rimsha glanced over her shoulder. Tommy was fighting the snake changeling, keeping it from biting him by wrapping his hand around its throat and pinning it to the van. Mr. Smith had run around the van and swiped at the bull changeling, helping his partner. Julien pushed Rimsha hard, and she turned to run.

The teens ran through the office, going for the bigger office in the back, where Mr. Cross had set up the transportation circle. Rimsha was in the back of the group, looking behind her. Maybe they should go for the vault? See if Mrs. Zheng wanted to use the transportation circle to get the sphere to safety? What if they used the circle, and something happened, and the others couldn't escape? Her thoughts were interrupted when she ran into Julien's back.

She looked around the taller teen and felt her blood turn cold. Kevin had been in front and stopped suddenly, Ichiro running into him, and Julien stopped before plowing into the other boys, all of them gaping at the sight in front of them. Something had broken the office window, cold air blowing in, the tiny silver of the moon revealing a bat changeling in the middle of the office. He had disturbed the crystals, either by accident or on purpose, Rimsha couldn't tell. His nightmarish face broke into a smile, showing pointed teeth the size of Rimsha's fingers.

He was chuckling, laughing. He lifted one mishappen hand and showed them a crystal. "Were you going to use this?" he asked. And then he puffed up and screeched, a horrible piercing sound that made Ichiro, Kevin, and Rimsha scream and cover their ears in pain. Julien, totally unaffected, saw their reaction and then pushed his way into the office. He grabbed a chair and tried to hit the changeling. The bat stopped screeching and jumped back, dropping the crystal.

"Run!" Julien yelled over his shoulder. "Vault!"

The boys turned around, and Rimsha followed them back to the warehouse's floor, rushing to the opened vault entrance. Rimsha glanced outside, and she could see Tommy fighting the bull changeling, taking swipes with his claws while staying out of the bull's punches. The snake changeling was fighting the hunters, ducking and weaving to avoid their swords, snapping at them when they got close.

Mr. Cross rushed up to the teens. "Where are you going?" he yelled.

Kevin pointed to the office. "Changeling... in the... office. It... destroyed the circle," he explained while panting. Mr. Cross scowled and then ran towards the office.

Kevin and Ichiro pushed Rimsha to climb down the ladder first, and she tore her eyes away from the fight. She tried to go down the ladder but yelped when she tried to use her left arm. "M-my arm," she told the boys. "I think it's broken."

Ichiro scrambled onto the ladder with Rimsha, putting his arm around her. "Down together!" he yelled. "Left! Right! Left!"

It was awkward for both of them to be on the ladder at the same time, but they quickly went down with coordinated steps. Rimsha felt hands on her back when they were halfway down, and she realized that Miss Hafeez and Mrs. Zheng were helping them. When they made it to the floor, Rimsha collapsed as her knees buckled.

"Who is it?" Mrs. Zheng shouted at Kevin as he descended the ladder, Ichiro and Rimsha panting too hard to answer her.

"Changelings!" Kevin cried. "Bat, bull, and snake! I think it's Camazotz, Yama, and Degei!"

"Are you seriously telling me three generals are here?!" Miss Hafeez asked him.

Suddenly, there was a howl, the unmistakable cry of a wolf, and Rimsha whimpered in fear. Kevin slipped on the ladder, but he was only a few feet off the ground, so he quickly recovered, looking up at the hole above them. "I think that's Fenrir," he said softly, a look of fear and awe on his face.

Mrs. Zheng looked at Miss Hafeez. "Help them," she ordered, and the younger hunter ran past the teenagers and climbed the ladder, scooping up her familiar to place him on her shoulders as she ascended. Mrs. Zheng started pushing the teens into the vault. "Get inside," she growled. "Get ready to close the doors when I tell you to."

"What about you?" Ichiro asked as Kevin helped Rimsha off the floor.

"Just go!" Mrs. Zheng yelled at them, giving the smaller boy a push into the vault.

They ran past all five opened doors, Kevin keeping an arm around Rimsha's shoulders. Ichiro stayed at the door while Kevin led Rimsha downstairs to one of the couches. Rimsha started to shudder when she sat down.

"Are you okay?" Kevin asked her. He didn't wait for her to answer and shouted at Ichiro. "Can you heal her?"

"Dude, I haven't taken a healing class!" Ichiro shouted back.

"It's okay," Rimsha told Kevin. "I'm more worried about the others. Do you really think it's the four generals?"

"Has to be," he whispered. He turned back to Ichiro. "Hear anything?"

"I think so?" Ichiro yelled back. "Some growling? That has to be Tomm—*wait!*" He started to bounce up and down. "Mr. Cross! Julien! *Come on!*"

Mr. Cross and Julien ran inside the vault, both leaning on the railing and panting. Mr. Cross saw Rimsha and flew down the stairs. "You alright?" he asked her as he looked her over.

"My arm. I think it's broken," she mumbled.

"A touch of shock, too, I would think," Mr. Cross replied.

Suddenly there was yelling and screaming from outside the vault. *"Retreat!"* Rimsha heard someone yell. "Inside the vault, *now!*"

Mrs. Zheng appeared, her hand hovering over the button which would close the vault doors. "Don't close it!" Ichiro shouted at her. She didn't answer, just staring grimly out of the vault.

All Rimsha could hear for several tense moments was yelling, growling, screaming, bellowing, cursing, and screeching. "Light!" Miss Hafeez shouted, and there was a flash of light so bright that they could see it, even in the vault. There were inhuman screams, and Ichiro started bouncing again. "Come on, come on!" he yelled, and Miss Hafeez flew through the door, Siad at her heels. Mr. Smith joined her at the railing a few seconds later, and he collapsed on the floor.

Mrs. Zheng ran out of the vault. "Close the doors!" she ordered. Miss Hafeez stepped up to the door and pressed the button that would close the doors from inside the vault.

"What are you doing?!" Ichiro screamed at her. "They are still out there!"

"We have to protect the sphere!" she shouted back.

The door was closing slowly, Rimsha praying for their safety and the safety of the others. She wanted to live, but not at the expense of others' lives.

Ichiro shouted joyfully, and three figures ran through the door just before it was too narrow for them to do so. Tommy and Mrs. Zheng were supporting Mx. Ellis, who was clutching their side, blood soaking their shirt and pants. The door closed with a hollow boom, and everyone seemed to relax a little, the space full of their pants and sighs.

They were safe.

Suddenly there was a bang, the sound of something hitting the first door. It sounded again and then again. The changelings were trying to destroy the door to get inside.

They were trapped.

．．．．．

Tommy and Smith brought Ellis to the first floor and deposited them onto a table. They looked pale as they tried to stop the bleeding from the wound on their side. Akrur looked around. Julien was covered in scratches, the worst ones on his arms where the bat bit him. Tommy had a cut on his temple where the buffalo changeling caught him with a punch. Smith and Hafeez both had claw marks on their arms. "Is anyone here a healer?" he asked.

"I can do it," Rimsha mumbled. She tried to stand up and then tumbled back onto the couch. She hit her arm and yelped. Akrur watched as Kevin helped her sit up. Her eyes almost fluttered shut. She was not in any condition to heal anyone. Smith took off his shirt and started to rip it into strips to wrap around his partner.

"What happened?" Zheng asked Ichiro.

"We stopped at the diner to grab some food," Ichiro explained. "And the changelings found us. Rimsha saw him sniffing us."

"They were looking for us," Kevin said. "We left the diner, and Rimsha said she needed to call Mr. Cross."

"But before she did, the changeling made us crash into a tree," Ichiro added.

"They were looking for Chrysta and Mr. Burke," Kevin said. "The snake changeling was going to hurt Julien if we didn't tell them where you guys were."

"And I made a deal," Rimsha said. She suddenly shuddered and let out a sob. "I said I would bring them here to the sphere if they didn't hurt us. I'm s-so sorry."

"Fuck," Tommy growled. He was helping Smith wrap the shirt around Ellis's middle, the injured hunter hissing in pain. "How did they know about all of this?"

"No way to tell," Zheng said, looking down from the upper floor. "Let's make sure we survive this to figure it out later."

"Oh, we know who it is," Hafeez growled. She pointed at Tommy. "It has to be him. He told them where to find us."

"If you didn't notice, they were trying to kill me as much as they were trying to kill you," Tommy shot back.

"He stopped Fenrir from eating your ass," Smith added. "So I trust him."

"With your life?" Hafeez asked with a scowl.

"Enough!" Tommy shouted, and everyone jumped. He glared at Hafeez and pointed a finger at her. "Last time I saw those assholes, they killed my mother in front of me! And now they will break down those doors and turn the sphere into dust, killing the only person who gives a damn about me, and those assholes will have to fucking kill me before I let that happen!"

The vault rang with silence after Tommy stopped yelling, and then there was a *BOOM* from outside the vault. The banging started again, closer this time. Zheng started to push Ichiro, Julien, and Hafeez to the lower floor. "Those doors are not going to hold," she announced as they went down the stairs. "We are going to have to make a last stand."

"What is your plan?" Akrur asked her.

Zheng didn't answer but went up to the sphere and gently picked it up. Then, she walked over to Kevin and held it out. "Hide this," she instructed the teen.

Kevin's eyes went wide, and he held his hands out, although he didn't take the sphere. "I'm not the best person to hold that," he muttered.

"Take it, hide it," Zheng continued, ignoring his hesitation. "When you place it down, place it at an angle. Neil will see the world at a tilt and bring them out. Do *not* tell anyone where it is."

Kevin nodded and then gently took the sphere, slowly and carefully going deeper into the vault and disappearing into the selves.

Zheng went to Tommy, and Cross and Hafeez joined them, glaring at the vault door as the booms sounded beyond it. "Three healthy hunters and one changeling against the four generals of the Golden One," Zheng murmured. She looked around at the frightened teens and Smith tending to his injured partner. "This will be a short battle."

"Do you have to fight?" Cross asked, not liking their chances.

"Until Neil and the girls are out of that sphere, we protect it," Zheng responded. "We have no other choice."

50

The day after the attack from the creature in the metal suit, Mr. Burke had Chrysta and Rosa gather some food and supplies. "I don't know how long we will be up there," he said. "It's mostly to satisfy my personal curiosity. It may be dangerous, Miss Torres. You don't have to come with us if you don't want to."

"Are you kidding?" Rosa asked with a grin. "I want to go. I can totally rub the fact I went to the castle into Ichiro's face."

They hiked up the mountain all morning and came to the red circle about midday. Mr. Burke paused before they went further. Even Poe landed in a tree far from the red circle, clicking his beak as the humans looked around. "Do you think you can pacify those automations if we come across another one, Miss Angelos?" the Headmaster asked.

"I think so," she said. She looked down at her arm, which had healed entirely on its own. "I rather not, though. I have to touch them to free them, and it hurts to touch them."

She took a deep breath and then entered the red circle, Rosa and Mr. Burke close behind her. "Chrysta!" Poe croaked as he took flight and followed.

After a few minutes of walking, they found the empty metal suit. Mr. Burke crouched down to inspect it. "This is a strong enchantment," he muttered to himself. "And to last this long. Someone extremely powerful must have created them."

"What was the thing inside?" Rosa asked.

"Black as night, moved like water, and hurt by light and fire," Mr. Burke said. He looked around. "A shadow demon?"

"Didn't the Golden One destroy them?" Chrysta asked.

"The Golden One obliterated their queen when she wouldn't bend the knee," Mr. Bure explained. He shrugged. "Metaphorically. The rest of the brood vanished. Sorcerers didn't know enough about them, so we assumed they couldn't live without their matriarch and evaporated." He stood up. "Let's continue."

They slowly and carefully trekked through the woods, the red trees continuing in front of them for miles. Suddenly Poe landed on a branch and started squawking. "Danger! Chrysta! Danger!" He took off to their right, and they saw what he was warning them about. A creature was coming for them, thumping through the forest.

"Mr. Burke?" Rosa asked in a frightened voice. "What do we do?"

"Run, Miss Torres," he responded. "And hope they can't approach the castle."

They ran, the metal monster following them. It started to pick up speed and catch up to them. When the creature grabbed a small red tree, ripped it out of the ground, and threw it at them, Rosa shrieked as it hit a tree next to her. Chrysta skidded to a stop and turned around, putting her hands up. She didn't want to touch it, but she wouldn't let it hurt anyone either.

The monster stopped, drawing its arm back to punch Chrysta. She could hear it screaming, the bright light hurting it, but there was anger in its voice, too, the overwhelming desire to harm the humans. She was steeling herself, getting ready to thrust her arm into the suit like she did with the first one when a black shadow came out of the woods and wrapped itself around the metal monster. It started to pull the struggling suit to the ground, tendrils shooting out and wrapping around trees for leverage.

attack, attack, attackattackattack, ATTACK!

Chrysta blinked in surprise and then shook herself out of her stupor. She scrambled over the floundering metal suit, reaching inside and feeling for the magical chains. She was quicker this time, already knowing what to look for. She destroyed the magical bonds, and the second creature fled, the suit collapsing as it emptied.

Chrysta retreated, and Mr. Burke grabbed her shoulder to inspect her arm. The first black creature melted off the suit, but it didn't run, fleeing to a nearby fallen log to get out of the light. "What is that?" Rosa asked as two shining blue eyes appeared, watching them.

"It's the creature from yesterday," Chrysta explained, panting. "I think it helped us because I freed it."

"Returning the favor and saving us," Mr. Burke said. "Shadow demons were reported to be intelligent."

"Look at those eyes," Rosa murmured. "My mom had a black dog. Beautiful thing with black fur and blue eyes. She called him Azul." She squatted down and held her hand out to the little black creature. "Would you like that name? Azul?"

"Don't touch it!" Mr. Burke warned Rosa, but it was too late. The shadow ran out from the log and stopped in front of her. It was currently the size of a small dog, but it ebbed and flowed, getting bigger and smaller as it inspected Rosa's hand. Finally, it abruptly shot up her arm and then perched on her shoulders. Blue eyes watched Chrysta, unblinking.

"It's cold!" Rosa cried, smiling. "Can I keep him?"

Mr. Burke scowled. "That is an ancient, dangerous, magical creature, Miss Torres. I seriously doubt you can keep it as a pet."

Azul started to make a rumbling noise. Rosa grinned. "I think he's happy to be one, Mr. Burke."

·····

Once Mr. Burke was sure that Chrysta wasn't injured, they continued to the castle. Azul flowed off of Rosa's shoulder and started zigzagging through the trees. He would go away and come back, wrapping around Chrysta's legs and then tugging her in another direction. "I think he wants us to follow him," she said after Azul did this for the fourth time.

"Maybe to stay away from the others?" Rosa asked.

"I don't know if we can trust it," Mr. Burke said. "But we will give it a shot."

They followed Azul's path, covering more ground and taking more time than if they went straight, but they did not run into any more metal guardians. Once they left the circle of red trees, Chrysta shuddered. "So you felt it too?" Mr. Burke asked her.

"Felt what?" Rosa asked. "What's wrong?"

"We just crossed a magical barrier," Mr. Burke explained. "One of the strongest I have ever felt. It is probably why no one can teleport into the castle, forcing them to go through the red circle." Finally, they came out of the tree line, and they all froze. "There it is."

The castle was built into the mountain, long and tall. Luckily the drawbridge was down, so they wouldn't have to cross the rushing river, which turned into a waterfall before flowing down the rest of the mountain to the lake. They walked across the drawbridge and used a bridge to get inside the walls. There was a small town just inside the walls, some wooden structures burnt and some untouched. It was silent as a tomb, Poe's croaking and their footsteps the only sound to reach their ears. Finally, after trekking for half a mile, they made it to the castle entrance. "Careful," Mr. Burke breathed. "We have no idea what magic is in play here."

The doors were massive, too big to move, but they were lucky that someone had left them open wide enough to walk through. The humans carefully walked inside, Poe settling on Chrysta's shoulder, Azul on Rosa's, and Willow sticking very close to Mr. Burke. The walls were set with windows that let in enough light. There were some signs of decay, stones that had fallen from the columns or the ceiling, a broken pane of glass in some of the windows. But the castle was in immaculate shape for the most part. The floor was dark marble, polished to a mirror finish so that Chrysta could see their reflection as they walked deeper into the castle.

A weird chandelier hung from the ceiling. It was almost as long as the ceiling was tall. It looked like the roots of a tree but was made of clear glass, catching the light and creating rainbows in the afternoon sun. "What is it?" Rosa asked.

"I have seen them before," Mr. Burke said. "When a lightning strike hits sand, it heats the sand until it melts and forms that shape. But they don't get that big naturally. So a powerful sorcerer must have constructed it."

The end of the hall had a short flight of stairs leading to a huge dais. There was a throne completely made of gold, glittering in the sunlight. They climbed the stairs and carefully approached the throne. Chrysta squinted at the back. There was writing there, and she started to read. "'Tremble, all ye who gaze upon my visage. Bow to the One who controls all, sees all, and knows all.'"

Mr. Burke's head whipped around, and he gaped at her. "You can read that?" he asked.

"Yes, of course," she answered. "Can't you?" She blinked and looked back at the throne, suddenly wondering why the writing on an ancient throne was in modern English.

"It looked like scratches to me," Rosa said, also squinting at the throne, not getting any closer. "And it looks like it's moving." She rubbed her eyes. "It hurts your eyes if you stare at it too long."

"The Golden One called it the language of the Angels," Mr. Burke explained, still staring at Chrysta in shock. "Only she could read it, and it covers most of her artifacts." He looked around them, at the throne, to the chandelier, the massive hall, and back at Chrysta. "I think we are in the castle of the Golden One."

.....

They sat down for a late lunch on the floor, not on the dais; none of them wanted to be too close to the throne. As they ate, Mr. Burke stared at the throne, forehead furrowed in concentration. Poe and Willow accepted some jerky, but Azul didn't seem to appreciate the portion Rosa gave him, playing with it like a cat playing with a toy.

"So, Strifelaughter makes this sphere," Rosa stated after a half-hour of quiet eating, "defeats the Golden One and then seals her castle inside it. But not her?"

"Maybe he killed her?" Chrysta pointed out.

"Then why take her castle?" Rosa asked.

"This castle is full of her secrets. Letting it fall into the wrong hands would be just as dangerous as the Golden One herself," Mr. Burke explained. He looked at Chrysta and shifted. "Presumably, most of the magic would have to be performed by someone who glows gold, just like she did. Studying the castle is only part of the key to unlocking her magic. Chrysta is the other part."

"So you're saying I should leave now and not explore this castle any further," Chrysta stated.

"Not necessarily," Mr. Burke admitted. "This sphere would have been yours eventually, Miss Angelos. The question is, what will *you* do with the knowledge when you possess it."

Chrysta looked around, studying the hall with its massive doors, windows, and glass chandelier, trying to gather her thoughts. "The book I read says that the Golden One may be the sorcerer who created the wasting curse."

"Correct."

"Tommy said that the Acolytes use wasting curses on sorcerers that stand up to them. But other sorcerers use them on people like Rosa because they believe that person is dangerous and shouldn't use magic.

"It's the same spell, but who can say using it one way is 'evil,' and the other way 'good.' Maybe both ways are wrong. Maybe if I can figure out how she made wasting curses, I can reverse them. Or maybe change the spell so people can limit their magic so they don't harm others."

She looked at Mr. Burke. "I would like to explore the castle some more. It's so big I doubt we can search the whole thing in the time we have left, but maybe we can come back someday. Learn more about the Golden One. Maybe what we find can help people."

She nodded at Azul, who was curled around Rosa's feet. "At the very least, I can help the other shadow demons trapped here. They are in pain and should be free."

Mr. Burke smiled. "Very well, Miss Angelos." He looked at both girls. "We will look around, but no one goes off alone. This castle is enormous and quite possibly still filled with dangerous magic." He looked up at the chandelier. "But I would be lying if I said I wasn't intrigued by this place."

.....

They took a day to explore and still didn't even cover half of the castle. They found a door that led to an underground cave full of swirling water from the river. There was a dungeon full of metal tools and weapons and barred cells, rusted with time but still covered in mysterious stains. There was a room full of bones, and Chrysta didn't consider herself an animal expert, but the bones and skulls looked weird, oversized, or twisted in unnatural shapes. A room full of gold and jewels and silver and precious stones lay behind one giant door. Mr. Burke had to grab Rosa's hand and shake his head, a silent command not to touch anything. A giant door was magically locked, and Chrysta felt like she could break the enchantment if she wanted, but when Chrysta put her hand on the wood, she heard screaming in her head and jerked her hand back in pain. There was a large room full of beds, some built like giant nests, full of feathers larger than Chrysta's arm. A second room was full of bones as well, but Mr. Burke identified it this time, saying it was a dragon's skeleton, its head so big that it could have swallowed all three humans whole.

But, finally, the second afternoon they were there, they found the library. They had wandered into a room where the wall was broken, pieces of the mural lying on the floor. Stepping over the rubble, they entered a large room full of books. Mr. Burke, holding a ball of light in one hand, held up a book and studied the spine. "Looks like you will be our translator, Miss Angelos." He handed the book to Chrysta, and she opened it up to a random page to read.

"'Today, the representative of Mali arrived with tribute. It was copper formed into bars. It will be useful in forming wires for the castle, but I told this man that I was displeased it was not gold. I cut out his tongue and sent him back to his people.'" Chrysta shuddered as she closed the book.

"Looks like we found the personal library of the Golden One," Mr. Burke murmured. He held his hand higher, and the light got brighter, Azul moving so he was hiding behind Rosa. The library wasn't tall, but it was deep, with piles of books lying everywhere. "If you hope to find the Golden One's knowledge, I believe we have found the mother lode."

Chrysta flipped through the book. "Let me grab a few and take them back to the hall." She picked up about a dozen books, but when she tried to walk out of the room, she tripped when the books froze at the door. "Um, Mr. Burke," she called out. "I don't think I can take these books out of the library."

Mr. Burke scowled, and he walked over to her. He took a book and then tried to take it out of the room. It stopped at the threshold, so he walked out of the room and tried to pull it, but it stayed where it was, blocked by an invisible barrier. He huffed. "Looks like we will be staying in here," he said.

.....

For the next four days, they camped in the great hall at night and would go to the library during the day. Mr. Burke was still uncomfortable with Rosa being alone, so she stayed just outside the library while Chrysta and Mr. Burke worked, throwing a ball to keep Poe, Willow, and Azul busy or practicing with her sword. They couldn't take the books out, but Mr. Burke wanted to at least catalog them. Chrysta would skim the books, figure out what they were about, and Mr. Burke would write a summary and leave it in the book.

"Most of them are journals," Chrysta explained the first day over lunch. "But they don't have dates, so it's hard to say when the events happened."

Meetings, the weather, what food she ate, and other mundane topics were mixed with torture scenes, tirades about people who angered her, spells she created, and her exploits. Chrysta felt like she was reading the journals of two different people sometimes, only it was in the same book and in the same handwriting, so it had to be the same person. Someone who was very disturbed in Chrysta's opinion.

The changelings were the main topic of a lot of her books. One morning, after studying a tome for a long time, Mr. Burke watched Chrysta as her look of concentration turned into horror. She pushed the book off of her lap and then ran out of the library. She went past Rosa and into a small courtyard nearby. "Miss Angelos?" Mr. Burke called out to her. "What is it?"

Chrysta paced back and forth, shaking her head. "I don't want to say," she murmured.

"You can share it, Miss Angelos," Mr. Burke told her, Rosa just silently nodding in agreement next to him. "It may be better to share than try to keep it all inside."

"It's not like Mr. Cross described it," Chrysta explained, still pacing. "The first changelings were too much like animals. When she was able to make them more human, she didn't know what their magical traits were, so she had to experiment." Chrysta stopped pacing and covered her eyes, feeling them prickle with tears. "She was seeing if they could heal faster than humans, so she took a young changeling and started to cut him. And she... s-she cut off his arm. And she didn't help him with the pain because she said in her journal that she punished him for screaming. The Golden One t-took his arm and left him screaming." Chrysta suddenly clamped a hand over her mouth and retched at the thought. Rosa rushed to her and held Chrysta's hair back as she doubled over, trying to hold onto her breakfast.

"Let's take a recess, Miss Angelos," Mr. Burke told her when she was calmer. "In fact... let's call it a day."

.....

The rest of the books were just as jumbled as the others, full of the mediocre and the profane. But Chrysta tried to get through them without letting the contents bother her. "This book is on solar crystals," she told Mr. Burke, passing him a book. "How to make them bigger?" She handed him another book. "This is a list of changelings she made, including the locations and animals used. Serapis wasn't always the leader of the changelings," she added as an afterthought.

"Really?" Rosa asked. "Who was in charge before him?"

"A jackal changeling named Anubis," Chrysta explained. "Serapis fought him for leadership and killed him."

"What did the Golden One think about all of this?" Mr. Burke asked.

"She encouraged it," Chrysta replied with a grimace. "She said she wanted the most powerful and ruthless creature to lead her army. She created Hel and made her a general in Anubis's place."

"Interesting," Mr. Burke murmured, inspecting the book like he could read it.

"What's this one about?" Rosa asked, and she handed a book to Chrysta. It was leather-bound and had a golden tree on the front cover.

Chrysta took the book and started to leaf through it, quickly skimming the pages. Her forehead furrowed as the minutes passed. "Well?" Rosa asked. "What is it about?"

"Her children," Chrysta said, and Mr. Burke's head whipped around to look at her in shock.

"The Golden One had children?" he asked, leaning over Chrysta's shoulder to squint at the book.

"Yes?" Chrysta said uncertainly. "Is that a secret?"

"The Golden One never had children as far as we know," Mr. Burke responded. "She was never pregnant, and she never claimed to have any. And no one else glows gold, so her powers didn't pass on to the next generation." He cocked his head to the side. "Unless they have been in hiding this entire time. Does she list any names?"

Chrysta flipped through the book, scanning for information. "It's weird, she talks about picking her partners, but they are all women." Her hand paused when she found a paragraph. "She... she turned herself into a man and impregnated women."

Rosa blinked. *"What?!"*

"She says she didn't want to become pregnant. It would be easier and faster for her to have other women carry her children. So she chose ten women, changed into a man, and then seduced them." She flipped a page. "She chose unmagical humans and then cursed their family line, so they could never have more than one child."

"Why?" Rosa asked.

"Insurance," Mr. Burke said. "With a living bloodline on this plane, it would always be an anchor if other sorcerers killed her. We know spirits need a living relative to converse with the living. But she didn't want to risk a child being born that could be as powerful as her."

"Does she say who her children were?" Rosa asked.

"There was a book... which had an enchanted page. It would write the names of her descendants as they were born. She planned to give it to the Acolytes so they would have the information if anything ever happened to her," Chrysta explained. She turned a page. "Oh! The mural outside this room has the same enchantment!" She got up and rushed out of the library, Rosa and Mr. Burke close behind her.

Chrysta looked at the stone on the floor, and her hands glowed, picking up the pieces and fitting them back on the wall. Once the mural was intact, Chrysta saw it was a golden tree covered in runes that only she could only read. She stepped up and started reading. "The Golden One," she murmured, running her fingers along the name on the tree trunk. Her fingers began to run through the branches. "The shortest ones are the bloodlines that are dead. People who passed away before having kids."

"What about the longest one?" Mr. Burke asked. "Is that bloodline still active?"

"Yes," Chrysta responded. "But, wait... this family, their last name is Angelos."

"Like your mom?" Rosa asked.

"Yes," Chrysta said. "The last person in the line is..." Chrysta froze as her fingers stopped at the last name, high above her head. "... is me."

"Wait, you mean..."

"I'm the last descendant of the Golden One," Chrysta said, stepping away from the mural.

Silence rang in the space. "Monroe said that the Acolytes were looking for pieces of paper," Mr. Burke said after several minutes passed. "They called it the Tree and never told him what information it possessed."

"The last bloodline of the Golden One," Chrysta murmured. "That must be why my father married my mother."

"He knew that a child from their union would be powerful, maybe as powerful as the Golden One herself. And with that power, the Acolytes could bring the Golden One back."

Chrysta put her hands on her face and moaned. "I'm the last descendant of the Golden One," she said again, feeling her eyes prickle with tears.

"So?" Rosa asked.

Chrysta whirled around to face her. "So everything that people will say about me will be true. I glow gold, and people will say I'm just like her. And maybe they will be right. She's my ancestor. I may become just like her."

"Chrysta, I just saw you almost throw up a few days ago because you read a book on how she created changelings," Rosa argued. "You're nothing like her. Glowing gold is not going to make you like her."

"Miss Angelos, I must agree with Miss Torres. I don't thin—" Mr. Burke started to say, but he paused. He was staring at something past the girls, and they glanced behind them. The ball Rosa had been playing with was where she left it, but it was rolling on the floor by itself. "Is that the first time it has done that, Miss Torres?"

"Um, yeah," she replied. "Maybe the floor is uneven?"

Mr. Burke didn't respond but reached into his shirt and took out his ring on the chain. He held it out and let it hang, but the ring didn't point at the floor but at an angle. "The sphere is tilting," he said in a stern voice. "We must go."

"Why, Mr. Burke?" Rosa asked.

"The sphere tilting is a sign from Jiao that something is wrong," he clarified. He started to stride out of the room, and the girls followed. "We must get outside of the barrier and transport ourselves out."

Chrysta paused and spun around, studying the mural for a few moments. She waved a hand, and the wall crumbled again, the tree gone for now. She hesitated until Rosa called her name, and then she turned around and rushed to join the others.

51

October 1855

Tommy was six-years-old, and he was happy.

He lived with his mother in the woods, and she said they could go live with other people when he could change into his other form. He saw his mother change all the time (the long black claws, the yellow fur with black spots, the golden eyes, the mouth full of sharp teeth), and he was never afraid of her when she was like that. She was still his mother, still his Mama. She would transform to go hunting, telling him to stay in their camp until she came back. And then she would come back with food.

He is Thomas Monroe, and she is Jemila Monroe, and they are changelings. He is not sure what that means, only that they look like other people, but his mother says they aren't, and one day he can change like her.

"When Mama?" he asked one morning. "When can I change?"

Her lips twitched into a smile, and she finished washing the last piece of clothing in the river and turned to him. "Soon," she said. She reached out and poked his forehead. "Most of us can change when we are your age."

"And once I change, we can go live with other people?" he asked.

She chuckled. "Yes, we can go live with other people. But remember..."

"Don't trust humans," Tommy recited from memory. "Don't trust sorcerers. Don't trust other changelings."

"That's right."

"How will I change, Mama?"

"You'll know," his mother replied with an amused smile.

One night, Tommy felt weird. His skin was itchy, and he started to pace in their small encampment. He didn't want to eat, but he was so hungry. His mother smiled and took him down to the river, the moon their only source of light. She led him close to the water and told him to sit on her lap, hugging him from behind. "You're ready to change," she told him. "So just change."

"I don't know how," he whined in frustration. "How do I do it?"

"Close your eyes," she told him calmly. He huffed in irritation but did what she asked, screwing his eye shut. "You will feel the change everywhere in your body," his mother explained.

"Does it hurt?" Tommy asked.

"Oh no," she replied. "It tickles." And suddenly, she tickled him with her fingers on his ribs. He giggled and laughed and wiggled, and suddenly he felt a weird tingle in his skin, his bones, his insides, and when it was gone, he opened his eyes and knew he was different. He leaned over to look at his reflection in the river.

Tommy didn't have his mother's yellow fur, but he had her snout, teeth, and spots. He brought a hand to his face and almost hit his eye with a claw, not used to having long black talons. Tommy curled his lips into a snarl, examining his teeth. One of his canines was missing, just like when he looked human. He turned around and looked at his mother, who was studying him with a smile on her face. "What do you think?" he asked her.

"Well, you have your father's skin," she said. "And look how big you are! I'm never going to be able to catch enough food to keep you full when you're older." Then, she changed, fierce claws and teeth, and she stood up, tugging him from the river's edge. "Well, come on. If you are old enough to change, you are old enough to start hunting for your dinner."

.....

Tommy was nine-years-old, and he was scared.

They found a settlement of people to live with. Most of the people lived in tents, his mother was one of the few people who could read, but there were farmers, herders, and a woman who could make medicine, although the changelings never needed her services. Tommy's mother hunted with the men while Tommy stayed in the settlement and helped with odd jobs. It was a hard life, but they were happy.

One night, Tommy woke up to the sound of screaming. His mother was up in a flash and covered him with her body. "Don't move," she hissed. They watched the chaos from their tent, men on horses tearing through the settlement with torches in their hands.

A torch landed on their tent, and they scrambled outside. Jemila kicked the torch away, and Tommy kicked dirt on the fire before it destroyed everything they owned.

A man galloped up and pointed a gun at them, laughing as Tommy's mother pulled him behind her. "Give us the boy!" he ordered.

Jemila gave out an inhuman growl in response, a sound Tommy hadn't heard in years, and the man's horse reared up in fear. The man cried and fell off his horse, and the changeling was on him before he could grab his gun. She punched him once, twice, and he was knocked out cold with the third punch.

The other men galloped off, yelling and hollering into the night. Tommy and his mother helped the people in the settlement, putting out fires and ensuring injured people were out of harm's way. By the time they finished, Tommy realized that some people were still screaming; but it was mostly the parents wailing. They gathered together, talking all at once.

"My daughter! They took her—"

"—just hit him with the gun and to—"

"—you seen him?! Have you seen my son?!"

Tommy's mother hauled the man she caught into the crowd, tying his hands behind him. The man wasn't scared; he was just laughing and hooting at the mob around him. Tommy studied him as the crowd screamed at him.

When his mother told him about white people, Tommy thought they would be paler, like the pages in a book. But the man was tan, darker than Tommy imagined, but lighter than any other person Tommy knew. His hair was dark, one of his ears looked like a cauliflower, and Tommy noticed he was missing some teeth as he smiled at the group of people screaming at him angrily.

"Just you wait!" he screamed back at them. "They will be back for me! They will be back to kill you, and *there is nothing you can do about it!*"

Tommy's mother sneered at him. "Shut your mouth!" she ordered the white man.

The white man blinked and then frowned. "Shut *my* mouth?! Wait until I get fr—" But before he could finish his threat, Jemila punched him again, knocking him out cold.

"Do you think the others will be back?" one man asked in the resulting silence.

"We can't risk it. We have to run."

"There wasn't more than ten of them. We outnumber them. We co—"

"We could what? Fight?! They had guns! Do you want to wake up at a slave auction?"

"I'll go."

The crowd fell silent, and everyone stared at Jemila in shock. She stood in the middle of the group, her chin held high while glaring at the white man at her feet. "I'll take this pig's horse and find the children," she said.

"How will you find them?" someone called out. "They could be anywhere!"

"He can tell me," she answered, kicking the unconscious man in the ribs. "And even if he doesn't, I should be able to track a group that large."

Jemila got dressed before dawn in a shirt and pants, what she wore every time she hunted with the men. She let the horse smell her and then got on its back, pulling the sleeping white man up so he was behind her, laying across the horse. "Give me two full days," she told one of the settlement's elders. "If I'm not back by then, move everyone deeper into the swamp to be safe."

"Mama," Tommy whispered. "What about me?"

His mother looked at him and then smiled. "I'll be fine, son." She pulled on the reins to point the horse in the direction the men had disappeared the night before. "I'll be back. You can count on that." She glanced at the elder. "Make sure our belongings are packed for when I return."

Tommy gave her a confused look. Why did he have to pack their belongings if she was coming back? Before he could ask her, though, the elder interrupted him. "One woman against ten armed men," the elder said. "Seems unfair."

Jemila smiled, something predatory that showed off a lot of teeth, and Tommy saw the elder jerk in surprise next to him. "I know. Those men won't know what hit 'em." And she dug her heels into the horse's side, and they were off.

Most of the settlement waited with Tommy, but some people who didn't lose their children moved deeper into the swamp like they didn't believe Jemila would return. Meanwhile, Tommy waited impatiently all day, a feeling of dread building in his stomach as time passed. "We will wait," the elder assured him as he picked at his dinner later that night, unable to eat.

Tommy tried to go to bed, worry robbing him of sleep. Dawn didn't reveal his mother returning, and Tommy spent the morning pacing back and forth in the settlement, watching the trees for any sign of his mother. *I will stay*, he thought to himself. *If they try to make me leave, I'll stay here. I'm not leaving Mama behind.*

Later in the morning, however, there were shouts of fear as a group appeared and walked out of the trees. But the screams turned into cries of joy when people saw who the group was. The children, several on horses, had returned, and they ran to their parents with tears on their faces. Tommy gave his own joyful yell when he saw his mother at the back of the group, galloping towards him.

Suddenly, the tone of the group changed. The children cringed when they saw Jemila coming. They cried and pointed at her in fear. Tommy then noticed that Jemila was covered in blood, her face, chest, and hands shining red in the sun. She had transformed, Tommy realized. It was the only way she could have stopped all those men at once. She had transformed, and the children saw it.

"Monster!" someone cried and pointed at Jemila, but she didn't react as she stopped in front of Tommy.

"Come on!" she cried, and he grabbed a bag full of their possessions, and then he climbed onto the horse behind his mother. As soon as he settled, she kicked into the horse's sides, and they galloped out of the settlement, away from the mob forming behind them.

They kept going, running for what felt like hours to Tommy. Finally, Jemila stopped, letting the horse drink from a river. She got down and started washing the dried blood off her face and hands. Tommy got down as well. "What happened?" Tommy asked.

"I think it's pretty clear what happened," his mother replied. "I gave those men a chance to meet their maker." She chuckled at her own joke, a dark sound.

"What about the others?" Tommy asked. He looked behind them, back to the settlement that had been their home for years. "Can we ever go back?"

"No, son," Jemila said softly. "I tried to do it at night when the children wouldn't see me... but they did. So we won't be welcomed there anymore."

"They should have thanked you," Tommy yelled, anger making him ball up his fists. "You said you would bring their children back, and you did! All by yourself! They should have *thanked* you!"

"They were scared, son," she explained. "Humans will always fear you when you show them what you are." She paused to throw more water on her face, getting the last of the blood off. "That's just the way it has to be."

"Then you shouldn't have done it," Tommy pouted, crossing his arms in front of him. "You shouldn't have done it if you knew that they would hate you for it."

"And let those children suffer? Knowing I could have done something?" his mother asked, and Tommy felt some of his anger toward her fade. She got up and walked to him, glaring at him. "I couldn't have lived with myself if I had done that." She sighed, her expression softening. "We will live for a very long time, son. When you get to be an adult, you can live your life the way you want. But make sure you don't regret your decisions. You won't be able to live with yourself otherwise."

She started to walk away. "Come on," she said. "Let's find a new home."

ᥴ 52 ᥐ

Tommy was eleven, and he was confused.

After the raid on the settlement, Tommy and his mother found an empty house on the great river, claiming it as their own. They fixed it up, built a dock at the water's edge, and made a home. There was a village nearby. Well, nearby in the sense that it took a day's walk to get there, and they had to stay the night before walking back, but they would make the trip once a month, Jemila taking furs and dried meat to trade in the small town. She used the money to buy books, clothes, and, after many months of saving, a violin that the general store happened to have.

"Do you know how to play?" Tommy asked her as she gently took the instrument out of its case.

"Of course," she replied.

"How did you learn to play?" he asked.

"A man taught me how," she explained. She put the violin up to her chin and gently ran the bow across the strings. "The same man who taught me how to read." She took the bow and hit his nose, making him blink in surprise. "The same man I named you after, to be honest. Would you like to play?"

He broke out into a grin. "Can I?!"

The town was where Tommy met a sorcerer for the first time. The man was in the bookstore with his family, and a smell of rotting food hung around them, which made no sense because they looked clean. His mother hit him on the back of his head and then dragged him outside. "Stop staring!" she hissed at him once they crossed the street and could watch the family unnoticed through the shop's window.

Tommy rubbed the back of his head. "Why did they smell like that?" he asked his mother.

"They're sorcerers," she explained, and Tommy's head whipped around to gape at the family. He had read some stories about wizards, so he assumed that sorcerers wore robes and pointed hats. But the man and his family looked ordinary, although richer than Tommy and his mother judging by their clothes.

"They look... normal," he said as the family left the shop, the children holding their books above their heads with excitement.

"Did you think they had three eyes?" his mother joked. "That sour smell you noticed is magic. It's stronger depending on how many spells they have on them."

Tommy watched the sorcerers walk down the street. "They don't know we are changelings?" he asked.

"No. Sorcerers can't smell how we are different than them. Some of their familiars can smell us." Tommy gave her a confused look. "Their pets. They can smell us. You see one of them sniffing the air, cover your scent." She looked at the family as they turned a corner, unaware of the changelings staring at them just down the street. "And if you see a sorcerer with a sword, you *run*. Those are hunters, and they are not to be messed with."

So they lived in isolation on the river, trading, hunting, and fishing. Tommy's mother taught him how to read, and they used most of their money for books and music, and they were happy. Tommy watched boats travel downstream, heading for the Gulf, a place he swore to visit one day. He wanted to see the beach and smell the salt air. Tommy watched the steamboats move upstream, powerful enough to fight the river's flow to the sea. He wanted to go with them too, visit the North, and see snow and the animals that provided the pelts that traders gave them.

He wanted to see the world, and one day he would.

.....

One day, they were leaving town when Tommy's mother suddenly scented the air. She always said to not act weird around humans, so smelling the air like an animal was so unlike her. "What is it?" he asked.

"Changeling," his mother murmured, looking around the crowd. "But it's faint. I can't tell who or what it is."

Tommy felt his stomach drop. "Do we... do we run, Mama?"

"No. They won't attack us while there are humans around," she said. She put a hand on his shoulder, and they started walking. "But there might be more of them, so stay alert."

They started their way home, every noise in the forest and swamp making Tommy jump. His mother kept her hand on his back so he couldn't turn around, but as the road twisted and turned, they got glimpses of a figure following them. The changeling stayed downwind from them so Tommy's mother didn't catch his scent again. At first, the road was busy enough that they didn't have to worry about an attack, but the traffic thinned as they got closer to home. They didn't stop to eat, eating while they walked. Nighttime was approaching, and the changeling was gaining on them, although they still couldn't see who he was.

"When I tell you to run, you run," his mother murmured.

"What about you?" Tommy asked.

"Don't worry about me," she said, voice low but using a tone to not argue with. "You run, you get home, and you lock the door behind you. If he gets there before me, what do you do?"

"Grab some fire and throw it at his face," Tommy murmured back.

"Good boy."

They were almost home, walking along the path only they used. Just one more bend in the river, and Tommy and his mother would be able to see the house. His mother took her hand off Tommy's back, and he tensed up, his heart pounding and his palms sweaty.

His mother suddenly dropped her bag and spun around, an inhuman growl rumbling from her chest. "Run!" she snarled, and Tommy ran on wobbly knees. The changeling behind them shouted, and Tommy fought the urge to turn around. Mama said to run, so he would run.

Jemila yelled, and he stopped running, almost falling as he skidded to a stop and turned to go back. He was not abandoning his Mama; he wouldn't let anyone hurt her. He ran back towards the changeling that was holding his mother up in the air. They were both in their human forms, but Tommy transformed as he ran, determined to do as much damage as possible. He slammed into the unknown changeling, trying to rip and tear with his talons. The man grabbed his shirt and picked him up with ease as Tommy hissed and kicked. The man brought him up so they were eye-to-eye. The man was smiling, but what gave Tommy pause was that his mother was smiling too, holding onto the other changeling's neck, leaning into him, *hugging* him. Tommy stopped fighting and stared dumbly at the other two changelings.

"Tommy, meet your father," Jemila said with a smile. "Niuhi, meet your son."

"Well," the changeling rumbled. "Isn't he something?"

.....

Tommy hated his father.

He was huge, almost as wide as he was tall. Their tiny house was nearly too small for him, and he constantly ran into things and knocked things over. Their furniture was tiny compared to him. He had to use two chairs when he sat at the table. He was noisy, always talking in a loud tone, making Tommy jump when he didn't expect it. He didn't read, so Tommy couldn't talk about the books they owned or the stories he knew. Niuhi stank of fish and saltwater, a scent so strong that Tommy wouldn't be surprised if even humans could smell him. When he worked, he sang at the top of his lungs, using a language Tommy didn't know. Not French, not Creole, not English. Sometimes Jemila would join him, singing or talking with the other changeling with a smile on her face.

That was the only thing Tommy didn't hate about his father: he made Tommy's mother very happy. She smiled and laughed and giggled like a little girl with Niuhi around. The giant changeling would kiss her, dance with her, listen to her play her violin, and talk with her the whole night through until it was dawn again.

A few days after he appeared, Niuhi loudly announced he was going fishing. Tommy watched as the changeling went outside, taking his clothes off as he walked. Tommy gaped as his father finished disrobing and continued stark naked down the dock.

"Mama!" Tommy hissed. "Someone will see him!"

"And?" she asked with a smile. "Who is going to stop him? You?"

Niuhi made it to the end of the dock, and he changed, leaning down so that he could lie on the dock as his legs fused together and became a tail. He was massive with grey skin with a long tail, although he kept his two arms which he used to pull himself down the dock. Tommy squawked and ran outside to help his father into the water. "You shouldn't change where humans could see you!" Tommy yelled.

"So what if they do?"

"They will get other humans, and they may hurt us!"

"Then I will eat anyone who sees me," Niuhi said with a grin, only now that he was in his other form, the smile was wide and full of nightmarish teeth.

Tommy blanched and then hissed as his father's skin tore into his hands. He turned to see his mother standing at the door, leaning on it as her shoulder shook in laughter. "Mama! He's going to eat a human!"

"No eating humans!" Jemila called out with a laugh.

Niuhi huffed. "No fun," he said with a rumble as he finally slid into the water.

It was several hours later when Niuhi reappeared. Tommy was at the end of the dock with his feet in the water when a fin broke the water's surface. He watched in fascination as the shark changeling got closer, grey form barely visible under the water but still massive enough to make waves. Tommy snatched his feet out of the water, generally not scared of gators or snapping turtles, but Niuhi swimming toward him spooked him. Finally, his father made it to the dock and started to haul himself out of the water, dragging a dead gator almost as big as Tommy behind him.

Niuhi started to force water out of his mouth and gills. "Water tastes bad," he rumbled as Jemila approached with his clothes.

"I would imagine so," Jemila said with a smile. "The river is mostly mud."

Tommy inspected the dead animal as his father transformed back. The shark changeling had bitten through the back of the animal's neck, breaking its spine but ruining its skin. "We can't use this hide," Tommy said as his mother picked it up.

"Sure we can," his mother replied. "And with something this big, we can eat good for a week."

"We?!" Niuhi cried. "I caught that beast for me!" he joked with a smile. Tommy glared at him and then followed his mother inside.

"He hates me," Tommy overheard his father say that night. Tommy slept in the loft by himself while his parents slept on the floor in front of the fire. They would murmur to themselves for most of the night, but Tommy could hear them if he concentrated on listening.

"He doesn't hate you," Jemila said. Tommy could only see their silhouette in the low light of the dying fire, but he could make out his mother running her hand through his father's hair. "He doesn't know you. And I have been telling him to avoid our kind for his entire life, so you have to assume he would be wary of you."

Niuhi hummed. "He shouldn't be afraid of his own kind, Jemila."

"Niuhi..."

"You shouldn't keep him away from his kind like this."

"Niuhi."

"He shouldn't be so... human-like."

"Niuhi," Jemila growled. Tommy saw the silhouette break up as his mother quickly sat up. "Enough!"

"Let me talk to him, Jemila," Niuhi responded, ignoring her outburst. "Serapis can be reasonable—"

"He is *not* reasonable," Jemila argued. "He is cruel and plays favorites, and if he knew about our son, he would *kill* Tommy."

Niuhi hushed her and then pulled her back down so that their silhouette was one massive form again. They stayed that way for so long that Tommy had almost fallen asleep before he heard his mother speak again.

"Promise me, Niuhi," she whispered. "Promise me you will keep Tommy a secret. Just give me a few more years, and he can live on his own."

"With the humans," Niuhi grumbled.

"Where he can be safe," Jemila argued.

Niuhi sighed. "Alright, *e ku'u aloha*. I promise."

. . . . .

Several weeks later, Niuhi left them, and Tommy watched him go with mixed emotions. He still felt that the other changeling was too loud, too big, too reckless. But his mother looked sad as she waved goodbye to his father, and Tommy hated to see her upset.

That night, Tommy watched his mother as she cooked. "Mama," he said suddenly. "What are we?"

"We're changelings," his mother responded.

"But what are changelings?" he asked.

His mother stopped stirring and turned around to look at him. "Well, I guess you are old enough to understand now," she muttered. She took the pot of gumbo off of the stove and brought it to the table, grabbing bowls and utensils and then spooning some dinner for Tommy.

Tommy waited for her to continue as she sat down with a sigh. She tore into a roll and took a bite, chewing thoughtfully. "A long time ago, a sorcerer called the Golden One made changelings. She created an army of our kind for herself to make other sorcerers listen to her. Other sorcerers banded together and killed her, but we changelings remained." Jemila scowled, an expression that Tommy remembered from the night the white men attacked the settlement. "The changelings now follow Serapis. And pray that you never meet him."

"Why?"

"The Golden One had a lot of rules, and Serapis follows them, no matter how weird or horrible they are. The biggest one is that there can only be 2,584 changelings alive at one time."

Tommy made a face of confusion. "Why?"

Jemila shrugged. "Don't know. As strange as it is, it is one rule Serapis enforces at all costs. A changeling can't be born until another one dies. Serapis picks the couple who can mate, but the child will never know who their parents were. Serapis says the children don't need a family, that we are all family. But he only chooses the couples he likes to have children. Or will kill changelings he doesn't like so that he can replace them with a younger changeling that will listen to him."

Tommy's mother took a bite of her gumbo and chewed her food. "When I found out I was about to have you, I refused to let Serapis decide if you would live or die. I wanted to have a child, my child, and live like a family. So I fled and had you, and you can go live by yourself when you are old enough, hopefully, hidden by the humans."

Tommy fell quiet and thought about what his mother had said. "So if Serapis finds out about me, he will hurt me?"

"Yes," Jemila confirmed.

Tommy felt a little bit of panic. "But we're safe here?"

"Yes, Tommy, we're safe."

"My father found us," Tommy argued.

"Because I told him where I was going, and he came looking for us. He promised not to tell anyone where we were. And I trust him with my life. And more importantly, your life."

Tommy nodded. He may not like Niuhi, but if his mother trusted him, Tommy would too. They ate for a few quiet minutes. Tommy thought of a question and looked at his mother. "Did you ever meet her? The golden sorcerer?"

Jemila smiled. "The Golden One. No. She died many years before I was born."

"So how were you made if the Golden One didn't make you?"

"The natural way."

"What's that?" Tommy asked.

His mother grinned. "Well, remember when we saw those two horses mating? And I told you how babies were made?"

"Yeah."

"My parents did that and made me."

Tommy nodded; it made sense. But he had another thought, and he dropped his spoon. "Wait, so is that how I was made?"

"Yep," his mother replied with an evil grin. "Me and your father."

"Ew!" Tommy yelled, putting his hand on his face, trying to block the mental image that flooded his mind. His mother laughed and took his plate away from him.

"If you have lost your appetite," she joked, "I'll just be taking this."

53

Tommy was thirteen, and he was terrified.

Tommy had grown over the last two years to the point he was almost as tall as his mother. He often remembered when his father visited them and the conversation he'd overheard between his parents. Someday, soon, he would be old enough to go off on his own. The thought was both exciting and frightening.

One day his mother came to him with the pack he wore when they went into town. "Do you want to go by yourself?" she asked.

Tommy blinked at her and then broke out into a grin. "Sure!" he cried, voice breaking slightly.

Jemila tossed the pack to him. "There is dried meat and furs to trade. You know what stores to take them to and how much money they should give you. You know the blacksmith will let you sleep in his barn. What else?"

Tommy racked his brain. "Hmm, avoid sorcerers. Don't let their pets—"

"Familiars."

"Don't let their familiars smell me. If I see a sorcerer with a sword, that's a hunter. I run."

"If someone tries to capture you?"

"Run. If I can't run, wait until I'm alone, transform, and get away."

"You forgot something," his mother joked. Tommy cocked his head to the side in confusion. "Don't eat humans."

Tommy laughed. "How could I forget that?" he replied, and his mother laughed. Jemila pulled him into a tight hug, and Tommy hugged her back.

"Leave in the morning and be back by the second night. I'm tracking you down and tanning your hide if you're late, understood?"

"Yes, Mama."

.....

Tommy was coming back from his trip. He had spent the last two days on high alert, worried that the bad things his mother had warned him about would happen. But it had been a fruitful and uneventful trip. No one tried to steal from him, no one tried to hurt or capture him, and he sold all of the goods. He had bought a few books and even found some sheet music for his mother in the bookstore. Maybe she would help him read it, and he could play her violin. It would be his birthday soon, after all.

As he went around the last bend of the river, night slowly falling, he slowed down. He could see the house but nothing else. He had expected his mother to be waiting for him, leaning in the front door with a massive smile on her face. But the house was dark, and he couldn't smell anything cooking.

Was he late getting home? Did his mother get worried and make good on her threat, leaving the house to look for him? He slowed down as he got closer to his home, unease building in his chest.

When he was about two dozen feet from the house, he caught the scent of something: fur and mud and unwashed human mixed together. He paused, the anxiety he felt getting worse. He thought he saw something moving in the house. "Mama?" he called out. "Mama, are you there?"

There was no response, but the air felt heavy like the whole world held its breath. Tommy debated what to do when he suddenly heard a bellow from the dark house. *"Tommy, run!"* a voice screamed, and Tommy turned around, dropped his pack, and started to run for the trees before even realizing that it was his mother yelling for him to escape.

Something came skittering after him, but Tommy tried to concentrate on running and not looking at whatever was chasing him. He had almost made it to the cover of the woods when something landed on his back. He cried as leathery membranes wrapped around him, and he was picked up so his feet dangled off the ground. The creature leaned forward to shove its face into Tommy's, and he jerked in surprise at the nightmare he saw. A bat with an upturned nose, large ears, and massive teeth grinned crazily at him. *"Vámonos, niño.* Mama is waiting for you."

The bat dragged him back to the house, and before they got through the door, someone struck a match and lit a lantern. By the time the bat pushed Tommy so he had stumbled to the floor, Tommy could see his mother struggling with a changeling that looked like a bull with black hair who restrained her with an arm across her chest. She had transformed, but the bull still held on, even as she bit and clawed at his bloody arm.

A third figure, the one who lit the lantern, sat at their dining table. He was in his human form, but Tommy could smell that he was a changeling. He looked older, with white skin and gray hair, wearing rumbled clothes. As the bat changeling landed on Tommy's back, pinning him to the floor, the man kept an air of boredom as he started picking at his nails. Tommy struggled to get free and was bitten. He stopped moving, and the bat changeling chuckled darkly in his ear.

"Well, well, well," the changeling at the table said with a leer. "Thomas. It is a pleasure to meet you finally." The bull changeling bellowed as Jemila bit his arm again. "Really, Yama? Get her under control, will you?"

Yama moved his hands to wrap them around Jemila's head and throat. She gave a yowl of pain as he squeezed, and Tommy saw red. He transformed and flipped over before the bat changeling could react. He started to rip and tear at the bat, making him shriek and let Tommy go. Tommy got to his feet and rushed at the bull, slamming into him with a snarl. It felt like hitting a wall, but Tommy started trying to climb up the bull changeling, planning on ripping his throat out if he could.

Yama just huffed and picked Tommy up by his throat. Both Tommy and his mother fought as the bull changeling started to squeeze harder, intent on choking them both. At the table, the man laughed. "You two are getting too old," he said with a chuckle. "Letting these two get the best of ya." He sighed as he got up slowly, lazily. "Alright, let me see him."

Yama lowered Tommy, and the man came close, inspecting him like he was an interesting object. Tommy tried to snap at the man, and Yama quickly let go of his throat to wrap a hand around Tommy's snout, slamming his jaws shut. The man leaned close and took a deep breath, and hummed. "Interesting. He smells like the sea." He tugged on the small patch of hair on Tommy's head, hard enough to rip out a few strands, holding them up and then rubbing his fingers to let them fall to the floor.

The bat changeling suddenly tackled Tommy with a hiss, wrapping his wings around Tommy and pinning his hands to his sides. The man used the opportunity to grab Tommy's head, studying it as he moved it around. He looked at his hands. "Sharkskin," he murmured. "Jemila, what little abomination have you made, hm?"

"He's not an abomination, you crazy bastard," Tommy's mother spat. Yama rumbled and tightened his grip, making Jemila wince and choke. The man didn't react to her insult, just studying Tommy while he stroked his chin.

"Tell me, Camazotz, which idiot do you think fathered this one?" the man asked, still calm, still examining Tommy like he was an inanimate object and not a person. "Since this mongrel has been living under your nose for the last thirteen years."

The bat changeling hissed. "I already told you, Serapis, she may be here, but I didn't kno—"

"Shut up," Serapis commanded cooly, and Tommy felt his stomach drop. He started looking the other changeling over, not believing that this unremarkable man was the dangerous changeling leader that his mother had warned him about for so many years. "You let this go on for too long, and now I'm here to fix it." He looked at Yama. "Kill him." Yama wrapped his hand around Tommy's throat again, and Tommy let out a wheeze as his throat was squeezed shut.

"Wait!" Tommy's mother cried. She changed to her human form, trying to pull Yama's fingers away from her face so she could talk. "Please, Serapis, please! Kill me instead! Tommy's big, strong, and will be a good fighter for you! Just *please,* spare him!"

Serapis gave her a cold smile and held his finger up like she was a naughty child. "You know the rules, Jemila, and you broke the biggest one. But, if you stay quiet, you may live to see tomorrow's dawn."

"You monster!" Jemila screamed, putting as much force into the shout as she could even as Yama kept his stranglehold on her. "You're killing our kind for the stupid rule of a dead, insane sorcerer!"

The other changelings froze, and they all glared at Jemila with identical looks of hatred. "Do not speak of the Lady, Jemila," Serapis growled.

"You're an idiot! A fool!" Jemila continued to scream, ignoring the changeling leader's warning. "She was a horrible woman, and instead of making our kind better, you just continue to make us worse!"

Serapis let out a growl from his chest and launched himself at Jemila, ripping her from Yama's grasp. He held her up by her throat. "You dare lecture me?" he hissed. His calm demeanor was gone, eyes wild as Tommy's mother struggled. "I was there at the beginning, made by her hand. You owe your life, your very existence, to her! And how do you repay her? By living like a filthy human!"

"Better than you," Jemila gritted through her bared teeth.

Serapis suddenly turned away, so Tommy couldn't see his mother anymore and could only see Serapis's back. But then, Serapis changed, and all Tommy could see was black fur covering board shoulders. However, there was something wrong with his head; it looked too large and misformed. "Maybe you should be the one to die tonight, Jemila," he growled, and suddenly Tommy's mother let out a scream that was cut off short.

Jemila was dropped to the floor, and Tommy started to fight as hard as possible to get free. Serapis changed back to his human form before turning around, and Tommy saw red when he realized the man was smiling. Serapis said something, and suddenly both changelings let him go. Tommy hurled himself at the changeling leader, but Serapis caught him before he could attack. Serapis shoved him to the floor, pinning his head so he couldn't bite. Serapis laughed as Tommy hissed and growled.

"Well, maybe you do have an ounce of fight in ya, huh, boy?" Serapis asked, but Tommy didn't answer. He looked at his mother and finally stopped fighting. She wasn't breathing, and realizing she was dead made him wail.

Serapis let him go, and Tommy transformed and scrambled to his mother. He gathered her body in his arms and started to cry.

"I'll make you a deal, Thomas Monroe, my boy," Serapis said several minutes later as he crouched down. Tommy didn't say anything, glaring at the other changeling with red eyes. "I'll let you live, and you can stay with the humans like your mother planned. And in a few decades, we will see if you want to join your kind or if I can kill you like the mongrel you are."

"I'll never join you," Tommy growled.

"We'll see about that."

Serapis got up, and he gestured to the other changelings. "Let's go, boys," he ordered. "We will leave Mr. Monroe to live as he pleases."

The changelings left then, and Tommy thought about following them, but in the end, he stayed with his mother, crying until the dawn came.

54

Akrur was able to heal Rimsha's arm, cursing at himself for not working with Abby more to improve his healing skills when he had the chance. It was no longer broken, but there was a lot of soft tissue damage, and the girl could break it again if she wasn't careful. *If only Abby was here,* he thought to himself, but he winced when he heard the second vault door fall, and the changelings started beating on the third one. No, it was good she wasn't here because he wasn't confident that they would survive this.

Rimsha, looking a little better, went to Ellis and tried to heal them. The hunter hissed as the wound closed. "I stopped the bleeding," the teen explained, "but it could start again, so be careful. We don't want you to start bleeding internally."

Ellis groaned. "I don't have a choice," they gritted out as they grabbed their sword and got off the table. "I have to fight."

"You are staying with the children," Zheng yelled from the front of the vault. She had kicked off her shoes and ripped her dress so she could move better. "No fighting unless absolutely necessary." Ellis opened their mouth to argue, but Zheng interrupted them. "That's an order!"

Ellis looked upset, but they nodded. "Yes, ma'am."

Akrur went to the front of the vault, gesturing at the kids to not follow him. Smith and Hafeez looked at the last vault door with identical grim expressions.

Akrur froze as the third door fell, and the pounding resumed on the fourth. Akrur walked up to the Director and glared at the door with the hunters. "I never thought those doors could fall," Akrur murmured.

"I assume you never planned on four changelings showing up to dismantle them," Zheng joked back.

Tommy, meanwhile, was pacing in the front of the vault. He had taken his boots off, and his bare feet slapped on the floor as he walked. Back and forth, back and forth, glowering at the last vault door. Akrur remembered going to the zoo as a child and watching a tiger pace in his enclosure in the same way. A predator, knowing it was trapped but preparing to fight once its prison was gone.

"What is the plan?" Akrur asked Zheng, watching Tommy pace back and forth.

"We will fight them. Hopefully, it won't be long before Neil, Miss Torres, and Miss Angelos are out of the sphere. Neil may be able to teleport some of us to safety once he does."

"Are we calling dibs?" Smith joked. "Cause I call dibs on Camazotz."

"You would," Hafeez muttered, and Smith glared at her. "We need to focus on Yama. He's the biggest threat," she announced.

"He's mine," Tommy growled.

"He has to have at least a thousand pounds on you," Smith said.

"I have a score to settle with him," Tommy said in a tone that didn't broker any argument.

"Fenrir will be your responsibility then," Zheng told Hafeez. "Remember, we have to help each other. This isn't the time for personal squabbles. It's the only way any of us will survive this."

"She means you," Smith told Hafeez, and she answered with a glare and a rude hand gesture.

"You hide with Ellis and the others," Zheng ordered Akrur, not commenting on the hunters' behavior. "If you see an opening to run and get out of the vault, you take it."

"Anything else?" Akrur asked, and everyone jumped as the fourth door finally failed.

"Yes," Zheng murmured as the changelings started beating the last vault door. "If you have any gods you pray to, now is the time."

Akrur nodded grimly. "Good luck," he said to the others, and he turned and hurried to the teenagers in the back of the vault.

"What do we do, Mr. Cross?" Kevin asked in a small voice as Akrur joined him and the others. They all looked so young and scared at that moment. They shouldn't be here either, he thought to himself. But he tried to put on a brave face.

"We will hide and stay out of the way," he replied. "And once the generals have their butts handed to them, we can leave."

Ichiro looked at Tommy and the three hunters at the front of the vault. "No offense, Mr. Cross, but I don't like their chances."

Akrur glanced behind him. "Right now, Mr. Takahashi, they are our only hope."

. . . . .

Tommy watched the final vault door as the changelings beat it down. Behind him, Hafeez and Smith had their swords out and at the ready. Zheng stood tall with her hand on the hilt of her sword. Three hunters and one changeling against the Golden One's generals. Zheng was right; they didn't have a chance. Tommy kept pacing, trying to keep his panic at bay. Smith was muttering to himself. "For he will command his angels concerning you, to guard you in all your ways..."

How many minutes had it been since Kevin hid the sphere? Five? Ten? He was about to ask Zheng if maybe someone should go inside it, look for Burke and the girls, and get them out, but it was too late. He stopped pacing and watched as the door was knocked off its hinges and hit the railing, teetering back and forth before falling to the lower floor below with a thundering *boom*. Several figures stepped through the hole, and Tommy growled in his chest. "You will tread on the lion and the cobra," Smith finished. "You will trample the great lion and the serpent."

"Amen," Hafeez answered back.

Yama and Degei were in their monster forms, Yama panting as he leaned over the railing. He had probably done all the work of beating down the doors. Good. Hopefully, he would be too tired to fight. Camazotz and Hel walked into the vault in their human forms. Camazotz leaned over the railing and grinned, transforming and turning into a nightmarish gargoyle. Hel was wearing a man's suit, her chest shining with sweat underneath her open shirt. And as the fifth figure walked up behind the generals, Tommy felt his stomach drop.

Serapis looked the same as he did so long ago, although his suit was modern but just as rumpled and dirty as the clothes he wore before. He was smiling, a cold grin that made Tommy's skin crawl. "Well, well, well," he called out in his thick Irish accent. "Look what the cat dragged in." He cocked his head to the side. "Thomas Monroe. I barely believed the others when they told me you were here. When I told you to live among the humans, lad, I didn't mean you should make friends with the hunters."

Tommy shrugged, trying to keep a calm demeanor. Keep the asshole talking; buy Burke and the girls some time. "They are better company than what I have been dealing with for the last few decades," he joked. He pointed at Hafeez. "And that one is trying to kill me."

"I can't let this go unpunished, Thomas," Serapis said. He actually looked sad as he leaned on the railing. "Tell me where that glass ball is, and I can consider having you return to the fold, lad. Don't betray Our Lady any more than you have."

Tommy looked down, trying to put a look of concentration on his face. Zheng glanced at him nervously, and he could feel Hafeez's glare boring into his back. "Monroe," Zheng growled. Tommy didn't answer but looked back up at Serapis straight in his eyes.

"That bitch is not my Lady," Tommy said, and the generals hissed at him in anger. Zheng seemed to sag in relief next to him, and Tommy could hear Smith chuckle behind him. Serapis, surprisingly, was grinning at Tommy again like he wasn't shocked by Tommy's statement.

"Serapis, let the children go, and I will go with you willingly," Zheng called out. Serapis focused his cold grin on her, and it turned into an obscene grimace. "I won't fight you."

"Jiao, no," Hafeez hissed.

"Oh, you'll fight," Serapis hissed. "You'll fight, and scream, and bleed, and die. I plan on making you pay for murdering Veles. I can promise you that. But first, I will find that ball and ground it into dust in front of you. Make sure that Burke is gone for good."

Hel leaned over and whispered something in Serapis's ear. He nodded. "No more stalling," he yelled. "If you won't help us, Thomas, we will just turn this vault upside down to find it. And kill anyone we find in the way. Is that what you want?"

"Bring it, asshole," Tommy replied.

Serapis smiled. He bent over the railing and said only one word.

"Hunt."

The generals growled and hissed as they hauled themselves over the railing, Fenrir the last one to transform. Tommy transformed and roared back, getting ready to launch himself at Yama when the buffalo changeling made it to the lower floor. Camazotz flung himself over their heads, and Tommy turned around to make sure the bat didn't attack them from behind, but he cursed when he saw what Camazotz was going after. Cross and Rimsha were in the middle of the vault, Cross trying to get the girl to run, but she was fighting him, watching the bat changeling coming at her with a scowl on her face. Camazotz was skittering on the tables in the middle, heading straight for them. Tommy had no choice but to go after him.

Camazotz had too much of a head start and was about to attack the humans, lunging with his mouth open and arms held wide, when there was a green flash of light. Tommy stopped as the smell of magic washed over him, and he opened his eyes again when he heard screeching. Rimsha had her hand on a tree, and Tommy realized it was Punchi, the small tree she had bought at the diner. Only now, it was a full-grown flowering cherry tree, its branches wrapped around the bat changeling as he struggled. Tommy smiled and joined Cross and Rimsha, punching Camazotz so he stopped moving. "Nice job," Tommy rumbled, and Rimsha gave him a smile.

The floor shook, and Zheng called out. "Monroe!" she screamed, and Tommy looked back. Yama had made it to the lower floor, and he, Fenrir, and Degei were advancing on the hunters. Serapis, the asshole, was still on the upper level, leaning on the railing and smiling. He would let the others fight and then join them once victory was in sight. Tommy looked at Cross and Rimsha. "Run," he hissed, and they finally ran to hide in the shelves.

Fenrir took swipes at Zheng while Degei squared up to Hafeez and Smith. Tommy growled and took a swipe at Yama. The buffalo was big but slow, and he bellowed as Tommy's claws left scratches on his chest. The buffalo tried to punch him, and Tommy ducked.

"Stay still," the buffalo changeling ordered Tommy, but he ducked another punch and hit Yama in the ribs. The buffalo left out a huff and swung, but Tommy stayed out of his range and hit the buffalo in the stomach. Yama grunted and shook his head, his horns cutting through the air. "Stay still!" he growled.

"Nope," Tommy said with a grin. He gave Yama an uppercut to the jaw, and the buffalo staggered. When Yama recovered, he dropped his head suddenly and tried to gore Tommy in the stomach, but he jumped back. Yama tried to swing his head the other way and catch Tommy, but he grabbed the buffalo's horns and pulled, making Yama almost fall forward. Instead of letting Yama recover, Tommy took the opportunity to wrap his arms around the buffalo's chest, pick him up, and throw him. Yama landed on a couch, breaking the furniture into two pieces.

Tommy heard Hafeez shout, and he turned around. Degei had knocked Smith to the ground, grabbed Hafeez by the arm, and pulled her close to bite her, fangs dripping with thick drool. Tommy snatched the other changeling's tail and tugged hard, making the snake changeling snap his jaws close. Degei glared at him and hissed. Siad jumped onto the changeling, hissing and spitting as he tore into the changeling's back. Degei grabbed the familiar by the scruff and threw him.

Tommy caught the yowling bundle of fur and then pulled on Degei's tail so hard that the snake changeling fell over, letting Hafeez go. Tommy kept pulling the changeling, dragging him so he couldn't recover, and Smith got up and stabbed at the snake. Degei saw the strike coming and jerked out of the way. The sword missed his head but embedded into his shoulder.

Degei was thrashing so hard that Tommy had to let his tail go, and as the snake changeling tried to get the sword out of his shoulder, Tommy dropped Siad. The familiar hurled himself at Fenrir, and the wolf changeling snapped his jaws at the cat tearing into his thigh. Zheng tried to run the changeling through as he was distracted, but Fenrir dodged the attack and grabbed her sword. One tug and the weapon went flying past Yama.

Zheng backed away from Fenrir, but before the wolf could attack her, Tommy landed on his back and picked him up. Tommy bit the wolf but got the meaty part of his shoulder, not his neck. Meanwhile, Degei had gotten Smith's sword out of his shoulder and tossed it. Degei got up from the floor and rushed at Tommy, wrapping himself around Tommy, pinning his left arm to his side, and making Tommy let go of Fenrir.

Yama had recovered and lowed as he stomped towards Smith and Hafeez. Hafeez got her sword ready, but Smith started running towards the changeling. Yama swiped at him, but he just phased through the changeling's arm, and Yama looked down dumbly as the hunter disappeared through him. Smith grabbed his sword and Zheng's and tossed the Director her sword. But before she could catch it, Fenrir caught it with a growl.

"Thank you," Fenrir growled, taking the sword and running it through Tommy's stomach. He roared in pain as Degei chuckled darkly in his ear.

Tommy's vision darkened, but he shook his head. He had to stay awake, or they were dead. He pushed backward and brought his feet up, using the claws on his feet to scratch at Fenrir's face. The wolf yelped and fell back. Degei twisted Tommy around and tightened his tail. Tommy winced as he felt the bones in his left arm grind together, and then he yowled as the arm broke.

Degei was laughing, still squeezing. Tommy realized he would continue to constrict until Tommy couldn't breathe, and he started to fight harder.

Zheng glowed purple, and Tommy saw a glow appear above them. Icicles were forming, and Tommy leaned forward so that Degei was shielding him. Zheng let the icicles drop, and Degei hissed as the icicles embedded themselves into his back. He let Tommy go and started to writhe on the ground, trying to remove the ice.

Zheng rushed to Tommy. "Are you alright?" she asked.

"Never better," Tommy rumbled. He grabbed the sword in his stomach and pulled it out, handing it back to her as the wound wept blood.

Meanwhile, Smith dodged Yama's punches as Hafeez approached Fenrir with her sword out. Unfortunately, Camazotz had gotten himself loose, and he suddenly threw himself at Smith, landing on the hunter's back and pinning him to the floor with a shout. Yama brought his fist up, aiming for the hunter's head. Tommy rushed to stop the changeling, only able to wrap his right arm around the buffalo changeling's throat and tear at his back with his feet. Yama started to twist in circles, trying to catch Tommy.

Degei finished getting the icicles off his back, hissing as he went after Zheng. The older hunter yelled as the snake knocked her sword out of her hands and picked her up, his talons tearing into her shirt. Hafeez made a fireball in her hand, but Fenrir rushed at her before she could throw it, grabbing her and pinning her to a table, the useless fireball fizzling out. Siad threw himself at Fenrir, but the wolf growled and backhanded him, making him fly into the shelves. "Siad!" Hafeez cried.

Tommy was trying to get his teeth into Yama's throat, but when he leaned forward, Yama grabbed him and pulled Tommy off his back. Then, he slammed Tommy to the floor and started throwing punches. At first, Tommy could dodge them, but Yama twisted Tommy's left arm, and he saw stars. Yama finally landed a hit, and Tommy's ears rang from the pain.

Smith was shouting, trying to guard his face as Camazotz bit his arms. "Camazotz!" Fenrir growled, holding a struggling Hafeez. "Find the children! We need that sphere!"

"Find them yourself!" Camazotz yelled back, turning back to Smith to lick at his wounds.

"The girl," Degei said, shoving Zheng to Fenrir. "We need the girl." He started to slither off, seizing Camazotz and making the bat changeling go with him.

Smith panted and then grabbed his sword, running at Yama and winding up to strike at the buffalo changeling. Yama saw him coming and hit the hunter, making him fly into the broken couch with a shout. Smith tried to get up but collapsed with a groan.

Tommy began fighting harder, but Yama just grabbed his left arm and twisted it. Tommy howled in pain and started to punch the buffalo, but Yama didn't react. Instead, Yama punched Tommy once, twice, and Tommy felt the world spin with the third hit. He growled and tried to shake his head, but the world just tilted in the other direction, and he panted, fighting to stay awake.

Tommy saw a figure walking down the stairs. Serapis came down now that the fighting was over, his bare feet slapping on the concrete. "Bet you wish you returned to the fold now, don't you, mongrel?" Serapis called out to him, but Tommy didn't answer as he lost consciousness.

.....

Akrur and the kids waited with Hunter Ellis as the sounds of the fight reached them. Ellis stood there with their sword out, but they didn't move as the others battled. Akrur realized they were in trouble when he heard Tommy yowl in pain, and then the vault fell silent. Akrur could hear grunts of pain and panting, but nothing else.

Suddenly, something popped down from the floor above them, and the kids yelped in surprise. It was Camazotz, smiling at them. "Found you," he said. He giggled madly as he used the metal grate above them to move along the ceiling.

Ellis got their sword ready, and Akrur pulled the kids behind him as they backed up. Suddenly the kids shrieked, and Akrur whirled around. Degei was behind them, grinning as he slithered up to the group. "Come now," he hissed. "Serapis would like an audience."

Ellis quickly pushed past the group to get between them and the snake changeling. Camazotz dropped from the ceiling and landed on all fours, chittering and clicking as the kids cowered from him. Ellis looked back and forth between the changelings and then chose to swipe at Degei. The snake changeling fell back, but only until he could punch Ellis in the stomach, right where Yama had gored them. Ellis made a wheezing noise as the air rushed out of them, and they weakly fought as Degei took their sword.

Camazotz perked up, sniffing the air. *"La sangre,"* he hissed, flinging himself at Ellis and landing on the hunter's back. He wrestled Ellis to the floor and started to drag them out of the shelves.

Degei hissed at Akrur and the kids. "Move, sorcerer," the snake changeling ordered. He brought up one hand and clicked his talons together. "I won't ask again."

They backed out of the shelves. Camazotz had dragged Ellis to the front of the vault and was tearing at their shirt, trying to get to the reopened wound on the hunter's torso. Poor Smith was moaning on the remains of a couch, and Hafeez and Zheng were in the clutches of Fenrir. Tommy was on the floor, knocked out cold, Yama standing over him. Yet, in all the chaos, a man smiled at them with an insane grin. Seeing him made Akrur's blood run cold.

Akrur tried to keep the fear off his face as he addressed the changeling in human form, although his voice shook slightly. "You must be Serapis, I presume?" he asked the man.

"Why yes, yes I am," the changeling replied with a smile. "I'm glad my reputation proceeds me. I don't have to kill any of you to make you behave."

"Let the kids go," Akrur said, trying to keep them behind him. "They don't know anything, and they aren't a threat."

"Ah, but the last time I let a pup go, he grew up and became a thorn in my side," Serapis replied with his cold grin, gesturing at Tommy, who was moaning and rubbing his head. "Besides, one of your pups brought us here."

Rimsha suddenly yelped as Degei wrapped his tail around her and started to pull her towards Serapis. Julien had to grab Kevin before he launched himself at the changeling leader. "Leave her alone!" Kevin yelled. Julien gave Akrur a grim look. *The vision coming true.*

Serapis ignored Kevin's outburst and grabbed Rimsha's upper arm when she was close enough. "Now, you brought my generals and me here, missy. Tell us where the ball is, and you will live."

Rimsha glanced towards Camazotz, who was struggling with Ellis on the floor. The bat was trying to lap at Ellis's wound, and the hunter desperately tried to kick the changeling away. "Y-you will let us all g-go?" Rimsha asked.

"Miss Khalil, don't listen to h—" Zheng started to say, but before she could finish her order, Degei punched her in the stomach. The hunter doubled over, coughing, Fenrir laughing as he held onto her hair so she couldn't drop to the floor.

"I will let you and your friends go," Serapis said, ignoring the coughing hunter. "But the mongrel and the hunters stay."

Poor Rimsha, shaking in fear, nodded her head. She pointed at Ellis and Camazotz, who were still wrestling on the floor. "You need to stop h-him first."

"Of course!" Serapis cried. He went over to the bat changeling and grabbed him by the back of his neck, hauling him off of the hunter. Camazotz hissed but cowered when he realized it was his leader holding him. "Calm down, Camazotz!" Serapis growled playfully. "You're scaring the children!" He tossed the other changeling like he weighed nothing, and the bat changeling scurried up Yama's body to perch on the buffalo changeling's shoulder. "Now, where is the ball, my dear?"

Rimsha looked around at the changeling generals, but she held one shaking hand up, pointing to the back of the vault, past the full-grown Punchi. At the iron maiden. Akrur felt his stomach drop. Did Kevin hide the sphere there? Did Rimsha see him hide it? "It's in there," she stated.

Serapis smiled and then looked at Camazotz. The bat changeling rushed to the torture device, sniffing it over. "Thank you," Serapis purred, and he gestured at the others to start dragging the humans to the back of the vault. Yama picked Tommy up, and Degei took a moaning Smith.

Camazotz looked up as they approached. "I smell magic," he said with a grin.

"Open it up," Serapis ordered, looking smug. Tommy moaned as Camazotz struggled with the iron maiden and started to open his eyes. Serapis smiled at him. "Looks like you chose the wrong friends to have, boyo."

Tommy blinked and suddenly surged at Serapis, actually escaping Yama's grasp for a split second. Yama had to grab him and slam his head on a table. Serapis just laughed at Tommy's poor attempt to get him.

The iron maiden screeched as it opened. "There is nothing here!" Camazotz yelled, leaning in to search the inside.

Serapis turned around to glare at the bat changeling, opening his mouth to say something, but before he uttered a word, Rimsha leaned forward and screamed. *"Close!"*

The iron maiden shut with a boom, and Camazotz's hand and arm were trapped inside. The bat changeling began to screech, a horrible sound that made Akrur's ears ring. Camazotz fought to get free, and Serapis let out an inhuman growl and seized Rimsha, slapping her before bringing her fact-to-face to him. "Do you think this is a game, girl?!" he yelled. Both Julien and Ichiro had to grab Kevin this time before he hurled himself at the changeling leader.

Suddenly there was a bright flash of white towards the front of the vault, the sound of pottery breaking from the shelves, and Akrur heard someone yell. Serapis looked up and growled again, pulling Rimsha in front of him.

"Oi! Burke!" Serapis called out in a high mocking tone. "Come out and play!"

55

hey made their way out of the castle, the world tilting more as they moved. They were able to cross the bridge, but by the time they finally made it to the woods, the world was at such a severe angle that the mountain's gentle slope was now a sheer mountain face that they couldn't walk on, but they had to climb. Trees, used to growing upwards, groaned now that they were at an angle, their limbs snapping with the new pull of gravity.

"Something is wrong," Mr. Burke growled. "Jiao is supposed to tilt the sphere, but not by this much."

"Should we teleport to the circle, Mr. Burke?" Chrysta asked.

"No, it's too risky. We could fall and hurt ourselves," Mr. Burke replied. He studied her face. "I know you are worried, Miss Angelos, but we must keep our wits about us." He started the climb down the mountain. "Come on. Time is of the essence."

They climbed, Mr. Burke going first and finding the safest route, the girls and Willow slowly following him. Poe and Azul kept to the trees, flying and flowing from tree to tree. They went through the red zone carefully, although none of the guardians appeared, either not finding the humans or unable to move with the sphere leaning as it was.

They stopped when night fell, although Chrysta wanted to keep going. She could feel something was wrong, and every hour they stayed in the sphere was time the others had to guard it on the outside. But Mr. Burke made them stop to sleep, using the trees as uncomfortable beds. "Eat, Miss Angelos," Mr. Burke told her. "Sleep. We will be no use to anyone if we don't."

They woke up before sunrise and continued their journey down the mountain. The angle was even more extreme than the night before, the mountain now almost ninety degrees. Trees, logs, and rocks fell, and they had to pause to make sure nothing hit them.

Mr. Burke slipped at one point, yelling as he lost his footing and started to crash through a leaning forest. Azul went after him, catching him and then wrapping around a tree to keep him from falling further as the girls carefully caught up.

"Apparently, I need to teach someone the meaning of 'tilt,'" he growled when Chrysta and Rosa joined him.

Finally, they made it to the foot of the mountain, where the ground still leaned but not as bad as the mountain did. They rushed through the forest and finally reached the stone circle with its stone sphere. The girls scrambled to the clearing and waited in the circle as Mr. Burke grabbed the tuning fork. He hesitated, studying the girls for a moment. "We don't know what is out there," he explained. "I need you two to promise, no matter what it is, to stay calm before you do anything. Especially you, Miss Angelos."

Both girls nodded, Chrysta feeling her stomach twist itself into knots. Maybe it was the Acolytes. Maybe it was her father. Maybe it was Guerra. What if they had hurt the others? Mrs. Zheng? Tommy?

Mr. Burke made sure his sword was secured at his side, and he hit the tuning fork. It rang, and he held it to the stone sphere. The light started to build, and Chrysta suddenly noticed that she was wearing the clothes that were in the elephant's vision, the red sweater and jeans. Her sense of dread built with the white light of the stone sphere, and it got so bright they had to look away, closing their eyes before they disappeared entirely.

. . . . .

There was a great amount of pressure, but not the pressure Chrysta felt when teleporting. It was almost too much to bear when suddenly, there was the sound of pottery breaking. Chrysta was falling, and then her feet connected to the ground, and she stumbled. Poe launched himself in the air, croaking loudly, and Rosa fell to her knees with a short shout of surprise. Mr. Burke and Willow appeared on the other side of a shelf. Azul slunk away, flowing through Chrysta's legs like water, getting away from the harsh electric lights.

Chrysta looked around and saw the sphere sitting in the remains of a pot, and she realized that someone must have hidden it there, and it broke when they came out.

The sphere started to roll, and it fell off the shelf. Luckily Rosa caught it before it hit the floor, and Chrysta let out a sigh of relief.

"You two alright?" Mr. Burke asked.

"Oi! Burke!" a voice called out in a high mocking tone before the girls could answer. Mr. Burke froze and scowled. "Come out and play!"

Mr. Burke pointed at the two girls. "Get behind me and don't say anything," he ordered, turning to go to the middle of the vault. Rosa stood and placed the sphere back on the shelf, making sure it was level and secure, and then they followed Mr. Burke.

The scene that met them made Chrysta's blood run cold.

Tommy was in his other form, bloody and bruised, fighting the buffalo changeling that pinned him to the floor. A wolf changeling held Mrs. Zheng and Hafeez by their hair, both of them wincing as the wolf changeling jerked them back. Poor Hunter Ellis was on the floor, their shirt soaked in blood, a bat changeling looming over them, a grimace on its face. Or maybe it was a smile. Chrysta couldn't tell. A snake changeling held Hunter Smith by the throat while his long tail wrapped around the Disaster Club, keeping them from moving.

Finally, in the middle of all of them stood a man restraining Rimsha. A little bit of blood came from Rimsha's mouth, tears trailing from her eyes. Rosa started to stalk toward the group, and Mr. Burke had to grab her arm to keep her from trying to fight the changeling all by herself. Willow was growling, and Mr. Burke took his sword out of its sheath with the hand not holding Rosa's arm. "Jiao," he called out, "are you alright?"

"Oh, she's fine," the stranger holding Rimsha answered. He smiled, showing almost all of his teeth in an unsettling grin. "We were hoping to find that glass ball before you came out of it, but maybe this is better. Let you watch as your partner, friends, and these kids die right in front of you."

Rosa surged forward, cursing in Spanish. Mr. Burke kept a vice-like grip on her arm, not letting her go. "Let them go, Serapis," Mr. Burke growled.

"No, I don't think so," the changeling leader said, a mad grin still frozen on his face. "You are outnumbered here, boyo. We will not be takin' orders from you."

Chrysta looked around and saw the vault door behind them ripped off its hinges. She looked back at the changelings and their hostages, standing at the back of the vault, quickly taking stock of who was where. She reached out and touched Mr. Burke's hand, the one holding his sword. He glanced at her and nodded, hopefully realizing what she planned on doing. "You only have a minute to concede," Mr. Burke commanded. "Otherwise, we will force you to comply."

Serapis blinked and then laughed, the other changeling chuckling with him. "Only a minute to 'concede?'" he barked. "And who will be forcing us, hunter? You?"

"No," Chrysta said, trying to keep her voice firm. "I will."

Serapis blinked again, but this time his smile faltered. He growled, making Rimsha flinch beside him. He suddenly threw his head back and laughed.

The other changelings seemed bewildered, not knowing how to react to their leader's antics. Serapis wiped at his eyes with the hand not holding onto Rimsha. "And who would you be, girly?" he asked, mirth still in his voice.

"Chrysta Angelos," Chrysta called out, feeling a weird sense of calm come over her. "You don't know me, but you may know who my father is. Jozef York?"

Serapis chuckled and cocked his head to the side. "Ah, yes, the acolyte brat," Serapis said. He turned his grin on her, and Chrysta felt her skin crawl, but she tried to keep her eyes on him and not cringe at his unnerving attention. "You may glow white like your father, girly, but you can't do anything to me and my kin."

"I don't glow white, Mr. Serapis," Chrysta said. "And I can do anything I need to do to keep my friends safe. So please let them go, and I don't have to hurt you."

All the generals laughed at her statement. Serapis looked around him, looking at the others. "Well, if you want to do something, Chrysta Angelos, now is the time. I want to see what you think you can do."

Chrysta held her hand out, concentrating on the changelings. Serapis was giggling, probably thinking that she was playing around and nothing would happen, but his chuckle died when her hand started to glow gold. Chrysta focused on the general's hands, bending back fingers and making their limbs move away from Tommy and the humans. The generals grunted and groaned in pain, their hands glowing gold as Chrysta made them move against their will.

"Serapis," the wolf changeling whimpered. "What is happening?"

Serapis didn't answer, glowering at his hands as they were forced to let go of Rimsha and move away from her. When Tommy wasn't pinned by the buffalo changeling anymore, he flipped onto his back and kicked at the buffalo's face. The buffalo huffed and then moved his head to run his horns into Tommy. Chrysta reached out her other hand and grabbed him, holding his head still. This seemed to be a sign to the other changelings, and the bat tried to bite Hunter Ellis, the wolf tried to bite Mrs. Zheng, and Degei tried to bite Hunter Smith. Chrysta stopped them all, flexing the magic so their mouths were clamped shut before they could hurt anyone, and the humans moved away from the changelings as they struggled.

Too much. There was too much movement, too many limbs, too much to keep track of and control. Chrysta shifted her feet, made sure she had a handle on all of the generals, and then lifted them in the air. "Don't touch them," she growled, using her anger to focus the magic, and she flung them towards the stairs in the front of the vault, Rosa and Mr. Burke having to duck as the changelings sailed past them.

The changelings hit the wall in a heap, yelping and crying out in pain. Chrysta let them go and panted, the gold glow fading from her arms as she let the magic dissipate. Rosa looked at her with wide eyes.

"Holy shit," Rosa said. "Remind me to never piss you off."

.....

Tommy felt a thrill in his chest, watching the generals get tossed like rag dolls across the vault. Finally, Serapis and his high and mighty assholes got what they deserved. It was a beautiful sight to see.

Chrysta, Rosa, and Burke rushed to the group, Chrysta's hands glowing gold before she crouched next to Ellis. She let her hands hover over their side, and they hissed. "Sorry," Chrysta said. "I'll try to make this quick." Ellis blinked and then pulled their shirt up. The wound was healing fast, and the injury was gone entirely by the time Smith got down to check on his partner. The only clue that it used to be there was the blood still on their skin and soaked into their shirt.

Burke was looking Zheng and Hafeez over, checking them for damage. Hafeez was staring at Chrysta, a look of wonder and awe on her face. Rosa ran to the Disaster Club, pulling a sobbing Rimsha into her arms as she looked the others over. Ichiro and Kevin were chattering loudly as Cross held Rosa's face and asked her something. She just nodded, a look of relief crossing her face.

Tommy slowly and carefully got up, but he fell. Maybe it was fatigue, his arm, or blood on the floor, but he slipped, and all Tommy could do was close his eyes and brace for impact with the floor.

He suddenly realized he wasn't falling anymore, held up by something. He cracked an eye open and realized it was Chrysta holding him up by the shoulders; although how she was able to support him with her tiny frame, he didn't know. She smiled up at him. "Hey, handsome, are you okay?" she asked.

He snorted. "Just fine, beautiful," he replied. Chrysta helped him sink to the floor and then moved her hands to cup his face. One hand moved to his snout, and he breathed in deeply. She smelled of woods, dirt, and dust, but underneath it all was her scent, warm cinnamon. She moved his feline head so they were touching, forehead to forehead, and then she started to glow. He should be smelling the magic, but nothing offensive hit his nose, just her scent. Tommy closed his eyes and let out a rumble as the pain in his body faded.

"What is she doing?" Tommy heard Hafeez ask Burke.

"Healing him," Burke explained.

"How? Changelings aren't affected by magic."

"They are by *her* magic."

Tommy felt a weird warmth spread all over his body. He groaned when he felt his arm knit itself back together, a bizarre but painless sensation. "Sorry," Chrysta murmured. "I'm almost done." When the feeling faded, Tommy opened his eyes, sight totally clear. Chrysta smiled up at him. "How do you feel?"

Tommy looked himself over. The wounds were gone; the only sign he had been in a fight was the ruined clothes he wore. Tommy held up his left hand, moving his fingers. Even the numbness he had been suffering from was gone. "Like a million bucks," he told her with a smile.

"You bitch!" Serapis screamed from the front of the vault. His voice was shrill, unhinged, and he held his fists at his sides in rage. Tommy looked at him and growled, his ears going back. "Imposter! False god!"

"I'm not a god, Serapis," Chrysta growled back. She looked angry, but her shoulders were set back, her chin held high. She was not afraid, and Tommy was so proud of her at that moment. "I'm just someone who can make sure you can't hurt my friends."

"You'll die in this vault!" Serapis screamed back, ignoring her statement, and the generals gathered around him, all growling and hissing.

Tommy growled back, and his ears went back as he stood up to his full height. Burke's hands glowed for a second, and the hunters' swords popped in front of them. The hunters joined Tommy, getting their swords at the ready, including Burke and Ellis. "Miss Angelos," Cross called out. "Come here before you get hurt."

"Actually, Mr. Cross, I can't," Chrysta replied. Her gaze was fixed on the changelings in the front of the vault. "I think I can force them back into their human forms, and that's the only way to make sure everyone stays safe."

Cross's jaw dropped open, and even Tommy glanced at her in shock. "How can you do that?" Cross asked.

Chrysta shrugged. "I glow gold. I'm sure I can figure it out." She bit her lip, finally looking a little uncertain. "I think I have to physically touch them, though."

"Do you want us to gift wrap them for you too?" Smith asked sarcastically.

"Get me her head!" Serapis roared, and the generals started moving toward them.

"Aw, shit!" Smith cursed. He looked at his partner. "Who we taking?"

"Degei," they growled, and they ran to meet the snake changeling, Smith close behind them.

"Camazotz is mine," Hafeez stated, and she vaulted over a couch with her familiar.

"Yama will be ours," Burke said.

"Just like old times," Zheng purred with a smile. "How romantic."

Burke shot his wife a look, then they ran at the buffalo changeling. Yama lowed at them as they swiped at him.

Fenrir stalked up to Tommy, growling. Tommy stepped in front of Chrysta, answering the wolf's growl with one of his own. The wolf's ears went back. "You worship a false idol, mongrel," he rumbled.

Tommy almost felt bad for the general, not knowing the difference between friendship and worship, but Fenrir snarled and snapped at Tommy before he could say anything. Suddenly one of the chairs nearby glowed gold and flew through the air toward the changeling. It hit Fenrir in the face, and the wolf changeling yelped. Tommy glanced at Chrysta to see her scowling at the general. "Like I said," Chrysta stated. "You're not hurting my friends."

Fenrir shook his head and then launched himself at Chrysta. Tommy caught him in the air and slammed the wolf changeling to the floor, going for his throat.

They fought on the floor, biting and clawing at each other, but any time Fenrir could, he pushed Tommy away and started to go after Chrysta. Tommy would grab the wolf changeling and pull him back, and the process would start all over again.

It was hard to watch the other generals while avoiding getting his eyes clawed out, but Tommy noticed that the other generals were doing the same thing. Degei used his tail to knock Smith and Ellis down and then, quick as lightning, went after Chrysta. Camazotz, after avoiding Hafeez and Siad, launched himself at the girl. And Yama, ignoring all the wounds Burke and Zheng were inflicting, just shouldered his way toward Chrysta.

Chrysta, for her part, was keeping herself safe, expression set in a frown as her hands glowed gold. Degei got another chair to the face, hissing as he almost fell backward. Camazotz went sailing as Chrysta allowed him to phase right through her. Yama lowed at her, but lightning arched between Chrysta's hands before he could reach her. "Stop!" she ordered the changeling, but he kept approaching her, probably thinking the lightning wouldn't affect him. Finally, she blasted him, and Yama bellowed and fell to one knee.

The kids cheered, and Camazotz hissed at them. He forgot Chrysta for a moment and started to scramble toward them with a nightmarish grin. The teens screeched and ducked behind Cross as the changeling went after them. Rosa made a useless fireball in her hand, but before anyone could try to stop Camazotz, a black creature came out of the shelves and tackled the bat changeling. Tommy thought it was a black jungle cat at first, but it started to ebb and flow as it wrapped itself around Camazotz, and the bat changeling squealed as he fought to get the weird creature off of him.

"Azul!" Chrysta cried, and her hand glowed even brighter for a second. All the generals glowed, and with a loud *pop*, they disappeared, reappearing in a heap in front of Serapis.

Serapis began screaming at his generals as they groaned and picked themselves off the floor. "Idiots! Useless, the whole lot of ya! All you have to do is get the girl!" He backhanded Fenrir, making the wolf changeling yelp, and then grabbed Yama's horns and roughly tugged on them, making the buffalo changeling grumble.

Tommy growled as he got off the floor. The generals were getting tired and weren't invulnerable to Chrysta's magic. The smart thing for Serapis to do would be to retreat, to get away while he could, but there was no way Tommy would let any of them escape tonight.

Serapis stopped berating the others and then looked behind him, towards the door, and then back to the group of hunters again, probably debating the same thing that Tommy was thinking. But he just adjusted his suit and squared his shoulders. "Well, if you want something done right, you have to do it yourself," he said with his mad grin, and then he transformed.

He was large and covered in black fur, which Tommy expected, but Serapis's head looked wrong, misshapen, and lumpy. It took Tommy a second to realize that it was because he had *three* heads, three canine heads with three sets of teeth, all three currently growling. Tommy felt some shock and disgust. He was a freak himself, with a leopard for a mother and a tiger shark for his father, but three fucking heads? How did the Golden One manage that?

There was a clatter, and Tommy looked over at Burke. He stared in shock at Serapis, even dropping his sword in surprise. "Sir?" Ellis said, looking between Burke and Serapis. "Are you alright?"

"The three-headed changeling," Burke breathed.

"Neil," Zheng said. She held her sword at the ready, but she was staring at her husband, not the generals. "Neil!"

Her shout finally got through to the Headmaster, and his look of shock melted into one of hatred. The sword disappeared from the floor and reappeared in front of him, and Burke snatched it out of the air. "He's mine," he growled. And then he launched himself at the changelings.

Tommy didn't know what Burke was thinking, taking on all of the generals by himself, but he swiped and cut through the generals with wild abandon. Tommy ran after him, grabbing Fenrir after Burke stabbed him to throw the wolf towards Zheng, punching Camazotz so he couldn't jump on Burke, and then tackling Degei to the floor. Yama tried to hit Burke, but the sorcerer didn't slow down, glowing white and grabbing the vault door with magic, flinging it at Yama so that the buffalo changeling flew into the shelves.

Serapis just watched all this with a grin on his multiple faces, showing off all his teeth and darkly chuckling. "Get the girl!" he roared as he squared up with Burke.

The generals immediately turned their attention to Chrysta again, trying to get to her while ignoring the hunters. Chrysta let Fenrir phase through her, blasted Camazotz with lightning, and then warily watched Yama pick himself off the floor. The buffalo changeling lowed at her but then glanced at the teens cowering towards the back of the vault.

"Azul!" Rosa cried, and the black creature got between the group and the buffalo changeling, electric blue eyes locking onto the changeling.

"Miss Angelos!" Cross called out. "We may need your assistance!"

"Teleport them!" Tommy yelled, but before Chrysta could do it, Degei punched Tommy and slithered towards Chrysta, quick as lightning.

Chrysta formed lightning in her hands, all of her focus on the snake changeling in front of her. She almost didn't see Fenrir about to attack behind her, but Poe squawked a warning, and Chrysta whirled, blasting Fenrir. Degei surged towards her, but Chrysta grabbed him with magic and forced his mouth shut, and Degei started to writhe on the floor, scratching at his snout.

Tommy heard a roar and looked behind him. Burke had stabbed Serapis, but the changeling leader backhanded him, so he stumbled to the floor without his sword. Serapis towered over the Headmaster, but Tommy looked back at Chrysta.

Burke needed help, but could Chrysta protect herself? Serapis growled and laughed, and Tommy decided to help Burke.

He attacked the changeling leader, grabbing one head so he could slam its jaw shut. That just meant there were now two heads to worry about now, snapping in his face. Tommy started throwing wild punches, avoiding their teeth. He tried to tear at Serapis with his feet, and Serapis did the same thing, blood beginning to splash on the ground below them.

Tommy grabbed Burke's sword and pulled it out, trying to do as much damage as possible. Serapis roared and punched him, and he didn't look that strong, but Tommy saw stars. Serapis grabbed his shirt, talons ripping the material, and then shoved Tommy so hard he stumbled. Before Tommy could recover, Serapis was on top of him, one set of jaws in each shoulder and tearing into Tommy's chest with his claws. Tommy yowled in surprise and pain.

"Tommy!" Chrysta screamed. Zheng was helping her husband up, so the other hunters had gathered around Chrysta to help her with the generals, who were still dismissing them and focusing on Chrysta. Chrysta formed two fireballs and threw them at Fenrir and Degei, both changelings desperately trying to put the fire out. Chrysta tried to move toward Tommy, her hands glowing, but before she could do anything, Yama bellowed and tried to punch her. She disappeared with a pop and reappeared on the upper floor, Yama's fist connecting with the floor.

Chrysta leaned over the railing, looking at Tommy so she didn't see the dark figure sneaking from the shelves behind her. It was Camazotz, grinning from ear to ear. "Chrysta!" someone screamed, maybe Rimsha or Rosa, but before she could turn around, Camazotz leaped at her. He wrapped his wings around her, then leaned back to open his mouth wide, sinking his teeth into her throat. He jerked his head back, blood flew, and Chrysta screamed. There was a flash of light, and Camazotz flew, tumbling to the lower floor, but it was too late. Blood flowed out of Chrysta's throat, and she stumbled as blood stained her sweater.

ෙ 56 ෙ

Tommy forgot about Serapis and the other generals as he watched Chrysta crumble. He'd failed her. He had been unable to protect Chrysta. Tommy had broken his promise.

Serapis watched Chrysta fall with a dark grin on all his faces, and then he turned to Tommy. "Looks like you can't keep the women in your life alive, boyo," he rumbled.

Tommy saw red, and he started to kick and bite at Serapis. He didn't even think about what he was doing; he just started fighting. He must have thrown Serapis because he was suddenly free and jumping to climb to the upper floor, not even bothering to run for the stairs.

He scrambled over the railing and then transformed, crouching next to Chrysta. Blood, so much blood. She was on her knees, bent over, and held one hand to her throat. "No, no, no, no," he moaned in despair. "Chrysta," he whispered. "Chrysta, can you hear me? Please, beautiful, talk to me."

"Ow," she said softly, and Tommy felt a rush of relief that made him go weak. If she was talking, then she was alive; if she was alive, there was hope. Tommy was about to look for Rimsha to get the teen to heal Chrysta, but Chrysta leaned back and took her hand off the wound. Tommy panicked and reached out to put his hand on the injury, but he paused when he got a good look at it.

Camazotz had ripped the sweater Chrysta was wearing, giving Tommy the perfect view of the wound knitting itself closed. He put his fingers to her throat, and she winced, but the wound was definitely disappearing on its own. "Spontaneous healing," she explained with a grin. "Any wounds on my body heal themselves. Looks like the elephant was wrong. I don't die today."

Chrysta reached up to the railing and stood, Tommy helping her. She swayed on her feet but stayed up. "You okay, Chrysta?" Cross called out.

"I'm okay, Mr. Cross," Chrysta replied.

"What did you do?!" someone screamed below them. Tommy looked down to see the generals gathered around Camazotz. He was in his human form, looking at his arms. He strained for a second and then stopped, panting.

"Camazotz, transform," Degei hissed at him. The hunters surrounded them, and Degei watched them, almost looking nervous.

"I'm trying," Camazotz whined. He strained again, but nothing happened. "I *can't*. She did something to me. I can't change."

"And I could make it permanent," Chrysta called out. She was looking at Serapis when she said it, her hand back at her throat. "I can make sure none of you can change ever again."

One of Serapis's heads whined, its ears going back on its head, but the other two growled. He looked at Camazotz, who was human, and back at the hunters that encircled them. He growled again. "Fall back!" he roared.

Fenrir and Yama looked at him in shock. "What?!" Fenrir asked.

"Retreat, dammit!" Serapis said again, and he started to run for the stairs.

Smith was in Fenrir's way, and the hunter wound up to swipe at the changeling. Fenrir caught the sword with a snarl and snatched it away. Smith got hit in the chest and went flying.

Yama was below Chrysta and Tommy, studying Camazotz dumbly. Chrysta looked at Tommy. "Think you can hold him still for me?" she asked with a smile.

Tommy grinned and transformed. "Anything for you, beautiful."

Tommy hoisted himself over the railing, landing on top of Yama. The bull changeling bellowed and started waving his arms wildly, trying to grab Tommy. Tommy caught Yama's arms and pulled them back, using the bull's horns to brace. Chrysta popped in front of them, her hands glowing. She put them on Yama's chest—

—and suddenly, Tommy was wrestling with a human. He was big and strong but fully human. Tommy smiled, put a foot to the man's backside, and kicked, sending him flying.

Yama recovered and turned around, scowling at Tommy and Chrysta. He actually stamped one bare foot and then started to stomp toward Chrysta. He lifted a fist to hit her, but before he reached her, Tommy punched him instead, and the man stumbled and fell over, knocked out cold.

Burke was still stunned on the floor, and Ellis was helping their partner, so Zheng and Hafeez were fighting Degei. The snake changeling was hissing and taking swipes at them. Suddenly he caught Hafeez and jerked her close, mouth wide to bite her, fangs gleaming. Siad landed on the snake changeling's back and started tearing at him. But Degei ignored the familiar, determined to bite and kill the hunter.

Tommy grabbed a piece of wood from the broken couch and thrust it at the snake changeling, so Degei bit it, not Hafeez. The snake changeling dropped the hunter, snatched the wood out of his mouth, and threw it. He rounded on Tommy and hissed, and Tommy answered with his own roar. Tommy jumped at the changeling and pinned him. Chrysta ran up to them, jumping over Degei's thrashing tail and putting her hand on his shoulder—

—and now Tommy was fighting a man with two legs and no fangs. The man started spitting something in another language, and Tommy may not know what language it was, but he knew the sound of cursing when it was directed at him.

"Out of the way!" Hafeez yelled, and Tommy let go of Degei. The man was up in a flash, spitting unknown insults at the hunter. Hafeez picked up her sword and went after the changeling.

There was a shout, and Tommy looked up to see Camazotz running at Zheng. The older hunter didn't even flinch but did a roundhouse kick when the changeling was close enough and sent him flying when her foot connected with his chest. The teens cheered, and Poe squawked.

Zheng looked up and suddenly pointed to the front of the vault. "Don't let them escape!" she yelled.

Tommy looked in the direction she was pointing to see Serapis and Fenrir running through the broken vault door. If they let Serapis get away, they may never see him again. Tommy growled, but before he could run for the stairs, Chrysta grabbed his arm. He looked at her in surprise. "Hang on," she said, and then they popped out of existence.

. . . . .

Chrysta tried to teleport in front of Serapis and Fenrir, but they reappeared above the two changelings as they ran through the printing presses instead. The *pop* was loud enough that both generals froze and looked up. Tommy landed on Serapis, and they started fighting, clawing and snapping at each other. Chrysta landed in front of Fenrir, and the wolf changeling leered at her.

"I'll rip your throat out," the wolf changeling rumbled.

"Just try," Chrysta replied, surprised at the strength in her own voice.

Fenrir howled and rushed at her, knocking Chrysta over. The wolf's talons tore at her already ruined sweater, and he pinned her hands to the floor. "I wonder if you would heal if I tore out your heart," he snarled.

Fenrir's jaws opened wide, and Chrysta could have teleported away, but she phased one of her hands from the wolf's grip and thrust her fist into the wolf's mouth.

Fenrir's eyes went wide, but before he could bite down, Chrysta felt the flex in her chest—

—and now it was a woman on top of Chrysta. Her now-blunt teeth scraped Chrysta's hand as she gagged and stood up. She was a handsome woman, blond hair going grey, with a square jaw, and beautiful blue eyes, but her beauty was ruined by the scowl she wore.

"I don't need my claws to tear you apart," she panted, looking around. She found a wrench as long as Chrysta's arm and grabbed it, bringing it over her head and aiming for Chrysta's face.

Chrysta held her hands out, stopping the wrench in the air. Hel grunted with the effort to bring it down and hit Chrysta with it, but Chrysta just flexed and sent the heavy tool in the opposite direction. It hit Hel in the face with a loud *thunk*, and the woman passed out and fell over.

Chrysta sprang up from the floor and watched as Tommy and Serapis fought. Tommy was larger but had trouble with all of Serapis's heads. They snapped and tore at him, and he couldn't keep them from biting and hurting him. Serapis kept pinning Tommy to the floor, and Tommy would have to fight to keep the heads from doing too much damage.

Chrysta felt the flex in her chest, and she used the magic to grab Serapis's heads and hands. The changeling leader growled and fought her, trying to jerk out of her grasp. Chrysta strained to keep him frozen.

"Chrysta!" Tommy roared, pointing at the wrench at her feet. She nodded and let Serapis go, but before he could start attacking Tommy again, Chrysta teleported the giant tool so that it would appear right in between the changelings. Tommy snatched it out of the air and swung it at Serapis.

THANG! The wrench connected with Serapis's right head, and the head fell unconscious, and the whole right side of Serapis's body went limp. The other two heads were still awake, but without the use of the right side of his body, Serapis crumbled to the floor, and Tommy flipped them so he was on top of the changeling leader.

The other two heads snarled and growled and barked, but they couldn't move. Tommy picked him up, and Serapis dangled in the air, entirely at Tommy's mercy.

Chrysta rushed over, and Serapis tried to grab her with his left hand, but Tommy bit his shoulder, and he roared in pain and tried to rip Tommy off of him. Chrysta put her hand on him, felt the magic inside of him that allowed him to change, turned it off, and—

—Serapis was human again, suit bloody and torn, the right side of his face bruised and swollen, and his shirt completely destroyed because of his other heads. "You bitch!" he cried, glaring at Chrysta. "I will never submit to—" But his insults were cut off when Tommy wrapped his long fingers around Serapis's throat.

Serapis's look of rage slowly melted and was replaced with his cold smile. He grinned at Tommy. "Alright, my boy," he wheezed. "You won. You know what has to come next."

Tommy growled. "I almost don't want to do this," he rumbled. "Part of me wants to make you suffer for a very long time." His hands started to tighten on Serapis's throat. "A quick death is almost too good for you."

"I will say hello to your mother," Serapis gasped, and Tommy's ears went back and, he snarled in the other changeling's face.

"Tommy, wait!" Chrysta cried. She put her hand on his arm. "Don't do it!"

"He deserves it, Chrysta," Tommy said. "He has hurt so many people, humans and changelings." The snarl on his snout softened slightly. "He killed my Mama."

Chrysta felt her heart break for him. "You shouldn't, Tommy. Killing him won't bring your mother back."

"I know that!" Tommy roared. Serapis grunted as Tommy jerked him closer. "But I'm still tearing his throat out."

"Don't!"

"Stop!" Tommy roared. "You have no idea what it feels like, Chrysta!"

"But I do!"

"How?!"

"Because I want to do the same to Guerra for killing my mom!"

Tommy froze and looked at her in shock. "The beads that Poe collected? They were from her necklace," Chrysta explained. "She was wearing it when Guerra killed her. Everyone told me she died in an accident, but when I touched one of her beads, I saw the whole thing. I watched her die."

"Beautiful, I'm sorry," Tommy replied.

Chrysta shook her head, fighting the tears that were burning her eyes. "I felt the same way when I found out. I wanted to get out of the sphere and go hurt Guerra like he hurt my mom. But Mr. Burke warned me not to become the monster I was trying to fight."

Serapis laughed. Or laughed as much as he could with his airway being crushed. "Don't listen to her, boy. She's weak. You beat me, so do it." He leaned in closer to Tommy. "Kill me, mongrel. It's the only way."

Tommy's ears went back, but he studied the man before him for several silent, tense moments. "Mama was right," he said after studying the changeling leader. "You are hurting our kind, not helping us."

"Kill me!" Serapis shouted. He almost sounded desperate. "What else could you do with me?"

Tommy growled and then smiled. "I think I know what I could do."

.....

Akrur scrambled up the ladder with Burke and Zheng, fearing what they would find. Hafeez, Ellis, and Smith were in the vault with the kids and the defeated changelings. Burke and Zheng went first, but they froze when they reached the top. Akrur pulled himself up and then froze with them.

Tommy and Chrysta were several feet away, Tommy leaning on one of the print machines in his human form while Chrysta's hands glowed gold as she healed him. They were both a mess, clothes torn and blood everywhere, but they were otherwise intact, and Akrur felt a rush of relief. "Are you alright?" he called out, and the couple looked at him.

"We're alright," Chrysta responded as her hands stopped glowing. Tommy wrapped his arms around Chrysta and tugged her into a hug. She smiled as she wrapped her arms around his neck, and Akrur just didn't have the heart to tell them to break it up.

"Where is Serapis?" Zheng asked sternly. "Did he get away?"

Tommy waved a hand towards the front of the warehouse. "Go see for yourself."

They moved as a group to the front, and Akrur couldn't help it when his jaw dropped open in shock. Hel and Serapis were on the bed of Smith's truck. Hel was knocked out cold, her hands tied behind her. Serapis was awake and sitting up, restrained with a chain. The crazy bastard was grinning from ear to ear, even with the right side of his face bruised and swollen. He chuckled as the hunters approached him. "You are going to regret letting me live," he said calmly.

Burke lifted his sword, leveling it so it pressed into Serapis's chest. He used both hands to hold the sword, ready to thrust. The changeling leader just kept grinning. "In 1945," Burke started to say, "my brother and I were hiking in the Irish wilderness. We were attacked by a man, who then changed into a three-headed monster."

"Ooooh, I think I remember that night," Serapis said, still smiling.

"I never *forgot* that night," Burke growled.

"What happened, Mr. Burke?" Chrysta asked in a small voice.

"A man ran into our camp, covered in blood, screaming about a monster. When we realized he wasn't hurt, he turned into a beast—a changeling. But he wasn't a type of changeling I had ever heard of before, with three heads. My brother was dragged into the night, never to be seen again." Burke shifted, but the sword didn't even twitch. "I survived, but no one believed me when I said I saw a three-headed changeling. I swore to become a hunter and find the monster that killed him."

"Your brother screamed so well that night," Serapis suddenly said, brightly and calmly, like he was commenting on the weather. "He was absolutely *delicious.*"

The look of rage that crossed Burke's face was the most frightening thing Akrur had ever seen, including the fight he had just witnessed in the vault below. Burke's body went rigid, and Akrur saw him get ready to run the changeling through with his sword. Tommy put a hand on his chest and pushed the Headmaster back. Burke allowed Tommy to do it, but he didn't break eye contact with the changeling leader. Serapis just kept smiling, unfazed by the threat on his life.

"Don't do it," Tommy said calmly. "I understand why you want to, trust me. But it's what he wants."

"What do you suggest we do with him?" Zheng asked. She put her hand on Burke's arm but didn't push her husband away.

"If we kill him here, he dies a hero. A martyr. Other changelings who think like him will just take his place and use his death as a rallying cry." Tommy looked at Serapis, whose smile was slowly fading. "But if you imprison him, put him on trial, let him be humiliated before he's executed..." Tommy shrugged. "Seems like a better idea than either of us getting to kill him here and enjoying a few minutes of joy."

"You understand what you are proposing, correct?" Zheng asked. She looked at Chrysta. "We can't just capture the five generals of the Golden One without people asking how and why. I can't ensure that your identity will remain a secret."

"I understand, Mrs. Zheng," Chrysta said. "But I think Serapis being on trial publicly will mean more for sorcerer's peace of mind than my privacy would." Cross reached out and squeezed her shoulder, and she gave him a smile.

"Oh, spare me," Serapis whined. "Kill me now, please."

Burke's face slowly returned to the usual neutral expression he always used. He looked at his wife and then at Tommy's hand on his chest. He raised an eyebrow and glared at Tommy, and the changeling took a step back and put his hands up in surrender. Burke slowly lowered the sword.

"Serapis, you are under arrest for murder and assault," Burke growled. "What say you?"

"I will make you wish you killed me," Serapis growled back.

"Noted," Burke drawled, and Akrur felt a slight sense of relief to see the Headmaster back to his old self.

"You flecking idiots," Serapis spat. "You think I need your *mercy*? Your *pity*? Weak, the whole lot of you." He stood up, trying to stand as tall as possible, even with the chain wrapped around his torso. "I will get free, and I will kill all that you love." He used a shoulder to gesture at Chrysta and Zheng. "Starting with these two bit—"

Before he could finish his threat, both Burke and Tommy punched him without warning, Tommy with his right hand and Burke with his left. Serapis was knocked out cold and dropped like a sack of potatoes. Both Tommy and Burke hissed in pain. "Aw, fuck," Tommy cursed as Burke rubbed his own hand. "I think I broke my hand on his nose."

Chrysta laughed. "Let me see," she said, grabbing Tommy's hand to inspect it.

Burke was scowling at his hand when his wife hooked a finger into his shirt and pulled him down. They shared a brief kiss. "Husband," she purred.

"Wife," he responded, a smile tugging at the corners of his lips.

"You were late," she growled.

"The sphere was at such a severe angle we couldn't travel safely," Burke explained.

"Good thing you came out when you did," Akrur admitted. "I don't even want to imagine what would have happened otherwise."

"I thought it was the Acolytes coming," Chrysta murmured. "How did the changelings find you?"

"They found the kids and forced them to bring them here," Akrur told her.

Zheng raised an eyebrow. "That doesn't explain how the generals found them to begin with."

Akrur frowned. "Blind luck?"

"Bullshit," Tommy growled. "They weren't just looking for sorcerers; they were looking for someone who knew Chrysta."

"For me?" Chrysta asked. She looked around at the group. "Wait a minute, how did they know about me?"

"There is a spy," Burke said, and they fell silent, looking at each other.

"One of the hunters?" Akrur asked.

"Or one of the teens," Zheng countered.

Akrur bristled at her tone. "None of the kids would dare, madam," he growled.

Burke put his hand up. "We will have to uncover that mystery later." He looked down at Serapis with a scowl. "For now, we have to call for help with this mess."

Zheng reached into an inner pocket in her dress and took out a beacon charm. "Once I break this, hunters will come running," she explained, looking at Chrysta. "Are you sure you want to drag this into the light?"

Chrysta looked down at Serapis. She reached a hand out, and Tommy took it, lacing their fingers together. She took a deep breath and then let it out in an explosive sigh. "Yes," she finally replied.

Zheng held up the beacon charm and, with the flex of her fingers, broke it in two.

www.ingramcontent.com/pod-product-compliance
Lightning Source LLC
Chambersburg PA
CBHW050916030726
47503CB00007BB/2317